for

Wicked Ta

Even Wickeder Tales

by Ed Wicke

Erin
Ciara
Iris

from
Ed Wicke
and
The Tooth Mice

Wicked

6 Rattees

Two rats kidnap an orphan baby and try to sell it. But the baby is more than a match for them, and joins in their life of crime. He would like to have a mummy of his own one day, and the Rattees might help his dreams come true...

27 Jack and the Cow

Don't swap your cow for a tin of beans, or a hat, or a talking chicken. You *know* it will all go wrong somehow, and you'll end up as Ogre Food, or worse.

54 The Gorilla and the Hunter

Big Bob the Hunter may have a jeep loaded with guns and a house stuffed with animal trophies, but he'll be no match for a jungle-wise little gorilla.

Tales Two

70 The Bad Tooth Fairy

If a fairy doesn't pass her fairy exams at primary school, she may end up with the second worst job in the world. But a naughty fairy won't care about that, so long as she gets enough fairy gold for Troll dances and chocolate.

111 Alicroc the Alien Scoutmaster

An alien with green, crackly skin and 272 fine white teeth becomes a scoutmaster. But can his Tiny Scouts beat Big Mike's Tough Scouts? Or will the call of the wild be too scary for them?

132 Easter Bunnies vs. Fairy G-Mother feat. Cinderella

When the Bunnies ride into town, they're in no mood to be pushed around - and especially not by a chavvy godmuvver in pink slippers and rubber gloves. As for Cinders, she *shall* go to the Ball... whether she likes it or not.

A note to the reader:

These stories are brilliant for reading out loud. Tell them to your little sister, your mum or your cat. Even better, get your mum to read them to *you*... and get the cat to read them to your little sister!

But whether you read them in your head or tell them out loud to your hamster, *you need to do the voices*. Just go for it! Make Alicroc sound like a hippy crocodile and make the Easter Bunnies talk like the cool bandit cowboys they are. Make the Tooth Fairy naughty and the Gorilla cheeky. Make the Fairy Grotmother as gloriously grotty as a Grotmuvver can be.

I've included a guide to the voices for each story. However, these are only *my* ideas, and there's no reason why the gorilla in your head should sound exactly like the one in mine...

And a note about pictures: In some stories I've given you choices. For instance, there are two versions of Cinderella & the Bunnies, two of the Gorilla, and nine of the Ssssnake. This is on purpose! I think the pictures in your head are the best, and I hope my illustrators in their different ways help to stir up your imagination.

This is my tenth book, and I hope you'll want to try the other nine as well, so I've told a little about each one at the end of this book.

Ed Wicke

Wicked Tales Two: *Even Wickeder Tales*

For little Ara Mutiny McKinstrie, who will one day be told these stories.

Published by BlacknBlue Press UK
13 Dellands, Overton, Hampshire, England
blacknbluepress@hotmail.com

Printed in Great Britain by:
Lightning Source
6 Precedent Drive, Rooksley, Milton Keynes MK13 8PR, England

ISBN 978-0-9840718-1-4

Rattees

The voices

The Rattees talk like gangsters. They even do a bit of Gangsta Rap on street corners while the baby crawls around tying the audience's shoelaces together. When the people try to walk away, they fall over and the Rattees pick their pockets faster than three blind mice can run from a farmer's wife.

The **Baby** is adorable and clever and talks in a high, sweet voice. He's a bit sad about not having a mummy or daddy, but otherwise he lives quite happily in his old doll's pram. He wishes people would always leave a couple of crisps at the bottom of the packets they throw away, for him to nibble.

The **Lady** wears pearls, talks in a marvellously middle-class manner, and is rather foolish. She's also a famous detective and sometimes watches herself solving crimes on television, when she can remember where she put her glasses.

The **Vet** is a rough and ready Jack-the-lad, and is rather rude to everyone. But he knows a cat from a baby and a baby from a rat, which in his opinion is ***all*** that matters.

The **Doctor** is young and pretty. She talks kindly to her patients, but uses a lot of very big words that no one understands – so they have to go and ask the nurse to explain.

Pussykins is a large and rather lazy cat who only comes to life when there are goldfish to watch.

The **Goldfish** say nothing, but they look very worried.

The story

Once upon a time there were two large, scruffy rats, known to their friends as Rattees.

The first scam: Baby-napping

The rats got tired of eating rat food and decided to make some money. So they went to a local supermarket and kidnapped a ginger-haired baby sitting outside the shop in an old doll's pram. He was wearing a tea towel as a nappy and had a ragged scrap of blue blanket wrapped around him.

Each time a mother came out of the shop, the Rattees would say to her:

'We've got your baby! And you can't have it back until you pay us loadsa money!'

Then the mother would peer at the baby in the ramshackle pram and shake her head.

The first mother said, 'This isn't my baby - my baby has *blue* eyes but this one has greenish grey eyes!'

The second said, 'This isn't my baby - my baby has *brown* hair but this one's hair is ginger!'

And every mother said it wasn't her baby.

Then the Rattees would ask, 'D'you wanna buy it, then? Only cost you a fiver!'

But one by one, the mothers shook their heads and said they didn't need another baby.

The first one added, 'This baby is rather dirty. I don't like dirty babies.'

The second said, 'This baby is a boy. I don't like boy babies.'

And no one wanted the baby, even though it looked up at the mothers very hopefully.

Finally the rats asked the baby, 'Where's your mother? Ain't she in the shop?'

The baby said sadly, 'I haven't got a mummy or a daddy!'

'What? Who looks after you, then?'

'I look after myself!'

The Rattees felt sorry for the baby. 'What do you eat?' they asked.

'Anything I can find,' he said. 'People drop lots of nice food. Look!'

He lifted the blanket and showed the rats his lunch. 'I've got a bread crust an old man threw away... the inside of a crisp packet to lick out... two old pieces of chewing gum, only a little bit chewed... and for pudding, I've got some sweets wrappers to suck on!'

'And what do you drink?'

'There's nice bits at the bottom of old bottles and cans that people drop. And when I can't find any of those, there's always slugs to suck... Yummy!'

'Poor baby,' said one Rattee. 'We gotta get you some real food.'

'Yeah, and I've got a plan,' said the other. 'See that old lady dozin' on the bench over there? Wot we do is this...'

They scampered over to the old lady and untied her shoelaces. They pulled them out of her shoes and fastened them to the old doll's pram.

A few minutes later, the pram was whizzing about the supermarket, pulled by the rats using the shoelaces they'd nicked. The baby was laughing and shouting, 'Go faster! Faster! Turn left here! Now stop! A bit further! ... Go again! Go!'

They went from shelf to shelf and the baby snatched things as they passed – sweets, raisins, cereal, bananas, a box of cat food –

'You don't want that!' said the Rattees.

'I *do!*' sulked the baby. 'I like crunchy cat food best of all!'

Then they charged for the exit, with the store staff chasing after them. They slid under a barrier and out the door.

'Faster! Faster!' shouted the baby.

They sped down pavements, making people and pigeons scatter. Behind them were running feet and angry shouts - and then the sound of a police siren.

'We got the fuzz after us!' shouted the Rattees.

'I don't want to go to prison!' the baby wailed.

'There's the police van! What'll we do now?'

'Down that hill!' ordered the baby.

The rats turned and started down a steep hill. The pram was rolling by itself now, so the rats jumped

onto the baby's lap and rode the pram down
and down
and
down....

... until they bounced across a path, rolled into the woods, bumped into a tree, and all fell out.

'Hooray!' shouted the baby. 'Do it again! Again!'

'Nah,' said the rats, who were lying on their backs watching the clouds and trees spin round and round. 'That's enough for one day.'

'Tomorrow then?'

'Yeah. Tomorrow.'

The slug scam

After a few weeks of nicking food from supermarkets, the Rattees had another idea. They went out just after dawn, pushing the baby in his rickety pram along the pavements of the better neighbourhoods.

As they went, they picked up the slugs they came across, until they had hundreds of them crammed inside an old cat food box, grey and black and orange and slimy.

'Yummy!' said the baby. 'Nice slugs to suck!'

'Yuk!' said the Rattees.

They came to a big house. 'This one'll do,' said a Rattee. 'It's a posh place and the lady here lives all by herself.'

They began flicking slugs about, until the walls were crawling with them. Then one Rattee climbed to the top of the pram handle and rang the doorbell.

A rich looking lady opened the rich looking door.

'Can I help you?' she asked in a rich sounding voice.

'Nah, but we can help **you**,' said the Rattees. 'You gotta real slug problem, lady.'

'Have I?'

'Yeah, just look up there.'

She came outside, looked back at the front of her house and screamed.

One Rattee said, 'See wot we mean? They's all over your place –'

'Climbin' the walls –'

'Tryin' to get in the windows –'

'Suckin' the bricks dry –'

'Fallin' in your hair when you comes out –'

(At this point, the baby secretly flicked some slugs into the air so that they landed on the lady's head).

'Oh no!' she shrieked, shaking slugs from her hair.

'And it'll get worse –'

'They lays a million eggs a day –'

'In a week they'll be all over your carpets!'

'What can I do?' the lady cried.

'Pay us a fiver a week, and we'll come do a slug hunt every day. Look – we'll show you how good we are at huntin'.'

The baby crawled about the lawn, snatching up slugs and dropping them into the cat food box while the rats scampered up the walls and knocked slugs down for the baby.

'I'm not sure...' said the lady. 'Five pounds is a lot of money for picking up a few slugs.'

The Rattees winked at the baby, and he secretly flicked twenty slugs through the open door.

'Look at your carpet!' shouted a Rattee. 'They's inside!'

The lady turned and gave another shriek when she saw the dazed slugs crawling about in her hallway.

'Get them out!' she begged. '*Please* get them out!'

'Fiver a week,' said the Rattees. 'In advance.'

'Oh, all right,' said the lady, taking out her purse.

The scam with the cat flap

Soon they had fifty houses paying them a fiver a week for Slug Services.

'But it ain't enough,' said one of the Rattees. 'We gotta save up for when the baby's old enough to go to playgroup.'

'What we need,' said the baby, 'is a house with a cat flap!'

'Why?' asked the Rattees.

'I'll show you!'

So next time, they tried the slug scam on a house with a cat flap. While the Rattees kept the lady busy with slugs that seemed to rain from the sky, the baby crawled around to the back door. He went inside through the cat flap and came out again, dragging something with him. He did this several times more.

As the lady paid the rats a fiver for slug hunting, one of the Rattees said, 'We've also got some cat food for sale. Real cheap it is, too.'

'Cat food?' the lady asked. 'I do have a cat, but he's very choosy about what he eats.'

The other Rattee looked at the pile the baby had dragged out. 'We got tins of King Kat,' he said. 'You want any of that?'

'That's just what my kitty likes best!' said the lady.

'And we got these nice saucepans. Quality, they are.'

'Oh!' she exclaimed. 'They're just like the pans *I* have! Yes, I'll buy those as well.'

'And we got these nice toys. You want any?'

'They're just the sort of toys my little boy likes!'

So they sold the lady her own toys, saucepans and cat food.

As the Rattees pushed the pram away, one of them asked the baby, 'What's that you're wearing?'

'My nappy was dirty,' said the baby. 'So I got a new one! I nicked a tea towel off the radiator.'

'What did you do with the old nappy?'

The baby said, 'I put it on the radiator I got the new one from. They never notice!'

More scams... The baby and the Rattees made up a new scam each week, such as:

Trolley scam where the baby pretended to fall out of his pram just as a lady came out of the supermarket. While the lady was helping the baby back into his pram, the Rattees raided her shopping trolley.

School scam where the Rattees pushed the baby to the school gates first thing in the morning. Any children who put their rucksacks down to play with the baby lost some sandwiches and found rude Rattee words scribbled in their school books.

Cream scam where the baby mixed up potions from the ends of old tubes and bottles he found in the ditch, and the Rattees sold them to ladies with wrinkles and men without hair. The Rattee Potion worked better than the expensive creams you can buy in shops (which don't do much anyway).

Star sign scam where they sold last week's star sign advice from magazines as if it was this week's. The Rattees added new bits like: *"Today you will meet a squirrel that will change your life."* or *"You need to run away and live as a tramp in the woods for a month."* The Rattee Star Guide was always truer and better than the star sign nonsense you find in magazines.

Knicker scam where they waited at the top of the hill for an old lady to toddle past, pulling her little shopping bag on wheels. The Rattees would hold up an old pair of big knickers as she passed and shout,

'Hey! Your knickers just fell off! Want 'em back?' When the lady stopped to check whether her knickers were still on, the baby would tie his pram to her wheelie bag and the Rattees would give the pram a push, and they would zoom down the hill with her bag.

The cat scam

One day the rats and baby were in a pet shop nicking some crunchy cat food for the baby's dinner, when a grey-haired woman with a sweet smile came into the shop. She was pushing an old doll's pram and appeared to be worried about something.

She parked her shabby pram next to the baby's own scruffy buggy. She didn't have a doll in hers, or a baby; she had a large, sleeping cat with ginger fur.

'I need two things,' she said to the shopkeeper. 'Firstly, do you have some tasty food for my kitty? He's stopped eating again.'

'Hello again, Miss Marple,' said the man. 'Why don't you feed him King Kat? My cat loves it.'

'I've tried that,' Miss Marple said. 'Pussykins just turns up his nose at it.'

'Kitty Krunchies?'

'He spits it out all over the floor and then rolls in it. Then he pushes the tins out the window!'

'Fishy Nibbles?'

'The last time I gave him that, he turned his bowl over and jumped up and down on it until it broke!'

The man scratched his head, thinking. 'I suppose you could try giving him some minced beef,' he said.

'He eats that if I cook it,' said Miss Marple. 'But it's

so expensive! Oh well… The other thing I wanted was a couple of goldfish. Mine keep escaping.'

The man went to a large fish tank and used a net to take out two plump goldfish, which he put into a plastic bag with some water. The cat in the pram opened his sleepy eyes and looked lovingly at the bag of goldfish the man was holding. He licked his lips and fell asleep again, purring.

The man said, 'I notice you buy a lot of these. How do they escape?'

'I don't know,' said Miss Marple. 'But I have to replace them because Pussykins loves watching them swim around. He sits by their bowl for *hours*. When they disappear, it puts him off his food all day!'

'Maybe it's herons doing it,' said the man. 'You

know – those tall birds with long beaks. They fly down and take fish from ponds. Some people put a plastic heron by the pond to scare them off.'

'I'll buy a plastic heron then!' the lady exclaimed.

She took out her purse and counted out the right money, which took a long time because she was very short-sighted and had to peer closely at each coin.

Then Miss Marple bustled out of the shop with a plastic heron under her arm and the bag of goldfish tied to a handle of the pram.

The Rattees watched her go and then turned to collect their own pram. But they stopped and stared, because in their pram was a fat, sleeping cat.

'She took the wrong pram!'

'She's got our baby!'

The rats ran down the road after the woman, who was chatting gaily to the ginger shape in the pram:

'So Pussykins, I've got two new fish for you to play with! But you must look after them carefully and make sure they don't disappear like all the others. I expect it *was* the herons getting them... though I don't know how the herons can get in through the living room window, it's awfully small you know...'

The Rattees caught up with them just as the woman was opening her front door, and ran inside with the pram. They were about to speak, when the baby said, 'Shhhhhh!'

'What did you say, Pussykins?' asked Miss Marple.

The baby looked up at the lady and said, '*Meow*!'

'Good kitty!' she said, stroking his ginger hair.

'Purrrrrrr,' said the baby happily.

'I'll go cook you a little mince,' said Miss Marple. She emptied the fish into a round goldfish bowl on a small table. She stood the plastic heron by the table and put the baby on the heron's back.

'What a big kitty you are, Pussykins!' she exclaimed. 'Stay there and watch the pretty fishies while mummy cooks you a lovely dinner!'

'Meow, purr, meow.'

When she had gone, the Rattees whispered to the baby, 'Jump down! And then we'll leg it before she finds out you're not Pussykins!'

The baby pouted. 'No!' he said. 'I want to stay here and have nice dinner and watch the fishies!'

'She'll try to feed you cat food!'

'I *like* cat food!'

A lovely meaty smell wafted through the house. The Rattees put their noses into the air, sniffed deeply and looked at each other.

'I'd like a bit of mince myself,' one said.

'And it'd be nice to have a proper bed,' said the other. 'I'm tired of sleeping under a pile of leaves in the woods.'

'Me too!' said the baby.

They looked around at the comfortable room with its big, old-fashioned settee, a fire hissing in the fireplace and lovely soft cushions everywhere.

'We just gotta keep that cat away,' said the Rattees.

The baby thought for a moment and then shouted, 'Quick! Go lock the cat flap! Then the nice lady will look after us forever!'

So the rats ran into the kitchen and turned the lock on the cat flap while Miss Marple was busy cooking the mince. Then they hid in the cat basket.

The baby had a lovely dinner, and left some mince in his bowl for the rats to gobble up. Then he sat in Miss Marple's lap and purred loudly while she peered at the television. From time to time there was a noise of a cat scratching at the cat flap, and then a cat appeared outside the window, yowling.

'Was that you, Pussykins?' asked Miss Marple.

'*Yowlllll!*' said the baby. Behind them, the Rattees quietly pulled the curtains shut.

Soon Miss Marple said, 'There, there – time to go into your cat basket, I think. Sleep tight, dear kitty!'

'*Mew... purr... snore snore.*'

Pussykins' revenge

A week later, Miss Marple noticed something. 'Pussykins!' she cried. 'Look! The fish are still there!'

'*Meow?*' asked the baby from his cat bed.

'Uh – Purr?' asked the Rattees tucked in beside him.

The lady said, 'This is the first time they've lasted a whole week. The man in the shop was right – it *was* herons eating them!'

'*Purr!*' said the baby.

'Yeah... Meow!' said the Rattees.

Miss Marple knelt beside the cat bed and stroked the baby's head. 'Oh!' she exclaimed. 'What's happened to your fur?'

'*Mew? Prrrrp?*'

'You've lost the fur from your ears! Oh, Pussykins –

poor kitty! I'll have to take you to the Vet's.'

In a moment she had swept the baby up into his pram and wheeled him to the back door. The Rattees chased after them and jumped into the pram just before the door shut.

A fluffy, bedraggled ginger cat was waiting outside the door and was knocked flying by the pram. Then it followed, growling, like a tiger stalking its prey.

Miss Marple marched straight to the Vet's and swept past the girl sitting at the desk.

'Emergency!' she shouted. 'Emergency! *Naked ears!*'

She wheeled the pram into the Vet's room, where the white-coated Vet was reading a book with his feet on the table.

Miss Marple took the baby from the pram and placed him on the table.

'Look!' she exclaimed. 'Pussykins is losing his fur! He's going naked!'

The Vet put down his book and came to see.

'You *silly* woman,' he said sternly to Miss Marple. 'This isn't a cat, it's a baby!'

'Of *course* it's not a baby,' she said. 'Babies don't have tails and whiskers!'

'Ha!' he said. 'Does *this* have a tail and whiskers?' He pointed at the baby wriggling on the table.

'*Meow?*' asked the baby hopefully.

Miss Marple peered at the baby. 'Oh... I see what you mean... Pussykins has turned into a baby!'

'Pah!' said the Vet. 'Take him away – and don't come back! You *silly* woman!'

'I'd better take him to the Doctor's then,' she said.

She gave the baby a big hug and put him back in his pram. 'I've got a *baby!*' she exclaimed. 'I've always wanted one of those!'

'Meow… purrrrrr… goo goo goo?' asked the baby.

.... To the Doctor

She wheeled him out of the Vet's and along the road at great speed. But as she passed through a dark alley, something furry and very, very angry leapt upon the pram and knocked the baby out of it, taking the baby's place.

Miss Marple didn't notice it except to say gaily, 'Now baby, stop that snarling and mewing. You're not a cat any longer, you know!'

The pram clattered along the pavement to the Doctor's. Twice there was a snarl and a hiss and a squeak as a Rattee was thrown out.

Miss Marple ran into the Doctor's surgery shouting, 'Emergency! Emergency! I've had a *baby!*'

People scattered as she charged through the waiting room and into the Doctor's office.

She exclaimed, 'Oh Doctor, I have the most wonderful news! I have a *baby* now!'

She snatched Pussykins from the pram, gave him a hug and placed him proudly on the Doctor's desk.

'Look! Isn't he gorgeous?' she cooed.

The Doctor put on her glasses and had a good look. 'This is definitely a feline quadruped,' she said.

'A what?' asked Miss Marple.

'A *cat!*' said the Doctor.

Miss Marple said, 'Oh no, you're wrong there, Doctor. He *used* to be a cat, but he's a baby now!'

The Doctor said severely, 'Look at this furry face and these whiskers! He is absolutely and incontestably a cat! And *you* are a very silly woman.'

Miss Marple had a closer look. 'Oh!' she said. 'The Vet said I was silly, too! But *he* was the one who told me that Pussykins was a baby! A *human* baby!'

The doctor said primly, 'I've never met the Vet, but he must be *a nitwit, a numskull, a noodle and a ninny* - and you can tell him I said that. Good day, and close the door on your way out!'

.... Back to the Vet

Poor Miss Marple sadly wheeled the pram back to the Vet's, saying to Pussykins, 'It's not *your* fault, kitty. It's the Vet's fault for tricking me into thinking you were a baby.'

As she passed through the dark alley again, there was another fit of hissing and fighting from the pram, and then a furry shape disappeared into the shadows, pursued by two smaller furry shapes.

At the Vet's office, she marched past the girl at the desk again, shouting, 'Emergency! I've been *tricked!*'

She barged into the Vet's room and announced, 'The Doctor says to tell you that you're *a nitwit, a numskull, a noodle and a ninny*. She says you don't know the difference between a cat and a baby!'

The Vet got up from his chair again and looked in the pram. He glared at Miss Marple. 'This *is* a baby, you silly woman,' he said. 'Just look at its cute little baby fingers and its sweet little baby nose!'

'Goo,' said the baby. 'Goo-googlе goo goo!'

Miss Marple said, 'But the *Doctor* says it's a cat. She says it's a cat with a furry face and whiskers!'

The Vet said firmly, 'I've never met the Doctor, but she must be *a dimwit, a dork, a dummy and a dingbat.* And you can tell her I said that! Now get out of my office and leave me alone!'

.... And back to the Doctor again

So Miss Marple took the pram back to the Doctor, after yet another pram battle in the alley. She ran through the waiting room again, shouting:

'Emergency! I've had *another* baby!'

She rushed into the Doctor's office a second time and insisted, 'Pussykins *is* a baby! The Vet says so! *And* he called you some rude names!'

The Doctor looked in the pram. 'This is definitely a cat!' she said angrily. 'What did that Vet call me?'

Miss Marple said brightly, 'He said you were *a dimwit, a dork, a dummy and a dingbat!*'

The Doctor turned a pretty shade of pink. 'That *does* it!' she said. 'I'm going to have words with that Vet!' And she followed Miss Marple along the road to the Vet's surgery.

.... And back the Vet again

As they passed through the dark alley, there was

another tussle in the pram and two snarling shapes rolled away into the shadows, fighting.

Miss Marple and the Doctor marched into the Vet's and past the girl at the desk. Miss Marple shouted:

'Emergency! Big fight coming up!'

They stormed into the Vet's office, where he was still reading a book with his feet on the desk. The Doctor pushed the pram up to him and said angrily:

'So you think you can call me *a dimwit, a dork, a dummy and a dingbat?* Look here! This is *not* a baby!'

The Vet stood up and replied every bit as angrily, 'And you think you can call me *a nitwit, a numskull, a noodle and a ninny?* Look yourself! This is *not* a cat!'

They both looked in the pram.

'You're right,' said the Doctor. 'It *isn't* a cat.'

'You're right,' said the Vet. 'It *isn't* a baby.'

'It's a couple of large rats!' they both exclaimed.

Then the Vet said to the Doctor, 'I'm sorry I called you a dimwit, a dork, a dummy and a dingbat.'

She replied, 'And I'm sorry I called you a nitwit, a numskull, a noodle and a ninny.'

'You're actually rather gorgeous,' said the Vet. 'Would you like to marry me?'

'You're actually very handsome,' said the Doctor. 'Of course I will.'

'But what about me?' asked Miss Marple.

'You're still a silly woman,' they both said. 'And you ought to wear your glasses.'

.... And home again, sadly

So Miss Marple wheeled her pram home quietly, wishing she had either a cat or a baby... and wishing that she *wasn't* silly.

But when she got the pram inside and found her glasses, she discovered to her excitement that she now had:

* One Pussykins
* Two Rattees
* Two worried goldfish
* And one baby.

'I'm not so silly after all!' she exclaimed.

She was so excited that she ran to the shops to buy a special dinner for them all. She left the baby in the cat's bed, the Rattees in the pram and the cat perched on the plastic heron watching the goldfish.

When she got back, she ran into the front room, wondering if it had all been a dream. But it wasn't! They were all still there!

.... Except for the goldfish.

And they all lived together happily ever after, but especially the baby.

Jack and the Cow

The voices

Jack's voice is friendly and always hopeful, as if he's expecting something good to happen soon.

Jack's Mother sounds worried, and you can tell from her voice that not much has gone right for her in the past twelve years. But when she meets the giant, she stands her ground and talks like the feisty teenager she used to be. (Your own mum does this when she goes to school reunions).

The Cow has a low, resonant voice, soft as milk and smooth as butter. She's a gentle and amiable beast, but rather scornful of anyone who doesn't have the right number of legs.

The Chicken is cheeky and cheerful. She copies every creature with a wink and a happy cackle.

The Hat knows how wonderfully wise it is, and sounds unbearably smug: like a rich kid with his own swimming pool.

The Giant speaks slowly and deeply. His voice makes the castle shake and would make your knees tremble. But when he talks to his own bad mother, he's like a little boy again; and when he comes face to face with Jack's mother, his voice goes all soft and soppy.

The Giant's Mother has a gruff, thuggish voice. You can tell that she would happily gobble up any child that came within reach. In fact, she fancies a bite of ***you*** right now. She's writing down your address on her greasy bib... she's setting off across the fields... what's that huge shadow on your bedroom wall?

The story

Once upon a time, there was a boy named Jack who lived with his mother in an old, broken-down cottage at the edge of town.

Jack had never seen his father, but his mother said Jack had been named after him and:

- ♣ He was big and handsome, and a prince....
- ♣ ... but Big Jack's mother, the queen, was a real ogre and wouldn't let him marry her...

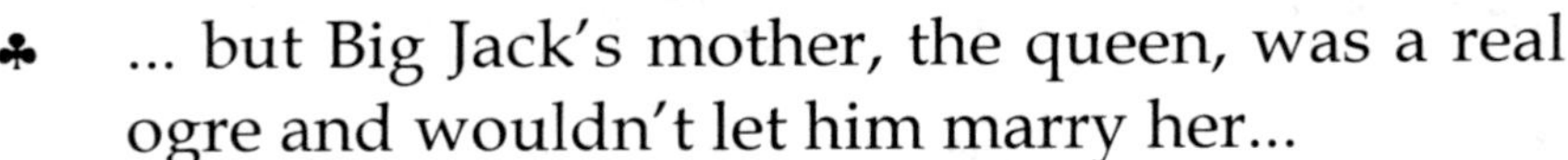

- ♣ ... so Jack's mother had run away, leaving Big Jack a message to come with her as they had agreed, but he hadn't turned up...
- ♣ ... and all men were horrid, horrid, horrid, and Big Jack was the most horrid of them all!

Jack and his mother didn't have very much, except for a cow. One day his mother told him to take the cow to the market and sell it so they could buy food.

'Do I have to go by myself, mother?' he asked.

'What if I meet bandits and robbers?'

'Don't be silly, Jack. You'll be quite safe - you're taller than me now! You're going to be big, like your father,' she sighed, 'like your big, *bad* father...!'

So Jack set off for the market, but sadly, for he liked the cow.

Magic beans

On the way to the market he met a man wearing a big cowboy hat. The man took the hat from his head and pointed at something inside it.

He whispered in a low, slow, lazy cowboy accent, 'Hey, boy – come look at this. I got me some magic beans in this hat. I'll swap you these here beans for that there cow. It's a *real* bargain!'

Jack went and looked in the hat. Inside it was an ordinary looking tin of beans. He said, 'Not on your life – I'm not *stupid*, you know!'

'Oh, yes you are!' the man crowed as he pulled out a gun, which he pointed at Jack. He took the cow and laughed as he led it away:

'Now you won't get the cow OR the beans! Ha! Ha! And by the way, the beans weren't magic anyway! I bought them at a shop this morning!'

Jack began walking home sadly, wondering how he could tell his mother. But a few minutes later he heard something galloping after him.

It was the cow, balancing the tin of beans on her head. She slid to a halt beside Jack and said, 'Good thing you didn't sell me, right?'

'You can talk!'

The cow gave him a puzzled look, 'Yeah... So? You can talk too, and *you've* only got two legs!'

She gave Jack the tin of beans.

'But I don't like beans!' Jack said.

'Don't say that,' said the cow. 'You'll hurt their feelings. Now come on – we need to run off before that man catches us.'

Magic chicken

Jack and the cow turned down a side road and went the long way round to the market. But before they got there, they met another man. This one was wearing a high top hat, the sort you see on magicians.

He took his hat off and made a low bow. He exclaimed in a showy magician's voice:

'In my hat, young man, I have... *a magic chicken*!'

A hen stuck her head up from the hat and said in a bored voice, 'Cluck... Cluck.'

The man said, 'This chicken is amazingly musical!'

The chicken sang, 'Cluck. *Cluckety.* Cluck.'

'This chicken is a wonderful mimic. She can copy any sound in the world!'

The chicken said, 'Woof. Meow. Baa. *Wuw*.'

'"*Wuw*"? What was *that*?' asked Jack.

'Goldfish,' said the man. 'Good, isn't she? Look, young man: I'll trade you this magic chicken for that ugly old cow. You can't lose!'

'Sorry,' said Jack. 'I won't swap a cow for a chicken. I'm not *stupid*, you know!'

The man laughed. 'Oh, yes you are!' he said.

He reached into the hat and brought out a big knife, which he pointed at Jack.

He crowed, 'Now you won't get the chicken OR the cow! And it wasn't a magic chicken anyway – I stole it from a farm this morning!'

He led the cow away, still laughing.

Once again Jack began walking home, looking at his tin of beans and wondering if they might taste all right if he put lots of tomato sauce on them.

A little later, there was the sound of a galloping cow again, this time with the chicken on its back.

'Run!' shouted the cow.

'Moo!' shouted the chicken. 'I mean – move it, kid!'

They turned down a winding road that led through narrow, tangled alleyways into a part of town Jack had never seen before.

'We've got away,' said Jack. 'But now we're lost.'

'I'm twice as lost as you,' said the cow.

'Why?'

'Because you've only got two legs, and *I've* got four.'

'I'm not lost at all,' said the chicken, 'because *I've* got... two wings!'

Magic hat

Just then an amazingly beautiful woman appeared in front of them, clothed in black and wearing a tall, pointy hat with a silver star on it.

'Halt!' she commanded. 'Did I hear that cow talk just now? And the chicken?'

'Moo?' asked the cow.

'Woof?' asked the chicken.

Jack didn't know what to say. She was the most beautiful woman he'd ever seen and was probably a witch - *and* she had a very long sword in her hand.

'Young Jack,' she said (*definitely* a witch!), 'please will you swap me your cow for *this?*'

She swept the hat from her head and held it in front of Jack.

Jack looked inside the hat. 'There's nothing in it,' he said, puzzled.

'Zilch,' said the cow. 'I mean, moooo....'

'Zero,' said the chicken. 'I mean, cluck!'

'It's the *hat* I want to swap!' snapped the amazingly beautiful woman.

'No thanks,' said Jack. 'My mother already has a hat.'

'But this is a *magic* hat!'

'Ooooo!' said the cow. 'I mean, *mooooo*!'

'Abracadabra!' said the chicken. 'I mean, *quack*!'

Jack said, 'Sorry, I still won't swap you the cow for a hat. I'm not *stupid*, you know!'

'Oh, yes you are!' said the amazingly beautiful woman. 'I wasn't going to swap anyway, I was just going to *take* the cow. Like this!'

She waved the enormous sword at Jack and led away the cow with the chicken still on its back. She shouted back over her shoulder:

'By the way, the hat wasn't even magic! I found it in a ditch this morning!'

This time Jack didn't start walking home. He waited a few minutes and then the cow came galloping down the road with the chicken on its back and wearing the magic hat on its head.

'Mooooove it!' called the cow.

'Scram! Skedaddadle! Meow! Woof! Cluck! Whatever!' crowed the chicken from its back.

'I strongly advise you to... RUN!' shouted the hat.

'The hat talks too!' exclaimed Jack.

'Yes,' said the cow. 'And that's really odd.'

'Why? Because it's got no mouth?' asked Jack.

'No. Because it's got no legs... How can you talk with no legs?'

'Slowly!' said the chicken.

'***I'm*** the Magic Hat of Good Ideas,' said the hat proudly. 'Good Ideas don't need legs, just brains.'

It was getting dark now, so Jack went home. His mother was waiting at the door.

She called out, 'Jack, what happened?'

'I'm sorry, mother. A man with a gun stole the cow, but she ran away and came back with this tin of beans. And then a second man with a knife stole the cow, but she came back with this magic singing chicken. And lastly a witch with a big sword stole the cow, but the cow ran away *again* and came back with this talking hat. And the cow talks, too!'

Jack's mother looked at the cow.

The cow said, 'Moo.'

The chicken said. 'Cluck... cluck... cluck.'

The hat said nothing at all.

'Oh, Jack!' sighed his mother. 'How can you make up such stories? You're as bad as your father was! *He* said he loved me, but he was only pretending!'

She took the tin of beans from him. 'At least we have something for supper,' she said.

'I don't like beans,' said Jack sadly.

'We don't have anything else,' she said, 'except of course…' She picked up a knife and went outside to catch the chicken.

The chicken ran about the yard, shouting, 'Don't eat me! I'm tough! I'm full of diseases! I've got swine flu and mad cow disease!'

She pointed the knife at the cow instead.

'Don't even think about it, lady,' said the cow. 'I've got cat flu and mad chicken disease.'

'You *can* talk!' she exclaimed.

'Definitely not,' said the chicken.

'It's just your imagination,' said the cow.

'I didn't hear anything,' said the hat. 'But maybe that's because I don't have any legs.'

So they had beans for supper, and very tough beans they were, too.

'Maybe they were magic beans,' said Jack. 'We should have planted them.'

'I'm the Magic Hat of Good Ideas,' said the hat primly, 'and I agree with you.'

'Meow to that!' said the chicken.

'Whatever,' said the cow, kicking the empty bean tin around the garden until it got stuck in the watery mud and sank from sight.

'I could have been a great footballer,' said the cow with a sigh. 'Twice as good as other footballers. They wouldn't stand a chance with *me* around!'

'I know why!' said Hat of Good Ideas. 'Is it because you've got four legs?'

'No,' said the cow. 'It's because I've got two horns.'

Magic beanstalk... sort of...

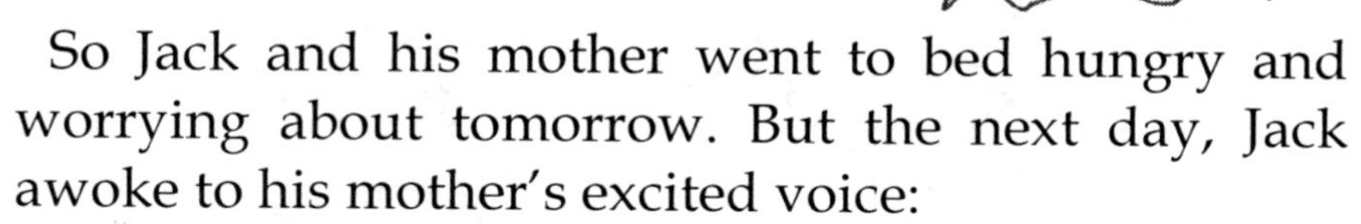

So Jack and his mother went to bed hungry and worrying about tomorrow. But the next day, Jack awoke to his mother's excited voice:

'Jack! Jack! The tin of beans was magic after all! Come see!'

'But mother, we ate all the beans!'

'Not the *beans*, Jack!' she exclaimed. 'The tin!'

When Jack looked out the window, he saw something astonishing: a shining metallic beanstalk that disappeared up into the clouds.

'Where does it go?' he asked.

His mother shook her head sadly. 'I'm afraid it goes to the kingdom of the giants,' she said.

'Do they have lots of gold?' asked Jack eagerly.

'Yes, but the older giants eat children and the men giants are heartless and cruel. Like *all* men!'

'Well, *I'm* not afraid,' said Jack. 'I'm going up to win my fortune!'

With that, he started climbing the silvery vine - which was a messy business because some of the soft, shiny leaves had tomato sauce on them.

As he paused to wipe his hands, he was overtaken by the cow climbing the vine with the hat on its head and the chicken on its back.

'You can climb!' exclaimed Jack.

'So?' said the cow scornfully. 'You can climb too, and *you've* only got two legs!'

They climbed a long way, up through the wet clouds and onto the mossy ground of the giant's kingdom. The chicken hopped off and they all walked up a winding road towards an enormous castle at the top of a hill.

The front door of the castle was twice as high as a normal door - and twice as wide - and twice as open. They crept inside and sneaked from room to room. Finally they found the giant in the kitchen, stirring a great pot while his old mother grumbled from a huge armchair in the far corner.

The giant was twice the height of Jack, with bushy brown hair and beard, and big, scary eyebrows. His hands looked like they could tear you apart as easily as you could tear apart a jam sandwich.

He wasn't as frightening as his mother, though. *She* was an ogress, and was as wide as she was tall.

'Gimme soup!' she growled. 'Want soup NOW!'

'Coming in a moment, dear Mummy,' said the giant. 'It's not warm enough yet.'

'Has it got bones in it?' she asked, sniffing the air. 'I smell *boys'* bones. Yummy!'

'No, Mummy,' he said. 'This is lovely potato soup. There haven't been any boys in our kingdom for fifty years now. You ate them all, remember?'

'I smell bones!' she grumbled.

'Fee fi fo fum
Look out children, here I come!

If you're alive, you'll soon be dead
When I grind your bones to make my bread!
Fee fi fum fo
I smell the bones of a little boy!
Be he alive or be he dead
I'll chew his legs and crunch his head!'

'That's not nice, Mummy,' said the giant, who was testing the soup against the back of his hand to see if it was warm enough.

'Don't care! Want bones!' she whined.

'Fee fum fo fi
Put his brains into a pie!
Make an omelette from his heart!
Bring me Boy and Apple tart!'

The giant took a big bowl of soup across to his mother and started to feed it to her. But she knocked the bowl of soup all over him and then threw the spoon across the kitchen, nearly hitting Jack who was peeking from behind some curtains.

She cried out excitedly, 'Want bones! I can smell a boy! GET ME THAT BOY!'

'Fum fo fi fee
Bring that little boy to me!
I'll give the child an Ogre Hug
And squash him like a little slug!'

The giant tried a second bowl, but his ogre mother threw that over him as well.

'You're upset, Mummy,' he said. 'Why don't you have a rest while I play you some music?''

He went to a high cupboard and took down a small golden harp. He sat down by his mother and began to play it, but she flicked soup at him, shouting:

'You can't play that thing! It's a human harp and your fingers are too big for it! You're rubbish naa naa naa naa naa you're rubbish!'

The giant put the harp on the floor and let it play by itself. However, the only tune it knew was Brahms' lullaby, and it played that over and over again, like a music box, until the ogress threw soup over it.

'I'll just go change my clothes and wash the soup from my hair,' said the giant. 'Try not to get soup on the ceiling, Mummy: you know how hard that is to clean off.'

As soon as he left the room, Jack turned to the others and whispered, 'I want to steal that harp. But I don't see how we can get it without the ogress seeing us.'

'I know!' said the cow. 'Ask her to close her eyes.'

'I know!' said the chicken. 'We'll pretend we're invisible!'

The hat said bossily, '*I'm* the Hat of Good Ideas! Let *me* do the thinking!'

... And the hat explained its plan...

The chicken crept out first and stood beneath the ogress's chair. It started making soothing, musical noises and very soon the ogress's eyes closed. Then Jack crept out and picked up the golden harp. He started to sneak away with it, but the harp began playing its lullaby again and the ogress's eyes flashed open.

She looked at Jack standing before her with the harp in his hands. 'A boy!' she said in a wondering voice. 'Can it be true? Or am I dreaming?'

A little voice sang from beneath her chair:

'You're dreaming, you're dreaming!
No plotting or scheming
Will bring a little boy to you:
It's just a dream, it isn't true!'

The ogress sighed. 'I wish it *was* true,' she said. 'I would *so* like to have a little boy to eat! And this little boy looks so real. Maybe it *is* true, after all.'

The hat whispered something to the cow, and the cow wandered out into the middle of the kitchen.

'A cow as well!' said the ogress. 'Maybe I *am* dreaming!'

'Meow, woof, cock-a-doodle-doo,' said the cow. It did a handstand and waggled its hind legs in the air.

The ogress said, 'Yep – I'm dreaming.' And she shut her eyes again.

Jack and the others ran out of the kitchen and along the corridors leading to the front door. They came into the final hallway and saw the door standing open before them. They galloped, flew and sprinted for it. They were almost there! They were –

SLAM!

The giant stepped out from where he was hiding by the door and looked down at them. He had a big club in his hand, and he looked very angry.

'How did *you* get in here?' he thundered.

Jack said, 'We climbed up a shiny magic beanstalk.'

'A likely story!' said the giant. 'I expect you'll tell me this chicken climbed up it as well.'

The chicken said, 'No. I came up on the cow.'

'I was the best at climbing,' said the cow. 'I've got the most legs, see.'

The giant looked at Jack. 'What's your name, boy?' he asked.

'Jack Smith.'

'Hmmm... Does your father know you're up here?'

'My father doesn't even know I exist,' said Jack.

'Have you got a mother, then? And does *she* know you're here?'

'My mother is Bessie Smith, sir. She tried to stop me but I came anyway.'

The giant looked Jack up and down. 'Tell me - is she thin like you, Jack?' he asked. 'Or is she plump maybe, with rosy cheeks?'

The hat whispered to Jack, 'Careful, Jack! He's trying to find out if she's good to eat!'

Jack said to the giant, 'She *used* to be plump and rosy. But she's much thinner now, because we've been poor for years. That's why I came here to find my fortune.'

'Did you, hey?' asked the giant. 'This is a dangerous place for boys. If my old mother catches you, she'll gobble you up like a sausage!'

'I'm not afraid,' said Jack.

'That's good!' said the giant. 'Because I won't let you go unless you promise to return. And if you *don't* promise, I'll feed all three of you to my old mother, one piece at a time!'

'I promise,' said Jack.

'Good boy. All you have to do is this: you must come back here within a month, and you must bring your lovely, plump, rosy-cheeked mother with you.'

'I'll try,' said Jack.

'Try?' roared the giant. 'You'll have to do better than that! In the meantime, the chicken stays here. She can sing to my mother and keep her quiet.'

'I'll come back as soon as I can,' Jack promised.

'You can take the harp,' said the giant. 'It's no use to me. And here's a gold coin. You can buy food with it until you return.' He gave Jack a gold coin big enough to buy food for a whole month.

Just then the ogress woke and started shouting from the kitchen, 'I can smell him! It's not a dream! Bring me the boy! Bring me bone soup NOW!'

'Uh-oh,' said the giant. 'She's getting upset. I'll have to give her something to keep her quiet.' He looked at the chicken and the cow.

'I'm tough,' said the chicken. 'And very small. And I haven't washed for *weeks*.'

'I'm invisible,' said the cow. 'So she won't be able to taste me. And besides, it's against the rules to eat anything with four legs.'

'What rules?' asked the giant.

'*My* rules,' said the cow.

'Want bone soup!' came the shout from the kitchen again, with the sound of someone heavy trying to get up from a chair.

The hat said hurriedly, 'It's my job to have ideas, and I've just had one. Why don't you saw off one of the cow's horns? That won't hurt the cow, and you can grind up the horn to put in your mother's soup.'

'I'll look silly with only one horn,' said the cow. '*That's* against the rules, too.'

'You'd look even sillier without a *head!*' growled the giant, 'and that's the only other option.'

So he got out a saw and removed one of the cow's horns. Then Jack and the cow went back down to the ground, but the chicken stayed and sang to the ogress while she ate cow horn soup and imagined it was boy bone soup instead.

Down to earth

When Jack and the cow and the hat got to the bottom of the beanstalk, Jack's mother was waiting for them. She threw her arms around Jack.

'Oh Jack!' she cried. 'I was so worried for you! Are you all right?'

'Yes, mother,' said Jack. 'The giant treated us very kindly –'

'- No he didn't!' grumbled the cow.

Jack added, '- and he gave me this golden harp.'

Jack's mother gasped, then exclaimed, 'That was your father's harp!' And then she fainted.

'Uh-oh,' said the Hat of Good Ideas. 'Now we know what happened to your father.'

'Chopped to pieces,' said the cow.

'Put in a pot with carrots and onions,' said the hat.

'Boiled for an hour?' suggested the cow.

'I agree,' said the hat. 'And then simmered over a low heat, without a lid, for two hours longer.'

'And served with brown bread and butter.'

'And a nice glass of red wine,' said the hat.

The cow looked at Jack. 'Our condolences about your father, Jack,' he said. 'But at least he made a good soup.'

Jack's mother came to herself and sat up. 'You're talking about soup?' she asked faintly. 'I'm sorry, Jack, but we've nothing left to make soup with.'

'That's all right, mother,' said Jack. 'I have this gold coin the giant gave me. We can buy some food now!'

'That's wonderful, Jack!' said his mother. 'But is that all the giant sent back with you? The harp and one little coin? Nothing more?'

'Yes, mother. That's all.'

'Then he's a very, very horrid giant and you must never talk about him again!'

As they set off for the market, Jack's mother looked at the little group and said, 'Something's missing.'

'The chicken,' said Jack. 'We left the chicken behind to sing to the giant's mother.'

They walked a bit further and she stopped again. 'Something else is missing,' she said. She looked at the cow, who was wearing the hat over the horn that wasn't there.

'Nothing's missing at all,' said the cow, offended.

'But your right horn! Where is it?'

'Under the hat of course,' said the cow. 'It's an Invisibility Hat, so you can't see the horn beneath it.'

'You look silly with only one horn,' she said.

'*You* look silly with only two legs!' snorted the cow.

A month passed, and they had run out of money again. Jack said to the cow and the hat:

'I promised the giant I would return with my mother. But she won't even talk about the giant. She just plays my father's harp all day and cries when I try to speak to her.'

'I know what to do! Don't go back,' suggested the cow.

'I have to! I promised!' said Jack.

'Then *do* go back,' the cow said.

'I can't, because I promised to take my mother, and she won't go!'

'Then… *don't* go back,' said the cow.

'But I have to!'

'Then *do* go back,' said the cow.

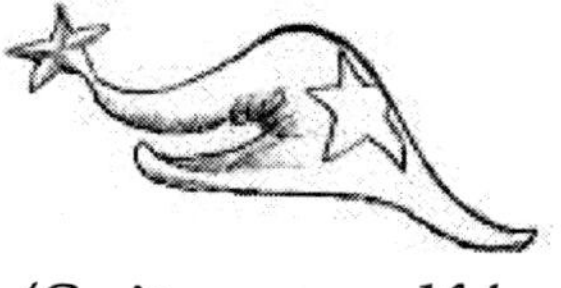

'Wait a minute!' cried the Hat of Good Ideas. 'Let *me* do the thinking for this!'

'Suit yourself,' said the cow grumpily. 'I was doing all right, I thought.'

The hat said, 'It's simple, Jack. You go back and steal the giant's teeth, and the ogress's teeth as well. Then they can't eat your mother!'

'That's a *silly* idea,' said the cow. 'You can't steal

teeth, unless you're the Tooth Fairy.'

'Okay,' said the hat. 'Then I have another clever plan: tell the giant he'll have to eat *you* instead!'

The cow said scornfully, 'That's an even sillier idea. I don't want to be eaten!'

'Not *you*,' said the hat. 'I was talking to Jack!'

'Oh,' said the cow. 'Eating *Jack*, you meant... I've changed my mind then. It's a *brilliant* idea!'

'But I don't want to be eaten,' Jack complained.

'You won't have to,' said the hat. 'Just challenge the giant to a duel.'

'But he's bigger than I am!' said Jack.

'Leave it to me,' said the hat smugly. 'I have a good idea about that, too…'

The good idea

So they climbed again to the giant's kingdom and ran to the great castle on the hill. They could hear the ogress shouting before they reached it, and they could guess what she was shouting about.

The door was open as before and the giant was feeding soup to his old mother while the chicken crooned a gentle lunchtime song from beneath her chair (that was the only place safe from being splattered with soup).

'Boy! I smell boy!' came her harsh voice. 'Put him in the soup NOW!'

'Fee fi fo fum
I shall bite him on the bum!
Fo fee fum fi
I'll suck out his little eye!'

'Calm down, Mummy,' said the giant. 'I expect it's just the wind blowing up from the land of the humans.'

'Ahhh!' she cackled. 'Human Land! I want to go there for my holidays this year! I can sit on the beach with my spade and bucket, and gnaw on boys' bones all day long!'

'Fum fee fi fo
To the seaside I will go!
Fi fo fum fee
I'll bite the swimmers in the sea!'

The giant left the ogress raving in her chair and flicking soup all around the room. He came through to the hallway and met Jack and the cow (with the magic hat sitting lopsided on its head).

'Where's your mother?' he boomed at Jack.

'I'm sorry sir, but I can't ask her,' said Jack. 'She sits around all day playing that harp and cries when I try to explain.'

'What's that to me?' demanded the giant angrily. 'We had a deal!'

'I can't do it,' said Jack. 'So I've come to challenge you to a duel instead. If *I* win, you let us all go back and never bother us again. If *you* win, you can eat me instead of my mother.'

'Eat you? Eat your mother?' roared the giant. 'What

are you talking about?!! No, Jack: if I win the duel, you'll go back and bring your mother to me, by hook or by crook. Do you agree?'

The hat whispered to Jack, 'Agree with him! You can't lose the duel – trust me!'

'I agree,' said Jack glumly.

'Then choose your weapon!' shouted the giant. 'Swords? Axes? Sledgehammers?'

'No,' said the hat. 'We choose… jigsaw puzzles!'

At this, the cow lifted the hat from its head, and there beneath it were two boxes containing the same jigsaw puzzle in each.

The cow counted, '3–2-1–Mooo!' and Jack and the giant emptied out their boxes onto the floor at the same time.

They began putting the pieces together, which was very hard for the giant because the hat had chosen a puzzle with very tiny pieces, and the giant's big fingers couldn't pick them up easily.

Soon Jack was half way done, but the giant had only ten pieces put together.

Then the cow sneezed.

Now Jack had only three pieces fitted, and half his puzzle was under the sofa. Jack worked away feverishly to catch up and soon had only ten pieces left, while the giant was only halfway through.

Then a big bowl of soup came flying out of the kitchen and landed on Jack's jigsaw.

Now half his pieces were coated with soup, and the rest were under the sofa again. Jack worked as fast as he could and soon he had five pieces left. But the giant was puzzling over his very last piece, turning it this way and that, and dropping it each time he tried to move it into place.

Jack had four pieces left, three, two…

'I think I'm going to sneeze again,' said the cow.

'Sneeze in the other direction,' suggested the hat. 'Towards the giant!'

'Why didn't *I* think of that?' asked the cow. 'Why-wh-wh-wh-y-y-y-y-y whssssssh!'

The cow sneezed and blew the last piece away from the giant's fingers - and it flew up into the air, flipped over twice, spun once and landed in the middle of the jigsaw, in exactly the right place.

'I won!' shouted the giant. 'Hooray! I won!' And he did a great stomping dance in the hallway, making the floor shake.

Jack was sitting on the floor with one piece – his last piece – still in his hand. 'Yes, you won,' he said sadly. 'So I guess I'll have to do what we agreed.'

'Yes!' exclaimed the giant. 'And if you don't keep your word this time, then I'll do something really horrible: I'll let my old mother loose and send her down to Human Land. And you know what she'll do if she gets there…'

Jack gulped. He knew.

Double Jack

But just then, there was a banging on the heavy door, followed by the voice of Jack's mother.

'Jack!' she was shouting. 'Jack! Open this door *right now!* Jack! I know you're in there!'

The giant pulled the door open, and there on the doorstep was Jack's mother glaring in at them, with her hands firmly on her hips.

'Jack?' she shouted. 'Jack??!!'

'I'm here!' Jack said from behind the giant. 'No need to shout!'

At that very moment, the giant also said, 'I'm here! No need to shout!'

'Jack!' she shouted again. 'I've had *enough* of this!'

'What?' asked the giant.

'What?' asked Jack.

She raged, 'I've waited twelve years – twelve years, do you hear me? – and not a *word* from you!'

'What?' asked the giant.

'What?' asked Jack.

'Golden coins?' she asked angrily. 'What do *I* care for golden coins? And you even sent back the golden harp I gave you! Jack, how *could* you?'

'I'm sorry,' said the giant, hanging his head.

'What?' asked Jack.

'Just a minute,' said the hat. '*I'm* the Hat of Good Ideas and I've just figured it out...'

'Dah dah *dah-**dah**-dah-dah-dah* ***Dah*** *dah-dah* ***dah*** *dah-dah* ***dah**!'* exclaimed the chicken, singing a Wedding March.

'Jack,' said Jack's mother. 'Meet Jack. Your father.'

'Oh,' said Jack.

'Oh,' said the giant.

'Oh?' stormed Jack's mother. 'Twelve years ago you abandoned me, and all you can say is "Oh"?'

'I didn't know where you were,' said the giant. 'I thought you just didn't want to see me again.'

'I left you a message, as we agreed!' said Jack's mother. 'I put it on your pillow!'

'I never saw it,' said the giant, shaking his head in puzzlement.

'I don't believe you!' said Jack's mother. 'Who else would have taken the message?'

Just then a voice boomed from the kitchen:

'With a fum and a fi and a fee and a fo
Off to human land I go!
With a fi and a fo and a fum and a fee
Look out children, 'cause I'm free!'

The ogress came hurtling past them, wearing an old apron and a very messy bib. The giant tried to stop her, but slipped in some soup and landed flat on his back.

Then because she was so fat, the ogress got stuck in the door. But she pushed and grunted and the door frame splintered, and off she ran down the path, leaving part of her apron behind her.

Jack's mother pointed at something. 'What's that?' she cried. 'What's in her apron pocket?'

A piece of paper was sticking out of one ripped pocket. It was old and stained with countless splashes of soup, but when Jack unfolded it they could still make out the words:

See you at the bottom of the hill at midnight.
If you love me, be there! Bessie XXX

'Oh...' said the giant. '*Mummy* took it. Naughty Mummy...'

Then he looked out the door and saw how far his mother had run already.

'We've got to stop her!' he shouted. 'She'll eat all the children!'

Soon they were running along the pathway and gaining on the ogress. She looked over her shoulder and saw them coming, and put on an amazing burst of speed for an old ogress. She got to the top of the beanstalk before them and started climbing

down, shouting excitedly, 'Little boys! Little girls! Lots and lots of BONES!'.

The giant ran to the edge and was about to climb down as well, when…

… when…

… when…

… there was a great rending, cracking noise as the beanstalk collapsed under the ogress's weight…

… and another enormous crashing, crunching noise as the ogress landed on Jack's house…

… and a final smashing, booming, crushing noise as the house collapsed on top of the ogress and then she and the house and the garden disappeared into a big hole in the ground.

'Poor Mummy,' said the giant, with a great tear rolling down his face. 'I'll miss her, even though she *was* rather badly behaved when it came to eating children.'

'I won't miss her at all,' said Jack's mother. 'She was a real ogre!'

'*And* she owes me a horn,' said the cow.

'She would have been a happier woman if she'd had a good hat,' said the Hat of Good Ideas.

'She would have been a happier woman if she'd had some more legs,' said the cow.

'Woof. Meow. Baa. Cluck. *Wuw!*' said the chicken. 'Whatever!'

'And they all lived happily ever after,' said Jack.

And he was right.

The Gorilla and the Hunter

The voices

Ernest the Gorilla is clever, cool and rather geeky. He talks in a lively manner – as if he's selling bananas on a market stall. He's always polite and finds life very amusing… even when it's also very dangerous.

Big Bob the Hunter is a big, important man with a big, important-sounding American voice. He's used to people calling him "Sir" all the time, even his own family. He likes big guns and big hats. He doesn't like children, and thinks his own grandchildren are crazy. He may be right about that…

The **King of the Jungle** speaks with a posh accent. He's not the cleverest animal you'll ever meet, and can get quite agitated about the tiniest thing. If you have a Great-Uncle Charles who wears a moustache and was an Officer in some war long ago, that's just what the Lion sounds like.

The **Lion's Wife** – the lioness – is a calm, intelligent lady who puts up with a lot.

The **Lion's family** really like their dad but also laugh at him a lot, because he's so funny when he gets annoyed.

The **Snake** has a lovely voice – musical, clear, sweet and a bit hypnotic in that scary snake way. You just know that if you listen to her for a few minutes, you'll fall asleep and then wake to find yourself inside a long, dark tunnel… But you can tell from the slightly wondering and hopeful tone of her voice that she's also just a little gullible, because she would SO love for someone to like her and believe in her.

The story

One day, Big Bob the hunter came to the jungle. Now, Big Bob already had:

- Coat hooks made from the antlers of a reindeer
- A letter opener which was a tiger's tooth
- A doorbell pull which was the tail of a yak
- And best of all, he had a waste-paper bin made from an elephant's foot.

But these weren't enough for Big Bob. He wanted a lion skin rug to put in front of his fireplace, and so he had come to the jungle to shoot a lion.

Not long after dawn, he drove to the edge of a grassy clearing and parked his jeep in the shade of some trees. He loaded his big lion guns and stood them on the seat beside him. He took his pistol out of his shoulder holster and placed it on his lap.

It was very hot, so he opened the front windows.

Then he pulled his jungle hat over his eyes and had a little doze.

A small gorilla named Ernest was on his way to school. If you've read a book called *Wicked Tales*, you'll know that Ernest often finds it difficult to get to school on time. Today was no different.

Ernest stopped when he saw the hunter's jeep. 'I've always wanted to drive one of those!' he exclaimed.

He climbed inside and looked around. Big Bob was asleep, so Ernest did his best to be quiet.

There was a plastic box full of cheese and tomato sandwiches. Ernest had never tried those, so he ate them but left the bread. And being a friendly gorilla, he hopped out of the jeep and went to find something tasty for the hunter to eat as well.

He found some lovely beetle grubs inside a rotten log, and some termites in a nest. He took them back to the jeep and put them inside the slices of bread.

He was thirsty now, so he drank the flask of water the hunter had brought. But then he thought how sad the hunter would be when he woke up and found there was nothing to drink: so he took the flask down to the river and filled it with water.

A few minnows got inside the flask with the water,

so he added some water weed for them to nibble and a few water snails for them to play with.

The hunter was still snoring, so Ernest played some games while waiting for him to wake up.

Banana game: He filled the barrel of one of the guns with banana. This was rather a sticky game, and Ernest had to wipe the gun mostly clean with the hunter's handkerchief, which he managed to put back in Big Bob's pocket without waking him.

Slug game: He tried to fit as many slugs as possible into a second gun. This was much harder, because the slugs kept trying to climb out again. He wedged them in with a very fat slug, number one hundred and twenty.

Worm game: He wondered whether worms would work better, but found that he could only get eighty-four worms into the third gun. Then he played with the tiny telescopes that were on the top of each gun and turned two of them the wrong way around.

Moth game: He picked up Big Bob's pistol and tried to take it to pieces. All the bullets fell out, so he threw them out the window and replaced them with some moths that were having a doze on a tree trunk.

Beetle races: Some of his gorilla friends turned up, and they had upside-down beetle races across the ceiling of the jeep. The beetles kept falling off and some of them went down the neck of Big Bob's shirt, but the snoring hunter didn't seem to mind.

Flick-golf: Then they invented the best game ever. They picked some small berries and played flick-golf with them. Big Bob's open mouth was the hole, but you got double points if you flicked a berry into his ear or up his nose.

Finally, one of the berries went down the hunter's throat the wrong way. Big Bob coughed and sat up suddenly, pulling his hat back from his eyes.

'Who? What?' he muttered dozily.

He looked around and saw Ernest and his friends sitting beside him.

Ernest smiled at Big Bob. 'Have a banana,' he said, holding one out to him.

But Big Bob didn't speak gorilla language. He grabbed his pistol and pointed it at the gorillas. They all ran away, except for Ernest who wasn't afraid of anything.

Big Bob laughed quietly. 'Okay, little gorilla,' he said. 'You're gonna die! And *then* I'm gonna stick your head on my library wall!'

He pulled the trigger.

There was a click, and then a scurrying noise along the barrel of the gun. A moth looked out and flew away. Big Bob pulled the trigger five times more. Five more moths fluttered out in turn.

Ernest patted the hunter on the head to show he was friendly and gave him a big smile, showing all his teeth.

'Can I drive your car?' he asked.

Big Bob panicked and jumped out of the jeep, leaving the driver's seat empty.

'Thanks!' shouted Ernest. He moved into the driver's seat and started turning the wheel left and right, making car noises and beeping the horn.

'Look at me!' he shouted. 'I'm driving the car! Neeeeeowwwww! Neeeeowwww!'

The hunter appeared at the other side of the car, with the sticky banana-filled gun pointed at Ernest. He looked very angry.

'Oh,' said Ernest. 'All right, Mr Grumpy. I've got to go to school anyway.' He jumped out of the window and ran off into the jungle.

Snakesong

Unfortunately, he ran straight into a snake, which wrapped itself around him and exclaimed:

'Yesssss! A tasssssty little sssssnack for my break-fassssst!'

But Ernest was too clever to be caught by a snake, even a poisonous lady snake.

'Pardon?' he asked. 'What did you say?'

'I sssssssaid you're a tassssty little sssssnack!' she hissed angrily.

'Sorry,' said Ernest. 'I can't understand you. That's a real shame, because you've got a lovely voice.'

'I have?' asked the snake.

'A *superb* voice,' said Ernest. 'I bet you can really sing up a storm!'

'Me? Sssssssssing up a sssssstorm? Sssssssssssuperb voicccccce?'

'Yes, you!' said Ernest. 'I can tell because – well, I expect you already know who I am.'

'No...' said the snake.

Ernest said, 'I'm Ernesto Caruso, the world famous jungle opera singer.'

'Opera... sssssssinger?'

'Yes, that's me. And I can tell that your voice is

truly something special. Go on – sing me a song.'

The snake thought a minute and sang:

'All thingssss bright and beautiful
All creaturessssssssss great and ssssssmalll
All thingsssssssssss wisssssse and wonderful
The Lord God made them all!'

Ernest nodded his head in time to the music. 'Such rhythm! Such feeling!' he exclaimed. 'It's a shame I can't be your singing coach, because I could teach you to get rid of all those hisses. Then your voice would really be top of the tree.'

'Sssssinging coach? To teach me to sssssing?'

'Yes, that's right. But if you're going to eat me, I suppose I won't be around to give you lessons…'

The snake said, 'I was jussssst teassssing about eating you. My little joke, you know.' And she loosened her coils so that Ernest could wriggle free.

'Come on, then!' said Ernest.

'Where to?'

'We'll go to my recording studio. I keep it near that grassy clearing where the lions sleep.' And Ernest led the snake back to the hunter's jeep.

Big Bob the hunter was peering out of the driver's window with his binoculars. The gorilla and the snake climbed in through the window on the passenger's side, and Ernest made signs for the snake to be quiet.

'This is my studio manager,' Ernest whispered. 'He's a brilliant singing coach, too. He's busy, so we'll wait a bit.'

Not far off, the lion family were waking up. The hunter saw the king of the jungle rise and shake himself, giving a great roar.

To the hunter, the roar was quite scary. But Ernest knew that the lion was shouting:

'Where's my hairbrush? Who – has – borrowed – my – hairbrush – without – asking???!!'

Through his binoculars, the hunter followed the lion's progress as he walked to and fro amongst his family, roaring a bit, biffing one with his left paw and boffing another with his right.

'Was it you?' he growled. 'Did you take it? I know I left it under that bush! One of you has *moved* it!'

The lioness roared in turn, and the hunter watched her walk over to the lion.

'You've got it stuck in your mane again!' she said, though all Big Bob heard was *'Growl! Roar!'*

The lion roared again, very angrily. 'Someone put it there!' he insisted. 'One of the children has been playing tricks on me! On *me*, the king of the beasts! I don't get *any* respect!' And he stormed off in a very sulky mood towards the trees where the jeep stood.

The hunter kept his binoculars fixed on the lion while reaching for one of his guns on the seat beside him. Ernest passed him the banana gun.

'Thanks,' said Big Bob. He put the rifle to his shoulder and looked through the telescopic sight. The lion looked very small, and smeary. The hunter wiped his eyes and looked again. The lion still looked small and smeary. But he couldn't be far away now. The hunter squeezed the trigger.

There was a loud ***bang***.

And a loud ***SQUELCH***.

The hunter looked up from the gun. The lion was still there, but he had changed. He seemed to have put styling gel all over his fur. And he wasn't happy. He was roaring again.

'Look what you've done!' he was shouting. 'You *naughty* children! Covered me with banana!' He turned and ran back to his family, cuffed a few more of them, then stalked away again. His children all growled with laughter, and his wife was looking at him in a very puzzled manner.

The hunter reached out his hand for his second gun. 'Thanks,' he said as it was passed to him.

He focussed the sight on the lion, who looked the

right size this time but still didn't look the right shape. The hunter pulled the trigger.

Bang!

SQUIDGE!

And now the lion was jumping up and down with rage as his children roared with laughter at his new coat of long, dazed worms stuck to the banana goo.

The hunter reached for the third gun.

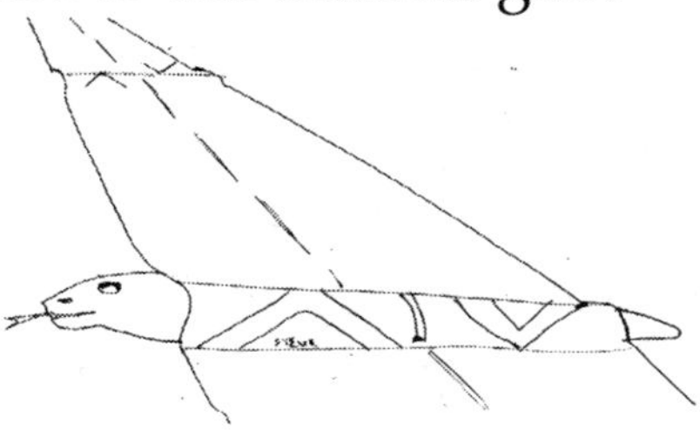

'Thanks.'

Bang!

SLURP!

The lion snarled at his family: '*Who* did that? Which one of you threw exploding slugs at me? Own up now, or you'll *really* be in trouble!' But no one could answer because the lioness and the lion cubs were all rolling about on the ground, helpless with laughter.

The lioness pointed towards the trees, and the lion peered into the shadows there. Then he gave a great roar and started walking towards the hunter's jeep.

The hunter began to shake with fear, and held out his hand for another gun.

Ernest handed him the snake.

'Thank you.'

The hunter pointed the snake at the lion. The snake kept drooping down, and he had to keep pulling its head up straight.

The lion came closer and closer. The hunter was trembling all over now. He felt for the trigger.... He felt for... *Where had the trigger gone?*

The lion was standing just outside the jeep now,

roaring his loudest.

'*You* did it!' he snarled. '*You* stole my hairbrush!'

'What?' asked Big Bob the hunter.

For the first time in his life, he understood what an animal was saying: and it was saying that he had stolen its hairbrush.

He stared at the lion. The lion was covered in slugs, worms and mashed banana. The hunter pointed the snake at it.

'I've got you now, lion!' he shouted. 'This time you won't get away!'

'Ha!' growled the lion. 'That snake's not loaded.'

'Of course it is!' insisted the hunter. 'I loaded it myself. I – *What did you say?*'

'You've made me look foolish in front of the children!' sulked the lion. 'First you stole my hairbrush, then you covered me with this mess, and now you're pointing an unloaded snake at me!'

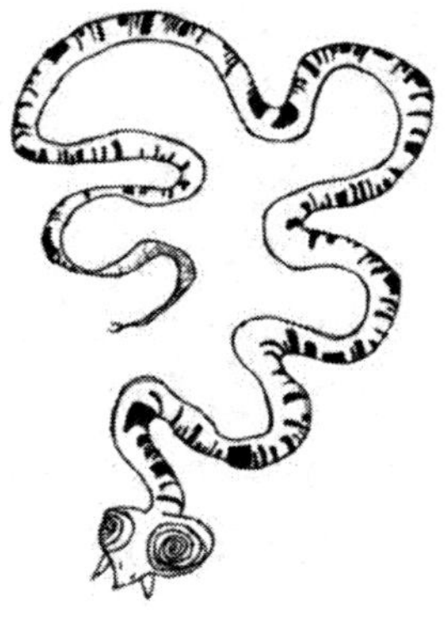

Big Bob the hunter looked down at the snake. The snake looked up at Big Bob.

'Are you the sssssstudio manager?' asked the snake hopefully. 'I've come for the sssssinging lesssssonsss!'

Big Bob screamed and dropped the snake. This was terrible. For the *second* time in his life, he understood what an animal was saying, and it was saying that it had come to him for singing lessons.

'A snake!' he shouted. 'A poisonous, talking snake!'

'No! A poisssonous, SSSSSINGING ssssnake!' the snake insisted.

Big Bob started the jeep and began to drive away. But a small gorilla hopped onto his lap and began turning the steering wheel this way and that, beeping the horn and shouting,

'I'm driving the jeep! Look at me driving! Yayyyyyy! NEEOWWWWW!'

The jeep went round and round in crazy circles as the gorilla and the hunter fought for control of the steering wheel. Finally, the jeep ran into a tree and stopped.

The lion jumped onto the roof of the jeep and scratched it with his claws, roaring and calling out proudly to his family:

'I've caught the hunter! Look, I'm paying him back for his tricks! Come here and you can each have a little piece of him!'

The snake slid into the passenger's side again and began singing to the hunter:

'Each little flower that openssssss,
Each little bird that sssssingsssss,
He made their glowing coloursssss,
He made their tiny wingsssss!'

Ernest said to the hunter, 'She's got great rhythm, don't you think? She's just got to get that hissing under control, and then she'll be the Mamba Mama of Snake Singers, right?'

Big Bob the hunter began to cry. On one side of him, a poisonous snake was singing Sunday school songs. On the other, a hungry-looking family of lions were gathering and licking their lips. And in his lap, a small gorilla was offering him a sandwich.

'Here,' said Ernest. 'I expect you're hungry now.'

Big Bob took the sandwich. The animals watched him eat it.

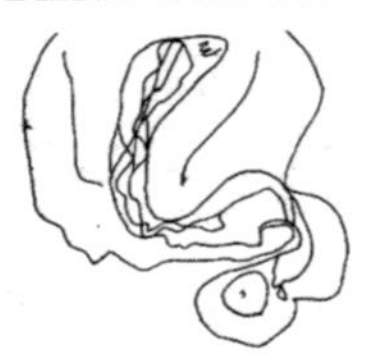

'The purple-headed mountain,
The river running by,
The ssssunssssset and the morning,
That brightensss up the ssssky!'

'*Sky*,' said Ernest to the snake. 'Only one S. The problem is that you keep sticking your tongue out. Touch the tip of your tongue to the roof of your mouth, then drop it back again. That's how you make a short S.'

'Ssssky,' said the snake. 'Ssky? Sky!'

'That's better!' roared the lion from the other side of the jeep.

One of the lion cubs asked, 'When's breakfast?'

'Do we get to eat the hunter now?' asked another.

'I get first bite!' said the lion. '*I* caught him!'

The lioness said calmly, 'Remember not to play with your food, children.'

The hunter could understand what all the animals were saying now, but he wasn't enjoying it much...

'Would you like another sandwich?' Ernest asked.

The hunter took a bite from the new sandwich.

'Tastes funny,' he said.

'That's the one with termites in it.'

The hunter suddenly felt very sick. He looked inside his sandwich, and some very unhappy termites looked back at him.

'What was in the first one I ate?' he groaned.

'Beetle grubs,' said Ernest. 'They're good for you. Lots of vitamins, my mum says.'

'I'm going to be sick!' the hunter gasped. 'I need water!'

'Here you are!' said Ernest, passing him the flask.

'The cold wind in the winter,
The pleasant summer sun,
The ripe fruits in the garden,
He made them every one!'

'Not a single hiss!' Ernest said. 'Well done!'

'You did it!' shouted the lion. 'Jolly good!'

'It was easy,' said the snake. *'I have a good teacher, you see: Ernesto Caruso the jungle opera singer!'*

The hunter coughed up a lot of water. 'This – is - disgusting!' he choked out.

'Oh! Did you swallow the minnows?' asked Ernest.

The lioness said kindly to the hunter, 'You've got to keep your teeth clenched and suck the water through them. That way, you can strain out the minnows and the water snails.'

'He's not very bright,' said one of the lion cubs.

'But I expect he's *very* tasssssty!' said the snake. 'I mean, tasty!'

'Yes!' the animals all shouted. 'TASTY!'

Big Bob began to cry again. 'Please let me go,' he begged.

'Not yet,' said Ernest. 'I have a better idea….'

So they opened the Jungle Zoo. It had only one animal in it, a hunter dressed in his underpants. But all the jungle animals came to see him.

The lion was the zookeeper, and he would take parties on a tour of the zoo, explaining how he had captured the Dangerous Hunter single-handed after a whole day of fighting.

His children would whisper a different story, and everyone would laugh.

The hunter was well looked after, but there were many things about the zoo that he didn't like.

- For instance, there was a sign up that said ***Do Not Feed the Hunter,*** but the visitors always threw Big Bob nice things to eat, such as fat, juicy spiders or rotten bits of fish.
- Nosy animals watched him when he went to the toilet.
- Unkind animals laughed at him.
- Silly animals tried to make him dance to jungle music.
- Hungry animals discussed loudly which bits

they would eat first - and said how easy it would be to break into the zoo after dark and have a nibble…

- And when no one was looking, the naughtier young animals would poke the hunter with sticks and call him rude names.

After a month, they let Big Bob get into his battered jeep and drive home. They'd become very fond of him and were sad to see him go. However, they kept some things to remember him by.

... So if ever you visit the jungle, ask to be taken to the Big Bob Museum. There you can see Big Bob's guns and his water flask, his sandwich box, the cage he stayed in, his hat, clothes and pistol holster…

… And they use one of his boots as a waste-paper bin!

The Bad Tooth Fairy

The voices

The Bad Tooth Fairy has a charming voice that makes you want to giggle. She's off the wall, scatty, full of fun and impossibly naughty. She could nick your fairy wand and sell it to the goblins, and you would just laugh when she told you what she'd done.

Amelia talks like the posh, pompous, selfish brat she is. She knows she's too important to listen to you.... **Her mother** is even worse: if you said hello to her, she would just give you a dirty look.

Amelia's father is a man of few words, mostly because Amelia and her mother don't let him say much. He doesn't like having yoghurt and cherry cola thrown at him, but puts up with it because he's a gentle and patient man. Please be kind to him: he can't help being an accountant.

The Fairy Inspector can sound rather severe at times, like your teacher. However, you can tell from his voice that he's friendly and rather shy... and that he quite likes the Bad Tooth Fairy, even when she's being incredibly naughty.

The Toenail Fairy looks a bit like a troll and talks like one too: low and slow and a little puzzled. He may be the stupidest fairy you'll ever meet, but he's also the nicest. You may have seen him at the seaside selling tasty crisps and sweets from a little stall, or sitting on the beach with his toes in the water, licking an ice cream and smiling at everyone.

Barbarella sounds like a lively Russian doll. For her, life is very simple: shoes, hairstyle, handbags, nail polish, shiny gun.

The story

First Bite: The Bad Fairy

Once upon a time there was a Bad Fairy. She failed all her exams at fairy primary school and annoyed the good fairies by nicking their wands at play time.

Fairies have to go out to work when they've finished primary school, but the Bad Fairy didn't want to do any work, so she stayed home watching Goblin TV all day and then went out to Troll Dances all night. Sadly, she soon ran out of the fairy money she'd saved.

Where did the Bad Fairy's money come from? From selling the wands she'd nicked!

So she ended up as a Tooth Fairy, which is almost the worst job in the world. Tooth Fairies have to take teeth of all sorts – pretty pearly ones, dirty slimy ones and nasty rotten ones. While they're rooting about under pillows, they get breathed on by children who haven't brushed their teeth and coughed upon by children with stinking colds.

Then they have to leave some money under the pillow. Good fairies who have passed their Tooth Exams use a magic spell to make pretend human money, which looks exactly like real money except that the head on it is smiling. The Bad Tooth Fairy could never remember the spell, so she usually nicked a few coins from the mother's purse.

At least being a Tooth Fairy is only the second worst job. The *very* worst job is being a Toenail Fairy. But more about the Toenail Fairy later....

The Bad Tooth Fairy was put in charge of all the children in London with names that started with an "A". Each evening she was given a Tooth List, which showed her every tooth that had fallen out that day.

This Sunday, it took her an hour to find the list because she was the second most untidy fairy in the world (the most untidy was a fairy called Magik Alice, but that's another story).

She found the list under the TV. She found the TV under the cat's bed. She found the cat's bed behind the laundry basket, which was full of books.

She read the list carefully.

'Oh, Fairy Flip-Flops!!' she shouted at the list. 'Not HER again!'

The fairy spread her wings and flew off in a very bad temper to the bedroom of one of the nastiest children in England, little Amelia Jane Argosy-Smythe.

Amelia was a minor royal person – a sort of second-hand princess. She was also the second snobbiest person in the world...

... And the snobbiest of *all* was her mother, who drove a different sports car every day of the week.

Second Bite: Tooth Hunting

You learn Tooth Hunting at Fairy School. It's not as easy as you might think...

First, the Bad Tooth Fairy used her wand to zap out the lights because she didn't want to be seen. If someone sees you and says the Gold Rhyme, they can have your fairy gold. The fairy didn't have any gold because she'd spent it going to troll dances, but she didn't like being seen by humans anyway.

Second, she threw some Fairy Dust into the air. This puts humans to sleep in seconds and keeps them that way for a few minutes.

Third, she put on her special Tooth Gloves. There are some teeth you really don't want to touch with your hands.

Then she flicked on her Fairy Light, which uses a pink light that humans can't see. She flew across to the bed, felt under the little girl's pillow and…

'Gotcha… oh, yuk! A dirty one! And it's as stinky as an ogre's armpit!'

The Bad Tooth Fairy glared at the dirty tooth. It had bits of slime on it… bits of food stuck in it… and a nasty jagged hole in one side.

'I've had it up to HERE with children who don't brush their teeth and parents who don't clean them before putting them under the pillow!' she said.

She gave Amelia's pillow a kick. Then she took out her magic marker…

A minute later she was off to the next house, and laughing wickedly as she flew.

When little Amelia Jane woke the next morning, she sat up, yawned, then remembered: *LOOK UNDER THE PILLOW!*

Excitedly, she felt for the money the tooth fairy should have left. But there was nothing except a rather smelly tooth.

'Mother!' she shouted. 'Mother, come here *at once!*'

Amelia's mother hurried in. 'Yes, my dearest girl?' she asked.

'Just look what the stupid tooth fairy did!' Amelia complained. 'She drew on my tooth! She put a big red "X" on it!'

Amelia's mother wasn't looking at the tooth, though. Instead she was staring, horrified, at her daughter. 'What's happened to your face?' she asked. 'There's something written on it backwards!'

Amelia ran to the mirror. Written across her big face was a message:

Your tooth was too disgusting to touch. From now on:

** No dirty teeth!*

** No stinky teeth!*

** No teeth with sharp edges!*

I'll be back tomorrow. If your tooth isn't sparkling clean, YOU'LL BE SORRY!

PS I can tell from your tooth that you eat and drink too many sweet things. You'd better stop that!

Amelia sneered and said, 'I'm not cleaning my old tooth. That's the tooth fairy's job!'

Her mother agreed, 'That fairy doesn't know her place! Expecting ***us*** to do the cleaning for her, is she? We're far too important for *that!* I shall report her!'

She took out her telephone but Amelia snatched it from her mother's hand and ran back into her room with it. She phoned the National Fairy Service and shouted at the Fairy Help Desk for a whole hour.

They put the horrible tooth under the pillow again that night. The next morning, the tooth was gone - but nothing had been left in its place.

'She's going to be in SUCH trouble!' exclaimed Amelia. 'Isn't she, Mother?'

'Of course, my darling. I shall write to the Queen about it immediately! That fairy stole your tooth and didn't pay for it!' Her mother rubbed her hands glee-fully. 'Maybe they'll put her in fairy prison!'

'Oh, I *do* hope so! Stupid fairy!' said Amelia.

They sat down for breakfast, and Amelia picked up her glass of cherry cola in one hand and her bar of chocolate in the other. She started stuffing chocolate into her big mouth and washing it down with cherry cola. She was halfway through swallowing when she began to choke.

'What's wrong?' cried her mother.

Amelia coughed... and out popped the nasty, dirty tooth from the night before.

'You put it in my glass!' wailed Amelia. 'Oh, you're

such a horrible mother! I'm going to phone the police and tell them! I'm going to make them put *you* in prison!' She ran for the phone and began dialling.

'I didn't!' her mother shouted back. 'You did it yourself!' She grabbed another phone and dialled a different number. 'I'm phoning your father to tell him to come home and deal with you! And then we'll send you away to Uncle Jack's farm, and you'll have to look after his pigs and live in a pigsty!'

'I *didn't* do it!' Amelia screamed, and threw cherry cola all over her mother.

'You *did!*' screamed her mother back, and flung her yoghurt all over Amelia.

It was just about to get even messier, when they both stopped and said at the same time:
'The fairy did it!'

Amelia finally got through to the police and shouted at them, 'You've got to come immediately because the tooth fairy has stolen my tooth and hasn't paid for it!'
'We can't come immediately,' said the police chief. 'We're busy solving murders and bank robberies.'
'But we're Very Important People!' Amelia raged. 'My father drives a Rolls Royce and my mother drives a Ferrari on Mondays, a Lotus on Tuesdays and lots of other sports cars too.'
The chief said, 'A Ferrari and a Lotus? Why didn't you say that to start with? We'll be over right away!'

Soon after that, Amelia's father arrived home. Amelia and her mother rushed out of the house and began shouting at him, mostly things like:
... 'You're late!'
... 'You're never here when we need you!'
... 'We don't love you any more!'
... 'You're useless!'
... and 'You're going bald!'
He said, 'Oh... but - '
They shouted at him for several minutes longer before he was able to add, 'I'm – I'm sorry, but -'
Then Amelia threw the tooth at him, and a full glass of cherry cola. Her mother threw some yoghurt over him as well, and then she and Amelia went back into the house, slamming the door.

He was still on the doorstep looking at the tooth in his hand, with cherry cola and yoghurt dripping from his head, when the police drove up in their black Minor Royals Trouble van.

The police jumped out of the van, shouting:

'That's the Tooth Thief! Get him!'

Amelia's father just stood there, holding the tooth.

'Put the tooth down!' the police shouted. 'Put it down *now!* And back away slowly!'

He carefully put the tooth on the doorstep. They ran across and handcuffed him.

'We're arresting you for stealing teeth from second-rate princesses!' shouted the chief of police.

'But it wasn't me!' said Amelia's father. 'It was the tooth fairy!'

The chief shook his head. 'The tooth fairy doesn't exist!' he said. 'Therefore I'm also arresting you for impersonating an imaginary being!'

They took Amelia's father away to jail and didn't let him out until the next morning.

Meanwhile, Amelia and her mother put the nasty, slimy tooth in the bin and wrote a nasty, slimy letter to the Fairy Police. But that wasn't the end of the tooth.

** On Tuesday it turned up in Amelia's chocolate mousse during school lunch.*

** On Wednesday her mother found it at the bottom of her coffee cup.*

** On Thursday it was in Amelia's chocolate sandwich.*

** On Friday it chased the cat and dog around the house.*

** On Saturday it crept around in Amelia's bathtub as she was having a bath.*

'That's enough!' shouted Amelia's mother. She grabbed the tooth and scrubbed it until it shone, then put it under the pillow.

The Bad Tooth Fairy arrived later that evening and checked under the pillow. She studied the tooth with her fairy light and then dropped it into her Tooth Bag with the other clean teeth. She made a note on her Tooth List and smiled to herself.

All across London, dirty teeth had been turning up in unexpected places.

** The Mayor found one in his soup at a posh banquet.*

** At one school, some teeth bit the dinner ladies and actually made one of them break into a run.*

** At the Queen's Garden Party there was a tooth on top of every fairy cake, and some of the guests were trying so hard to be polite that they swallowed theirs.*

But at least some parents in London learned to scrub dirty teeth before hiding them under pillows.

Third Bite: The Fairy Inspector

(**Note:** This is a LONG story. If you're reading it out loud to someone, do what *I* do: leave out the three visits by the Fairy Inspector)

However, Amelia's mother kept complaining and soon there was a knock at the fairy's tiny door.

It was the Fairy Inspector. He was tall and thin and had a serious frown on his face and a twinkle in his eye. He was carrying a long shiny case made of copper, and every fairy knows what that means.

'Come in!' called the Bad Tooth Fairy brightly. 'I'll find you a chair. There used to be one underneath that pile of dishes.'

He asked, 'Why don't you wash the dishes?'
'Because the dishwasher's full of dirty clothes.'
'Why not put the clothes in the laundry basket?'
'That's where I keep the bread, silly!'

The Fairy Inspector sat down and took out an important looking notebook and a magic fairy pencil. He asked, 'What's Fairy Rule Number Five?'

'Can't remember!'

The Fairy Inspector wrote this down in his notebook... *"Can't... remember!"*

He explained, 'Rule Five says *"Fairy shouldn't play tricks on humans"*. But I'm told you've been playing tricks with the teeth. You're a very naughty fairy!'

'Don't care!' said the Bad Tooth Fairy.

The Fairy Inspector wrote this down, too... *"Doesn't... care!"* He added:

And you haven't been cleaning the teeth yourself. You've been making the humans do it.'

'Can't be bothered!' she pouted.

The Fairy Inspector wrote this down as well... *"Can't... be... bothered!"*

'You're a very, very naughty fairy!' said the Fairy Inspector, shaking his head gravely. He picked up his copper case.

'In this magic case,' he said, 'I have my copper punishment wand. Are you willing to say you're sorry?'

'Fairy Flip-Flops,' said the Bad Tooth Fairy, 'with knobs on them!'

'I warned you!' exclaimed the Fairy Inspector. 'Now I'll have to turn your wings into two slimy slugs attached to your back. *Then* you'll be sorry!'

He unfastened the magic locks and took out a long fairy wand made of copper. He checked what he had written on his notepad.

'Now let me see – you said you can't remember, don't care and can't be bothered, right?'

'Did I?' asked the Bad Tooth Fairy with an innocent smile. 'Or did I say I can't remember why I care about being bothered all the time?'

'What?'

'Or did I say I'm really bothered when people don't care about their teeth? Or that I care *so* much about people that I just don't want to bother them?'

'Pardon?'

'Or maybe I said I couldn't remember the last time I was so caring about how bothered people were about their teeth?'

'Come again?'

'I might of course have said that no one bothers more than me about remembering how to care for teeth. By the way, would you like a cup of tea?'

The poor Fairy Inspector looked at his note pad, crossed out what he had written, and said, 'Yes please.'

So the Bad Tooth Fairy gave him a lovely cup of tea, with fairy cakes she had baked herself. And he had two cups and said he'd never tasted such good fairy cake.

He stayed a long time, talking and laughing with the Bad Tooth Fairy. And when he left, he didn't notice that his special copper wand case was lighter than it had been when he came....

Fourth Bite: Tooth Money

It was several months later, and the Bad Tooth Fairy was bored. She had no fairy money left to go to Troll Dances with, and no money for chocolate.

Tooth fairies only get paid if they bring back a hundred teeth a night. The Bad Tooth Fairy always intended to do a hundred, but she usually got fed up after fifty and started playing tricks on the children instead, like wiring up their computer game stations backwards so that all the games ran in reverse.

But one day she had a brilliant idea:

Mice! She would use mice to collect the teeth!

This isn't as silly as it seems. In some countries (such as Chile) the mice have always collected the teeth. In England however, the fairies always turned up their noses at that idea.

The fairy called a meeting of all the mice in her

area. About a thousand mice arrived and nibbled happily at the tiny cheese and peanut butter sandwiches she'd made for them.

'We don't mind nicking teeth,' said the king mouse. 'But what's in it for us?'

'What would you like best?' asked the fairy.

'Nuts!'

'Chocolate!'

'Cheesy nuggets!

'Toffee popcorn!'

The Bad Tooth Fairy made a note of this on a fairy notepad.

The king mouse said sadly, 'But you gotta have human money for that stuff, and then someone's gotta buy it. They don't let mice buy things. That ain't fair, is it?'

The fairy said, 'I know where we can get the money. And I'll find a way to do the buying...'

She explained her plan, and the mice thought it was brilliant.

All the mouse tooth collections went like clockwork, until Amelia's next tooth fell out.

The tooth was properly cleaned this time, and was waiting for collection under her pillow. The only problem was a doll named Barbarella.

You see, Amelia Jane didn't have expensive cars like her parents. But she did have toys.

She had enough toys to fill a ten ton truck.

She also had a doll's house – no, not just a doll's house, but a doll's *castle* on the back lawn. This is where she kept most of her toys. But Barbarella lived in the main house, and even had her own bed next to Amelia's.

Barbarella was the most special doll in the world. She cost ten thousand pounds.

Not only was she dressed like a princess most days, but she was as tall as a princess, too.

She knew a hundred thousand songs. If Amelia pressed a button on her special Doll Controller, Barbarella would dance and talk and sing - and sometimes (if you pressed the buttons in the wrong order) she would dance, talk and sing backwards as well.

This night, a dozen mice sneaked into Amelia's house through an open window. Some of them scurried off to Amelia's room, but most went to the find the living room.

Why did they go to the living room? That was the Bad Tooth Fairy's clever idea.

You see, in a living room there will be a settee, or

an armchair or a couch. And when somebody sits in a settee, money often falls out of their pockets and gets stuck down the back and sides.

The mice had a great time in Amelia's house because there were three living rooms. Very quickly they filled their tiny loot bags with coins and dragged them back through the house to the window they'd come in by. Then they waited for the other mice to come back from Amelia's room.

But the other mice were having a bad time. One of them had stepped on the Doll Controller and Barbarella had come to life. She sprang up from her doll's bed and looked down at the mice.

'I have lovely hair,' she said. 'Would you like to brush it?'

The mice shook their little heads.

'No thanks, lady. We don't do hair. Just fur.'

'Look!' she said. 'My face is fresh and free from wrinkles because I rub it with special cream. Would you like to try some?'

One of the mice said, 'No thanks. We don't get wrinkles.'

'Oh,' said Barbarella, puzzled. 'Do you like shoes? I have a hundred pairs! Shall we count them?'

'We hate shoes!' the mice squeaked. 'They step on us.'

'That's scary,' said the doll. 'I just wet myself! Would you like to change me?'

'Yuk!' said all the mice.

'We just came for your teeth, lady,' said one.

'Did you want to brush them for me?' asked Barbarella. 'Look how shiny they are!' She smiled at the mice and a special light came on inside her teeth.

'We can use my special toothbrush!' she said, reaching into her handbag. 'Look! Oh... *that's* not my toothbrush. It's my shiny black gun! Do you like it?'

She pointed a wicked looking gun at the mice, who squeaked with fear and ran away – except for the cleverest mouse, who saw by the light of Barbarella's smile that a girl was asleep on the other bed, so he crawled under her pillow and found the tooth.

Unfortunately, Amelia woke just then and opened her eyes to see – by the light of the doll's smile – a scruffy rodent with her tooth in its paws.

She screamed.

The mouse squeaked.

Barbarella announced, 'I've wet myself again!'

The mouse ran away and Amelia chased after it, shouting for her mother and father. She was just in time to see the final bags of jingling coins being tossed out the window and the last mouse leaping out, her tooth hugged to its chest.

She ran to the phone, called the police and shouted, 'We've been attacked by Robber Rats!'

The policeman yawned and asked, 'Can you describe them?'

'They have evil eyes and long furry tails,' she said.

'They can't be rats if their tails are furry,' said the policeman.

'I don't care! You have to come *now!*' she shouted.

'We can't,' he answered. 'We're very busy arresting bad people and taking away their knives and guns.'

Amelia screamed down the phone, 'If you don't come now, you'll be in big, BIG trouble! We're Very Important People! I'm Amelia Jane Argosy-Smythe and my mother drives a Porsche on Wednesdays and a Lamborghini on Thursdays and lots of other sports cars too!'

'A Porsche and a Lamborghini? Why didn't you say that to start with?' asked the policeman. 'We'll come at once!'

'You'd better!' shouted Amelia and slammed the phone down. Then she shouted, 'Daddy! Mother! Come here *now!*'

Her father and mother came running, with Barbarella following close behind.

'What is it?' they asked.

'Robber Rats stole my tooth so I've phoned the police, and they're coming,' she said.

'Will they dance with me?' asked Barbarella. 'We can be princes and princesses at the Ball!'

'I don't think so,' said Amelia's mother. She whispered to Amelia's father, 'You'd better take out the doll's batteries and put her back in her Doll's Box!'

So when the police came in their big van, the first thing they saw was Amelia's father in the upstairs window with a big screwdriver in his hand, trying to unscrew Barbarella's head to get to the batteries. And when her head wouldn't come off, he picked her up and carried her away.

'It's that Tooth Thief again!' one of them shouted. 'Get him!'

They ran upstairs and found Amelia's father sitting on a big box, with his wife and daughter standing by and shouting at him.

'Aha!' exclaimed the chief of police. 'So we meet again, Mr Tooth Thief! You couldn't keep away from the scene of the crime, hey?'

'But – but - I *live* here,' said Amelia's father.

'A likely story,' scoffed the chief. 'And I bet you're going to tell me there isn't a girl in that box.'

Amelia's father said, 'Of course there isn't –'

But just then the lid of the box began to shake and Amelia's father fell backwards as Barbarella rose from the box. Her head wasn't on quite straight.

'Aha!' the police chief exclaimed again. 'We've caught you red-handed!'

'You don't understand,' said Amelia's father. 'She's just a –'

Barbarella burst into song: *'I'm just a crying, talking, sleeping, walking, living doll!'* Then she sang the rest of the song as well.

The police all stared at her.

'Do you want to play with me?' Barbarella asked. 'You could take turns dressing me as a princess!'

'Uh... no...' said the policemen.

Amelia said, 'Barbarella and I were the only ones who saw the Robber Rats.'

'We'll have to ask you both some questions then,' said the chief.

Barbarella looked at them with her head tilted crookedly to one side, She said, 'I have fingers you can pull off. Would you like to paint them for me?'

'*What?!*' asked the chief of police.

'She doesn't mean that,' said Amelia. 'It's only her fingernails you can take off. She's talking nonsense because Daddy's pulled her head loose.'

The policemen all looked at Amelia's father and one of them took out some handcuffs.

The chief said to him, 'You'll have to come down to the police station with us, even though you've got a Rolls Royce.'

He turned to Barbarella and asked, 'So what do *you* know about the Robber Rats?'

Barbarella said sadly, 'They didn't want to brush my hair. Would *you* like to style it for me?'

'Uh.... No.'

'I can be sick!' she said proudly. 'Would you like me to puke up all over the floor?'

'No... but I think you'd better come with us.'

'Okay!' She beamed happily at the chief with her little head tilted to one side. 'But which shoes should I wear? The pink ones that go with my dress? The gold ones that match my hair? Or the grey ones that match the bits of fluff in my belly button?'

So they took away both Barbarella and Amelia's father and questioned them throughout the night, but then gave up and sent them both home again.

Fifth Bite: What Tooth Fairies Do with the Teeth

The Bad Tooth Fairy had the tooth collection well sorted now. The mice took the teeth and put a few coins under the pillows. They gave the rest of the money to the fairy, who bought them cheese and chocolate and nuts and other things that mice like.

But why do fairies collect teeth in the first place?

Tooth fairies are very important because they stop the world from filling up with second-hand teeth. If we didn't have tooth fairies, there would be tooth mountains in every town.

However, a tooth fairy's job isn't over when she puts the teeth in her Tooth Bag. Next, she has to take them to the Tooth Counter to be counted and stamped with an official counting mark.

Then she has to turn them into tooth sand.

Then she has to use a detoothing spell.

Then she has to take the sand and spread it somewhere that already has a lot of sand, such as a beach or a sandpit.

The Bad Tooth Fairy sometimes didn't bother with changing the smaller teeth to sand – that was too much trouble. And therefore when children went digging on the beach, sometimes they found an old tooth in the sand, looking up at them hungrily.

Even when she remembered to turn the teeth into sand, the Bad Tooth Fairy usually forgot to de-toothify the sand.

The detoothing spell makes the tooth sand forget it used to be teeth. If a fairy doesn't use the spell, the sand tries to gobble up anything it finds. You may have heard of quicksand, which swallows you alive. Quicksand is simply large pockets of tooth sand that fairies in the olden days didn't detoothify properly.

Some of Bad Tooth Fairy's bad tooth sand got to the beach, where it bit children's toes. Some of it she dropped into children's sandpits, where it waited patiently until someone got in, and then...

GULP!

...it swallowed them whole!

She did feel bad about the children who were gobbled up by their own sandpits.

Soon after this, there was another knock at the fairy's tiny door.

It was the Fairy Inspector. He was carrying a long shiny case made of silver, and every fairy knows what that means.

'Come in!' called the Bad Tooth Fairy. 'Sorry you can't have a chair this time, but I had to rescue the cat from the roof so I stacked up all the chairs and used them as a ladder. But you can have one of the big cushions I've been using as a trampoline.'

The Fairy Inspector sat down on a cushion and took out his notebook and pencil.

'What's Fairy Rule Number Three?' he asked.

The Bad Tooth Fairy said, 'Rules are silly!'

The Fairy Inspector wrote this down and said, 'Rule Three says *"Fairies must look after the world better than the humans do."* It's a very good rule.'

The Bad Tooth Fairy gave him a fairy shrug, which fairies do with their wings instead of their shoulders.

The Fairy Inspector said, 'Five children got their toes nibbled on the beach yesterday. You haven't been doing the detoothing spell properly, have you?'

'Can't be bothered.'

'You *must* bother from now on. It's important!'

'Can't remember the spell,' she said.

'Look it up in the Spell Book!'

'Lost it,' she sulked.

'Get a new one!'

'Haven't got any fairy money,' she sighed.

'Why not?'

She said, 'I spent it on dances and chocolate. But I lost my last bar of chocolate behind the settee.'

'Why don't you look behind the settee then?'

'Because I've lost the settee as well! Did you bring any chocolate with you? Have you got some in your funny pencil case?'

'In this magic case,' he said, 'I have my silver punishment wand. I don't want to use it because I quite like you. But this is your last chance. Are you sorry?'

'Fairy Flip-Flops,' said the Bad Tooth Fairy, 'with great big fluffy feathers on them!'

The Fairy Inspector gave a large and very sad sigh. 'I warned you!' he said. 'Now I'll have to turn your lovely fairy hair into snakes. *Then* you'll be sorry!'

He unfastened the magic locks and took out a long fairy wand made of silver. He checked what he had written on his notepad.

'Now let me see – you said rules are silly, you've forgotten your spells, and you've spent all your fairy money on chocolate. These are all very, very bad things to do.'

'Did I say that?' asked the Bad Tooth Fairy with a puzzled sigh. 'I do sometimes get things mixed up, you know. Perhaps what I meant was that I'm so silly that I sometimes forget how to spell "chocolate"?'

'You didn't say anything like that!'

'Or maybe I said it's very silly for fairies to forget the spells for making chocolate money?'

'I don't think –'

'And I may have meant that fairy rules are like sweet chocolate, and are worth their weight in fairy gold.'

'No, I –'

'Of course I *might* have said that I always make it a rule not to waste my fairy money on silly things like chocolate. Would you like a cup of tea? '

The poor Fairy Inspector looked at his notepad, crossed out what he had written and said:

'Yes please.'

So the Bad Tooth Fairy gave him a lovely cup of tea, with chocolate cake this time. The Fairy Inspector stayed a long time, talking and laughing with the Bad Tooth Fairy. And when he left, he didn't notice that his special silver wand case was lighter than it had been when he came....

Sixth Bite: A better way

The Bad Tooth Fairy was feeling guilty about the number of children being bitten by teeth on the beach or swallowed whole in their own sandpits.

She was earning a lot of fairy money now, and had a sack bulging with fairy gold. But even when she was having a good time at Goblin discos and Troll dance clubs she would remember, all of a sudden, that she hadn't done anything about the bags of teeth waiting to be processed.

She didn't mind so much about doing the spells, which the Fairy Inspector had written out for her again. But she hated having to take the tooth sand to the beach and spread it about.

That was *boring!*

Early one morning – after a night of tooth collecting - she was at the park playing on the slides with the Tooth Mice, when she noticed a large, warty fairy clomping past with a big bag over one shoulder.

It was the Toenail Fairy, returning from his own night's work.

The Toenail Fairy has an important job, too. He collects all the bits of toenail that come off your feet, grinds them to powder and takes them far away to be dumped in the desert. If he didn't collect the toenail scraps – and the full toenails that sometimes fall off – your room would soon be full of nasty, smelly bits of toenail. Even so, he sometimes misses a few.

.... As you might have guessed, there are other fairies that look after fingernails and dandruff and belly button fluff. But the Toenail Fairy has the worst job of all, and he's usually the stupidest fairy in the city.

'Good mornin'!' shouted the Toenail Fairy. 'Did ya have a good night's huntin'?'

'Yes!' the Bad Tooth Fairy shouted back. 'The mice collect most of the teeth for me, so it doesn't take so long these days. What about you?'

The Toenail Fairy shrugged his great shoulders and came to sit on a swing next to the Bad Tooth Fairy.

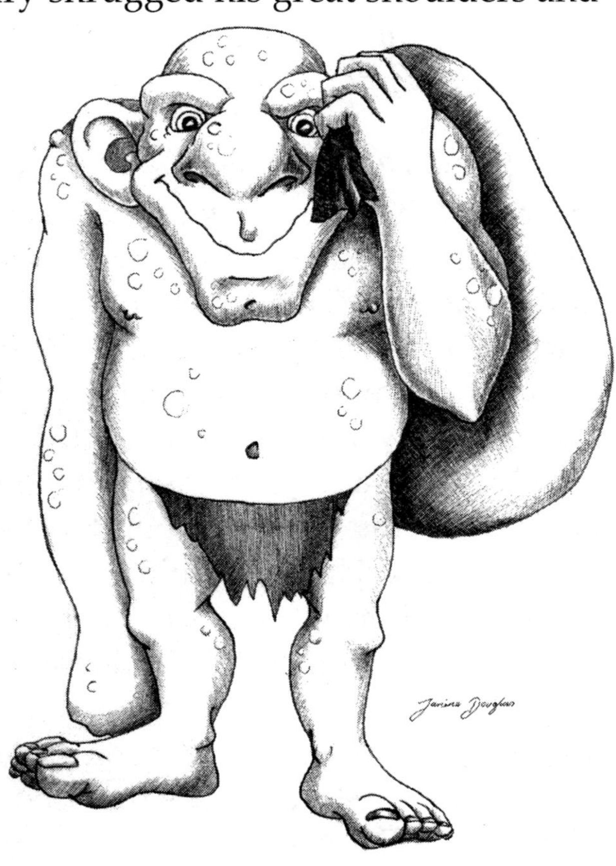

'I don't mind pickin' up all dem toenails,' he said, smiling. 'Dat's fun! It's a *biggg* adventure! You gotta *hunt 'em down!* But I hates havin' to take 'em all the way to the nearest desert, cos dat takes a long time and I'd rather be at the seaside. I likes buildin' sand castles, see. And I likes to sit wiv my feet in the water, eatin' ice cream and countin' all the pretty waves. Dere's *millions* of 'em!'

The Bad Tooth Fairy's eyes lit up suddenly. She

asked, 'Why don't we do a swap? You could take my tooth sand to the seaside and I'll look after your toenails for you.'

'Oooh,' said the Toenail Fairy. 'I don't know about dat. How're you gonna take 'em to the desert?'

'Maybe I won't,' said the Bad Tooth Fairy. 'Maybe I have a better idea, which will make us both some money.'

'Oooh,' said the Toenail Fairy again. 'Does dat mean I can buy more ice cream?'

So the Bad Tooth Fairy went out and bought a deep fat fryer, which she took to the Toenail Fairy's house. They mixed the toenail powder with a little water and some salt. Then they squirted the gloopy mess into the deep fat fryer and made Toenail Crisps.

And that's why the Toenail Fairy goes to the seaside once a week, with a sack of tooth sand over one shoulder and a sack of Toenail Crisps over the other. He spreads the tooth sand on the beach and sells the packets of crisps to children. Then he buys ice creams for himself and sits happily by the sea, licking ice cream from a cone and smiling at everyone.

However, very soon there was another knock at the fairy's tiny door.

It was the Fairy Inspector. He was carrying a long shiny case made of gold, and every fairy knows what that means.

'Come in!' shouted the Bad Tooth Fairy from inside. 'You'll have to climb in by the window though, because I've lost the door key.'

The Fairy Inspector crawled through the window.

'You'll have to share a chair with the cat,' said the Bad Tooth Fairy. 'I've had to tape him to the seat to stop him from chasing the hamster.'

'Why don't you put the hamster in its cage?'

'Don't be silly!' said the Bad Tooth Fairy. 'I've put the cage over the goldfish bowl to keep the fish safe from the parrot that escaped from the bathtub.'

'What was the parrot doing in the bathtub?'

'Having a bath, of course! I couldn't use the washing machine because it's full of bread rolls, you see.'

So the Fairy Inspector squeezed in next to the cat and took out his notebook and pencil. He asked, 'What's Fairy Rule Number Seven?'

The Bad Tooth Fairy groaned, 'There are too many Rules!'

The Fairy Inspector wrote this down. He said, 'Rule Seven says "*Fairies should try to bring peace and happiness to the world.*" It's my favourite rule.'

The Bad Tooth Fairy made a face at this.

The Fairy Inspector said, 'You've caused chaos at some houses! Remember when you didn't pay for little Amelia Jane's tooth?'

The Bad Tooth Fairy laughed and said, 'Bad humans like them deserve to be turned upside down and given a good shake!'

'That doesn't matter. Fairies should be good to everyone, whether they deserve it or not!'

'I bet *that's* not in the Rule Book,' she scoffed.

'It's Fairy Rule Nine.'

'Then it's a crazy rule,' she said.

The Fairy Inspector gave a great sigh.

'I do like you a lot,' he said. 'But you can't make fun of the Rules.'

He picked up his gold case. 'In this magic case,' he said, 'I have my gold punishment wand. I don't want to use it. Just say you're sorry.'

'Fairy Flip-Flops!' said the Bad Tooth Fairy. 'Great big pink furry ones with a thousand knobs on them!'

'I did warn you!' said the Fairy Inspector, shaking his head sadly. 'Now I'll have to turn your lovely fairy ears into earwigs. *Then* you'll be sorry!'

He unfastened the magic locks and took out a long fairy wand made of gold. He checked what he had written on his notepad.

'Now let me see – you said there are too many rules, you like turning people's lives upside down, and you think the Goodness Rule is crazy. These are all very, very bad things to say.'

'Did I say all that?' asked the Bad Tooth Fairy with a puzzled sigh. 'Perhaps what I meant was that I'm crazy about the Rules and there's too much wrong with the world and I want to put it right?'

'You didn't say anything like that!'

'Or maybe I said I know a fairy who's crazy about you and you've turned her heart upside down but you keep talking to her about boring Rules?'

'I don't think –'

'And I may have meant that you can never have too many slices of pineapple upside down cake, and you would be crazy not to eat it when it's lovely and warm from the oven, and there ought to be a Rule about not wasting any more time talking when there's cake to eat.'

'No, I –'. The Fairy Inspector paused. 'Did you say pineapple upside down cake? Ready now?'

'With cherries on top,' said the Bad Tooth Fairy.

'Let's have a cup of tea then,' he suggested, putting down his wand.

The Fairy Inspector stayed a long time, talking and laughing with the Bad Tooth Fairy. And when he left, he didn't notice that his special gold wand case was lighter than it had been when he came....

Seventh Bite: Disaster

Just as the Bad Tooth Fairy thought she had everything sorted, the very worst thing happened.

It started one Sunday when Amelia Jane's final baby tooth started to wobble, while she was counting the fivers in her piggy bank.

'Mother!' she shouted. 'Mother, come here *at once!*'

When her mother arrived, Amelia asked, 'How much do the common children get for their teeth?'

'The same as everyone else,' said her mother.

'But that's not fair!' shouted Amelia. 'I should get *more*, shouldn't I?'

'Of course you should, dear. After all, we're worth so much more than common people.'

'Exactly! Now Mother, I've had a clever idea: I know how we can get what we deserve...'

Amelia explained her clever, nasty plan and soon

they were both laughing about how rich they would be, and how foolish the Fairy would look.

The next weekend, the Bad Tooth Fairy was doing her rounds – going to a house, taking money and a tooth from the Tooth Mice waiting there, dropping it into her Tooth Bag and ticking off a child's name from her list. She got to Amelia's mansion and found a group of unhappy mice waiting for her.

'Can't do it,' one of them squeaked. 'They've got a dozen cats in there. Big ones!'

'And traps,' said another. 'Wiv proper mouse food in 'em. Wot mouse can resist cheesy nuggets?'

'Bodger couldn't,' said a third. 'Poor Bodger...'

All the mice bowed their little furry heads and whispered sadly, 'Poor Bodger...'

'You'll have to do this one,' said the first mouse. 'Sorry.'

The Bad Tooth Fairy tucked her Tooth List into a pocket and took out her fairy wand. 'That's okay,' she said. 'Little Amelia's last tooth is going to be one to remember. I'll show *her* who's boss!'

She flew through the air and landed on Amelia's window ledge. The window was shut, but that doesn't stop a fairy: one wave of a wand, and they can step through glass.

She put on her gloves and took out her fairy dust.

Stepped through the window.

Zapped the lights.

Threw the dust through the gap in the curtains.
Turned on her fairy light and flew to Amelia's bed.
Felt under the pillow...

Amelia was breathing slowly and deeply, her face turned away from the window. Her special doll Barbarella was seated against the wall by the bed, with her eyes closed.

The fairy was feeling about for the tooth, which must be hidden far beneath the pillow. And then –

'Barbarella!' Amelia shouted. 'NOW!'

Barbarella's eyes suddenly lit up, shining directly at the Bad Tooth Fairy. At the same moment, Amelia turned over and looked straight into the fairy's eyes.

Amelia was wearing an odd plastic mask. 'Ha!' she shouted through the mask. 'Gotcha!'

'I can see you, fairy:
I've looked into your eyes.
And since I see you, fairy
You can't tell me any lies!
So tell me how much gold you have
And fetch it instantly.
I can see you, fairy,
And your gold belongs to me!'

The Bad Tooth Fairy's heart sank. Not only had Amelia caught her, but she had said the Gold Rhyme. It was a dirty trick.

But how had Amelia done it? The plastic mask over her mouth and nose was attached to a diver's air tank. The fairy dust couldn't get to her!

'Your gold!' Amelia gloated through the mask. 'Give me your fairy gold *now!'*

The Bad Tooth Fairy glared at Amelia. But it was no good. She was powerless to refuse.

'I'll have to go get it,' she said.

'No!' shouted Amelia. 'Just wave your wand and make it appear!'

'It doesn't work that way,' said the Bad Tooth Fairy. 'I'll have to go home and put it into a big bag and bring it back.'

'How much have you got?' asked Amelia greedily.

'I suppose it's worth about a hundred thousand of your human money. Maybe more.'

'Yes!' shouted Amelia, jumping up and down on her bed, still wearing her mask. 'I did it! I fooled the tooth fairy! And now I get all the gold! I'm *sooooooo* worth it!'

The Bad Tooth Fairy stood there, twitching her wand and wishing she could turn Amelia into a frog. But she had no choice. Sadly, she flew to the window and out into the night.

It was a dreary journey back home, and an even drearier time packing all her fairy gold into a large bag. But it had to be done. She had just zipped the bag when there was a knock at the door.

It was the Fairy Inspector. 'The mice came and found me,' he said. 'They told me you'd been caught by a human, so I've come to see if you're all right.'

The Bad Tooth Fairy said sadly, 'I got caught by the most horrible human child in the world. Can't I turn her into something slimy?'

'I'm sorry,' said the Fairy Inspector. 'You can't. But Rule Eight says –'

'No more Rules!' shouted the Bad Tooth Fairy. 'I

want *Revenge!* I want that greedy little girl to suffer! I want to wipe that snobby smirk off her nasty sneering face! I want to see her *cry!* I want her to lie on the floor and kick her heels in a great big tantrum!'

'That would be very pleasant, I agree,' said the Fairy Inspector. 'But Rule Eight –'

'Not - another - word!' roared the Bad Tooth Fairy. 'You might at least try to be helpful!'

'I *will* be helpful,' said the Fairy Inspector. 'I'll carry the bag for you.'

So they set off across London towards Amelia Jane Argosy-Smythe's house, with the Bad Tooth Fairy fuming and complaining every inch of the way.

'I don't mind so much losing my fairy gold,' she said. 'But I hate losing it to *her!* She's too rich already! AND she's such a snob!'

'Rule Eight –' began the Fairy Inspector.

'Fairy Flip-Flops with enormous golden knobs on!' shouted the Bad Tooth Fairy. 'Never mention Rule Eight to me again!'

'Then I'll just have to show you,' said the Fairy Inspector calmly.

He stopped by an alleyway and unzipped the bag of fairy gold. He took out a few coins. 'Follow me,' he said.

There were some tramps sleeping in the alley and he woke each one in turn.

'Please would you tell me you want a gold coin?' he asked each one.

'Er – yes – I would like a gold coin,' each one said. So he gave them a coin each and then threw a pinch of fairy dust at them, so that they fell into a deep slumber, happily clasping their gold.

'There's another group a few streets down!' he called to the Bad Tooth Fairy. 'Come on!'

When they ran out of people sleeping rough, they called in at some shelters for homeless people. Then they knocked at the doors of the poorer houses and did the rounds of the all-night cafes.

Final Bite: Just desserts...

Finally they got to Amelia's house and the Bad Tooth Fairy flew up to the window by herself. When she landed, she found Amelia and her mother waiting for her in a very bad mood.

Amelia shouted at the fairy, '*You* took your time!'

'Rule Eight,' said the Bad Tooth Fairy. 'I was held up by Fairy Rule Number Eight. It's a very important rule, apparently.'

'Don't tell me about Rules!' said Amelia with a sneer. 'Rules are for *poor* people! Rich people like us make our *own* rules!'

Her mother rubbed her hands excitedly. 'How much gold is there?' she asked.

The fairy said, 'I started off with about a thousand little gold coins. That's the same as a hundred thousand of your human money.'

'*Started off*? What do you mean?'

The Fairy said, 'On the way here, we met some people who wanted a gold coin each. You have to give them one if they ask, you see. That's Rule Eight. You can't refuse to help every human who asks, but you can only help them a little each time.'

'You gave them some of MY gold?' gasped Amelia. 'I hate you!'

Her mother said, 'It's all right, darling, they only got a coin each.'

'But they should have NOTHING!' shouted Amelia. 'It's MY money!'

'What's left is all yours,' said the fairy. 'Here it is.'

She turned the bag upside down. One tiny gold piece fell out and rolled across the floor.

'We met quite a few people on the way,' she said with a sweet smile.

Amelia Jane threw herself upon the floor and kicked her feet, sobbing and shrieking and screaming and swearing. Her mother did the same.

Barbarella picked up the gold coin and swallowed it. 'I'm worth my weight in gold now!' she said.

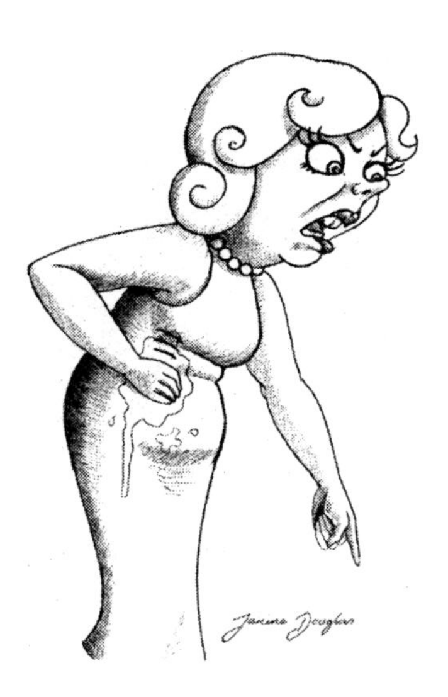

When the Bad Tooth Fairy had gone, Amelia got up from the floor and fetched a bucket of water, which she threw over her mother.

'You're a bad mother!' she shouted. 'You let the fairy cheat me out of my gold!'

'I didn't!' screamed her mother. 'You did it yourself!' And she got a bucket of water and threw it over Amelia.

'It's Daddy's fault!' shouted Amelia. And they *both* filled a bucket of cold water, went into the bedroom where Amelia's father was sleeping, and threw the buckets of water over him.

Then Amelia shouted at her mother, 'I'm going to get you for this!' She locked herself in her room and began phoning people and telling them what a bad mother she had.

'You're a very bad daughter!' her mother shouted back, and began phoning people too.

The next day, a ten ton truck arrived from a charity shop while Amelia was at school, and began loading up her toys.

'Take them all,' said Amelia's mother. 'Take the doll's castle, too. Amelia doesn't need them any more. Her uncle is picking her up from school today and taking her to live on his farm, with only pigs to play with. *Ha!*'

The men from the truck came to Barbarella's box and began to lift it. But the doll sat up and smiled at them.

'Have you come to brush my hair?' she asked. 'I have lovely hair!'

'Uh – no.'

'Have you come to paint my toenails?'

'Uh – no.'

'Are you going to change me then? I can wet myself, you know!'

'No, lady. We've come to take you away.'

Barbarella shook her head. 'You aren't!' she laughed.

'Oh yes we are.'

'Oh no you aren't!'

'Oh yes we are! After all, you're just a talking doll.' The moving men flexed their muscles and stepped forward to pick up her box again.

Barbarella took something from her handbag.

'Look - I have a gun!' she said brightly. 'It's a very nice gun. It's black and shiny. I like my gun. Do you want to see me shoot it?'

'Uh – no.'

'I think you *do!*'

She pointed the gun at the men, who dropped the box and ran away. She frowned.

'Spoilsports!' she shouted after them. Then she pulled the trigger. A shower of water came out.

Meanwhile, a crack team of army commandos was crawling across the immense lawns that surrounded the mansion.

They watched the lorry full of toys drive away at top speed.

'Leave them, men,' said the commander. 'We know the spy is still in the house...'

A few minutes later they smashed down the door and surrounded...

... Amelia's mother.

'You can't arrest me!' she said. 'I drive a BMW sports car on Fridays and a turbo-charged Saab racer on Saturdays. And I'm so important that I can't even *remember* what I drive on Sundays!'

'But you're a spy,' they said. 'Spies are *bad*. And if you don't confess, we're going to take away all your cars and give them to poor people.'

'All right! I surrender!' she shouted. 'I've been a spy for years! But who told you? Who *ratted* on me?'

The soldiers all shrugged their shoulders.

'It can't have been a rat, though,' said one. 'They can't talk.'

And the soldiers took her away.

... and happy endings

However, it turned out to be a happy ending for Amelia's mother. She became a Double Agent, which meant she could spy for several nations at once and have a different set of cars in each country.

Amelia loved being with the pigs, and they totally adored her. They spent all day eating together and playing in the mud. And the pigs *loved* it when she shouted and threw food at them.

It was an even happier ending for the Bad Tooth Fairy. She gave the wands back to the Fairy Inspector and they got married and moved into a big house at the better end of the fairy woods, with all the

Tooth Mice living in the west wing of the house and the Toenail Fairy living in the east wing - except when he was at the beach eating ice creams and selling toenail crisps to children.

They all went together to Troll Dances every Saturday night, Ogre Church on Sunday, and watched Goblin TV every weekday morning.

When Amelia's father came home, only Barbarella was there to greet him.

'The bad people have all gone away!' she exclaimed.

'Oh,' said Amelia's father.

'***I*** will look after you from now on!'

'Oh,' said Amelia's father again, looking puzzled. 'What happened to Amelia Jane?'

'She is with the pigs. She will be happy there.'

'And my wife?'

'She was a spy, so I told the soldiers and they took her away.'

'Oh... I suppose things will be different now,' said Amelia's father. 'No more shouting?'

Barbarella said, 'I will sing lovely songs to you. I know a hundred thousand of them!'

'That would be better than being shouted at.'

'And maybe we can count my shoes together?' she asked hopefully.

'I would like that,' he said. 'I'm good at counting. I'm an accountant, you see.'

'*And* I won't throw water over you,' she promised. 'Or yoghurt or cherry cola.'

'That would be so kind of you,' he said.

She said shyly, 'If you wish to get wet, we can shoot each other with water pistols. I like my water pistol. It's black and shiny! '

'That's an excellent idea. I'll buy a black and shiny one for me as well.'

Barbarella smiled at him.

'Would you like to brush my hair?' she asked.

'I'd love to,' said Amelia's father.

Alicroc the Alien Scoutmaster

The voices

Alicroc is cool and calm and crazy, and talks like an American hippy. He's so smooth that you don't even notice the 272 fine white teeth, the green skin or the spiky tail. He talks in a laid-back but upbeat way that makes you think he's completely in control of the situation, even when he hasn't the slightest idea what he's doing. Which is most of the time.

Big Mike is a big guy with a big, show-off voice. He's so tough that puppies wet themselves when they see him. He thinks *everyone* should be tough like him... He thinks he's really cool... He thinks Big is Best... He thinks winning is all that matters... He thinks a lot of nonsense.

The **Tiny Scouts** are a crazy bunch of four years olds. Some of them speak in whispers, some shout everything, some cry whenever Big Mike appears. Some sound like your little brother or sister, if you have one. They all sound like they would very quickly drive you mad.

The **Big Scouts** all try to talk like smaller versions of Big Mike, even the girls. But you can tell that most of them are actually just bigger versions of the Tiny Scouts, and they would be fun to have around if they weren't always trying to look tough and mean.

The **Ponies and Alligators** don't say anything, but they do whinny or grunt in a very surprised manner when being lassoed or wrestled or used as stepping stones.

The **Chickens** were eaten last time, and aren't in this story. But if they *were* here, they would sound like chickens again.

The story

Once upon a time there was an alien named Alicroc who had green crackly skin and 272 fine white teeth. He lived in a galaxy far, far away and had only visited the earth once, which had been a frightening experience for him because he'd ended up teaching a class of four year old children.

That story is told in the first book of *Wicked Tales*.

'Never again!' Alicroc said afterwards. '*Never!*'

But one morning - a month or two after returning home - he received a letter through the Intergalactic Post Office. It read:

Deer mer alee cwoc

Wenow be tine scots ant r scotmast win 2 wuds butty met a bare an only back a foot. The scots pitshun stars x month and we wont 2 win but kneed a new scotmast and u was the best teecher everso please come morrow.

Class 1A

Although Alicroc was an alien, he understood four year old English and knew that they were trying to say something like this:

Dear Mister Alicroc
We are now in the Tiny Scouts and our scoutmaster went to the woods but he met a bear and only his foot came back. The scouts competition starts next month and we want to win but we need a new scoutmaster and you were the best teacher ever, so please come tomorrow.
Class 1A

Alicroc shook his head and repeated, 'Never again!'

He was just about to throw the letter in the bin when he saw something written on the other side:

PS The big scots laff at us an call us loosers.

'What?!' he thundered. 'Big kids laughing at *my* class? How dare they!' And a minute later he was zooming to earth in his big black Alienmobile.

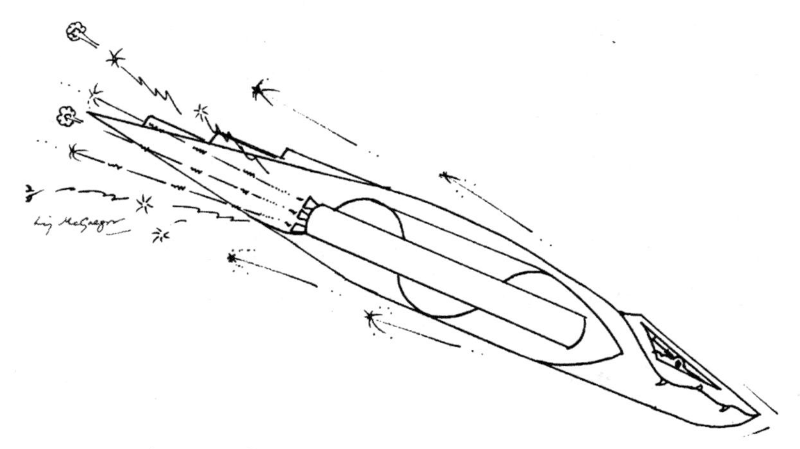

It was early Friday evening and he drove about the little streets near the nursery school, looking for the children. But some bigger scouts saw him first, and threw an egg at his car.

The bigger scouts were laughing as the egg hit the Alienmobile... they were still laughing as the egg bounced back from the car... then they stopped laughing as a hundred eggs followed and splattered them from head to foot.

Alicroc screeched to a halt and shouted out the window, 'Hey, kids! Have you seen any Tiny Scouts around here?'

One of the big scouts wiped egg from his face and pointed towards some small trees near the road.

'You can't miss them!' jeered one of the big girl scouts, and they ran away, laughing nastily.

Alicroc walked up a little hill to the trees. There were ten trees, and each tree had a tiny scout tied to it, upside down.

'Mister Ali-cwoc!' they all shouted.

'- We're playing a game with the big scouts!'

'- We're playing Hide and Seek –'

'- But they didn't want us peeking while they hid –'

'- So they said we had to be tied up -'

'- Upside down -'

'- And I get sick upside down –'

'- They're not very nice, Mister Ali-cwoc...'

'Kids!' said Alicroc. 'This is no time to be playing games. We've got a competition to win!'

Big Mike and the Big Scouts

Alicroc and the Tinies went to the Scout Hut.

'Okay, Tinies,' said Alicroc. 'What have we got to

do for this competition?'

'We gotta climb a mountain.'

'Easy!' he said.

'We gotta cross a big river.'

'Easy!' he said.

'We gotta walk through a big forest at night.'

'Easy again! Kids, we're going to *win*! What are we going to do?'

'***Lose!***' they shouted back.

'- They're older than us!'

'- And meaner than us!'

'- And bigger than us!'

'- And their scoutmaster is enormous!'

'- Like a gorilla!'

'- An elephant!'

'- A 'nocerous!'

'- Like a gorilla and an elephant *and* a rhinocerous all stuck together!'

Just then there was a knock on the door, and a big man came in, with a group of Big Scouts behind him.

Big Mike was big and tough, with a large head, a square chin and a crewcut. He was built like a bear. ***No*** - he was built like a bear that went to the gym every day and pumped iron until its muscles bulged.

'So you're the new scoutmaster for these Tinies?' he sneered in a loud, slow, show-off voice. 'What are you gonna to do with them? Teach them how to tie their shoelaces?'

He laughed at his own joke, and the Big Scouts joined in.

But Alicroc exclaimed, 'What a *great* idea! Is there a

Shoelaces Badge?'

'No!' said Big Mike. 'And if there was one, your stupid scouts would never get it! They're ***losers***, every one of them. My pack could beat your pack with their eyes closed and both hands tied behind their backs.'

'Yeah!' shouted all the Big Scouts from behind him.

'Hey!' said Alicroc. 'That's *another* great idea! Shall we try that? Come on – let's tie all your hands behind your backs! And then we'll *wrestle!*'

'Uh... no...' said all the Big Scouts.

Big Mike said proudly, 'My pack can do *anything!* We're big and tough and mean. Aren't we, kids?'

'Yes, sir!' shouted all the Big Scouts.

'And we're a Team. Aren't we, kids?'

'Yes, sir!' they shouted.

'And I'm a really cool guy, aren't I, kids?'

'Uh... yes, sir!' they said, not so loudly this time.

Big Mike said, 'The kids and I hang out together most weekends. Don't we, kids?'

'Yes, sir!' said all the Big Scouts again, but not so happily this time.

Big Mike said, 'I've got a big boat, Mister Ali. A *really* big boat. It's a *yacht!* I take my Team out on it sometimes. Have *you* got a yacht, Mister Ali?'

'No,' said Alicroc. 'All I have is an Alienmobile.'

Big Mike just laughed at him. 'Yeah, yeah,' he said. 'I've seen your little black car. My Off Road Monster Truck could eat it for breakfast!'

All the Big Scouts laughed at Big Mike's joke.

Big Mike added, 'I'm taking my scouts out on my yacht tomorrow. What are *you* doing, Mister Ali?'

Alicroc said, 'Hey – I've got an idea! *We* could come on the yacht too! Have you got room for us?'

Big Mike said proudly, 'I've got *plenty* of room. It's the biggest boat in town! But your scouts are all wimps and scaredy-cats and babies, and I don't allow wimps on my boat. I only want kids who are big and tough and brave!'

He marched out of the hut with his scouts following him, chanting a tough scout marching song. When the first scout reached the door, the Big Scouts all turned and threw something at the Tiny Scouts.

'Balloons!' shouted one Tiny. 'Hooray!'

SQUELCH!

'... Oh yuk! Balloons filled with *custard*!'

'- Mister Ali-cwoc – I got custard on my head!

'- I got it on my clothes!'

'- I got it in my underpants!'

From outside came the booming laughter of Big Mike and his Big Scouts.

Alicroc looked at a blob of custard that had landed on his arm. He licked it.

'Hey kids!' he shouted. 'This tastes *good!* Anyone know how to make it?'

Sharing the Custard

So Alicroc went out that night and with his intergalactic credit card, he bought some huge saucepans, a hundred pints of milk, dozens of eggs, and plenty of sugar and vanilla. And the next morning, he and the children made buckets and buckets of lovely, gloopy yellow custard.

The children said, 'We can't eat all that!'

'- We'll get fat!

'- And I'll be sick, Mister Ali-cwoc!'

Alicroc nodded. 'You're right, kids. We can't eat it all. And if you've got too much food, the right thing to do is share it, don't you think?'

'Yes, Mister Ali-cwoc!'

He said, 'Yeah – *care and share!* Do you remember how the big scouts shared their custard with us?'

'All over our faces, Mister Ali-cwoc...'

'- And my shirt!'

'- And down my underpants!'

Alicroc said, 'Hey, kids - they shared their custard with us, and that was kind of them. So we're going to share *our* custard with *them!*'

'Hooray!!!'

Alicroc opened a flap on the side of his big black Alienmobile and poured the buckets of custard inside until it spilled out of the tank and ran down the sides of the car. Then he pressed a button on his intergalactic wristwatch. Three black posts rose from the roof of the Alienmobile.

The first one was shaped like the body of a snake, and had a glass front.

The two behind it were also shaped like snakes, and had little nozzles at the front that made them look like guns.

Alicroc called, 'Okay kids, hop in!'

'But there's ten of us!

'- We won't all fit inside!'

'- There won't be enough seat belts!'

'- I get car sick!'

But they all climbed in and looked around. It was a very weird car.

- *Outside, it was the size of a large car. Inside, it was as big as a school bus.*
- *There were soft black leather chairs with big arm rests.*
- *In front of each chair was a computer screen and keyboard and joysticks, and you could play a computer game as the car drove along.*
- *Next to each chair was a little fridge with your favourite food inside.*

Alicroc started the engine and the car glided smoothly along the road towards the river.

'Mister Ali-cwoc, what are the sticks on the roof for?'

Alicroc pressed a button and a picture of the roof appeared on their computer screens.

'See that first stick, kids? That's called a periscope. You have them on submarines. When you're underwater, you can look through them and see what's above you.'

He pressed another button. 'Like this!'

On their computer screens, they were looking through the periscope now. They could see the river coming closer... closer... closer...

'Windows up!' ordered Alicroc.

And then the Alienmobile drove off the road and straight into the river. Everybody screamed.

An hour later they were cruising underwater, chasing the fish and alligators. The Tiny Scouts took turns driving. Then Alicroc put up the periscope and scanned the surface.

'There they are!' he shouted.

They could see a yacht in front of them, with the name 'Big Mike's Big Boat' on its side. Alicroc brought the Alienmobile close to it and then pressed another button.

⊕ Each computer screen now had a picture of the big white yacht in the middle of a circle, with a cross through it, as if you were lining it up through the sights of a gun. ⊕

'Okay, kids!' said Alicroc. 'The big scouts played a custard game with us, and now we're gonna play one with *them*! You each have a turn. When your own screen lights up, you're in control of one of the Custard Guns for one minute. See how many big scouts you can hit!'

Two screens lit up and two Tinies started firing.

On board the yacht, the Big Scouts were sitting on the deck in the sunshine, eating their barbecued food and drinking something cold and fizzy. Suddenly two thick yellow streams of custard cut through the air and nailed two of them.

Each computer screen showed a close-up of the hit, then cut to an overhead view of the boat. Big Scouts were running to and fro, and Big Mike was shouting at them. Then two streams of custard floated through the air and filled Big Mike's big mouth.

⊕ ⊕ ⊕ ⊕ ⊕ ⊕ ⊕ ⊕ ⊕

After half an hour, the custard tanks were empty and the deck of the yacht was slippery with custard. The Alienmobile rose from the water and ran up the Tiny Scouts flag before speeding away back to shore.

Going Wild

Next week, the scout troops met at the scout hut again and they went for a hike together. The Tiny Scouts gave the big ones some alien sweets from the Alienmobile, and some of the Big Scouts started being friendly. But some other Big Scouts pushed the Tinies into the nettles and brambles.

Big Mike laughed at the screams of the Tiny Scouts. He said to Alicroc, 'Little kids shouldn't be allowed in the scouts. Scouts have to be hard and mean. They have to be real men like me!'

'Even the girls?' asked Alicroc.

Big Mike growled, 'They *all* have to learn to be tough! This weekend I'm taking them to a real ranch. I'm gonna show them how to ride horses and tie knots and make fire without matches and sleep on the ground. We're gonna be like old time cowboys!'

He marched away, with all his scouts stepping together and chanting:

'Left right, *one two*, left right, *three four*, lefty righty, we are mighty, *one two three four...*'

Alicroc watched them go, then said to his Tiny Scouts, 'Kids! *We* could do that, too!'

'But Mister Ali-cwoc, we don't *know* left and right!'

'- Or up and down!'

'- Or in and out!'

'- I get sick when I count things!'

Alicroc said, 'Not that stupid marching thing, kids! I meant we could try being cowboys!'

'But that's scary, Mister Ali-cwoc!'

'- I don't like horses!'

'- I always fall off!'

'- I always get sick!'

Alicroc said, 'It'll be *fun!* Leave it to old Alicroc...'

That Saturday, Alicroc collected the Tinies from their houses at dawn. They drove to some woods and he took out some long coils of rope from the back of the Alienmobile.

'Okay kids,' he said. 'Big Mike is teaching the Big Scouts how to tie little knots. I'm gonna teach *you* how to use .... the lasso!'

'Hooray! Hoo- *What's a lasso*?'

So they spent all morning learning how to make a big loop at the end of some rope, and then throw the loop over a target that Alicroc set up.

They weren't very good at it. They caught:

- Flowers
- Beetles
- Tree branches
- Each other
- Alicroc several times
- *- And finally, they caught the target.*

'Okay, kids – part two!'

They drove out into the wilderness and chased down some wild ponies in the Alienmobile, and the Tinies lassoed them until they had ten ponies, one for each child.

'Tomorrow, kids, we have part three!'

'What's that?'

'We learn to ride them!'

The next day, late in the afternoon....

.... The Big Scouts were all feeling tired. It had been a hard weekend. They rode their horses slowly along the path, following Big Mike on his Big Horse. They were almost back at the ranch. They took the final turn. They could see the ranch house. They could smell the barbecued chicken. They could see the tables loaded with food and drink. ***At last!***

Then they heard a scary noise: a noise of hooves pounding and little voices screaming.

Ten wild ponies flashed past, with ten wild Tiny Scouts clinging to their backs and swinging ropes. One of the scouts was sick over his shoulder as he passed the Big Scouts.

The Tinies were stripped to the waist and had strange, red markings painted all over them. The ponies were neighing and kicking up dust.

The ponies charged past the tables of food, the lassos whipped through the air, and the barbecue was whisked away and disappeared into the sunset.

Getting Tough

Next Friday, the Tinies brought the wild ponies to the scout hut and let the Big Scouts ride them. They all had a good time, except for Big Mike.

'You think you're *tough*, hey?' he said to the Tinies. 'My scouts can beat you at anything! Football, running, fighting, *anything*!'

One Tiny said, 'That's 'cos they're bigger than us!'

Big Mike said, 'Yeah, but *big* is good! *Tough* is good! We're gonna win the annual scout competition, and *you're* gonna come last!'

Alicroc said, 'Maybe we *will* come last. But we're going to have fun! That's what matters!'

'Fun?' asked Big Mike with a big laugh. '*Fun??* Are

you crazy? You can't have fun unless you win!'

'Hey!' said Alicroc. 'Losing is cool, too. A good loser beats a bad winner *any time*!'

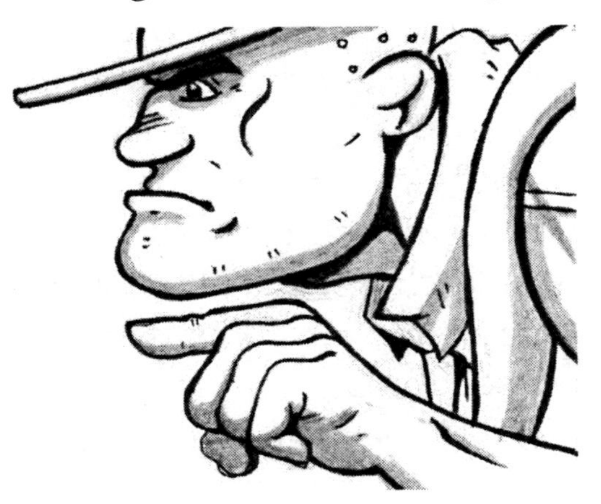

Big Mike put a finger to the side of his head and made crazy-type circles with it. 'You're a loony!' he said. 'Winning is *all* that matters! We're going to a big Scouts Wrestling Competition tomorrow, and we're gonna win that! But *your* scouts couldn't win a wrestling competition with a *worm!*'

The Tiny Scouts looked up at Alicroc. 'Why don't *we* learn to do something tough?' one of them asked.

'Okay,' said Alicroc. 'What do you want to do?'

'I want to wrestle worms!' said one.

Alicroc said, 'That's too easy.'

'- I want to wrestle puppies!'

'That's cruel.'

'- I want to wrestle elephants!'

'That's stupid,' Alicroc said.

'- I want to wrestle mud!'

'You *can't* wrestle mud.'

'- But my mother does mud wrestling!'

'Yeah?' asked Alicroc. 'Well, your mother's a head case. Kids, leave it to me!'

So next weekend, Alicroc took his scout troop down the river in a big canoe. They turned off into a swamp and climbed out of the boat onto a wet, grassy bank. The sun was hot, the flies were buzzing and the brightly striped water snakes were looking at the Tiny Scouts' toes and licking their snaky lips.

'Kids,' said Alicroc, 'Big Mike has taken the Big Scouts off to do some wrestling against other scouts. Well, we're going to do something better. We're going to wrestle....

...... *Alligators!'*

'Hooray! Hoo – ***WHAT??'***

'It's easier than you think, kids. Trust me!'

He took some large rubber alligators out of the canoe and let the children try to wrestle them. But even though the alligators were made of rubber, they still beat the children.

'Okay, kids,' said Alicroc. 'Let me show you two secrets about alligator wrestling. First, you've got to look them in the eye. Like this!'

He grabbed a rubber alligator and showed the children how to stare down their opponent.

'Then you use the Alligator Peace Grip. Like this!'

He reached out and held the alligator's mouth shut with a thumb and one finger.

The children practiced all morning on rubber alligators. After lunch, Alicroc caught some tiny alligators for them to try.

An hour later, after he had bandaged all their bites, he caught some bigger alligators.... and then bigger ones... and then alligators more than twice the size of the children.

'Remember, kids! Once you've used the Peace Grip, the alligator will do whatever you tell it to!'

Helpfulness badges

The next time at the scout hut, the big ones showed off the trophies and medals they had won, and the little ones showed off their alligator bite marks.

Big Mike scoffed at them. 'I know what you kids have really been doing – you've been fighting *kittens!* And the kittens won!'

All the scouts laughed and jeered at the Tinies.

Big Mike said, 'You little kids just get in the way! Now, *my* scouts all have their Helpfulness Badges. Last week, they cut the grass in the park and I fed it to my big horses. Tomorrow they're going to help some stupid old people across the road.'

'Helping people is a good thing,' said Alicroc. 'I'd like my scouts to do that, too. Can we join you?'

Big Mike sneered at him. 'You can't!' he said. 'Your scouts aren't big enough to get Helpfulness Badges! All *they'll* ever get is *Uselessness* Badges!'

The Tinies shook their heads sadly, and the Big Scouts laughed at them again.

But after that, everywhere the Big Scouts went, they kept meeting the little scouts Being Helpful.

- *The big ones went to the zoo, and the Tinies were feeding the animals and cleaning their cages.*
- *The big ones went to the cinema, and the Tinies were running the projector...backwards.*
- *The big ones went to the circus and the Tinies were riding the circus ponies dressed as clowns.*
- *The big ones went to the beach and all the Tinies were there as Lifeguards, trying to save the jellyfish.*
- *The big ones went to help old ladies across the*

street, only to find that the Tinies were driving the old ladies around in little golf carts.

The Competition

Finally the Scouts Competition came. All the scouts camped out in the hills and sang scout songs around their campfires. Everyone had a good time, except for Big Mike. He couldn't enjoy the songs and games because he was thinking all the time about *Winning*.

He made his scouts think about it all the time, too. He even made them sing songs about Winning!

The first competition was a race to the top of a long, high hill. The scouts all had to carry big packs on their backs, and the packs were so big that the Tinies could hardly stand up. The other scouts laughed as they passed the Tinies on the road, and some of them "accidentally" pushed the Tinies over.

'It's okay, kids,' said Alicroc. 'We're going to let them go past, and then we're going to...

.... take out our lassos!'

They caught some wild, smelly mountain goats and rode them to the top of the hill - *and got there first!*

Big Mikes' team was only second, and he wasn't happy about that...

The second test was a race across the river. All the teams had long canoes with their scoutmaster sitting in the middle.

They were all bumping into one another, splashing one another, and snatching the other teams' paddles - especially from the poor Tinies.

And then, when the Tinies got their canoe halfway across, they found that someone had made holes in it. They started to sink... and started to scream.

'Mr Ali-cwoc, we're going down!'

'- I can't swim!'

'- I can't count!'

'- I'm gonna be sick!'

Alicroc said calmly, 'Don't panic, kids. I've made some arrangements, just in case. Follow me!'

He stepped out of the boat and stood up. 'Okay, one at a time,' he said. 'Quick march!'

Each scout got out nervously and found a line of dark green alligators waiting by the boat. As they walked forward, the alligator at the back of the line would swim ahead to the front, and so the line kept moving forwards, one alligator at a time.

Alicroc said, 'Like I told you, kids: once you've used the Peace Grip on an alligator, he'll do anything you ask!'

The other boats were still fighting one another, so the Tinies walked through them - *and got to the other side first!*

Big Mike's team was second again, and he wasn't happy about that...

Lastly, there was a night-time hike through a deep, dark wood. Every troop started in the middle of the wood and had a different path out to follow, using a map, a compass and three small lights.

As darkness fell, each troop opened its instructions to find out which way to go. The Tinies had to go out on a path to the West, and Big Mike's Big Scouts had to go East. The other scouts went off in different directions: North, South and everything in between.

It took the Tinies much longer to read their instructions and put on their backpacks, because:

- most of them couldn't read
- most of them couldn't put on their packs by themselves
- and none of them could tie their own boots.

'Mr Ali-cwoc, I can't find my light!'

'- I can't find my hat!'

'- I can't find my boots!'

'- I can't find my sick bag!'

'Okay,' said Alicroc. 'We won't be the fastest team tonight, and maybe I'll have to carry one or two of you, but we'll get out of the woods somehow. We'll probably be last this time, but that doesn't matter so long as we do our best. Now, who's got the map?'

But the map wasn't there. In its place was a piece of paper, on which was written one word:

LOSERS!

One Tiny said, 'Big kids must have taken the map when we were packing our bags, Mister Ali-cwoc!'

'I guess you're right,' said Alicroc.

'Let's go anyway, Mister Ali-cwoc! We can be explorers!'

'- Pirates!'

'- Adventurers!'

'- Cannibals!'

'- Rabbits!'

'- Worms!'

Alicroc shook his head. 'No, kids,' he said. 'It's not safe to wander around the woods in the dark without a map. We'll have to make camp here.'

'But we'll lose!'

Alicroc said, 'That's right. We're going to lose, and Big Mike's team is probably going to win. But we're going have *fun* losing! We'll build a big fire and eat sausages and drink lemonade and tell stories and sing songs!'

'Hooray!'

An hour later the woods were ringing to laughter and singing around a campfire, and even some of the woodland animals had crept close to listen. There was a wonderful smell of food, and the shadows cast by the fire were deep and mysterious.

'Wait a minute!' said Alicroc suddenly. 'What's that noise?'

The Tinies held their breath and listened. It was the sound of marching feet and a weary song:

'Left right, *one two,* left right, *three four,* lefty righty, we are mighty! *One two three four*! Left right...'

All of Big Mike's troop marched into the camp, and the biggest boy and girl came forward.

'We're sorry we took your map,' they said. 'Big Mike said we had to. But we've brought it back.'

'And your lights...'

'And this hat...'

'And this pair of boots...'

'And this sick bag...'

Alicroc said, 'That's okay, kids. Would you like some sausages?'

So they all sat around the campfire eating sausages and marshmallows and telling stories. Some of the stories were so scary that everyone shivered. Some of the stories were so funny that everyone laughed until tears ran down their faces.

Then they took turns acting out little plays, making up songs, and reciting silly poems.

And the Big Scouts said it was the best time they'd ever had in the scouts.

... But Big Mike was so angry with them that he drove away in his Off Road Monster Truck and was never seen as a scoutmaster again....

... And Alicroc enjoyed being a scoutmaster so much that he stayed for a whole year.

Easter Bunnies vs.

Fairy G-mother feat. Cinderella

The voices

The Bunnies are a tough bunch of desperados. They talk like cops from the mean side of town who have woken up one morning and found they've been turned into cowboys. They truly believe their leader was snared by the evil, scheming Snow White and you can feel the anger and puzzlement in their voices as they speak about it.

The Fairy G-mother's voice is low and rough, just like her. She growls a bit when she's angry (which is often) and shouts when she's annoyed (which is almost always). But she does have a soft side... a *very small* soft side... and her voice goes rather shaky and sweet when she's thinking about the stupid, hunky princes.

The Stupid, Hunky Princes have rawther luvly accents, don't you know? They are absolutely spiffingly certain they're right about everything, and will marry a girl in a flash if the shoe fits somewhere on her body, or else they'll have her head chopped off if she doesn't know how to curtsey properly.

Cinderella is young and sweet and very, very tired. Her gentle and kind voice has an edge to it, because (1) she *knows* you're going to ask her to clean something and (2) she *knows* she's meant for better things – such as robbing banks.

Her **Stepsisters and Stepmother** sound bossy. They are.

The story

1: The Bunnies hit town

Long ago - so long ago that nothing much had been invented, not even hot cross buns - the Six Easter Bunnies rode into town. They wore colourful ponchos over their shoulders and dusty cowboy hats on their heads.

They tied up their horses outside Trader Jon's bar and went inside. Heads turned as they pushed through the swinging wooden doors: heads with plenty of scars, and eyes that narrowed as they looked up from their gambling chips.

The bunnies took off their hats, and several men choked on their drinks.

One bunny said politely to the barman, 'We'd like seven carrot cocktails, please.'

Trader Jon sneered at them. 'That drink hasn't been

invented yet!' he said.

One of the men at a table spoke up: 'And we don't like rabbits in this town!'

Six machine guns suddenly appeared from beneath the ponchos.

One bunny pointed his gun at the bartender. 'Maybe you're gonna invent that drink now,' he said softly. 'I like mine with a stick of celery in it.'

The bartender pointed a shaking finger at the machine gun. 'What in tarnation is *that*?' he asked.

'This is a machine gun. It can fire a hundred rounds of high velocity, low melting point confectionery in five seconds.'

'A hundred *whats*?'

'A hundred Easter eggs which melt as they're fired and cover the target with a variety of fillings. Which filling would you like to try first? We have coffee cream, vanilla, nut crunch, marshmallow, chocolate chip and Easter Surprise.'

'What's an Easter Surprise?' asked one of the cowboys at a table.

One of the Easter bunnies threw him something wrapped in foil. 'This,' he said.

The man slowly unwrapped the egg-shaped lump of chocolate. 'Smells good...' he said.

'... Tastes good, too...' he added, taking a big bite.

'... Except –' and then he ran outside to be sick on the road.

'Yep,' said the Bunny. 'A nice, crunchy snail in every egg. ***That's*** the Surprise!'

The bartender poured seven drinks with a hand that shook. He said, 'You guys look a little warm, and I can see you're upset. Does that mean you're that dangerous gang that goes by the name of – '

'Don't say it!' shouted the bunnies. '**DON'T** say it!'

The bartender put his hands up shakily and said, 'I wasn't gonna say nothin'. It's just that I –'

Six guns pointed at his face, six trigger fingers twitched, and he stopped dead. He watched quietly as the rabbits downed their drinks in one gulp.

But one man made the mistake of saying, 'Hey - you rabbits can't count! There's seven drinks and there's only six of you! There's only -'

Six guns pelted him with quick-drying chocolate, and in a moment there was a small black statue where a man used to be.

'Anybody else want to complain about how many drinks we have?' snarled a bunny. 'Anybody?'

The men all shook their heads.

'That's good, because if we had to tell you how our boss married a double-crossing, bunny-snatching Princess, it would make us very upset and we would have to shoot everybody in this bar. Understand?'

One very stupid cowboy put up his hand and said, 'Excuse me, but you just told us the very thing you said you would have to shoot us for –'

Half a dozen guns spoke again and another chocolate statue appeared.

One Easter bunny looked around at the slightly smaller group of men. He asked, 'Has anybody ***else*** got something to say about the way our boss was snared by Snow White and left us sad and angry, so that we travel around the countryside picking fights?'

'No,' they all whispered.

'Good,' he said, 'Because ***we ain't gonna tell you!*** Bartender, pour us another seven carrot cocktails!'

The bartender mixed another seven drinks and placed them before the bunnies.

'We – ummm – don't see many bunnies around here,' he said.

One bunny nodded. 'Yeah. We've come to town because it's nearly the day that would be Easter, if Easter had happened yet. We've brought presents for the children: Easter eggs. *And* we've brought presents for any dumb cowboys we meet: also Easter eggs.'

A dumb cowboy held up his hand. 'Excuse me!' he said. 'What's the difference between the eggs for the children and the eggs for the cowboys?'

'This,' said one of the bunnies, and opened fire. Another cowboy turned into a chocolate statue.

'Yep,' said a bunny. 'That's the difference: about a hundred miles an hour... or it would be a hundred and sixty kilometres per hour, if kilometres had been invented yet.'

'Oh,' said all the cowboys that weren't statues.

'Have another drink,' suggested the bartender.

'A toast!' shouted the cowboys.

'A toast!' shouted the bunnies.

'Long live the King!' shouted the cowboys, and

slurped their drinks.

'May your chewing gum never go hard!' shouted the bunnies, and slurped theirs.

There was silence while the cowboys looked at one another. 'Long live the Queen?' they tried next.

'Always brush your teeth before going to bed!' shouted the bunnies, downing their cocktails.

'Um... Long live the three Princes!' shouted the cowboys. 'And all the cute Princesses!'

'Don't scratch a mosquito bite!' shouted the bunnies.

Just then there was a noise of marching feet outside, and a soldier wearing a red uniform and a furry hat shouted through the window:

'I heard you! You didn't toast the King and Queen and the Royal Children properly. You must be those notorious rebels called –'

'Don't say it!' shouted six voices.

'Okay. But you bad bunnies had better come outside!' the soldier ordered.

'Why?' asked the bunnies.

'Because we'll make a mess of Trader Jon's windows if have to shoot arrows through them.'

The bunnies shouted, 'You can't make us come out! We've got six machine guns!'

'So? *We've* got a hundred bows and lots of arrows.'

One bunny shouted back, 'So? ***We've*** got a ***bomb!'***

The soldier shouted to the other soldiers, 'They've got a bomb!'

There was a stunned silence, and then someone asked, 'What's a bomb?'

'It's one of these,' said a bunny, pulling out a very large Easter egg and holding it up to the window.

The soldier shouted back to the others, 'It's a big egg thing with shiny wrapping!'

'We're not afraid of eggs!' they shouted back.

One bunny shouted, 'But this egg blows things up!'

'Ohhhh.... it blows things up... You mean, like a balloon? Like a balloon you blow up at parties?'

'No!'

'Ohhhh... like a feather, then. Like when a feather floats down and you blow it back up again?'

'***No!***

'Like what, then?'

The bunnies looked at one another. 'It blows things up like – like a ***bomb***,' they said.

'What's a bomb?' the soldiers asked again.

The bunnies sighed. 'One of these,' said a bunny, and rolled it out the door.

There was a brief silence. Then someone said, 'Awww, look how shiny it is! Ain't it pretty?'

There was a loud noise.

Someone said, 'Oh... *That's* blowing up!'

Someone else said, 'I'm covered in chocolate.'

'Tastes good, though.'

'Stop licking me!'

2: Cinderella cleans up

The bunnies ran out the back way and didn't stop running until they came to a large house at the bottom of the hill, below the palace. They broke into the garden, ate all the lettuces, and fell asleep in a big shed. After a while some chocolate-covered soldiers marched past and went back to the palace.

The next morning they were woken at dawn by someone sweeping the paving stones. They went back to sleep but were woken again by someone washing the windows of the house.

Then they were woken by someone washing the roof of the house. *Then* they were woken by someone emptying the bins. And as they were dozing off again, someone started scrubbing down the carriage, and singing as she scrubbed.

The bunnies got up and were eating carrots in the garden when a loud, unpleasant voice shouted from the big house:

'Cinderella! Come wash my dress!'

Then another voice, equally loud and obnoxious, shouted, 'No! Come clean my shoes first!'

A third and older voice shouted, 'But only after you've mopped the kitchen floor!'

'- And cleaned my bathtub for me!'

'- First you've got to carry me to the dining room! The floor's cold and I can't be bothered to put my slippers on!'

'- And then take the coal down into the cellar!'

Cinderella shouted back, 'But Evil Stepmother, we don't *have* a cellar!'

'Oh.... Then *dig* one!'

And so it went on all day, until Cinderella's stepmother and stepsisters went out to a party, leaving Cinderella to wash the dishes and put away the garden furniture. She opened the shed door and...

... There were six bunnies inside, trying to hide beneath six big cowboy hats.

'I can see you!' she said.

'Bother!' said one bunny crossly.

'Oh!' said Cinderella. 'You're in a bad mood. Does that mean you're that gang of angry desperados they call the –'

'Don't say it!' Six machine guns appeared.

Cinderella put her hands on her hips and looked at them sternly, saying, 'I *know* guns haven't been invented yet, but you'd better not fire those in here! I spent all Saturday getting this place tidy!'

The bunnies meekly put down their guns and one bunny begged, 'Please don't tell the palace guards we're here. They want to kill us, especially after we covered them with exploding chocolate outside Trader Jon's.'

'That must have been messy,' said Cinderella. 'Did you clean it up afterwards?'

'No,' said one bunny. 'We were too busy running away.'

'Okay,' said Cinderella with a sigh. 'I'd better get a broom... and maybe a shovel as well. And some hot soapy water to wipe down the walls.'

'*You* don't have to clean it up!' said the bunnies.

'Well, *someone* needs to do it! Tell me - did any of the chocolate get on the windows? Windows are a real nuisance to clean. They go all streaky, don't they? You really need something that just scrapes the soapy water off, and doesn't scratch the glass.'

The bunnies looked at one another. 'We'll invent a squeegee for you,' said one of them. 'That's like a big letter T with a strip of leather along the top, and you use it for cleaning windows.'

Another added, 'Yeah, and we'll make a sweeping machine to clean up the mess in the road. We haven't got any fuel, so we'll have to hook it up to a bicycle.'

Cinderella asked, 'What's a bicycle?'

'Uh... We'll invent one of those, too.'

When a month had passed, Cinderella also had a vacuum cleaner, a washing machine and a dishwasher. Electricity hadn't been invented yet, so she had to run them off a bicycle, and therefore she now had very strong legs as well.

She also had an automatic car wash you put coins in, when it would spray soapy water all over the carriage and rub it down with big rotating fluffy rollers. She put the horses through it, too. They liked it.

The one invention she didn't like was the television. Cinderella's stepsisters were both lazy slobs, and they insisted on sitting in front of the television for hours while Cinderella pedalled away on the bicycle to make it work.

And since no one had ever made any TV programmes, all you saw on the television was other people sitting in their own homes watching *you*. Only six homes had TV, so you had six channels, one of which was your own.

But at least there was Royalty Channel One. If you turned to this, you could see the Royal Family in the palace, eating off plates made of gold in the Dining Room or having someone's head chopped off in the Chopping Room. And on Friday nights, the Channel showed you the Royal Ball - or as they called it, "Royalty Come Dancing". This went on for hours.

Royalty Come Dancing was incredibly boring. It wasn't nearly as good as "Royalty Come Get Your Head Chopped Off" on Saturdays, but the two stepsisters used to watch it every Friday night, starting at 9 pm and finishing at about 3 in the morning. They would drool over the hunky but stupid Princes and the beautiful but stupid Princesses, and exclaim over all the silly dresses and hats, and copy the waltzes, foxtrots, polkas and tangos until Cinderella got so tired and bored that she fell asleep and fell off the bicycle.

When this happened, the two stepsisters would throw their popcorn and ice cream at her until she woke up. (They were too lazy to get off the sofa). Then she would climb wearily back onto her bicycle and start pedalling again.

Of course, what the stepsisters wanted most of all was to go to the Ball themselves and appear on TV, so that other silly people could drool over *them*.

And what Cinderella *also* wanted most of all was for the stepsisters to go to the Ball, so that she could have a good night's sleep on Fridays.

One Friday morning, Cinderella was chopping down a tree on the front lawn to build a boat for one of the stepsisters when a Royal Messenger came to the front door. He had a big envelope in his hand.

He raised his hand to the big, shiny brass door knocker… But before he could touch it, the door was flung open and the stepmother snatched the envelope from the messenger's hand and ripped it open, scattering pieces all over the doorstep for Cinderella to pick up.

'An invitation to the Ball tonight!' the stepmother screeched. 'Two invitations! Three! *Four!*' She counted them again and then ripped one into tiny pieces which she threw into the air.

'Like I said, *three* invitations! Cinderella?'

'Yes, Evil Stepmother?'

'Cinderella, put that tree back in the ground and come help your stepsisters get ready for the Ball. We have a lot to do. And *you're* going to do most of it!'

Cinderella spent all day helping the others get ready for the Ball. Finally they went off in the family carriage, leaving Cinderella looking at piles of shoes, clothing, makeup, shoes, dirty teacups, shoes, tissues, shoes, plates, pots, pans, broken tennis rackets and... shoes.

'I'll never get all this cleaned up before they come back at 3 am!' she complained. 'What I need is a Fairy Godmother!'

And as if by magic... nothing happened.

When the six Easter bunnies turned up a few minutes later, they found Cinderella sobbing next to a pile of shoes.

This was serious! So they set to work, and within an hour they had tidied the whole house. Two bunnies did the washing up, two sorted the clothes and spent half an hour putting makeup on each other, one did the vacuuming and one bunny took charge of the shoes.

'That was amazing!' said Cinderella an hour later. 'How on earth did you manage to match up all those shoes and put them back into the correct shoeboxes so quickly?'

The bunny looked out into the garden, where a big shoe-and-shoebox bonfire was burning merrily. 'Ummm... we're just talented that way,' he said. He crossed his ears as he spoke, because bunnies can't cross their fingers.

Finally they all sat down with a cup of tea and seven carrot cocktails.

'Why seven?' asked Cinderella.

'We can't tell anyone,' said one of the bunnies.

'Yeah – no one must find out our secret sorrow.'

'No one must know that our great leader kissed the evil, heart-breaking bunny-hugging Snow White.'

'Yuk!' said all the bunnies.

'And then married her.'

'Double Yuk!' said all the bunnies.

'And now lives happily ever after in married bliss.'

'Triple Yuk!' said all the bunnies.

'Oh,' said Cinderella. 'I won't ask you about that, then.'

3: The Fairy G-mother

Just then – as they were sitting happily before the fireplace, where a log and shoe fire was crackling – as they were sipping their drinks – as they were talking happily of this and that – ***Suddenly*** –

There was a flash of light.
There was a roll of thunder.
There was a puff of smoke.
There was a smell of soap.

And out from the smoke stepped a fairy. A big fairy. A tough fairy. A fairy who could beat you at arm-wrestling with both arms tied behind her back. She looked like an Olympic weightlifter, but with

lots of long wavy hair, two wings and a tiny wand.

'Greetings!' she cried. 'I am your Fairy Grotmother!' She had a very deep voice and didn't speak posh like the other fairies. In fact, what she said came out as: *'Greetins! Oi am yer Ferry Grotmuvver!'*

Cinderella leapt to her feet with a shout of joy. 'You've come at last! Oh, I always *knew* you would! But what took you so long?'

The Fairy Grotmother looked shifty. 'I wuz... busy. Loadsa fings to do, y'know. Meetins and… fings.' She shrugged her shoulders and twiddled her wand.

It was an odd shape for a fairy's wand - a sort of wooden spoon shape…

… and her wings looked like two great oven gloves stapled to her back…

… and her fairy dress looked suspiciously like an apron with gravy stains down the front…

… and beneath her apron she was wearing a pink velvety tracksuit that needed a good wash….

… and on her feet she had fluffy pink slippers.

She was the chavviest fairy you ever saw.

Cinderella sighed, 'I always *knew* my Fairy Godmother would come and rescue me!'

'You wuzn't listenin',' complained the Fairy Grotmother. 'No one ever *listens!* I'm *not* your Fairy Godmother. I'm your Fairy ***Grot***muvver.'

'But – but – I thought –'

The Fairy Grotmother explained, 'Fairy Godmothers turn up once in a blue moon and give you magic slippers and rubbish fings like that. But we Grotmuvvers is more practical, right? We look after you all yer life.'

'All my life? But I'm eighteen, and this is the first time I've seen you!'

The Fairy snarled, 'Yeah, ***so****?* I been busy, I said.

But I've been lookin' after you, right? I mean, who d'ya fink has been sendin' you all this work to do? All this cleanin' and scrubbin' and mendin' and boat buildin'? You fink the Fairy Godmother done that? Nah – it was *me*!'

'But I don't *like* cleaning!'

'Cleanin's good for you. Healthy, innit?'

Cinderella frowned. She asked, 'But at least you've come now, and it's all going to be different, isn't it?'

The Fairy Grotmother shrugged her mighty shoulder. 'Sort of,' she said. Then she raised her wooden spoon wand and said in a dramatic voice:

'Cinderella – you *shall* go to the Ball!'

Cinderella sighed. 'That's very kind of you,' she said, 'but I'd rather stay home. I've been working nonstop all week, and all I want now is a long hot bath, a good book and an early night. I've waited *weeks* for the chance to have an evening on my own!'

The Fairy Grotmother shook her head. 'You weren't listenin'!' she growled. 'Why does no one ever *listen*? I didn't say you *can* go to the Ball. I didn't say you *may* go to the Ball. I said you *shall* go! It ain't a matter of choice, sweetheart!'

'Oh,' said Cinderella. 'But why can't I stay home?'

'Because I got a contract.'

'A what?'

'A contract. I've agreed to get all the cleanin' done at the palace tonight. You fink these Balls clean themselves? I get paid a hundred gold pieces, but the girl what was gonna do the cleanin' is sick. So you *shall* go to the Ball, and you *shall* take your mop and bucket wiv you!'

She pointed her wand at Cinderella, in a threatening way.

The six Easter bunnies had been listening to all this quietly, but when the Fairy Grotmother turned her wand on Cinderella, six machine guns appeared and were aimed precisely at an x-shaped gravy splash in the middle of the Fairy Grotmother's apron.

'Drop that wand, Fairy!' one bunny shouted. 'And back away from it reaaaaaal slow!'

The Fairy Grotmother laughed at them and twitched the wand once. The machine guns seemed to melt in the bunnies' hands, and turned into dainty little brooms.

'And *you're* goin' to the Ball as well, bunnies!' she sneered. 'All ... uh... one – two – free – uh, free and a bit... (she tried to count them).... uh... *all* of you!'

'Bother!' said all the bunnies. 'Botheration!'

The Fairy Grotmother looked at them. 'Just a minute,' she said. 'You're all hot an' bovvered. Does that mean you're the dangerous gang that bakes those little cakes at this time of year and goes round pushin' 'em through letter boxes, strikin' terror into people's hearts, that gang known as the –'

'***Don't say it!***' shouted the bunnies crossly, pointing their brooms at her. 'Don't say it, or we'll do bad things to you with these brooms!'

The Fairy Grotmother thought about what they might do with the brooms.

'Orl right,' she said. 'Cool it, bunnies.'

Then Cinderella folded her arms, stamped her foot and said crossly, 'I *won't* go! I *won't* do the cleaning at the Palace!'

'Won't you, sweetheart?' asked the Fairy Grotmother. There was an evil look upon her face. 'Tell me: do you like teddy bears?' she asked.

'I *love* teddy bears!' exclaimed Cinderella.

The Fairy Grotmother reached into an apron pocket and took out a dear little teddy.

'You see this teddy?' she growled. 'See its little teddy smile?'

The teddy beamed up at them all.

'Yes,' said Cinderella. 'It's a very happy teddy. Can I give him a hug?' She reached out for the bear.

'No you can't!' the fairy shouted.

The Fairy Grotmother reached into another apron pocket and took out a needle and some thread. She said, 'You see this needle and thread? Yeah? Well, do you know what I'm gonna do if you won't go to the palace? I'm gonna take this needle and thread, and sew a great big frown on his happy little face. I'll make this the saddest teddy you ever met!'

The teddy looked very, very worried.

'And then,' gloated the Fairy Grotmother, '*then* I'm gonna cut off his ears and sew them to his bum!'

'No!' shouted Cinderella. 'Please don't do that! I'll do anything, *anything*! Just don't hurt the teddy!'

The Fairy Grotmother put the teddy back in her pocket, led them all outside and waved her wand. One of the bunnies' Easter eggs grew to the size of a carriage and sprouted candy-coated wheels, a door and windows with elegant white chocolate curtains.

'Horses,' she muttered. 'Need some horses.' She looked at the bunnies and raised her wand again.

'Wait!' said one bunny. 'Give us five minutes and

we'll invent something.'

'Orl right.' Then she looked at Cinderella. 'You ain't half dirty,' she said. 'You're sweaty, grimy, greasy, blotchy and smelly.'

'Well, of course I am!' said Cinderella indignantly. 'I've been slaving all day, haven't I? I just need a long, hot bath!'

'No time for that,' said the Fairy Grotmother. 'You got a car wash outside, right? I saw it as I came in.' And she waved a wand and put Cinderella through the carriage wash machine.

Cinderella came out the other side spluttering and gasping for breath, but a lot cleaner.

'Now for your Ball gown!' Another swing of the wand, and Cinderella was clothed from head to toe in the most beautiful...

... maid's outfit, complete with feather duster, rubber gloves and sensible shoes.

'I *hate* sensible shoes!' shouted Cinderella. 'Give me back my lace-up boots!'

'No chance!' said the Fairy Grotmother and pushed Cinderella into the carriage, climbing in beside her.

'Why are *you* coming?' asked Cinderella, holding her nose because the Fairy Grotmother smelled very strongly of soap.

The Fairy Grotmother turned pink. Her voice went a bit shy and giggly. 'I like lookin' at Princes,' she said. 'I fink they're really fit, like.'

Then she cracked a whip at the bunnies and shouted, 'Gee up there!'

The six bunnies climbed onto the bicycle, now fitted with seven sets of seats, handlebars and pedals.

'Why *seven* seats?' the Fairy Grotmother asked.

'Don't ask!' the bunnies shouted.

The carriage smelled delicious and the Fairy Grotmother ate the door handles and half the windows on the way. And when Cinderella and the Fairy Grotmother got out, they simply reeked of chocolate... and soap.

4: Midnight at the palace

Cinderella spent all evening cleaning at the palace, and the bunnies had to help her. The Fairy Grotmother just sat around and watched the Princes, but the others worked their little socks off.

As Cinderella was collecting empty plates, the youngest Prince ran over to her and took her hand. 'Come dance with me!' he cried.

'Why me?' asked Cinderella.

'Because you're wearing sensible shoes! *And* you look so *clean!* You look like... like a car that's just gone through a car wash - even though cars haven't been invented yet! And you smell like...'

The Prince took a big sniff.

'... like soap and chocolate. It's gorgeous!'

So Cinderella and the Prince danced for an hour. But then she heard the clock chiming midnight.

'I must go!' she said.

'Don't!' the Prince cried.

'I must - the bunnies are waiting for me on their bicycle!' she insisted.

'What???'

The Prince released Cinderella and backed away from her nervously. 'Did you say some bunnies were waiting for you on a bicycle?'

'Yes. They invented it last week.'

The Prince backed away a little further... a little further... too far... and fell down two flights of stairs.

Cinderella watched him bounce to the bottom of the staircase, and then ran down the stairs towards the waiting carriage.

As she passed the Prince at the bottom of the staircase, he grabbed at her leg but she gave him a good kick and got away...

... all apart from one sensible shoe which he pulled off her foot. He hugged it close and sighed happily. It smelled of...

'Soap and chocolate!' he exclaimed. 'It's *her* shoe!'

5: If the shoe fits...

Sadly, no one knew who the beautiful cleaning girl was. So the Prince went out with ten soldiers, a royal shoe holder, a royal door knocker and a royal head chopper. They began knocking on doors and inviting women to try on the shoe, and chopping off the heads of those who didn't pass the Curtsey Tests.

'It's *soooo* important to keep up standards!' said the Prince, sentencing yet another girl to appear on the next 'Royalty Come Get Your Head Chopped Off.'

Finally they came to Cinderella's house.

'I'm looking for a beautiful girl I danced with at the Ball,' said the Prince. 'She smelled of soap and chocolate and I want to marry her.'

'That was me!' said the older stepsister.

The Prince leaned close and sniffed. 'No,' he said. '*You* smell of fried chicken.'

The younger stepsister ran upstairs and rubbed soap all over her neck and sprinkled chocolate in her hair. She ran down and shouted, 'It was *me!*'

The Prince had a sniff. 'Could be,' he said. 'See if the shoe fits.'

The stepsister tried to get the shoe on, but her foot was too long.

'Just a moment!' she said. She ran to the kitchen, got a knife and chopped off her big toe.

She tried the shoe again and it fitted perfectly, though blood kept dripping out of the end of it.

'You're the one!' exclaimed the Prince. 'Marry me!'

Just then there was a flash of light and puff of smoke, and the Fairy Grotmother appeared, pulling Cinderella by the arm.

'You got it all wrong,' she growled. 'Here's the girl you danced with. Marry *her!*'

The Prince looked at Cinderella's feet. 'It can't be *her*,' he said. 'She's wearing lace-up boots!'

'What?' asked the Fairy Grotmother. 'You danced wiv her for an hour! Didn'tcha look at her face?'

'No,' said the Prince. 'Of course not! It's the *shoes* that matter. And the curtseying, of course.'

Cinderella stamped her foot. 'I don't want to marry a stupid Prince anyway!' she shouted.

The Prince said, 'I'm *not* stupid. I'm very clever, and I *know* you can't be the right girl because *you* don't smell of soap and chocolate - you smell of dirt and sweat and bicycle grease! And that's *impossible,* because bicycles haven't been invented yet!'

(So later that year the youngest Prince married the youngest stepsister, but she always had to wear soap and chocolate perfume, which she hated. *And* she had to cut off her other big toe as well, so both her feet always hurt and she never danced again. *Which served her right!*)

6: Midnight strikes again

The next month, they were all invited to another ball, and once again Cinderella had to help them dress, and once again the Fairy Grotmother turned up, and once again Cinderella refused to go.

The Fairy Grotmother reached into another apron pocket and took out a sweet little rat.

'You see this rat? He's darlin', right?'

'Squeak!' said the rat, looking cute and cuddly.

'He's a very dear little rat,' Cinderella agreed. 'Can I pet him?' She held out her hands to hold him.

'No you can't!' growled the Fairy Grotmother. 'Now, his name is Rocky: Rocky the Rat. Good name, innit?'

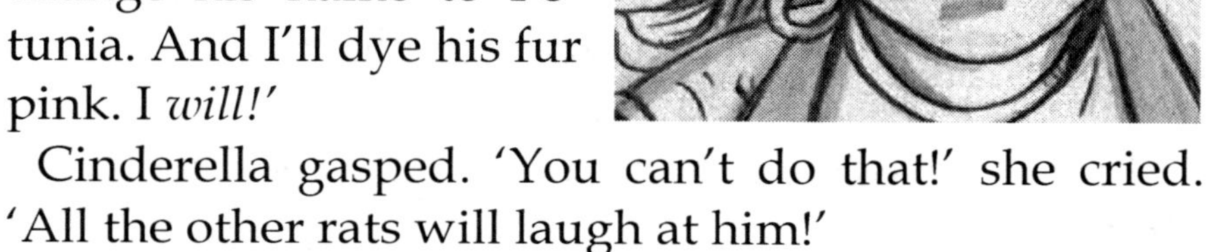

'Oh yes. It really suits him!' Cinderella said.

'Well, if you don't go to the Ball, I'm gonna change his name to Petunia. And I'll dye his fur pink. I *will!*'

Cinderella gasped. 'You can't do that!' she cried. 'All the other rats will laugh at him!'

The rat nodded its little head, and tears came into its cute little rat eyes.

The Fairy Grotmother laughed scornfully. 'But I *will* change his name and dye his fur, if you don't go to the Ball! He won't never have no friends after that, and it'll be *your* fault!'

So of course Cinderella went to the Ball again and spent the evening cleaning up after the guests, danced with the *middle* Prince, watched *him* fall down the stairs, lost *another* sensible shoe and got to the carriage just in time.

The older stepsister was ready for the middle Prince the next day and was wearing chocolate lipstick and had bits of soap stuck to her hair. She passed the smell test and then tried on the shoe.

'It's a little loose,' said the Prince unhappily.

'Just a moment!' she said and went into the kitchen.

She found the big toe her sister had chopped off and glued it to the end of her own toe. She came back and tried on the shoe again. It fitted perfectly.

'My darling!' exclaimed the Prince. 'Come kiss me!'

Just then there was a flash of light and a puff of smoke and soap as the Fairy Grotmother appeared, dragging Cinderella with her once again.

'You stupid Prince!' she shouted. '*Here* is the girl you danced wiv last night!'

The Prince looked at Cinderella. 'Can't be,' he said. 'The one I danced with had nice clean hands. This girl's hands are quite, quite yukky.'

'But the *face*! Look at the face!' exclaimed the Fairy Grotmother.

'Right face, but wrong hands,' said the Prince. 'Sorry!' He turned and took the hands of the older stepsister. 'See?' he said. 'These are lovely clean hands. And the shoe fits. So it *must* be her!'

As the Fairy Grotmother dragged Cinderella away in a huff, the Prince looked at the stepsister's face again. He frowned.

'Now that I think of it, though,' he said, 'your ears are too big. I'm sure they were smaller last night!'

'Just a moment!' said the stepsister and went into the kitchen again. She came back with...

... a felt tip pen...

... and a pair of scissors.

She gave the pen to the Prince. 'Maybe they stretched overnight. What size did you think they were?' she asked.

He marked each ear with the pen.

'Come back in a few days,' she said, sharpening the

scissors. 'I promise they'll be back to normal then.'

'Wait a minute!' he said. 'I'm sure your nose was a bit longer. And those kneecaps aren't right, either...'

(So the middle Prince eventually married the older stepsister, but only after she had changed most of her body. And then, every few weeks, he would remember something else that he thought was different, so she ended up with twelve fingers, no hair, one leg longer than the other and a nose that twisted round like a corkscrew. *And it served her right!*)

7: And once more...

There was one Prince left – the oldest, richest, handsomest and stupidest of the three. And one day a royal messenger came with four invitations again.

'*Three* invitations,' said the stepmother firmly, ripping one up. 'Cinderella has a lot of cleaning to do, *and* she smells like ... well - like a woman who does a lot of cleaning. Cinderella, you shall *not* go to the Ball!'

'I bet I do,' whispered Cinderella sadly. And she was right. Just as she and the bunnies had finished cleaning the house, the Fairy Grotmother popped out of another puff of smoke.

'Rose Red has the measles,' she announced, 'and Sleeping Beauty's out like a light. It's you and me again, Cinders.'

'You and me?' asked Cinderella. 'But *you* never do anything!'

'I watch,' said the Fairy Grotmother. 'It's hard work, watchin'.'

'You don't watch me, you only watch the Princes,' scoffed Cinderella. 'Why don't you dance with them yourself?'

The Fairy Grotmother turned bright red. 'I got hairy legs,' she said. 'No one's gonna dance wiv a girl wiv hairy legs.'

'Well, I'm *not* going!' Cinderella shouted. 'I've had enough of cleaning up after other people! The bunnies and I are running away and living as bandits!'

The Fairy Grotmother just laughed and reached into her apron pocket. She took out a tiny kitten.

She put the kitten on the kitchen table.

'Mew?' asked the kitten, looking very sweet.

The Fairy Grotmother held it firmly with one big, tough hand. 'See this cute little kitten?' she asked.

'Yes,' said Cinderella. 'It's an *adorable* kitten. Can I stroke it?' She held out her hands for it.

'No you can't!' The Fairy Grotmother shouted. She took something else from an apron pocket.

'See this big sharp knife?' she asked.

Cinderella gasped. 'Oh no!' she said. '*Please* don't hurt the kitten!'

The Fairy Grotmother laughed evilly. 'You know what I'm gonna do? Hey? If you don't do the cleaning tonight, I'm gonna *cut off the kitten's whiskers!*

And worse than that –' she dropped her voice to a cruel whisper. 'I'm gonna cut off the whiskers *on only one side!'*

'Mew!' said the kitten, looking very worried.

'No!' cried Cinderella. 'Not its dear little whiskers!'

So once again Cinderella had to go and clean at the Palace. And this time the eldest Prince came and demanded a dance with her.

He and Cinderella were dancing sweetly at the top of that long, steep staircase when midnight began to chime and Cinderella pulled away.

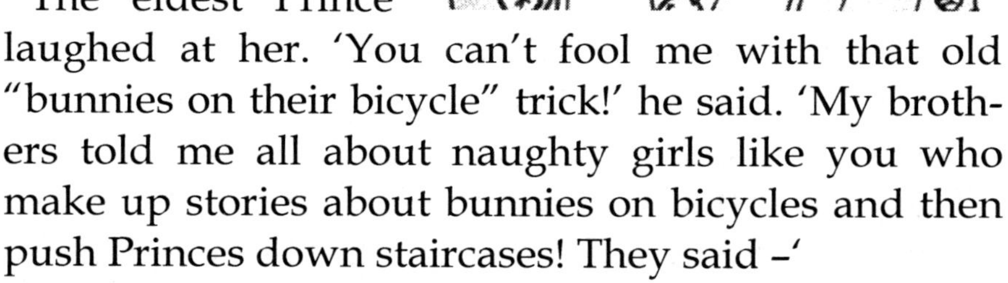

'Please stay!' he begged her.

'I can't!' she said. 'The bunnies are waiting for me on their bicycle!'

The eldest Prince laughed at her. 'You can't fool me with that old "bunnies on their bicycle" trick!' he said. 'My brothers told me all about naughty girls like you who make up stories about bunnies on bicycles and then push Princes down staircases! They said –'

Just then there was a noise of a bicycle bell being rung. The Prince turned and saw six bunnies on a bicycle made for seven, cycling up the stairs.

The Prince's jaw dropped as he stared at the bunnies on the bicycle. He took a step away from Cinderella... and another... and one too many... and fell all the way down the stairs.

As the Prince was bouncing down the staircase, the bunnies arrived at the top of the stairs, panting and sweating.

They all stood looking down at the Prince: Easter bunnies, Cinderella and Fairy Grotmother.

Then the bunnies grabbed the Fairy Grotmother, snatched her wand, tied her wings and threw her down the stairs as well.

It was a clever move: a move they had practiced for weeks. It was all over in a second, and the Fairy Grotmother was soaring through the air just they way they'd planned, down, down and down –

... and then landed with a *thump* in the arms of the eldest Prince, who was still lying on the floor.

'Oh!' she gasped.

'Oh!' said the Prince. 'You smell of soap and chocolate! Have you got sensible shoes on?'

The Fairy Grotmother pulled up the hem of her scummy pink tracksuit and showed him a pink, furry slipper.

'Oh, wow!' said the Prince. 'Pink slippers - that's *so* classy! *And* you've got hairy legs! *Double wow!*'

The Fairy Grotmother turned red.

'Sorry 'bout that,' she muttered.

'Oh, but I *like* them!' exclaimed the Prince. 'They're simply gorgeous! Will you marry me?'

'Spect so,' said the Fairy Grotmother with a shrug of her mighty shoulders. 'Wotever.'

And she smiled.

At the top of the stairs, the bunnies jumped back on

the bicycle.

'Hop on!' they shouted to Cinderella.

Together they pedalled furiously around the palace, nicking anything small and valuable and throwing it into the bike's baskets.

8: The Bunnies ride again

A few months later a long, gleaming motorcycle roared through the dusty streets. Its turbo-charged engines throbbed and its seven handlebars gleamed.

It came to rest by Trader Jon's bar and seven cowboys climbed off. They were all dressed in white leather and wore big white cowboy hats.

One of the cowboys was much taller than the others and led the way inside. The six bunnies took off their hats, and some of the men sitting inside choked on their drinks.

The tall cowboy took off *her* hat, and *all* the men choked.

She went to the bar and threw some gold pieces to the bartender. 'Seven Carrot Slammers,' she ordered, 'and put some ice in them!'

The bartender said unhappily, 'That drink hasn't been invented yet –'

Six automatic weapons appeared from beneath six leather jackets, and one mean-looking wand was pulled from the top of a knee-high lace-up boot. They were all pointed at the bartender.

He said, 'I'll invent it right away, Ma'am.'

His hands trembled as he mixed the drinks.

'Tell me,' he said. 'You guys look like you've ridden a long way -'

'We have.'

One of the men at a table added, '- and you look kinda hot -'

'We are.'

Another said '- and, well, you look like you're angry at everything –'

'That's us!' shouted the Bunnies.

' – so does that mean you're that low-down gang of desperados and bandits who go around the country stealin' from the rich and givin' to the poor –'

'- and shootin' anyone that gets in their way –'

'- and shootin' people who look at you funny –'

'- or call you names –'

'- or make fun of your ears –'

'- or just happen to be wearing sensible shoes?'

'Yep!' said Cinderella, swallowing her Carrot Slammer in one gulp. 'That's us. We're the ***Hot Cross Bunnies***. You wanna make something of it?'

'Uh... No.'

'Then pour us seven more Carrot Slammers - and hop to it!'

…………………

... and if you're wondering about how the Easter Bunnies came into existence, and how Snow White (in the picture here) is mixed up in it all, you can always read about that in *Wicked Tales*.

Some other books by Ed Wicke for ages 9 and over...

WICKED TALES

Nine crazy stories. Did you know that the bears think *Goldilocks* is a stupid story and have their own version? Or that lightning is made by a family of trolls living in the clouds? What happens when Alicroc the Alien becomes a teacher at a nursery school? How does a dancing horse save a fairy from a witch? Why does Snow White team up with the 7 Easter Bunnies, and why do they have machine guns?

BILLY JONES, KING OF THE GOBLINS

Billy Jones has the same sort of problems you have – a grandma who's loopy, a school bully who wants to thump him, and a mean teacher who insists he'll have to do the school's country dancing display dressed as a girl! But on his tenth birthday he's woken at midnight by a group of weird goblins who tell him he's now their king. You *know* it's going to get crazier by the minute...

AKAYZIA ADAMS AND THE MASTERDRAGON'S SECRET

A school visit to London Zoo causes Kazy Adams to swap the rough streets of London for a new world of magic, adventure and danger. And in Old Winsome's Academy, there's an ancient mystery to solve: the disappearance of nine pupils during the Headship of the Masterdragon Tharg, at the time of the Goblin Wars.

AKAYZIA ADAMS AND THE MIRRORS OF DARKNESS

The second adventure of Akayzia Adams and her friends starts with one mirror and ends with another. In between, there are three worlds of magic, a squadron of werewitches, a fistful of trolls, and one annoying little lizard with a taste for chocolate. And in the Academy, there are thousands of spiders... some of them not actually spiders at all.

MATTIE AND THE HIGHWAYMEN

It's 1845. Recently orphaned and running away from her bullying aunt, 13-year-old Matilda Harris finds herself down in The Devil's Eyeball with an eccentric, well-spoken highwayman; his gang Lump, Stump, Pirate and Scarecrow; and two young "brats" who have escaped from the notorious Andover Workhouse. Oddly enough, she comes to enjoy it.

BULLIES

The only book in the world with a fairy who conducts anti-bully warfare using beetles, a snowman that talks in riddles, a school assembly taken by a talking bear, a little sister who starts a pirate mutiny at school and a boy who turns into a bird after Christmas lunch! A book packed with poems and riddled with riddles. A book that's serious about bullying... but *crazy* about everything else!

NICKLUS

There's a mad scientist who wants to destroy all the cats in England, and nobody can stop her – except Nicklus and Marlowe. Nicklus is a nine year old boy who hardly talks at all. Marlowe is a talking cat, the "coolest cat in England". Together they set out on an adventure to find Nicklus' missing mother and save the cats.

Lightning Source UK Ltd.
Milton Keynes UK
UKOW031827181011

180524UK00001B/2/P

Engaging with Learning in Higher Education

Engaging with Learning in Higher Education

First published in 2012 by Libri Publishing

ISBN 978 1 907471 53 7

A CIP catalogue record for this book is available from The British Library

Cover design by Helen Taylor

Design by Carnegie Publishing

Printed in the UK by Berforts Information Press Ltd

Libri Publishing
Brunel House
Volunteer Way
Faringdon
Oxfordshire
SN7 7YR

Tel: +44 (0)845 873 3837

www.libripublishing.co.uk

Contents

Introduction

The idea of student engagement has become somewhat of an enigma in higher education in that it has come to be interpreted and applied in a number of differing ways. Through policy, assurance and practice, student engagement has become a valuable tool in examining and enhancing the experience of students. Praxis around student engagement therefore deserves critical examination. This book aims to provide a contemporary synthesis of practice and research on student engagement from various parts of the world, in several disciplines, and across the lifetime of the student.

The collection of writings from practitioners and researchers in the field of student engagement locates in one volume a number of authoritative perspectives on the subject, some of which cross discipline and international boundaries. The aim is to satisfy a need for broader scholarly writing on an increasingly important and studied area of higher education learning and teaching, and quality assurance. Much of the writing reports empirical research of various methodologies and draws together other phenomena not necessarily recognised in contemporary student engagement measures and concepts, such as professional identity, support of non-standard entry students, and students of the 'third age'.

The writings are organised under four sections: the nature of student engagement (including antecedents and current applications); pedagogy of engagement (exemplified by focus on particular aspects of the student experience); engagement in context (with examples from various disciplines); and policy and implications (looking at local, national and international priorities related to engagement and its use as a proxy measurement of quality).

The discussion of the nature of student engagement is introduced in the opening chapter, where the editors briefly describe the history of two major paradigms related to the quality of student learning as a background to the rest of the book. The first paradigm is that of *approaches to learning*; the idea that students approach their studies with varying intentions that result in qualitatively different approaches and outcomes. The second paradigm is *student engagement*, a term that is widely used but that has various underlying concepts and antecedents. The chapter concludes with an attempt to rationalise the two paradigms into a single relational model.

Chapter 2 by Colin Bryson and Christine Hardy records UK student voices to illustrate perceptions about 'being a student' at university. The authors are keen to stress the broad and changing nature of engagement and how it can vary over time and relative to various influences: some academic and some not so. Their findings suggest that one of the most important factors in student engagement is the relationship the student has with his or her communities, academic or social. Most importantly, they show how social communities did more than any other to support students during moments of doubt and crisis.

Chapter 3 is by Glen Newbery, an Australian psychologist specialising in motivational theory. He sets out to characterise student engagement in terms of a relation between things (the student and the object in question) and as having cognitive, emotional and motivational categories. These categories have been applied elsewhere in the corpus on student engagement leading some authors in the book to promote an ontological pedagogy in support of engagement. Newbery examines this call and what it might actually mean in a pragmatic sense, concluding that the pedagogy of critical enquiry holds much promise.

Chapter 4 by Sue Gordon, Anna Reid and Peter Petocz compares and contrasts the views of engagement held by students and staff from three different disciplines – statistics, teacher education and music. In doing so they illustrate, again, variation in quality of engagement relative to various factors, in this case the conception of engagement held by students and staff, with broader conceptions leading to deeper engagement. Of course, this then has some significant implications in terms of the potential mismatch in levels of engagement between the relevant parties. They also illustrate how the discipline in question may have some bearing on the student's level of engagement.

Chapter 5 by Ed Foster and associates applies the concept of 'doubt' to the student engagement debate, seeking to find what lessons might be learned from students who have doubted their choice of study but have stayed the course, and the potential impact programme teams might have on retention. The work was part of a major UK research project on Higher Education Retention and Engagement (the HERE project, also discussed by Becka Colley in Chapter 16). Doubting seems to offer another useful perspective on student engagement and can be shown to change over time relative to support factors within the student's experience such as programme and professional support but more importantly the curriculum and a sense of belonging. This theme is picked up again in the next chapter on student transitions into university.

The next section of the book focuses on the pedagogy of student engagement. In Chapter 6, Karen Nelson, Sally Kift and John Clarke detail significant work undertaken at Queensland University of Technology to model and apply a 'transition pedagogy' at the whole-of-institution level. In doing so they suggest six principles and explore the systemic variables that need to be in place for such a pedagogy to impact positively on the success of students regardless of equity group and student background. Access to higher education for all is thus enhanced at a time when universities around the world have widening participation as a major imperative.

Chapter 7 explores another contemporary university phenomenon, that of generic attribute or capability development. Elizabeth Reid and Ian Solomonides report empirical research into first-year students' experience of engagement (or not) with capabilities as espoused within an Australian university. Through interviews with students, they show how sensitivities to various capabilities change relative to the experience of the student and the discipline being studied. This illustrates the need to recognise student diversity, motivation and experience when setting broad university objectives for student learning outcomes.

In Chapter 8, Beverley Webster and Wincy Chan from the University of Hong Kong describe the rapidly changing nature of Hong Kong higher education policy and the move to an outcomes-based curriculum. This has promoted an increased emphasis on evaluation of the first-year experience relative to transition, the learning environment, approaches to study, and learning outcomes. Applying a survey instrument, Webster and Chan show how the experience of successive cohorts of students has changed within the new policy framework and following several initiatives at the university.

Chapter 9, by Kay Sambell from Northumbria University in the UK, discusses the promotion of Assessment for Learning across the university. Lamenting a legacy of instrumental assessment, she calls for a strategic rethink of assessment practices in order to promote deeper student engagement, and in turn less surface approaches to study and alienation. In doing so she reasserts the importance of the affective dimensions of learning in assessment and higher education theory more broadly.

Miriam David from the Institute of Education in the UK is well known for her work on widening participation in higher education and on issues relative to social diversity and difference. In Chapter 10 she embeds the concept of student engagement in approaches to equity and widening participation in global higher education. She describes how sociological approaches to understanding global higher education expansion and related policy debates have tended to ignore wider cultural issues such as gender, ethnicity and race. At the pedagogical level, therefore, it is important to develop practices that are meaningful to both genders to enhance engagement.

Linda Leach and Nick Zepke from New Zealand have been researching aspects of student engagement for over a decade. In Chapter 11 they draw on the wealth of research literature to present a conceptual framework of student engagement, which they then investigate empirically. They identify six perspectives and related indicators for student engagement. These provide useful criteria that institutions and teachers can draw inspiration from and against which they might judge their efforts to foster student engagement.

Various studies of engagement in context comprise the third section of the book. Chapter 12 evokes themes of student agency and authenticity, and therefore engagement, in discussing the work of the Reinvention Centre at the University of Warwick, UK. The Director of the centre, Paul Taylor, and his associates critically examine the characterisation of students as 'consumers', developing instead the concept of the 'student as producer'. This places students as integral to the development of (and engagement with) the curriculum and its pedagogies. A case study illustrates the student-as-producer approach that, not without risk, offers some exciting possibilities for the reformatting of teaching and learning in higher education.

Expanding with the changes to global demography is engagement with learning by older people. In Chapter 13, Garnet Grosjean from British Columbia, Canada, discusses this phenomenon and the nature of lifelong engagement with learning. Grosjean presents a case study of community-based research respectful of a number of critical factors affecting learning for senior adults. The educational programme he describes has a wider bearing on civic engagement as the community-based learning the students undertake is applied to the health and wellbeing of successive 'students', other members of the community.

Chapter 14 by Michelle Sisto (Monaco) and Peter Petocz (Australia) describes collaborative project-based learning in the support of student engagement. Sisto and Petocz are teachers of statistics, a discipline not well known for project-based approaches and often viewed as of peripheral importance by students. The authors take a practical approach to engagement and use the project-based pedagogy to good effect, showing profound changes to ways in which students (and teachers) experienced the teaching and learning of the subject.

Another discipline to apply principles of engagement is music, as shown in the case study described by Peter Dunbar-Hall in Chapter 15. Dunbar-Hall calls the international fieldwork undertaken by his pre-service teacher-training students 'ethnopedagogy'. The students' experiences in Bali have a significant impact on their understanding of music as a cultural phenomenon and more importantly on their conceptions of how music is taught. This engages the learners directly with their understanding of their own and their future students' pedagogies.

The explosion of social media in the early twenty-first century means that their affordances to student engagement deserve some attention. In Chapter 16, Becka Colley and Ruth Lefever (also participants in the HERE project described earlier, in Chapter 5) illustrate the strategic application of social media to supporting students in the university lifecycle. Social media were successfully used to augment student support interventions in the University of Bradford's *Develop Me!* programme. Two further illustrative case studies show how individual practitioners have incorporated Twitter, Facebook and email into their work with students. From these, Colley and Lefever extrapolate a number of activities that universities and teachers might consider applying in their own contexts.

We return to the issue of student agency as a foundation of engagement in Chapter 17. Janice Kay, Derfel Owen and Elisabeth Dunne also critique the 'student as consumer', preferring instead to develop the idea of the student as 'change agent' and one who is integrated into various institutional practices as a partner in the institutional endeavour. They illustrate this with two small case studies and thereafter discuss the logical conclusion to this level of student engagement, the role of students in quality assurance and enhancement.

The final section of the book focuses on policy aspects of student engagement and their implications. The National Survey of Student Engagement (NSSE) has been applied extensively in North America and Canada and modified versions are now being applied in South Africa, Australasia and China. In Chapter 18, Heidi Ross and Yuhao Chen, from Indiana University, USA (the 'home' of the NSSE), discuss the development and implementation of the NSSE-China against the political and institutional contexts of a country with a higher education system expanding at an exponential rate. The process of introducing and applying the instrument has yielded several benefits in national and international collaborations on student engagement, vocalising the student experience, and in an evidenced-based approach to quality assurance and enhancement.

In Chapter 19, Theresa Winchester-Seeto, Agnes Bosanquet and Anna Rowe present some fascinating analysis of graduate capability statements published by Australian universities over the last 15 years and in doing so set out to explore the engagement of students through the intended, enacted and experienced curriculum. They warn that it is easy to articulate grand ideas for student learning and somewhat harder to turn these into practice. Winchester-Seeto and associates do, however, show examples of some curriculum designs that foster both capability development and student engagement.

Having conversations with practitioners and students about

engagement is one of the practical things that can be done in order to enhance the engagement of both teachers and learners. In Chapter 20, Angela Voerman and Ian Solomonides reflect on the piloting of the Australasian version of the NSSE (the AUSSE) in their institution and on a project they undertook to promote conversations about engagement. They conclude that there is an inevitable tension between the potential of engagement as a conversational focal point and the measurement of engagement through a survey with inherent norms about learning and teaching.

The final invited chapter comes from Kerri-Lee Krause, well known in Australia and elsewhere for her work in the development of the First Year Experience Survey, amongst other things. In Chapter 21, she considers engagement through the lens of higher education policy and advises us to look beyond instruments like the NSSE and AUSSE and, in doing so, into the diversity of cultural, linguistic and social experiences impacting on the engagement of our students. Krause explores the 'wickedness' and the 'messy' problems and policy challenges promoted by changes in higher education policy and by governments keen to 'measure' student engagement. Moreover, she casts a critical eye at institutional policy with many institutions espousing the importance of the student experience whilst failing to refer to engagement in their documentation.

In the concluding chapter, the editors return to the paradigm of student engagement and ask what has been discovered in this book. There is no doubt that opinions vary on the application and utility of student engagement. It is indeed an enigmatic phenomenon. Nevertheless, there are a number of emergent metaphors for engagement that are worth noting. We describe these metaphors in the summary and reflect on the book as a whole, cross-referencing the chapters with each other in highlighting the major findings.

SECTION 1: THE NATURE OF STUDENT ENGAGEMENT

Chapter 1

A relational model of student engagement

Ian Solomonides[1], Anna Reid[2] and Peter Petocz[1]

[1] *Macquarie University, Australia*
[2] *Sydney Conservatorium of Music, Australia*

There are a number of influential concepts and trends in the literature and in practice that focus attention on the *quality of student learning* and *student engagement*. Most significantly, for example, in the European arena, quality has been linked to what is known as '*student approaches to learning*', whilst in the American and Canadian contexts there has been more emphasis on '*student engagement*'. The students' experiences of university learning, teaching and assessment have generally been seen to be at the heart of these concepts. Likewise, there has been an emphasis on trying to understand how students act or react within particular contexts of learning. This chapter gives a very brief overview of the history and status of the two paradigms – *approaches to learning* and *student engagement* – before presenting a new model that attempts to merge them. Throughout the rest of this book, various authors explore, not always in harmony with each other, aspects of academic engagement – a truly complex phenomenon.

At one time, research into student learning was dominated by a paradigm of information processing, advocated by researchers such as Craik and Lockhart (1972), Gagne (1977) and Schmeck (1983). Then, in the late 1970s and '80s, a movement emerged in Europe and Australasia together with a paradigm to describe patterns of learning and the intentions that underpinned that learning. This paradigm became known as student approaches to learning, or study. Somewhat confused with information processing because of the original references to 'surface' and 'deep levels of processing', the work of Marton and Säljö (1976) and thereafter Biggs (1976), Svensson (1977), Entwistle and Ramsden (1983), Gibbs, Morgan and Taylor (1984), Dahlgren (1984) and many others began to unpack the differences or similarities between the cognitive, information-processing view of student learning and the view now offered by phenomenographic studies of student learning in context. This latter view has ascended to give us the now familiar, but sometimes misunderstood, concepts of 'deep' and 'surface' approaches to learning. Sometimes erroneously described as a learning style, the approaches to learning paradigm has been one of the most significant descriptions of patterns of learning and studying in higher education. At the heart of approaches to learning is the idea that learning is comprised of 'how' the student learns or structures a task and the quality of 'what' he or she achieves. Here the departure from 'processing' is finally made and a picture of student learning emerges where the student approaches a task with a particular intention. Why a student would do this and the aim he or she may have with respect to education and life within the institutional context became the focus of other studies (Gibbs, Morgan and Taylor, 1984; Biggs, 1987).

A key reason students may approach their learning in qualitatively different ways may be due to the various conceptions they have of learning itself. Following the work of Säljö (1979), students' conceptions of learning – their beliefs and understandings of what learning is – were broadly described as 'transforming' and 'reproducing' by Entwistle and Entwistle (1991). Elsewhere, Laurillard (1979) and Fransson (1977) studied the relationship between approaches to learning and certain motivational aspects of the learner. Laurillard (1979) suggested that students make decisions about how to approach a task based on their perception of its importance and their interest in it. Following this, Gibbs, Morgan and Taylor (1984) proposed that students have various 'orientations' to study based on their vocational, academic, personal or social reasons for being in higher education.

Through the student approaches to learning (or study) research briefly outlined above, an appreciation has emerged of the interrelationships between the various concepts included in the paradigm and quality of academic outcome. According to the approaches-to-learning theorists, an implied systemic relationship between concepts is evident. Approaches to study are formed in relation to the context of learning and will interrelate with other foci of student attention. Approach to study is therefore a function of the interrelationship between student-based factors and teaching-based factors, including assessment. The effect of context on student approaches to learning has been widely demonstrated by researchers such as Newble and Clarke (1986), Trigwell and Prosser (1991), Meyer (1991), Eley (1992) and Tang (1994).

There are specific geographical origins of research into and explication of student approaches to learning. By and large this has been located in institutions with what might be described as European heritage, including Australia. The student approaches to learning paradigm was not so overtly and enthusiastically adopted in the United States, where it can be argued other, equally cogent series of studies were building towards a description of student learning and behaviour now known as 'student engagement' – without doubt a concept that now has international interest in higher education research and practice.

Student engagement has its roots in the work of Pace (1979, 1982), Astin (1977), Chickering and Gamson (1987), Tinto (1987) and others. Pace (1979) developed the College Student Experience Questionnaire containing 14 'quality of effort' scales and came to the conclusion that, "once students got to college, what counted most was not who they were or where they were but what they did" (Pace, 1982, p.20). It is perhaps worth reflecting on some of Pace's original work and the parallels with arguments today when he says that:

> Excellence, efficiency, productivity, accountability – these are all common words in much of the rhetoric about higher education today. But more often than not, the rhetoric has been one sided. It assumes that leaving college before getting a degree is a sign of failure, when in many cases it may be a prudent and well-informed decision. It assumes that professors produce learning. It assumes that the college, not the national economy, controls the job market. It assumes that if you don't benefit from college it's their fault. It assumes that the student is buying a product and therefore entitled to value for that product. It is a curious line of thinking because actually a student at a later point in time is the product!
>
> (Pace, 1982, p.3)

Pace's arguments were that learning involves investment of time and effort by the student, where effort is defined as the quality of the work students put into curricular and co-curricular activities. The emphasis students feel is given by the institution to academic, vocational, cultural and intellectual competencies further influences this, as do personal relationships with students, teachers and staff.

Following previous publications on the college environment, student dropout and predicting academic performance, Alexander Astin published books in the late '70s, revisited in the '90s, discussing 'what matters in college?' (Astin, 1977, 1993). His work studied undergraduates in the '60s and '70s (who were also the focus of follow-up work by Pascarella and Terenzini in 1991). Astin's main concern was to identify and isolate 'college impact' and to understand how undergraduates were affected by where they studied and the type of experiences they had there. Most interestingly, Astin contributed the idea that the educational impact of institutions is mediated by variables such as student peer-group relationships and 'involvement'. In other words quality of learning is positively correlated with involvement in study, with teaching staff, and with peer groups. Again there are interesting reflections from this study for today's university economy and culture:

> The characteristics and behaviors of faculty also have important implications for student development. For instance, attending a college whose faculty is heavily research oriented increases student dissatisfaction with various aspects of college and has negative impacts on most measures of cognitive and affective development... Attending a college that is strongly oriented toward students and their development shows the opposite pattern of effects.
>
> (Feldman, 1994, p.618)

Astin (1984) declared 'student involvement' as being a theory based on the work described above, stating that it refers to the "amount of physical and psychological energy that the student devotes to the academic experience" (Astin, 1984, p.518), remembering of course that 'academic experience' in this sense includes, inter alia: study, time on campus, student associations, interaction with other students, and interaction with faculty staff. Moreover, involvement has quantitative and qualitative characteristics. Astin also suggested that student learning and development is directly proportional to student involvement, and that the effectiveness of policy and practice is related to the capacity of that policy and practice to increase involvement. Like Pace (1982), Astin is clear that his theory "directs attention away from subject matter and technique and toward the motivation and behaviour of the student", and that, "college personnel... can assess their own activities in terms of their success in encouraging students to become more involved in the college experience."

Pascarella and Terenzini (1991, 2005) support Pace and Astin in determining that the "impact of college is largely determined by individual effort and involvement in the academic, interpersonal, and extracurricular offerings on campus" (2005, p.602). Impact in this context is a wide range of cognitive, social, emotional and economic outcomes that benefit the college graduate, and the authors distinguish broadly between developmental and environmental factors that influence such outcomes. Pascarella and Terenzini are therefore focusing on the contexts, circumstances and conditions that are most likely to maintain student involvement when they suggest that, "institutions should focus on the ways they can shape their academic, interpersonal, and extracurricular offerings to encourage student engagement" (2005, p.602), and that:

> The greatest impact may stem from the student's total level of campus engagement, particularly when academic, interpersonal, and extracurricular involvements are mutually supporting, reinforcing, and relevant to a particular educational outcome. Not only do students develop holistically, the sources of influence on their development are similarly holistic.
>
> (Terenzini, 1999, p.43)

Taking a similar holistic view, Chickering and Gamson (1987, 1991) developed their well-publicised 'seven principles' for good practice in higher education. The seven principles for staff and institutions are: encourages contact between students and faculty; develops reciprocity and cooperation among students; encourages active learning; gives prompt feedback; emphasises time on task; communicates high expectations; and respects diverse talents and ways of learning. The values and forces that underpin these principles are: activity, diversity, interaction, cooperation, expectations and responsibility. The seven principles have come to be associated with research and dialogue around student engagement, especially in America through the work of George Kuh and associates (see Kuh et al., 2005).

It is through the far-reaching work by Kuh and the development of the National Survey of Student Engagement (NSSE) that the concept of student engagement has reached most recent prominence. The NSSE was developed in 1998 by George Kuh and others at Indiana University Bloomington and has defined engagement as a measurable property and a proxy measure for quality to be evaluated through a survey instrument.

The NSSE is in part based on the work of Pace, Astin, and Chickering and Gamson. It also has items related to Bloom's (1956) Taxonomy of Educational Objectives. Underpinning the NSSE is the idea that engagement is manifest in student action and participation in curricular and co-curricular activities. Subsequent to the NSSE, there has since been the development and application of the South African Survey of Student Engagement (SASSE) (Strydom, Kuh and Mentz, 2010) and the Australasian University Survey of Student Engagement (AUSSE) (ACER, 2008; Coates, 2006); the development of the National Survey on Student Engagement-China (NSSE-C) is described by Ross and Chen (Chapter 18, this volume). The NSSE and its derivatives report against five main clusters or benchmarks of effective educational practice. According to the student-engagement paradigm and the previous research described above, the benchmarks describe concepts supportive of student engagement. The five benchmarks are: level of academic challenge; active and collaborative learning; student–staff interaction; enriching educational experiences; and a supportive campus environment. Broadly, these stances may be thought of as focusing either on student behaviour, including effort, time on task and use of resources (Kuh, 2006; Coates, 2006), or on socio-cultural factors, including a perceived sense of belonging to, or lack of alienation from, the group (Tinto, 1993; Astin, 1999; Mann, 2001). Hu and Kuh suggest that:

> The most important factor in student learning and personal development during college is student engagement, or the quality of effort students themselves devote to educationally purposeful activities that contribute directly to desired outcomes.
>
> (2002, p.555)

'Engagement', then, is a term that has been widely used to describe various relationships between the student, study and the institution, including the campus. Student engagement is referred to extensively in contemporary higher education and there are survey instruments designed to evaluate levels of student engagement as a proxy for quality. A scan of the research literature shows engagement is seen variously as: some relationship between students and their studies, some aspect of student behaviour, quality, motivation (intrinsic and extrinsic), something that is promoted by teaching, a passive or active approach and a level of interest (Reid and Solomonides, 2007). The concept has reached holistic levels of definition, appropriated at various times and with divergent aims to practices such as the ability or inability of universities to deal effectively with issues such as contact hours, extra-curricular activities or campus life, students' patterns of study and working (individually or collaboratively), the curriculum, staff–student ratios, distractions to study including paid part-time employment, inclusivity, the research–teaching nexus, work-integrated learning, greater student heterogeneity, et cetera.

At the heart of these issues is the emphasis on engagement and what it may mean in the academic setting. Harris et al. (2004) provide perhaps the most incisive of definitions when they say that:

> Academic engagement is defined as engaging in the activities of a course programme with thoroughness and seriousness. Indicators of academic engagement are cognitive (organising and planning his/her own work, entering deeply into learning on his/her own), affective (being motivated, persevering, taking pleasure in the course, being interested), conative (giving the necessary energy and time) and relational.
>
> (2004, p.1)

This also hints at an important point: that when we consider academic engagement we need to go beyond the definition and measurement of engagement to include holistic and philosophical arguments similar to the phenomenographic studies more typical of the approach to learning paradigm. In other words, epistemology and ontology should be brought to bear on this important concept and neither the approach to study paradigm nor the student-engagement paradigm has primacy over the other. Approach and engagement are inextricably linked through epistemology and ontology, what Barnett calls the 'will' of the student:

> The student's being, her will to learn, her strong self, and her willingness to be authentic: all these are a set of foundations for her knowing and her practical engagements. Without a self, without a will to learn, without a being that has come into itself, her efforts to know and to act within her programme of study cannot even begin to form with any assuredness.
>
> (2007, p.70)

This book argues there is an inclusive nature to engagement that implies that we are considering the ontological in addition to – rather than instead of – the epistemological aspects of learning. Engagement in this sense has a pivotal role in the student's approach to study:

> A 'deep' orientation towards her studies is a personal stance on the part of the student in which she invests something of herself as a person; in a 'surface' orientation, by contrast, the student lacks such a will and subjects herself passively to her experiences. That is, underlying the apparently cognitive level on which the 'deep'–'surface' distinction works, is an ontological substratum.
>
> (Barnett, 2007, p.18)

The authors have developed a relational model (Figure 1.1) of student engagement based on phenomenographic empirical research (Solomonides and Reid, 2009), which attempts to illustrate some of the major categories researchers might focus on in understanding the student experience of engagement.

The central 'hub' of the model represents the senses of 'self' students have expressed in relation to academic engagement, whilst the outer components represent student expressions of engagement that contribute to their understanding of self. Sense of Being describes the way in which students think about themselves and their study that emphasises confidence, happiness, imagination and self-knowledge (Barnett, 2004, 2005, 2007). Sense of Transformation is the means through which Sense of Being is enhanced and expanded (Dall'Alba and Barnacle, 2007). In other words, the student experience of engagement relies on their own ontological dimensions of Sense of Being and Sense of Transformation, which are in a dynamic relationship with three main components:

- Sense of Being a Professional involves students as initiates into a

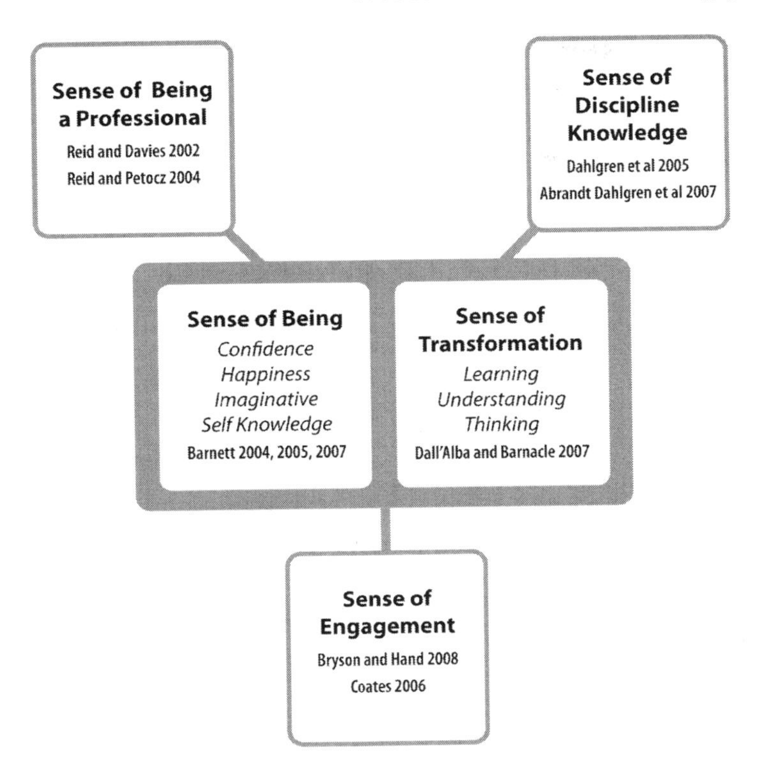

Figure 1.1: A relational model of student engagement

specific professional community, exposed to the rituals, practices and practitioners of that community (Reid and Davies, 2002; Reid et al., 2011)

- Sense of Discipline Knowledge represents the legitimate activities, skill and knowledge of the discipline. These might be described as rational and substantive (having utility within the discipline or transferable between contexts), and ritual (the context-free exchange value of knowledge) (Abrandt Dahlgren et al., 2008; Reid et al., 2011)
- Sense of Engagement is promoted by affording learners the opportunity to engage creatively with the task in hand. Engagement is encouraged as students become more aware of the epistemology and ontology of the subject and adopt moral and philosophical stances relative to it (Bryson and Hand, 2008)

According to this relational model of engagement, students have a variety of foci of attention that influence their Sense of Being and Sense of Transformation. Consequently, curriculum developers and practitioners should carefully consider the constitution of Being and Transformation in specific disciplines and how these relate to the other elements described above. In any event, student happiness and confidence appear integral to the application and appreciation of discipline knowledge and student capacity for critical reflection.

> Taking this perspective means that we must be cautious about focusing too narrowly on one facet of learning – such as deep v. surface, or learning styles or orientations, or motivation – however insightful they appear, because they are insufficient to describe holistically the full individual experience of learning. We propose that engagement might be such a holistic concept.
>
> (Bryson and Hand, 2008, p.8)

There is an increasing competition for status, resources and students in higher education. Consequently, universities and colleges are looking at student engagement and transition issues from pedagogic, institutional and strategic perspectives. An underlying imperative for the development and enhancement of student engagement relates to the nature of the core mission of the university. Another goal is the fundamental one of securing resources, resources that are intrinsically linked to student satisfaction, retention and progression.

Student academic engagement may vary over time and relative to experience, exposure and the student's position in the lifetime of their study but it is essential for transformative learning. Dall'Alba and Barnacle (2007, p.689) conclude that learners need to "transform as people" in order to become professionals – and that this requires "educational approaches that engage the whole person: what they know, how they act, and who they are." Engagement can refer to a sense of belonging fostered by such things as extra-curricular activities, and the blurring of the boundary between formal and informal student life. As such, universities might seek ways in which a community of learners can be established around both co-curricular and extra-curricular activities. This might be as simple as enabling students to work in groups or to feel part of an identifiable cohort; students who struggle often work alone or do not have a sense of belonging. Unfortunately, it is sometimes difficult to inculcate a sense of belonging and inclusion; residential education might be very beneficial in this respect but it is far from normal practice in many institutions. Similarly, with the increasing absence of structures that encourage student unionism there may be less incentive to be involved socially with university. The impedimenta of modern university teaching may also mean staff have less time to devote to supporting engagement. Student engagement will involve and require staff engagement as well as interaction, including student to staff and peer to peer. Academic engagement may be developmental. It might be encouraged by negotiation and choice and involvement in significant pieces of work. This book seeks to explore not only the concepts of student academic engagement but also its applications and the conditions that support it with evidence drawn from international studies.

References

Abrandt Dahlgren, M., Reid, A., Dahlgren, L.O. and Petocz, P. (2008) 'Learning for the Professions: Lessons from Linking International Research Projects', *Higher Education*, 56/2, pp.129–48.

ACER (2008) *Attracting, Engaging and Retaining: New Conversations About Learning*, Australian Student Engagement Report (Melbourne: Australian Council for Educational Research).

Astin, A.W. (1977) *Four Critical Years: Effects of College on Beliefs, Attitudes, and Knowledge* (San Francisco: Jossey Bass).

Astin, A.W. (1984) 'Student Involvement: A Developmental Theory for Higher Education', reprinted in *Journal of College Student Personnel*, Sept–Oct 1999, 40/5, pp.518–29.

Astin, A.W. (1993) *What Matters in College? Four Critical Years Revisited* (San Francisco: Jossey-Bass).

Astin, A.W. (1999) 'Involvement in Learning Revisited: Lessons we have Learned', *Journal of College Student Development*, 40/5 pp.587–98.

Barnett, R. (2004) 'Learning for an Unknown Future', *Higher Education Research and Development*, 23/3, pp.247–60.

Barnett, R. (2005) 'Recapturing the Universal in the University', *Educational Philosophy and Theory*, 37/6, pp.785–97.

Barnett, R. (2007) *A Will to Learn: Being a Student in an Age of Uncertainty* (Maidenhead: Society for Research in Higher Education, Open University Press).

Biggs, J.B. (1976) 'Dimensions of Study Behaviour: Another Look at the ATT', *British Journal of Educational Psychology*, 46, pp.68–80.

Biggs, J.B. (1987) *Student Approaches to Learning and Studying* (Hawthorn: Australian Council for Educational Research).

Bloom, B.J. (1956) *Taxonomy of Educational Objectives* (New York: David McKay).

Bryson, C. and Hand, L. (2008) *Student Engagement – SEDA Special 22* (London: Staff and Educational Development Association).

Chickering, A.W. and Gamson, Z.F. (1987) 'Seven Principles for Good Practice in Undergraduate Education', *American Association of Higher Education Bulletin*, 39/7, pp.3–7.

Chickering, A.W. and Gamson, Z.F. (1991) 'Applying the Seven Principles for Good Practice in Undergraduate Education', *New Directions for Teaching and Learning*, 47, pp.63–9.

Coates, H. (2006) *Student Engagement in Campus-based and Online Education: University connections* (Abingdon: Routledge).

Craik, F.M. and Lockhart, R.S. (1972) 'Levels of Processing: A Framework for Memory', *Journal of Verbal Reasoning and Verbal Behaviour*, 11/6, pp.671–84.

Dahlgren, L.O. (1984) 'Outcomes of Learning', in Marton, F., Hounsell, D. and Entwistle, N. (eds) *The Experience of Learning* (Edinburgh: Scottish Academic Press) pp.19–35.

Dall'Alba, G. and Barnacle, R. (2007) 'An Ontological Turn for Higher Education', *Studies in Higher Education*, 32/6, pp.679–91.

Eley, M.G. (1992) 'Differential Adoption of Study Approaches within Individual Students', *Higher Education*, 8/4, pp.381–94.

Entwistle, N. and Entwistle, A. (1991) 'Contrasting Forms of Understanding for Degree Examinations: The Student Experience and Its Implications', *Higher Education*, 22/3, pp.205–27.

Entwistle, N. and Ramsden, P. (1983) *Understanding Student Learning* (London: Croom Helm).

Feldman, K.A. (1994) 'What Matters in College? Four Critical Years Revisited – Review Essay', *Journal of Higher Education*, 65/1, pp.615–22.

Fransson, A. (1977) 'On Qualitative Differences in Learning IV: Effects of Intrinsic Motivation and Extrinsic Test Anxiety on Process and Outcome', *British Journal of Educational Psychology*, 47, pp.244–257.

Gagne, R.M. (1977) *The Conditions of Learning* (New York: Holt, Reinhart, Winston).

Gibbs, G., Morgan, A. and Taylor, E. (1984) 'The World of The Learner', in Marton, F., Hounsell, D. and Entwisle, N. (eds) *The Experience of Learning* (Edinburgh: Scottish Academic Press) pp.165–88.

Harris, R., Bolander, K., Lebrun, M., Docq, F. and Bouvy, M.T. (2004) 'Linking Perceptions of Control and Signs of Engagement in the Process and Content of Collaborative E-Learning', paper presented at the *Network Learning Conference*, Lancaster, UK, April. Retrieved from <http://www.networkedlearningconference.org.uk/past/nlc2004/proceedings/symposia/symposium10/harris_et_al.htm>

Hu, S. and Kuh, G.D. (2002) 'Being (Dis)engaged in Educationally Purposeful Activities: The Influences of Student and Institutional Characteristics', *Research in Higher Education*, 43/5, pp.555–75.

Kuh, G.D. (2006) 'Making Students Matter' in Burke J.C. (ed.) *Fixing the Fragmented University: Decentralization with Direction* (Bolton: Jossey-Bass) pp.235–64.

Kuh, G.D., Kinzie, J., Schuh, J.H. and Whitt, E.J. (2005) *Student Success in College: Creating Conditions That Matter* (San Francisco: Jossey-Bass).

Laurillard, D. (1979) 'The Process of Student Learning', *Higher Education*, 8/4, pp.395–409.

Mann, S.J. (2001) 'Alternative Perspectives on the Student Experience: Alienation and Engagement', *Studies in Higher Education*, 26/1, pp.7–19.

Marton, F. and Säljö, R. (1976) 'On Qualitative Differences in Learning: 1, Outcome and Process', *British Journal of Educational Research*, 46, pp.4–11.

Meyer, J.H.F. (1991) 'Study Orchestration: The Manifestation, Interpretation and Consequences of Contextualized Approaches to Study', *Higher Education*, 22/3, pp.297–316.

Newble, D.I. and Clarke, R.M. (1986) 'The Approaches to Learning of Students in a Traditional and in an Innovative Problem-Based Medical School', *Medical Education*, 20/4, pp.267–73.

Pace, C.R. (1979) *Measuring Outcomes of College: Fifty Years of Findings and Recommendations for the Future* (San Francisco: Jossey-Bass).

Pace, C.R. (1982) *Achievement and the Quality of Student Effort, Report to the Department of Education* (Washington: Department of Education).

Pascarella, E.T. and Terenzini, P.T. (1991) *How College Affects Students: Findings and Insights from Twenty Years of Research* (San Francisco: Jossey Bass).

Pascarella, E.T. and Terenzini, P.T. (2005) *How College Affects Students: Vol. 2 A Third Decade of Research* (San Francisco: Jossey-Bass).

Reid, A. and Davies, A. (2002) 'Teachers' and Students Conceptions of the Professional World', *Improving Student Learning Theory and Practice – 10 Years On*. Retrieved from <http://www.arts.ac.uk/docs/cltad_DesignAHRB.pdf>

Reid, A., Abrandt Dahlgren, M., Petocz, P. and Dahlgren, L.O. (2011) *From Expert Student to Novice Professional* (Dordrecht: Springer).

Reid, A. and Solomonides, I. (2007) 'Design Students' Experience of Engagement and Creativity', *Art Design and Communication in Higher Education*, 6/1, pp.25–39.

Säljö, R. (1979) *Learning in the Learner's Perspective: 1 Some Common Sense Conceptions*, Reports from the Department of Education (Goteborg: University of Goteborg).

Schmeck, R.R. (1983) 'Learning Styles of College Students', in Dillon, R. and Schmeck, R.R. (eds) *Individual Differences in Cognition* (New York: Academic Press) pp.233–279.

Solomonides, I. and Reid, A. (2009) '*Understanding the Relationships Between Student Identity and Engagement with Studies*', paper presented at the 32nd Higher Education Research and Development Society of Australasia (HERDSA) Annual Conference – The Student Experience, Darwin Australia, July. Retrieved from <http://www.herdsa.org.au/wp-content/uploads/conference/2009/papers/HERDSA2009_Solomonides_I.pdf>

Strydom, J.F., Kuh, G.D. and Mentz, M. (2010) 'Enhancing success in South Africa's higher education: measuring student engagement', *Acta Academica*, 42/1, pp.259–78. Retrieved from <http://www.sabinet.co.za/abstracts/academ/academ_v42_n1_a10.html>

Svensson, L. (1977) 'On Qualitative Differences in Learning: III, Study Skill and Learning', *British Journal of Educational Psychology*, 47, pp.233–43.

Tang, C. (1994) 'Effects of Modes of Assessment on Students' Preparation Strategies', in Gibbs, G. (ed.) *Improving Student Learning: Theory and Practice* (Oxford: The Oxford Centre for Staff Development) pp.151–70.

Terenzini, P.T. (1999) 'Research and Practice in Undergraduate Education: And Never the Twain Shall Meet?', *Higher Education*, 38/1, pp.33–48.

Tinto, V. (1987) '*The Principles of Effective Retention*', paper presented at the Maryland College Personnel Association Fall Conference, Prince George's Community College, Largo, MD.

Trigwell, K. and Prosser, M. (1991) 'Improving the Quality of Student Learning: The Influence of the Learning Context and Student Approaches to Learning on Learning Outcomes', *Higher Education*, 22/3, pp.251–26.

Chapter 2

The nature of academic engagement: what the students tell us

Colin Bryson[1] and Christine Hardy[2]

[1] *Newcastle University, UK*

[2] *Nottingham Trent University, UK*

This chapter examines the nature of academic engagement and the key influences that appear to foster or diminish it. We shall draw from the students' own voices through evidence gathered from two major studies on student engagement conducted in a UK university with undergraduates. This has provided rich and detailed evidence about their perceptions of 'being a student'. The study focuses on the whole undergraduate experience, from just before they start until the end of the final year. Although not all of the students in the study stayed until the end of their course, this nonetheless provides interesting insights into the nature of student engagement.

The opening chapter has explored the development of the notion of student engagement and a number of differing and related concepts that describe what engagement might be. We agree that engagement is a multi-faceted and dynamic concept that is closely linked to the student's sense of identity and purpose in being a student in higher education. However, many teachers and educational managers focus mainly on academic engagement. There are a number of reasons for this:

- It is via direct curricular activities (for example, in the classroom) or as outcomes of assessment that teachers interact with students

- It is hard for teachers to get to know students well in a mass higher education system: they lack the time or perhaps the disposition to do so (Lahteenoja and Pirttila-Backman, 2005)
- Many teachers share the view that an engaged student is one who espouses the same values and beliefs as the teacher and has the same intense interest in the subject – being, in short, a mirror image of what the teacher was like as a student (or imagined themselves to be) (Brennan et al., 2010).

Whilst we may not agree that engagement can be described so narrowly, and there are several crucial aspects missing in such a model, there is much evidence to show that students who manifest the sort of academic engagement that is demonstrated in instruments such as the National Survey of Student Engagement (NSSE) and the Australasian University Survey of Student Engagement (AUSSE) do achieve good academic outcomes. In contrast to these instruments (of which four out of the five benchmarks concern academic engagement of some kind), academic engagement was only seen as one of the seven dimensions of engagement proposed by Krause and Coates (2008). The body of evidence we have gathered here, though, goes far beyond that which such surveys can obtain. Students have told us not only what they do but also why (or at least why they think) they behave or respond in these ways. They have also told us about their backgrounds and aspirations, and their broader experiences whilst in higher education. Therefore we will not only investigate what influences academic engagement but also what shapes and underpins these influences.

Empirical evidence about academic engagement from the study

In our first study on engagement (Bryson and Hand, 2007a), which was focussed on what students considered to be good learning and teaching, we noted that there were different spheres/locations of academic engagement, for example:

- Within a classroom or in undertaking a particular task or assignment

- Within/to a particular module
- Within/to and across the course/programme of study
- Within/to the university or higher education.

This tells us that students may be engaged differentially to different aspects of their education. Some spheres may be more salient overall, and the aspects may affect each other.

That study went beyond teaching delivery, encompassing curriculum and assessment design and teachers' dispositions and behaviour, with such questions as "what is it that teachers do (or not do) that influences engagement?" From this, we found five key influences on academic engagement (and teachers are significant agents within these), as follows (Bryson and Hand, 2007b):

1. A student perception that their expectations are being met to a sufficient degree (thus fit with intrinsic motivation, and sense of relevance of curriculum, coherence, centrality of degree and study, and 'level of service')
2. Ensuring an appropriate level of challenge but not excessive workload for the student
3. A sufficient degree and balance of choice, autonomy, risk and opportunities for growth, and that learning is enjoyable
4. Appropriate trust relationships (staff with students, students with other students, and staff with staff)
5. Discourse, or at least communicating for understanding and dialogue.

We do not claim this is novel as other studies have identified one or more of these influences: however, we felt that we had only observed the tip of the iceberg and our research approach had only scratched the surface. We needed a much more focussed, in-depth, longitudinal, qualitative approach. There are few such studies of this type since the work of Perry and Baxter Magolda in the 1990s (recent examples include Askham, 2008; Fung, 2006; Weatherston and Lawrence, 2008).

Our second study began in 2007 with the selection of 24 individual students drawn from several degree programmes across the schools of

Business, Art and Design, and Arts and Humanities in a large post-1992 UK university. We interviewed each student using an in-depth semi-structured approach: three times in first year, once in second year, once in the final year, and in a group interview just before graduation. This has produced rich accounts from the students on their perceptions and reflections of their experiences – in the order of 60–70,000 transcribed words per individual.

We have selected five cases for presentation here that reflect both shared and diverse student perceptions and experiences. The summaries are structured with reference to the five key influences on 'academic' engagement above but also any emergent salient influences too. The cases include two students who left their studies before completion.

Ella

Ella commenced a degree in business management at 18 years old. Her degree involved a normal full-time first year, then she spent years two and three in a placement role in a company, returning to university for four study blocks. Each cohort consisted of only 20 students studying their modules not shared with other courses. Ella preferred drama but chose this degree at the last moment – "it was a spur of the moment, out of the blue, decision to choose business" – as she did not want to move too far from home. Although she had good grades she worried that she was not "as clever" as other students. She much preferred experiential learning and rather struggled with first-year modules that involved theory, "So long and boring... it was mind boggling". Social cohesion on the course was of great importance to her and the course had a residential induction event: "best holiday trip I have ever been on".

She scraped through first year, doing lots of socialising and building strong relationships with peers on the course. She engaged with the integrated team-project approach because this combined her interests in the practical and the social: "Yeah [I know] everyone, I love them all... I think we've just developed as people and you get to know people... and I've spent a lot of time with them in the business project." But she did not form a rapport with staff at this stage. So although she felt, "very comfortable with all of them", she relied on peers: "I would ask for help from other students any day".

Her lack of confidence and low self-perception contributed to her nearly not gaining a placement: "they said that sometimes I can come across girly and have no substance... I think they just thought that, you know, like, blonde bimbo kind of thing." Ella did, at the last moment, find a placement near London. This was very daunting, as she had to move so far away from home. She kept in touch with her family returning almost every weekend, and drew on her father as proofreader for her assignments.

Although Ella found the study blocks intense she started to meet the academic challenge, beginning to understand what was required to get good marks. She relished the independent aspect of the learning, was much more organised and really enjoyed it, "Because our course is all about on-the-job learning; we learn ourselves, we learn it through the companies we are in". She took the integrating and coordinating role in group work. Ella did get to know the course leader (who was also her dissertation supervisor) in the final year; to the extent that they almost developed a discourse, if only about the assignments. Ella developed a "100 per cent engagement with the course" and a very strong identity with her peer cohort: "We are in the same boat together... sharing this unique experience... we are all so motivated".

The exposure in the placement to a different set of role models, and the sense it gave her of being part of a professional community, built Ella's confidence. She equated herself with the lead character in *Legally Blonde* (a 2001 film directed by Robert Luketic which seeks to break the stereotype of the 'blonde' by demonstrating that outward appearance can mask excellent capability). "She's got more to herself than pink and blonde... she's got the ability to get on with anyone, she communicates effectively in and out of work, and she's quite well, not clever, clever but she's not stupid." Her academic competence improved to the extent that she achieved a strong, upper-second-class degree classification and has stayed at her placement company.

Martin

Martin applied unsuccessfully to study the same in-company degree as Ella so he entered the general business degree at 18 years old. His ambition was to become a stockbroker and he intended to work hard to achieve this, believing he could get a first-class degree. He considered himself to be a "versatile learner" who enjoyed discussion and debate, evaluation, and synthesis, and claimed to thrive on pressure. He expected to keep ahead with the work, to make a lot of friends, and that tutors would be like his former teachers.

Academically, he found that the first year was neither challenging nor demanding; rather it was a similar standard to A-levels (university entry qualifications). He attended most lectures and seminars and felt that although the workload increased in terms of assessments, the work got somewhat easier due to familiarity with the process. In the second year, Martin became critical of his academic experience: the lack of contact time, unfamiliar teaching and learning, and increased workload and pressure as marks now contributed to the final degree classification.

> The step up in learning that I was craving for in the first year came in such an ambiguous manner that it was fairly... it was nothing that I was anticipating at all... I thought it would be harder but I thought we might have a little more contact time. I thought we might be a little bit better prepared for it.

He disliked his subjects, even being offended by one of them: "hard selling is immoral". He felt that he did not gain a lot from lectures or seminars and stopped attending most of them. He did not "catch up" and struggled to cope with assessment. Martin felt that the course throughout was "constrained" in terms of choice and lacked autonomy, "being told what to write, what to learn"; and when you did not "play the game" then marks suffered. The experience was in direct contrast to his college experience where discourse was encouraged. He was disappointed with the lack of participation by peers in seminars.

All tutors were "friendly and helpful" and he felt he was a "popular" student with staff, as he asked questions. Establishing a relationship with the tutors was important: "I always try and speak my mind and if I've had a problem I've gone to the tutors about it". During the second year he found it increasingly difficult to establish relationships due to having a lot of different tutors, large class sizes and little time to "get to know them properly".

In group work, Martin took the role of leader working with the same group of people throughout the first year – although he did not socialise with them – but in the second year he worked with new people and never even got to know their names. There was no opportunity for him to meet new people on the course as the lectures were so big and in the seminars there is "always at least one person [I] know and so I sit with them, not meeting other people".

Martin made a lot of friends in first year but not with people on the course. During the second year the shared house did not work out as planned and he had financial problems. He became increasingly socially isolated:

> I drift between friends and [have] a couple of close friends... my closest friends I did not actually see that much 'cause they all have jobs in the week and go back home or things like that.

Martin then suffered from depression but received no support, "from tutors, friends or the campus doctor". It was not until his mother intervened that a tutor gave Martin support during the last term. He was "considering leaving... I literally am doing it [the course] because I'm already in 12 grand's worth of debt, I should really finish it off." Martin could have returned for his third and final year, but decided not to. He wanted to repudiate his student identity:

> I don't really like the person I've been becoming over the past few years... my big problem with university is that people will take you on first impressions and... that's what you get stuck with.

Kelly

Kelly was 23 when she came from Korea to study fashion textile management, after two years studying law at university. She wanted to study fashion so that she could have her own shop. She was the first amongst her friends to study in the UK and came alone to study for a three-month course in professional English, sharing a flat with another Korean student. Her initial confidence was undermined by concern about her English language skills. She did not attend any university welcome-week events; her first experience of the university was the induction.

The tutorial system was one reason for studying in the UK, promoting particular expectations from UK higher education regarding relationships with tutors:

> This is very attractive and I have already experienced in the professional English course and there are some tutorial times, so that was very nice. I was given feedback from tutorial and that was very nice for me. This system is very nice, in Korea it is not.

Ironically she found lectures difficult but comfortable as she, "knew what to expect". The seminars were a challenge, due to a lack of confidence and understanding of what both the tutor and other students were saying: "whenever I go to the class seminar, I always hesitate. Sometimes I really don't want to go to class because I should talk and give opinions or ideas to other students."

Group work created problems for her. She was surprised at the way British students work together; she found it "very individual" with little contact, just an exchange of information "at the last minute". In addition she did not feel accepted as a member of the group. In the first two terms, Kelly felt isolated, as she did not make any friends on the course, worked very hard and found the course very stressful, challenging and demanding.

> The course is getting harder and harder, so it has been difficult... Actually, I studied every day and even on weekends, but [there] is not enough time because it takes quite a long time to preview and review and do assignments.

She was overwhelmed by the workload and studying a technical subject where she did not understand the terminology. The stress actually caused ill health in mid-year.

Kelly did not establish a trust relationship with tutors and felt that when she did approach a tutor the feedback she got did not help her to improve, but that she received platitudes:

> When I show my work to tutor and they gave me feedback, but every person just say, "it's very nice idea, and you can just keep going and you will be fine", and every, actually every tutor said very same "you will be fine"; actually I was not fine.

Therefore Kelly sought help and support with her work from her professional-English tutor, as she had known him quite a long time and had an established relationship. In the final term she made some friends on the course and started to socialise, which offered emotional support, increasing her confidence. Conversely she stopped attending classes regularly. She found little subject discourse with either peers or tutors and found it unhelpful to discuss the detail of her assignments with them, instead "sort[ing] it out [herself] by reading". Kelly scraped past the final assessments and said she intended to return for the second year, but did not, offering the reason that the economic downturn prevented this

Ryan

Ryan was studying fine art. He dropped out of his first degree in science and after doing a foundation course returned to university at 32 years old. In the first year he was commuting from home, but in years two and three he shared accommodation. He intended to treat university as a job and on average spent 40 hours a week studying, most of it in the studio. Sometimes it was difficult for him to stay focussed on his studies, having to "juggle" them with paid employment (first and second year) and his social life. Ryan was reflective and kept a journal; he wanted to work hard and had few expectations: "I am a sponge; I just want to soak it all up. Expectations, there aren't any, I just want to take it as it comes and live it and experience it as I know I have the opportunity." Ryan really enjoyed his degree, finding it intellectually challenging but coped throughout by reflecting that if it were easy, he would be bored: "It's great; I love it, absolutely living it. It's just what the doctor ordered, it's perfect for me, it's the right institution, the right course, and it's at the right level. I love it."

He took advantage of many extra-curricular activities such as attending shows and exhibitions, visiting other art programmes in the area, working with local artists and becoming a course representative and buddy to other students. Ryan revelled in the academic environment; lectures, tutorials and the studio; he felt it was a safe environment to work in and to make mistakes, and that, within the constraints of the degree, he had absolute freedom on the course to express his creativity. He believed that he was not only learning about his practice but also himself: "I think being in this environment has allowed me... has given me the confidence to look at what fires me, what turns me on, what makes me tick, what I'm interested in." Throughout, he felt that the tutors were "superb" and although there was not much tutor contact at the beginning, if you wanted help you just had to "ask for it".

Contact did increase, particularly informal contact, and he developed working relationships with the tutors based on "mutual respect". Reflecting on these relationships over the three years:

> We used to look at the tutors speaking to the third years when we were first years and think "oh God, look how tight they are", you know "they're really in with them... will I have a relationship with my tutors like that?" And this year it just seems natural.

From the beginning he drew on peer feedback constantly, particularly in the studio. His relationship with peers was influenced by the age and attitude difference – he did find some of them rather immature – however, he gained considerably from group work in the first two years, working with those who he perceived were "good attenders", "hard working", "clever" and "interesting". Towards the end of the degree he reflected on his current position and the future:

> My practice is changing quite a lot, I'm changing quite a lot and I think that is feeding into the practice... but also I think... that what I'm making is art and it's just not playing at it. You know, I am an artist, I'm not an art student, and I'm not an art wannabe... [I've] not outgrown university, but I feel I've grown to fill my space here, you know, and I'm ready to see what the next steps are.

Ryan achieved a first-class honours degree.

Keith

Keith, an only child from a local town, studied for a joint degree in history and European studies at 18 years old. He had an intellectual and emotional attachment to history, particularly military campaigns, relating them to his own family. Throughout his degree he had paid employment, living in his family home for financial reasons and to study "without distractions". He felt proud to get into university, wanting to give something back to his parents by getting a good job. His expectations were vague; he enjoyed the ambiguity of history, was confident he could cope and was determined to work as hard as was needed.

He found the first year a "big jump from A-level" but worked steadily and coped well with the demands and challenges. He found the work satisfying as it was more "in depth" and broadened his horizons in history.

During the second year he struggled to stay motivated as the work was more challenging – a move from the narrative to criticality – and there was an increase in workload and pressure:

> I just felt drained, sort of isolated from everyone... I just found it difficult to concentrate and to find motivation especially with the amount of work that we had... everything [came] at once...

His friends played a large role in him continuing at university:

> This year [it is] especially important to have friends to help you through it more than anything... We've decided, as a group, to motivate ourselves, motivate each other, sort of drag ourselves through it if needs be.

He looked forward to his final-year dissertation, where he could be creative, and started working on it in the second year, visiting archives in London over the summer. This external sourcing of information and the importance of time management were the main differences from the first two years. He achieved both and did not feel "stressed".

At the beginning of his degree, he had no relationship with tutors, finding them "intimidating"; he did not "have that much time to connect with them". As his confidence increased, he asked questions and by the second year relationships with many of the tutors changed. Keith felt that they were more "directed towards helping you without necessarily being spoken to first" and that they were more "accepting". In the final year, mutual relationships had been established with the history lecturers, "so you can have a good talk with them, have a laugh with them". No relationships were established with his European studies lecturers but he was "not bothered", as he did not find the subject that interesting. The relationship with the dissertation tutor is of particular note as it was based on mutual respect and Keith feels that this was:

> Partly because he wants to learn about it [the subject] as much as I do... some of the stuff I'm digging up is new to him and he's finding it really interesting to mark my work and read through it... and he's trying to get me to do a master's in it as well.

Working in small groups was useful for his learning, gathering alternative perspectives and encouraging a sense of involvement in the subject. He found larger groups quite intimidating. In the small amount of group work, Keith worked well with the same friends; and he was part of a study group sharing resources for assessments and revising together for examinations. Although he did not feel this was important for his learning, it was for support. Keith achieved an upper second-class degree, was looking forward to leaving university and starting "his life".

Discussion

Ella, despite her rather uncertain start and lack of self-belief, developed into a very engaged student who felt involved with the course and community of students, and assimilated into the professional community in her placement. The factors at play here include:

- The opportunities in this course to build strong social cohesion and belonging, such as the residential induction and team projects – these provided a community resource to enable Ella to overcome some difficult challenges
- The curriculum design focus on connecting to relevant and 'real' business practice engaged students like Ella and allowed a smoother transition into the placement
- As her confidence and competence developed she started to develop intellectually and achieve more academically – a virtuous circle.

Her positive engagement emerged less from a direct academic context and much more from her experiences on placement. The strong support she got from a good social network gave her the foundation to overcome challenges. At the end of her first year, the situation was not so good but, once the placement began, she moved on and was positively transformed by her experiences. Although not all experience was positive (she criticised some aspects of the study blocks and the lack of feedback), other dimensions – such as the opportunity for students to study a common curriculum in small cohorts and to share a common experience – lends support to Astin's (1993) contention that this approach provides common ground and social and learning interaction. Although Ella had little interaction with staff, her strong identification with peers enabled meaningful interaction with them, which contributed in a major way to her powerful sense of engagement.

At the beginning and throughout his first year, Martin seemed highly engaged and destined for success. He appeared to make a rapid and successful transition to higher education and was apparently full of confidence. The fragility of this engagement was demonstrated by the implosion he suffered in the second year. At the root of this was the fracture of his social relations exacerbated by his academic experience, with almost every academic engagement aspect alienating him yet further. The social situation went from being strongly involved in a large 'disparate community' in first-year halls to loneliness and depression in the second year. On reflection, signs of this emerged in the first year, as at this stage he had:

- Adopted an instrumental vocation converse to his intrinsic interests
- A general sense of disengagement with academic aspects of the course (despite apparently high participation)
- Never got really involved with peers or staff on the course.

A major problem for Martin was that he was attending a large anonymous course in which the infrastructure did not serve to build community and relationships – quite the opposite in fact. Dubet (1994) has proposed that there are three dimensions that underpin "ways of being a student" in the current mass higher education system: the nature of the personal project (why the student is studying at university), the degree of integration into university life and the level of intellectual engagement with the subject. Martin's personal project was always a bit of an illusion (or self-delusion) and he did not really have a genuine interest in the subjects he was studying. Thus although the integration aspect mitigated for a period, it then began to come apart.

Dubet (1994) ascribes those who have a negative orientation to all three dimensions as being in a state of "anomy". Jary and Lebeau (2009) used Dubet's conceptual map in their study of UK sociology students. They found evidence of the other seven archetypes described by Dubet but not this one. Perhaps surprisingly, they concluded that these seven orientations of students were viable in leading to being 'sufficiently' engaged to be successful. Anomy is an accurate descriptor for Martin, who left university in order to recover and rebuild an identity with which he felt more comfortable.

Martin also illustrates some of the themes of Mann (2001) who identified alienating forces in HE: to be successful, students are forced to adopt some strategies as they enter an unfamiliar culture with different values and beliefs, and with too much focus on performance and academic discourses that constrain student identities. These issues caused discomfort to Martin but proved to be very alienating to Kelly.

Kelly had a strong personal project (her aspiration to have a fashion shop) and an intrinsic interest in the subject, but she found it hard to integrate and did not appear to have sufficient social and cultural capital or to be able to find the resources to overcome these problems (David, 2009; Reay, David and Ball, 2005). Her communication difficulties and lack of confidence meant she found many potentially positive influences on engagement to have the opposite effect: the workload and challenge were too much for her; group work and seminars (which she had looked forward to) turned out to be very stressful; and relationships with staff did not develop. Therefore she struggled to integrate, both socially and academically (Tinto, 1993). It was just too much to do both and in the second half of her only year on the course she opted to focus on the social. The real reason for her withdrawal is not known but she did not develop any strong engagement to almost any aspect of her university experience on the course, despite retaining her aspirations and interest in the subject – which challenges Jary and Lebeau's (2009) assertion previously noted. Kelly illustrates an example of a type of disengagement proposed by Krause (2005), who argued that in addition to "inertia" (inactivity or non-involvement) there is also a scenario of students trying to engage but finding that this is a "battle" with unfamiliar values and cultures.

Ryan exemplifies the Dubet archetype of strong personal project ("becoming an artist"), love of the subject and early and strong integration into university life. His journey through higher education was very much an "identity project" (Holmes, 1995) and both his goal and development were all about "becoming rather than having" (Fromm, 1978). His university experience was not perfect but he made light of any course issues and overcame some difficult social issues. He was able to tackle these issues – some of which were quite challenging – because his sense of engagement was so strong and he never lost confidence. He brought maturity and experience with him as well as no expectations. It is notable that across our study, expectations only became an issue for students when things started to go badly wrong; otherwise, for all the others, expectations – which were much more about settling in socially than academic issues – simply ceased to matter (Bryson and Hardy, 2009).

Ryan developed a 'virtuous circle' of engagement, where everything integrated together to strengthen mutually and to enable him to make the most of all opportunities: academic aspects of delivery and curriculum, relationships and extra-curricular experiences. There was a special factor that can only have assisted this: as Ryan was studying art, the studio was central in his student life and became a key part of his identity. It offered an academic community and sense of belonging through spending most days with peers and staff, interacting in informal ways and being a 'safe' place to take risks and try things out.

Keith entered university with a "readiness to engage" (Handley, Price and Millar, 2011). His personal project was more vague and he was only strongly committed to one of the subjects of his joint degree. He had already developed a strong sense of responsibility and this sustained him well in the first year, which for him was mainly about settling in. At this stage he made a few, but quite close, peer relationships but no staff relationships. Keith had a crisis in second year when he felt overcome by the workload and when the conclusion of the degree was so far away. He managed to overcome this through:

- Support from his social network – his friends on the course
- Maintaining his 'will to learn' (Barnett, 2007) by making an early start on his dissertation – a task which held strong personal interest for him and offered desired autonomy.

McCune (2009) contends that students' "willingness to engage" is influenced by their perception that they are involved in "authentic learning experiences" – for Keith, the dissertation served such a purpose. The dissertation was a catalyst to improve his relationships with staff; working closely with a supervisor encouraged Keith to see staff differently. That gave him the confidence to approach other staff, although he thought the staff were more receptive to final-year students anyway; the implications of that (echoed by other students) need to be considered further.

It was readily apparent that Ella, Keith and Ryan developed intellectually (Perry, 1999) during their courses and the foundation for this was their relatively stronger (or growing) engagement. This supports the notion that assimilating new and more advanced "ways of knowing" (Baxter Magolda, 1992) is uncomfortable and if the individual is not strongly engaged it simply will not happen.

Conclusions

So what does this tell us about the nature of academic engagement? We certainly did not set out to diminish our own earlier proposals on what the key 'academic' influences on engagement were. Although at least some of these academic factors have played a role in enhancing (or reducing) engagement and relationships have emerged as most salient, other 'non-academic' dimensions have been equally, if not more, important. What the student 'brings' influences their readiness and willingness to engage. Although all the students had personal projects – that is, "why were they here, what purpose did university serve for them?" – some projects were much better founded than others and therefore maintained. The roles of social factors, and a sense of belonging and becoming a member of communities (academic and otherwise), were very important. Indeed, it was strong social networks that sustained the students during moments of doubt and crisis, and a lack of such networks that led to withdrawal. Other commentators have emphasised the importance of communities (Perry, 1999; McInnis, 2005) and Tinto has argued that social integration is equally vital to academic integration (1993) and questioned whether "the social, is, for many students, a developmental precondition for addressing the need for intellectual engagement?" (1997, p.618). We have explored these social and community dimensions arising from our research study in more detail elsewhere (Bryson and Hardy, 2010; Hardy and Bryson, 2010).

A holistic view of engagement needs to take account of all the issues in the broader student experience, particularly the social and other 'external' mediating influences. Our own research and a consideration of the relevant literature have made us develop a more comprehensive definition of student engagement (Bryson, Cooper and Hardy, 2010, p.15):

> Student Engagement [SE] is about what a student brings to Higher Education in terms of goals, aspirations, values and beliefs and how these are shaped and mediated by their experience whilst a student. SE is constructed and reconstructed through the lenses of the perceptions and identities held by students and the meaning and sense a student makes of their experiences and interactions. As players in, and shapers of, the educational context, educators need to foster educationally purposeful SE to support and enable students to learn in constructive and powerful ways and realise their potential in education and society.

This concept is very much rooted in a constructivist notion of learning. We take issue with commentators who state that engagement is amenable to measurement as it is manifest and demonstrable through what a student does. This underplays the 'pattern-centred' rather than 'variable-centred' nature of engagement (Fredricks, Blumenfeld and Paris, 2004). We note that this measurement approach also often relies on closed survey instruments administered to students at a single point during a three- or four-year experience. Our longitudinal research has demonstrated that the level of engagement varies for individuals at different points of time and may be both resilient and fragile in rather unpredictable ways.

Teachers, academic curricula, delivery methods and structures do enhance engagement. However, these influences can be limited or rendered ineffective if other factors are not taken into account. Hockings (2010) notes that even pedagogic approaches designed to raise engagement do not work with all students; indeed, this group of students found this approach even more alienating than the traditional approaches, echoing earlier work from Honkimaki, Tynjala and Valkonen which found that "not even pedagogical innovations can make all students do their best"

(2004, p.447). Hockings argues that a more personalised approach is required, taking into account the views and position of the individual student.

Kuh (2008) identified particular curricular and extra-curricular opportunities associated with higher engagement. They share the common feature that learning is 'owned', at least in part, by the student (Harris, 2008). So the academy can make a difference, but that needs to be though a sharing approach that avoids alienating effects, with a discourse between the parties. It was so disappointing to observe, in some of this research, how indifferent the staff (and systems) seemed to be to students, particularly in the early part of a degree, and how they made little attempt to establish any sort of engaging relationship. This infers that too many staff perceive that lack of engagement is a "problem with the students" (Zyngier, 2008).

This point illustrates why academic engagement may indeed be so salient. This is the territory where staff interact with students, and too many staff are wasting this opportunity or even exacerbating the problem by alienating students through their own behaviour. Staff being 'distant' is one issue but even worse is the antipathy or authoritarianism which some students experience. Our earlier research (Bryson and Hand, 2007b) demonstrated that even some 'student-centred' staff seem to be constantly 'disappointed' by students not meeting their expectations. Yet, there is much talk in higher education of 'managing student expectations'. This pejorative view of students must change to ensure that student engagement is conceived as a joint enterprise, as doing so is a fruitful path to achieving the true purpose of higher education for all parties.

References

Askham, P. (2008) 'Context and Identity: Exploring Adult Learners' Experiences of Higher Education', *Journal of Further and Higher Education*, 32/1, pp.85–97.

Astin, A.W. (1993) *What Matters in College: Four Critical Years Revisited* (San Francisco: Jossey-Bass).

Barnett, R. (2007) *A Will to Learn: Being a Student in an Age of Uncertainty* (Maidenhead: Open University Press and Society for Research in Higher Education).

Baxter Magolda, M. (1992) *Knowing and Reasoning in College: Gender-related Patterns in Students' Intellectual Development* (San Francisco: Jossey-Bass).
Brennan, J., Edmunds, R., Houston, M., Jary, D., Lebeau, J., Osborne, M. and Richardson, J. (2010) *Improving What is Learned at University* (London: Routledge).
Bryson, C. and Hand, L. (2007a) 'The Role of Engagement in Inspiring Teaching and Learning', *Innovations in Teaching and Education International*, 44/4, pp.349–62.
Bryson, C. and Hand, L. (2007b) 'Do Staff Conceptions of Good Teaching and Learning Approaches Align with Enhancing Student Engagement?', paper presented at Higher Education Research and Development Society of Australia Conference, Adelaide.
Bryson, C. and Hardy, C. (2009) 'An In-Depth Investigation of Students' Engagement Throughout Their First Year in University', paper presented at UK National Transition Conference, London.
Bryson, C. and Hardy, C. (2010) 'What Students Tell Us about what Influences Their Engagement with Communities within HE', paper presented at SEDA Conference, Leeds.
Bryson, C., Cooper, C. and Hardy, C. (2010) 'Reaching a Common Understanding of the Meaning of Student Engagement', paper presented at SRHE Conference, Newport, Wales.
David, M.E. (ed.) (2009) *Improving Learning by Widening Participation in Higher Education* (London: Routledge).
Dubet, F. (1994) 'Dimensions et Figures de l'Experience Etudiante Dans l'Universite en Masse', *Revue Francaise De Sociologie*, 35/4, pp.511–32.
Fredricks, J., Blumenfeld, P. and Paris, A. (2004) 'School Engagement: Potential of the Concept, State of the Evidence', *Review of Educational Research*, 74/1, pp.59–109.
Fromm, E. (1978) *To Have or to Be?* (London: Jonathan Cape).
Fung, D. (2006) 'Telling Tales: A Fresh Look at Student Experience and Learning in Higher Education', paper presented at BERA Conference, Warwick, September.
Handley, K., Price, M. and Millar, J. (2011) 'Beyond "Doing Time": Investigating the Concept of Student Engagement with Feedback', *Oxford Review of Education*, in press.
Hardy, C. and Bryson, C. (2010) 'The Social Life of Students: Support Mechanisms at University', paper presented at Society of Research into Higher Education Conference, Celtic Manor, Wales, December.

Harris, L. (2008) 'A Phenomenonographic Investigation of Teacher Conceptions of Student Engagement in Learning', *The Australian Educational Researcher*, 35/1, pp.57–79.

Hockings, C. (2010) 'Reaching the Students that Student-centred Learning Cannot Reach', *British Educational Research Journal*, 35/1, pp.83–98.

Holmes, L. (1995) 'Competence and Capability: From Confidence Trick to the Construction of the Graduate Identity', paper presented at the Higher Education for Capability Conference, UMIST, November.

Honkimaki, S., Tynjala, P. and Valkonen, S. (2004) 'University Students' Study Orientations, Learning Experiences and Study Success in Innovative Courses', *Studies in Higher Education*, 29/4, pp.431–49.

Jary, D. and Lebeau, Y. (2009) 'The Student Experience and Subject Engagement in UK Sociology: A Proposed Typology', *British Journal of the Sociology of Education*, 30, pp.697–712.

Krause, K. (2005) 'Understanding and Promoting Student Engagement in University Learning Communities', keynote address at James Cook University Symposium, Queensland.

Krause, K.L. and Coates, H. (2008) 'Students' Engagement in First-Year University', *Assessment and Evaluation in Higher Education*, 33/5, pp.493–505.

Kuh, G.D. (2008) *High Impact Practices: What They Are, Who Has Access to Them and Why They Matter* (Washington: Association of American Colleges and Universities).

Lahteenoja, S. and Pirttila-Backman, A.-M. (2005) 'Cultivation or Coddling? University Teachers' Views on Student Integration', *Studies in Higher Education*, 30/6, pp.641–61.

Mann, S. (2001) 'Alternative Perspectives on the Student Experience: Alienation and Engagement', *Studies in Higher Education*, 26/1, pp.7–19.

McCune, V. (2009) 'Final Year Biosciences Students' Willingness to Engage: Teaching, Learning Environments, Authentic Learning Experiences and Identities', *Studies in Higher Education*, 34/3, pp.347–61.

McInnis, C. (2005) 'Reinventing Student Engagement and the Learning Community: Strategic Directions for Policy, Research, and Practice. Enhancing the Student Experience', keynote address to the HEA Conference, Edinburgh.

Perry, W. (1999) *Forms of Intellectual and Ethical Development in the College Years: a Scheme* (New York: Harcourt Brace).

Reay, D., David, M.E. and Ball, S. (2005) *Degrees of Choice, Social Class, Gender and Race in Higher Education* (Stoke-on-Trent: Trentham Books).

Tinto, V. (1993) *Leaving College: Rethinking the Causes and Cures of Student Attrition* (Chicago: University of Chicago Press).

Tinto, V. (1997) 'Classrooms as Communities: Exploring the Educational Character of Student Persistence', *Journal of Higher Education*, 68/6, pp.599–623.

Weatherston, D. and Lawrence, F. (2008) 'Changing Lives: Perspectives from a Study of Six Music Undergraduates in Their First Year', in *Proceedings of the European First Year Experience Conference*, Wolverhampton, pp.205–211.

Zyngier, D. (2008) '(Re)conceptualising Student Engagement: Doing Education Not Time', *Teaching and Teacher Education*, 24, pp.1,765–76.

Chapter 3

The psychology of being engaged and its implications for promoting engagement

Glen Newbery

University of Western Sydney, Australia

No-one could seriously doubt that student engagement and its promotion always has been, and always will be, a key concern of the *genuine* educator. In view of this, the recent upsurge of interest in the concept of student engagement may be deemed somewhat curious. This upsurge of interest can be understood, however, when considering it within the context of the more general forces of change impacting on contemporary higher education institutions.

These changes have been well documented in the higher-education research literature during the past decade. Hockings, Cooke and Bowl (2007) refer to "a changing world in higher education – changes that encompass student funding, the school curriculum, government policies to widen participation, and the 'massification' of higher education." (p.721) Dall'Alba and Barnacle (2007) point to:

> the largely instrumental function universities are seen to have within contemporary societies and to trends within contemporary universities such as an emphasis on 'quality assurance' and accountability... increased marketing of university programmes locally, nationally, and internationally, and areas of study showing strong student demand or attributed high status.
>
> (p.680)

Ahlfeldt, Mehta and Sellnow (2005) note that, "As our world evolves and students' attention spans change, educators must also adapt to meet the changing needs of their students." (p.5)

As the last quote makes particularly clear, survival within the changing higher-education landscape requires adaptation to those changes. It is this 'evolutionary pressure' that has produced the increased interest in student engagement, for innovative approaches to engagement provide one means of adaptation. For instance, confronted by a student cohort for which the average attention span is markedly lower than for previous cohorts, the educator is interested in how to engage such a changed student cohort; that is to say, he or she is interested in how to 'adapt to meet the changing needs' of such students. And it is no longer just the educator who is confronted with the challenge of engaging students: non-academic university staff also feel the pressure to adapt, so they too have an interest in engagement and its promotion. Marketing officers are concerned to engage prospective students so that they will attend their university rather than one of the other institutions comprising the competition. Managers within the university are concerned to engage first-year students so as to meet a key expectation attached to state funding, namely, student retention and completion (Yorke, 2006). Hence, there is both an increased number and a growing diversity of those interested in the concept of student engagement.

In view of this greater diversity of interest, it is not surprising that the term 'engagement' has been employed in a variety of ways. As Reid and Solomonides (2007) point out, "engagement is a term used widely to describe all manner of relationships between the student and the institution, program of study, task, et cetera..." (p.28). However, despite the wide usage of the term, there is evidently agreement that engagement is a *relation*.

This characteristic of engagement is worth elaborating. Engagement is a relation between at least two things, where one thing (typically, a person) is in the state of *being engaged* (let us call this the *subject* of the engagement relation) while the other thing can be considered *engaging* (let us call this the *object* of the engagement relation). The particular meaning of engagement, then, will depend on the nature of both the subject and the object of the engagement relation. In the case of '*student* engagement', the student is obviously the subject of the relation, but the object of the engagement relation can vary, which is the main reason why the term 'student engagement' can be used to "describe all manner of relationships between the student and the institution, programme of study, task, et cetera...".

There is, of course, more to the concept of student engagement than its relational component. Four additional components can be extracted from the various definitions of engagement that have been put forward by researchers in the field: the behavioural component; the affective (or emotional) component; the cognitive component; and the conational (or motivational) component. These components are set out in the following definitions of student engagement:

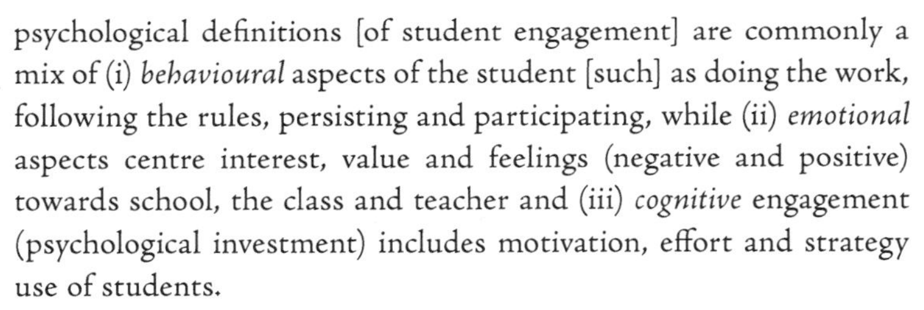

> psychological definitions [of student engagement] are commonly a mix of (i) *behavioural* aspects of the student [such] as doing the work, following the rules, persisting and participating, while (ii) *emotional* aspects centre interest, value and feelings (negative and positive) towards school, the class and teacher and (iii) *cognitive* engagement (psychological investment) includes motivation, effort and strategy use of students.
>
> (Zyngier, 2008, p.1,769)

> Academic engagement is defined as engaging in the activities of a course programme with thoroughness and seriousness. Indicators of academic engagement are **cognitive** (organising and planning his/her own work, entering deeply into learning on his/her own), **affective** (being motivated, persevering, taking pleasure in the course, being interested), **conative** (giving the necessary energy and time) and **relational**.
>
> (Harris et al., 2004, p.2)

Motivation, emotion and cognition are the three traditional psychological categories (Anderson, 1934) and are (in interaction) the key determinants of behaviour. Their inclusion in definitions of student engagement, then, makes it clear that student engagement is (correctly) considered to be a *psychological* relation. Yet there is some confusion regarding the psychological categories in the student engagement literature. As can be seen above, Zyngier (2008) observes that cognitive engagement commonly appears in psychological definitions of engagement and that "cognitive engagement (psychological investment) includes motivation". Thus, it would appear that there is a tendency to conflate cognition and motivation in psychological definitions of engagement. Harris et al. (2004) claim that indicators of academic engagement are cognitive, affective, conative and relational, but they also state that affective indicators include "being motivated" and "persevering", thus conflating the categories of emotion and motivation.

Before student engagement can be effectively promoted, there must first be a sound understanding of the psychology of 'being engaged'. That is to say, there must first be a sound understanding of the dynamic interplay of motivation, cognition and emotion in the determination of engaged behaviour. Such an understanding can be established via a critical examination of Deci and Ryan's (1985, 1991, 2008) account of intrinsic and extrinsic motivation – forms of motivation that figure prominently in discussions of student engagement (see Pintrich, 2003; Harris et al., 2004; Reid and Solomonides, 2007).

The psychological dynamics of engaged behaviour

In their Self-Determination Theory (SDT), Deci and Ryan "distinguish between different types of motivation based on the different reasons or goals that give rise to an action" (Ryan and Deci, 2000a, p.55). The most fundamental distinction is between *intrinsic motivation* and *extrinsic motivation*. Intrinsic motivation is defined as the doing of an activity for no reason other than the rewards in the activity itself (Ryan and Deci, 2000a). An intrinsically motivated person, then, sees the activity as an end in itself.

Extrinsic motivation, on the other hand, is manifest when a person performs an activity because it is a 'means to an end'. As Deci (1998) puts it:

> *extrinsic motivation* refers to doing something for a separable consequence, whether that consequence is in the environment or is a specific cognitive 'reward' one gives oneself after completing the

> activity. To do something for a material reward is to be extrinsically motivated; to do something for approval is to be extrinsically motivated; to do something so you can tell yourself you are a worthy person is to be extrinsically motivated. In each case the activity is instrumental to the 'reward' rather than being the source of a spontaneously satisfying experience.
>
> (p.147)

Examination of both these types of motivation reveals much about the psychological dynamics of engaged behaviour. Since intrinsic motivation is commonly considered to be the paradigm case of student engagement, it is worth making this the initial focus of attention. By examining Deci and Ryan's account of intrinsic motivation, the dynamic interplay of motivation, emotion, and cognition in engaged behaviour will be clarified and this, in turn, will make it clear why intrinsic motivation is commonly regarded as the zenith of student engagement.

Intrinsic motivation and student engagement

While most contemporary motivation theorists accept the important role of biological drives such as hunger, thirst and sexuality, they maintain that human behaviour is also motivated by a set of 'growth' needs (Reeve, 2005). According to Deci and Ryan (2008), intrinsically motivated behaviour has its source in three such growth needs: the need for competence (that is, the need to feel effective; to feel capable of producing desired outcomes); the need for self-determination (that is, the need to experience an internal locus of causality; to feel that one's actions originate from the self); and the need for relatedness (that is, the need to experience a satisfying and coherent involvement with others) (Deci and Ryan, 1991). Deci and Ryan (1985) have the following to say about the motivational function of these three intrinsic needs:

> The intrinsic needs... motivate an ongoing process of seeking and attempting to conquer optimal challenges. When people are free from the intrusion of drives... they seek situations that interest them and require the use of their creativity and resourcefulness. They seek challenges that are suited to their competencies that are neither too

> easy nor too difficult. When they find optimal challenges, people work to conquer them, and they do so persistently.
>
> (pp.32–3)

Drawing together the strands of Deci and Ryan's account, it is possible to spell out the dynamic interplay of motivation, emotion and cognition in intrinsically motivated activity. In *seeking* optimal challenges, cognition serves motivation (that is, the needs for competence, self-determination and relatedness), insofar as it guides the person to an event that can satisfy that motivation. This shows that, contrary to popular belief, cognition is not 'cold' but 'hot', insofar as it involves motivational processes (see Pintrich, 2003). When the person finds an optimally challenging task and attempts to conquer it, he or she satisfies his or her innate psychological needs and, as a consequence, experiences positive emotional states such as enjoyment and interest; that is, has a spontaneously satisfying experience. These positive emotional states are the so-called 'intrinsic rewards', that is, the rewards in the activity itself. They play a role in guiding future behaviour; the *knowledge* that participation in an activity has produced positive emotional states functions as a *reason* for participating in that activity again (so, as mentioned before, intrinsic motivation is doing an activity for no reason other than the rewards in the activity itself).

This account of the psychological dynamics of intrinsically motivated behaviour makes it clear why intrinsic motivation is commonly regarded as the highest form of student engagement. Key indicators of student engagement are interest and enjoyment (Harris et al., 2004; Reid and Solomonides, 2007; Zyngier, 2008): interest and enjoyment are inherent rewards that emerge spontaneously as a person participates in an intrinsically motivated activity. Student engagement is characterised by independence (that is, the student organises and plans his or her own work) and perseverance (Harris et al., 2004; Handelsman et al., 2005): intrinsic motivation, "keep[s] people involved in ongoing cycles of seeking and conquering optimal challenges" (Deci and Ryan, 1985, p.33). Student engagement has been associated with high-quality learning (Australasian University Survey of Student Engagement, 2010): Ryan and Deci (2000a) claim that "intrinsic motivation results in high-quality learning and creativity" (p.55).

It is certainly the case that *some* students are intrinsically motivated in the sense described above. Consider, for instance, a study conducted by Kim and Merriam (2004). They examined motivations for learning among older adults and found that the most commonly reported reasons for studying included "to learn just for the joy of learning" and "to seek knowledge for its own sake". Unfortunately, however, this ideal state of student *engagement* is typically the exception rather than the rule in contemporary higher education institutions. The following passages provide an insight into the type of motivational orientation that is most common amongst the university students of today:

> Typically, students enter courses possessed of one main problem: *what must I do to pass (or do well) in this subject?* Some students combine this subjective interest with a second: *what skills will this course give me?* Such a view sees education as a preparation for *something else*, something beyond the course itself.
>
> (Michell, 1996, pp.15–16)

A so-called strategic approach to study (see Chapter 1) involves the student using deep and surface approaches to learning as he or she deems appropriate. Hence a deep approach might be adopted, say, to parts of the study programme seen as vital, whereas a surface approach might be used for a more peripheral component... "One might characterise being strategic as 'playing the game' to best personal advantage" (Yorke, 2006, p.5).

Today's university students, then, are typically *extrinsically* motivated. That is to say, they see their university studies as being instrumental to the achievement of a reward that is external to study itself (for example, skills that will help them secure relatively well-paid future employment). This being the case, and given the popular view that extrinsic motivation is a "pale and impoverished" form of motivation (Ryan and Deci, 2000a, p.55), it may seem that the prospects for promoting student engagement in contemporary universities are rather bleak.

However, extrinsic motivation is *not* necessarily impoverished. Consideration of the development of extrinsic motivation further enhances understanding of the psychological dynamics underlying engaged behaviour, for it shows that extrinsic motivation takes various forms. As will be discussed below, these forms range from relatively immature states characterised by a feeling of being 'controlled', to more mature states characterised by autonomy and authenticity. The autonomous forms of extrinsic motivation produce high levels of engagement; in fact, the most autonomous form of extrinsic motivation is indistinguishable from intrinsic motivation. Yet, some level of engagement can also be generated by the 'controlled' forms of extrinsic motivation, thus indicating that student engagement is not an either–or phenomenon, but rather a matter of degree.

Extrinsic motivation and student engagement

If there were no obstacles to the satisfaction of motivational states, people would participate in only those activities that naturally interest them. Perhaps regrettably, the reality is that there are obstacles to motivation. Many obstacles. This is nowhere more evident than in the process of socialisation.

As Deci and Ryan (1985) note, this process is one that every person is inevitably subjected to because "there are many behaviours, attitudes, and values that are neither natural nor intrinsically motivated, but that are important for effective functioning in the social world" (p.129). In socialisation, social forces and regulations come to bear upon people such that they adopt those behaviours that, while not naturally interesting, are socially valued. From a motivational perspective, socialisation produces conflict within the person; the person does not want to engage in socially valued activities if they are not naturally of interest but at the same time he or she *does* want to be accepted by the social group. According to Deci and Ryan (1991), this is a conflict between the need for relatedness and the need for autonomy: "The need to be related is fundamental and basic, and the social context in which approval is made contingent upon particular behaviours can bring a person's needs for autonomy and relatedness into opposition" (p.272). Conflicts of motivation are resolved in favour of the behaviour that maximises pleasure overall (this is the hedonic principle, a key assumption underlying all motivation theories). In the case of the conflict between the needs for relatedness and autonomy, the former need naturally wins out, for the process of socialisation has its most important psychological impact during infancy and early childhood, a period during which the person is dependent on the primary caregivers (who are normally the primary agents of socialisation). So, in order to preserve the approval of the primary caregiver (and thereby maximise pleasure overall), people compromise their 'need for autonomy' and become extrinsically motivated to participate in certain socially valued activities. Going to school would, for most people, be a case in point. Getting a job would be another. But the degree to which autonomy is compromised by extrinsically motivated behaviour varies. In other words, people differ in the degree to which their extrinsically motivated behaviour is *authentic*.

When a behaviour is authentic (or 'autonomous') the person feels that the action really originates from him or herself. As Ryan and Deci (2006) put it, "Authentic actions are those for which one takes responsibility; they are not half-hearted or disowned... for an act to be autonomous it must be endorsed by the self, fully identified with and 'owned'" (p.1,561). The degree to which extrinsically motivated behaviour is autonomous depends on the extent to which the relevant social regulation has been *internalised* and *integrated*. Internalisation is the psychological process by which a person actively transforms external regulations into internal regulations, while integration is the psychological process by which a person fully assimilates a new internal regulation by conducting a self-examination that brings the new internal regulation into congruence with his or her other guiding beliefs, values and needs (Ryan and Deci, 2000a). The more completely a social regulation is internalised and integrated, the more a person moves away from infantile feelings of being 'controlled' and towards an adult state of autonomy and authenticity. Deci and Ryan maintain that four types of extrinsic motivation can be distinguished on the basis of the degree of internalisation and integration (and hence, the degree of autonomy) involved in each.

The least autonomous form of extrinsic motivation is called *external regulation*. Here, behaviour is performed either to obtain a reward or to avoid punishment (for example, a student stays up all night to complete an assignment only because he will receive a late penalty if it is not submitted the next day). As the term external regulation suggests, the relevant social regulations have not been internalised. Consequently, the externally regulated person has an external perceived locus of causality; that is, he or she does not feel any ownership of the behaviour, but instead experiences it as alienated. This is why Deci and Ryan class external regulation as controlled (Ryan and Deci, 2000b).

A second type of extrinsic motivation – called *introjected regulation* – is also classed as controlled. In this case, the social authority that rewards and punishes has been internalised such that it assumes an independent existence in the person's psyche. As a result, behaviour is performed to avoid guilt and anxiety, or to attain ego-enhancements, that is, to attain self-approval (for example, a student strives for high grades because he would not feel worthwhile otherwise). In this type of extrinsic motivation, then, behaviour is undertaken out of a sense of obligation (that is, the person feels he or she *should*) and/or performance is accompanied by a feeling of pressure (that is, the person always feels that he/she has to live-up to some ideal standard) (Ryan and Deci, 2000a).

The remaining two types of extrinsic motivation in Deci and Ryan's taxonomy – *identified regulation* and *integrated regulation* – are classed as 'autonomous'. In identified regulation, the relevant social regulation has been fully internalised. In other words, the person has identified with the personal importance of the behaviour. For instance, a student who takes a course in functional grammar because she views it as relevant to her life goal of becoming a creative writer would have identified with the personal importance of this course of study. As this type of extrinsically motivated behaviour is consciously valued and self-endorsed, it is performed with less conflict and tension (Deci and Ryan, 1995). The most autonomous form of extrinsic motivation, however, is integrated regulation. In this type of regulation, identified regulations are brought into congruence; that is, integrated with other aspects of the self. When regulations are integrated, behaviour is "*authentic* in the full sense of emanating from the 'author', of displaying full self-endorsement" (Deci and Ryan, 1991, p.257). Thus, this type of extrinsic motivation shares many qualities with intrinsic motivation. Deci (1998) states that the distinction between integrated regulation and intrinsic motivation "is somewhat subtle" (p.149). In fact, close analysis of the matter reveals that the most autonomous form of extrinsic motivation generates a level of engagement that is indistinguishable from intrinsic motivation. According to Deci (1998):

> Intrinsic motivation and integrated regulation are different in that intrinsically motivated behaviour is done because it is interesting, while integrated behaviour is done because it is personally valued.
>
> (p.149)

This distinction is not cogent, for to 'personally value' a task *is* to take an interest in it. Deci must mean that intrinsic motivation and integrated behaviour differ insofar as the former involves *personal interest,* whereas the latter involves *situational interest.* Certainly, motivation theorists generally associate personal interest (that is, an individual's enduring disposition to enjoy a particular activity) with intrinsic motivation, and situational interest (that is, a psychological state of interest elicited by the nature of the activity) with extrinsic motivation (Pintrich, 2003). Deci (1998) says that "a situational interest can become a personal interest as the organismic integration process functions to bring it into coherence with one's self" (p.157). This is effectively to say that the quality of interest involved in extrinsically motivated behaviour can, if the regulations are integrated, become the same as that involved in intrinsic motivation. Thus, the most autonomous form of extrinsic motivation produces a level of engagement that is the same as intrinsic motivation.

Given that integrated extrinsic motivation and intrinsic motivation share many qualities, and given that intrinsic motivation is the highest form of student engagement, it is clear that extrinsically motivated students whose regulations are integrated can exhibit a high level of engagement – indeed, a level that is indistinguishable from intrinsic motivation. What is perhaps less clear, however, is that each of the other types of extrinsic motivation could also produce some level of student engagement. Like the extrinsically motivated student whose regulatory style is integrated, the extrinsically motivated student whose regulatory style is identified consciously values and self-endorses his or her studies. Hence, the 'identified student' would also display a high level of engagement; the level of engagement would only be diminished were the student to experience tension between the identified regulations relevant to his or her studies (in which case, the most likely impact would be on the affective indicators of engagement). Students whose extrinsic motivation is introjected behave to avoid guilt or to attain ego-enhancements. Consequently, they experience pressure during performance and would be both less likely to enjoy their studies and less likely to enter deeply into learning. Still, they would typically attend classes and submit the required work. Indeed, those motivated to attain ego-enhancements tend to be particularly adept at 'playing the game', so that the work they submit is usually awarded relatively high grades. Thus, while these extrinsically motivated students may be relatively deficient with respect to the affective and cognitive components of student engagement, they may nevertheless display the behavioural markers of student engagement. Even students whose extrinsic motivation is of the least autonomous form (that is, external regulation) may present the behavioural indicators of student engagement (although, to be sure, they are likely to do their work with resentment and resistance). It is not the case, then, that a student is either engaged or disengaged; rather, there are varying levels of student engagement. Where the level of student engagement is relatively low, only behavioural indicators are presented. Higher levels of student engagement are characterised by affective and cognitive indicators in addition to behavioural indicators. The crucial point with regard to the psychology of engagement is that a student's level of engagement is a function of the extent to which he or she has transformed from the state of being controlled (a vestige of infantile dependency) to an adult state of owning his or her learning behaviour. That is to say, a student's level of engagement is a function of the extent to which his or her learning behaviour is autonomous.

There is experimental support for the notion that the level of student engagement is a function of the autonomy of learning behaviour. In fact, studies have found that more autonomous extrinsic motivation is associated not just with greater engagement but with better performance, less dropping out, higher quality learning and greater psychological wellbeing (see Ryan and Deci, 2000a). The applied implication of this is obvious; given the prevalence of extrinsic motivation amongst contemporary university students, attempts to promote engagement should focus on fostering the highest level of autonomy within extrinsic motivation – a level, as I have argued, that merges with intrinsic motivation.

But how exactly can this applied goal be achieved? Ryan and Deci (2000a) state that for a person to internalise a regulation fully and become autonomous with respect to it, he or she "must inwardly grasp its meaning and worth" (p.64). This appears to be consistent with Pintrich's (2003) suggestion that student motivation can be facilitated by providing "tasks, material, and activities that are relevant and useful to students" (p.672). But this kind of suggestion could be applied in a way that actually diminishes authenticity in a university (that is, scientific) course of study or in any course of study that cultivates an objective interest in what is *really* the case, independent of extraneous interests (see Michell, 1996). Consider again the interests of the contemporary university student as described earlier: he or she is interested in the skills that can be acquired from a course, because he or she is interested in attaining relatively highly paid future employment. A teacher may, in light of this, attempt to make course content 'relevant and useful' to students by emphasising how it will help them with respect to future employment; how it will, as it is often put, help them in the real world. Such an approach would, however, encourage students to view learning as a means to an end rather than as an end in itself, which would diminish their authenticity with respect to scientific study by undermining their objective interest in what is really the case.

As Michell (1996) observes, the instrumentalist attitude (the view that learning is a means to an end) may be appropriate with vocational courses but it is not appropriate with scientific courses, because discovering what is *useful* is not the same thing as establishing what *is really the case* (see Anderson, 1980; MacIntyre, 1964). What is called for, then, is an approach to making course content personally meaningful to students that does not reinforce the instrumentalist view of learning. In this regard, the recent movement in higher education away from "epistemology in itself to epistemology in the service of ontology" (Dall'Alba and Barnacle, 2007, p.684) appears promising. Not only is it put forward as a reaction against the dissolution of the university ideal by trends such as increasing instrumentalisation and vocationalisation (Thomson, 2001; Dall'Alba and Barnacle, 2007) but its pedagogical goals include "helping students to gain the self-confidence that comes from being authentic and the transformation of the person into an autonomous thinker" (Petocz and Newbery, 2010, p.139). Certainly, closer consideration of the ontological approach is warranted to establish whether it is really an appropriate vehicle for the promotion of student engagement.

Promoting engagement: pedagogy for autonomy and authenticity

Drawing upon the thinking of postmodern philosophers and their predecessors – in particular, Martin Heidegger – an increasing number of researchers have called for an *ontological* approach to higher education

(Hyde, 1995; Thomson, 2001; Barnett, 2004, 2005; Dall'Alba and Barnacle, 2007; Lundie, 2009). These researchers are united by the belief that the acquisition of knowledge (epistemology) is necessary but no longer sufficient for contemporary higher education and that, this being the case, higher education must take an "ontological turn" (Barnett, 2004; Dall'Alba and Barnacle, 2007). In the following section, a descriptive overview of the ontological position will be provided in order to establish both why it is supposed that an ontological turn is required and what an ontological turn entails for a pedagogy that promotes autonomy and authenticity. Since Barnett (1997, 2000, 2004, 2005) is particularly influential amongst current advocates of the ontological approach, the focus will be on his work.

The promise of an ontological pedagogy

Barnett (2005) observes that the postmodern world is one in which relativism has led to "the promotion of new and rival frameworks of understanding" (p.788), so that "no doctrine, no value and no principle can be upheld with absolute assurance" (p.787). This postmodern predicament provides the platform for his notion of 'supercomplexity':

> We now live in a world of radical contestation and challengeability, a world of uncertainty and unpredictability. In such a world, all such notions – as truth, fairness, accessibility and knowledge – come in for scrutiny. In such a process of continuing reflexivity, fundamental concepts do not dissolve but, on the contrary, become systematically elaborated. In this process of infinite elaboration, concepts are broken open and subjected to multiple interpretations; and these interpretations may, and often do, conflict. As a result, we no longer have stable ways even of describing the world that we are in... We are entitled to call this a world of proliferating and even mutually contesting frameworks a world [sic] of *supercomplexity*: amid supercomplexity, there can never be any complete resolution of the contestability of our frameworks.
>
> (Barnett, 2005, p.789)

The uncertainty (or strangeness) engendered by supercomplexity is said to impact not just epistemologically, but ontologically. That is, the impact of 'uncertainty' is not merely intellectual; rather, the "generalised understanding that the world is forever beyond any clear uncontestable understanding" engenders a sense of *personal* destabilisation that, in turn, produces "existential angst" (Barnett, 2004, pp.252, 260). It is on account of this, Barnett maintains, that higher education must take an 'ontological turn':

> Under these conditions of uncertainty, the *educational task is, in principle, not an epistemological task*; it is not one of knowledge or even knowing per se. It is not even one of action, of right and effective interventions in the world. For what is to count as a right or an effective intervention in the world? Amid supercomplexity, *the educational task is primarily an ontological task*. It is the task of enabling individuals to prosper amid supercomplexity...
>
> (Barnett, 2004, p.252)

In order to enable students to prosper amid supercomplexity, higher education programmes involving "risk, uncertainty and transformation of human being itself" are required (Barnett, 2004, p.258). An ontological pedagogy would involve risk and uncertainty by presenting "awkward spaces to and for students" (Barnett, 2005, p.795) or, as Dall'Alba and Barnacle (2007) put it, by providing "a forum for challenging taken-for-granted assumptions" (p.689). Barnett admits that an epistemological pedagogy can also involve risk and uncertainty; he states that a pedagogy that is a largely epistemological journey "will be one of encountering strangeness, of wrestling with it, and of forming one's own responses to it" (2004, p.257). However, while both epistemological and ontological pedagogies can involve "exposure to dilemmas and uncertainties", only in an ontological pedagogy will the exposure "widen such that human being itself is implicated" (ibid., p.257).

According to Barnett, an ontological exposure to dilemmas and uncertainties fosters in students an authentic form of being that is characterised by "self-belief, self-confidence, and self-motivation" (2004, p.254), as well as by "carefulness, thoughtfulness, humility, criticality, receptiveness, resilience, courage, and stillness" (2004, p.259). This authentic being is clearly consistent with high levels of student engagement, so the ontological approach would appear to be an appropriate vehicle for the promotion of student engagement.

It is regrettable, then, that a lack of clarity in the articulation of the ontological approach presents an impediment to its implementation. Barnett himself observes that an ontological pedagogy eludes adequate description:

> If we are to capture the kind of pedagogy that is [ontological]... then a quite different language is required... It may be a poetic language, a language that speaks to human being. It might be a language of love, of becoming, of disturbance, or of inspiration. What is it for human beings to be encouraged, to be brought forth, out of themselves?
>
> (2004, p.258

Since an ontological pedagogy cannot be clearly articulated, it is obviously the case that "practising a pedagogy of this kind is not a set of practices that we readily understand" (Barnett, 2004, p.260).

However, it seems to me that the ontological approach to pedagogy cannot be readily understood because its foundational assumptions about the status of knowledge are confused. Once these confusions are dispelled, the ontological position's promise for the promotion of student engagement can be put into proper perspective.

Ontological pedagogy from a realist perspective

The central claim of the ontological approach is that the acquisition of knowledge (that is epistemology) is necessary but no longer sufficient for contemporary higher education. Knowledge is deemed to be insufficient on the basis of two assumptions. Firstly, it is assumed that there can be no foundational and absolute (that is, *objective*) knowledge. Secondly, it is assumed that knowledge cannot effect a transformation of the human being itself. As will be demonstrated, neither assumption withstands critical scrutiny.

The denial of objective knowledge is a standard postmodern position that has been encouraged by the growth of relativism. Barnett exemplifies this postmodern relativist stance when he states that the growth of relativism has produced "a multiplication of incompatible differences of interpretation", so that we now inhabit a postmodern world, which "is radically unknowable" (2004, pp.249, 254). But there have been well-known and long-standing objections to relativism. One of these objections is that relativism is self-refuting. Take the central relativist claim that there is no objective truth: this is a statement about what is really the case and hence assumes the very objectivity that it explicitly denies. Barnett's assertion that the world is radically unknowable is self-refuting in the same way: in denying that the world can be known he effectively professes to know something about the world. Plainly, the realist view that there *can* be objective knowledge is a precondition of making any meaningful assertion about the way things are. Still, relativists persevere in the face of this. They argue that, since there are incompatible differences of interpretation, and since nothing can be asserted with certainty, then there can be no objective knowledge. However, this attempt to rescue relativism fails. Contrary to postmodern opinion, the realist position on knowledge accepts that there can exist incompatible differences of interpretation. But it correctly denies both that this entails the impossibility of objective knowledge and that, where there are incompatible interpretations of the one event, more than one of them can be true. Further, the realist position does *not* claim that objective knowledge supplies certainty; rather, it acknowledges both that any contingent statement can be doubted and that this does not prohibit objective knowledge. Hence, the claim that there can be no objective knowledge is not justified, and so it cannot provide support for the claim that the acquisition of knowledge is insufficient for contemporary higher education.

As noted above, there is a second assumption underlying the claim that knowledge is insufficient for contemporary higher education, namely, that knowledge cannot bring about a transformation of human being itself. Barnett's distinction between "contestability" and "challengeability" sheds light on why it is supposed that only an ontological pedagogy can "disturb the human being as such":

> *Contestability,* we may take it, refers to that state of affairs in which a proposition or framework might be subjected to the counter punch of a rival proposition of [sic] framework. It indicates a situation in which competing voices might wish to be heard or can be heard. *Challengeability,* in contrast, refers to that state of affairs in which our orientation to the world is subject to counterintuitive experiences. Suddenly, something takes our breath away: we have the

> stuffing knocked out of us. The assumptions on which we depended, but of which we were hardly aware, are – in the same moment – both revealed and found to be inadequate. While their conceptual territories overlap, contestability occupies the more epistemological position while challengeability stands in the more ontological position.
>
> (2005, p.794)

Hence, it is only the ontological approach that can "disturb the human being as such", because only this approach elicits a somatic response. In other words, only an ontological approach to "dilemmas and uncertainties" that "spring from complexities within a field" (Barnett, 2004, p.257) can "knock the stuffing out of us". An epistemological approach to such dilemmas and uncertainties, on the other hand, elicits a mere intellectual response – a mere "epistemic delight" (Barnett, 2004, p.258).

It appears, then, that proponents of the ontological approach consider knowledge to be insufficient because it is a cognitive phenomenon and, as such, can only transform a student cognitively; it can be a means by which a student "comes to live in a new cognitive universe" (Barnett, 2004, p.258) but it cannot elicit the kind of bodily response which brings about an existential transformation of the entire person.

However, this thinking is premised on the notion that there is a separation between cognition and bodily processes. Such dualist notions are very common. In psychology, for instance, the notion that reason (cognition) and the passions (motivations and emotions generated by physical processes) are separate realms has been popularly held from Plato through to the present day (Leahey, 2004; Newbery, 2011). However, the notion that cognition is separate from bodily processes is mistaken. As demonstrated earlier, cognition is not 'cold' but 'hot' insofar as it involves motivational processes. Far from being situated above bodily processes in some executive control function, cognition works in the service of motivation, for it guides the person to objects in the environment that can satisfy the prevalent motivational state. Indeed, it is the pressure exerted by motivational processes that has led to the evolution of the relatively sophisticated cognitive capabilities possessed by human beings (see Freud, 1915). Thus, there is no justification for the claim that knowledge is existentially inferior. Given that cognition is embodied, any interested student whose beliefs regarding a topic are challenged will experience a disturbance that is at once cognitive, emotional and motivational. A cognitive transformation, then, *is* an existential transformation of the entire person. In fact, granting that assumptions are cognitive, Barnett himself inadvertently admits that a cognitive transformation *is* an existential transformation when he says (in the passage just cited) that a challenge to core *assumptions* is sufficient to "take our breath away" and to "knock the stuffing out of us".

Divesting the ontological position of its confusions regarding the status of knowledge shows that a quite different language is *not* required in order to realise its potential for the promotion of student engagement. Viewed from a realist perspective, the ontological approach to pedagogy is consistent with an approach to learning that is based on *critical enquiry*.

A realist approach to the promotion of engagement

The approach to learning based on critical enquiry is certainly not new; it has its origins in the Socratic method (Anderson, 1931; Leahey, 2004). Still, it bears all the marks of the contemporary ontological approach, bar the postmodern jargon. Like an ontological pedagogy, the critical-enquiry approach to learning provides a forum for challenging taken-for-granted assumptions and encourages students to form their own responses to dilemmas and uncertainties. More specifically, in adopting a critical enquiry approach, the teacher confines him- or herself primarily to asking questions; and through this persistent questioning students are led to clarify their thoughts, to sharpen their criticisms and to develop their own, distinctive views (Leahey, 2004; Michell, 1996). Such free exercise of critical enquiry stands in direct opposition to dogmatic and authoritarian education (Michell, 1996). Hence, the critical-enquiry approach to learning provides the autonomy support that helps students gain the self-confidence that comes from being authentic. Moreover, because it cultivates an objective interest in what is really the case, the critical-enquiry approach makes course content personally meaningful without nurturing an instrumentalist view of learning. It is, therefore, an appropriate vehicle for the promotion of student engagement.

As with an ontological pedagogy, a critical-enquiry approach to learning "requires relatively open relationships between teacher and taught" (Barnett, 2004, p.258). Hence, it creates an educational situation in which teachers put themselves as much at risk as do students. In fact, the forces of change impacting on contemporary higher education institutions intensify the pedagogical risk for teachers, for they set up a conflict between subjective interests and the objective interest in what is really the case. As Michell (1996) observes:

> faced with students' demands for 'right' answers and with the institutions' and the professions' demands for marketable skills, it takes considerable courage to resist them and foster the interest in objective, critical enquiry.
>
> (p.20)

It also takes considerable courage to conduct research with critical rigor when there is substantial pressure to produce quantity rather than quality. Faced with such conflict, most academics compromise to some extent, else they would not survive within the changing higher education landscape. But this conflict and inevitable compromise need not impede a critical-enquiry approach to teaching. Teachers can help students to see where aspects of a discipline have "arisen not from the requirements of science per se but from social, political, and other forces" (Petocz and Newbery, 2010, p.139). Doing so would be consistent with the openness required of the critical enquiry approach, and would constitute a positive disillusioning of students – positive in the sense that it involves, "challenging and dispelling their illusions" (Petocz and Newbery, 2010, p.139) Thus, critical enquiry stands as a vehicle by which to navigate the current crisis in higher education while simultaneously providing the ontological autonomy support that promotes both high levels of student engagement and student self-transformation.

References

Ahlfeldt, S., Mehta, S. and Sellnow, T. (2005) 'Measurement and analysis of student engagement in university classes where varying levels of PBL methods of instruction are in use', *Higher Education Research and Development*, 24/1, pp.5–20.

Anderson, J. (1931) 'Socrates As an Educator', in Anderson, J. (ed.) *Studies in Empirical Philosophy* (Sydney: Angus and Robertson) pp.203–13.

Anderson, J. (1934) 'Mind As Feeling', in Anderson, J. (ed.) *Studies in Empirical Philosophy* (Sydney: Angus and Robertson) pp.68–78.

Anderson, J. (1980) *Education and Inquiry* (Oxford: Blackwell).

Australasian Survey of Student Engagement (2010). Retrieved from <http://www.acer.edu.au/ausse/seq.html>

Barnett, R. (1997) *Higher Education: A Critical Business* (Buckingham: Open University Press).

Barnett, R. (2000) *Realising the University in an Age of Supercomplexity* (Buckingham: Open University Press).

Barnett, R. (2004) 'Learning for an Unknown Future', *Higher Education Research and Development*, 23/3, pp.247–59.

Barnett, R. (2005) 'Recapturing the Universal in the University', *Educational Philosophy and Theory*, 37/6, pp.785–97.

Dall'Alba, G. and Barnacle, R. (2007) 'An Ontological Turn for Higher Education', *Studies in Higher Education*, 32/6, pp.679–91.

Deci, E.L. (1998) 'The Relation of Interest to Motivation and Human Needs – The Self-Determination Theory Viewpoint', in Hoffmann, L., Krapp, A., Renninger, K.A. and Baumert, J. (eds) *Interest and Learning: Proceedings of the Seeon Conference on Interest and Gender* (Kiel: IPN) pp.146–62.

Deci, E.L. and Ryan, R.M. (1985) *Intrinsic Motivation and Self-Determination in Human Behavior* (New York: Plenum).

Deci, E.L. and Ryan, R.M. (1991) 'A Motivational Approach to Self: Integration in Personality', in Dienstbier, R. (ed.) *Nebraska Symposium on Motivation 1990: Perspectives on Motivation* (Lincoln: University of Nebraska Press) pp.237–88.

Deci, E.L. and Ryan, R.M. (1995) 'Human Autonomy: The Basis for True Self-Esteem', in Kernis, M.H. (ed.) *Efficacy, Agency, and Self-Esteem* (New York: Plenum Press) pp.31–49.

Deci, E.L. and Ryan, R.M. (2008) 'Self-determination Theory: A Macrotheory of Human Motivation, Development, and Health', *Canadian Psychology*, 49/3, pp.182–5.

Freud, S. (1915) 'Instincts and their Vicissitudes', *The Standard Edition of the Complete Psychological Works of Sigmund Freud*, vol. XIV (London: Hogarth).

Handelsman, M.M., Briggs, W.L., Sullivan, N. and Towler, A. (2005) 'A Measure of College Student Engagement', *Journal of Educational Research*, 98/3, pp.184–91.

Harris, R., Bolander, K., Lebrun, M., Docq, F. and Bouvy, M.T. (2004) '*Linking Perceptions of Control and Signs of Engagement in the Process and Content of Collaborative E-Learning*', paper presented at the Network Learning Conference, Lancaster, April. Retrieved from <http://www.networkedlearningconference.org.uk/past/nlc2004/proceedings/symposia/symposium10/harris_et_al.htm>

Hockings, C., Cooke, S. and Bowl, M. (2007) '"Academic Engagement" Within a Widening Participation Context – A 3D Analysis', *Teaching in Higher Education*, 12/5–6, pp.721–33.

Hyde, B. (1995) 'An Ontological Approach to Education', paper presented at the annual conference of the Western States Communication Association, Portland, February. Retrieved from <http://www.eric.ed.gov:80/PDFS/ED381380.pdf>

Kim, A. and Merriam, S.B. (2004) 'Motivations for Learning Among Older Adults in Learning in a Retirement Institute', *Educational Gerontology*, 30, pp.441–55.

Leahey, T.H. (2004) *A History of Psychology: Main Currents in Psychological Thought* (Upper Saddle River: Pearson Education International).

Lundie, D. (2009) 'A Theory of Motivation and Ontological Enhancement: The Role of Disability in Student Empowerment and Institutional Change', *Educational Philosophy and Theory*, 41/5, pp.539–52.

MacIntyre, A.C. (1964) 'Against Utilitarianism', in Hollins, T.H.B. (ed.) *Aims in Education* (Manchester: Manchester University Press) pp.19–21.

Michell, J. (1996) 'Introduction: J.P. Sutcliffe as a University Teacher', in Latimer, C.R. and Michell, J. (eds) *At Once Scientific and Philosophic: A Festschrift for John Philip Sutcliffe* (Brisbane: Boombana Publications) pp.13–20.

Newbery, G. (2011) 'Drive Theory Reconsidered (Again!)', in Mackay, N. and Petocz, A. (eds) *Realism and Psychology: Collected Essays* (Leiden: Brill) pp.839–71.

Petocz, A. and Newbery, G. (2010) 'On Conceptual Analysis as the Primary Qualitative Approach to Statistics Education Research in Psychology', *Statistics Education Research Journal*, 9/2, pp.123–45.

Pintrich, P.R. (2003) 'A Motivational Science Perspective on the Role of Student Motivation in Learning and Teaching Contexts', *Journal of Educational Psychology*, 95/4, pp.667–86.

Reeve, J. (2005) *Understanding Motivation and Emotion* (Hoboken: John Wiley and Sons).

Reid, A. and Solomonides, I. (2007) 'Design Students' Experience of Engagement and Creativity', *Art, Design and Communication in Higher Education*, 6/1, pp.27–39.

Ryan, R.M. and Deci, E.L. (2000a) 'Intrinsic and Extrinsic Motivations: Classic Definitions and New Directions', *Contemporary Educational Psychology*, 25, pp.54–67.

Ryan, R.M. and Deci, E.L. (2000b) 'Self-determination Theory and the Facilitation of Intrinsic Motivation, Social Development, and Well-Being', *American Psychologist*, 55/1, pp.68–78.

Ryan, R.M. and Deci, E.L. (2006) 'Self-regulation and the Problem of Human Autonomy: Does Psychology Need Choice, Self-Determination, and Will', *Journal of Personality*, 74/6, pp.1,557–85.

Thomson, I. (2001) 'Heidegger on Ontological Education, Or: How We Become What We Are', *Inquiry*, 44/3, pp.243–68.

Yorke, M. (2006) 'Student Engagement: Deep, Surface, or Strategic?' keynote address, in 9th First Year in Higher Education Conference, Brisbane. Retrieved from <http://www.fyhe.com.au/past_papers/2006/Keynotes/Yorke.pdf>

Zyngier, D. (2008) '(Re)conceptualising Student Engagement: Doing Education Not Doing Time', *Teaching and Teacher Education*, 24, pp.1,765–76.

Chapter 4

Students' and lecturers' views of engagement in higher education

Sue Gordon[1], Anna Reid[2] and Peter Petocz[3]

[1] *University of Sydney, Australia*
[2] *Sydney Conservatorium of Music, Australia*
[3] *Macquarie University, Australia*

> Mathematics is what you make of it – it can be artistic, practical, creative or routine.
>
> (Quote from student survey)

Introduction

The student comment above succinctly captures the idea that the way students engage with a discipline shapes the very nature and quality of their learning in that field of study. Yet there has been much debate on the exact meaning of the term 'engagement' at the university level. It can be interpreted in different ways: time on task and participation in extra-curricular activities, the quality of academic effort devoted to studies, or the student's "will to learn" (Barnett, 2007) and ontological commitment to learning. It can be affected by students' own views of their discipline, their learning and their expectations for their future professional work. The first chapter of this book examines the range of notions of engagement that can be found in the literature, together with the ways in which such engagement can be assessed and measured. These notions suggest that engagement is a complex and multi-dimensional concept, and, viewed as a process (Krause and Coates, 2008), can be dynamic, contextualised and varied.

In this chapter we will investigate empirically the views about engagement held by participants in the process of higher education. In particular, we will contrast the views of students and lecturers, and compare views expressed in three quite different discipline areas – statistics, teacher education and music. Hodkinson (2005, p.119) points out that while education communities within specific disciplines have the strength of shared identity and belonging, they also risk fragmentation into "separate boxes that seldom talk to each other, sometimes replicate each others' work, and sometimes fail to understand what others already know." We aim to broaden understanding within disciplines and develop areas of connection between disciplines concerning engagement.

The empirical data that we draw on consist of transcripts of several sets of interviews with students and lecturers, collected in separate projects carried out by the authors during more than a decade of research into learning and teaching in diverse discipline areas. Each set of data was collected to address specific research questions and analysed using qualitative research approaches appropriate to those questions, usually thematic analysis or phenomenography (Marton and Booth, 1997). In each set of transcripts, participants illustrated implicitly – and sometimes explicitly – their views about engagement, an indication of the importance of the topic in teachers' theories in use (Schön, 1987) and students' perceptions and reflections about learning and teaching. We present these views in the form of a series of case studies in the next section of the chapter.

We have investigated the relationship between students' engagement and their conceptions of their discipline, their learning and their future profession (Reid et al., 2011, Chapter 6). There we presented a model of engagement that was derived from consideration of views of professional learning and knowledge for a profession. This model described three categories of engagement, from narrowest to broadest:

- *Formal:* a physical presence and a willingness to do what is required (by teachers, employers)
- *Disciplinary:* a meaningful interest in and interaction with the artefacts of the discipline, a desire to understand the profession

- *Essential:* a personal commitment to and involvement with the discipline, a personal identification with the profession.

When students focus on the technical aspects of a discipline and are unclear about the meaning of disciplinary knowledge, their engagement is likely to be at the *formal* level emphasising techniques. When they direct their learning towards specific artefacts and focus on meaningful substantive knowledge, their engagement tends to be *disciplinary*. When they make a strong personal connection with their discipline and future profession, and broaden their views of knowledge in the discipline to include generic as well as substantive aspects, students display an *essential* level of engagement. The broader and more inclusive categories include the narrower and more limited categories both logically and empirically.

An important aspect of this model is that it is not based on quantity of engagement but rather on quality. We will illustrate the model in the case studies that follow, and make an overall assessment in our conclusion.

Statistics

Our first case studies are in the area of statistics and investigate the experiences and aspects of engagement of three students. Many students at the tertiary level study some statistics – for most it is a compulsory, and often unwelcome, part of studies in another discipline. Students' lack of engagement with learning statistics as a service course is legendary. Possible reasons for this include a dislike or fear of mathematics (which often plays a large part in statistics courses), a lack of connection between the statistics curriculum and other areas of their primary discipline and the shortage of trained practitioners in these disciplines with specialised knowledge of statistics (Gordon, 1995; Onwuegbuzie and Wilson, 2003). Negative affective reactions may be exacerbated by the large size of some statistics classes and the key role played by statistics in accreditation of professional courses such as psychology (Swingler and Bishop, 2008). The three students introduced in this section are studying in areas that make extensive use of statistics – psychology and finance – and so there is a strong motivation for them to engage with their statistical studies. Like many students, they show an initial disinclination to include statistics in their studies; one of them describes it as useless and dull. Their narratives are informative in illustrating the different aspects of engagement and how, in some cases, students overcome barriers and achieve success in their endeavours.

Sandra

The first statistics case study illustrates the way Sandra, a second-year psychology student at an Australian university, overcame her reluctance to engage with learning statistics (Gordon, 1993). Sandra reported that at school she was bored and confused by mathematics. She attributed this to having gone to fourteen different schools, in different countries, where the educational systems did not match. Her perception of statistics was that it was "useless and dull". She initially appraised the statistics lecture notes as "daunting" and described herself as "resistant" to learning statistics. Her engagement with statistics seems to have been focused on the technical aspects at this stage. However, Sandra's concern that she would not be able to understand statistics led her to take action in a determined and methodical manner to broaden her engagement with the study and overcome difficulties:

> I worked through my lecture notes at the same time as the lecturer did. I just wanted to get a broad-brush stroke, a picture and then more detail with the tutorials. I went to three tutorials, one at the beginning of the week, one in the middle and one at the end. Each time it became a little clearer. By the third time I was feeling on top of it. And then I was coming here (to the Mathematics Learning Centre) twice a week as well. And I was working with Norman and Alice and my husband as well. We worked through examples for hours, our tute sheets [tutorial exercise sheets], to learn how typical these things are, to understand.

It appears that Sandra's initial grappling with statistics – her strong engagement with the material, initially at a formal and technical level – took place when she interacted with others: her teachers, colleagues or husband. Sandra's comment, below, shows that working collaboratively on statistics helped her to overcome some of her anxiety:

> I didn't work a great deal on my own, although I did at the end. I had to go through it on my own – but I felt frightened working on my own.

Sandra reported an increase in confidence during the year she studied statistics. She noted that "it is possible to learn stats successfully". Her perseverance led ultimately to a high grade in statistics but in the examination she had constantly to fight against her own resistance.

> I had this constant overwhelming desire to put down my pen and say: "I can't be bothered carrying on with this!" It was very difficult.

At the end of her intermediate year, Sandra's account of learning psychology reflects a far-reaching and personal perspective on her academic learning. She explained:

> While a lot of course material is not relevant for counselling, a lot of the attitudes that you learn are important. A sense of professionalism in your approach, not a knee-jerk reaction to things, but sitting back and assessing it. The [psychology] course teaches you to take many theories in and assess the different theories – not what is right and wrong but hold many different theories in mind at once.

To Sandra, an exceptional student, evaluation of learning statistics was in terms of the quality of learning and self-development she felt she had achieved, enabling her to broaden her outlook and gain insights on the particular facts and skills which she had learned.

> It's almost like two separate things in the statistics course we've just done. You could have actually just got the steps and maybe not understood why you were doing it. I wanted to understand what I was doing... By the end of the year I thought, it doesn't really matter how I go in this examination. I'm not going to let the exam mark dictate to me my knowledge. Because I knew I had a better grasp at the end of the year and I really felt that if I was doing experimental work I could work out what to do with my stats.

Sandra's persistence with her study resulted in a deeper engagement with statistics at an essential and personal level. Her interview traced her broadening focus from the technical details, through the statistical aspects of psychological theories, to the important role of statistics in her future professional life.

Hung

We interviewed Hung towards the end of his third year of study in a mathematics and finance degree at an Australian university (Reid and Petocz, 2002). The interview focused on his ideas about statistics and learning statistics. We have found that students' conceptions of statistics can be described in three levels, from the narrowest view that statistics is all about techniques, through a broader view of statistics as analysing and interpreting sets of data, to the broadest view of statistics as a way of making sense of the world and developing personal meanings (Petocz and Reid, 2010). In much of his interview transcript, Hung seemed to show the most limited conception of the discipline, focusing on individual statistical techniques. For instance, in several diverse statements he identifies the most interesting aspects of statistics:

> Just the different problems you get or the real-life application of regression analysis. I find that the most interesting... It is interesting to fit models to data... Just building models, financial models, understanding how it all works and how everything is put together into a model... The basic fundamentals of it like the derivation of things is interesting and if you learn how to do things from first principles it's pretty good.

Even Hung's statement about fitting models to data shows a view of statistics in terms of its techniques. While he mentions financial models, he seems to have only a generic idea in mind and gives no details of the process of explaining aspects of finance using statistical models. At this stage of his degree, he still has some difficulty explaining how statistics will help him in his career, and is only able to express this in general terms.

> I think in understanding more things in real-life problems. I suppose if you understand the statistics and how it works, that is what is most helpful in your career.... I haven't really joined the work place; it's really limited. I am not really sure.

Such a view of the discipline and its utility suggests a formal and technical engagement, and this is supported by Hung's comments on his learning of statistics. The following exchange illustrates this:

> *What do you aim to achieve when you learn statistics?* Probably furthering my career. I mean it has hopefully some aspects of finance, statistics to go further on with my career. *How do you know you have learnt something in statistics?* If I can keep doing different questions relating to the same problems over and over again without having to look back or getting any mistakes in them.

When we asked him what he expected of his lecturers, he was able to identify features that did not help his learning.

> They just keep writing unnecessarily and at the end of the lecture you have just written 20 pages or whatever and you've just got nothing out of it... Sometimes it just gets really boring and you just have basic rote learning type questions and you really want to expand and do more practical questions. It just stops at the theoretical questions, and that's pretty boring.

Yet his suggestions for improvements seemed to be focused on the formal aspects of his assessment.

> Before the final exams they have an outline of the final exam, like just specific points of what the final exam would cover. At the beginning of the course then you can actually relate all your study towards that, understand work related to the final exam. If they are going to cover a lot of the course in the final exam then it is probably better if they give out points relating to that at the beginning of the course.

Hung is a struggling student who seems to have progressed towards the end of his degree in mathematics and finance with only the narrowest conception of one component, statistics, as techniques. His approach to learning seems to be as narrow, focusing on basic aspects such as taking notes, repeating problems and preparing for exams. His motivation seems almost completely extrinsic and his engagement is correspondingly narrow, at the formal level of being physically present and carrying out the prescribed activities. Yet he describes statistics as "the most practical of all the subjects we cover" and says that he studies statistics "hoping it will help me get further in the workplace, but also for my enjoyment." This is an interesting inconsistency, in that perceiving a subject such as statistics as enjoyable is often seen as a desirable result of engagement; yet Hung seems to show only the narrowest level of engagement.

Jessica

Jessica is a student in the same mathematics and finance degree as Hung; we interviewed her at the end of her first year of study, after she had taken her first course in statistics. In her interview, Jessica shows the broadest conception of the discipline as an approach to life and a way of making sense of the world, an immediate contrast with the views put forward by Hung. For instance, she says of statistics:

> It's pretty relevant in lots of things. Like, they might compare cultures or something like that, and just the statistics involved in... for example, in our exam there was a question about drugs, and it's just interesting just what they get out of statistics and how they analyse people and things and life in general from statistics. I find that interesting.

At this stage of her course, she is clearly aware of the wide applicability of statistics and its importance to her future studies and professional work:

> It just gives you a clearer understanding of things going on, like, when you're working with figures or whatever, it just gives you a more scientific, like a solid evidence towards what you're trying to look at, if you're looking for some sort of answer... I didn't think statistics was that important before, I didn't relate it to... because I didn't know much about the subject, but then when I started learning about it, I thought "gee, it's basically everywhere", especially in consumer things, it's there in research and everything academic, I guess.

When we asked her what she thought was important to learn in statistics, she answered with the same broad focus, passing over the idea of learning specific techniques, and beyond the idea of the discipline of statistics itself, to the notion of making connections with other disciplines and life in general.

> Critical to learn now is probably how you can relate what you're learning to what you're... you've got to relate what you're learning to something else, like to a field, I don't know, you should relate what you're learning to different areas, like medicine, like manufacturing, everything, so you've got a subject and you can relate it to different things. That's what I think is important.

Jessica, unlike Hung, appears to view statistics in the broadest way, as a key to understanding the world, and displays a broad and mature view of her learning in statistics. Both these aspects set up the best conditions for her engagement with statistics – she believes in the importance and applicability of the subject and she approaches her learning of it with the aim of making connections to other areas of interest. At the same time, she makes an obvious personal connection with statistics, initially for her current and future studies, but also by implication for her future professional work – and this despite the fact that she has only completed the first year of her degree.

Given her overall approach, it is not surprising that the aspects of her lecturer's help that she values the most concern personal interactions with students and the practical applications of the subject itself. Talking of her views of lecturers' responsibilities, she describes her lecturer's approach:

> Like, he comes up and helps; it's personal, so it's not... you're not so detached from your work and you feel like getting into it. I think it's good when you've got a lecturer that gives you motivation, and gives the interesting side to the subject, and things like that, and helps you out.

Throughout her interview, Jessica shows the strong 'will to learn', the desire to be an authentic student, that is described by Barnett (2007). She shows the broadest conception of her discipline, views her learning in a correspondingly broad way, and, unlike Sandra, seems able to relate them to future professional opportunities, even in this early stage of her studies. Her engagement is at the essential level and she is able to appreciate and benefit from the personal engagement of her lecturer.

Teacher education

Our next two case studies contribute to understanding about engagement in learning from the perspectives of teachers – indeed, from specialists in education (Loughran and Russell, 2007): teacher educators. One unique feature of teacher education courses is that the participants are in the dual roles of student (at present) and teacher (in the future), and these roles are further mixed by periods of concurrent practical placements in schools. Lecturers in teacher education seem very aware of the modelling that can take place in their own classes and the opportunities for heightened engagement that occur in such authentic learning situations. Here we present case studies introducing two such lecturers, the first in the area of creative arts and the second in educational psychology. We show how the teacher educators engage their students and enable them, in turn, to think about engaging their own students with their schooling.

Dolphin

Dolphin (her choice of pseudonym) is a teacher educator in the general area of educational psychology at a university in South Africa. We talked with her by email using a protocol we developed for such interviews (Reid, Petocz and Gordon, 2008) in a study investigating the ways in which university teachers introduce their discipline to their students and how they understand and acknowledge diversity in their classes (Reid, Petocz and Gordon, 2010). Since her area, life orientation and inclusive education, is "all about people and their needs", Dolphin introduces students to her discipline area by "telling real life stories – we go to the theory with continuous reference to the practice". Her approaches to engaging students in this area of psychology and pedagogy are varied and include "discussions, co-operative learning and group work, video clips, music, case studies, real life situations. Not a lot of direct teaching. If I do that my students are allowed to interrupt me for questions or comments."

Throughout her interview, Dolphin showed an engagement with her discipline and her students at the essential and personal level. Her articulated belief in the importance of inclusive education was clearly passed on to her students. She describes the effects on students of telling real-life stories in this way:

> It usually opens their eyes to reality. Gets them out of the tunnel vision many of them have because of the safe and comfortable environments they grew up in. Most of the time it changes attitudes towards people/children with disabilities or learning difficulties... Although we have done the theory it made them understand these learners' physical and emotional experiences better. They also could apply the theory much easier.

By using visual and auditory aids, group discussions and also individual assignments, Dolphin attempts to accommodate students' different learning styles. She further explains that by "allowing students to ask questions and make comments, different needs are also identified."

> They are allowed to say if they don't feel comfortable with a topic and then it is attempted to address it in a different way. They are also prepared beforehand if we discuss sensitive topics... When students start chatting about it, it removes stereotypes and encourages respect and understanding. In an inclusive lecture having real people or video clips of disabilities opens their minds to see that these are normal people/children who experience problems, as we are all people with different problems.

Dolphin adds that a difficult task for her is to encourage all students to participate in discussions about differences, even those who may be reticent in coming forward.

> We (lecturer and students) try to agree on basic class rules where things like listening with an open mind, respect, confidentiality, and judging behaviour not the person, are essential. Because students agree together on these rules they remind each other to adhere to it. The most important thing is to treat students as adults with their own opinions, but to encourage them to think about their opinions... Students are not forced to verbalise their opinion, but the discussions sometimes get so stimulating that they cannot help but give their opinion.

Dolphin emphasises that using the real world as a classroom helps students to apply what they have learned.

> Although we are a university where the theoretical aspect is emphasised we train teachers to teach children to become whatever they want to become. However, by becoming what they want to become they need to assess what is going on in the real world.

Above all, Dolphin's own essential engagement with teaching underpins her philosophy and approach.

> I love teaching at a tertiary institution – simply because you can reason with the students and make them think. I hope that somewhere I make an impact on their attitudes towards teaching in a positive way – including all learners.

The excerpts from this interview illustrate a view of engagement that includes developing students' active participation and involvement with both theory and practice and, further, also encourages students to respect and understand the varied and individual needs of their own future students.

Klauss

Klauss is a teacher educator in the area of visual, expressive and creative arts at an Australian university preparing her students for their professional work as primary school teachers. We interviewed her by email as part of the same study in which Dolphin participated (Reid, Petocz and Gordon, 2010). She has several ways in which she encourages her students' engagement – and these model ways that her students could use in their own teaching to encourage their own students to get the most out of their art classes. The first of these is direct and overt – getting students to participate gladly in the work, individually and with their colleagues:

> They actually draw or paint or work with clay, et cetera. Some never have or have forgotten how much fun it is or how fulfilling it is to express themselves visually. They also share their work and ideas with others and get time to create an artwork individually, which is not assessed so non-threatening although it is displayed for the others to see.

Another aspect of the modelling is that Klauss herself is carrying out her own artistic work, explicitly offering it for the consideration and comments of her students.

> The art room is a typical art space, a bit messy, lots of work areas where students can come in out of lecture time and work or talk to each other. My tutor and I are always around, I often do my own painting in the same area... I think it is helpful for them to see that I continue to reflect on my teaching, not accepting taken for granted 'truths' and encouraging them to challenge what they are told also. It seems to be of interest for them to see me putting the theory into practice and working on my art, demystifying the art, talking about what I am up to and why, what works and what doesn't and why and linking it to teaching.

Klauss also encourages the personal connection that is necessary for students to engage essentially with their studies. She asks students to do this explicitly, and models the process by adding her own openness about her own artistic work.

> Students are required to keep a reflective journal. They are asked to record their memories of past experiences in art (good and bad). They reflect on their beliefs about art at the beginning and then have to write weekly reflections on their experiences during the workshops. We discuss how our past shapes the way we will do things in the future. I talk about my research which is an auto-ethnographic study done in the form of a self-portrait constructed from the words of my study. The aim was to try to understand why I teach what I do and why I think it is important.

Through Klauss's words, we can see clearly how her students are involved with their work, and how they develop the approaches to encourage the involvement of their own students.

> Mostly they write about how they feel empowered, they feel they have taken risks, done things they never would have in the past, realise how great they feel and want to pass it on to their students... They mention the 'buzz' in the art room when people are involved in their work and they seem to get excited about transferring this to their class. Some

> write about how bad their own teachers were and some say they are guilty of doing some of the things we talk about, such as correcting a child's work instead of guiding them to see for themselves.

Students have identified another important aspect of Klauss's teaching that contributes to their interest in the discipline:

> Student evaluation of my teaching consistently mentions teacher passion for the subject matter as being very important for their learning and even though they only have six weeks to learn about teaching art in primary school they say they value art more after the experience, after being able to 'do it' for themselves and feel good about what they achieved.

Although most of her students don't seem to need convincing, Klauss has thought about how to challenge those who are less interested in the creative arts to engage more fully with them and, once again, model the process so that they can engage their own students:

> I hope to alter that view, at least to convince them that art has some use; for designing, influencing, helping to be more creative and to 'see' with better clarity... Thinking about how to interest [their] students. What would make them want to learn? Thinking about the different ways people learn, different ways of making meaning. Just opening up their approaches, and using the arts is a very effective way to do this.

And the overall effect of this approach is indicated by Klauss's report of a discussion between several of her students towards the end of their course of study:

> The discussion indicated that they felt changed by the experience, they began to realise (sounds corny but...) the power of art, and the feeling of satisfaction and achievement that was generated by participating.

Klauss's personal and essential engagement with the pedagogy of art seems to help her students to make their own commitment to the discipline and in turn inspire their own students towards such an engagement.

Music

Our final case studies of engagement combine the views of teachers and students and are situated in the discipline of music education. The study from which we have taken them aimed to investigate students' and teachers' ideas about music and its teaching and learning (Reid, 1997, 2001). At the level of tertiary studies in a conservatorium, the most common form of pedagogy is the one-to-one lesson between an experienced professional musician and a student. In most other disciplines, this is only common at the postgraduate level. Here we investigate the views of Brenton, a teacher of flute, and two of his students, Kaitlyn and Simon. Writing about this triad allows us to link the views of a teacher about his students, and the views of two students about their teacher. This gives an opportunity to investigate participants' ideas about music and the music profession from both sides of the pedagogical divide and, at the same time, illustrate the range of engagement with musical studies.

Brenton

Brenton is a teacher of flute at an Australian conservatorium of music. He is an expert flautist with many years of professional experience behind him and he is able to use this background as a resource for teaching his flute students in their individual lessons. He explains his approach of breaking down his professional experience of music into small manageable portions that his students can utilise.

> I am the sort of person who looks at the details and I believe if the details are all right, I compare it to a jigsaw puzzle. So if each little piece is perfect then we put it all together and we have a picture... The technique of the instrument is being able to do what you want to do with that instrument. And whatever may not be just what you want to do, but what somebody else wants you to do, and then you can approach the music. Of course we are using the music as a means to an end, playing an instrument.

Brenton's engagement with music focused on the technical problems that needed to be addressed and overcome. When we asked him about teaching his students about musicality, he equated this with technical development. It was this experience that he intended to pass on to his students. His professional experience as an orchestral musician contributed to his idea that there are things that simply have to be known so that they can be produced on demand. In his music lessons this experience accounts for the strong emphasis on technical know-how.

As a teacher, he focused on his part of the encounter, the teaching. He seemed to regard students as passive clients who would learn by being informed about his musical experiences and could base their development on his approaches. When we asked him what he aimed to achieve with a particular student, Kaitlyn (whom we will meet soon), he was at first unsure who the student was and then unsure about specifying how the lesson would progress:

> I am not sure I can differentiate between students... Well, the student would play, and sometimes I'll, look, with a more advanced student I would have to, it's very hard to say, I'm afraid... Well, she might play a phrase or a few lines of a piece of music and then we would go back and perhaps analyse a few things that I didn't think were quite right. I would think to myself, "that phrase doesn't really make any musical sense." Now the first thing that I do is ask the student to explain to me "what is a phrase?" The first thing they say is "it's a sentence." I say, "No, it is not a sentence, it is a phrase, what is the difference between a phrase and a sentence?" They have a lot of trouble with that.

Although Brenton was an expert musician, his engagement with music was essentially at a technical level, and his engagement with his teaching role was likewise narrow. His difficulty in recognising a particular student may be common in some disciplines where lecture classes consist of several hundred students, but it seems unusual in his context of small numbers of individual students. And his description of how his lesson might unfold indicates a formulaic approach that does not engage with the individual aspects of each of his students.

Kaitlyn

Kaitlyn is a second-year student of flute at the same conservatorium, taking individual lessons from Brenton and another teacher. Her overall approach to music was to try to discover the composer's intentions for a particular work and the inherent meaning of the piece, determined by musical analysis and an understanding of the style of the period. Her engagement with music was in terms of the music itself, built first on the technical background and then on the inherent musical meaning of a work, encapsulated by the composers' intentions and style.

> As I said earlier, you can't do particularly much if you don't know the notes. I don't feel like I can do much if I don't know the notes. And then if the composer's written dynamics on the page he intends that to be... unless it is an Urtext [composer's original] edition, but if it is in the arranging of it, then maybe that is not necessarily true. But normally if the dynamics are there, that's how it is meant to be played.

She expected that her teachers would be able to help her uncover the meaning of the music that she was studying, based on their professional experience and knowledge of the pieces. Her views about learning and the role of her teachers in her learning are shown in this collection of short extracts from her interview:

> I think they should know what they are talking about... They either know the pieces or they don't... I think at that level you go to a teacher because you know they can give you what you want and therefore that is another of their responsibilities. They have already done it in their years of study... I think learning is a combination of watching and imitating and going away and thinking about it... You can learn what works and what doesn't. You learn through experience, you learn through the teacher too. All sorts of different ways. It just depends on the teacher too.

In her music lessons, Kaitlyn was aware that she produced what she thought each teacher expected from her. At the same time, she was aware of her own autonomy as a learner and a musician, and her ultimate responsibility for the interpretation.

> So I let him have his way in his lesson and her way in her lesson... then I weigh up both and what I think is right... You need to be an individual. You need to be able to express things in your own way...

> therefore I think that that music becomes more me, or a combination of all of us rather than just one person's interpretation all the time.

Nevertheless, her engagement remained focused on the interpretation of the piece of music, even if it was her own view or combination of views. She seemed aware that her teacher had a narrower focus but she was able to use his expertise as a component of her approach. She says of Brenton:

> He's a meticulous person, he's very precise and I am not... I wouldn't want to learn from him for more than two years because I think he restrains you as a person. I can pick the students who learn from him because they all play in the same way. Everything was precise and perfect and totally rounded and there were no loose ends anywhere, but it was very small and undynamic... not greatly adventurous, it stays in the bounds of what is safe.

Simon

Simon is another flute student of Brenton, in his final year of studies. He saw music as having a personal quality and his aim was to seek out ways in which he could give meaning to the music from his own experience. His overall engagement with music was at a personal and essential level.

> A lot of the time I try and approach a new piece by myself first. Of course, along the way, you hear other people along the way who are playing the piece that you're working on and that has some kind of effect and I try not to let that affect me too much. I'd rather come up with my own sort of version... I believe that music is something that comes from everyone and that's why we can have such a variety of musicians because everyone has something personal to give.

Simon's intentions for learning incorporated the technical aspect of memorising the music, and the uncovering of the meaning inherent in the score itself. But above all he sought to find his own personal interpretation of the music, an interpretation that was not static but could change depending on context.

> A lot of learning an instrument will be learning the scales and time exercises and tonguing exercises to enable you to carry out the ideas that you have in your head... The purpose of the music is a good place to start when you're looking at how to interpret at piece of music... But a lot of things change as my life changes. Like feeling different on a different day, a phrase changes like that. I suppose music is the same as with a person and how you relate to a person. Although music doesn't change and a person can, the way that you relate to the music changes, and you change as a person.

Simon, a reflective student, engages with his music learning as part of his personal need to grow, change and understand. His entire focus for learning the flute was to enable his own personal growth to be expressed through the medium of music. Although his engagement was at a broader level than Brenton's, Simon was able to use and appreciate his teacher's expertise, even aspects of which his teacher seemed unaware.

> I find that a lot of the time the teacher just points the student in the right direction, picks up a few technical tricks. Few will get down to how a student will approach it personally. But a good teacher, and this is the case with Brenton, lets the student's own ideas develop, which I think is essential. Otherwise you end up as a clone of your teacher. It was very encouraging of Brenton to encourage my own ideas and when I do come up with something he's been open minded to it.

At the same time, he was aware of his teacher's limitations, and even turned them into opportunities to practice professional skills.

> It was fairly clear to me that Brenton had got into a pattern of teaching. And a little phrase that he would say for this and certain things that he would say for that. So after four years of learning, especially if you went each week with a lot of questions, you got to know the typical way that he wanted you to do things, to satisfy him. In fact, in order to be flexible you have to be able to play in any way that you're asked to, whether you want to or not.

Brenton's two students provide contrasting views: Kaitlyn described her learning as a means of discovering musical meaning; Simon described his as a way of developing personal expression. Each had different expectations of themselves as learners and of their teacher. Their perceptions of the contribution of their teacher seemed at times at odds with the aims described by Brenton himself. Although Kaitlyn was looking for help with understanding the meaning of the music, she viewed Brenton's teaching as a demonstration of his techniques and experience, which she also needed to acquire. Simon appreciated Brenton's teaching that encouraged him to explore his own ideas and musical self-expression, though Brenton seemed unaware of this aspect.

Discussion and conclusion

In our case studies, we have explored how students and teachers in three distinct disciplines view the concept of engagement. On the basis of these results, we now discuss the pedagogical implications with the aim of investigating what lecturers can do to enhance their students' engagement with their studies, the core activity of higher education. This includes the aspect of what students can do about their own engagement with their studies; lecturers can and should talk to students about the importance of engagement and the ways of enhancing it. Barnett (2007, pp.18–19) talks about the 'will to learn' and makes its essential role very clear: "Without will, too, the idea of a student cannot seriously have meaning. A student is someone who gives something of herself, who throws herself into her studies... Where the will is present, everything is possible. Where the will is absent, nothing, educationally speaking, is possible."

But it is not always easy for students to maintain this will to learn and it seems that, at times, engagement "denotes a battle and a conflict in the lives of students for whom the university learning environment is a foreign and sometimes alienating one" (Krause, 2005, p.4). Sandra's struggle to learn statistics is an example of just such a battle and illustrates that engagement may be built out of uncertainty and conflict. Indeed, engagement is strongly connected with the ontological aspects of higher education – who the student really is and what he is becoming during the process of his studies. Hung's interview points out the importance for engagement of such essential questions that go beyond notions of 'working hard' and repeating questions until you can get the 'correct answers'.

This brings up a fundamental question; is engagement a quantitative idea or a qualitative one, or maybe a combination? If a student spends more time with their studies, or maybe with associated extra-curricular activities, does that mean they are more engaged than a student who spends only a limited amount of time? Our interview with Hung challenges the quantitative notion that doing more work results in more engagement: Hung told us that he spent lots of time "doing different questions relating to the same problems over and over again" but, nevertheless, we felt that his engagement was at the most limited level. The model that we have presented of qualitative levels of engagement links with our research on the relationships between students' conceptions of discipline, learning and profession (Reid et al., 2011). A conclusion from the model is that the same pedagogy that encourages students towards the broadest conceptions of discipline, learning and profession also encourages students towards the broadest level of engagement.

Such pedagogy begins by making explicit the range of conceptions of discipline, learning and profession held by students, then proceeds by utilising teaching approaches and materials that encourage students towards the broadest conceptions – for instance, by using group learning approaches and authentic learning contexts – and takes every opportunity to point out the links between students' studies and their personal and professional world. Our case studies have several examples of variations on this theme but the interviews with Dolphin and Klauss are outstanding examples.

Finally, can we say anything about differences between disciplines in terms of engagement? There is not enough data here for any more than general speculation. However, the case studies we have presented challenge some obvious assumptions: for instance, that music students are always deeply engaged in their studies while students of statistics, especially those majoring in another area, are only minimally engaged with learning statistics. Indeed, we have indicated that all levels of engagement can be present in any discipline and in students of any year level – and even in their teachers. Our music case studies have shown situations where there is a mismatch between levels of engagement between teachers and their students. In the larger collection of interviews that we have undertaken, in music and other disciplines, we have seen that teachers at the broadest level of engagement will tend to 'pull' their students up with them. By contrast, teachers at the narrowest level of engagement may constrain learning but – as our two music students show – may also give students an opportunity to take control of their own studies, to express their 'will to learn'.

References

Barnett, R. (2007) *A Will to Learn: Being a Student in an Age of Uncertainty* (Maidenhead: Society for Research in Higher Education and Open University Press).

Gordon, S. (1993) 'Mature Students Learning Statistics: The Activity Theory Perspective', *Mathematics Education Research Journal,* 5/1, pp.34–49.

Gordon, S. (1995) 'A Theoretical Approach to Understanding Learners of Statistics', *Journal of Statistics Education,* 3/3 Retrieved from <http://www.amstat.org/publications/jse/v3n3/gordon.html>

Gordon, S., Reid, A. and Petocz, P. (2010) 'Educators' Conceptions of Student Diversity in Their Classes', *Studies in Higher Education,* 35/8, pp.961–74.

Hodkinson, P. (2005) 'Learning as Cultural and Relational: Moving Past Some Troubling Dualisms', *Cambridge Journal of Education,* 35/1, pp.107–19.

Krause, K. (2005) *'Engaged, Inert or Otherwise Occupied? Deconstructing the 21st Century Undergraduate Student'*, keynote paper, James Cook University Symposium: Sharing Scholarship in Learning and Teaching – Engaging Students, September. Retrieved from <http://www.griffith.edu.au/gihe/staff/kerri-lee-krause>

Krause, K. and Coates, H. (2008) 'Students' Engagement in First Year University', *Assessment and Evaluation in Higher Education,* 33/5, pp.493–505.

Loughran, J. and Russell, T. (2007) 'Beginning to Understand Teaching As a Discipline', *Studying Teacher Education,* 3/2, 217–27.

Marton, F. and Booth, S. (1997) *Learning and Awareness* (Mahwah: Lawrence Erlbaum).

Onwuegbuzie, A. and Wilson, V. (2003) 'Statistics Anxiety: Nature, Etiology, Antecedents, Effects and Treatments – A Comprehensive Review of the Literature', *Teaching in Higher Education,* 8/2, pp.195–209.

Petocz, P. and Reid, A. (2010) 'On Becoming a Statistician: A Qualitative View', *International Statistical Review,* 78/2, pp.271–86.

Reid, A. (1997) 'The Meaning of Music and the Understanding of Teaching and Learning in the Instrumental Lesson', in Gabrielsson, A. (ed.) *Proceedings of the Third Triennial ESCOM Conference* (Uppsala University) pp.200–5.

Reid, A. (2001) 'Variation in the Ways That Instrumental and Vocal Students Experience Learning in Music', *Music Education Research*, 3/1, pp.25–40.

Reid, A., Abrandt Dahlgren, M., Petocz, P. and Dahlgren, L.O. (2011) *From Expert Student to Novice Professional* (Dordrecht: Springer).

Reid, A. and Petocz, P. (2002) 'Students' Conceptions of Statistics: A Phenomenographic Study', *Journal of Statistics Education*, 10/2 Retrieved from <http://www.amstat.org/publications/jse/v10n2/reid.html>

Reid, A., Petocz, P. and Gordon, S. (2008) 'Research Interviews in Cyberspace', *Qualitative Research Journal*, 8/1, pp.47–61.

Reid, A., Petocz, P. and Gordon, S. (2010) 'University Teachers' Intentions for Introductory Professional Classes', *Journal of Workplace Learning*, 22/1/2, pp.67–78.

Schön, D.A. (1987) *Educating the Reflective Practitioner: Toward a new design for Teaching and Learning in the Professions* (San Francisco: Jossey-Bass).

Swingler, M. and Bishop, P. (2008) 'Enhancing Self Efficacy in Experimental Design and Statistics Using E-Learning Technologies: An Interactive Approach', *Practice and Evidence of Scholarship of Teaching and Learning in Higher Education*, 3/2, pp.164–80.

Chapter 5

HERE to stay? An exploration of student doubting, engagement and retention in three UK universities

Ed Foster[1,2], Sarah Lawther[1], Ruth Lefever[2], Natalie Bates[3], Christine Keenan[3] and Becka Colley[2]

[1] *Nottingham Trent University, UK*
[2] *University of Bradford, UK*
[3] *Bournemouth University, UK*

Introduction

Not every student who is unhappy with his or her course, accommodation or social life withdraws from university. The decision to persist or not depends not just on the experience but also upon the student's reaction to it. Castles (2004) notes that some students have to overcome great personal hardships to remain on their course, others disengage after minor illnesses. The Higher Education Retention and Engagement (HERE) Project was a UK-based tri-institutional research project to explore those factors that helped students to remain at university despite encountering difficulties. Our work concentrated on two areas. Firstly, what can we learn from students who have doubted that they are on the right course but have chosen to remain? Secondly, what impact can individual programme teams have on retention? Throughout our analysis, we repeatedly found that student engagement was one of the factors closely associated with doubting and retention. Student doubters were less satisfied with their experience, less engaged and, ultimately, more likely to withdraw from their studies. Conversely, those students with better rates of progression appeared to be more satisfied and more engaged with their institution. This chapter explores the relationship between doubting, engagement and retention. At the end we share a number of programme-level strategies for reducing doubting, improving engagement and supporting doubters to cope.

Doubting

We have used the term 'doubter' to describe a student who has doubts about being on the right course or at the right university that are serious enough to lead him or her to consider withdrawing. Previous studies into doubting suggest that many more students doubt than actually withdraw. Two UK institutional studies found between 21 per cent (Rickinson and Rutherford, 1995) and 39 per cent of students (Roberts et al., 2003) had doubts. ACER (2008) reported that 33 per cent of students answering the AUSSE survey seriously considered leaving. Yorke and Longden (2008) found that 40 per cent of students with little, or no, prior knowledge of their programme were doubters, whereas only 25 per cent of those who felt they were better informed had doubts. In the UK, early withdrawal rates are fairly static with approximately 10 per cent of students leaving early in the first year (National Audit Office, 2007). This suggests that there is a large body of students who have doubts but, through personal drive, adaptation or other reasons, remain.

Mackie (2001) studied the differences between students with doubts who withdrew (leavers) and students with doubts who stayed (doubters) on a UK business studies degree. She interviewed leavers and doubters and both groups expressed similar levels of satisfaction with the social, organisational and external factors. She found that the main difference between leavers and doubters was that doubters appeared to have a stronger internal sense of drive and could talk positively about staying at university. Roberts et al. (2003) found that the main factors that helped student doubters stay related to personal self-esteem, goal orientation and the ability to adapt to a new environment.

Throughout this chapter, we have used the term 'non-doubters' to describe those students who have not considered withdrawing. Our evidence suggests that these students are more likely to be engaged both academically and socially, and therefore it seems that the term 'engagers' might also be appropriate. However, as we cannot absolutely state that all engagers have not doubted we have retained the use of the term 'non-doubters'.

Student engagement

Probably the most widely used description of student engagement derives from Kuh (2001) who describes it as the "level of academic challenge, time on task, and [participation] in other educationally purposeful activities" (p.12). However, our research suggests that student engagement also takes place outside the curriculum and we are therefore interested in definitions that encompass the whole student, not just the student as learner. Hardy and Bryson (2010) suggest that student engagement is a multi-dimensional and complex interplay between students and institutions. They found that both a sense of belonging and emotional engagement amongst peers and between peers and tutors were particularly important.

The two major surveys of student engagement both offer a comprehensive means to measure different aspects of students' academic engagement. In the US, the National Survey of Student Engagement (NSSE) explores five themes: challenge, enriching educational experiences, collaborative learning, support and interaction (Kuh et al., 2008). The Australasian University Survey of Student Engagement (AUSSE) measures seven themes: five broadly the same as the NSSE and also online and extra-curricular activities (Krause and Coates, 2008).

Bryson and Hand (2008) invite us to consider student engagement as a continuum. At one end of the spectrum there will be highly engaged students who, as Adams (1979) suggests, will engage "in the activities of a course with thoroughness and seriousness" (see Willis, 1993). McInnis (2005) also argues that these students are likely to adopt beliefs of the academy and take on approaches akin to those of their tutors. At the opposite end of the spectrum are those students who are struggling to engage at all, who are scarcely participating in lectures, with assessments and the institution, and face the concomitant risk of early withdrawal.

Bryson and Hand (2008) identified two groups of students who had adopted engagement strategies somewhere between these two extremes. They describe the first group as false engagers; these students were engaged with achieving a particular grade, not with the curriculum or the wider learning experience. They describe the second group as disengaged; these students were simply seeking to achieve a pass and no more. We would suggest that a more useful phrase might be 'minimally engaged'. To us, disengaged implies the absence of engagement and might more usefully be used to describe students falling away and even departing from their studies.

Retention

We would argue that retention is the baseline from which all other engagement starts. If a student is present, they at least have the potential to be engaged, whereas if they have withdrawn, logically they cannot. Both of the major surveys of student engagement, NSSE and AUSSE, show that engaged students are more likely to progress than those students who are not. Kuh et al. (2008) reported that:

> Student engagement in educationally purposeful activities during the first year of college had a positive, statistically significant effect on persistence, even after controlling for background characteristics, other college, experiences during the first year, academic achievement and financial aid.
>
> (p.551)

They also reported that the impact of positive student engagement appears to have a greater benefit to the retention of academically weaker students when compared to their more capable peers. Similarly, the Australian Council for Educational Research (ACER) (2008) found in the AUSSE 2008 survey that where students perceive that they are both academically challenged and well supported, academic performance increases and the intention to withdraw decreases.

Tinto's longitudinal model of institutional departure (1993) suggests that retention is based upon the interplay between a student's personal characteristics, their goals and their experiences of being a student. His model proposes that if a student engages they are more likely to persist. Importantly, his model stresses the importance of engagement with the academic faculty and the multiple social communities within the institution. Palmer, O'Kane and Owens (2009) suggest that this process is not a smooth linear one. They suggest that engagement comes as a response to turning points, for example participating in a rewarding or enjoyable seminar. They also argue that this process is reversible: negative experiences, such as failing an assignment, can reduce a student's feeling that they belong to the institutional community.

Lowis and Castley (2008) devised a course survey using Chickering and Gamson's (1991) seven principles of good undergraduate teaching. They measured students' expectations in each of these themes at the start of term and then measured students' actual experience of each in week nine. In all areas, experience rated lower than expectations. Students who withdrew early tended to report lower levels of satisfaction in all seven areas. Yorke and Longden (2008) found that of the twelve most frequent reasons cited by UK first-year students for withdrawing, the top eleven related directly to engaging with the course. For example, the most commonly cited reason was that "the course was not as I expected" (p.41) and the fourth was an explicit admission of a lack of personal engagement with it.

The HERE Project

The HERE Project (Higher Education Retention and Engagement) was a research project to investigate strategies for improving student retention at English universities. Funded jointly by the Higher Education Funding Council for England (HEFCE) and the Paul Hamlyn Foundation (PHF), the project was one of seven under the banner 'What works? Student Retention and Success'. There were three partners: Nottingham Trent University (NTU), Bournemouth University (BU) and the University of Bradford (UoB). All three are members of the University Alliance, a group of 23 business-focused universities in the UK, and offer broadly similar course portfolios.

The HERE Project focused primarily upon first-year students and investigated two questions: "What can we learn from students who have doubts but stay?" and "What impact can individual programs have on retention?"

Methodology

Between March and May 2009, all first-year students at the three partner universities were invited to complete an online student transition survey. NTU had the highest response rate (656 students or nine per cent of the first year) and so for quantitative analysis we have used the NTU data (although it must be stressed that the results from the Bournemouth University and the University of Bradford are broadly similar). Where we have used qualitative data, we have drawn from all three partners. Completion of the survey was voluntary and so our sample did not perfectly match the profile of the first year. As may be expected, more female students (62 per cent) responded to the survey than males (38 per cent) and only female students were prepared to engage in the subsequent focus groups. Business and law students were under-represented in the survey as were part-time and non-European Union international students. Nonetheless, we believe that the survey offers us a reasonable basis to explore doubting.

The survey asked students to rate 17 student experience items such as "Feedback on my work is useful" (see appendix). Students were asked to rank these statements on a scale of 1 to 5 (where 1 indicated that they disagreed strongly, 5 that they agreed strongly). Students were asked to rate both the importance and the actual experience of each item. They were also asked whether or not they had doubted and, if they had, what had helped them to stay. Students were also asked to give us permission to track their progress. From May 2009 onwards, a series of focus groups and interviews were conducted with groups of respondents to clarify the data from the surveys further. In December 2009, partway through the following academic year, students' progression was reviewed to see what impact doubting had on retention.

Using themes arising from these data, the team devised a programme survey tool to investigate the impact of individual programmes on retention. Ten programmes were investigated: staff were interviewed, students surveyed and documentary evidence reviewed. The programmes were chosen as they were either very good at retention or were tackling particular issues; for example, one programme had a very high proportion of mature and other non-traditional entrants. The final stage, a second transition survey, was conducted in spring 2011, unfortunately too late for inclusion in this chapter.

Findings

In total, 37 per cent of NTU's student respondents had considered withdrawing at some point during the first year. In comparison, 45 per cent of Bournemouth University students were doubters. When progress was monitored, 96 per cent of non-doubters and 91 per cent of doubters progressed into the second year. At the University of Bradford, 29 per cent of students had doubts; 100 per cent of non-doubters and 91 per cent of doubters progressed. In December, we monitored the progress of all 370 students who granted us permission to do so and 37 per cent of this subset were doubters. Progression from the first year was as follows in Table 5.1.

Student Type	Progression Outcome	Notes
Non-doubters (n=234)	Still at the institution (n=230) 98.3 percent retention	These students had progressed to the second year, were repeating the first year or had transferred to another course within the university.
	Withdrew early (n=4)	
Doubters (n=136)	Still at the institution (n=124) 91.2 percent retention	These students had progressed to the second year, were repeating the first year or had transferred to another course within the university
	Withdrew early (n=12)	

Table 5.1: Summary of progression statistics

Doubters were therefore more likely actually to withdraw than their non-doubting peers. This overall pattern of withdrawal appears to support Ozga and Sukhnandan's (1998) departure model, in which they suggest most students withdraw due to a gradual realisation that there are problems or issues of compatibility with their course, rather than due to a sudden crisis. In other words, early leavers appear to be accruing doubts as the year progresses that eventually lead them to withdrawing. Overall, the rate of progression for students in our study was better than that of the institutional benchmarks. We suspect that this is largely due to the voluntary nature of the survey; it appears that being interested enough to answer perhaps indicates a higher level of engagement with the institution.

Reasons for doubting and staying

We note that the reasons for considering leaving and for choosing to stay are not simply polar opposites of one another. This may be particularly interesting in the light of Tinto's (1993) departure model. The most common reasons cited by our respondents for considering leaving are in Tinto's "academic system" (p.114) and relate to academic studies. For example, 112 of the 263 reasons cited by NTU doubters related to their course. When further analysed, anxieties about coping accounted for almost half of these responses. "Lifestyle" issues and "finance" were the next-most-frequently mentioned, but far less often. When asked what had helped doubters to stay, the most frequently cited responses were in Tinto's "social system" (p.114) and related to "support from friends and family". Friends made at university made up the largest component group. Students also reported the importance of "future goals", "determination and personal drive" and "starting to adapt to their studies"

Is there a relationship between doubting and engagement?

It appears that there is. When the 17 student experience factors (for example, "feedback on my work is useful") were reviewed, there were stark differences between the responses of doubters and non-doubters. In most instances, all students rated the importance of a factor more highly than their experience of it. For example at NTU, on average, 78 per cent of students rated the importance of each factor as either 4 (important) or 5 (very important) out of 5. Only 65 per cent of students rated their actual experience as 4 (positive) or 5 (very positive). However, the gap between importance and experience was far higher for doubting students than their non-doubting peers. Non-doubters reported an 8 per cent gap between importance and experience, doubters a 21 per cent gap. This appears to show that non-doubters appear better able to understand and engage with their new learning environment.

Academic engagement

To make the student experience factors more manageable we carried out a factor analysis (rotated component matrix) to create three underlying factors: "academic experience", "support, resources and future goals" and "student lifestyle". These three factors were then tested using a logistic regression to identify which would be the strongest indicators for doubting. We also tested the variables of "age", "gender", "first family member at university", "living independently for the first time" and "arriving at university through the university clearing system".

The variables of "age", "living independently", "first family member at university" and "arriving via clearing" did not have a statistically significant impact on doubting. However, "academic experience", "support, resources and future goals", "student lifestyle" and "gender" all did. The academic experience factors showed a very clear pattern. Those students with the lowest scores in this factor were twelve times more likely to be a doubter when compared to those with the most positive scores. Furthermore, each of the individual academic factors was also rated lower by doubters. Therefore, non-doubting students reported that they felt more valued by their tutors, found their subject more interesting, encountered more enthusiastic lecturers and appeared to gain greater meaning from both the assessment and feedback processes. Very importantly, they also appeared far more confident than their doubting peers that they were actually coping.

As confidence about coping was so frequently cited as a reason to doubt, we also tested a number of variables to see which other factors might have a positive relationship with it. The following factors were tested: "do you have a personal tutor?" and four academic factors, "lecturers are accessible", "the feedback I receive about my work is useful", "I would know where to go in the university if I had a problem" and "my fellow students are supportive". Feedback emerged as the most important factor; that is, if a student reported a higher level of satisfaction with their feedback, it was also highly likely that they would report being more confident about coping. The next most important factors were "supportive peers" and "accessible lecturers".

Students who felt that they did not understand the differences between the prior stage of education and higher education were also more likely to be doubters. Once here, if they reported finding their studies "very difficult" or "very easy", again they appeared more likely to have doubts. Similarly, those students who reported that they were working "very hard" or "not working hard at all" felt the same. Non-doubters were more likely to report that they were finding their studies fairly difficult and were working fairly hard. It therefore appears that non-doubters perceive that there is a sufficient challenge in their programme to engage them with their studies, but not too much so as to cause them unnecessary anxiety.

In the original 2009 survey we did not ask for entry qualifications, so have been unable to test the impact of this variable on doubting. However, it does appear that there is a relationship between doubting and academic performance. Researchers at the University of Bradford found that non-doubting students achieved better grades than their doubting peers. They found that 66 per cent of non-doubters achieved a grade of 60 per cent or higher, whereas only 33 per cent of doubters did so. The final academic factor of note is how much students enjoyed their studies. Students were asked "how much have you enjoyed your course so far?" and once again non-doubters rated the experience more highly than doubters. Doubters who subsequently left had the poorest level of personal enjoyment.

Social engagement

In the NTU focus group interviews that followed the transition survey, a number of differences emerged between doubters and non-doubters, primarily regarding social engagement and a sense of belonging. Thirteen students were interviewed either individually or in groups of between two and six. The six non-doubters appeared more likely to have joined clubs and societies and they were able to explain a time when they felt that they had started to belong to the institution. Importantly, they also felt that there was a member of staff within the university they could talk to if they had a problem, either a personal tutor or a lecturer. The seven students who had expressed doubts about being at university appeared less connected to the institution. Although they expressed different reasons and degrees of disconnection they tended to report feeling more distant from their peers and tutors than did non-doubters. One student reported, "I don't seem very involved with the university to be honest". Others felt highly anonymous, one commenting that, "probably if I see my tutor on the road, he wouldn't recognise me".

Demographic factors

Demographic factors do appear to have influenced doubting, the most important of which was gender. Female students were more likely to have doubts than their male peers, ten per cent more so at NTU (Foster and Lefever, 2011). However, male students were more likely actually to withdraw. It appears that the important difference between the two sexes is that whilst female students are more likely to have doubts, they also appear to be better able to deal with those factors causing them to do so. Whilst fewer male students expressed doubts, doing so appears to be far more serious and much more likely to lead to withdrawal. Students with disabilities and part-time students were also more likely to doubt and more likely to withdraw, although in our study the numbers of student respondents were low. Student ethnicity and age provided a more mixed picture: there were no clear patterns across the three universities.

Developing a dual approach to retention

Our research indicates that doubters are more likely to leave early when compared to non-doubters. It also strongly suggests that non-doubters are more academically engaged with their institution. They appear to have a better understanding of the learning and teaching environment, have found an appropriate work level and are achieving better academic grades. This offers the possibility of developing preventative strategies for improving retention. If we can prevent students from doubting in the first place by engaging them meaningfully within the learning environment, we ought to be able to reduce doubting and improve retention. Our research also suggests that institutions ought to develop a second complementary approach and find ways of supporting doubters to manage doubting. Several sub-themes were identified that suggested possible strategies to achieve these goals, for example, relationships and communication with staff.

Throughout 2009–10, researchers at the partner institutions surveyed ten academic programmes to find examples of these sub-themes in practice. The opinions of staff and students were sought about themes that our evidence suggested might help. In 2010–11, the project team wrote a retention toolkit designed for programme teams to self-assess their practice and consider approaches for improving retention.

The toolkit has three basic stages. Programme teams are invited to reflect on their current position and prioritise areas for exploration. We suggest initially investigating one theme to reduce doubting ("transition into higher education") and one to support doubters ("social integration"). Users are encouraged to action plan and set review dates. Where possible, we suggest that they explore further themes that appear relevant to them.

Programme-level strategies

This next section is based largely upon survey work conducted with programme teams and students. We have identified a number of practices that programmes use to help students engage.

First approach: reducing doubting and increasing engagement

Our evidence suggests that programme teams intended to help reduce doubting and increase engagement can adopt the following strategies. The words in brackets indicate whether they are primarily academically oriented, socially oriented or mixed according to Tinto's (1993) model.

Transition into higher education (academic)

It appears that there are significant differences between learning in the first year and students' previous education (Foster, Lawther and McNeil, 2011). The HERE Project research suggests that non-doubters have been more successful at making the transition between the two educational systems. One of the most important starting points is helping students to understand these differences. Therefore, we suggest that programme teams start by reviewing their approach to helping new students engage with the curriculum. The programme teams used a variety of methods prior to arrival, during induction and throughout the first year to help students understand the differences. The second area to consider is building students' confidence that they can cope in this new environment. Our research suggests that confidence is most influenced by feedback and supportive peers. We would suggest that programme teams review how they engender good practices in these areas throughout the first year.

Engaging students (academic)

Our programme surveys suggest that where programmes were successful at retention, both staff and students agreed that lecturers were passionate about teaching. Furthermore, staff interviewees often placed great emphasis on recruiting the most suitable people to teach first years:

> I like the lectures – [it's] easy to learn from staff who are passionate about their subject.
>
> (Bournemouth University (BU) student)

Students also appeared to respond well to a range of teaching approaches, for example:

> There are many practical classes. These classes are one of my favourite aspects as they help consolidate and reinforce the theory taught in lectures.
>
> (University of Bradford (UoB) student)

Our evidence suggests that courses can be made more enjoyable for students by encouraging active learning, providing opportunities for students to gain different perspectives on subjects and using technology to enhance teaching and learning. Students appear to feel engaged when their course offers variety in content, structure, delivery and assessment.

Choosing the right course and early communication (academic)

In the NTU transitions survey, those students who found the pre-arrival information about the university to be inaccurate were extremely likely to have doubts. Some of the programme teams interviewed stated that it was important for them to start the process of acculturation as they engaged with students during open days and other pre-arrival communications. This enabled students to make more informed decisions about which courses to choose and also started to help students understand what to expect.

Relationships and communication with staff (academic/social)

In the 2009 student transition surveys, a lack of support appeared to be one factor that led students to consider leaving. In the subsequent interviews with student doubters, support from individual staff was seen to be extremely important helping individuals to stay.

> Being here I have received all the help and support I've needed and more, this has made me want to continue and see the degree through to the end!
>
> (BU student)

At the University of Bradford, "feeling valued", "having accessible lecturers", "knowing where to go for support" and "the course being well organised" were all more important to doubters than non-doubters. Yet doubters reported that their experience of these factors was more negative than non-doubters. As we have stated earlier, doubters appear less confident in their own abilities and these findings suggest that as a consequence of lower confidence, doubters may be more reliant upon the views of their tutors. Doubters appear grateful for the support and reassurance provided by staff.

> This period of crisis where I didn't really know what to do and if I was managing with my studies, I guess getting that tutor support... that kind of broke some barriers that I had in my head.
>
> (UoB student)

The programme explorations suggested that programme teams could make a positive impact on retention and engagement by fostering positive relationships with students, communicating clearly with them, particularly about staff roles and responsibilities and being coherent and consistent in their communication with all students.

Second approach: supporting doubters

We have found that the following strategies have all been used by programmes to support doubters:

Social integration (social)

Social support appears to be one of the factors that can act as a shock absorber for student doubters, not only offering a buffer against disappointments and anxieties but also making the experience more enjoyable. Friendships are developed through all manner of social opportunities, although Wilcox, Winn and Fyvie-Gauld (2005) found that the course was only the third most useful place to develop friendships after accommodation and clubs and societies. However, we would contend that there are many excellent opportunities to build community and individual friendships within the programme. In programme interviews we encountered a number of strategies that had proved effective in increasing social integration. These included pre-arrival tasks such as Stepping Stones 2HE (Keenan, 2008), use of social media, effective use of icebreakers during induction, small group work and particularly overnight fieldtrips.

> I have never been so homesick as I was that weekend... but what it did was really pulled [together] our friendships... because we were feeling a bit out of our depth... then when you come back after then, you really felt that you knew people.
>
> (BU student)

Central student support (academic/social)

Although knowing where to go for help was ranked relatively lowly in overall importance (for example, being ranked 10th of 17 student experience factors at UoB) it was a factor in which doubters appeared more concerned than their non-doubting peers. Moreover, for those students who have needed and successfully accessed specialist support, it appears to play an extremely positive role.

> [The] Learner Development [unit]... has been the biggest support ever, I couldn't, I wouldn't be here without [them] that's it...
>
> (UoB student)

Overall, the data suggested three possible programme-level approaches to consider. These were: ensuring clarity of understanding amongst the programme team about services available; promoting the services to students; and ensuring that programme staff have the most up-to-date information possible.

Belonging (social/academic)

Belonging appeared to stem from a student's feeling of involvement, feeling comfortable with the campus and feeling valued, or at the very least recognised. It was often articulated through identification or interaction with others. Making and having supportive friendships featured very strongly as a reason to stay at university and these social connections appeared to have influenced whether students felt engaged:

> I feel a great sense of belonging amongst my group and my friends.
>
> (UoB student)

It appeared that developing a sense of belonging was one factor in the process of moving from doubting to non-doubting

> I feel better now because I feel like I know where everything is and I always see someone walking around that I know if I want to stop and talk to them.
>
> (NTU student

Our programme interviews suggest that belonging can be developed by, as Yorke and Longden (2008), suggest, "treating the curriculum as a social milieu" (p.4). Programme teams might also consider their use of campus space, both physical and virtual, and promote student success within the cohort.

Motivation, goals and determination (academic/social)

Motivation and future goals appear to be important to helping doubters stay; for example, at NTU they were the reason second-most-frequently cited by doubters for staying. At both Bournemouth and Bradford, "completing my degree will help me achieve future goals for example, career" was the most important of the student experience factors. For example:

> I know what I want out of it and it will be better for my future career!
>
> (BU studen

Internal drive and determination also featured strongly; at UoB it was the third-most-frequently cited reason. Student comments included:

> It is a course that I really want to do, and even though it has been hard sometimes I know that in the end it is definitely worth it.
>
> (BU student)

Where programmes were seen to be successfully engaging students' future aspirations, this was often by helping them consider their career options, or widening their horizons.

> It's widening my opinion on life in general. It also opens my eyes to new things and I can start to explain things around me by applying things from which I have studied.
>
> (UoB Student)

Our programme work suggests that programme teams cultivate students' motivation by involving students in decision making, celebrating success and helping students to understand how the course can enable them to achieve future goals.

Conclusion

We believe that doubting offers another useful perspective on student engagement. If student engagement creates a virtuous cycle with a positive impact upon retention, the failure to engage, at the very least, appears to lead students to question their decisions about choice of course or university. Furthermore, as doubters are more likely to leave early there is also a financial imperative upon programme teams and institutions to reduce doubting. However, doubting is not fixed: student doubts can fade away. Time and professional support can have an impact but, perhaps most importantly, engagement with the academic curriculum and developing a sense of belonging within university social communities appear to play a positive role in reducing doubting. Finally, we have seen that individual staff members and programme teams can implement positive strategies that reduce doubting and improve engagement.

Appendix – complete list of student experience items

Students were asked to rate both the importance and their actual experience of each of the following items. The items are arranged in the three groups identified by the factor analysis.

A. Academic experience

- My subject is interesting
- My course is well organised
- I have enthusiastic lecturers teaching on my course
- My taught sessions (such as lectures and seminars) are interesting
- Lecturers are accessible
- I feel valued by teaching staff
- The assessment on my course is what I expected it to be
- The feedback I receive about my work is useful
- I feel confident that I can cope with my studies

B. Support, resources and future goals

- My fellow students are supportive
- My family is supportive
- I have easy access to University resources (for example, computers, library books that I need)
- Completing my degree will help me achieve my future goals

C. Student lifestyle

- I like the house/flat/halls that I am living in

- I have an enjoyable social life
- I am confident that I will have enough money to cope

An outlying item, "I would know where to go within the University if I had a problem", did not fit well with any other factors.

Acknowledgements

Thanks to Dr Nick Foard for help with the statistical analysis.

References

Australian Council for Educational Research (ACER) (2008) *Engaging Students for Success* (Melbourne: Australian Council for Educational Research).

Bryson, C. and Hand, L. (2008) 'An Introduction to Student Engagement', in Hand, L. and Bryson, C. (eds) *Student Engagement: SEDA Special 22* (London: Staff and Educational Development Association) p.7.

Castles, J. (2004) 'Persistence and the Adult Learner: Factors Affecting Persistence in Open University Students', *Active Learning in Higher Education*, 5/2, pp.166–79.

Chickering, A. and Gamson, Z. (1991) *New Directions for Teaching and Learning: Vol 47. Applying the Seven Principles for Good Practice in Undergraduate Education* (San Francisco: Jossey-Bass).

Foster, E., Lawther, S. and McNeil, J. (2011) 'Learning Developers Supporting Early Student Transition', in Hartley, P., Hilsdon, J., Keenan, C., Sinfield, S. and Verity, M. (eds) *Learning Development in Higher Education* (London: Routledge) pp.79–90.

Foster, E. and Lefever, R. (2011) 'Barriers and Strategies for Retaining Male Students', in Berry, J. and Thomas, L. (eds) *Male Access and Success* [Conference Discussion Paper] (York: Higher Education Academy) see <http://www.heacademy.ac.uk/assets/York/documents/events/academyevents/2010/06_july_Ed_Foster_Presentation.ppt>

Hardy, C. and Bryson, C. (2010) 'Student Engagement: Paradigm Shift or Political Expediency?', *Networks*, Spring, pp.19–23.

Keenan, C. (2008) 'Students Getting Down to Work Before They Start University: A Model for Improving Retention', in Crosling, G., Thomas, L. and Heagney, M. (eds) *Improving Student Retention in Higher Education: The Role of Teaching and Learning* (Padstow: Routledge) pp.82–87.

Krause, K. and Coates, H. (2008) 'Students' Engagement in First-Year University', *Assessment and Evaluation in Higher Education,* 33/5, pp.493–505.

Kuh, G.D. (2001) 'Assessing What Really Matters to Student Learning: Inside the Story of Student Engagement', *Change,* 33/3, pp.10–66.

Kuh, G.D., Cruce, T., Shoup, R., Kinzie, G. and Gonyea, R. (2008) 'Unmasking the Effects of Student Engagement on First-Year College Grades and Persistence', *Journal of Higher Education,* 79/5, pp.540–63.

Lowis, M. and Castley, A. (2008) 'Factors Affecting Student Progression and Achievement: Prediction and Intervention: A Two-Year Study', *Innovation in Education and Teaching International,* 45/4, pp.333–43.

Mackie, S. (2001) 'Jumping the Hurdles – Undergraduate Student Withdrawal Behaviour', *Innovation in Education and Teaching International,* 38/3, pp.265–76.

McInnis, C. (2005) 'Reinventing Student Engagement and the Learning Community: Strategic Directions for Policy, Research and Practice', keynote presentation at Higher Education Academy Conference, Edinburgh.

National Audit Office (2007) *Staying the Course: The Retention of Students in Higher Education* (Norwich: The Stationery Office).

Ozga, J. and Sukhnandan, L. (1998) 'Undergraduate Non-Completion: Developing an Explanatory Model', *Higher Education Quarterly,* 52/3, pp.316–33.

Palmer, M., O'Kane, P. and Owens, M. (2009) 'Betwixt Spaces: Student Accounts of Turning Point Experiences in the First Year Transition', *Studies in Higher Education,* 34/1, pp.37–54.

Rickinson, B. and Rutherford, R. (1995) 'Increasing Undergraduate Retention Rates', *British Journal of Guidance and Counselling,* 23/2, pp.213–25.

Roberts, C., Watkin, M., Oakey, D. and Fox, R. (2003) *Supporting Student 'Success': What Can We Learn from the Persisters?* Retrieved from <http://www.ece.salford.ac.uk/proceedings/papers/cr_03.rtf>

Tinto, V. (1993) *Leaving College: Rethinking the Causes and Cures of Student Attrition* (Chicago: University of Chicago Press).

Wilcox, P., Winn, S. and Fyvie-Gauld, M. (2005) 'It Was Nothing to Do with the University, It Was Just the People: The Role of Social Support in the First-Year Experience of Higher Education', *Studies in Higher Education,* 30/6, pp.707–22.

Willis, D. (1993) 'Academic Involvement at University', *Higher Education,* 25/2, pp.133–50.

Yorke, M. and Longden, B. (2008) *The First Year Experience of Higher Education in the UK* (York: The Higher Education Academy).

SECTION 2: THE PEDAGOGY OF STUDENT ENGAGEMENT

Chapter 6

A transition pedagogy for student engagement and first-year learning, success and retention

Karen Nelson, Sally Kift and John Clarke

Queensland University of Technology, Australia

> Engagement matters and it matters most during the critical first year of [university]...
>
> (Tinto, 2006–7, p.4)

Introduction

Student engagement "is increasingly understood to be important for higher education quality" (Australian Council for Educational Research [ACER], 2008, p.1). As a broad phenomenon, student engagement includes both the academic and non-academic activities of the student within the university experience and is a key factor in student achievement and retention (Krause and Coates, 2008; Tinto, 2010). More pragmatically, student engagement may be defined as "students' involvement with activities and conditions likely to generate high quality learning" (ACER, 2008, p.1) or, equally, as "the time, energy and resources students devote to the activities designed to enhance learning at university" (Krause, 2005, p.3). Nevertheless, as the opening quote from Tinto highlights, student engagement in the first undergraduate year is critical, not only for making quality learning outcomes possible for commencing cohorts, but also because it is the central enabling element for student learning, success and retention (ACER, 2008; Tinto, 2009).

This chapter argues that higher education institutions (HEIs) must direct coordinated, whole-of-institution attention to changing, both culturally and structurally, the fundamental and prevailing character of the first-year experience (FYE). It leverages evidence from the sector (Nelson, Kift and Clarke, 2011), from research-led practice in our institution (for example, Kift, Nelson and Clarke, 2010; Nelson et al., in press) and from research conducted under an Australian Learning and Teaching Council Senior Fellowship (Kift, 2009a, 2009b, 2009c) to assert that student engagement and success should not be left to chance, particularly those aspects such as curriculum design and enactment that are within our institutional control.

To set the scene for the remainder of this chapter, the Australian higher education context – which is in the midst of its second radical change in two decades – is briefly described. Next the concept of "engagement" is more fully discussed and a theoretical model of engagement is presented, followed by an examination of the role HEIs perform in

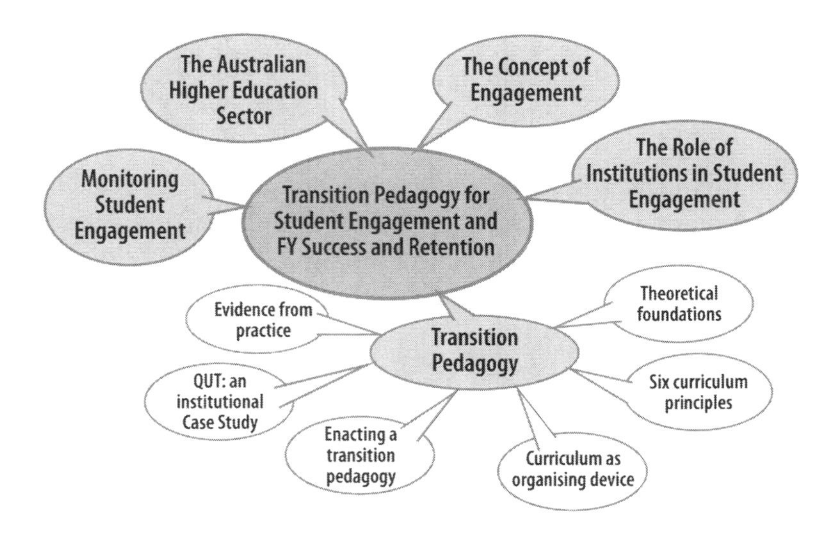

Figure 6.1: Chapter concepts and préci

facilitating engagement for student success. The focus of the chapter then turns to a discussion of the theoretical underpinnings, research base and application of the concept of a transition pedagogy, which is presented as the organising framework for student engagement with a particular focus on its role in facilitating engagement for first-year success and retention. This section highlights the central role that curriculum design and enactment play in engagement and student success, and the next section presents a persuasive argument for actively monitoring student engagement and making support interventions with those students who may be at risk of disengaging. This précis is summarised in Figure 6.1.

Pressures in the Australian higher education sector

The perennial issues of student engagement and retention in higher education have been on the Australian agenda for many years and they have become more visible since the move from what was an elite system to a mass higher education sector under the Dawkins' reforms (Dawkins, 1998). Recently, they have gained further prominence in the sector following Bradley's review (Bradley et al., 2008) and the federal government's response (Australian Government, 2009) that is pushing the sector further towards Trow's (1970) notion of universal higher education. Participation and achievement targets have been set to drive these reforms. However, it seems to be the performance-based funding linked to improvements in the student experience and achievement (particularly for low socio-economic status [LSES] cohorts) articulated in mission-based compacts* that has galvanised the attention of the sector and, in particular, of university managers.

The goals set by the Australian government for increasing the participation of groups currently under-represented in higher education and for increasing the percentage of the population aged 25–40 who have at least a bachelor's degree will only be achieved if appropriate and balanced attention is given to two strategies: building aspiration for and pathways to higher education for social groups currently under-represented in the sector; and increasing the success and retention of these students once enrolled.

---

* See http://www.deewr.gov.au/HigherEducation/Policy/Pages/Compacts.aspx

Implementation of this second strategy cannot be directed solely at certain cohorts: firstly because that approach problematises students and their previous circumstances (over which they may have had little or no control) and secondly because the international research evidence clearly shows that it is learning engagement that enables success and retention. Therefore, this second strategy must be located where the engagement occurs, in the curriculum. For the second strategy to be successful it needs to be designed not only to scaffold learning and provide assessment for learning, but also to be inclusive of all students and to incorporate and mediate all of the elements necessary for student engagement.

In a mass higher education sector, student engagement may be seen as "a practical lens for assessing and responding to the significant dynamics, constraints and opportunities facing higher education institutions" (ACER, 2008, p.vi). The concept of engagement and how it is interpreted in higher education is examined next.

The concept of engagement

The notion of engagement underpins student learning in terms of persistence, achievement and retention (see, for example, Crosling, Heagney and Thomas, 2009; Lodge, 2010; Scott et al., 2009; and Simeoni, 2009, for recent reviews). Previous research and notions about the concept of student engagement have been discussed in the opening and previous chapters of this book.

The issue of first-year engagement has always been one of critical significance and more recently, particularly for the Australian context with its focus on widening participation, it has become an even greater focal point for international thinking. Across the globe, commencing undergraduate students are becoming increasingly heterogeneous, are being deliberately recruited from more diffuse backgrounds, and exhibit diverse and changing patterns of engagement. Yorke (2006) has found that "the engagement of students in higher education is influenced by a number of factors – for example, how they finance their studies; how they balance studies and part-time employment; and what they see as their aims in undertaking a program of study" (p.1). Other frequently mentioned factors include, for example, students' educational, linguistic and socio-cultural background and experiences, their paid work and

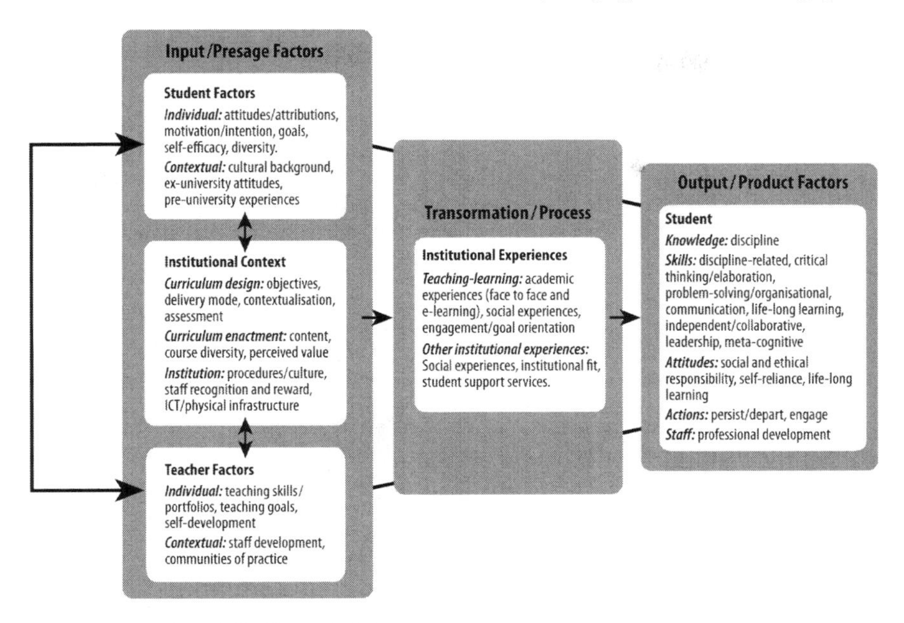

Figure 6.2: The IICISRE Model

other life commitments, and importantly, their perceptions of the relevance of university learning to achieving their personal future career goals (Krause, 2006). Consequently, to facilitate student engagement in ways that are strategic and scalable for institutions as well as relevant for students, universities must take into account the diverse reality of commencing cohorts' lives and external commitments.

The theoretical framework of engagement presented in Figure 6.2 attempts to bring together all of the factors implicated in student engagement. Essentially, it is an adaptation of the Biggs' Presage-Process-Product (3P) model (Biggs, 1999). This framework specifically focuses engagement through the lens of the 'transition-in' to university experience because engagement and subsequently retention are regarded as crucial indicators of success in that experience. Existing models conceptualising retention (Bean and Eaton, 2000; Tinto, 1993) and engagement (Dart, 1994; Krause, 2006) were synthesised onto Biggs' 3P model to identify the individual and institutional characteristics that influence student retention and engagement. This framework was then augmented with recent developments not envisaged when the contributing models were developed (for example, the role of ICTs in teaching and learning, increased student diversity and curriculum innovations) and by the inclusion of aspects such as graduate attributes.* The IICISRE (Individual and Institutional Characteristics Influencing Student Retention and Engagement) Model that emerged from this process is summarised in Figure 6.2.

As Figure 6.2 shows, it is the transformation process that has the potential to engage students successfully. The role of the transformation process is to provide the *institutional experience* and to mediate the *teacher factors* and *student factors* that can impact on the transformation, which here represents student engagement. Figure 6.2 also implies that learning, if situated in an inclusive and intentional curriculum, may be the key to first and subsequent year student success and engagement. The transformation process will therefore exhibit characteristics such as:

- Challenging learning opportunities, designed to develop learning proficiency and discipline knowledge and skills
- Relevant, structured assessment for learning, accompanied by timely constructive feedback on that learning
- Opportunities to participate in peer-to-peer social and learning communities
- Timely, adequate and equitable access to life and learning support services (Kift, Nelson and Clarke, 2010).

While many of the factors influencing student engagement are related to individual attributes of the students – for example, how students finance their studies and their lack of personal commitment to study (Yorke, 2006; Yorke and Longden, 2008) – the responsibility for the transformation or student retention and engagement does not reside solely with commencing students: institutions and their teaching and support staff have an obligation to provide the necessary "conditions, opportunities and expectations" for such engagement to occur (Coates,

* See Barrie, Hughes and Smith (2009) for a recent analysis of the contribution of graduate attributes to curriculum design and the assessment of learning outcomes. An overview of the minimum academic standards being developed for disciplines in anticipation of the new quality and regulatory regime, the Tertiary Education Quality and Standards Agency (TEQSA) can be found online at <http://www.deewr.gov.au/HigherEducation/Policy/teqsa/Pages/Overview.aspx>

2005, p.26). As discussed above, the curriculum is the element that enables student engagement and facilitates the transformation or transition of new students into experienced students and ultimately graduates. Consistent with this view, it is proposed below that institutions focus their student engagement efforts, particularly for commencing students, on and within the curriculum.

The role of institutions in facilitating engagement: especially in first year

It is now without doubt that student success in higher education is largely determined by student experiences during the first year (for example, Upcraft, Gardner and Barefoot, 2005) and that their first year is complex, challenging and constantly changing (Harvey, Drew and Smith, 2006). There is also an increasing body of evidence that factors beyond the control of individual students influence retention and success (Gale, 2009) and a general acceptance that "it's our job as politicians and educators to ensure we do everything we can to overcome such disadvantage" (Gillard, 2010, p.13).

Consistent with these views, Reason, Terenzini and Domingo (2005, 2007) have argued that the personal, social and academic competences of students have to be addressed by institutionally initiated engagement activities. Similarly, the Scottish Quality Assurance Agency for Higher Education, in its recent work on the FYE, framed its Quality Enhancement Theme inquiry around both engagement and the "transformational process" of "empowerment", the latter being defined as:

> equipping the first-year student with the competency to learn effectively... with the skills, capacities and knowledge to be effective as independent learners for the rest of their programme, and for their subsequent employability, professional development, and, for that matter, lifelong learning.
>
> (Mayes, 2009, p.4)

Reflecting this, as any scan of FYE-related journals and conference proceedings attests, there are many reported pockets of excellence in individual institutions and in various discrete programmes and subjects of study. However, as Krause and her colleagues noted in 2005, this essentially "piecemeal approach" of discrete first-year initiatives is rarely if ever linked across an institution and "effort now needs to be directed at moving practice towards more holistic and sustainable institution-wide approaches and enhancements" (Krause et al., 2005).

The commitment of institutions to student engagement and success is clearly a critical factor in retention. Universities need to initiate, support and promote student personal, social and academic engagement, particularly in first year (Nelson, Kift and Clarke, 2008). Tinto (2010) maintains that institutions should not only take some responsibility for but also encourage student involvement, while Nelson, Kift and Clarke (2008) contend that universities need to instigate, sustain and promote student personal, social and academic engagement, particularly for those students who face the greatest challenges in transition.

Hence, while student engagement might primarily be conceived of as the "student's commitment and motivation to study" (Mayes, 2009, p.4), it seems clear that the responsibility for student engagement does not reside solely with commencing students and that the responsibility therefore for providing an environment where all students have the opportunity to make the most of their higher education experience rests firmly with HEIs.

Tinto (2009) challenges institutions to:

> Stop tinkering at the margins of institutional academic life and make enhancing student success the linchpin about which they organise their activities… and establish those educational conditions on campus that promote the retention of students, in particular those of low-income backgrounds.
>
> (p.2)

The question for HEIs is how to do this for cohorts of students who enter their programmes with greater diversity in preparedness and cultural capital than ever before.

The next section proposes that a "transition pedagogy" (Kift and Nelson, 2005) provides the capacity to mediate the learning experiences of diverse commencing cohorts. The transition pedagogy has been investigated for the sector (Kift, 2009a) and implemented in our institution (Kift, Nelson and Clarke, 2010; Nelson et al., in press). The construct and the six curriculum principles that underpin it and enable it to be operationalised are first described. Then evidence of its implementation at the Queensland University of Technology (QUT), in Brisbane, Australia, is used to illustrate the proposal.

Transition pedagogy

Kift and Nelson's (2005) conceptualisation of a transition pedagogy has been posited as a useful concept to assure first year student engagement. In this conceptualisation, transition pedagogy is a guiding philosophy for intentional first-year curriculum design and support that carefully scaffolds and mediates the first-year learning experience for contemporary heterogeneous cohorts. Transition pedagogy is framed around the identification of six *First Year Curriculum Principles* that stand out as supportive of first-year learning engagement, success and retention (Kift, 2008, 2009a). Further support for this position is the alignment between the independently developed six curriculum principles and the six engagement scales of academic challenge, active learning, student and staff interactions, enriching educational experiences, supportive learning environment and work-integrated learning identified and measured by the Australasian University Survey of Student Engagement (AUSSE) (ACER, 2008). A transition pedagogy seeks to attend to each aspect of student engagement in a coherent, embedded and integrated way, utilising the curriculum to mediate as much as possible of the student–institution interactions to enhance the broader student experience. The sections below discuss the research and evidence base for a transition pedagogy and identify strategies for harnessing the curriculum as the academic and social "organising device" and the "glue that holds knowledge and the broader student experience together" (McInnes, 2001, pp.9 and 11).

Six curriculum principles

The development of the six curriculum principles that underpin the transition pedagogy and examination of their applicability for the Australasian sector has been discussed in detail elsewhere (Kift, 2009a). Statements for each of the curriculum principles are available online at http://www.fyhe.qut.edu.au/transitionpedagogy/firstyearcur/ and are presented below for the context of this chapter.

Using the curriculum as the organising device for first-year engagement

In all their first-year diversity, what students have in common is that they come to higher education to learn. It is within the context of that learning that diverse and frequently time-poor students are entitled to expect academic and social relevance and engagement. The first-year curriculum must therefore bear the load of inspiring and supporting (engaging) students as they acquire not only a sense of belonging to the discipline but also a foundation for their later-year learning success and transition to professional practice.

Adopting this approach, the first-year curriculum, and the pedagogical principles that inform its design and delivery, should be privileged as a critical influence on positive early student engagement (Kift and Field, 2009). In this way, the curriculum becomes the "totality of their learning experience with us – academic and social" (Kift, 2009b, p.9) designed to engage students with their new programme of tertiary study. Curriculum, in this sense, is the "educational conditions in which we place students" (Tinto, 2009, p.2) and incorporates as much as possible of the academic, social and support aspects of the student experience, often referred to as curricular and co-curricular activities. There is general agreement about the activities that fall under the co-curricular banner (for example, learning support, orientation events, peer programmes, academic advising, social activities and enrichment programmes) and that students should be encouraged to engage with these. However, it is more challenging to regard these activities – which are crucial to student engagement – as part of the curriculum, as is proposed here.

While it might seem like common sense to propose a joined-up view of curricular and co-curricular activities, a detailed analysis of the literature over the last decade (2000–11) has shown conclusively that, until very recently, most first-year interventions and student engagement research has tended to be focused around the curriculum, or in support of it, and have only recently come in from the curriculum's periphery to sit within an intentional and holistic conceptualisation of first-year curriculum design and enactment (Kift, 2009a; Nelson, Kift and Clarke, 2011).

Enacting a transition pedagogy: a third generation approach to the FYE

As foreshadowed above, enacting a transition pedagogy for optimal first-year engagement requires a shift from interventions which sit around or in aid of the curriculum – commonly referred to as co-curricular activities – to a focus on enhancing the student learning experience within the curriculum through pedagogy, curriculum design, and learning and teaching practice in the physical and virtual classroom. A classification of evolving FYE research and practice, facilitated by Wilson's (2009) notion of "generations" of FYE approaches, provides a useful framework to describe this shift. In this classification, traditional co-curricular interventions and initiatives are classified as first generation approaches to the FYE (Wilson, 2009, p.10) and those that focus on curriculum interventions constitute second-generation approaches. Although the literature reveals reasonable consensus about what activities are classified as first generation, second-generation interventions – those within the curriculum – have been variously articulated. Wilson (2009) presents the second-generation approach as consisting of specific curriculum-related activities and strategies: "the core practices of education (for example, teaching quality, course design, et cetera) [with] common examples including engaging course and assessment design, formative assessment tasks, and community building in the classroom" (p.10). The view presented above focuses more explicitly on an integrated holistic approach: intentionally blended curricular and co-curricular activities (broadly "curriculum" in this conceptualisation) with a "focus squarely on enhancing the student learning experience through pedagogy, curriculum design, and learning and teaching practice in the physical and virtual classroom" (Kift 2009a, p.1).

Whereas the first generation is broadly around or in aid of and the second generation is within curriculum, a third-generation approach is characterised by Lizzio (Australian Learning and Teaching Council, 2009) as "a coordinated whole of institution partnership and consistent message about the first-year experience across the university" (p.14) and even more explicitly and operationally by Kift (2009a) as "whole-of-institution transformation" (p.1).

This definition is consistent with the current state of maturity of FYE at QUT and what was previously theorised as a transition pedagogy. We have argued elsewhere (Kift, Nelson and Clarke, 2010; Nelson, Duncan and Clarke, 2009) that institutional practices designed to foster student engagement should reflect a "whole-of-person" or holistic approach and, to that end, present a summary of evidence from our institution, QUT, as a case study of implementation of third-generation FYE student engagement programmes and practice. Before the case study is discussed in detail, the rationale for QUT's institution-wide approaches to student engagement and first-year learning, success and retention are explored to provide context.

Rationale for adopting a transition pedagogy

Forty per cent of QUT students are the first in their family to attend university. They have complex lives which include working off-campus for 10 per cent more time than their peers nationally; spending on average six hours per week travelling to and from classes; spending less time on classes; and relying heavily on learning technologies to provide anytime, anywhere access to course and learning materials. Approximately 33 per cent of all QUT students belong to one or more equity groups, with the largest concentrations being students from rural and regional backgrounds (19 per cent) and LSES backgrounds (14 per cent) (ACER, 2009; James, Krause and Jennings, 2010). In the next five years, the diversity of the student cohort is expected to increase as QUT responds to the Federal government's widening participation agenda.

Given this context and the fragility of disparate initiatives that are often dependent on local champions, the focus at QUT has been on establishing sustainable institution-wide approaches to student engagement, success and retention so that student take-up of these is not left to chance. In the face of increasing diversity, equal opportunity for success delivered through the curriculum is within our institutional control and will ensure that the opportunities for learning, success and retention in higher education are not predicated on social or cultural background, previous educational or economic advantage. Put quite simply, delivering equal opportunity for success is a legal and moral responsibility.

Queensland University of Technology: an example of transition pedagogy in action

The tables and figures that follow summarise QUT's adoption and implementation of a transition pedagogy. The claim here is not that all institutional student engagement, success and retention activities are at this stage of maturity at QUT, but rather that the infrastructure is in place and there is evidence of the transition pedagogy in action in all faculties and divisions. Table 6.1 presents the strategic goals and guiding strategies used to implement the transition pedagogy while Table 6.2 present a chronology of the emergence of transition pedagogy practice as QUT's student engagement, success and retention strategy has matured over the last decade.

Transition Pedagogy	Description
Overarching Goal	To enable students to make a successful transition into university study and to enhance all students' engagement with their studies and maximise their success as learners by: Achieving universal change across all academic, professional and administrative areas of QUT in support of the FYE our commencing students in all their diversity, and Acknowledging the reality of our students' learning needs and lives in the design of academic, administrative and social programs and decision making processes.
Guiding Strategies	Assessment, pedagogy and teaching practices must engage learners in their learning and mediate support for that learning. This is assisted by: • sustainable institution-wide partnerships between faculties and divisions and professional and academic staff • students' awareness of and timely access to QUT support services; and by • creating for learners a sense of belonging through involvement, engagement and connectedness with their university experiences.

Table 6.1: Transition curriculum principles

Timeframe	Summary of activities	Outcomes & Evidence
2000–2002	High levels of attrition recognized. Interventions with students resulted in increased retention of "at risk" students.	QUT, FYE *Issues Papers* developed Three core principles identified FYE Program Coordinator (professional staff) appointed.
2002–2005	Renewed attention on peer-led strategies for orientation and peer mentoring.	Increased attendance at orientation. Systematic approaches and resource for peer mentoring (1st Gen). Pockets of curricular excellence emerging (2nd Gen).
2005–2006	*Enhancing Transition at QUT* Project (ET@QUT) – aim to create a blueprint for the FYE at QUT.	Blueprint for the FYE at QUT and eight sub-projects refined QUT's approach to the FYE. Academic-professional partnerships now identified as necessary for institution-wide impact (Nelson, Kift, Humphreys & Harper, 2006).
2007	Academic Director, FYE position established with academic staff seconded from Law (2007) and then Science and Technology (2008-2010) DVC(A) sponsored FYE Program consisting of 5 projects.	FYE Policy, Orientation and Transition policy, FYE Survey, FY curriculum design principles, institution-wide approach to orientation agreed.
2007–2009	DVC(A) commissioned *Transitions-In Project* (TIP) builds capacity for FYE across the institution. Student Services Engagement Team established (Nelson, Smith et al. ,in press).	*Student Success Project* (SSP), curriculum design resources and evaluation frameworks, First Year Experience (practitioners) Network established. Orientation & Transition Coordinator position established and extended. Policy protocols and guidelines developed.

Timeframe	Summary of activities	Outcomes & Evidence
2010	Director and FYE team Director now contributing to broad range of institutional projects, activities and committees as divisional academic leader.	FYE web site (external) and FYE wiki (internal) established as public and staff resources. Embedding of FYE in: curriculum advisory, curriculum design and approval, curriculum review and improvement. SSP extended in scope and reach and operationalized.
2011	Director, FYE role changed to Director, Student Success & Retention (SS&R). QUT drafts new blueprint with KPIs for student engagement, success and retention aligned with compact process.	Portfolio of SS&R activities and initiatives including work integrated learning, learning support, peer programs, intercultural competence, and staff development related to these.

Table 6.2: A timeline and brief summary of the development and current stage of maturity of activities

Figure 6.3 illustrates diagrammatically the six Curriculum Principles and the strategies used to implement them at QUT within the transition pedagogy concept. Table 6.3 describes key interventions against each of the implementation strategies.

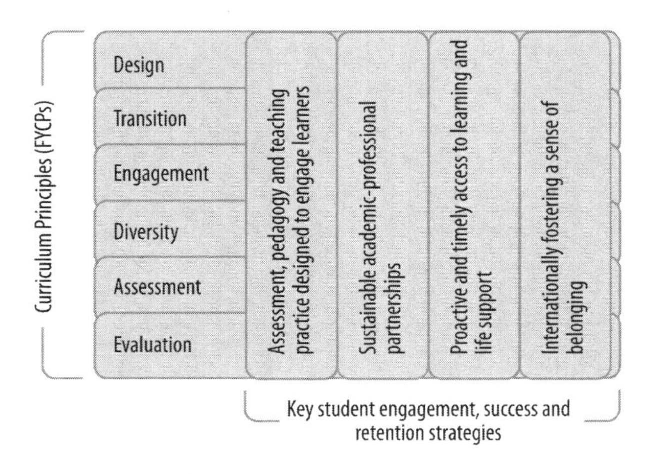

Figure 6.3: Transition Pedagogy Implementation Model

Guiding strategy	Strategic priorities	Operational activities
Assessment, pedagogy and teaching practices must engage learners	Implementation of curriculum design principles in new programs through integration in the QUT Curriculum Framework. Review and redesign of programs to align with principles where there is high commencing or continuing attrition. Integration of transition pedagogy principles and approach in academic staff development programs. The QUT FYE Policy sets out the intention of adopting the transition pedagogy.	Implementation guidelines and operational "checklists" for each of the principles are available. Major curriculum reform in all seven faculties has taken place to align with curriculum principles. Concepts included in professional and academic staff development programs.
Sustainable institution-wide partnerships	Academic Director, SS&R and Director, Student Support Services work in partnership on University T&L committee. Two uni-wide committees (FYE and Retention, Student Experience Management Committee).	Key academic-professional partnerships for orientation, student experience and engagement, peer programs, SSP, learning support. Communities of practice for key T&L initiatives (FYE, WIL & Capstone)
Proactive, timely access to support services	Monitoring and support of students' engagement in learning through the SSP. Universal for all commencing students and at risk cohorts.	Six campaigns established through the SSP that span all key orientation, academic and administrative milestones.
Intentionally fostering a sense of belonging	Enactment of orientation and transition as a process that occurs over time embedded in FYE Policy. Enhancement of peer programs.	Coordinated, multi-campus, whole-of-institution learning enhancement focused orientation events 2008-2011. New peer programs (learning communities and mentoring) for at-risk courses and cohorts.

Table 6.3: Key strategic and operational interventions against each strategy

There is a large collection of policy and practice, and strategic and operational, levels that exemplify the enactment of the transition pedagogy. Some examples of that activity are shown in Table 6.4. Acronyms in the table identify specific examples drawn from QUT's seven faculties where: BEE = Faculty of Built Environment and Engineering; BUS = QUT Business School; CIF = Creative Industries Faculty; ED = Faculty of Education; FAST = Faculty of Science and Technology; HEALTH = Faculty of Health; and LAW = Faculty of Law and Justice. To provide some sense of scale and scalability, the numbers of students impacted by these activities are provided where possible.

Key Strategy / TP Principles	Assessment, pedagogy and teaching practice	Academic-professional partnerships	Timely access to support	Sense of belonging
Design	Assessment for learning is a key component of QUT's developmental curriculum design framework.	Responsibility for the student engagement & success and particularly the FYE seen as "everyone's business" is articulated in policy.	Learning support sessions aligned, integrated or embedded in most course "core" or mandatory units (300-1700 students).	Institution-wide enactment of orientation and transition as an ongoing process from point of offer until the end of week 4. (11,000 commencing students in 2011)
Transition	Transition intensive for all students as part of commencing program. (LAW - approx 200 students)	Peer learning communities in threshold skills units (HEALTH, BEE, ED - 1,000 students)	Monitoring engagement of entire commencing cohort (LAW, BUS, BEE, CIF - approx 8,000 students).	On-campus orientation for external students (LAW) On-line peer learning community (ED – 50 students).

Diversity	Campus-wide FYE & retention program to support widening participation strategy (600 students).	Language and Learning Advisors embedded in faculties (HEALTH & BUS).	Post-admission diagnostics for information literacy and communication skills (BEE, BUS - 3,000 students).	Peer mentoring for mature-age advanced standing cohorts (ED – 80 students).
Engagement	Exploration of self, profession and careers (CIF, FAST - 2,000 students).	Academic performance and supplementary assessment procedures support learner progression.	Cohorts and students at greater risk of disengagement monitored for participation and academic activity.	Integration of work integrated learning activities and profession/ industry relevant curriculum within the FY of most programs.
Assessment	Early/formative assessment items for all commencing cohorts.	Information literacy integrated into early assessment items.	Program of learning support/skills workshops for EAL and FY students (BUS - 1,500 students).	Peer learning advisers assigned to known threshold skills units (ED, HEALTH - 1,000 students).
Evaluation & Monitoring	Course QA processes include student experience surveys, measures of student experience & retention and individual and consolidated course reporting.	Course exit survey has measures for all aspects of students' experience.	Monitoring academic activity to identify students at-risk of disengagement.	Annual orientation survey. Participation in AUSSE & FYEQ. Course quality assurance processes.

Table 6.4: Examples of the transition pedagogy in action organised by FYCP and guiding strategies

It appears that the concept of transition pedagogy, which has now been taken up and implemented across the institution, is robust enough to guide the transformation and engagement of not only commencing undergraduate students but also all students in all types of programmes.

Monitoring student engagement

As student populations become increasingly diverse, the issues surrounding student engagement and success will become more closely scrutinised. It stands to reason then, that if engagement is the linchpin of student success and retention, HEIs need to monitor and measure the extent of student engagement – particularly in the first year – and most importantly intervene with students exhibiting signs of disengaging from their studies. Importantly for the widening participation agenda, it will be critical that these initiatives are consistent with the concepts of social justice and do not problematise individual students or cohorts, nor make any assumptions about why disengagement may be indicated.

James, Krause and Jennings (2010), reporting in an Australian tertiary context, concluded that "there is perhaps no greater challenge facing the sector than that of identifying and monitoring the students who are 'at risk' of attrition or poor academic progress" but simultaneously noted that "limited inroads have been made into this problem" (p.102). Similar concerns have been expressed globally, for example in North America: "In spite of the attention paid to retaining students, we have made very little progress. ... Our efforts... have been less than successful" (Coley and Coley, 2010, p.2); and in the United Kingdom: while "higher education in England achieves high levels of student retention... there is scope for some further improvements" (National Audit Office, 2007). In Australia, "the importance for institutions of implementing carefully designed monitoring and preventative procedures that can track student progress, identifying at risk students, and putting in place conditions which may support and inspire student success" (ACER, 2009, p.44) have been noted.

In 2007, a pilot study at QUT investigated the effectiveness of monitoring and providing personalised contact with first-year students deemed to be at risk of disengaging from their studies (Duncan and Nelson, 2008). A gap analysis of the systems, processes and resources required to identify, monitor and provide support interventions to at-risk students, at an institution-wide scale, recommended implementation of a systematic approach to data collection and highly tailored, individualised and purposeful support for such students.

An initiative called the Student Success Program (SSP) was piloted in 2008 and subsequently implemented as part of the Transitions-In Project (TIP) (Nelson et al., in press). The purpose of an intervention of this scale is to promote student engagement proactively and systematically by providing purposeful, timely interventions tailored to meet the needs of individual students. The activities in the SSP are organised into a series of campaigns, each of which is related to key engagement and success milestones. Each campaign identifies students exhibiting behaviours that indicate potential disengagement before they fail a unit or, worse, drop out of university studies. The goal is that the SSP monitors the engagement of all commencing (undergraduate) students and supports students and cohorts in units and courses where there are historically high levels of disengagement or failure and attrition. At the time of writing, the SSP is well on the way to achieving this goal, having supported the engagement and success of more than 30,000 students since its inception in 2008 (Nelson et al., in press).

Two key systems, a custom-built Contact Management System (CMS) and a knowledge base, support the SSP. The CMS interfaces to key corporate systems (for example, student information and academic systems) to collect descriptive data about students and their course (degree programme) and to receive input from other systems about students' academic behaviour and performance (for example, attendance at orientation or in class, assignment submission or marks). The CMS allows call lists of at-risk students to be constructed and facilitates evaluation of the impact of the SSP's campaigns and reporting of outcomes. The knowledge base stores information about each campaign and its call lists, the types of services available for specific cohorts or courses, information related to each campaign, links to university information (support services, policies and administrative procedures), as well as templates and resources for the SSP Advisers. The knowledge base is used as a resource to personalise the calls and to construct the action plan that follows each call, which is sent via email to each student who appears on a call list. The SSP campaigns are organised around key engagement and success milestones including:

- Pre-semester – follow-up with students who are late to accept an offer or who have not enrolled correctly
- Early semester – welcome (and welcome back) calls to equity cohorts and other cohorts where corporate data has indicated high levels of course attrition. Follow-up with students who were not able to attend their faculty orientation (attendance rolls)
- During semester – learning engagement campaigns where first year or other units are harnessed as a vehicle to create and gather academic performance data (for example, post-entry diagnostic evaluation or non-submission of assignments) and to make purposeful support interventions for those students
- End of semester – international students and first-year students who have a failing grade-point average or are identified as entering probation or exclusion processes are contacted to promote help-seeking behaviour.

Detailed evaluations have been conducted of the effectiveness of the SSP initiative (Nelson, Kift and Clarke, 2011) but, in summary, there is compelling sustained evidence that the SSP has had a positive impact on student engagement as indicated by academic success, improving student progression rates and declining attrition rates at QUT.

Conclusion

The value of higher education in terms of opportunities for improved social and economic outcomes for individuals, community and countries is well recognised (Australian Government, 2009). All equity groups are under-represented in higher education and, despite comparable outcomes (p.14), students from LSES backgrounds have not enjoyed the same opportunities afforded to members of the population who come from economically and educationally better circumstances. Achieving equity in higher education – the hallmark of a civil and just society (Bradley et al., 2008) – will require institutional attention to student engagement, particularly in first year, as well as to improved access and recruitment, because these are the elements that are implicated in learning success (Nelson et al., in press). Research from the United Kingdom argues persuasively that "the changes to curriculum provision and learning, teaching and assessment, which have occurred alongside the transition from an elite to a mass participation HE sector, benefit all students and can have a positive impact on higher level and critical thinking skills" (Shaw et al., 2007, p.48). This chapter has proposed using a transition pedagogy to leverage student engagement and as the mechanism by which first-year student success can be enhanced.

The current pressures on HEIs to meet equity targets and maintain quality, accompanied by tensions brought about by perceptions that "accommodating equity... is in clear opposition to excellence" (Gale, 2009, p.10), provide a critical opportunity for informed pursuit of a new conceptualisation about curriculum not only with a view to social equity but also to assure high academic quality.

The opportunity now is for university educators to design and enact the transition pedagogy with its underpinning six curriculum principles, and to implement key strategies contextualised for individual HEIs. This will require vision, institutional commitment, resources and practical advice. All the elements of the transition pedagogy are critical to maintain and enhance academic standards, to enrich the learning environment and to ensure that the opportunities for student learning engagement, success and retention in higher education are not predicated on social or cultural backgrounds or on previous educational advantage or economic wealth.

Swing (2003) has cautioned that it may take as long as ten years to achieve embedded institutional change. In this context, the evidence presented here is a chronicle of what has happened over the last decade as QUT's student engagement programme has matured. As action learning research, the findings may be instructive, while the models and various initiatives described here may provide practical approaches on which others can build to grow and refine their own institution's policy, practice and procedures.

References

Australian Council for Educational Research (ACER) (2008) *Attracting, engaging and retaining: New conversations about learning. Australasian Survey of Student Engagement report* (Melbourne, Australia). Retrieved from <http://www.acer.edu.au/documents/AUSSE_ASER-Report.pdf>

Australian Council for Educational Research (ACER) (2009) *Doing more for learning: Enhancing engagement and outcomes. Australasian Survey of Student Engagement report* (Melbourne, Australia). Retrieved from <http://ausse.acer.edu.au/images/docs/AUSSE_2009_Student_Engagement_Report.pdf>

Australian Government (2009) *Transforming Australia's higher education system* (Canberra: DEEWR). Retrieved from <http://www.deewr.gov.au/HigherEducation/Documents/PDF/Additional%20Report%20-%20Transforming%20Aus%20Higher%20ED_webaw.pdf>

Australian Learning and Teaching Council (2009) Ensuring a successful transition to first year, *Communique*, 2/14.

Barrie, S., Hughes, C. and Smith, C. (2009) *The National Graduate Attributes Project: Integration and assessment of graduate attributes in curriculum* (Sydney, Australia: Australian Learning and Teaching Council).

Bean, J.P. and Eaton, S.B. (2000) 'A psychological model of college student retention', in Braxton, J.M. (ed.) *Reworking the student departure puzzle*, 1st ed. (Nashville: Vanderbilt University Press) pp.48–61.

Biggs, J.B. (1999) *Teaching for quality at university* (Buckingham: Open University Press).

Bradley, D., Noonan, P., Nugent, H. and Scales, B. (2008) *Review of Australian higher education: Final report* (Canberra: DEEWR). Retrieved from <http://www.deewr.gov.au/he_review_finalreport>

Coates, H. (2005) 'The value of student engagement for higher education quality assurance', *Quality in Higher Education*, 11/1, pp.25–36.

Coley, C. and Coley, T. (2010) *Retention and student success. Staying on track with early intervention strategies* (Malvern: SunGard Higher Education).

Crosling, G., Heagney, M. and Thomas, L. (2009) 'Improving student retention in higher education: Improving teaching and learning', *Australian Universities' Review*, 51/2, pp.9-18.

Dart, B.C. (1994) 'A goal-mediational model of personal and environmental influences on tertiary students' learning strategy use', *Higher Education*, 28, pp.453–70.

Dawkins, J.S. (1988) *Higher education – A policy statement* (Canberra: Australian Government Publishing Service).

Duncan, M. and Nelson, K.J. (2008, June–July) 'The Student Success Project: Helping students at risk of failing or withdrawing from a unit – a work in progress', paper presented at the 11th Pacific Rim First Year in Higher Education Conference, 'An Apple for the Learner: Celebrating the First Year Experience', Hobart, Australia. Retrieved from <http://www.fyhe.qut.edu.au/past_papers/papers08/FYHE2008/content/html/sessions.html>

Gale, T. (2009) 'Towards a southern theory of higher education', keynote address presented at the 12th Pacific Rim First Year in Higher Education Conference, 'Preparing for Tomorrow Today: The First Year Experience as Foundation', Townsville, Australia. Retrieved from <http://www.fyhe.com.au/past_papers/papers09/ppts/Trevor_Gale_paper.pdf>

Gillard, J. (2010) Address to the Universities Australia Annual Higher Education Conference. Retrieved from <http://www.deewr.gov.au/Ministers/Gillard/Media/Speeches/Pages/Article_100303_102842.aspx>

Harvey, L., Drew, S., and Smith, M. (2006) *The first year experience: A literature review for the Higher Education Academy*. Retrieved from <http://www.heacademy.ac.uk/assets/York/documents/ourwork/research/literature_reviews/first_year_experience_full_report.pdf>

James, R., Krause K. and Jennings, C. (2010) *The first year experience in Australian universities: Findings from 1994 to 2009* (Melbourne: Centre for Studies in Higher Education).

Kift, S.M. (2004) *Organising first year engagement around learning: Formal and informal curriculum intervention*, keynote address presented at the 8th Pacific Rim First Year in Higher Education Conference, 'Dealing with Diversity', Melbourne, Australia. Retrieved from <http://www.fyhe.qut.edu.au/past_papers/Papers04/Sally Kift_paper.doc>

Kift, S.M. (2008) 'The next, great first year challenge: Sustaining, coordinating and embedding coherent institution-wide approaches to enact the FYE as everybody's business', keynote address presented at the 11th Pacific Rim First Year in Higher Education Conference, 'An Apple for the Learner: Celebrating the First Year Experience', Hobart, Australia. Retrieved from <http://www.fyhe.com.au/past_papers/papers08/FYHE2008/content/pdfs/Keynote%20-%20Kift.pdf>

Kift, S.M. (2009a) *Final Report for ALTC Senior Fellowship Program* (Sydney: Australian Learning and Teaching Council). Retrieved from <http://www.altc.edu.au/resource-first-year-learning-experience-kift-2009>

Kift, S.M. (2009b) 'A transition pedagogy for first year curriculum design and renewal', paper presented at the FYE Curriculum Design Symposium 2009, Brisbane, Australia. Retrieved from <http://www.fyecd2009.qut.edu.au/resources/PRE_SallyKift_5Feb09.pdf>

Kift, S.M. (2009c) 'A transition pedagogy: The First Year Experience Curriculum Design Symposium', *HERDSA News*, 31/1: 3–4. Retrieved from <http://www.herdsa.org.au/wp-content/uploads/herdsa-news-311-april-2009.pdf>

Kift, S.M. and Field, R. (2009) 'Intentional first year curriculum design as a means of facilitating student engagement: Some exemplars' ,paper presented at the 12th Pacific Rim First Year in Higher Education Conference, 'Preparing for Tomorrow Today: The First Year Experience as Foundation', Townsville, Australia. Retrieved from <http://www.fyhe.com.au/past_papers/papers09/content/pdf/16D.pdf>

Kift, S.M. and Nelson, K.J. (2005) 'Beyond curriculum reform: embedding the transition experience', in Brew, A. and Asmar, C. (eds) *Higher Education in a changing world: Research and Development in Higher Education*, 28, pp.225–35.

Kift, S.M., Nelson, K.J. and Clarke, J.A. (2010) 'Transition pedagogy: A third generation approach to FYE – A case study of policy and practice for the higher education sector', *The International Journal of the First Year in Higher Education*, 1:1, pp.1–20.

Krause, K. (2005) *Understanding and promoting student engagement in university learning communities* (Melbourne: Centre for Studies in Higher Education). Retrieved from <http://www.cshe.unimelb.edu.au/pdfs/Stud_eng.pdf>

Krause, K. (2006) 'On being strategic about the first year', keynote address presented at the Queensland University of Technology First Year Forum, Brisbane, Australia. Retrieved from <http://www.fye.qut.edu.au/fyeatqut/KrauseQUTPaper.pdf>>

Krause, K. and Coates, H. (2008) 'Students' engagement in first-year university', *Assessment and Evaluation in Higher Education*, 33/5, pp.493–505.

Krause, K., Hartley, R., James, R. and McInnes, C (2005) *The First Year Experience in Australian universities: Findings from a decade of national studies* (Melbourne: Centre for Studies in Higher Education).

Lodge, J. (2010, July) 'The benefits of using social networks to increase student engagement – Not so obvious?', paper presented at the HERDSA 2010 International Conference, Melbourne, Australia.

Mayes, T. (2009) *Overview of the Enhancement Theme 2006–08: The aims, achievements and challenges*, The Quality Assurance Agency for Higher Education, Quality Enhancement Themes: The First Year Experience. Retrieved from <http://www.enhancementthemes.ac.uk/documents/firstyear/FirstYearOverview.pdf>

McInnes, C. (2001) *Signs of disengagement? The changing undergraduate experience in Australian universities* (Melbourne: Centre for Studies in Higher Education). Retrieved from <http://repository.unimelb.edu.au/10187/1331>

National Audit Office (2007) *Staying the course: The retention of students in higher education.* Retrieved from <http://www.nao.org.uk/publications/0607/student_retention_in_higher_ed.aspx>

Nelson, K.J., Duncan, M. and Clarke, J.A. (2009) 'Student success: The identification and support of first year university students at risk of attrition', *Studies in Learning, Evaluation, Innovation and Development,* 6/1, pp.1–15.

Nelson, K.J., Kift, S., and Clarke, J.A. (2008, June–July) 'Expectations and realities for first year students at an Australian university', paper presented at the 11th Pacific Rim First Year in Higher Education Conference, 'An Apple for the Learner: Celebrating the First Year Experience', Hobart, Tasmania. Retrieved from <http://www.fyhe.qut.edu.au/past_papers/papers08/FYHE2008/content/pdfs/6a.pdf>

Nelson, K.J., Kift, S.M. and Clarke, J.A. (2011) 'An analysis of Australasian First Year Experience literature 2000–2010', *The First Year in Higher Education Centre Research Series on Evidence-based Practice,* Volume 1 (Brisbane: FYHE Centre).

Nelson, K.J., Kift, S.M., Humphreys, J. and Harper, W. (2006, July) 'A blueprint for enhanced transition: Taking an holistic approach to managing student transition into a large university', paper presented at the 9th Pacific Rim First Year in Higher Education Conference, 'Engaging Students', Gold Coast, Australia. Retrieved from <http://www.fyhe.com.au/past_papers/2006/Papers/Kift.pdf>

Nelson, K.J., Quinn, C., Marrington, A.D. and Clarke, J.A. (in press) 'Good practice for enhancing the engagement and success of commencing students', *Higher Education.*

Nelson, K.J., Smith, J.E. and Clarke, J.A. (in press) 'Enhancing the transition of commencing students into university: An institution-wide approach', *Higher Education Research and Development.*

Reason, R.D., Terenzini, P.T. and Domingo, R.J. (2005) 'First things first: Developing academic competence in the first year of college', *Research in Higher Education*, 47/2, pp.149–75.

Reason, R.D., Terenzini, P.T. and Domingo, R.J. (2007) 'Developing social and personal competence in the first year of college', *The Review of Higher Education*, 30/3, pp.271–99.

Scott, G., Shah, M., Grebennikov, L. and Singh, H. (2009) 'Improving student retention: A University of Western Sydney case study', *Journal of Institutional Research*, 14/1, pp.9–23.

Shaw, J., Brain, K., Bridger, K., Foreman, J. and Reid, I. (2007) *Embedding widening participation and promoting student diversity: What can be learned from a business case approach?* (York: Higher Education Academy).

Simeoni, R.J. (2009, June–July) 'Student retention trends within a health foundation year and implications for orientation, engagement and retention strategies', paper presented at the 12th Pacific Rim First Year in higher Education Conference, 'Preparing for Tomorrow Today: The First Year Experience as Foundation', Townsville, Australia. Retrieved from <http://www.fyhe.com.au/past_papers/papers09/content/pdf/2B.pdf>

Swing, R.L. (2003, June) 'First-year student success: In search of best practice', keynote address presented at the 7th Pacific Rim First Year in Higher Education Conference, 'Enhancing the Transition into Higher Education', Brisbane, Australia. Retrieved from <http://www.fyhe.com.au/past_papers/keynote2.htm>

Tinto, V. (1993) *Leaving college: Rethinking the causes and cures of student attrition*, 2nd ed. (Chicago: University of Chicago Press).

Tinto, V. (2006–7) 'Research and practice of student retention: What next?', *Journal of College Student Retention*, 8/1: 1–19. Retrieved from <http://www.uaa.alaska.edu/governance/facultysenate/upload/JCSR_Tinto_2006-07_Retention.pdf>

Tinto, V. (2009, February) 'Taking student retention seriously: Rethinking the first year of university', keynote address presented at the FYE Curriculum Design Symposium 2009, Brisbane. Retrieved from <http://www.fyecd2009.qut.edu.au/resources/SPE_VincentTinto_5Feb09.pdf>>

Tinto, V. (2010) 'From theory to action: Exploring the institutional conditions for student retention', in J.C. Smart (ed.) *Higher Education: Handbook of theory and practice* 25 (New York: Springer) pp.51–89.

Trow, M. (1970) 'Reflections on the transition from mass to universal higher education', *Daedalus*, 99, pp.1–42.

Upcraft, M.L., Gardner, J.N. and Barefoot, B.O. (eds) (2005) *Challenging and supporting the first-year student* (San Francisco: Jossey-Bass).

Wilson, K. (2009) 'The impact of institutional, programmatic and personal interventions on an effective and sustainable first-year student experience', keynote address presented at the 12th Pacific Rim First Year in Higher Education Conference, 'Preparing for Tomorrow Today: The First Year Experience as Foundation', Townsville, Australia. Retrieved from <http://www.fyhe.com.au/past_papers/papers09/ppts/Keithia_Wilson_paper.pdf>

Yorke, M. (2006) 'Student engagement: deep, surface or strategic?', keynote address presented at the 9th Pacific Rim First Year in Higher Education Conference, 'Engaging Students', Brisbane, Australia. Retrieved from <http://www.fyhe.qut.edu.au/past_papers/2006/program.html>

Yorke, M. and Longden, B. (2008) *The first-year experience of higher education in the UK: Final Report* (York: Higher Education Academy). Retrieved from <http://www.heacademy.ac.uk/assets/York/documents/resources/publications/FYEFinalReport.pdf>

Chapter 7

Student engagement with capability development

Elizabeth Reid and Ian Solomonides

Macquarie University, Australia

Introduction

Student engagement is currently of great interest in higher education. In Australia for example, this has resulted in the development of the Australasian University Survey of Student Engagement (AUSSE) (Coates, 2006; ACER, 2008). The AUSSE is based on the National Survey of Student Engagement (Kuh, 2001) but there are other instruments that 'measure' engagement such as the Academic Engagement Form (Foster, Long and Snell, 1999). In these surveys, student engagement is represented as an holistic concept combining participation, involvement, effort, affiliation and quality of learning. It relates to the full range of experiences and practices of being a student and of learning in a university. It is a description of the behaviour toward, relationship with, and commitment to learning. Engagement is supported by a sense of belonging, fostered by aspects such as high-quality learning and teaching, co-curricular and extra-curricular activities, and the blurring of the boundary between formal and informal student life. As yet there is little qualitative evidence from students regarding their experience of co-constructing and critiquing the formal and informal activities that support engagement with capabilities. This chapter discusses engagement of students with the capability agenda of a major Australian university.

The early concept of capability was developed by Sen (1979) with Stephenson (1992, 1998) later introducing the notion of graduate capability, suggesting that capability is about "fitness for specified purpose" or capacity to function a certain way. Such graduates would have the ability to integrate knowledge, skills, personal qualities and understanding in their personal and professional lives. They would be capable human beings and their capability could be observed by their confidence and ability to take effective and appropriate action; communicate their perspective; live and work effectively with others; and continue to learn from their experiences as individuals and in association with others, in a diverse and changing society (Stephenson, 1992). According to Walker (2006), capability is "what we are actually able to be and do."

Like many other universities, Macquarie University in Sydney, Australia, has attempted to codify – in its case into a 'framework' – general learning outcomes into graduate capabilities to be incorporated into the curriculum. But how is this translated into actual practice and the student experience? In reviewing its undergraduate provision, Macquarie University (2008) established curriculum review working parties, representative of University stakeholders with a mission to develop a set of principles for curriculum renewal and design. As part of this, courses were expected to 'map' where the opportunities for students to engage with capabilities are within the curriculum. But knowing where things are is manifestly different from a student making personal meaning of them. Nevertheless, at the forefront of this drive from a curriculum standpoint was the promotion of four 'principles' and nine graduate capabilities, presented as a framework shown in Figure 7.1. Students are expected to be aware of and informed about espoused capabilities through course materials such as course guides, learning outcomes, teaching and learning activities and assessment. However, as described by Winchester-Seeto and colleagues (Chapter 19, this volume), there are tensions between the intended, enacted and experienced. Similarly, staff are encouraged to 'teach to' the capabilities, as a compulsory question within the feedback gathered from students explicitly asks the extent to which learners feel "This unit contributed to my development of one or more of the Macquarie Graduate Capabilities". Within this context, this chapter reports on empirical research based on 17 interviews that investigated what, if any, awareness of the framework first-year students have; and allied to this, whether they feel any of these capabilities are being enacted and then experienced in their studies.

A distinct feature of the framework in Figure 7.1 and of provision at Macquarie is the three Ps at the centre of the framework, representing People, Planet and Participation units of study. These PPP units are unique to Macquarie and are taken by all students regardless of discipline. In achieving an undergraduate degree each student will experience 'People' units of study with a focus on what it means to be engaged and ethical local and global citizens; 'Planet' units designed to promote understanding of the nature of science and the challenges and issues facing the world at present; and 'Participation' units that contain work experience and, particularly, service-type learning with the intention of promoting social and cultural sensitivity and engagement with community. Every undergraduate will be expected to have completed a People, a Planet and a Participation unit during their study and there are a variety of such units available and 'owned' by subject teams across the University. As shown in Figure 7.1, laying between the core of the PPP units and the guiding principles are the mix of capabilities – cognitive, personal and social dispositions to be expected of the Macquarie graduate.

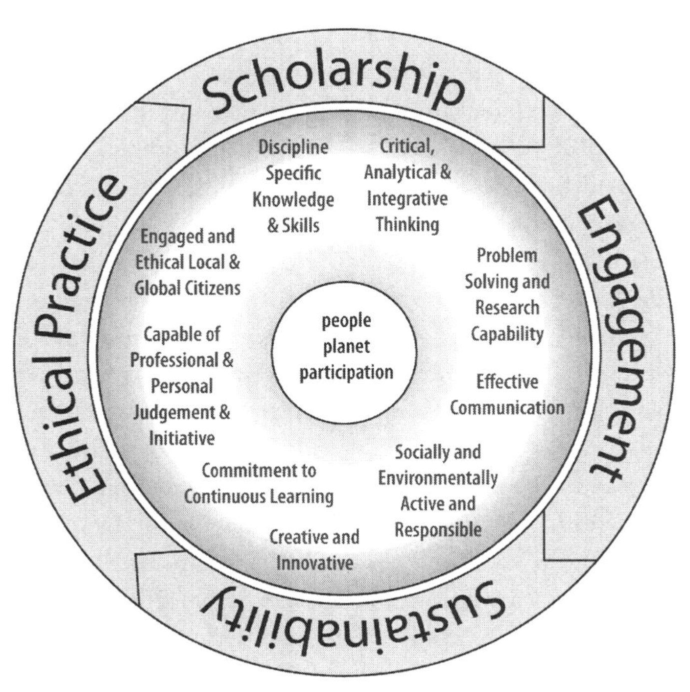

Figure 7.1: Macquarie University Graduate Capabilities Framework

Many institutions strive to demonstrate their promotion of generic graduate outcomes to stakeholders through their development of graduate capability statements or frameworks. These function as a guide for curriculum design and indicate, often to employers as well as to students, what graduates can expect to be able to do, know and value as a consequence of study. Gibbs (2010) describes inherent tensions within this as trying to educate and develop capabilities for a continually changing market that would require expertise demanded by employers as well as adaptability enabling efficiency in new and unpredictable situations. The student participants of this study also voiced similar sentiments.

Despite there being little academic agreement as to the meaning of 'capability development' (Barrie, 2004, 2006), capabilities have been promoted as essential in the modern curriculum (Yorke and Harvey, 2005). Surprisingly, only minimal research exists broadly to support links between student academic engagement as conceptualised in the opening chapter and graduate capabilities. There have been some studies into aligning capabilities in the curriculum (Treleaven and Voola, 2008), the 'mapping' of capabilities using some form of taxonomy across the curriculum (Oliver, 2010) and, perhaps most promisingly, the negotiated inclusion of capability statements, criteria and the mediated evaluation of them by students and their assessors (Thompson, 2008). Elsewhere, studies provide empirical support for discrete capabilities and the efficacy of student learning. These include studies on information literacy (Jones, Evans and Magierowski, 2007) and 'research type' attributes, described by the Quality Assurance Agency, Scotland, as critical understanding, awareness of knowledge creation, problem solving, evidence-based application and creativity (QAA Scotland, 2009). Brew (2010) also provides strong advocacy for the inclusion of research and inquiry in the undergraduate curriculum. Whatever is emerging as desirable, appropriate or efficacious in the capability domain, students' engagement and the effort they devote to these desired outcomes remain the most important factor in student learning (Hu and Kuh, 2002; Kuh 2008). Consequently, by examining the ways in which capability development is presented to and experienced by students, universities will be in a better position effectively to encourage student effort and engagement with capability development.

The empirical study

Student participants were recruited from each of Macquarie's four faculties with four students from Arts, four from Business and Economics, five from Science and four from Human Sciences. Interviews were carried out using a semi-structured method. Participants were provided with two prompts: a copy of the Graduate Capabilities Framework (Figure 7.1) and a list of ten pedagogic principles that support academic engagement:

- Collaborative and active learning, assignments and projects
- Choice and negotiation in assessment
- First-year experiences that ease and enable effective transition
- Common and shared experiences that foster belonging
- The promotion of learning communities and identifiable cohorts
- Undergraduate research and experiential learning
- Good teaching, including consistency, organisation and the promotion of common values
- Learning with and about diversity
- Community and service learning
- Culminating projects, expositions and capstones.

The framework implies that the University places equal weighting on each of the capabilities. Participants were invited to reflect on how these capabilities had been encouraged or otherwise promoted. The interviews were initially held with 17 participants in 2009 and 12 of them agreed to a repeat interview in 2010 to identify any changes in their perspective. The interviews were transcribed and thematically analysed using the software tool NVivo. Thematic analysis (Boyatzis, 1998) focuses on themes and patterns emerging from (usually) ethnographic data. Following a six-phase approach detailed by Braun and Clarke (2006), analysis of students' responses to the two prompts revealed the role they considered capability development to play in their engagement with study and the weighting they placed on particular capabilities. As the interviews were confidential, the students' names in this chapter have been replaced by an abbreviation of their faculty (*Arts, Bus, Hum* or *Sci*) and a number.

In discussing their approach to the capabilities, interviewees introduced a number of common considerations:

- Identifying the capabilities which seemed most applicable to their degree and career goals
- Identifying the context in which the development of different capabilities does/should occur
- Considering the extent to which these capabilities should be developed prior to university.

The participants talked about their personal motivations for studying and the way these influenced the significance they placed on each of the capabilities. The capabilities students were most interested in varied according to their personal aims for study. One of the most prominent distinctions drawn by students across the interviews was between *Scholarship*-driven capabilities and those focused on *Ethical Practice* and *Sustainability*. Most students treated these concepts as though they sat at opposite ends of a spectrum and so aligned their motivations for study more strongly with one or the other. Students' opinions on this division varied depending on age group and faculty of study. *Effective Communication* and *Commitment to Continuous Learning* were two capabilities which students from all faculties highlighted as applicable to the aims of their degree and developing throughout their studies. Analysis of student interviews revealed patterns in students' approaches and ambitions according to two primary variables: the faculty in which the students were located and their age and life-experiences prior to their current study. Unsurprisingly, students exhibited enthusiasm and a greater level of engagement with the development of capabilities in which they had particular interest. The following discussion has therefore been organised to provide an overview by faculty of the outcomes whilst maintaining an overarching interest in the mature-aged/recent-school-leaver dichotomy.

Faculty results: Faculty of Arts

The Arts students interviewed recognised that the capabilities as a whole improved their future employability and enhanced their experience by supporting their learning processes. More than other disciplines, they were inclined toward a positive view of the ethics and sustainability capabilities. They considered these qualities, which were developed in both a social and formal context on campus, to be essential qualities for an 'educated person'. However, some students considered them as important yet distinct, as they were developed in other spheres; critical thinking and academic expression might be developing in class whereas ethical practice might be achieved through involvement in clubs and societies. One international student described how clubs and societies helped him to strengthen his sense of security, to balance his life-style and to "grow up" (in terms of social and communication skills). In terms of prior experience with the capabilities, one student referred to cultural sensitivity as "half a pre-requisite, and then half you develop by studying."

The societal focus of the new degree led some students to expect the incorporation of community work. *Arts4* also noted that the promotion of volunteering opportunities during lectures encouraged students to consider ways of developing ethics through independent practical experience:

> I don't know necessarily if it's something that first years would engage in just because they are still acclimatising themselves to what university is, but if anything it's sowing a seed for later on.

Arts4 therefore saw community service as a personal choice but recognised the university's role in encouraging and preparing students for such actions. Many students, across the faculties, had difficulty identifying direct associations between university and the outside community.

Thinking about ethics in an academic context, *Arts1* expressed his early anxieties and growing awareness of the ethical dimensions of essay writing:

> I was nervous mainly about the research and how to... reference. Each time I used a source, I just opened the webpage of the steps that you have to follow in order not to be considered as plagiarism...

Academic integrity, demonstrated though correct referencing, was one experience that caused a few of the recent school-completers to merge the concepts of ethics, communication and scholarship. Group work was another such area where *Arts2* argued:

> It can be bad but I think the dynamic is good most of the time and people have to learn how to deal with that kind of stuff anyway because it's a fact of life that you can't just go through life doing your own thing when social interaction is like key.

Arts2's decision to attend university was motivated by a desire to strengthen his résumé and because "it would have been a waste of doing the HSC (High School Certificate) and everything if I didn't use my UAI [matriculation mark] to go somewhere." He felt that his chosen career required practical experience, which was unobtainable in a university context, thus making the scholarship capabilities, particularly the discipline-specific skills, less relevant for his goals. His interests and approach to gaining what he could from university favoured the other capabilities. He wanted to learn about ethics and global citizenship, to improve his communication skills, to start working with the tools of his chosen field and to be "creative and innovative". Despite his approval of the well-rounded nature of the capabilities (extending beyond "knowledge"), the fact that he was only interested in a portion of the capabilities led him to regard them as globally less applicable to himself. He suggested instead that the framework was for "people who want to go down a very strict path."

Arts3 approved of the ethics capabilities because they were crucial to being "an educated person" and were "what you need to get through life as a good person." Others (predominantly mature-aged students) made the same observation but concluded that these skills were, therefore, incompatible objectives for a university education. *Arts3*'s use of the phrase "educated person" emphasises that she considered the capabilities belonged in a university context. She believed they were "relevant to everyone" and that:

> University is not just about teaching you a specific – knowledge about a specific field or a specific subject, it's more about putting you in a new environment... getting you ready for the real world.

Her reference to the 'real world' relates to a previous argument she made, that ethical capabilities were "developed at high school but uni is meant to really nourish that, enrich it so you're ready for afterwards". There is a difficult discrepancy to reconcile between the overall outcomes sought by recent school-completers and those of the mature-aged students, who tended to be less interested in the university 'preparing' them for life beyond formal education. When asked if she thought these capabilities were appropriate objectives even for people who felt they had developed them elsewhere, *Arts3* answered:

> I think so, yes... Whilst you should be picking it up in your everyday life, maybe people don't... because all they've done is go to school [where] there's not a lot of social variation... So by pushing it they're making you think about it if you never have before. And if you've thought about it before then that's great, it's not going to bother you 'cause you know all these things.

Arts4 saw "developing self belief" as the intrinsic personal outcome of the complete set of graduate capabilities. "If you're doing well scholarly and you feel as though you're engaged and you feel as though you're relating to the world around you, then I think that that will instil confidence in you." In terms of the projected application of the capabilities, *Arts4* highlighted effective communication as vital to his ambition to teach. He hoped to gain a well-rounded perspective and so approved of the University's interest in "people being active and engaged global citizens". He noted an increase in the University's attention to ethics and sustainability over his first year. However, his overall approval did not result in placing equal weighting on each point. Although he considered ethics important he was not alert to its role in his coursework in the same way as research or critical thought:

> If you're talking about something as an ethical issue, then that's bringing it to the forefront... that brings something to what you're learning, but I don't think that is something that you consciously think about all the time.

Faculty of Business and Economics

The theme which resounded throughout the Business and Economics interviews was the extrinsic drive to obtain a job that informed the students' differing attitudes toward discipline-specific skills and ethics. Several students discussed the importance of taking on work outside the University, not for the sake of money but in order to inform their degree and improve their practical skills. They suggested that such skills development should be encouraged or incorporated into the degree rather than being sought independently. For all of these students, the complete sets of capabilities on the framework were important; however, they differed in their opinions of whether the development of ethics should occur in class, on campus or outside University. The students all supported their argument by referring to international communications, global economics and employability.

Discipline-specific skills were the most important to *Bus1* because the "point of doing a degree was to get a job within that discipline". The capabilities on the list that she did not see as relating to this objective seemed to detract from her primary goal. On viewing the range of graduate capabilities, she admitted, "I'm a little bit worried that I'm going to get a very broad degree and I'm going to graduate and not really be... specialised." She cited the global economic crisis as an additional reason for courses to be structured in a way that was sympathetic to the needs of an employer. She suggested the University should encourage internships to avoid situations where graduates become disillusioned when their chosen field turns out to be different from what they had imagined and strived for.

Bus2 argued that his field changes too quickly for discipline-specific skills to be relevant to students (particularly those in their first year), who will not be joining the workforce until they have completed their degree. He therefore argued that it "doesn't really matter about what you learn in uni" and "we know that what we learn in uni is not going to be real, real world outside". By contrast, the communication and ethical skills he was developing were "all about society... how to deal with people, how to deal with resources" and so would be applicable and would "stay in your head for life". He expressed concern that his course was "still focused on the dollar sign" and that his lecturers never talked about "how to make choices ethically". Both *Bus1* and *Bus2* indicated that what they had learnt about ethics they had learnt through volunteer work rather than encouragement received on campus.

The fact that *Bus3*'s lecturers skipped over ethics examples in class (because "it's not examable" [sic]) encouraged her belief that ethics was not relevant to her degree. She did, however, appreciate the opportunity to engage with sustainability and environmental issues on campus outside class. She acknowledged that the experience of university was "not just about academic work" occurring in the classroom and that other skills which may seem irrelevant to the degree could be acquired by participating in a wider university community.

The idea that social interaction outside class or in group work provided the primary context for developing ethical and cross-cultural communication skills was popular among the participants of this project. *Bus3* showed that this was not always the case, saying:

> I just get a feeling like people are pretty much grouped in their own group... I don't think it's about racism though, it's more about the gap or the communication problems... new students in this uni and in this country as well, so they just define themselves, I'm international student, I don't belong to Australia; I don't belong to uni; I'm here just for my degree.

Cross-cultural communication, ethics and sustainability were also important to *Bus4*, who noted that he "seems to bring everything back to being a global citizen". He argued that in an international industry, cultural sensitivity was vital. However, although a recent school leaver, he felt that these were skills he already had and so he looked to university to develop the scholarship skills he would need in his future career:

> I feel I already have, so just the whole ethical, sustainability side of things, so understanding my position in the globe as well as being creative and innovative. But in the degree in particular, especially in uni, I'd like to develop the scholarship side of things, so being able to apply the knowledge and skills I get, being able to analyse situations I'm going to be in, to be able to integrate what I learnt at uni in the workforce hopefully.

This student's own ambition was to "work for companies with more corporate social responsibility". He observed that students already had their own ethical code and so the University should aim to refine those skills in conjunction with discipline-specific skills to develop students' awareness of the application of ethics in their field.

Faculty of Science

Four out of the five interviewees from Science were mature-aged students (though this doesn't reflect the proportion in science as a whole) who argued that one should develop ethical capabilities prior to university through life experience. One suggested that the University's mission to address such skills in a degree was "patronising". As a whole, the science students were primarily interested in developing their scholarship capabilities. Some suggested that the other capabilities were those that they would expect to be addressed in an arts degree or a degree with a particular focus on the environment rather than being incorporated into *every* degree and that generic skills would broaden the degree to the detriment of students' discipline-specific knowledge.

For *Sci1* it was important that the different capabilities supported one another as they developed:

> You can't get better problem-solving skills and research capability without improving your critical thinking, without improving the discipline-specific knowledge and without the want to continuously learn... you can't improve one without the other parts of it.

Here he focused on the skills identified with his own goals. He considered ethics and social skills in general to be of a different ilk. For example, he argued that social skills were "a personal thing" and that scholarly capabilities would not go under-developed as a result of non-social or non-communicative behaviour. When asked about the role of ethics and sustainability in his degree, he replied "I don't really notice much along those lines." However, he clarified this saying "I can see that it's there. I just don't think I'm at the point where it's something that I engage with much." In fact he noted a decrease in ethical and sustainability skills development since attending university:

> I'm probably less engaged with local and global citizens, ethical local and global citizens now than I was when I was at work... There's more of a flow of people around but you're still sort of segregated from those people... Socially, environmentally active and responsible: when we were at work... you always got a lot of training on how to deal with the public and in the environment, how to look after it... I've still got all that knowledge there so I still employ it but I don't, I'm not actively building on it as fast as I used to be. The things that are changing now, the discipline-specific knowledge, they're the things I'm really noticing big changes in.

The scholarship skills addressed *Sci2*'s expectations of university and he recognised the potential relevance of the engagement skills, which he was conscious of developing. However, he found it hard to identify crossover between the ideas he was concerned with in his degree and the concepts of ethics and sustainability. He believed sustainability was an issue belonging in an "environmental degree". He was only able to identify his engagement with sustainability in his second interview after it was directly tackled in an assignment. He indicated that it was a rare situation rather than an issue relating to his daily practice. *Sci2* was "more familiar with" and comfortable talking about "problem solving and research because that's relevant to what I'm studying and the critical and analytical section". Interestingly, *Arts3* had initially also suggested that sustainability was irrelevant to her degree until she participated in a science unit and argued instead that "environmentally responsibility is a huge thing… 'cause it's science so it's always – by nature it's a wasteful industry."

When asked if he had discussed matters of ethics in his classes, *Sci3* answered:

> No. I don't really have the time to socialise in the classroom… I don't have the time to just go down with other people and talk about their backgrounds or where they're from or what they're doing.

This answer indicates the student's immediate association of ethics with social interaction rather than ethics as a component of his discipline. *Sci3* provided an interesting perspective as he was a first-year student but also a full-time worker, completing a degree to advance his career. He argued that the aims of the University to produce graduates with a focus on sustainability would face difficulties in that:

> You can change the mentality of the students here as well, but once they go out and find a job, they will be reporting to a manager who perhaps has different views or different perspectives, and everything changes from there.

Younger students (from all faculties) expressed a hope that practical experience could be incorporated into their course. Mature-aged students, likewise, talked about the greater depth of understanding they felt they achieved by relating what they learnt to their practical experience. *Sci3* gave examples of the ways his study had altered his approach to work, including a higher level of analytical thinking and a greater consciousness of sustainability:

> Instead of going there like a robot and fixing it and get it to work the same way, I go with a different perspective. Try to understand why is it working that way, why is it behaving that way and could we get it to work better or save energy?

Sci1 had also commented on the way he engaged with the information he was learning through a new analytical appreciation for the machinery of his previous workplace:

> We used to use a lot of equipment at work which used that physics... we just got taught how to use them. But now that I'm learning the things behind them... I could effectively use them better... so I can see the practical placement.

Career aspirations made scholarship and communication appear to be the most important skills to *Sci4*. This student had initially done an arts degree and had chosen to return to university for a science degree. This seems to have informed her viewpoint in such a way that she identified arts with "nice to have" capabilities (those she had already developed) and science with the scholarship bracket (addressing those discipline-specific capabilities which inspired her return to study). She argued that arts students could learn more from the sciences than science students could learn from the arts. Her justification for this stance indicated that she identified science with applicable facts saying arts students "need, maybe, a bit of science", whereas arts have more to do with the development of social consciousness which "you don't really need it for science" apart from "some of the less adjusted kiddies [who] could use it".

For *Sci5*, giving back to the community (associated with ethics and sustainability) was a matter of human nature and not a motivation for a degree. She argued that, for the purposes of a degree, the scholarship capabilities were "by far the most important", followed by engagement:

> Maybe the least important, engaged and ethical, local, global citizens, not because I don't think that that's an important point but I

> don't think that you should have to do [them in] a degree that you undertake and pay for at university.

Voluntary experiences on campus might inform existing sustainability and ethical consciousness but *Sci5* believed it would be presumptuous for the University to try to instil values in its students who were at university for an education in a particular discipline.

Faculty of Human Sciences

The Faculty of Human Sciences at Macquarie takes in departments that in other universities might be spread between Humanities (such as Education) and Science (such as Psychology). It is telling, then, that the results of the interviews show a greater division of opinion than those from the previously discussed faculties. More than any other discipline, the Education students interviewed discussed ethics as conceptually inseparable from discipline-specific knowledge and skills. This was because they recognised that ethical practice was a constant component of their projected careers as teachers. They saw ethical skills being developed primarily through tutorial discussions and assignments as well as social integration. For the other students interviewed, ethical practice remained predominantly a personal matter although the University's social environment was considered particularly influential for developing those personal capabilities.

Humanities students, as well as students from Arts and Business and Economics, pointed out how much they could learn by talking to international students and those from different parts of Sydney. *Hum1* listed some of the capabilities she considered were developed through group discussions in her tutorials:

> Effective communication, being able to really kind of understand what other people are thinking and why they might say certain things. Socially active and responsible... by having the group discussions... [we] become a little bit more active in how we all communicate and get along together. Engaged and ethical local and global citizens... We're engaged in how the rest of the world is. Like it's not just this little insular Sydney bit, it's you know, we've got people from all over the place... I think that's great especially for ethical practice.

Hum1 was a little concerned that, following her initial introduction to university life, what she was learning about ethical practice and cultural variation was via a theoretical discussion about its application in a classroom rather than as a spontaneous communication between herself and her peers.

The attention that the University appeared to dedicate to 'being a good person' surprised *Hum2*. He remarked that "If I wasn't going to learn discipline-specific knowledge and skills I wouldn't come to uni" and he felt that very few of the skills listed actually addressed that aim. Even students who were concerned that in-class discussions of ethics and sustainability would diminish the time dedicated to scholarly skills approved of such issues being addressed in a separate sphere on campus. *Hum3* was positive about most of the capabilities; however, as she was aiming for a career as a teacher, the skills she valued most were those that she knew she would apply at work. She considered practices belonging predominantly in an academic context to be the least useful for her future career. When asked what skills would remain important following her degree she answered:

> Maybe not so much the essay writing but for some of my assignments like the one I've just been doing I had to plan lessons and things like that, which will be really helpful... [and] safety aspects.

Nevertheless, she recognised that her skills associated with writing, specifically critical thinking, were improving:

> I never had to do that in high school and that was one thing that at first I was taken aback by, but I've gotten so much better at it. And putting specific knowledge into different areas, because I used to be really vague and just try to chuck everything in just to show that I did know it.

Hum4 said that nothing had changed between her two interviews: however, the emphasis in her discussion of ethics and of discipline-specific skills indicated that her balancing of these concepts had continued to shift. Having the opportunity, in her first interview, to reflect on her experience in relation to the capabilities wheel made her realise how her attitude toward university had changed over time. She had enrolled in university with the aim "to learn and then get out", with a focus on acquiring discipline-specific knowledge and skills. Nevertheless, when looking at the list of student capabilities she saw that university was about "building people to not just do what they want to do but do what they want with respect to everyone else". She realised that having been exposed to a range of different people and ideas "rather than having just a piece of paper being the goal, it's your experience and anything else you can pack in there along the way is what it's really about now".

In her second interview, *Hum4* indicated that the way her course was taught led her to divide the capabilities more distinctly between what was interesting and what was relevant. She discussed the continual development of discipline-specific skills and research capability as essential to her objectives. She pointed out that her communication should, likewise, continue to improve as a result of class participation and assignments. Ethics, on the other hand, had not been presented as a continually relevant component of her education, with only scattered references from her lecturers and tutors, and she concluded that she didn't feel it was an integral part of her degree. Earlier in her second interview she spoke with approval of the incorporation of 'people and planet' subjects to the degree (providing languages units were offered). This indicates her continued interest in cultural awareness and engagement with the wider world despite the attitude she picked up from her lecturers that appeared to lead her to downplay its importance within university education.

Discussion

The picture that emerges from this modest study is the differential responses of students of various ages concerning what they frequently termed "personal capabilities". Mature-aged students often argued that many of the listed capabilities would more appropriately be engaged with through life-experience rather than university. Macquarie University's White Paper, 'Review and Renewal of Postgraduate Curriculum' (2009), indicates awareness of these students' concerns in a postgraduate context:

> The graduate capabilities developed through undergraduate education cannot be assumed as a starting point since postgraduates enter from many different points and with a wide variety of skill sets and experiences... which the curriculum should serve to enhance.

The six mature-aged students interviewed all indicated that it was also inappropriate to assume undergraduates were at the starting point of their own committed, ethical and professional lives; indeed, some suggested the implication within the initiative was patronising. Herein lies an example of the "messy policy challenge" alluded to by Krause (Chapter 21, this volume). Even a number of recent school-completers, although generally more comfortable with the inclusion in the graduate outcomes, argued that the ethics and sustainability capabilities were not new to them. The younger international students, without a previously established social circle in the country, tended to support the inclusion of these capabilities. They argued that these formed a part of the effective structure necessary for engaging with their study, building a social support group on campus and so helping them to develop skills which were "not just academic but how to do life and how to make decisions" (*Bus2*). Recent school-completers as well as mature-aged student *Hum4* noted that the university environment provided new opportunities to develop and apply their ethical perspectives (through discussions and friendships made within a wide social demographic) and identified resulting positive changes in their social and cultural outlook. Therefore, the extent to which the considerations of the curriculum review and renewal could effectively be carried over into the university's approach to undergraduate students is complicated by the wide range of undergraduate needs and the prominence of students who have only recently completed high-school.

The findings have implications for the promotion of such frameworks, which by their very nature are broad paradigms that cannot hope to correspond with the wide variation in attention and importance that students place either on the capabilities or university itself. Analysis of the interviews revealed students' tendency to establish particular contextual realms in which it would be more (or less) common or appropriate to engage with different capabilities. Social interaction outside class and in group discussions was considered by participants across the faculties to be vital for the development of ethical and communicative skills. Despite the importance a number of students placed on the development of their social consciousness, they continued to suggest that matters of ethical practice and sustainability were most appropriately developed through activities outside class. It could be argued, therefore, that the majority of students interviewed saw these as personal capabilities which, although they may be developed as a component of a university experience, are an optional feature which may or may not suit the current needs of particular students rather than being overall issues addressed seriously throughout all students' degrees.

Students primarily objected to the ethics and sustainability principles of the framework when they considered them irrelevant to their discipline. They seemed to believe that time would be taken in teaching to address 'how to be a good person' rather than considering ethics and sustainability as a component of their discipline. This explains why students who were opposed to ethics education as a part of the degree still approved of sustainability prompts on campus or the development of ethical skills which spontaneously occurred through group work and social interaction.

Viewed by faculty, the Arts students were the most supportive of the concept that a well-rounded education should include ethics and sustainability capabilities. The Business and Economics students displayed greatest interest in those skills that they argued would best prepare them for a successful career. Science students were more strongly opposed to the inclusion of ethics and sustainability (though we must also take into consideration that this group made up the largest number of mature-aged students). They contrasted these capabilities with the scholarly skills that they aligned more directly with their own objectives and their own discipline. The Human Sciences group exhibited a combination of these views, predominantly depending on the application of different skills within their particular department. Arts, Science and Human Science students particularly were inclined to use arguments concerning the different levels of (moral) responsibility they considered the University to have in relation to their scholarly, engaging, ethical and sustainable development.

Students' personal explanations of their purpose for studying go a fair way towards explaining their attitude to and engagement with different capabilities represented in the framework. Employability and realistic projected application of the capabilities play a large part in the value they consider each to have. *Sci4*'s original answer that what she wanted from her degree was "a degree" was similar to *Bus2*'s aim to "get a good mark and move on" and *Hum4*'s "learn and then get out". These comments suggest that first-year students display a product-versus-process dichotomy and are initially more interested in their own broader picture – what their *completed* degree would mean for their future destination – rather than actively taking time to consider the progress of their capability development throughout the act of completing their degree.

The nature of the interviewing process meant that students were encouraged to reach their opinions of the University's capability framework through reflection. Many of their answers indicate that these matters were not in the forefront of their minds. *Hum2* said that he thought the listed capabilities were "important things looking at them but I don't really think about them in general". When encouraged to consider these capabilities, however, some students (such as *Hum4*) did identify an unexpected and unexplored change in their personal motivations for studying. Throughout her interviews, *Hum4* became increasingly enthusiastic and excited as she continued to identify the deeper levels to her learning experience that she had not paid attention to previously. *Arts1*, similarly, talked about taking more from his experience by reflecting on previous on-campus experiences and feedback which made him appreciate both the effort he had put in and the improvements he was making.

Irrespective of the capability in focus, it was clear that the interviews (and therein the opportunity to frame the capability discussion and reflect on their achievement) were a useful exercise, without which many of these students would have had no real cause to reflect on engagement and capability. This indicates that although students can develop the capabilities 'accidentally', reflection does help them to engage in a more meaningful way with their degree and to develop the "confidence" and "self belief" referred to by *Arts4*. It also suggests that some caution needs to be taken in developing policy as, no matter how well intentioned, these types of one-size-fits-all framework have a whiff of the deficit model about them; a presumption that students have not had these experiences, do not have these capabilities and perhaps can only achieve them through university provision. This illustrates, therefore, the importance of recognising student diversity, individual motivations and prior experience at both the macro (policy) and micro (teaching and assessment) levels. As argued elsewhere in this book, this is especially important in the first year of study where engagement and, it seems, capability cannot be presumed as one thing or another.

References

ACER (2008) *Attracting, Engaging and Retaining: New Conversations About Learning*, Australian Student Engagement Report (Melbourne: Australian Council for Educational Research).

Barrie, S.C. (2004) 'A Research-Based Approach to Generic Graduate Attributes Policy', *Higher Education Research and Development*, 23/3, pp.261–75.

Barrie, S.C. (2006) 'Understanding What We Mean by the Generic Attributes of Graduates', *Higher Education*, 51, pp.215–41.

Boyatzis, R.E. (1998) *Transforming Qualitative Information: Thematic Analysis and Code Development* (Thousand Oaks: Sage).

Braun, V. and Clarke, V. (2006) 'Using Thematic Analysis in Psychology', *Qualitative Research in Psychology*, 3, pp.77–101.

Brew, A. (2010) 'Enhancing Undergraduate Engagement Through Research and Inquiry', *Australian Learning and Teaching Council National Teaching Fellow Report*. Retrieved from <http://www.altc.edu.au/resource-enhancing-undergraduate-engagement-research-enquiry-macquarie-2010>

Coates, H. (2006) *Student Engagement in Campus-based and Online Education: University Connections* (Abingdon: Routledge).

Foster, S., Long, G. and Snell, K. (1999) 'Inclusive Instruction and Learning for Deaf Students in Postsecondary Education', *Journal of Deaf Studies and Deaf Education*, 4, pp.225–35.

Gibbs, G. (2010) *Dimensions of Quality* (York: The Higher Education Academy). Retrieved from <http://www.heacademy.ac.uk/assets/York/documents/ourwork/evidence_informed_practice/Dimensions_of_Quality.pdf>

Hu, S. and Kuh, G.D. (2002) 'Being (Dis)engaged in Educationally Purposeful Activities: The Influences of Student and Institutional Characteristics', *Research in Higher Education*, 43/5, pp.555–75.

Jones, S., Evans, C. and Magierowski, R. (2007) 'A Vertically Integrated, Embedded Curriculum Enhances the Information Literacy Skills of Science Undergraduates', in *Enhancing Higher Education, Theory and Scholarship* (Proceedings of the 30th HERDSA Annual Conference, Adelaide) pp.285–92.

Kuh, G.D. (2001) 'Assessing What Really Matters to Student Learning: Inside the National Survey of Student Engagement', *Change*, 33/3, pp.10–17.

Kuh, G.D. (2008) *High Impact Educational Practices: What They Are, Who Has Access to Them and Why They Matter* (Washington: Association of American Colleges and Universities).

Macquarie University (2008) 'Review of Academic Programs' (White Paper, Sydney: Macquarie University). Retrieved from <http://www.mq.edu.au/provost/reports/docs/FINALWHITEPAPER_revised_17102008.doc>

Macquarie University (2009) 'Review and Renewal of Postgraduate Curriculum' (White Paper, Sydney: Macquarie University). Retrieved from <http://www.mq.edu.au/provost/reports/docs/WhitepaperFinal.pdf>

Oliver, B. (2010) *Assurance of Learning for Graduate Employability*. Retrieved from <http://web.me.com/beverleyoliver1/benchmarking/About.html>

QAA Scotland (2009) *Research-Teaching Linkages: Enhancing Graduate Attributes, Key Findings and Recommendations*. Retrieved from <http://www.enhancementthemes.ac.uk/documents/ResearchTeaching/leaflets/RTLKeyfindings.pdf>

Sen, A. (1979) 'Personal Utilities and Public Judgements: Or What's Wrong with Welfare Economics?', *Economic Journal*, 87, pp.537–58.

Stephenson, J. (1992) 'Capability and Quality in Higher Education', in Stephenson, J. and Weil, S. (eds) *Quality in Learning: A Capability Approach in Higher Education* (London: Kogan Page). Retrieved from <http://www.johnstephenson.net/qinlch1.pdf>

Stephenson, J. (1998) 'The Concept of Capability and Its Importance in Higher Education', in Stephenson, J. and Yorke, M. (eds) *Capability and Quality in Higher Education* (London: Kogan Page) pp.1–13.

Thompson, D.G. (2008) 'Software as a Facilitator of Graduate Attribute Integration and Student Self-Assessment', in Duff, A., Quinn, D., Green, M., Andre, K., Ferris, T. and Copeland, S. (eds) *ATN Assessment Conference 2008: Engaging Students in Assessment* (Adelaide: Australian Technology Network) pp.234–46. Retrieved from <http://reviewsecure.com/index.php?option=com_content&task=view&id=12&Itemid=6>

Treleaven, L. and Voola, R. (2008) 'Integrating the Development of Graduate Attributes Through Constructive Alignment', *Journal of Marketing Education*, 30/2, pp.160–73.

Walker, M. (2006) 'Towards a Capability-Based Theory of Social Justice for Education Policy-Making', *Journal of Education Policy*, 21/2, pp.163–85.

Yorke, M. and Harvey, L. (2005) 'Graduate Attributes and Their Development', *New Directions for Institutional Research*, 128, pp.41–58.

Chapter 8

First-year experience and effects on student learning outcomes: an Asian perspective

Beverley Webster and Wincy Chan

University of Melbourne and University of Hong Kong

Introduction

Hong Kong's economic wellbeing depends heavily upon its ability to become a knowledge-based economy. It is well accepted that human capital is its single most important asset and that the higher education sector is a key source of impetus for the development of this asset. Whether young people can face up to the challenges of a changing world depends significantly on the learning experiences during formal education. The Hong Kong government has initiated a major and bold territory-wide curriculum reform for the public education system. As a result of this reform the undergraduate curriculum will include an additional year and an outcomes-based curriculum. Universities in Hong Kong understand that the first year is a critical development stage for undergraduate students and so helping students to transit through the academic, psychological and social adjustments is a priority for universities as the new curriculum is implemented and evaluated.

Research on the quality of student learning in higher education strongly indicates that students develop deep learning approaches and achieve better learning outcomes when expectations of the course are clear to them and when teaching and learning activities are aligned to the stated learning outcomes (Biggs, 1996; Wilson and Fowler, 2005). Recent research shows this is also evident in Hong Kong (Webster et al., 2009). One of the most important initiatives of the current curriculum reform is the mandatory implementation of an outcomes-based approach to student learning in the undergraduate curriculum. The student approach to learning perspective focuses on how expected outcomes relate to the teaching and learning activities and the assessments of students in higher education. The focus shifts from what the teacher will deliver to what the student will learn. The approach is aligned with those aspects of the learning environment that encourage students to adopt deeper approaches to their learning (Andrich, 2002; Biggs, 1996).

In addition to academic performance, university graduates are expected to be equipped with the ability to think and act beyond their discipline knowledge. In Hong Kong, as elsewhere, this expectation has been highlighted by employers as not being very well met (Barrie, 2007). Providing students with learning experiences that promote the development of graduate attributes from the very beginning of their undergraduate education should be equal to the development of disciplinary knowledge. While there are ongoing debates relating to empirical measurements of generic outcomes, the positive influences of clear conceptualisation and communication of expectations for generic graduate attributes in the curriculum are evident in Hong Kong (Prosser and Trigwell, 1997; Chan, 2010). This aligns well with the implementation of an outcomes-based approach in the new curriculum.

In this chapter we will discuss a recent project in Hong Kong involving an investigation into the experiences of the first-year transition, course learning environment, approaches to learning and learning outcomes.

First-year experience

Existing research on the first-year experience (FYE) at universities suggests that first-year students' integration into the academic and social communities at university impacts greatly on their persistence in their undergraduate programme as well as on their intellectual, social and emotional wellbeing (Tinto, 1987; Tinto and Goodsell-Love, 1993). Central to understanding the phenomena of transition from secondary school to higher education is that first-year experiences can shape and influence the remaining experiences as an undergraduate. Latham and Green (1997) viewed the first year as a significant episode in which many changes are encountered while the student moves from a familiar environment to an unknown one. First-year experience research portrays this initial year of university as a critical stage of adjustment and substantial intellectual development (Harvey, Drew and Smith, 2006; Kuh et al., 2006; McInnis, 2001; Tinto, 1987; Tinto and Goodsell-Love, 1993). The difficulties in transition and adjustment coupled with the high withdrawal rate in some countries (particularly Australia, the US and the UK) have attracted extensive research about undergraduate education and the first-year experience (Harvey, Drew and Smith, 2006; Hurtado, Carter and Spuler, 1996; Tinto, 1987; Tinto and Goodsell-Love, 1993; Yorke and Longden, 2007).

Hong Kong institutions of higher education do not experience the high rates of student dropout seen in other countries, so retention is not a major concern. However, the student transition to higher education issues – such as the transition in relation to teaching and learning styles, induction to specific disciplinary knowledge, and academic and personal achievement of goals, which influence the student learning experience and student outcomes – are particularly salient in a time of such major curriculum reform and in a country where secondary education is still very much examination driven and teacher centred.

Tinto (1987) suggests that students undergo three stages as they move to higher education: (i) the disconnection from past communities (the secondary school, family and/or workplace), (ii) the transition between school and university, and (iii) incorporation into the university community. Existing studies generally confirm that first-year students are seriously challenged in the academic transition to university, having to shift from old study habits and styles of learning to those demanded by university. For example, Lowe and Cook (2003) found that first-year students struggled with academic demands, their workload and the need for more independent learning styles. Asmar et al. (2000) also found that transitional difficulties could be both intrinsic (personal responsibilities and adjustment difficulties) and extrinsic (lack of feedback on assessment, timetabling and the lack of access and availability of lecturers and tutors). Lam and Kwan (1999) found similar intrinsic and extrinsic factors including a lack of interaction with teachers and peers, teachers' lack of interest in a broad-based curriculum, insufficient space/resources for individual and collaborative work, difficulties with workload and a lack of interest in the subject. These factors all hindered first-year Hong Kong undergraduate students achieving their expectations of university.

Existing studies on academic induction have primarily focused on orientation programmes and study skills workshops offered to first-year students (Yorke and Longden, 2004; Krause et al., 2005). Such studies are normally not concerned with how first-year students are being inducted into their academic discipline and the extent to which they have acquired the academic discourse and gained understanding of the key concepts of the discipline. Crawford et al. (1994) researched students' conceptions of the discipline they are about to study and how that relates to their approach to study within the discipline. This showed that students are more likely to adopt surface approaches to learning if they enter first year with a less-sophisticated understanding of the discipline they choose to study. Others have studied the nature of teaching and learning in the courses they are entering and how this relates to student learning approaches (Minasian-Batmanian, Lingard and Prosser, 2006). Students entering first-year problem-based learning courses without prior conceptions of this mode of curriculum delivery were more likely to adopt more surface approaches (Duke et al., 1998; Hendry et al., 2006). More systematic approaches in orienting first-year students will result in positive learning experiences and outcomes (Krause et al., 2005).

Student learning in higher education

It is widely supported in the higher education literature that undergraduate students' perceptions of the learning environment and their approaches to study can influence student learning outcomes (Kreber, 2003; Lizzio, Wilson and Simons, 2002; Wilson and Fowler, 2005; Wilson, Lizzio and Ramsden, 1997). A deep approach to learning has been shown to enhance student outcomes such as better understanding, better conceptions of academic material and greater development of generic skills (Lizzio and Wilson, 2005; Lizzio, Wilson and Hadaway, 2007; Lizzio, Wilson and Simons, 2002; Trigwell and Prosser, 2004; Wilson and Fowler, 2005). Researchers into university student learning experiences have established a correlation between student approaches to learning and the quality of learning outcomes (Prosser and Trigwell, 1999; Ramsden, 2003). The relationship with course experiences, approaches to learning and academic outcomes was conceptualised in a 3P (presage, process, product) model by Biggs (1989). Biggs suggested that the relationships between the elements in the 3P model are best conceived as an interactive system. Prosser and Trigwell (1999) proposed a model where student perceptions of the course are represented by an interaction between certain characteristics of the student and the context of the course, and that students approach their studies in relation to these perceptions which in turn influences the outcomes (see Figure 8.1). They argue that the interpretation of the interactions in this model does not demonstrate a causal chain but that they are simultaneously present in the awareness of students.

There appears to be little argument that a deep approach to learning is desirable in higher education (Biggs and Tang, 2007; Wilson and Fowler, 2005). Apart from students' characteristics such as their motivations and prior experiences, students' learning approaches and learning outcomes are powerfully influenced by their perceptions of the learning context, such as perceptions of the teaching, workload and assessments (Gow and Kember, 1990; Prosser and Trigwell, 1999; Ramsden, 1991, 2003). Some studies have found relationships between student approaches to learning and the design of the curriculum in their courses (Hilliard, 1995; Newble and Clarke, 1986; Richardson, 2005). Students in medical

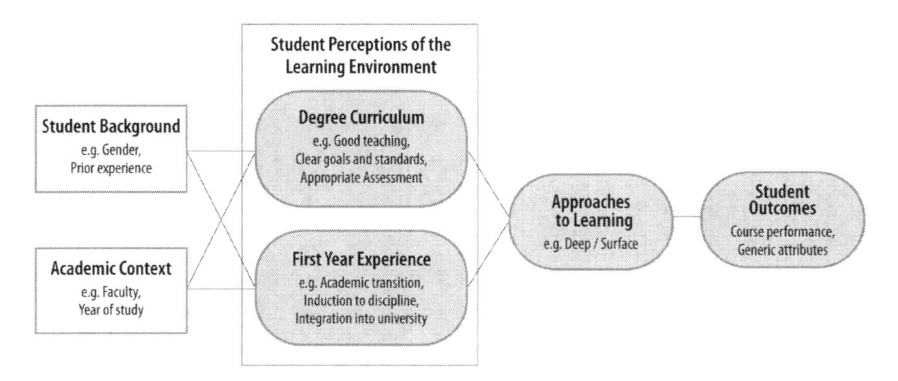

Figure 8.1: Influences of first-year experiences on undergraduate student learning and student outcomes

schools displayed more surface learning in first year where a traditional content-based curriculum is delivered, compared with those students in problem-based learning programmes who showed more deep learning approaches in these courses (Prince, 2004). According to Kember and Gow (1991), students will adopt a surface approach to learning if the curriculum demands it. So aiming for a curriculum, particularly in the transition stages, which demands a deeper approach has to be desirable in higher education.

Compared with Western students, Chinese students in secondary school experience much more rote learning, learning of model answers and preparation for extensive public examination systems. The delivery of the curriculum is well known for its didactic and transfer characteristics.

Conceptual framework for first-year experience in Hong Kong

An initial exploration has recently been conducted in a university in Hong Kong by a research team (Yang, Webster and Prosser, 2011) involving 42 students who, at the end of their first year of undergraduate study, participated in a series of focus groups to reflect on their learning experiences. The purpose of the exploratory focus groups was to identify common ways in which students experienced, conceptualised, perceived and understood various aspects of phenomena in their learning in the first year. The results of these focus-group interviews, although not able to be generalised, showed some interesting findings worthy of further research in the Chinese context. In relation to induction to the discipline, it was evident that by the end of the first year many of these students were not able to provide much evidence of an understanding of their discipline. Many students indicated difficulties in the transition in terms of teaching and learning styles that confronted them as new undergraduates and of how these differed markedly from secondary school. The induction process for these students was more of an orientation to university and, although appreciated, it was perceived to be of little help in relation to disciplinary academic induction.

Based on these results, the researchers developed a survey of first-year experiences. They initially piloted it with 200 students and then with a larger sample (N=1,092), focusing on teaching strategies, achievement

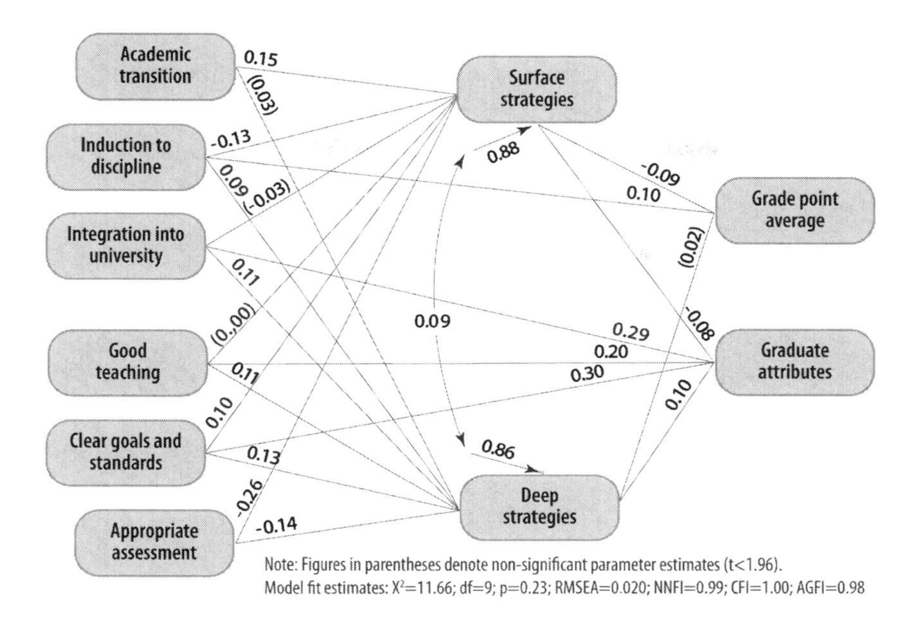

Figure 8.2: Structural model for first-year experience on student learning and outcomes

goals and elements of a cooperative learning environment (Webster and Yang, 2009). The survey included the well-known constructs of the Course Experience Questionnaire (Wilson, Lizzio and Ramsden, 1997) and the Study Process Questionnaire (Biggs, 1986), in addition to a set of items intended to be indicators of students' perceptions of their transition to university, such as induction to the discipline, academic transition and achievement of academic and personal goals. The initial analysis provided some evidence that these issues of transition could be related to perceptions of the course learning experience. Taking the previous discussion and Chinese context into account, the following conceptual model (see Figure 8.2) is presented as a basis for this proposed research study.

In this model, student transition experiences will include difficulties in the transition to academic study, induction to the academic discipline and integration into the wider university community. Transition experiences are believed to be an important part of the total first-year university experience. While students' perceptions of the academic course are a function of how students go about their learning, transition experiences are hypothesised to interact with student approaches to learning in a similar way. As we begin to provide scientific evidence to support this hypothesis we can encourage teachers of first-year undergraduate courses to focus on these transition issues.

The present study

The present study involved the application of three major surveys and the collection of student outcome measures. The Student Learning Experience Questionnaire (SLEQ) was developed by a team of academics and researchers and tested among students to provide feedback to faculties as part of a quality assurance exercise. The SLEQ provides evidence to support teaching and learning initiatives at a particular time of major curriculum reform. The SLEQ has been administered annually and undergone several revisions based on feedback from faculties and students. The SLEQ is administered to all first- and final-year students in the university. The survey is not compulsory and students have the option of completing the survey online or on paper. The SLEQ consists of the following sections: 'students' perceptions of the learning environment', 'approaches to learning' and 'student learning outcomes'.

Perceptions of the learning environment were measured by the Student Course Experience Questionnaire (SCEQ; Ginns, Prosser and Barrie, 2007). The SCEQ is found to be a valid measure for university students' perceptions of 'good teaching', 'clear goals and standards' and 'appropriate assessment' in Hong Kong (Webster et al., 2009). The SLEQ includes an additional three scales to examine the different dimensions of the 'first year transition experience' (FYE). The FYE scales were developed and validated locally (Webster and Chan, 2009; Webster and Yang, 2009). Webster and Chan (2009) also found that positive transition experiences were linked to deep learning approaches and positive academic performance. The present study included an 'academic transition scale' (5 items), 'induction to discipline scale' (5 items), and 'integration into university scale' (5 items).

Student approaches to learning were measured by a shortened version of the Study Process Questionnaire (SPQ; Biggs, 1987). It examines deep and surface-level learning in terms of motive and strategy. Webster et al. (2009) found that, for both Science and Humanities first-year undergraduates in Hong Kong, those who perceived teaching as good and goals and standards as clear were those who used deeper strategies in learning, whereas those who rated assessment tasks and workload as inappropriate were also those who were likely to use surface learning strategies. These relationships were consistent with those found in Western samples (for example, Prosser and Trigwell, 1999; Lizzio, Wilson and Simons, 2002).

Student learning outcomes included the cumulative grade-point average at the end of the first year (Range from 1.0 to 4.0) and eight items relating to the development of graduate attributes. These items measured students' perceptions of their development of generic attributes including 'analytical skills', 'problem solving', 'lifelong learning', 'self-reflection', 'collaboration', 'empathy', 'cultural understanding' and 'global citizenship'. Students were asked respond to such items on a 5-point scale, from 1=strongly disagree to 5=strongly agree.

The sample

The sample included all first-year undergraduate students of a research-intensive university in Hong Kong in the 2008–9 academic year. Data were collected from 1,765 students. The response rate here was 56.3 per cent. Respondents represented all faculties and included the humanities- and science-related disciplines. The analysis for this chapter included 734 cases with no missing variables.

Data analysis

Confirmatory factor analysis was performed using LISREL 8.80 (Jöreskog and Sörbom, 1996) to test the measurement models. A robust maximum likelihood (RML) approach was used to estimate the goodness-of-fit indices between the data and the specific models based on an asymptotic covariance matrix. A weighted measure of composite reliability (r_c) was estimated for each of the scales using the RML regression estimates and error variance estimates from the LISREL output (Rowe, 2006). Structural equation modelling was used to test the hypothesised model (see Figure 8.1). Assessment of model fit included the conventional χ^2 test of significance, rejected at $p<0.05$ level; the comparative fit index

(CFI; Bentler, 1990) and non-normed fit index (NNFI; Bollen, 1989); the adjusted goodness-of-fit index (AGFI; Jöreskog and Sörbom, 1982), for which values >0.90 and >0.95 indicate moderate and good fit to the data, respectively; and the root mean square error of approximation (RMSEA; Steiger, 1990), for which values <0.50 and <0.80 reflect good and moderate fit to the data, respectively. Independent samples t-tests were used to compare the scale means between the sample and student responses from the preceding year.

Results

Goodness-of-fit of measurement models

Goodness-of-fit statistics showed that the measurement models are a good fit with the data (Table 8.1). The significant covariances between pairs of independent variables in the models were specified (Byrne, 1998) and the number of parameters being observed was explained by the degrees of freedom. The composite reliabilities (r_c) estimates indicated a moderate to good reliability for the nine scales.

Scale	$\chi 2$	*df*	p	RMSEA	NNFI	CFI	AGFI	r_c
Academic transition	3.40	3	0.334	0.013	1.00	1.00	0.97	0.850
Induction to discipline	1.37	4	0.850	0.000	1.00	1.00	0.99	0.885
Integration into university	4.92	3	0.178	0.030	0.99	1.00	0.98	0.809
Good teaching	3.81	4	0.433	0.000	1.00	1.00	0.97	0.905
Clear goals & standards	1.64	2	0.440	0.000	1.00	1.00	0.99	0.698
Appropriate assessment	2.26	1	0.132	0.042	1.00	1.00	0.98	0.816
Graduate attributes	23.28	17	0.141	0.022	1.00	1.00	0.96	0.802
Surface strategies	2.210	1	0.137	0.041	0.99	1.00	0.98	0.656
Deep strategies	0.190	1	0.662	0.000	1.01	1.00	1.00	0.663

Table 8.1: Fit estimates of one-factor congeneric measurement models

Relationships between student outcomes and learning experiences and approaches

LISREL analysis confirmed that the hypothesised model was a good fit to the data. The results showed that those students who were well inducted to the academic discipline and well integrated into the university community were more likely to adopt deep strategies in their learning. Positive induction to the discipline was also found to promote better academic performance, while there was a positive relationship between integration into university and development of graduate attributes. At the same time, good teaching and clear goals and standards were found to influence deep learning directly, as well as directly and indirectly promote positive development of graduate attributes. Not surprisingly, surface learning strategies were found to be negatively associated with both academic and generic student outcomes. Students who perceived their first-year transition into academic study as difficult were also those who used surface strategies to approach their learning. Students who felt they had been adequately inducted into the academic discipline were less likely to develop surface strategies and more likely to achieve better academic outcomes. Clear goals and standards were found to be positively associated with both surface and deep learning strategies. On the other hand, appropriate assessment was found to be negatively associated with both surface and deep strategies.

Enhancement in student learning experiences

Compared to their counterparts from the previous year, first-year students perceived significantly more positive experiences in regards to induction into the discipline and integration into university; however, the effect sizes of these differences are small (see Table 8.2). These students also considered the teaching to be significantly better with clearer goals and standards. The perception of the development of graduate attributes was also significantly higher for this group of students.

	2008-09		2007-08		t-test		effect size
Scale	mean	SD	mean	SD	t	p	d
Academic transition	3.50	.753	3.58	.738	1.86	0.063	.11
Induction to discipline	3.60	.571	3.52	.586	2.33	0.020	.14
Integration into university	3.70	.604	3.56	.630	4.18	<0.001	.23
Good teaching	3.27	.689	3.14	.651	3.33	0.001	.19
Clear goals & standards	3.31	.723	3.03	.752	6.81	<0.001	.38
Appropriate assessment	3.00	.805	3.04	.735	0.94	0.347	.05
Graduate attributes	3.62	.462	3.56	.435	2.25	0.025	.13
Grade point average	2.94	.610	2.91	.495	1.01	0.312	.05

Table 8.2: t-Test results of mean differences

Discussion

When considering the first year of undergraduate education experience and the relationships evident in the conceptual model, we see confirmation of existing and well-known phenomena, such as that the students who perceive the teaching to be good and the goals and expectations to be clear are also those students who adopt deeper approaches to their learning. In addition, these students feel they have more opportunities to develop graduate attributes even in their first year of study.

Much attention is paid to the issues of transition from secondary school to tertiary education and the differences that students experience in relation to the teaching and learning environment, types of assessment, workload and modes of learning. These issues did not have significant effects on student approaches to learning or learning outcomes within this study. It was observed, however, that students who indicated more difficulties with these issues of transition were also students who adopted more surface approaches to learning. There was a strong and significant effect of induction into the discipline and academic achievement: those students who felt they had a better understanding of their specific discipline area were also students who did academically better. This suggests there should be a focus on promoting a better understanding of the discipline and its key concepts, the areas of the relationship between the courses students take, the connection between individual courses and the overall programme. It is well known that students who do not feel a sense of belonging to the institution are more likely to struggle, to drop out and/or to do poorly in their first year. In this study, students who had a better experience of being integrated, in terms of fitting in, feeling positive and having meaningful interactions with staff and other students, were also those students who indicated they had opportunities to better develop graduate attributes directly and indirectly through adopting deeper approaches to learning. In this study we included items about being intellectually stimulated by academics and peers as part of the measurement of integration and it is recognised that, whilst integration can occur in class, it can also be a product of co-curricular activities. It seems that it is also in these extra-curricular activities that undergraduates have more opportunities to develop graduate attributes.

When we look at the differences in the data from the two years of this study, whilst the size of the differences is not large, we still see some interesting but explainable results. For each of the constructs of interest in this chapter, there is a difference between the first- and second-year data. In the second year there are improvements in the students' perceptions in all areas. The most noticeable difference is in the clarity of the goals and standards, which can be clearly explained by the implementation of an outcomes-based approach to the curriculum where a significant focus is on the student's understanding of the course, its outcomes and the assessment tasks and what the connections are between them. There is also a medium-sized difference in the perception of the quality of teaching; again, this could be explained by, firstly, the outcomes-based implementation and, secondly, the university's emphasis on quality issues related to teaching and learning (in the most part a result of a government quality assurance exercise of teaching and learning in higher education). This university has channelled many resources into teaching and learning and a significant amount of professional development has occurred in recent semesters. Another area where we see improvement in student perceptions is integration into the university, where students feel they are more positive, have a greater sense of belonging and consider that interactions with peers and teachers are intellectually stimulating. At this university there have been many initiatives in relation to the broadening of the curriculum to include more opportunities for experiential learning, the taking of general education courses and participation in activities and courses from outside the student's own faculty. These will all help to make students feel more integrated into the university as a community and the research results could be a reflection of these particular initiatives.

There is evidence of some small changes in student perceptions of the opportunities to develop graduate attributes. At this university there are a set of university-level outcomes which have been articulated, passed at senate level and published on the university website. All students are presented with these in their course outlines and they are included in the student learning experience survey. It is possible that all these activities can account for some of the changes in perceptions about graduate attributes and the changes might be more about awareness raising than actual attainment. However, it is considered important that students are aware of the attributes that the university is promoting and that students can see where in the curriculum these opportunities are being afforded. It is a requirement that all programmes articulate the set of university-level outcomes throughout the courses that make up the programme.

In summary, we can see that there are positive effects of the changes on student approaches to learning and student learning outcomes. The introduction of an outcomes-based approach has been presented as a plausible explanation for these positive changes in conjunction with the raising of the profile of teaching and learning at this particular institution.

References

Andrich, D. (2002) 'A Framework Relating Outcomes Based Education and the Taxonomy of Educational Objectives', *Studies in Educational Evaluation*, 28, pp.35–59.

Asmar, C., Brew, A., McCulloch, M., Peseta, T. and Barrie, S. (2000) *Report on the First Year Experience Project* (Sydney: The University of Sydney, Institute for Teaching and Learning).

Barrie, S.C. (2007) 'A Conceptual Framework for the Teaching and Learning of Generic Graduate Attributes', *Studies in Higher Education*, 32, pp.439–58.

Bentler, P.M. (1990) 'Comparative Fit Indexes in Structural Models', *Psychological Bulletin*, 107, pp.238–46.

Biggs, J.B. (1986) *Student Approaches to Learning and Studying* (Melbourne, Victoria: Australian Council for Educational Research).

Biggs, J.B. (1987) *Student Approaches to Learning and Studying* (Hawthorn, Victoria: Australian Council for Educational Research Melbourne).

Biggs, J.B. (1989) 'Approaches to the Enhancement of Tertiary Teaching', *Higher Education Research and Development*, 8, pp.7–25.

Biggs, J.B. (1996) 'Enhancing Teaching through Constructive Alignment', *Higher Education*, 32, pp.347–64.

Biggs, J. and Tang, C. (2007) *Teaching for Quality Learning* (Buckingham: Society for Research into Higher Education and Open University Press).

Bollen, K.A. (1989) *Structural Equations with Latent Variables* (New York: John Wiley and Sons).

Byrne, B.M. (1998) *Structural Equation Modeling with LISREL, PRELIS, and SIMPLIS: Basic Concepts, Applications and Programming* (Mahwah: Lawrence Erlbaum Associates).

Chan, W.S.C. (2010) 'Generic Skills Development in the Students' Approaches to Learning Paradigm', paper presented at the International Symposium on Higher Education Quality Assurance, Macao Polytechnic Institute, Macau.

Crawford, K., Gordon, S., Nicholas, J. and Prosser, M. (1994) 'Conceptions of Mathematics and How It Is Learned: The Perspectives of Students Entering University', *Learning and Instruction*, 4, pp.331–45.

Duke, M., Forbes, H., Hunter, S. and Prosser, M. (1998) 'Problem-based Learning (PBL): Conceptions and Approaches of Undergraduate Students of Nursing', *Advances in Health Sciences Education*, 3, pp.59–70.

Ginns, P., Prosser, M. and Barrie, S. (2007) 'Students' Perceptions of Teaching Quality in Higher Education: The Perspective of Currently Enrolled Students', *Studies in Higher Education*, 32, pp.603–15.

Gow, L. and Kember, D. (1990) 'Does Higher Education Promote Independent Learning', *Higher Education*, 19, pp.307–22.

Harvey, L., Drew, S. and Smith, M. (2006) *The First Year Experience: A Literature Review for the Higher Education Academy* (Heslingon, UK: The Higher Education Academy).

Hendry, G.D., Lyon, P.M., Prosser, M. and Sze, D. (2006) 'Conceptions of Problem-based Learning: The Perspectives of Students Entering a Problem-based Medical Program', *Medical Teacher*, 28, pp.573–5.

Hilliard, R.I. (1995) 'How Do Medical Students Learn: Medical Student Learning Styles and Factors That Affect These Learning Styles', *Teaching and Learning in Medicine*, 7, pp.201–10.

Hurtado, S., Carter, D. and Spuler, A. (1996) 'Latino Student Transition to College: Assessing Difficulties and Factors in Successful College Adjustment', *Research in Higher Education*, 37, pp.135–57.

Jöreskog, K.G. and Sörbom, D. (1982) *LISREL V: Analysis of Linear Structural Relationships by Maximum Likelihood and Least Squares Methods (Program Manual)* (Chicago: International Educational Services).

Jöreskog, K.G. and Sörbom, D. (1996) *LISREL 8 User's Reference Guide* (Chicago: Scientific Software International Inc.).

Kember, D. and Gow, L. (1991) 'A Challenge to the Anecdotal Stereotype of the Asian Student', *Studies in Higher Education*, 16, pp.117–28.

Krause, K., Hartley, R., James, R., and McInnis, C. (2005) 'The First Year Experience in Australian Universities: Findings from a Decade of National Studies', <http://www.griffith.edu.au/centre/gihe/aboutus/klk_publications/FYEReport05.pdf>, assessed 10 August 2007.

Kreber, C. (2003) 'The Relationship Between Students' Course Perception and Their Approaches to Studying in Undergraduate Science Courses: A Canadian Experience', *Higher Education Research and Development*, 22, pp.57–75.

Kuh, G.D., Kinzie, J., Buckley, J., Bridges, B. and Hayek, J. (2006) *What Matters to Student Success: A Review of the Literature. Final Report for the National Postsecondary Education Cooperative and National Center for Education Statistics* (Bloomington: Indiana University Center for Postsecondary Research).

Lam, B.H. and Kwan, K.P. (1999) 'Student Expectations of University Education', in Jones, J. and Kwan, K.P. (eds) *Evaluation of the Student Experience Project* (Hong Kong: Center for the Enhancement of Learning and Teaching, City University of Hong Kong) pp.11–20.

Latham, G. and Green, P. (1997) 'The Journey to University: A Study of the First Year Experience'. Retreived from <http://ultibase.rmit.edu.au/Articles/dec97/greenlath1.htm>

Lizzio, A. and Wilson, K. (2005) 'Self-managed Learning Groups in Higher Education: Students' Perceptions of Process and Outcomes', *British Journal of Educational Psychology*, 75, pp.373–90.

Lizzio, A., Wilson, K. and Hadaway, V. (2007) 'University Students' Perceptions of a Fair Learning Environment: A Social Justice Perspective', *Assessment and Evaluation in Higher Education*, 32, pp.195–213.

Lizzio, A., Wilson, K. and Simons, R. (2002) 'University Students' Perceptions of the Learning Environment and Academic Outcomes: Implications for Theory and Practice', *Studies in Higher Education*, 27, pp.27–52.

Lowe, H. and Cook, A. (2003) 'Mind the Gap: Are Students Prepared for Higher Education', *Journal of Further and Higher Education*, 27, pp.53–76.

McInnis, C. (2001) 'Researching the First Year Experience: Where to From Here', *Higher Education Research and Development*, 20, pp.105–14.

Minasian-Batmanian, L.C., Lingard, J. and Prosser, M. (2006) 'Variation in Student Reflections on Their Conceptions of and Approaches to Learning Biochemistry in a First-year Health Sciences' Service Subject', *International Journal of Science Education*, 28, pp.1,887–904.

Newble, D.I. and Clarke, R.M. (1986) 'The Approaches to Learning of Students in a Traditional and in an Innovative Problem-based Medical School', *Medical Education*, 20, pp.267–73.

Prince, M. (2004) 'Does Active Learning Work? A Review of the Research', *Journal of Engineering Education*, 93, pp.223–31.

Prosser, M. and Trigwell, K. (1997) 'Using Phenomenography in the Design of Programs for Teachers in Higher Education', *Higher Education Research and Development*, pp.41–54.

Prosser, M. and Trigwell, K. (1999) *Understanding Learning and Teaching: The Experience in Higher Education* (Philadelphia: Open University Press).

Ramsden, P. (1991) 'A Performance Indicator of Teaching Quality in Higher Education: The Course Experience Questionnaire', *Studies in Higher Education*, 16, pp.129–50.

Ramsden, P. (2003) *Learning to Teach in Higher Education* (London: RoutledgeFalmer).

Richardson, J.T.E. (2005) 'Students' Approaches to Learning and Teachers' Approaches to Teaching in Higher Education', *Educational Psychology. Special Issue: Developments in educational psychology: How far have we come in 25 years?*, 25, pp.673–80.

Rowe, K. (2006) 'Paper 6: School Performance: Single-level and Multilevel Analyses of Australian State/Territory Comparisons of Students' Achievements in International Studies', paper presented at the ACSPRI Social Science Methodology Conference.

Steiger, J.H. (1990) 'Structural Model Evaluation and Modification: An Interval Estimation Approach', *Multivariate Behavioural Research*, 25, pp.173–80.

Tinto, V. (1987) 'The Principles of Effective Retention', paper presented at the Maryland College Personnel Association Fall Conference, Prince George's Community College, Largo, MD.

Tinto, V. and Goodsell-Love, A. (1993) 'Building Community', *Liberal Education*, 79, pp.16–21.

Trigwell, K. and Prosser, M. (2004) 'Development and Use of the Approaches to Teaching Inventory', *Educational Psychology Review. Special Issue: Measuring Studying and Learning in Higher Education – Conceptual and Methodological Issues*, 16, pp.409–24.

Webster, B.J. and Chan, W.S.C. (2009) 'First Year Transition Experiences and Effects on Student Outcomes', paper presented at the 32nd HERDSA Annual Conference, Darwin, Australia.

Webster, B.J., Chan, W.S.C., Prosser, M.T. and Watkins, D.A. (2009) 'Undergraduates' Learning Experience and Learning Process: Quantitative Evidence from the East', *Higher Education*, 58, pp.375–86.

Webster, B.J. and Yang, M. (2009) *Transition, Induction and Goal Achievement: First Year Experiences of Hong Kong Undergraduates*. Manuscript submitted for publication.

Wilson, K. and Fowler, J. (2005) 'Assessing the Impact of Learning Environments on Students' Approaches to Learning: Comparing Conventional and Action Learning Designs', *Assessment and Evaluation in Higher Education*, 30, pp.87–101.

Wilson, K., Lizzio, A. and Ramsden, P. (1997) 'The Development, Validation and Application of the Course Experience Questionnaire', *Studies in Higher Education*, 22, pp.33–53.

Yang, M., Webster, B.J. and Prosser, M.T. (2008) *Exploring the Variation in First Year Undergraduates' Induction into Their Academic Discipline*. Manuscript submitted for publication.

Yang, M., Webster, B. and Prosser, M. (2011) 'Exploring the Variation in First Year Undergraduates' Induction into their Academic Discipline', *International Journal for the Scholarship of Teaching and Learning*, 5.

Yorke, M. and Longden, B. (2004) *Retention and Student Success in Higher Education* (Maidenhead: Society for Research in Higher Education and Open University Press).

Yorke, M. and Longden, B. (2007) *The First Year Experience in Higher Education in the UK: Report on Phase 1 of a Project Funded by the Higher Education Academy* (York: The Higher Education Academy).

Chapter 9

'This was really different!' Alternative perspectives on the student experience of assessment: alienation and engagement

Kay Sambell

Northumbria University, UK

From 'assessment of learning' to 'assessment for learning'

This chapter focuses on students' experiences of engagement in the context of assessment. It explores one case study, which formed part of a university-wide attempt to promote Assessment for Learning (AfL), based on strong arguments in the research literature that higher education assessment practices need to be rethought and renewed. The case for reform (Birenbaum, 2003; Segers, Dochy and Cascaller, 2003; Boud and Associates, 2010; Carless, 2005; ASKE, 2010) has been predicated on the view that dominant discourses of assessment as 'measurement' (the assessment of learning) have left us with a legacy of assessment methods which might well serve the purpose of producing numerical marks and differentiating between students, but are of much less value in developing and evaluating authentic and worthwhile performances of understanding, application, creativity and commitment.

In response, holistic and complex models of AfL have begun to emerge in university education (see, for example, Carless, Joughin and Mok, 2006; Gibbs and Simpson, 2004; Nicol, 2009). These tend to be based upon educational principles rather than specific techniques, with a view to re-engineering learning and teaching environments to promote students' active engagement with summative and formative assessment tasks. They suggest that assessment can be used to foster effective conditions for learning by placing student involvement, effort and activity at the heart of assessment design. There is a close match between the philosophical premises of AfL and the principles of engagement that Chickering and Gamson (1991) promote to staff, which include contact, reciprocity, active learning, prompt feedback, time on task, communication of high expectations and respect for diverse talents and ways of learning.

The Northumbria model of Assessment for Learning

At Northumbria University our particular model of AfL (McDowell, Sambell and Davison, 2009) has developed from a significant foundation of empirical research investigating the students' experience of assessment. Our approach means that students benefit from assessment that does far more than simply test what they know. Figure 9.1 illustrates our Centre for Excellence in Teaching and Learning (CETL) model in a form that has been used to stimulate review and development of assessment practice across the university.

The six inter-related principles view learning as an active, dynamic process, in which students learn by actively making connections and organising learning into meaningful concepts and understandings (Barkley, 2009). A presiding belief is that, appropriately framed, assessment practices can help us move strongly away from overly didactic or transmission-based teaching methodologies, thereby encouraging our students to focus on developing an enduring understanding (Sadler, 2009) and to share responsibility for learning with their teachers (Black and Wiliam, 2009). The ultimate goal is to develop students' abilities to direct their own learning, evaluate their own progress and support the learning of others. Student engagement in assessment is, then, of paramount importance.

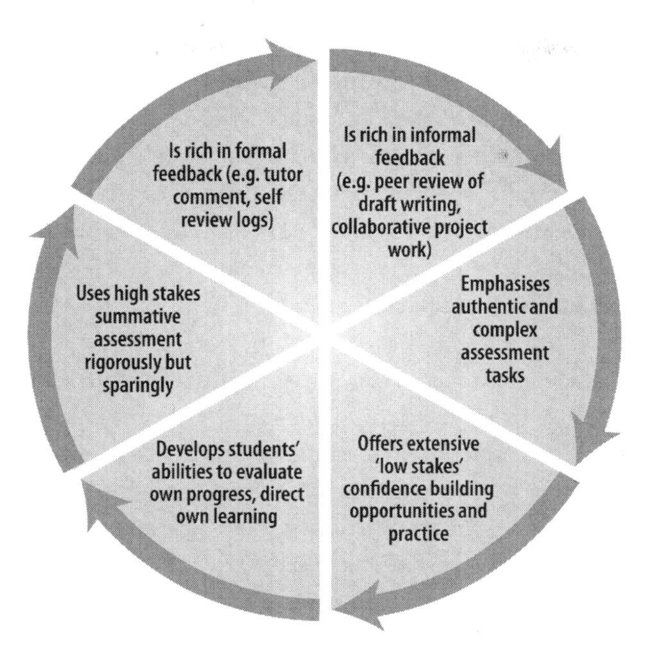

Figure 9.1: Northumbria University AfL model

The dominance of the metaphors of 'deep' and 'surface' approaches to learning

Assessment reform often seeks to use assessment to promote deep approaches to learning. Within the literature and in teachers' discourse, this metaphor has come to epitomise the core values of higher education (Case, 2008; Haggis, 2003) and can be seen as equivalent to engagement. A deep approach is broadly characterised by a learner's intention to understand material, to look for integrating principles and ideas, to question and make new sense of a subject area. Within this framework, when we say individuals 'understand' something within a particular domain, what we are really saying is that they are capable of relating to a context in the way that a specialist in that discipline does (Ramsden, 2003).

Research on student learning, however, has consistently revealed that students often tend to adopt either a surface approach to study, typified by a focus on rote learning, memorisation, regurgitation, a lack of reflection and a preoccupation with task-completion (Marton and Säljö, 1976), or a strategic approach, characterised by a focus on assessment requirements and lecturer expectations, and a careful organisation of time and effort focused on the intention to gain high grades (Ramsden, 2003; Biggs and Tang, 2007; Marton, Hounsell and Entwistle, 1997). This is a cause for concern, because it suggests that the student is not actively involved in trying to understand the subject or in the process of study itself. In other words, a surface approach represents a lack of engagement.

Summative assessment, in particular, has frequently been seen as a significant feature with regard to surface – or disengaged – approaches to learning. From the 1970s, studies began to show that students' perceptions of the demands of assessment influenced their approaches to learning more heavily than teaching. Snyder (1970), for instance, explored the ways in which the formal curriculum emphasised high-order educational goals, such as independent thinking, analysis, problem-solving ability and originality, but from the student viewpoint, assessment and teaching procedures suggested that memorising facts and theories were what was really needed to achieve success.

Anxiety about the backwash (Watkins, Dahlin and Eckholm, 2005) of assessment on students' approaches to learning has driven much assessment reform. For example, Ramsden (1992, p.68) warns that "unsuitable assessment methods impose irresistible pressures on students to take the wrong approach to learning tasks." Gibbs and Simpson (2004, p.25) draw attention to the influence of the design of assessment tasks and "the quality of student engagement," highlighting the dangers of assessment designs which embody "low level demands" and result in "surface approaches to learning." Nicol (2009) advises that assessment tasks should "engage students in deep not just shallow learning activity" and "promote students' productive engagement in learning". Our own research (Sambell and McDowell, 1998; Sambell, McDowell and Brown, 1997) highlighted the extent to which students typified 'traditional' assessment tasks as valuing surface approaches to learning, whilst 'innovative or alternative' assessments endorsed deep approaches.

Often, carefully designed 'authentic' assessment (Torrance, 1995; McCune, 2009) is regarded as a powerful means of fostering the features and characteristics of deep approaches to learning. Here, lecturers seek to match the assessment of educational courses to the key aims and intended outcomes of their courses, so that the students find tasks inherently meaningful. Additionally, instead of tasks being designed in isolation, or tacked onto learning as an afterthought, effective assessment is integrated as fully as possible into the learning experience. This helps students see the point of all the learning activities they are required to do leading up to a high-stakes assessment task. Biggs (1996) has referred to this process as an attempt to achieve 'constructive alignment' between our learning, teaching and assessment approaches. The notion of 'constructive alignment', like the metaphors of deep and surface approaches to learning, has exerted a powerful hold on the discourses of teachers and educational developers in higher education, presumably because it implies that the power to generate 'good' learning – or engagement – lies within the reach of staff.

Case study: designing an authentic assessment task to improve student learning

This chapter focuses on staff and student views of authentic and integrated AfL assessment practices in a second-year option that students from a range of discipline areas on a joint honours course could elect to study. Its topic was educational theory, although there was no supposition that students would ultimately become teachers. The module designer wanted to encourage her students to engage with educational concepts and philosophies and think about what they might mean in practice, especially in relation to promoting effective approaches to learning. Twenty-six students elected to take the module, which ran over one semester. The course was organised around a series of interactive lectures, workshops and a project, in which students were asked to produce some learning materials that might help first-year students to appreciate the nature of effective study.

The summative assessment required the production of guides to learning which would be suitable for first-year undergraduates. Students chose a variety of formats, including booklets, catalogues, DVDs, games and leaflets. Learners could decide to work alone, or with others, to produce these materials. The guides took shape gradually and, as the module progressed, 'teaching' sessions were given over to their design and development, with ample opportunity for student–student and staff–student dialogue. Each individual submitted a brief reflective commentary that theorised the materials.

The lecturer (who is also the author of this chapter) was interviewed and observed by a researcher working on the CETL research programme. When the interview data were analysed by the research team, she routinely used the metaphors of deep and surface approaches and the principle of constructive alignment to describe the rationale for her AfL assessment design. For instance, she claimed to have devised the assessment task in the hope that students would experience it as "challenging, relevant and meaningful in its own right" because she wanted them "to understand and take a deep approach to the subject, applying the concepts, rather than putting in huge undigested swathes of secondary reading" to their assignments. She also wanted them to "get a sense of why the subject matters," by applying ideas in context, rather than "superficially going through the motions by including stuff from the reading list." She explained that she had specified a "real audience" for the guides to "push students into making their own sense of the subject," because she felt strongly that "authenticity matters." The concept of authenticity is, of course, a relative one (Gulikers, 2006). The teacher in this case study defined authenticity as "faithfulness to the discipline... being able to see and think about things in the ways that researchers in this area do" (Meyer and Land, 2006). In interview, she also explained how she issued the assessment brief at the very beginning of the module, so all her classes supported "formative activities" which she hoped would help students to experience "getting involved" in "discussing, thinking about and understanding" the topic in increasingly sophisticated ways.

Researching the student experience of assessment in the case study

The module became a case study in the Centre's four-year research project. Data were also gathered in order to illuminate students' perspectives of the new assessment practices being introduced in different AfL initiatives. Students' views were generated with reference to the CETL's six AfL principles, which offered the conceptual framework within which to review AfL practices in each case study.

In overall terms, the Centre's research approach was predicated on the claim that the activities of learning and teaching are best understood if they are investigated as activities in their natural context, rather than on the basis of 'experimental' interventions, so the research was situated within the socio-cultural context. Multiple methods of data collection were used within an interpretive approach to the generation of meaning, drawing upon a range of perspectives. Instruments included semi-structured interviews with individuals and groups of students, participant observation, student diaries and other documentary evidence.

Most of the students in this case study were so-called 'non-traditional' students: many were first-generation entrants who were not from historically advantaged socio-economic backgrounds and who held diverse entry qualifications. All were female. Student volunteers were sought to participate in interviews and six came forward. They included mature students as well as school-leavers.

The findings, reported below, explore the meanings that, in interview, this small group of students attributed to the authentic assessment task. It should be noted, however, that the students who volunteered for interview seemed particularly enthusiastic about the module. All were relatively high-achievers on this (and other modules). This must be borne in mind when interpreting the findings. It means, however, that this specific piece of research highlights interesting ways in which these particular students – who were accustomed to 'doing well' in all their assignments – perceived a substantial difference between what they saw as 'normal' assessment practices and the assessment as embodied on this module.

Data were analysed using an emergent approach, drawing themes from the data during the process of analysis. We were aware of the criticisms levelled against the kind of approach to data analysis that "seeks merely to identify broad themes in the qualitative data, then illustrate them with random quotes" (Asmar, Ripeka Mercier and Page, 2009, p.152). For this reason, the research team used NVivo to carry out a systematic analysis and this was completed well before the selection of quotes (Bazeley, 2009).

In this particular case study, data were analysed from the viewpoint of approaches-to-learning frameworks and from the alternative perspectives of alienation and engagement. This was done to set the research in a constructivist paradigm (Case, 2008) by actively looking for the complexities of location and context when considering students' views of assessment. Interestingly, this analytical approach revealed aspects of student engagement which might remain largely invisible if viewed exclusively from the perspective of the approaches to learning framework.

Alternative perspectives on the student experience: alienation and engagement

Mann (2001) offers an alternative theoretical framework that usefully complements the approaches-to-learning model. Informed by concepts from critical theory, postmodernism and post-structuralism, she uses perspectives drawn from, for example, Marx, Foucault and Lacan to understand the student experience in a way which places attention on the salience of socio-cultural, rather than principally cognitive, aspects of learning.

In particular, Mann suggests that it is useful to associate the characteristics of surface and strategic approaches to learning with the concept of alienated experience. As in the dominant model of approaches to learning, she continues to view learning as a *relationship* between the learner and a context. Alienation, however, represents a learner's sense of *disconnection* between themselves and a given context.

Mann makes a persuasive case that powerful forces in the broader socio-cultural context of higher education present barriers to student engagement. They include: an over-emphasis on the utilitarian 'value' of education; the way that academic discourse constructs and constrains student identity; the student feeling an outsider in the academic world or constructed in a deficit model; and university customs and practices offering contexts which demand compliance rather than creativity. Mann, like many approaches to learning researchers, also importantly singles out assessment practices as crucial mediating factors. However, she views them within a wider perspective, framing them as a means of exerting control and power over students, promoting conformity, obedience and docility. Her framework, then, broadens out from a sharp focus on individual student learning (Trowler and Trowler, 2010) and draws attention to more general feelings of powerlessness, subservience, meaninglessness, exclusion, social isolation, cultural disorientation and identity.

Case (2008) argues that Mann's approach provides useful insights into why students frequently have difficulty in embracing the core values of higher education as epitomised by deep approaches to learning. She, like

Bryson and Hand (2007), has employed the framework of alienation and engagement to explore undergraduates' experiences of their general relationships with their subject, their classmates and life beyond the classroom. We will also use it in what follows, this time to examine the student experience of learning by looking for evidence of students' sense of connection or disconnection with assessment practices in the context of the case study.

Students' views of the differences between 'normal' university assignments and authentic assessment as represented in the case study

All the students who were interviewed felt strongly that the 'new' assessment – the act of preparing the guide – felt very different from the 'normal' experience of doing what one called "bog-standard assignments". There was considerable evidence that 'normal' assignments were, from these learners' viewpoints, frequently framed in terms of alienation. For instance, all the students expressed the view that the new assessment practice offered more than 'just marks'. To illustrate this, they referred to a variety of ways in which they experienced other assignments as tasks that they undertook mainly to conform to the expectations of the system.

This manifested itself in a range of ways, all of which resonate with Mann's critique. For instance, all the students claimed that, when they did 'normal' assignments, the 'need' to gain marks was foremost in their minds. As one said, "You're trying to write to pass, let's face it." This positions the business of 'doing' an assessment task within a utilitarian perspective: fuelled by the socially constructed 'need' to acquire credit. For example, the following student constructed this 'need' in terms of gaining a particular percentage. She saw the percentage as her passport to further study, with little attention paid to engagement with the subject itself: "I have my 2:1 in mind, I need a 60 per cent for my postgrad course, and that's what I am writing for." This was an extremely dominant characteristic attributed to 'normal' assignments. In all the students' minds this located control outside the student and in external others' demands and success criteria. Further, all the students also expressed the view that 'normal' assignments were characterised by 'pressure' and anxiety. The general feeling was one of isolation and exposure. The following student, for instance, discussed the ways in which producing an assignment on her own failed to correspond with the value she placed on her relationships with her peers and the social learning environment she inhabited beyond the classroom. Instead, she felt, "writing a normal academic assignment, it's very isolating".

Interviewees frequently talked about how they interacted in particular ways with their peers when it came to 'assignment time'. On these occasions the student social culture did not focus on discussions of the subject matter in question, but on feelings and emotions about the impending deadlines:

> Doing assignments is pure pressure. People go around in a daze, saying to each other, "How are you managing to sleep at night?"

They felt this had some significant backwash effects on their approaches to learning. As one student said, this feeling normally caused her not to write "for herself", but for an external other:

> I don't write it for me. I don't think I write my academic assignments for myself. I'm writing them for the person who is reading them – the marker.

The notion of feeling compelled to conform to culturally alien writing practices and customs was also powerfully expressed. From this viewpoint, the 'new' assessment seemed very different from the ways in which students felt they usually had to express their learning:

> We wanted our guide to be fun, to hit a particular target... [not] end up another assignment. I am sick of doing assignments. The terminology you use, the formality of the words and the formality of the sentence structure.

By contrast, the students all saw the process of producing the guide as 'fun'. In one sense, this was framed as a case of being free from the usual pressure and compulsion to perform which assignments represented:

> We knew the guide would be more fun. I didn't want to go down that kind of road; a 2,000 word assignment. I was looking for something different.

The backwash of the new assessment format: ameliorating alienation

Mann argues that faculty can try to ameliorate alienation by consciously seeking to foster closer staff–student relationships. In one sense, the students in this case study felt strongly that the new assessment established different rules of engagement with assessment. Their typifications were framed as 'doing things differently' or 'working in a different way'. For example, students felt that having a 'real' audience, which was specified by the lecturer, repositioned them in relation to their approach to their assessment performance. They also talked of trying to understand key principles and concepts so they could 'get the message over' to the implied audience for their work. This, they felt, deeply affected the ways they approached the business of writing. In part, they gained a feeling of authorial control, which could be seen as fostering their creativity, rather than compliance:

> We were conscious that we wanted to use different ways of getting the point over rather than just a load of writing. That would have bored them rigid.

Having the sense that they needed to communicate ideas contrasted strongly with their view that 'normal' assignments had no 'real' audience. The following student, for instance, talked about her lack of knowledge about what happened to her assignments once she had handed them in: "I don't know. They get read and they get sent back." She expressed this as a feeling of being 'churned through' a factory-like process, which had little point beyond the system. This had an impact on her view of writing:

> There is no obligation, you're writing for a set task and set thing and once it has been achieved then that's it.

By contrast, producing the guide seemed different:

> It's more analytical, isn't it? You are thinking on your feet for a start so you're trying – you're thinking – thinking about producing something that gets the message over.

Other views included finding personal meaning in writing the guides, which also extended beyond utilitarian criteria. Four students talked, for instance, about how far the new assessment acted as a catalyst which prompted them to think critically and reflectively about their own experience. For one student, the process of writing about her own experiences was framed as a sharp contrast to the usual experience of assignment writing. She expressed the latter as a means of disciplining her behaviour (Tan, 2004). Producing the guide formed a stark contrast:

> I used it to think through the things [in educational settings] that had happened to me. It was about me, which my assignments aren't normally. I just normally check what they're asking and put bits in on each criteria [sic].

This student was not alone in drawing a clear distinction between, on the one hand, the feeling of 'putting in bits' to try and comply obediently to others' demands and expectations and, on the other, using the new assessment as a space to think about her own experiences. Another interviewee claimed she felt her personal experience was legitimised by the authentic assessment task: "[I drew on] my own observations of what we have learnt so far about being a student."

Whilst most of these comments relate to deep, as opposed to surface, approaches to learning, others more strongly resonate with the concepts of alienation and engagement in Mann's sense. In complementing traditional sightings of these students' experience of assessment, they help us develop a fuller understanding of why some students struggle to view assessment in terms of the core values embodied by deep approaches to learning.

The values and principles, which Mann proposes as factors, which might ameliorate alienation – hospitality, safety, redistribution of power and solidarity – were extremely important factors in these students' sense of connectedness with the new assessment. From this standpoint, the new assessment provided an environment that felt more welcoming than hostile. This helped dissolve feelings of disconnection and exclusion. The salience from the student viewpoint of being 'allowed' to work collaboratively enabled them to call, for instance, upon emotional support. The importance to these students of a sense of 'fun' and safety should not be underestimated. Their sense of normally struggling in isolation with assessment tasks was ameliorated by:

> Having a lifeline; we were on the phone every five seconds. And when we started writing the guide, we had such a laugh! At times, I had a pain laughing!

This sense of safety and fun was important:

> When something is fun it takes the pressure off... So I didn't feel the usual pressure. No, I didn't feel the pressure at all.

Time and again in the interviews, the students' sense of social cohesion and feelings of being part of the group emerged as an antidote to a sense of alienation from university practices and customs. As one put it:

> We actually had fun. You know, normally university is so serious! You're not supposed to laugh. But we do. We take the Mickey out of each other – and life – all the time!

All the students were extremely conscious of the 'different sort of writing' the new assessment represented. They saw this as 'friendly' and welcoming, rather than unfamiliar and a way of 'othering' (Jones, 2009) the student:

> Normally you would have to form an academic speak and you would have to form an academic structure. We didn't want to do that. We wanted to go the opposite way on. Conversational and friendly. Different to academic writing. I enjoyed the guide more.

They attributed this to the sense of having an authentic, more accessible and knowable designated audience for the work. This meant they felt they had 'permission' to use a more familiar voice, which led them to draw upon more familiar informal vernacular multi-literacy practices based in popular culture, which are rarely engaged in formal assessment (Ivanic et al., 2007).

This seemed to be associated not just with safety and hospitality but with a sense of sharing power and developing identity. It focused on a sense of being and becoming, rather than simply 'doing' assessment. This is the focus of the next section of the chapter, which explores the ways in which the students experienced a sense of engagement and agency that extended well beyond the teacher's assessment design and her intentions in relation to the official curriculum.

First, though, it is important to draw attention to the ways in which, although the students claimed to feel a sense of personal pride and engagement in creating their guides, they still felt a compulsion to produce an artefact that met their teacher's requirements. One student, for instance, worried about whether her guide was "too risky", because it moved beyond the parameters of what she viewed as normal academic discourse. She talked about feeling unsure about what the assessors were really prepared to tolerate. So her feelings were mixed as she handed her assignment in. On the one hand, she said she "felt proud and thought this is really good"; but she also "worried whether it was in the ethos of what the teacher wanted".

Other students also claimed not to 'stray too far' with their guides:

> The approach is different but the construction remains very much the same. So you are writing to a format, you are writing to an academic standard. I was quite conscious that we are still writing to an academic standard because we read a lot and I read stacks of stuff.

At root, of course, students find it impossible to escape from the multiple functions assessment performs. This means, perhaps, that although the way staff design assessment might begin to ameliorate students' feelings of alienation, broader structural factors beyond the control of individual teachers necessarily involve some level of compulsion to perform assessment tasks when and how the system requires. As Trowler and Wareham (2008) acknowledge, wider structural social forces are typically in play in higher education. They argue, though, that while structural factors are hard to shift, there is always a residue of agency that allows would-be innovators leeway. They assert that setting up "new, alternative structures" (ibid., p.8) assists in any attempts to reformulate existing practices.

The chapter will now turn to indicate briefly the ways in which the students in this case study seemed acutely aware of the module as providing a new alternative structure which visibly devolved power to them, to the extent that it reformulated their own social practices more radically than the lecturer anticipated. This factor appeared to have an equally, if not more, profound effect upon the students' learning experiences than did the official curriculum designs (Bloomer, 1997).

Being and becoming: creating 'support from below'

All the interviewees became acutely aware of the novel roles they felt they occupied as authors of student guides. The sense of acting on the first years' behalf was, for all of them, very keenly felt. Indeed, for some, the main advantage of their involvement in the new assessment practices was the possibility of having a positive impact by achieving change within the first-year community. This felt like a realistic goal and a sense of agency emerged as a key theme.

All the interviewees seemed strongly motivated by a powerful drive to help others. Their interest owed as much to altruism and a sense of responsibility to others as to personal gain. For instance, one said she'd really enjoyed the module because:

> For once, it's not just a pass or a fail or a number in a box. There's other important things like satisfaction, there's recognition. There's the feeling that it is going to help other people.

While these feelings of engagement began with the injunction to produce the guides, they extended well beyond this. Students hoped their guides would 'really get used'. Four actually volunteered, unsolicited, to become involved in first-year teaching sessions:

> We'd like to go and introduce it to the first years, in Study Skills. If it helps someone – great!

Concepts of authenticity became framed, then, in terms of the students themselves making a difference and helping address issues of alienation, rather than joining the lecturers' academic subject community in terms of appropriating their ways of thinking and practising (Meyer and Land, 2006) per se.

Within this dimension, the salience of the affective and social dimensions of learning emerged as a strong theme. These became attached to powerful feelings of sympathy and expressions of pity for the first years:

> I feel really sorry for them. They do need a bit of help, because the group sizes are so big. You see them in the library. Sheer panic. I just want to say "it's OK!"

Much of this sympathy stemmed from the students' own recollections of the emotional 'roller-coaster' of the first-year experience (Christie et al., 2007). This included the trauma of trying to 'get a feel for the place'. It concerned the difficulties of feeling unfamiliar with, isolated from or overwhelmed by university practices (Bensimon, 2009; Forsyth and Furlong, 2003; Krause and Coates, 2008). Assessment practices were particularly singled out as alienating elements. In response, the interviewees sought to help the first years overcome the 'pain barrier' of assessment:

> They need something most when they're going through the pain barrier of having to do assignments, and they see their marks are good, bad or ugly!

They recalled feeling agonisingly out of step with the acceptable self at university when they were first years themselves. This came to a head in relation to assessment, because of its power to exclude individuals, literally and metaphorically, from staff and student communities:

> I think the same insecurities went through everyone: my work is not good enough. I will fail. Everyone else gets it, but me!

What emerged, in response, though, was a pressing sense of social responsibility. This took the form of a powerful and personal desire to help the first years survive these alienating experiences. The interviewees began to attach huge personal significance to their sense of growing 'obligation'. This took the guise of an ethical duty to assume some responsibility for creating social networks that could offer "support from below" (Moronsou, O'Donovan and Handley, 2010). All the interviewees set great store by student–student, not student–staff relations. They saw student–student relationships and personal ties as vital to joining and 'sticking with' university study. They sought to create forms of support for others that they "wished we'd had when we were in the first year". The forging of personal ties, informality, feelings of belonging and a sense of the humane were hugely important features.

As before, these features of engagement were embodied in the principles of hospitality, solidarity, safety, and the sharing of power, which these students located firmly within an ethical framework. They talked, for instance, of their moral responsibility to 'pass on the baton' to the first years:

> I think that it is part the peer thing we talked about earlier. Mentoring. If we do this and have fun it is proof that there is life after a 2,000-word assignment! That there is something fun and you can achieve something!

Their sense of social justice occasionally spilled over into the real 'lived experience' of their student social lives. Some began to interact with the first years in the library to offer support:

> We have gone into the library and they [the first years] have been sitting around the table and you can see their faces: panic. And I've actually got a hold of them and said are you alright? And they say "do you understand this?" Sometimes you do and sometimes you don't. But just let them chat.

Of course, this could be interpreted as a matter of gaining a sense of personal identity and power by asserting one's essential difference from the first years. However, the ways in which interviewees talked about it inclined more towards a view that was embedded in empathy and sharp recollections of their own painful transitions. They were keen to reassure others that it was worth the struggle but were also keen to show solidarity about the ways in which students, themselves included, generally failed to match up with the 'ideal':

> We know what students are like because we're students! We all want to be deep learners but sometimes we're not. We go to the pub when we shouldn't!

Conclusions

Hopefully, these insights into students' viewpoints help to frame assessment issues in broader terms than are sometimes acknowledged in the research literature. The findings draw attention to the salience of the socio-cultural realm and the part it plays in the student experience of our assessment practices. It is useful to acknowledge that feelings of alienation and belonging in relation to assessment are, in part, socially induced. Accounts that dwell solely on the rational and cognitive interactions with subject material do not tell the whole story. The affective dimension of learning, for instance, is deeply powerful (Tinto, 1993). As a rule, though, assessment research and development has tended to downplay the affective dimensions of learning, and the role of emotions has tended to remain under-theorised in higher education (Beard, Clegg and Smith, 2007).

Our research into students' perspectives draws attention to the extent to which these learners experienced assessment practices holistically and multi-dimensionally. Many of their views about the nature of their involvement in assessment extended well beyond their academic engagement with subject matter, for instance, and placed a premium on assessment's power to foster a sense of being and becoming, and a sense of connectedness and assimilation into the academic and social culture of the university (Nicol, 2009). Further, issues concerning identities, roles and interactions frequently assumed dominance. Moreover, the salience of social engagement to students when it comes to designing assessment practice should not be underestimated. This all suggests that, pedagogically speaking, one challenge the AfL movement faces is how best to design assessment practices which are able to create situated contexts and conditions that matter for involvement in an holistic sense (Astin, 1997; Kuh et al., 2005), by acknowledging the varying dimensions and interrelated concepts which contribute to fostering student engagement.

Finally, it may be salutary to acknowledge the keen desire for some students to feel more fulfilled and, as one put it, "get involved in a something, rather than just doing a degree". This has spurred us on to design a model of 'Learning Leadership' (Sambell and Graham, 2010), a large-scale scheme that is currently in its first year of operation. The scheme is voluntary and based on a blend of the principles and values underpinning

Supplemental Instruction (PASS, 2010) and our own model of AfL. Learning Leadership has become a 'summative free zone' to create a clear demarcation between 'high stakes' and 'low stakes' (Knight and Yorke, 2003) assessment environments.

Student second- or third-year volunteers are trained by a Student Development Officer to become Learning Leaders who support first-year students within their discipline. Learning Leadership is designed to adapt to local contexts in a bespoke manner, so that each new version or uptake has a focus that emerges from a consultation process with staff and students in the particular area. The idea is that assigning students a degree of power to effect pedagogic change and facilitate others' learning might help position the student leader with a sense of agency within the university milieu.

Contrary to the enduring myth that students will not do anything unless it is marked, our new Learning Leadership scheme has proved extremely popular with students from a range of disciplines. It has been running with large numbers in subject areas as diverse as Law, Information Sciences, Nursing and Allied Health. Moreover, whilst it might be argued that the case study reported in this chapter ran in predominantly female, community-focused types of courses, which could explain some of our findings, there are strong indications that the model of providing 'support from below' is similarly popular with diverse courses and very different student profiles. The will, it seems, is there on the part of our students to "invest themselves in their engagement with thinking, self and action" (Mann, 2001 p.18).

References

Asmar, C., Ripeka Mercier, O. and Page, S. (2009) '"You Do It From Your Core": Priorities, Perceptions and Practices of Research Among Indigenous Academics in Australian and New Zealand Universities', in Brew, A. and Lucas, L. (eds) *Academic Research and Researchers* (Maidenhead: McGraw-Hill/Open University Press) pp.146–60.

Assessment Standards Knowledge Exchange (ASKE) (2010) *Assessment Standards Manifesto.* Retrieved from <http://www.brookes.ac.uk/aske/manifesto.html>

Astin, A. (1997) *What Matters in College? Four Critical Years Revisited* (San Francisco: Jossey Bass).

Barkely, E. (2009) *Student Engagement Techniques: A Handbook for College Faculty* (New York: Jossey Bass).

Bazeley, P. (2009) *Analysing Qualitative Data: More Than 'Identifying Themes'.* Retrieved from <http://www.researchsupport.com.au/More_than_themes.pdf>

Beard, C., Clegg, S. and Smith, K. (2007) 'Acknowledging the Affective in Higher Education', *British Educational Research Journal,* 33/2, pp.235–52.

Bensimon, E.M. (2009) 'Foreword', in Harper, S.R. and Quaye, S.J. (eds) *Student Engagement in Higher Education* (New York: Routledge) pp.xxi–xxvi.

Biggs, J. (1996) 'Enhancing Teaching through Constructive Alignment', *Higher Education,* 32, pp.1–18.

Biggs, J. and Tang, C. (2007) *Teaching for Quality Learning at University: What the Student Does* (Maidenhead: Open University Press).

Birenbaum, M. (2003) 'New Insights into Learning and Teaching: Their Implications for Assessment', in Segers, M., Dochy, F. and Cascaller, E. (eds) *Optimising New Modes of Assessment: In Search of Qualities and Standards* (Dordrecht: Kluwer Academic) pp.13–36.

Black, P. and Wiliam, D. (2009) 'Developing the Theory of Formative Assessment', *Educational Assessment, Evaluation and Accountability,* 21, pp.5–31.

Bloomer, M. (1997) *Curriculum Making in Post-16 Education: The Social Conditions of Studentship* (London: Routledge).

Boud, D. and Associates (2010) *Assessment 2020: Seven Propositions for Assessment Reform in Higher Education* (Sydney: Australian Learning and Teaching Council).

Bryson, C. and Hand, L. (2007) 'The Role of Engagement in Inspiring Teaching and Learning', *Innovations in Education and Teaching International,* 44/4, pp.349–62.

Carless, D. (2005) 'Prospects for the Implementation of Assessment for Learning', *Assessment in Education: Principles, Policy and Practice,* 12/1, pp.39–54.

Carless, D., Joughin, G. and Mok, M. (2006) 'Learning-Oriented Assessment: Principles and Practice', *Assessment and Evaluation in Higher Education,* 31/4, pp.395–8.

Case, J. (2008) 'Alienation and Engagement: Development of an Alternative Theoretical Framework for Understanding Student Learning', *Higher Education,* 55, pp.321–32.

Chickering, A.W. and Gamson, Z.F. (1991) 'Applying the Seven Principles for Good Practice in Undergraduate Education', *New Directions for Teaching and Learning*, 47, pp.63–9.

Christie, H., Tett, L., Cree, V., Hounsell, J. and McCune, V. (2007) '"A Real Rollercoaster of Confidence and Emotions": Learning to Be a University Student', *Studies in Higher Education*, 33/5, pp.567–81.

Forsyth, A. and Furlong, A. (2003) 'Access to Higher Education and Disadvantaged Young People', *British Educational Research Journal*, 29/2, pp.205–25.

Gibbs, G. and Simpson, C. (2004) 'Conditions Under Which Assessment Supports Students' Learning', *Learning and Teaching in Higher Education*, 1, pp.3–31.

Gulikers, J. (2006) *Authenticity Is in the Eye of the Beholder: A Five Dimensional Framework for Authentic Assessment* (Milton Keynes: The Open University).

Haggis, T. (2003) 'Constructing Images of Ourselves? A Critical Investigation into "Approaches to Learning" Research in Higher Education', *British Educational Research Journal*, 29/1, pp.89–104.

Ivanic, R., Edwards, R., Satchwell, C. and Smith, J. (2007) 'Possibilities for Pedagogy in Further Education: Harnessing the Abundance of Literacy', *British Educational Research Journal*, 33/5, pp.703–21.

Jones, P. (2009) *Rethinking Childhood* (London: Continuum).

Knight, P. and Yorke, M. (2003) *Assessment, Learning and Employability* (London: Society for Research into Higher Education and Open University Press).

Krause, K. and Coates, H. (2008) 'Students' Engagement in First-Year University', *Assessment and Evaluation in Higher Education*, 33/5, pp.493–505.

Kuh, G.D., Kinzie, J., Schuh, J.H. and Whitt, E.J. (2005) *Student Success in College: Creating Conditions That Matter* (San Francisco: JosseyBass).

Mann, S.J. (2001) 'Alternative Perspectives on the Student Experience: Alienation and Engagement', *Studies in Higher Education*, 26/1, pp.7–19.

Marton, F., Hounsell, D. and Entwistle, N. (1997) *The Experience of Learning* (Edinburgh: Scottish University Press).

Marton, F. and Säljö, R. (1976) 'On Qualitative Differences in Learning: 1, Outcome and Process', *British Journal of Educational Research*, 46, pp.4–11.

McCune, V. (2009) 'Final Year Biosciences Students' Willingness to Engage: Teaching-Learning Environments, Authentic Learning Experiences and Identities', *Studies in Higher Education* 34/3, pp.347–61.

McDowell, L., Sambell, K. and Davison, G. (2009) 'Assessment for Learning: A Brief History and Review of Terminology', in Rust, C. (ed.) *Improving Student Learning Through the Curriculum,* Proceedings of the 2008 16th International Improving Student Learning Symposium (Oxford: Oxford Centre for Staff and Learning Development) pp.56–64.

Meyer, E. and Land, R. (eds) (2006) *Overcoming Barriers to Student Understanding: Threshold Concepts and Troublesome Knowledge* (London: Routledge).

Morosanu, L., O'Donovan, B. and Handley, K. (2010) 'Seeking Support: Researching First-Year Students' Experiences of Coping with Academic Life', *Higher Education Research and Development,* 29/6, pp.665–78.

Nicol, D. (2009) *Transforming Assessment and Feedback: Enhancing Integration and Empowerment in the First Year* (Mansfield: Scottish Quality Assurance Agency for Higher Education).

PASS (2010) *University of Manchester.* Retrieved from <http://www.campus.manchester.ac.uk/tlso/studentsaspartners/peersupport/pass/training/>

Ramsden, P. (1992) *Learning to Teach in Higher Education* (London: Routledge).

Ramsden, P. (2003) *Learning to Teach in Higher Education* (2nd edn) (London: Routledge Falmer).

Sadler, D.R. (2009) 'Indeterminacy in the Use of Preset Criteria for Assessment and Grading in Higher Education', *Assessment and Evaluation in Higher Education,* 34/2, pp.159–79.

Sambell, K. and Graham, L. (2010) *Enhancing Staff–Student Dialogue About Assessment and Learning Practice,* presented at the European First Year Experience conference, Belgium, 26–28 May.

Sambell, K. and McDowell, L. (1998) 'The Construction of the Hidden Curriculum: Messages and Meanings in the Assessment of Student Learning', *Assessment and Evaluation in Higher Education,* 23/4, pp.391–402.

Sambell, K., McDowell, L. and Brown, S. (1997) '"But Is it Fair?" an Exploratory Study of Student Perceptions of the Consequential Validity of Assessment', *Studies in Educational Evaluation,* 23/4, pp.349–71.

Segers, M., Dochy, F. and Cascaller, E. (eds) (2003) *Optimising New Modes of Assessment: In Search of Qualities and Standards* (Dordrecht: Kluwer Academic).

Snyder, B.R. (1970) *The Hidden Curriculum* (New York: Alfred A. Knopf).

Tan, K. (2004) 'Does Self Assessment Empower or Discipline Students?', *Assessment and Evaluation in Higher Education,* 29/6, pp.651–62.

Tinto, V. (1993) *Leaving College: Rethinking the Causes and Cures of Student Attrition* (Chicago: University of Chicago Press).

Torrance, H. (1995) *Evaluating Authentic Assessment* (Buckingham: Open University Press).

Trowler, V. and Trowler, P. (2010) *Student Engagement Evidence Summary* (York: Higher Education Academy).

Trowler, P. and Wareham, T. (2008) *Tribes, Territories, Research and Teaching Enhancing the Teaching-Research Nexus*, project report (York: Higher Education Academy).

Watkins, D., Dahlin, B. and Eckholm, M. (2005) 'Awareness of the Backwash Effect of Assessment: A Phenomenographic Study of the Views of Hong Kong and Swedish lecturers', *Instructional Science*, 33/4, pp.283–309.

Chapter 10

Student engagement and equity issues for policy, practice and pedagogies in global higher education

Miriam David

Institute of Education, University of London, UK

Introduction

"Student engagement" is a concept that is embedded in approaches to equity and widening participation in global higher education. It is not, however, always articulated or defined as engagement, and ranges over concepts of involvement and participation. Moreover, notions of widening participation have encompassed concepts of access and/or recruitment without the necessary consideration of academic development, but rather with a relatively new conceptual focus on education as forms of learning and teaching. Over the last decade, many countries of 'the global north' have developed evidence-based policies and practices to try to ensure 'fair access' and participation of a range of disadvantaged or previously excluded groups, including women, in higher education.

The question of how to theorise and understand the massive changes in global economies and their implications for, and effects upon, higher education has become a huge research field in the twenty-first century. (For a so-called balanced review see Brown, 2010.) Mass higher education is now a global phenomenon, although inequities between countries of the global north and the south remain and indeed have become entrenched (Altbach, 2010, pp.48–50; Rhoads and Torres, 2006; Shavit, Arum and Gamoran, 2007; Slaughter and Rhoades, 2004). Both the concepts and contexts for equity and widening participation as forms of student engagement in the policies and practices of global higher education have been open to challenge, debate and question. Feminists have been at the forefront of developing critiques of policies and practices and have campaigned for greater engagement of women as students in higher education, as well as challenging pedagogical practices whilst also developing feminist and inclusive pedagogies (David, 2003; Leathwood and Read, 2009).

Official or government policies have developed globally around competing and divergent concepts of equity and widening participation (known colloquially as WP in some contexts in the UK). The focus has largely been on fair access or what might be called recruitment to higher education, rather on than retention or participation throughout higher education leading to equity in results or academic achievements. Whilst "student engagement" as a concept has been embedded in these developing practices it has not been central to the policy debates; these have focused more on questions of the disadvantaged or previously excluded groups. It is this challenging and complex arena of debate about diverse forms of equity and engagement that I wish to illuminate by reference to my own research and coordination work for the UK's Economic and Social Research Council's Teaching and Learning Research Programme (David, 2009a). In this research work, we drew together studies of equity and widening participation in UK higher education and developed critiques of policies and practices around access or recruitment and participation or retention. Our work, in keeping with UK policy developments, was largely around socio-economic disadvantage or working-class students rather than gender.

In the UK, for some policy makers and practitioners the focus is about 'new' and diverse groups being able to access or enter higher education, or *recruitment*; for others it is about a more inclusive notion of participation or engagement within and across forms of higher education: *retention and degree results*. How might equity be considered in terms of progression or continuation through higher education, and achievements in terms of degree results, for instance? There is also the question of developing appropriate inclusive pedagogies to ensure academic or educational engagement and progression.

Perhaps even more importantly, there has been huge debate about which are the *key new groups* to be the focus of attention – those from low social classes (such as the working class), or socially disadvantaged as low socio-economic group or status (SES), or other markers of socio-economic position such as income or employment? (David, 2009b) Here, too, questions have been raised about parental education as well as parental employment, concentrating attention on school leavers and young people rather than those who are non-traditional students in terms of age of potential participation and access. The policy debate has been quite narrowly focused upon a particular way of conceptualising lack of participation, ignoring wider cultural issues, such as the additional questions of ethnicity or race.

Changing contexts

As higher education has expanded in relation to changing forms of the knowledge economy and society, the question of the meanings of the new forms of post-compulsory schooling as higher education or universities has been brought into focus. There has been a key question about equity within expanding systems of higher education, and how that might be accomplished to ensure greater student engagement. The debate both globally and locally has wavered between a simple focus on the traditional, elite versus the newer, more-comprehensive universities. This has been especially around the role of research in relation to teaching in higher education, with a traditional core assumption being that research should underpin academic teaching. In the UK, this has meant a focus on either the elite, or Russell Group, research-intensive universities, aiming for their success in the international league tables; or a broader focus on the range of universities to include the smaller research groupings (for example the UK's 1994 group), new (post-1992) universities and other institutions of higher education.

Whilst there has been intensive debate about which types of higher education institution to include in the question of equity and widening participation, there has been virtually no interrogation of anything other than initial undergraduate or first degree student participation or engagement. Wakeling and Kyriacou (2010) made this point strongly in their recent UK research synthesis entitled *Widening Participation from*

Undergraduate to Postgraduate Research Degrees. Given this paucity of interest and research (with, for example, the exception of Leonard, 2001), in this chapter I will only be concerned with engaging first or undergraduate degree students, although the notion of enhancing student engagement might also be usefully and creatively developed for postgraduate- and research-degree students.

Despite feminist contestation (Evans, 2004; Hey, 2004; Morley, 2003) there is an assumption in mainstream UK public policies that gender equality has been 'achieved' for women students and that the problem is now one of male disadvantage (HEFCE, 2005; Bekhradnia, 2009). There has indeed been a significant 'closing of the gender gap' (Arnot, David and Weiner, 1999) not only in UK higher education enrolments or recruitment but also in participation and progression across UK higher education (HEFCE, 2005; Bekhradnia, 2009). Where gender is now acknowledged, for example in government-funded studies, the question of the reverse 'gender gap' is raised: how to ensure male access or recruitment and attainment or results rather than female equality in participation and attainment in higher education.

The question of gender (meaning women) has been sidelined in this UK policy agenda (David, 2009c; Leathwood and Read, 2009). Yet as Leathwood and Read (2009) show, this represents a fear of a feminist future rather than its achievement. Together with Weiler and David (2008, p.435), I argued that:

> Given the growing social diversity among students in terms of social class, ethnicity, race and gender, feminist ideas challenge us to think more deeply about pedagogies and practices and to develop new theories which critique essentialist notions of classed, racialised and gendered subjectivities and at the same time retain the original political vision of the women's movement.

A traditional student in elite universities was not clearly typified but more recently has been characterised as a "young, white and middle class man" (David, 2009a, p.13). White working-class boys or young men have become a major focus of attention in their lack of access to and participation in post-compulsory education and training for skills, as much as for higher education. Whilst the question of gender or women's participation had been the original concern in the 'global north' (that is, the UK and US), particularly through feminist campaigning and research, the policy debates have recently been normalised to be about working-class men (Morley and David, 2009). It could be argued that women's engagement in higher education, as students, has been accomplished successfully.

Indeed, it has recently been argued that on average more women than men participate as undergraduate and first degree students in UK higher education. Altbach suggests that this is also part of a global phenomenon (2010, p.50, my italics): "Widening access opens higher education to people from an array of social class and educational backgrounds, but *one of the most dramatic results of greater access is the expansion of enrolments by women, who now comprise a majority in many countries.*"

There is also policy-informed evidence about women's participation across forms of UK higher education (Bekhradnia, 2009). In *Male and Female Participation and Progression in Higher Education,* Bekhradnia (2009) argues that, given changed gender balances in undergraduate or first degree students, there is no longer any issue about female participation and concern should now centre on male access and participation. Given the recent transformation of the policy debates through the classification of subject areas by the three categories of STEM subjects (science, technology, engineering and maths, including medicine), arts and humanities, and the social sciences, it has also been claimed that women's participation in STEM subjects is greater than men's.

Indeed, national governments have increasingly sought to embed higher education or universities in their policies for national developments. An example here is the New Labour government's white paper published in November 2009 entitled *Higher Ambitions: the Future of Universities in a Knowledge Economy.* This was an attempt to show how transformative and transforming universities could be and how they might be used for future policy purposes. However, a report of a UK government Cabinet Office committee a few months previously also showed how limited UK universities had been in achieving social mobility especially into graduate professions (Cabinet Office Strategy Unit, 2009 – the 'Milburn Report'). Most serious were their limitations in extending opportunities for women's participation in graduate labour markets. Milburn argued that there remained a glass ceiling for women in graduate professions.

Recent policy and public media debates illustrate the dilemmas about how to understand and further transform higher education, given that it is now considered to be mass higher education. Recruitment to UK higher education has increased dramatically: the Higher Education Initial Participation Rate (HEIPR) for individuals aged 17–30 shows that now 43 per cent of each generation receive higher education. Whilst debate at the beginning of the twenty-first century focused upon questions of equity in the context of increasing diversity of cultures and groups, and measures to secure such equity, the neo-liberal agenda has dominated to such a degree that there is now far more acceptance of forms of inequality between institutions and individuals. The Equality Challenge Unit, the UK higher education equality body, was originally funded by government and is now a semi-autonomous body, illustrating the dominance of a neo-liberal approach. Nevertheless, it is still committed to what it calls "accelerating equality in higher education" across both individuals as students and academics and institutions.

As one of its first measures in 2010, the UK's coalition government sought to reduce the size and scope of higher education, based on its perceived funding and fiscal crisis in the context of the global recession. In implementing the Browne report (2010), "An independent review of higher education and student finances" entitled *Securing a Sustainable Future for Higher Education*, the government has decided to raise tuition fees to £9,000 p.a. for undergraduate students in higher education from 2012–13, payable after the completion of higher education. At the same time cuts in higher education funding for arts, humanities and social sciences in universities were also announced to take effect from 2011–12. Both of these measures are likely and, indeed, intended to have major consequences for equity in undergraduate student engagement in higher education, especially for women and disadvantaged groups.

Foreshadowing this, Philip Altbach writing in the UK's *Times Higher Education* (23 September 2010, p.48) argues that:

> It might seem a contradiction that widening access would bring inequality to higher education, but that is exactly what happens. Institutions that cater to mass access provide vastly different quality, facilities and focus than do elite institutions, and this gulf has widened as access has expanded worldwide. Furthermore, mass

higher education has, for the majority of students, lowered quality and increased dropout rates.

He goes on to argue that:

> Mass higher education is a worldwide phenomenon. More than 150 million students are enrolled in universities worldwide, an increase of 53 percent in just a decade... Even in much of the developing world, enrolments are increasing dramatically... massification has moved largely from the developed countries, which have achieved high participation rates to the developing and some middle income nations. In fact, the most growth in the coming decades will take place in China and India. China now enrolls about 23 percent of the traditional university-going age cohort, and India around 12 percent. The region with the lowest enrolment rate, sub-Saharan Africa, which in 2007 was educating only 6 percent of the age group, is expanding access, but still has a long way to go...

Altbach concludes very fatalistically and pessimistically that:

> The reality of greater access to higher education in an era of fiscal constraint, combined with ever-increasing costs, is that inequality within higher education systems is here to stay... these issues constitute a deep contradiction for 21st century higher education. As access expands, inequalities within the higher education system also grow...

He offers no remedies for these various kinds of inequities but seems to accept the inevitability of a stratified system of higher education globally and nationally, embedded within an unequal global knowledge economy. He does, however, raise challenging questions about the nuances and specificities of different higher education systems, from the quality of schooling to the qualities of teaching and academic life within higher education, to issues about retention and completion or non-completion rates, and to the systems of private versus public forms of higher education. He also points to some of the ways in which new, diverse groups including women are now engaged in higher education.

In the UK, many policy measures for mitigating the worst effects of inequalities in both student *access and participation, or engagement,* have been proposed for undergraduate education but these have been addressed to particular disadvantaged socio-economic groups or low SES with a specific institutional focus (Thomas, 2010). Under the UK's New Labour government, a panoply of measures was developed in the aftermath of the Higher Education Act, 2004. For example, *Aimhigher,* a scheme targeted at schoolchildren to try to raise their aspirations and expectations about particular forms of higher education, was inaugurated. Individual institutions across the higher education system have also developed their own support networks for these schemes, ranging from student ambassadors to mentors, aimed at increasing and improving access and entry to universities, almost invariably about low SES rather than ethnicity or gender.

In addition, as a result of policy changes and legislation, the financing of student participation in higher education was changed towards student fees, with higher education institutions able to charge an array of fees for undergraduate study. To redress problems here, an Office for Fair Access (OFFA) was created, under the leadership of a former university vice chancellor, Professor Sir Martyn Harris, to act as a form of quality control on the operation of institutional measures on bursaries and plans for widening access and participation. Thus, in addition to an undergraduate student-focused agenda, there has also been an institutional agenda all of which has been targeted at socially disadvantaged (SES) students.

Most recently, UK higher education institutions (HEIs) have been required to develop Widening Participation Strategic Assessments and report about them. These (129) reports have been analysed to unpick the cultural, economic, social, familial and educational issues underpinning the criteria used by institutions for their widening participation agendas (Thomas, 2010). Thomas argues that the vast majority (127) of HEIs targeted 'disabled students' in their schemes, without providing any clear definition, whilst over two-thirds also targeted young people from low socio-economic backgrounds and families (NS-SEC 4-7). This report confirms the developing emphasis on SES, or social class, in national policy-making (see also National Audit Office, 2008).

This is also the emphasis that has been taken by the Australian government as a result of its Bradley Review (Bradley et al., 2008) and the creation, in 2008–9, of a National Centre for Student Equity in Higher Education at the University of South Australia in Adelaide (Gale et al., 2010). This centre has been assiduous in developing critiques of policies and practices in institutions in Australia, including reporting upon a research study about rural schools in South Australia (Gale et al., 2010).

Changing concepts of equity and widening participation for student engagement

Through the UK Teaching and Learning Research Programme (TLRP) I have developed an analysis of the UK government's commitment to public policies on widening access to, and participation within, higher education (David, 2009b). In 2005, the government, through its Higher Education Funding Council for England (HEFCE), and the Economic and Social Research Council (ESRC), commissioned the TLRP to undertake seven projects on widening participation in higher education. These projects covered issues about diversity and equity in participation, including gender, and questioned how to develop inclusive pedagogies and practices for engaging a diversity of students in higher education. This UK research programme illustrates Slaughter and Rhoades' (2004) analysis of how mass, global higher education has become important in national and global economies. These two American scholars argued that "the academic capitalist knowledge/learning regime in the early twenty-first century is in the ascendant, displacing but not replacing public good knowledge or liberal learning regimes" (2004, p.305).

The concept of 'academic capitalism' is particularly useful, providing a conceptual framework for understanding the complexities of increased access for women (Brine, 2006; Deem, 2001, 2004; Langa Rosado and David, 2006) intersected with diversity, pedagogies and the implications of access for the curriculum (Mirza, 2008). Maher and Tetreault (2007), two American feminist scholars, used it to explain how the discourses of racism and sexism remain entrenched in US universities despite the incorporation of notions of diversity, meaning ethnicity and gender, meaning women into higher education.

More traditional sociological approaches to understanding the expansions of global higher education do not incorporate either a feminist or a gender perspective. Shavit, Arum and Gamoran (2007), American sociologists, undertook international case studies, focused on notions of social stratification and mobility, using concepts of equity and diversity, without regard to gender: "The key question about educational expansion is whether it reduces inequality by providing more opportunities for persons from disadvantaged strata, or magnifies inequality by expanding opportunities disproportionately for those who are already privileged" (ibid., p.1).

They compared and contrasted 15 different countries and classified them as *diversified* systems such as Israel, Japan, Korea, Sweden, Taiwan and the US; *binary* systems such as Great Britain [sic], France, Germany, the Netherlands, Russia and Switzerland; and *unitary* and other systems such as Australia, the Czech Republic and Italy (Shavit, Arum and Gamoran, 2007, pp.1–35). Their focus was the 'global north' and excluded other countries of the Americas, whereas Rhoads and Torres (2006) did consider the influence of globalisation on universities in Latin America. They also excluded Africa, China and India. Shavit, Arum and Gamoran (2007, p.29) conclude that 'persistent inequality' remains across all the 15 countries. Their conclusions match those of other sociologists of education (Halsey et al., 2000; Lauder et al., 2006) and Altbach's (2010) recent analysis. They also footnote the fact that they omitted gender from their analysis, which is only of higher education enrolments, recruitment or access to higher education, rather than academic success or achievements in terms of retention or results within higher education.

There has been a systematic occlusion of feminist perspectives from recent research about equity and diversity and so I question, from a feminist perspective, where women are located and the engagement of diverse women. What is the research evidence drawn from seven interdisciplinary projects commissioned by HEFCE on the UK government's policies to widen access to, and participation within, higher education, as presented in *Improving Learning by Widening Participation in Higher Education* (David, 2009a)? We focused upon concepts of equity and diversity but mostly around access or recruitment to and participation within higher education, largely avoiding discussion of degree results. Specific consideration was also given to pedagogies for improving academic engagement for diverse students.

Given the context of academic capitalism and the nature of the research funding, none of the researchers took an explicitly feminist or even a gender focus but the evidence provides a significant picture of how gender is embedded and intersected with diversity and equity in recruitment and retention. The research teams comprised feminist and gender researchers, with four of the main grant-holders being senior women researchers and each of the teams including several well-known feminist researchers. This represents a significant shift in the demography of UK research grant holders over the past decade, evidence of the contradictory processes of academic capitalism.

This research evidence makes for a significant picture of gender in the diverse practices of higher education, using a range of methods from qualitative, ethnographic studies to quantitative datasets (David, 2009c). No one concept of equity underpinned all the studies although concepts about learners' identities and backgrounds of social class, socio-economic disadvantage, ethnicity, increasingly multicultural communities and gender were used. Given the English policy focus, definitions of widening participation concentrated upon socio-economic disadvantage or working class and diversity rather than more multi-cultural questions about ethnicity, race or the newly emerging issues concerning international students, whether from Africa, Asia, Europe or the other UK nations. UK public policy concerns about 'working class' entry to elite universities (defined in terms of international university league tables) underpinned the initial research focus and designs.

Evidence about student engagement from the UK studies

The findings emphasise the diversity of student participation in a diverse, inequitable and stratified higher education system. They address participation across the life course, and question the international league table approach to higher learning and the relevance of higher education to people across their lives. They also address the appropriate national and international policy contexts for post-compulsory education for a more equitable system across a diversity of subjects and higher education institutions in the twenty-first century, given the expansions of academic capitalism. It is amply demonstrated that recent UK government policies have led to increasing, if not widening, opportunities for learners from diverse families and disadvantaged socio-economic backgrounds (David, 2009c).

The policies have not led to fair access or recruitment to all types of higher education or to equal benefits in the graduate or professional labour markets in contexts of academic capitalism. Nevertheless, it is shown that policies have also provided opportunities for new institutional practices and pedagogies to *engage* diverse students, including gendered and racialised students for the twenty-first century (David, 2009a, Chapter 7). We see how influential feminist pedagogies have been, and what the potential for inclusive pedagogies might be in a changed policy environment.

The research team, led by Parry (David, 2009a, Chapter 2), studied policies to broaden participation by offering higher education in further education colleges and provided the contextualisation of these policies, practices and strategies. In England, the higher and further education sectors have different and separate funding and quality regimes. Government policy has expanded higher education in the further education sector to make it easier for colleges to operate within two funding systems. Rather than identify a special or specific mission for colleges in higher education, these compete and collaborate with universities in the same markets for college students.

The team link English policies on widening participation and institutional differentiation to wider international debates about the role of lower-tier colleges in the democratisation of access and the so-called diversion of demand. They show that English policies militate against such new open systems given asymmetries of power and advantage. They provide a clear map of systemic and systematic differentiation in higher education and demonstrate how this leads away from equalising opportunities and outcomes for diverse gendered and racialised students towards different regimes of practice. In other words, we argue that higher education has become stratified, especially for low SES and women students.

We also consider forms of engagement on student progress and progression around 'seamlessness and separation' between higher education offered in further and higher education institutions (David, 2009a, Chapter 3). We explored how the boundary between further and higher education is experienced, mediated and managed by gendered and diverse students and staff in 'dual sector' colleges. A 'seamless' system of tertiary education may be desirable and possible but our research evidence suggests that institutions, staff and students treat further and higher education as separate enterprises, affecting the practices of students and tutors at various stages in the student lifecycle and the imagined futures at the end of college study. The 'logic of practice' throughout these various stages is related to implicit and explicit awareness of the gendered, stratified and differentiated nature of higher education. Here, the critique of seamlessness, and the emphasis on separation between the more privileged higher education institutions, such as Russell group universities, at the expense of the less-privileged and lower-status colleges illustrates how there are different institutional forms of academic or educational engagement.

Similarly, three other projects focus on individual first degree and undergraduate students and their pathways into and through higher education. Vignoles' team (David, 2009a, Chapter 3) undertook a large-scale quantitative cohort study (young people aged 16 in state schools in 2004–5) of students' access, participation and disadvantage in higher education using an innovative linkage of newly available official datasets and sophisticated modelling techniques. As already noted, recruitment to UK higher education has increased dramatically: women especially have increased their participation relative to 'traditional' students, defined as male, white and middle class, and now outnumber men. This team focused particularly on the extent to which differences in university participation between advantaged and disadvantaged students are driven by their very different prior educational experiences. Male and female children from poor (low SES) backgrounds remain far less likely to go to university than more advantaged children. However, controlling for individual characteristics, such as gender, reduces the gap and, once prior attainment is controlled for, the disparity disappears. In other words, females have higher attainment than males whatever the SES and are more likely to participate in higher education. When poor students, mainly female, participate they attend lower-status universities (in league-table terms). This finding again shows how educational engagement in school leads to different practices at university.

The socio-economic gap in higher education participation is because poorer pupils do not achieve as highly in secondary school as their more socio-economically privileged counterparts. Ethnic minority students are significantly *more* likely to participate in higher education than their white British peers of the same socio-economic group, confirming the success of longstanding policy measures to widen participation to ethnic minority groups. Vignoles' team shows that the issue of equal or fair access to old and research-intensive universities does not have its origins in higher education recruitment, but rather in the prior educational experiences in different types of state schools.

Fully to reap the rewards from a university education in the labour market, poorer students need also successfully to complete a good class of first degree. The English university system has historically had low levels of student 'drop-out' (i.e. high retention) but as it has expanded, non-completion has risen (David, 2009a, Chapter 5). Disadvantaged male and female recruits to higher education have a lower probability of retention, taking full account of their level of prior achievement. However, mature students, the majority of whom, in the UK, are women, appear less likely to drop out than their younger peers, and are more likely to achieve a higher class of degree result. They remain engaged in higher educational processes.

The under-representation of low SES students in the UK implies that if differences in educational achievement emerge early in the educational process then policies that only target interventions at the point of entry into higher education (for example, bursaries) are not likely on their own to produce large increases in university participation amongst poorer students. Clearly, it is critical that if educational inequalities emerge early in the education system (certainly by age 11), it is necessary to raise children's expectations – especially those of boys from disadvantaged families, as they were found to be amongst the least likely to continue.

Hayward's team (David, 2009a, Chapter 3) looked at learners' transitions from Vocational Education and Training (VET) to higher education to demonstrate similar gendered patterns of recruitment, retention and results. This analysis reveals that the proportion of students entering full-time higher education with vocational rather than GCE Advanced level qualifications increased between 1995 and 2004 from 18 to 25 per cent. This growth is due to an increase in those combining vocational and academic qualifications, up from 4 to 14 per cent. Over the same period, the proportion of students entering full-time higher education with only vocational qualifications decreased from 14 to 10 per cent. Including students from VET backgrounds *widens* instead of simply increases participation – that is it alters the SES composition of the student population – but compared to traditional A-level students, those with VET qualifications have a much higher risk of not obtaining a place and of dropping out after their first year. The majority of these students were young men and these VET students are heavily under-represented in higher-status universities. This uneven distribution is a result of individual and institutional processes. First-year students who had undertaken VET before they started higher education describe their transition into university as a complex, often difficult process including family commitments (especially for the women) and the jobs needed to finance their studies. Students need to be able to draw on support to overcome these difficulties but existing mechanisms of retention are often not appropriate to deal with the complexity of issues faced by students with a VET background.

Crozier's team studied how socio-economic circumstances influence the challenges facing working-class students entering university, where the majority are women (David, 2009a, Chapter 3). This project drew on questionnaires and interviews (51 female, mainly white British) with middle- and working-class students (defined either by their being the first in the family to go to higher education or through their parents' occupations) who were studying a range of subjects, and in-depth case studies at four contrasting 'colleges' or universities (an elite, a high-status and a new university and a further education college). The students adopted a strategic attitude to their studies, the process of navigation through and engagement with the university, their subject and the nature of study. For the working-class students, not only are their financial resources limited but so too is their route map through higher education. They start out with limited knowledge of what to expect or what is expected of them and little understanding of the structure and overall requirements of their course or what might be at their disposal to further their studies. The team explored how the students accessed the means by which they would succeed, to explain the dynamics of the students' learning negotiations. Whilst the predominantly female students are not richly endowed with 'cultural capital' (Bourdieu, 1992), they are resourceful, determined, persevering and strongly focused. Having overcome significant challenges to get to university, such women students are determined to succeed and achieve good degree results. These students are fully engaged with educational processes.

Pedagogies for student engagement

Two projects concentrated specifically on pedagogies and equitable practices to *engage* diverse gendered and racialised students (David, 2009a, Chapter 4). Hockings' team focused on teachers' strategies to engage diverse students, especially learning and teaching for social diversity. Using the concepts of 'academic engagement' and 'ways of knowing', they explore the conditions under which students engage with or disengage from learning in two contrasting universities (a high-status and a new university) and across six different subjects – bioscience, business, computing, history, nursing and social work. They found that student diversity is multi-faceted and students do not fit simplistic constructions of being 'traditional' or 'non-traditional' but come from a range of social, cultural and educational backgrounds, in which the majority are women and mature students. Drawing on data from classroom videos, interviews, focus groups and questionnaires, similarities and differences in teachers' pedagogic practices were found. These differences were influenced by the teachers' beliefs about their students, their own educational experiences and the ways of knowledge generation in their subject and professional communities. Student-centred and inclusive pedagogies were found to engage thoughtfully with student diversity. This is clearly pedagogical attention or recognition of the needs of diverse students.

Williams' team (David, 2009a, Chapter 4) focused on how diverse students learn mathematics for university study of science, technology, engineering or medicine (STEM). They showed how mathematics is inflected slightly differently from VET around student identities and questions of pedagogy. They drew on surveys, qualitative case study data from further education classrooms and 44 (only 15 female) learners' narratives of their mathematical trajectories gleaned from serial interviews. They found a picture of students 'aiming higher' with high expectations of going to university. Their subject choices, however, were gendered, classed and subject to strong ethnic trends. Students used ideological values to present themselves as certain kinds of people. Although the team found the majority aspired to university, the choice of institution and kind of higher education was culturally influenced, with white British working-class and Asian female students indicating preferences for staying in their local areas. Students' decisions to participate in post-compulsory education were strategic: mathematics must be 'useful' and meaningful. A measure of success, somehow construed as 'value' by the gendered student, is an essential outcome if students are to persist in recruitment to universities.

The study also shows that different pedagogies can make a real difference to students. An inclusive approach to mathematics involves mathematicians literally devaluing mathematics as an abstract approach and making it more social. For use value, these propositions or concepts are the opposite: engaging socially in shared consumption of mathematics as a communicative practice can be satisfying for learners and teachers, and can even become a pleasure shared. Thus a 'connectionist' teaching approach by contrast with a 'transmissionist' (teaching to the test) pedagogy is of more value to students' dispositions and understanding (especially for those with lower grades). The former is akin to reflexive and critical pedagogies as opposed to ones that, with the current cultures of performativity in colleges, can be damaging to students.

Fuller's team (David, 2009a, Chapter 5) uniquely focused on non-participation in higher education and how adults think about their educational and social identities, given that they are qualified to participate in higher education but do not all choose to participate. They looked at social networks, or 'networks of intimacy', that influence individuals' decisions about participation across the life course. They questioned how decisions are made within families and social networks about study at university, and when this decision is made, using a critical and feminist framework. Those adults with the qualifications to enter higher education but who have not yet chosen to do so are seen as 'potentially recruitable' and as a pool to be tapped to deliver government participation targets. Research has not focused on mature adult decision-making about education and careers and little is known about their values about formal learning or the relevance of higher education to their lives. Fuller's team showed that, although the 'potentially recruitable' men and women might be likely to participate, given the example of their younger 'participation pioneers', they are living comfortable, stable lives and usually see little need for higher education. However, the mature (women) learners want high-quality, work-related and employer-supported provision, and the recognised qualifications that offer economic and social returns. Choices are then clearly related not only to employment or economic benefits but also to the fit with family lives and circumstances.

Pedagogies and practices for 'meaningful' student engagement

These seven TLRP studies have demonstrated how equity and diversity are currently played out in the processes of diverse UK higher education, leading to inequitable pathways for individual, diverse or disadvantaged (low SES) and mainly female students through highly stratified systems of higher education (defined in terms of international league tables). Nevertheless, the pedagogies and institutional practices can lead to *meaningful educational engagements* across the life course. The diverse practices and pedagogies across subjects may sustain *or* reverse patterns of differentiation and inequity. The learning outcomes through and across the life course illustrate that higher education *can* be meaningful in people's lives, authentic, practical and relevant, and as social as well as work or economic experiences. In other words, as already noted, policies for equity and widening participation in UK higher education have not achieved either fair access or equal participation and achieving degree results in a diversified and highly stratified system of higher education. Whilst the concept of educational or academic engagement was not foregrounded across the seven studies, it is clear that it is crucial for equity and widening participation policies. Moreover, the two studies that focused on pedagogies for student engagement drew on the wealth of theories and evidence from feminist and critical studies about how to engage students in their learning.

Conclusions

We in the TLRP argue that national and international policy frameworks around fair access or recruitment need to be adjusted to take account of prior and current educational experiences, especially for low SES. We also argue that it is crucially important to develop pedagogies and practices in higher education that are meaningful to male or female participants (as students and teachers) and that enable them to engage more effectively in higher education. It is clear that gender is deeply embedded and entwined with diversity in both the processes of knowledge production and the knowledge that has been produced. Women are taking an increasingly active role as students in higher education and as teachers, developing creative and inclusive pedagogies. Although gender is often implicit rather than explicit, policies and practices have included gender and feminist scholarship and pedagogies.

Gender is indeed deeply embedded within the processes of innovative knowledge production and the findings themselves, just as the policies and practices have included an array of equity issues, including especially gender and feminist scholarship (David, 2009a, chapters 6 and 7). Our work suggests that women as students and as academics or teachers are now important in producing this knowledge and the evidence-base for developing new policies and practices for global mass higher education. The academic labour market within the UK as an example of the theory of 'academic capitalism' has been dramatically and yet subtly transformed but this is rarely acknowledged in the policy processes and institutional practices.

It is not merely the acknowledgement of gender that is important but how gender and feminist perspectives contribute to reducing socio-economic and ethnic inequalities, and how they are based upon ethical principles that value and respect contributions from a diversity of people. Feminist and gender-sensitive work (for example, Morley et al., 2010) is particularly useful and important for embedding such gender-sensitive approaches to policies, pedagogies and practices. Finally, a vision for women in the global academy, despite academic capitalism, would surely incorporate the uses of feminist pedagogies, including developing inclusive and critical pedagogies to ensure that people's lives across the life course were enhanced and improved. This would not only entail the production of knowledge or research evidence, such as that from the TLRP, for policy but collaborative approaches for the twenty-first century, including incorporating a diversity of women in the processes of ensuring that the inclusive and flexible curricula have a strong impact upon learning outcomes and success. If we value inclusion, teachers, practitioners and policy makers should maintain high expectations of all students, as learners, whilst recognising the diversity of their needs, cultures and identities.

References

Altbach, P. (2010) 'Trouble with Numbers', *Times Higher Education*, 23 September 2010.

Arnot, M., David, M. and Weiner, G. (1999) *Closing the Gender Gap: Postwar Education and Social Change* (Cambridge: Polity Press).

Bekhradnia, B. (2009) *Male and Female Participation and Progression in Higher Education* (Oxford: Higher Education Policy Institute).

Bourdieu, P. (1992) *An Invitation To Reflexive Sociology* (Cambridge: Polity Press).

Bradley, D., Noonan, P., Nugent, H. and Sacles, B. (2008) *Review of Australian Higher Education Final Report* (Canberra: Department of Education, Employment and Workplace Relations). Retrieved from <http://www.deewr.gov.au/HigherEducation/Review/Pages/ReviewofAustralianHigherEducationReport.aspx>

Brine, J. (2006) 'Locating the Learner within EU Policy: Trajectories, Complexities, Identities', in Leathwood, C. and Francis, B. (eds) *Gender and Lifelong Learning: Critical Feminist Engagements* (London: Routledge/Falmer) pp.149–79.

Brown, R. (ed.) (2010) *Higher Education and the Market* (London: Routledge).

Browne, J. (2010) *Securing a Sustainable Future for Higher Education: An Independent Review of Higher Education Funding and Student Finance*. Retrieved from <http://www.independent.gov.uk/browne-report>

Cabinet Office Strategy Unit (2009) *Unleashing Aspiration: Summary and Recommendations of the Full Report*, the Panel on Fair Access to the Professions (Milburn report). Retrieved from <http://www.agcas.org.uk/assets/download?file=1204&parent=465>

David, M.E. (2003) *Personal and Political: Feminisms, Sociology and Family Lives* (Stoke-on-Trent: Trentham Books).

David, M.E. (ed.) (2009a) *Improving Learning by Widening Participation in Higher Education* (London: Routledge).

David, M.E. (2009b) *Effective Learning and Teaching in Higher Education: A Commentary by the Teaching and Learning Research Programme* (London: TLRP).

David, M.E. (2009c) *Transforming Global Higher Education: A Feminist Perspective*, Inaugural professorial lecture (London: Institute of Education).

Deem, R. (2001) 'Globalisation, New Managerialism, Academic Capitalism and Entrepreneurialism in Universities: Is the Local Dimension Still Important?', *Comparative Education*, 37/1: 7–20.

Deem, R. (2004) 'Sociology and the Sociology of Higher Education: A Missed Call or Disconnection?', *International Studies in the Sociology of Higher Education*, 14/1, pp.21–46.

Evans, M. (2004) *Killing Thinking: The Death of the Universities* (London: Continuum).

Gale, T., Hattam, R., Comber, B., Tranter, D., Bills, D., Sellar, S. and Parker, S. (2010) *Interventions Early in School As a Means to Improve Higher Education Outcomes for Disadvantaged Students* (Adelaide, National Centre for Student Equity in Higher Education, University of South Australia).

Halsey, A.H., Lauder, H., Brown, P. and Wells, A.S. (eds) (2000) *Education: Culture, Economy and Society* (Oxford: Oxford University Press).

Hey, V. (2004) 'Perverse Pleasures: Identity Work and the Paradoxes of Greedy Institutions', *Journal of International Women's Studies*, 5/3, pp.33–43.

Higher Education Funding Council for England (2005) *Young Participation in Higher Education* (London: HMSO).

Langa Rosado, D. and David, M.E. (2006) 'A Massive University or a University for the Masses? Continuity and Change in Higher Education in Spain and England', *Journal of Education Policy*, 21/3, pp.343–65.

Lauder, H., Brown, P., Dillabough, J. and Halsey, A.H. (eds) (2006) *Education, Globalisation and Social Change* (Oxford: Oxford University Press).

Leathwood, C. and Read, B. (2009) *Gender and the Changing Face of Higher Education* (Maidenhead: SRHE and McGraw-Hill/Open University Press).

Leonard, D. (2001) *A Woman's Guide to Doctoral Studies* (Maidenhead: Open University Press).

Maher, F.A. and Tetreault, M.K.T. (2007) *Privilege and Diversity in the Academy* (New York: Routledge).

Mirza, H. (2008) *Race, Gender and Educational Desire: Why Black Women Succeed and Fail* (London: Routledge).

Morley, L. (2003) *Quality and Power in Higher Education* (Buckingham: SRHE and Open University Press).

Morley, L. and David, M.E. (2009) 'Introduction: Celebrations and Challenges: Gender in Higher Education', *Higher Education Policy*, 22, pp.1–2.

Morley, L. et al. (2010) *Widening Participation in Higher Education in Ghana and Tanzania: Developing an Equity Scorecard: Research Report*, January (University of Sussex: An ESRC/DFID Poverty Reduction Programme Research Report).

National Audit Office (2008) *Widening Participation in Higher Education*, report by the Comptroller and Auditor General HC 725 Session 2007–8, 25 June. Retrieved from <http://www.nao.org.uk/publications/nao_reports/07–08/0708725.pdf>

Rhoads, R.A. and Torres, C.A. (eds) (2006) *The University, State and Market: The Political Economy of Globalization in the Americas* (Stanford, CA: Stanford University Press).

Shavit, Y., Arum, R. and Gamoran, A. (eds) (2007) *Stratification in Higher Education: A Comparative Study* (Stanford: Stanford University Press).

Slaughter, S. and Rhoades, G. (2004) *Academic Capitalism and the New Economy: Markets, State and Higher Education* (Baltimore: Johns Hopkins University Press).

Thomas, L. (2010) 'Presentation to the Society for Research in Higher Education's Access and Widening Participation Network on Widening Participation to Research Degrees', 21 September 2010.

Wakeling, P. and Kyriacou, C. (2010) *Widening Participation from Undergraduate to Postgraduate Research Degrees: A Research Synthesis* (York: National Coordinating Centre for Public Engagement and Economic and Social Research Council, University of York).

Weiler, K. and David, M.E. (2008) 'The Personal and Political: Second Wave Feminism and Educational Research, Introduction', *Discourse*, 29/4, pp.433–5.

Chapter 11

Student engagement in learning: facets of a complex interaction

Linda Leach and Nick Zepke

Massey University, New Zealand

Introduction

Student engagement is a complex interaction. The last decade has seen considerable growth of interest in student engagement as one way to increase student retention, outcomes and success. In this chapter we explore some understandings of the complexity of the interactions referred to as student engagement. We do this in three sections. First we introduce a conceptual framework of student engagement drawn from the research literature. Next we investigate this framework empirically by using research findings from a project in New Zealand with students enrolled in higher and further education programmes. Finally we consider some implications for practice emerging from our conceptualisation and investigation of student engagement.

Conceptualising student engagement

Student engagement is a complex construct that is understood in a variety of ways. Research has been conducted worldwide, primarily in North America and Australasia, but also in South Africa and the UK. Early definitions focused on what students and institutions do: "the time and effort students devote to activities that are empirically linked to desired outcomes of college *and* what institutions do to induce students to participate in these activities" (Kuh, 2009, p.683). More recently, Trowler (2010) identified three axes of engagement, each having a positive and negative pole. The first axis focuses on individual student learning such as the extent to which students actively participate in learning. The second axis covers issues of structure and process, which includes student representation, their role in governance and student feedback processes (most evident in the UK). The third spotlights issues of identity, understood as a sense of belonging for students, and how to engage specific groups of students – usually those considered 'under-represented' or 'non-traditional'. She also identifies three dimensions of engagement: behavioural, emotional and cognitive.

Initially, engagement research focused on what students did to enhance their learning: the time, effort and commitment they put into their study; the use they made of the resources and opportunities provided for them; the intentions they brought to their study. Notions like quality of effort, time on task and conceptions of learning were evident. A shift of focus recognised that institutions and teachers also contribute to student engagement, that they provide the context in which engagement occurs and, therefore, influence engagement both positively and negatively. The student engagement questionnaires currently used in several Western countries (for example, the USA National Survey of Student Engagement, the Australasian University Survey of Student Engagement, and the South African Survey of Student Engagement) acknowledge this dual responsibility, exploring both what students do and what institutions do to enhance engagement.

However, we suggest that student engagement is more complex than this. As part of a Teaching and Learning Research Initiative (TLRI) project on student engagement, we reviewed international literature, developed a conceptual organiser for student engagement, tested it with data from the project and consequently revised it (Leach and Zepke, 2011). The revised conceptual organiser identifies six perspectives on student engagement and includes some suggested indicators for each of the perspectives (see Table 11.1). One perspective relates to what the student does and four to what the institution and teachers do. The sixth incorporates a third kind of perspective: the non-institutional factors that influence engagement.

Perspectives on engagement	Chosen indicators
Motivation and agency (Engaged students are intrinsically motivated and want to exercise their agency)	*A student feels able to work autonomously* *A student feels they have relationships with others* *A student feels competent to achieve success*
Transactional engagement (Students engage with teachers)	*Students experience academic challenge*
	Learning is active and collaborative inside and outside the classroom
	Students and teachers interact constructively
	Students have enriching educational experiences
Transactional engagement (Students engage with each other)	*Learning is active and collaborative inside and outside the classroom*
	Students have positive, constructive peer relationships
	Students use social skills to engage with others
Institutional support (Institutions provide an environment conducive to learning)	*There is a strong focus on student success*
	There are high expectations of students
	There is investment in a variety of support services
	Diversity is valued
	Institutions continuously improve
Active citizenship (Students and institutions work together to enable challenges to social beliefs and practices)	*Students are able to make legitimate knowledge claims*
	Students can engage effectively with others including the 'other'
	Students are able to live successfully in the world
	Students have a firm sense of themselves
	Learning is participatory, dialogic, active and critical
Non-institutional support (Students are supported by family and friends to engage in learning)	*Students' family and friends understand the demands of study*
	Students' family and friends assist with e.g. childcare, time management
	Students family and friends create space for study commitments

Table 11.1: A conceptual organiser for student engagement

The first perspective focuses on students and what they bring to engagement in learning – their motivation and agency. It assumes students are agentic, constructivist learners. Studies informing this strand show that student motivation is an important explanatory factor in whether students engage (Ainley, 2006; Scheutz, 2008) and that a variety of motivations influence engagement (Caspi et al., 2006; Yorke and Knight, 2004). Scheutz (2008) found that Self-Determination Theory (SDT) (Deci and Ryan, 2000, see also Newbery, Chapter 3, this volume) was an excellent fit with findings from the Community College Survey of Student engagement (CCSSE). While not specifically about engagement, SDT enables a synthesis of findings about how motivation and learner agency lead to engagement. It focuses on agentic individuals who have set clear performance and learning goals, have positive self-theories and interact with their social environments in both positive and negative ways. SDT suggests that understanding human motivation requires an appreciation of innate psychological needs for competency, autonomy and relatedness (Deci and Ryan, 2000).

The second engagement perspective highlights transactions between teachers and students in educationally purposeful activities. Research conducted in the NSSE by Kuh and his associates is dominant[*], though findings from other countries are increasing[†]. Effective transactional practices include academic challenge, active and collaborative learning, student–teacher interaction and enriching educational experiences (Kuh et al., 2005). Key to successful transactions is the relationship between teacher and students. Teachers who establish inviting learning environments, demand high standards, challenge and are available to discuss students' academic progress, engage students (Bryson and Hand, 2007; Mearns, Meyer and Bharadwaj, 2007; Umbach and Wawrzynski, 2005). Research also identifies practices that disengage (Hockings et al., 2008; Hu and Kuh, 2002), create passivity (Coates, 2007) and alienation (Case, 2007). Students without the required social capital experience engagement as a battle (Krause, 2005).

Also an institutional one, the third perspective concerns transactions between students. Findings suggest that active learning in groups, peer relationships and social skills engage learners. Peer interaction has a strong predictive capacity for engagement and outcomes (Moran and Gonyea, 2003). Co-operative learning, cognitive challenge and the

---

* See <http://nsse.iub.edu/>

† For example, <http://ausse.acer.edu.au/>

development of personal skills (Ahlfeldt, Mehta and Sellnow, 2005) as well as active and collaborative experiences contribute to student engagement and learning (Lambert, Terenzini and Lattuca, 2007; Umbach and Wawrzynski, 2005). Working in learning communities is positively associated with students' personal and social development, practical competence, greater effort and deeper engagement (Zhao and Kuh, 2004) and enhances their sense of belonging (Krause, 2005). However, risk and safety considerations could hinder engagement unless students receive appropriate support (Lizzio and Wilson, 2006). Student–student transactions are also important in online learning with peer interaction improving engagement (Jung et al., 2002).

The fourth perspective features institutional support. According to Kuh et al. (2005), successful institutions have cultures focused on student success, highlight student learning in their mission, establish high expectations, aim for continuous improvement, value diversity and difference, prepare students for learning in higher education and invest money in support services. However, spending money by itself did not improve student engagement. What mattered was institutional culture and mission (Pike et al., 2006; Porter, 2006). The first year is very important (Pittaway and Moss, 2006). A comprehensive, integrated and co-ordinated approach to the first-year experience engaged students (Reason, Terenzini and Domingo, 2006). Diversity is also important. Students must feel they belong (Deci and Ryan, 2000). 'Non-traditional' students often feel uncomfortable in traditional institutions and do not engage (Laird et al., 2007). However, more students are now in paid employment so engagement cannot be assumed and must be negotiated (McInnis, 2003).

The fifth perspective, also an institutional one, we call active citizenship – a deeper, socially aware form of engagement that is less common in the literature. It was informed by two sources: McMahon and Portelli (2004), who promote a democratic-critical conception of engagement that goes beyond strategies, techniques or behaviours to engagement that is participatory and dialogic; and Barnett and Coate (2005), who distinguish between operational engagement and ontological engagement. The former incorporates conservative and student-centred engagement; the latter incorporates three projects: knowing how to make knowledge claims; acting constructively in the world; becoming aware of themselves and their potential. However, some students lack the social capital required to engage as active citizens (Case, 2007; Krause, 2005). Further, Read, Archer and Leathwood (2003) argue that traditional higher education culture inhibits engaging for active citizenship and students from 'non-traditional' backgrounds are particularly disadvantaged by an institutional culture that places them as 'other'.

The sixth perspective, non-institutional support, suggests there is a third aspect to student engagement that is often overlooked and goes beyond what the students and the institution do. For example, Coates (2006, p.173) identifies 23 things institutions can do to enhance student engagement. None recognise non-institutional support as an influence. Factors such as personal or family health, financial pressures, family support or lack of support, family and community responsibilities also influence students' willingness and ability to engage in their learning – positively and negatively. Almost half the students in one study considered withdrawing because of external pressures (Zepke, Leach and Prebble, 2005). Yorke and Longden (2008) identify two non-institutional reasons for early departure: problems with finance and employment; and social integration problems. In another study, over half of the students in part-time employment give family reasons for being employed (Krause et al., 2005). Some want independence while others are supporting families.

Investigating the six perspectives empirically

We now investigate these perspectives further by presenting selected findings from the TLRI project. The project used a mixed method, quantitative dominant approach in nine institutional case studies to investigate the research question *how do institutional and non-institutional learning environments influence student engagement with learning in diverse tertiary settings?* Data-gathering methods included a survey of students enrolled for a first time in the institution (1,246 responses) and follow-up semi-structured interviews with 72 students and a survey of teachers (376 responses). The student survey used Likert scales, for example, very important, important, little importance, no importance; strongly agree, agree, disagree, strongly disagree and not applicable. Details of the project and findings are accessible at <http://www.tlri.org.nz/learning-environments-and-student-engagement-their-learning-tertiary-settings>.

Motivation and agency

Following Scheutz (2008) we developed questions for one section of the student survey around Deci and Ryan's (2000) SDT. This section was made up of 24 questions, eight for each of the three SDT needs: agency, relatedness and competence. Analysis revealed that competence was of high importance to 65 per cent of students and of little importance to 1 per cent; agency was of high importance to 47 per cent and of little importance to 1 per cent; and relatedness was of high importance to 44 per cent and of little importance to 6 per cent of students. This suggests that competence is the most important motivational need in student engagement and relatedness the least important to these students. However, it is also important to note that all three of the needs were seen to be of at least some importance to most students: competence 99 per cent, agency 99 per cent and relatedness 94 per cent. In interviews students provided examples of each need:

> What I'm finding with this course is that it is very news focused. News doesn't blow my hair back... That's not my interest in journalism. I'm interested in cultural stuff, like events, travel, so I'm thinking I may be able to influence the content somehow.
>
> (E9)

> But my teacher keeps saying, "Just listen and don't look it and think ahh" – it's actually straightforward. There is that fear that I won't get it right. I just take my time, listen, pay attention, read properly, don't think it's so hard. Once you get into it, it becomes easier and easier.
>
> (H8)

> I was a bit scared first. I was at college for seven years and then coming here, I was quite scared, but definitely feel at home now.
>
> (I2)

More detailed analysis of the survey data also identified interesting variations between case-study institutions (Zepke, Leach and Butler,

2010a). For example, in one institution the three needs were quite similar with both agency and competence rated of high importance by 89 per cent of students and relatedness by 81 per cent of students. In another institution, relatedness was rated of little importance by 15 per cent of students; in four other institutions more students rated relatedness than agency to be of high importance to them, though in two the difference was less than 2 per cent. The highest importance given to competency was by 89 per cent of students in one institution, the lowest by 69 per cent in another. The range for agency was from 89 per cent to 47 per cent and for relatedness from 81 per cent to 32 per cent. These data show significant institutional differences.

Teacher–student interactions

The student survey included 26 items about what teachers and institutions do to engage students (Zepke, Leach and Butler, 2009). Many related to specific teacher–student interactions. For example, 'teachers being enthusiastic about their subject', 'encouraging me to work independently', 'providing opportunities to apply my learning', 'recognising I have family and community responsibilities'. Students were asked how important each item was to their learning and how well they thought their institution was performing.

Data show some remarkable similarities. Of the 26 items, 13 were considered to be of high importance to over 80 per cent of students in all nine institutions. Of these 13, eight were about specific teacher–student interactions. For example, 'teachers providing prompt feedback', 'providing feedback that improves my learning', 'challenging me in helpful ways', 'making themselves available to discuss my learning' and 'teaching in ways that help me learn'. Three other items may involve teacher and student interaction, for example, 'receiving helpful guidance and advice about my study'. Only six items were considered to be of low importance in any institution. Of particular interest, 'teachers encouraging me to work with other students' was of low importance in four institutions and 'having my cultural background respected' in three.

There were also differences between institutions. One did not meet student expectations on any of the 26 items; on 23 the difference between importance and performance was significant. In another, significant differences showed expectations were met on 15 items and not met on three. Of interest were items students rated as 'low importance'. In three institutions no item was so rated; in one institution four items were. These data suggest that students had high expectations of their teachers and that a variety of teacher and student interactions are very important to students' engagement in their learning. In interviews, students explained their views:

> Teachers are creative and create a friendly atmosphere. It all feels like a big family... Teachers change the way they are telling you something if I don't understand.
>
> (G6)

> Certainly the better lecturers make it more interesting and more entertaining and give you more desire to attend the lectures. Some lecturers are more supportive than others... Approachable people are good too because you feel free to come up with dumb questions... And with some you can't keep your eyes open, they are so boring and you are falling asleep.
>
> (A10)

> One tutor used to read from the screen notes and then never finish the sentence... I made sure I went to the other lecturer's tutorials because they were more engaging. I used to run a mile if she was lecturing.
>
> (D5)

Student-to-student interactions

Under 'motivation and agency' above, we presented findings that suggest students were motivated more by autonomy and competence needs than by a need to belong. Nevertheless, relatedness was very important to 44 per cent of students. Positive social and academic interactions and relationships with other students build relatedness. Items related to student–student interactions were in three survey questions. 'Feeling I am valued as a person' was very important to 36 per cent of students and 'feeling comfortable with other students' to 33 per cent. However, 'joining in social occasions' was very important to only 13 per cent; 'knowing how to help other students with their learning' to 17 per cent; 'making social contacts with other students' and 'wanting to learn alongside other students' to 20 per cent of students. While 26 per cent thought 'teachers encouraging me to work with other students' was very important, for 22 per cent this was of little importance, and for 4 per cent of no importance. Students reported they 'make social contact with other students' every day (38 per cent) and not at all (27 per cent); they 'join in cultural events run by my institution' not at all (71 per cent); and 'join in sporting events run by my institution' not at all (78 per cent). Conversely these three items were rated as very important by 21 per cent, 7 per cent and 6 per cent of students respectively.

These data suggest students have mixed views on the value of student–student interactions, social and academic. Interview data showed a similar mix. Some students discussed the value of academic and social interactions with other students:

> I have a study buddy and we help each other. We are both older students and him and I we bounce off each other.
>
> (H5)

Others made it clear that they preferred to learn independently:

> I don't really like team work because other people frustrate me and I tend to think I can do it faster myself.
>
> (C11)

> When we were given a group exercise and put into groups and I couldn't cope with it because they were all mucking around and carrying on, not doing the job.
>
> (C1)

Institutional support

Institutional support comes in many forms. While research suggests the institutional culture is influential (Porter, 2006), students tend to think in terms of services provided for them. Two survey items related to institutional culture: 'staff creating a pleasant learning environment' was rated very important by 51 per cent of students and 'having my cultural background respected' by 35 per cent. Data show students value several forms of institutional support. 'Having access to the learning resources I need' was very important to 61 per cent, 'receiving helpful guidance and advice about my study' to 57 per cent and 'knowing where to get help' to 51 per cent. For these first-time-enrolled students, 'knowing how to contact people to get help' was very important to 49 per cent, 'being given information on how systems work' to 42 per cent and 'knowing how to find my way around' to 40 per cent. Interestingly 'knowing how to use the library to support my learning' was very important to fewer students (36 per cent), as was 'knowing how to access learning support services' (31 per cent). However, 'learning support services being available at the times I need them' was very important to 42 per cent. Overall, support services were important, as fewer than 2 per cent of students rated any of 'no importance'. "The main support service I go to is the cultural support committee on campus. They can provide you with a tutor and I had one for computer science. That's the main service. I went to the learning skills centre once and have joined some clubs" (A7). The most frequently used services were library, computers for Internet access, learning support and health services.

How well were these services provided? Forty-one per cent of students rated the nine institutions' performance 'very well' on 'having access to the learning resources I need', with 39 per cent on 'knowing how to contact people to get help' and 36 per cent on 'knowing how to find my way around'. The worst performance was on 'being given information on how systems work' (29 per cent), though fewer than 3 per cent of students rated institutions' performance 'poorly' on each of the services. Some questions gauged students' willingness to take action to get support they need. Thirty-five per cent responded that they 'actively seek help' once a week and 17 per cent 'not at all'.

Active citizenship

We included items on active citizenship in order to gauge the importance of and performance on this emerging perspective on student engagement. Items were included in three questions. 'Learning to effect change in the community/society' was rated 'very important' by 28 per cent of students; 'knowing how to draw attention to what needs changing' by 25 per cent; 'talking to students with views different from my own' by 20 per cent. Two items sought students' views on questioning their teachers. 'Questioning teachers about their teaching' was rated 'very important' by 17 per cent of students with 32 per cent reporting it was of 'little importance' to them. But responses to the item 'I question teachers' revealed that 28 per cent think this is very important and 31 per cent reported that they questioned teachers 'once a week'; 24 per cent 'not at all'. Perhaps the difference lies between questioning teachers' teaching, and questioning teachers in order to understand the subject. Two further questions sought students' responses to being involved in student leadership. 'Taking a leadership role in student affairs' was 'very important' to only 8 per cent of students; 'I take a leadership role' was very important to only 10 per cent; and 53 per cent 'took a leadership role' 'not at all'. Institutional performance was sought on one of these active citizenship items – 'learning to effect change in the community/society'. Twenty-one per cent of students rated performance 'very well', a further 41 per cent as 'quite well'. This suggests that, although active citizenship is not so important to students, institutions are performing well overall. A third of students interviewed made comments that suggest they engage in active citizenship: for example, "now I feel much more open-minded" (A10); "I may be able to influence the content somehow" (E9).

It is clear that the active citizenship items were less important to students' engagement than many others, in particular the teacher–student interaction and motivation and agency items.

Non-institutional support

A non-institutional support perspective is not well-recognised in engagement research. To address this gap we wrote 12 items for the student survey addressing issues such as family support, the influence of social activities, friends, work, family expectations, cultural expectations, health and the ability to self-organise.

The four statements students most 'strongly agreed' with were: 'my family supports me studying' (61 per cent), 'I organise myself to succeed in my study' (41 per cent), 'my family has high expectations of me' (30 per cent) and 'work commitments make studying difficult' (17 per cent).

The four most strongly disagreed with were: 'my friends don't want me to study' (39 per cent), 'cultural commitments interfere with my study' (19 per cent), 'commitments to my religion affect my study' (17 per cent) and 'health issues affect the time I have for study' (15 per cent).

The items which most affected students' success were: 'I organise myself to succeed in my study' (60 per cent), 'my family supports me studying' (51 per cent), 'my family has high expectations for me' (29 per cent) and 'finances make it hard for me to study' (22 per cent). Those with least effect were 'my friends don't want me to study' (45 per cent), 'cultural commitments interfere with my study' (34 per cent), 'health issues affect the time I have for study' (27 per cent) and 'commitments to my religion affect my study' (27 per cent). In the interview data comments on family support were most frequent:

> I try to work things out with my husband and even my extended family have had the kids to stay... so I can get things done.
>
> (D5)

These data suggest that non-institutional factors impact on some students' engagement, at least at times. In the next section we consider key messages for practice emerging from the six perspectives on student engagement and the TLRI data.

Implications for practice

It is clear from the literature and the TLRI data that student engagement is a complex concept. It is understood and implemented in quite different ways by teachers and researchers (see Solomonides, Reid and Petocz, Chapter 1, this volume; Trowler, 2010). Further, as Stefani (2009, p.11) points out, "Given the heterogeneity of any student body, it is quite likely that 'engagement' will mean different things to different students." Hardy and Bryson (2009), synthesising these views, are calling for a reframing of the concept, arguing that "normative conceptions of good educational practices vary amongst institutions, programmes of studies and student subcultures. There can be no one 'quick fix' solution, it is a multi-faceted, social constructivist concept that should take account of students' sense of self and aspirations and the context they are in" (p.1).

We have added to that complexity by identifying six perspectives on student engagement. These perspectives include, for example, both psychological and sociological approaches to engagement, taking account of both individual and social power dimensions (Ball and Perry, 2011); the behavioural, emotional and cognitive dimensions identified by Trowler (2010); the emerging active citizenship perspective (McMahon and Portelli, 2004; Barnett and Coate, 2005); and the non-institutional factors that impact on students' engagement (Zepke, Leach and Prebble, 2005; Zepke, Leach and Butler, 2011). Hardy and Bryson (2009) recognise this, pointing out that engagement is both "within and outside of the institution's sphere of influence" (p.6). We agree with Hardy and Bryson's (2009) comment that "student engagement is dynamic and multifaceted (and not amenable to fitting neatly into any dimension)" (p.6). Boundaries between the perspectives are porous and not tightly contained. They configure an open, changing network in which both connections and distinctions emerge (Zepke, 2011).

Building on the conceptual and empirical foundations laid in the chapter, we now sketch out some implications for practice by using the indicators listed in Table 11.1.

Teachers can use extrinsic motivators to enhance student engagement

Motivation is a key factor in engagement. It focuses on what the student does, their 'quality of effort' (Pace, 1988, cited in Coates, 2006, p.22) and recognises that engagement requires the agency of the individual student (Krause and Coates, 2008). Self-Determination Theory is a good fit for student motivation to engage in higher education contexts (Scheutz, 2008). Data from the TLRI study support this. Students reported they were motivated by the three needs – autonomy, relatedness and competence (Deci and Ryan, 2000). Very few students indicated these needs provided little motivation for them: 1 per cent for competence and autonomy and 6 per cent for relatedness. This suggests that these needs provide motivational impetus for most students. However, they were motivated more by competence and autonomy needs than relatedness needs. This confirms Deci and Ryan's (2000) finding that, "Although autonomy and competence have been found to be the most powerful influences on intrinsic motivation, theory and research suggest that relatedness also plays a role, albeit a more distal one"(p.235).

Teachers lament that not all students are intrinsically motivated. However, Deci and Ryan (2000) identified a continuum of six types of motivation ranging from extrinsic to intrinsic. While intrinsic motivation maps most closely to feelings of wellbeing and engagement, some forms of extrinsic motivation do too. Teachers can encourage extrinsic motivation in addition to devising learning activities that will meet students' needs for autonomy, relatedness and competence. For example, teachers could devise tasks and activities that enable students to feel competent without glossing over weaknesses; provide feedback on completed tasks that is timely, specific, reinforces strengths and provides guidance on how to address weaknesses; and develop group activities that encourage interdependence, a sense of belonging.

Teachers are very important to student engagement

A second key factor in student engagement is what teachers and institutions do (Kuh, 2009). Teachers are especially important. As Umbach and Wawrzynski (2005, p.173) reported: "Our findings suggest that faculty do matter. The educational context created by faculty behaviours and attitudes has a dramatic effect on student learning and engagement." Kuh et al. (2006) place teachers and teaching at the heart of engagement, reporting:

> Virtually everyone agrees that student–faculty interaction is an important factor in student success (p.34) [and] Good teachers are knowledgeable about their subject matter, are enthusiastic, encourage students to express their views through discussion, and interact with their students, both in and outside of class.
>
> (p.68)

Students in the TLRI study confirm this. When comparing the importance of teaching, motivation and non-institutional influences on engagement, we found that five of the top ten items, including the top two, were from the teaching scale (Zepke, Leach and Butler, 2010b).

Two related to approaches to teaching, two to subject matter and one to teacher–student relationships. Teacher influence was rated as 'high importance' by more students than motivational and non-institutional influences. This held across all sub-populations: female, male, Maori Pasifika, European, 20 and under, 21 and older, part-time and full-time students.

We cannot underestimate the influence of teachers on student engagement. Teaching that ensures indicators for successful teacher and student interactions are met (Table 11.1) is most likely to engage students. For example, offering students academically challenging experiences, planning for active and collaborative learning activities and enriching educational experiences, and interacting constructively with students.

Collaborative learning needs to be promoted with some students

Collaborative learning is a feature of much literature on engagement (Lambert, Terenzini and Lattuca, 2007; Umbach and Wawrzynski, 2005), a feature sometimes described as working in learning communities (Kuh et al., 2006). Coates' (2006) typology of student engagement styles includes one called 'collaborative'. Collaborative learning "involves students learning through appropriately situated conversational interaction about knowledge with their peers" (pp.55–6) and is reported to have many benefits:

> Furthermore, when students collaborate with others in solving problems or mastering difficult material, they acquire valuable skills that prepare them to deal with the messy, unscripted problems they will encounter daily during and after college.
>
> (Kuh et al., 2005, p.193)

Some even suggest "encouraging, even requiring, students to study in groups" (Markwell, 2007, p.18) because "a particular study habit shared by almost all students who are struggling academically [is that] they always study alone" (Light, 2001, cited in Markwell, 2007, p.7).

However, data from the TLRI project is conflicted. The item 'wanting to learn alongside other students' was of high importance to only 20 per cent of students; 'teachers encouraging me to work with other students' was of high importance to only 26 per cent but was of 'little' or 'no importance' to 26 per cent. In contrast, 'teachers encouraging me to work independently' was of high importance to 34 per cent, of 'little' or 'no importance' to 17 per cent. These students were divided over the value of collaborative learning to their engagement. If we believe that there are real benefits in collaborative learning for students, we must explain those benefits clearly to some students. Additionally teachers might organise and support group activities in which students solve authentic problems related to the subject; learn more about and create formal learning communities; and even form smaller groups and learning communities within large classes. But teachers might do well also to listen to students who exercise an informed choice to continue to work independently.

Institutional support is important to student engagement

Student engagement is a shared responsibility (Trowler and Trowler, 2010). It is the institution's responsibility to create a supportive environment within which students will use their agency to engage in learning. This is the culture of the institution (Porter, 2006) or the institutional conditions, which include resources, educational policies, programmes and practices and structural features (Kuh et al., 2006, p.8). Also part of institutional support are the variety of support services available to students (McInnis et al., 2000) and the interactions they have with all staff: "faculty members, academic administrators, and student affairs professionals can influence the extent to which students perceive that the institutional environment values scholarship and intellectual activity by communicating high expectations" (Hu and Kuh, 2002, p.570–1). As Markwell (2007, p.18) concluded: "student engagement requires staff engagement".

Students in the TLRI study thought institutional support was important to their engagement. Several of the support services seemed to be related to their status as students enrolled for a first time in the institution, as they found their way around the institution, worked out what help was available and how to access it, and got information on their study programme. The most important support, however, was access to learning resources. Knowing how to use the library and access learning support seemed to be less important at this stage.

It seems that support services are essential to the engagement of some students. If services are not retained, the cost will possibly be lower student completion rates (McInnis et al., 2000). But teachers have an important and continuing role in making students aware of support services. Actions may include being familiar with the range of support services the institution offers students; being an advocate for services and, where necessary and possible, helping out; and planning ways to organise support services for the students they teach.

Active citizenship could be encouraged in institutions

McMahon and Portelli's (2004) critical-democratic conception of engagement reflects "an education which engenders personal empowerment and personal and social transformation guided by principles of equity, social justice and inclusion" (p.72). This includes engagement for equality and social justice, for example by widening participation for 'non-traditional' students (Trowler, 2010); student participation in institutional governance (Lizzio and Wilson, 2009); and a wide variety of extra-curricular activities (Trowler, 2010), some with political agendas (Slocum and Rhoads, 2009). Research shows that engagement in active citizenship activities is beneficial for students (Kuh, 2009); McMahon and Portelli (2004, p.73) argue that "policy makers have the moral obligation to create polices that move beyond lip service to preparing students for democratic citizenry".

In stark contrast to this literature, students in the TLRI project were not engaged by activities related to active citizenship. Few thought 'taking a leadership role in student affairs' was very important (8 per cent) and a majority (53 per cent) responded 'not at all' to 'I take a leadership role'. Only a quarter thought that 'knowing how to draw attention to what needs changing' and 'learning to effect change in society' were very important. Clearly there is a mismatch here. Is active citizenship a misfit in a society increasingly focused on the individual? Or does this mean that active citizenship is even more important than in the past? We believe the latter. So we see advantages in every teacher taking an affirming position on active citizenship activities. Our ideological position is that this emerging perspective be incorporated into curricula and practices to help prepare students for their future roles in democratic societies. The idea is to help students make legitimate claims about knowledge in a world of uncertainty and negotiate challenges to such claims; act constructively in the world by identifying ethical and political issues affecting their subject; and become aware of themselves and their potential to effect change in a world that is open, fluid and contested.

Non-institutional support deserves to be recognised in student engagement

Influences outside the direct control of the institution, which we call non-institutional support, are recognised by few in the student engagement literature (Yorke and Longden, 2008; Zepke, Leach and Butler, 2011). Yet such support, for example, from partner, children, family, friends or employer, can enable students to engage with their study even when the going gets tough. Alternatively, unsupportive social networks can be the reason a student disengages and withdraws. Similarly, personal or family ill health or financial difficulties can interfere with engagement, even when the student is motivated and achieving. In New Zealand we saw the effect the Christchurch earthquakes had on students. As one student wrote, "it is difficult to study when you are spending more time under the desk than sitting at it!"

Data from the TLRI study show that family high expectations and support are important positive influences on engagement. Financial issues and employment issues had the most negative impact. While few students reported that cultural or religious issues affected their time for study (3 per cent), Pasifika students are affected more than other groups by non-institutional influences (Zepke, Leach and Butler, 2010b). Institutions and teachers need to recognise non-institutional influences on student engagement, both their positive impact and the issues they create. We cannot just ignore them, arguing they are outside our control. While that is true, we can acknowledge the positive effects and take action to reduce their negative impact. Our understanding of and caring about these impacts is important to students. Most frequently, some flexibility with assessment deadlines is all they need to remain engaged while they deal with issues external to the institution. Institutional systems need to have some flexibility, particularly around deadlines for reporting results – although we acknowledge this may become more difficult as governments partially fund on completion.

Conclusion

In this chapter we have done three things. We introduced a conceptual organiser for student engagement that embraces six perspectives we found in the literature: motivation and agency; teacher–student transactions; student–student transactions; institutional support; active citizenship; and non-institutional support. We then used this conceptual organiser as a framework to present an overview of findings from a TLRI project on student engagement. Finally we drew on the literature that informed the conceptual organiser and the TLRI data to introduce six implications for practice. As Markwell (2007, p.4) concludes:

> All these factors point unmistakeably to the importance of students engaging actively in their own learning, engaging with each other, engaging with those who teach them, engaging with and through a range of available learning resources, and engaging in extra-curricular activities – all this within an academic community to which they have a real sense of belonging.

We would add engaging with non-institutional support and in active citizenship activities; and we suggest that engagement be researched in individual institutions to identify the specific engagement needs of students enrolled there. We end with a question for institutions and teachers: what are you doing, and what more could you do, to foster students' engagement in each of the six perspectives?

Acknowledgements

We warmly acknowledge the Teaching and Learning Research Initiative, for funding the project this chapter is based on, as well as our research partners in each of the nine institutions for their involvement in the project: Helen Anderson, Alison Ayrton, Philippa Butler, Jerry Hoffman, Peter Isaacs, Judy Henderson, Jill Moseley, Catherine Ross, Barbara Russell, Gloria Slater, Kiri Solomon, Stewart Wilson, Adelle Wiseley.

References

Ahlfeldt, S., Mehta, S. and Sellnow, T. (2005) 'Measurement and Analysis of Student Engagement in University Classes Where Varying Levels of PBL Methods of Instruction Are in Use', *Higher Education Research and Development*, 24/1, pp.5–20.

Ainley, M. (2006) 'Connecting with Learning: Motivation, Affects and Cognition in Interest Processes', *Educational Psychology Review*, 18, pp.391–405.

Ball, I. and Perry, C. (2011) 'Differences in Student Engagement: Investigating the Role of Dominant Cognitive Processes Preferred by Engineering and Education Students', *Education Research International*. Retrieved from <http://www.hindawi.com/journals/edu/2011/414068.html>

Barnett, R. and Coate, K. (2005) *Engaging the Curriculum in Higher Education* (Maidenhead: Society for Research into Higher Education and Open University Press).

Bryson, C. and Hand, L. (2007) 'The Role of Engagement in Inspiring Teaching and Learning', *Innovations in Education and Teaching International*, 44/4, pp.349–62.

Case, J. (2007) 'Alienation and Engagement: Exploring Students' Experiences of Studying Engineering', *Teaching in Higher Education*, 12/1, pp.119–33.

Caspi, A., Chajut, E., Saporta, K. and Beyth-Marom, R. (2006) 'The Influence of Personality on Social Participation in Learning Environments', *Learning and Individual Differences*, 16, pp.129–44.

Coates, H. (2006) *Student Engagement in Campus-Based and Online Education* (Oxford: Routledge).

Coates, H. (2007) 'A Model of Online and General Campus-Based Student Engagement', *Assessment and Evaluation in Higher Education*, 32/2, pp.121–41.

Deci, E. and Ryan, R. (2000) 'The "What" and the "Why" of Goal Pursuits: Human Needs and the Self-Determination of Behavior', *Psychological Inquiry*, 11/4, pp.227–68.

Hardy, C. and Bryson, C. (2009) *Student Engagement: Paradigm Change or Political Expediency?* Retrieved from <http://www.adm.heacademy.ac.uk/resources/features/student-engagement-paradigm-change-or-political-expediency>

Hockings, C., Cooke, S., Yamashita, H., McGinty, S. and Bowl, M. (2008) 'Switched Off? A Study of Disengagement Among Computing Students at Two Universities', *Research Papers in Education*, 23/2: 191–201.

Hu, S. and Kuh, G.D. (2002) 'Being (Dis)engaged in Educationally Purposeful Activities: The Influences of Student and Institutional Characteristics', *Research in Higher Education,* 43/5, pp.555–75.

Jung, I., Choi, S., Lim, C. and Leem, J. (2002) 'Effects of Different Types of Interaction on Learning Achievement, Satisfaction and Participation in Web-Based Instruction', *Innovations in Education and Teaching International,* 39/2, pp.153–62.

Krause, K. (2005) *Engaged, Inert or Otherwise Occupied? Deconstructing the 21st Century Undergraduate Student,* keynote paper at the Sharing Scholarship in Learning and Teaching: Engaging Students Symposium, James Cook University, Townsville, September.

Krause, K. and Coates, H. (2008) 'Students' Engagement in First-Year University', *Assessment and Evaluation in Higher Education,* 33/5, pp.493–505.

Krause, K., Hartley, R., James, R. and McInnis, C. (2005) *The First Year Experience in Australian Universities: Findings From a Decade of National Studies.* Retrieved from <http://www.cshe.unimelb.edu.au/pdfs/FYEReport05KLK.pdf>

Kuh, G.D. (2009) 'What Student Affairs Professionals Need to Know About Student Engagement', *Journal of College Student Development,* 50/6, pp.683–706.

Kuh, G.D., Kinzie, J., Buckley, J., Bridges, B. and Hayek, J. (2006) *What Matters to Student Success: A Review of the Literature.* Retrieved from <http://nces.ed.gov/npec/pdf/Kuh_Team_Report.pdf>

Kuh, G.D., Kinzie, J., Schuh, J., Whitt, E. and Associates (2005) *Student Success in College: Creating Conditions That Matter* (San Francisco: Jossey-Bass).

Laird, T., Bridges, B., Morelon-Quainoo, C., Williams, J. and Salinas Homes, M. (2007) 'African American and Hispanic Student Engagement at Minority Serving and Predominantly White Institutions', *Journal of College Student Development,* 48/1, pp.39–56.

Lambert, A., Terenzini, P. and Lattuca, L. (2007) 'More Than Meets the Eye: Curricular and Programmatic Effects on Student Learning', *Research in Higher Education,* 48/2, pp.141–68.

Leach, L. and Zepke, N. (2011, in press) 'Engaging Students in Learning: A Review of a Conceptual Organiser', *Higher Education Research and Development.*

Lizzio, A. and Wilson, K. (2006) 'Enhancing the Effectiveness of Self-Managed Learning Groups: Understanding Students' Choices and Concerns', *Studies in Higher Education,* 31/6, pp.689–703.

Lizzio, A. and Wilson, K. (2009) 'Student Participation in University Governance: The Role Conceptions and Sense of Efficacy of Student Representatives on Departmental Committees', *Studies in Higher Education*, 34/1, pp.69–84.

Markwell, D. (2007) *The Challenge of Student Engagement*, keynote address at the Teaching and Learning Forum, University of Western Australia, 30–31 January. Retrieved from <http://www.catl.uwa.edu.au/__data/page/95565/Student_engagement_-_Don_Markwell_-_30_Jan_2007.pdf>

McInnis, C. (2003) *New Realities of the Student Experience: How Should Universities Respond?*, paper presented at the 25th annual conference of the European Association for Institutional Research, Limerick.

McInnis, C., Hartley, R., Polesel, J. and Teese, R. (2000) *Non-Completion in Vocational Education and Training and Higher Education*. Retrieved from <http://www.dest.gov.au/archive/research/docs/final.pdf>

McMahon, B. and Portelli, J. (2004) 'Engagement for What? Beyond Popular Discourses of Student Engagement', *Leadership and Policy in Schools*, 3/1, pp.59–76.

Mearns, K., Meyer, J. and Bharadwaj, A. (2007) *Student Engagement in Human Biology Practical Sessions*, refereed paper presented at the Teaching and Learning Forum 2007, Curtin University of Technology, Perth.

Moran, E. and Gonyea, T. (2003) *The Influence of Academically-Focused Peer Interaction on College Students' Development* (ERIC Document Reproduction Service No. ED478773).

Pike, G., Smart, J., Kuh, G.D. and Hayek, J. (2006) 'Educational Expenditures and Student Engagement: When Does Money Matter?', *Research in Higher Education*, 47/7, pp.847–72.

Pittaway, S. and Moss, T. (2006) *Contextualising Student Engagement: Orientation and Beyond in Teacher Education*, refereed paper presented at the 9th Pacific Rim First Year in Higher Education Conference, Griffith University, Gold Coast Campus, July.

Porter, S. (2006) 'Institutional Structures and Student Engagement', *Research in Higher Education*, 47/5, pp.531–58.

Read, B., Archer, L. and Leathwood, C. (2003) 'Challenging Cultures? Student Conceptions of "Belonging" and "Isolation" at a Post-1992 University', *Studies in Higher Education*, 28/3, pp.261–77.

Reason, R., Terenzini, P. and Domingo, R. (2006) 'First Things First: Developing Academic Competence in the First Year of College', *Research in Higher Education*, 47/2, pp.149–75.

Scheutz, P. (2008) 'A Theory-Driven Model of Community College Student Engagement', *Community College Journal of Research and Practice*, 32, pp.305–24.

Slocum, J. and Rhoads, R. (2009) 'Faculty and Student Engagement in the Argentine Grassroots Rebellion: Towards a Democratic and Emancipator Vision of the University', *Higher Education*, 57/1, pp.85–105.

Stefani, L. (2009) 'Designing the Curriculum for Student Engagement', *All Ireland Journal of Teaching and Learning in Higher Education*, 1/1, pp.11.1–11.13.

Trowler, V. (2010) *Student Engagement Literature Review* (York: Higher Education Academy). Retrieved from <http://www.heacademy.ac.uk/assets/York/documents/ourwork/studentengagement/StudentEngagementLiteratureReview.pdf>

Trowler, V. and Trowler, P. (2010) *Student Engagement Evidence Summary* (York: Higher Education Academy). Retrieved from <http://www.heacademy.ac.uk/assets/York/documents/ourwork/studentengagement/StudentEngagementEvidenceSummary.pdf>

Umbach, P.D. and Wawrzynski, M.R. (2005) 'Faculty Do Matter: The Role of College Faculty in Student Learning and Engagement', *Research in Higher Education*, 46/2, pp.153–84.

Yorke, P. and Knight, P. (2004) 'Self-Theories: Some Implications for Teaching and Learning in Higher Education', *Studies in Higher Education*, 29/1, pp.25–37.

Yorke, M. and Longden, B. (2008) *The First Year Experience of Higher Education in the UK: Final Report*. Retrieved from <http://www.heacademy.ac.uk/assets/York/documents/resources/publications/FYEFinalReport.pdf>

Zepke, N. (2011) 'Understanding Teaching, Motivation and External Influences in Student Engagement: How Can Complexity Thinking Help?', *Research in Post Compulsory Education*, 16/2, pp.1–13.

Zepke, N., Leach, L. and Butler, P. (2009) 'The Role of Teacher–Student Interactions in Tertiary Student Engagement', *New Zealand Journal of Educational Studies*, 44/1, pp.69–82.

Zepke, N., Leach, L. and Butler, P. (2010a) 'Engagement in Post-Compulsory Education: Students' Motivation and Action', *Research in Post-compulsory Education*, 15/1, pp.1–17.

Zepke, N., Leach, L. and Butler, P. (2010b) *Student Engagement: What Is It and What Influences It?* Retrieved from <http://www.tlri.org.nz/assets/A_Project-PDFs/9261–Zepke/9261–Introduction.pdf>

Zepke, N., Leach, L. and Butler, P. (2011) 'Non-Institutional Influences and Student Perceptions of Success', *Studies in Higher Education*, 36/2, pp.227–42

Zepke, N., Leach, L. and Prebble, T. (2005) 'Now You've Got Them, Can You Expect to Keep Them? Factors That Influence Student Departure and Persistence', *New Zealand Journal of Educational Studies*, 40/1&2, pp.181–99.

Zhao, C. and Kuh, G.D. (2004) 'Adding Value: Learning Communities and Student Engagement', *Research in Higher Education*, 45/2, pp.115–38.

SECTION 3: STUDENT ENGAGEMENT IN CONTEXT

Chapter 12

Reinventing engagement

Paul Taylor, Danny Wilding, Alex Mockridge and Cath Lambert

University of Warwick, UK

> There is abundant evidence that the most effective higher education environments are ones in which students are diligently involved as part of a community of learners. As part of this engagement, they work together with academics to enhance teaching, assure quality and maintain standards. In these contexts, they understand themselves as active partners with academic staff in a process of continual improvement of the learning experience.
>
> (Ramsden, 2008, p.16)

> This research experience has not only taught me valuable research skills, it has opened my eyes to different styles of teaching. Being treated as an equal from day one was a novel experience and facilitated a learning and research environment in which people were stretched to their potential, were given the responsibility of making their own decisions and therefore produced insightful pieces of research, that one person could not have produced on their own.
>
> (Sarah [undergraduate researcher] in Mockridge et al., 2009, p.20)

Prelude

As we write, across the UK students and schoolchildren are taking to the streets. They are (for the most part) peacefully occupying university buildings and council chambers in protest at devastating cuts by central government to the public sector[*]. They are remonstrating against: proposals (fast becoming policy decisions) to cut a vast proportion of the state's contribution to university teaching and learning budgets, to treble university tuition fees[†] and to cut the Educational Maintenance Allowance (EMA) for 16 year olds[‡]; the removal of funding from the AimHigher programme which opens the doors of higher education (HE) for many who would not otherwise consider it[§]; the very real threat of closure to many arts, humanities and social science departments and the effective privatisation of educational provision (Finlayson, 2010). In a useful summary of some of the protests, Mablin (2010) declares on behalf of students and young people: "We are no longer the post-ideological generation; we are now the generation at the heart of the resistance". These vocal protests are significantly contributing to a growing angry voice speaking against the politicians who, propelled by what many see as a myopic neo-liberal drive to demolish state provision of central services, continue to suggest that cuts are unavoidable without considering alternatives (for illustrations see Bowman, 2010; Daily Politics show, 2010). The national papers provide excited commentary and dramatic footage of children and young people waving banners, occupying public spaces, causing damage, being 'kettled' and restrained by police. Although not so well reported in the national press, several universities have ongoing peaceful occupations by students, supported by many of their lecturers (see for example Amsler, 2011). Critical commentaries evoke Paris 1968 (Toynbee, 2010). In short, students have rarely seemed so engaged.

---

* The UK General Election of May 2010 resulted in a hung parliament in which no party won enough votes to be a clear winner. The Conservative and Liberal Democratic parties formed a Conservative-led coalition under David Cameron. Their first term of office began with the implementation of brutal cuts across the public sector in order to cut the country's financial deficit. Higher Education has been particularly badly hit. For further discussions see Callender, 2010.

† The latest policy information regarding the implementation of student fees is available at <http://www.bis.gov.uk/policies/higher-education/students/student-finance>

‡ The Educational Maintenance Allowance (EMA) was a means-tested grant for 16–18 year olds who stayed on in Further Education. For information about the protests to prevent the EMA from being cut, see <http://emacampaign.org.uk/>

§ Further information on AimHigher is available at <http://www.direct.gov.uk/en/EducationAndLearning/UniversityAndHigherEducation/DG_073697>

The student as producer

We begin with this bigger picture as an important context in which to locate our case study of student engagement at the University of Warwick in central England. In this chapter, we aim to demonstrate how it is possible (indeed, we would argue, necessary) to involve students actively in all processes of the university, including organisation and administration, curricula design and development, research and pedagogy. This engagement brings, we would suggest, localised gains for students and the institution. However, we also present a wider argument for a model of engagement in which students, despite the putatively incontestable machinations of political and economic forces, are able to resist the powerless subject position of 'consumer' and are enabled to become creators and producers of ideas, knowledge and meaningful outputs. The leadership and participation of students and young people in opposing current political interventions in state education helps underline that this is an achievable proposition, not a pipe dream. At the same time as mobilising students to find their (individual and collective) voice(s), the dramatic policy developments currently taking place in UK higher education have served to reignite important debates about the role of the university in contemporary society: What should be the purpose of a university education? What is or should be the role and status of undergraduate students within the higher education sector? The discussion in this chapter aims to contribute to these debates.

In particular, we offer a direct challenge to the limiting role and subject position of the student as an educational 'consumer'. Under the New Labour government (1997–2010), there has been a growth in the notion of students as "choosier and more demanding consumers of the higher education experience" (Mandelson, 2009) and this has only accelerated under the present coalition government. Although we offer evidence from the UK (and in particular, England), these trends are evident in many other national contexts. Within this consumerist discourse, students are engaged in education as nothing more than customers of whom the university must take account when selling its educational product. New-managerialist strategies reinforce this relationship "through the deployment of performance indicators and league tables which strengthen the hand of consumers by providing information to aid choice" (Naidoo and Jamieson, 2005, p.4). This opens up the question of the market power of students and their forces in shaping the curriculum. Naidoo and Jamieson (2005, p.5) suggest that:

> the pedagogic relationship is likely to be transformed into one that is dependent on the market transaction of the commodity. Education is likely to be reconceptualised as a commercial transaction, the lecturer as the 'commodity producer' and the student as the 'consumer'... consumerist mechanisms may be seen as a device to reform academic values and pedagogic relationships to comply with market frameworks.

Against this (damaging) trend, the Reinvention Centre for Undergraduate Research[*] has developed the powerful concept of the 'student as producer' (see Neary and Winn, 2009; Lambert, 2009[†]). This focus on the student as producer (re)locates the university itself as an important public institution engaged with, and contributing to, wider social, political and economic concerns. Students do not shut themselves away for three years in order to 'consume' a degree that may (if they are lucky) earn them a place in the labour market from whence they can pay back their debt. The university is a workplace and the development of critical, creative and collaborative citizens is its business. Neary and Winn (2009, p.126) argue that this reconstruction of the student as producer entails:

> undergraduate students working in collaboration with academics to create work of social importance that is full of academic content and value, while at the same time reinvigorating the university beyond the logic of the market.

The case study which forms the empirical basis of this chapter is not therefore an isolated project; rather, it is an example of business-as-usual

---

* The Reinvention Centre for Undergraduate Research was a collaborative Centre for Excellence in Teaching and Learning (CETL) based between the Department of Sociology at the University of Warwick and the School for the Built Environment at Oxford Brookes University, both in the UK. The Reinvention centre covers a range of progressive pedagogies. This chapter represents the specific views of the authors.

† For practical examples see <http://www.warwick.ac.uk/go/reinvention>; <http://studentasproducer.lincoln.ac.uk/>;<http://www.universityofutopia.org/critical-theory>

for students and staff from the Reinvention Centre, providing a rich resource for illustrating our key arguments that: (a) students can and should be integral to the research and pedagogic endeavours of their departments, disciplines and institutions, and (b) collaboration between students and staff is an appropriate and productive means of carrying out both practical and intellectual work, particularly work relating to pedagogy and curriculum.

The case study that forms the substance of the following discussion draws on collaborative (student–staff) research undertaken as part of the Kings–Warwick project (2009–10). The focus of Kings–Warwick was to investigate the possibilities for creating 'an active and outward facing curriculum' for 'research-intensive' universities (such as Kings College and the University of Warwick) with a view to generating a 'blueprint' for use in other similar settings. Given the opportunity to contribute, the Reinvention Centre saw this as an ideal forum for involving students in curricula review and reform. The overall investigation and research findings were substantial, and only selected aspects of it are utilised in the following discussion.*

We begin by paying critical attention to the concept of 'engagement' before turning to the Kings–Warwick project. After introducing this project, we present our methodology, with a focus on the implications of these choices for student engagement. The discussion then considers one aspect of the research: a qualitative study of the design and implementation of a new interdisciplinary module, 'The Faust Module', at the University of Warwick. The investigation into the planning, curriculum and pedagogy of this course raises a number of issues around student engagement in the production of knowledge and we consider these in turn before concluding with the argument that, despite the many and real challenges posed by active student involvement, the university which neglects or refuses to create meaningful spaces for student engagement is failing to acknowledge and make use one of their most valuable resources, with negative consequences for both students and the universities of the future. But first, we consider what it means to be 'engaged'.

---

* A comprehensive overview of the Reinvention research team's findings together with the summary report are available at <http://www.warwick.ac.uk/go/reinvention/fundingopps/centreprojects/graduatepledge/>

Reinventing engagement

Alongside the characterisation of students as consumers in an educational market, there has been increased currency of the idea of 'student engagement'. This is not an unproblematic term. Many different authors use it in a variety of ways. For some, engagement is narrowly defined and measured in terms of the completion of data-gathering exercises designed to get feedback. For example, the CHERI (2009, p.4) report on Student Engagement in England concluded that:

> Institutions view student engagement as central to enhancing the student experience, but more emphasis seems to be placed on viewing students as consumers and rather less on viewing students as partners in a learning community. For student unions, the emphasis tends to be on the latter aspect. ...The majority of HEIs [Higher Education Institutions] and FECs [Further Education Colleges] rate their student engagement processes, comprising a basic model of student feedback questionnaires and student representation systems, as reasonably or very effective; student unions are less likely to do so.

The authors of the CHERI (2009) report's representation of the dominant model of engagement used in universities is as a *cycle* in which – drawing on the 'student feedback cycle' in Brennan and Williams (2003, p.7) – the institution makes itself accountable through 'consumer' feedback and then decides on, and implements, changes in response. Such a cycle implicitly alienates students from their institution, since they are not involved in the productive part of the cycle[*]. A more participatory version of engagement is proposed by the UK's Quality Assurance Agency (QAA), who have introduced mechanisms for student involvement in quality and enhancement processes within HE institutions, including recruiting students onto audit teams[†]. However, this model, too, is limited in that students are invited to participate in the implementation of existing structures, frameworks and regimes whose principles and processes have already been established without student input. The

* There have also been critical responses to the reliability and validity of data produced by this method – see Cheng and Marsh (2010) and Holmwood (2011).

† see <http://www.qaa.ac.uk/students/studentengagement/>

scope for creative and intellectual input is circumscribed by the strictures of audit itself. Similar concerns could be levelled at mechanisms such as Staff–Student Liaison Committees (SSLCs), which enable students' opinions to be heard via representatives and allow for 'consultations' on matters affecting students whilst the instigation of ideas and concerns, final decisions and the operational discourses are all initiated and dominated by administrative and/or academic staff.

In contrast, we are working with a dynamic concept of engagement which recognises students as productive and responsible agents in the generation and development of all aspects of the university. We have previously remarked on the opposition between alienation and engagement, drawing on the work of Sarah Mann (2001). For Mann (2001 p.8) alienation can be defined as "the state or experience of being isolated from a group or an activity to which one should belong or in which one should be involved" and often characterises the undergraduate's experience of their university education. In Taylor and Wilding (2009 p.1) we defined 'engagement' in opposition to this, as 'involvement' or 'participation' in, with an additional notion of *commitment*, drawing on an older meaning of engagement as a 'pledge' (see French *engagé*)*. For us, then, engaged and committed students will be productively involved in their institution, with mechanisms for dialogue and negotiation replacing structures aimed at accountability and compliance. In our presentation and analysis of the case study that follows, we demonstrate both the potential and the challenges of implementing such a model of student engagement.

The case study: the Kings–Warwick project

> Rather than academics doing research on students, in this study students are researchers of their own environments. This provides viewpoints that may be different from the ones that are mostly conveyed in academic publications... our learning processes developed in a dialogue with each other. Not only do we look back on different research experiences, but also how our respective disciplinary backgrounds shaped our understanding of the environment

* We are, however, alert to possible oversimplifications of 'participation' – see Lambert (2009).

> that we are researching whilst we find ourselves within it at the same time: the university.
>
> (Mockridge et al., 2009, pp.15–16)

> Six people from different disciplines – four undergraduate researchers, one postgraduate researcher and one postdoctoral researcher – forming a research team, framing and specifying research questions, deciding upon a research methodology, carrying out the research and putting together a first, preliminary research report. This was an immensely steep learning curve for everyone involved.
>
> (Elisabeth [post-doctoral researcher] in Mockridge et al., 2009, p.24)

In 2009, the University of Warwick, in collaboration with Kings College London, embarked on a major curriculum review project, funded by the Higher Education Funding Council for England (HEFCE). The aim of the project was to explore graduate capabilities developed in the teaching and learning practices at two Russell Group universities* with the intended outcome being a 'blueprint' for research-led teaching to inform policy in other HE institutions. These 'graduate capabilities' were defined from the outset as being the experience of: a research-led learning environment; inter-disciplinary study; a globally-oriented curriculum; community engagement and academic literacy. The project was organised into research strands on the basis of these five themes, working across both institutions†. The initial proposal claimed that "student engagement will be a major strength. The initiative offers many opportunities for students to take a more active part in shaping their own academic growth and in negotiating curriculum choices and the focus of projects." The Reinvention Centre was asked to be involved in the research and we saw this as an exciting opportunity for further putting the principles of the student as producer into practice.

---

* The Russell Group, in its own words, "represents 20 leading UK universities which are committed to maintaining the very best research, an outstanding teaching and learning experience and unrivalled links with business and the public sector". See <http://www.russellgroup.ac.uk/>

† Details of the Kings–Warwick project, including access to the final report, can be found at <http://www.kingslearning.info/kwp/>

We proposed that there would be critical student engagement and commitment at the outset and throughout the project. Our model of student engagement aimed to deliver meaningful research results in relation to the curriculum and provide an action research setting to explore and demonstrate how students can critically explore and intervene in the pedagogic and curricular processes of their universities. In keeping with these aims, and the principles outlined above, a collaborative research team comprising students and staff was established. The core research team was made up of four undergraduates from different year groups and from different disciplines, one postgraduate researcher and one post-doctoral researcher[*]. The undergraduate students were recruited via a competitive open invitation circulated to the entire student body. This research team of six worked together with members of academic staff from the Reinvention Centre to devise research questions and methodological approaches. Technical and administrative members of the Reinvention Centre also supported them. The research team met weekly to discuss progress and share work and ideas, with input from others as necessary. The result was a lively and productive model of collaboration across many of the usual institutional divides (for example, staff–student, arts–science, academic–administrative, research–teaching-and-learning). Such a model was not unusual for the Reinvention Centre[†] but, as Kings–Warwick was a high-profile cross-institutional project, with national funding, it brought our distinctive working practices into a more 'public' (and traditional, hierarchical) research and administrative space. Significantly, the research team were involved in *all* aspects of the project, including report-writing and other outputs such as seminar papers. This chapter is co-authored by two members of academic staff and the two student researchers who remained at the University at the time of writing[‡].

The Reinvention research consisted of two phases. In phase one, the team carried out content and discourse analysis of the University

* Details about the team members can be found at <http://www.warwick.ac.uk/go/reinvention/fundingopps/centreprojects/graduatepledge/atwarwick/>

† See <http://www.warwick.ac.uk> for details of other projects; for critical discussion see the WASS Collective (2007).

‡ The Reinvention Centre actively promotes students engaging either independently or collaboratively in academic writing and in 2007 established *Reinvention: a Journal of Undergraduate Research*, a peer-reviewed, interdisciplinary and international journal for the publication of undergraduate research. See <http://www.warwick.ac.uk.go/reinventionjournal/>

of Warwick's web pages (its public face) in order to examine and map evidence of a research-led learning environment; interdisciplinary study; a globally-oriented curriculum; community engagement and academic literacy. A sample of nine departments was selected, three from each of the University's faculties, and also five cross-institutional services (the Library, the Learning and Development Centre, the Careers Service, the Student–Staff Liaison Committee and the Students' Union). The research team explained their approach as follows:

> Two researchers investigated all of the selected departments. Each person was the primary researcher for one graduate capability as well as the primary researcher for two departments and cross-disciplinary institutions in the university. Every theme and department had a second person being responsible for co-analysing the material. The key advantage of this procedure consisted in the creation of an interpretive and discursive space amongst the researchers that further enhanced the quality of the interpretation. In this manner, our different disciplinary affiliations and thus potential interpretative leanings towards a specific side were confronted with an alternative viewpoint.
>
> (Mockridge et al., 2009, pp.14–15)

In phase two, four in-depth case studies were carried out on the Chemistry Department, the Theatre Studies Department, the History Department (with a focus on a study visit to Venice) and on a new module, the Faust Project (Interdisciplinary and Creative Collaboration). The investigations were divided amongst the research team who utilised mixed qualitative methods, including interviews with students and staff, focus groups, participant observation of classroom activities, reflexive diaries, documentary analysis and questionnaires. The team continued to meet weekly to share progress, findings and analysis and made use of a shared web space to upload their data. In the quote at the beginning of this section, Elisabeth Simbuerger, postdoctoral researcher on the team, wrote in the summary report about the "immensely steep learning curve" that the team experienced. This is central to understanding what it means for students to be engaged in shaping and understanding the university. Such engagement is not easy nor indeed painless and, significantly, the challenges are not just felt by the students but by "everyone involved".

We turn now to focus on one specific area of the data that concerned the study and analysis of a new collaborative module at the University of Warwick, the Faust Project. The module was selected as being of relevance to the 'graduate capabilities' outlined above, in particular because of its unusual commitment to interdisciplinarity. It also turned out to provide, as the following discussion illustrates, an exciting glimpse at the generally unrealised potential for students to be actively and creatively engaged in curricula and pedagogic development.

Faust: student engagement in the curriculum

The Faust module ran at the University of Warwick in the academic year 2009–10 with the help of an Academic Fellowship from the Reinvention Centre*. It was devised and convened by Dr Paul Prescott in the English Department. Prescott (2010) describes the module as being:

> distinctive for three main reasons: 1) it is open to all second-year students from across the University, regardless of degree course; 2) it is delivered by an 'ensemble' of teachers from a range of departments; 3) it attempts to take seriously the notion of interdisciplinary learning and seeks to establish how feasible – logistically and philosophically – such learning is at the University of Warwick, and, by extension, at similar institutions across the UK.

The module was designed to be open to students from all disciplines, offering the curricular space for students to analyse a single topic from the perspective of many different academic fields. The topic for the year 2009–10 was the Faust myth. Our research of the module led us to discover how the issues surrounding student engagement in higher education come into play in the setting of a module specifically designed to reinvent some of the established positions in teaching and learning environments. We can see both the challenges involved in setting up

* Between 2005 and 2010, academic fellowships of up to £10,000 were available to staff at the universities of Warwick and Oxford Brookes in order for staff to reinvent curricula and pedagogy and make it more research based. Further information on all the funded projects can be found at <http://www.warwick.ac.uk/go/reinvention//fundingopps/fellowships/>

and implementing such a module as well as the potentially dramatic results.

A statistics undergraduate student, Alex Mockridge, carried out this research. Alex undertook analysis of module documentation, observed some seminars, conducted an interview with the convenor, Paul Prescott, and held a focus group with the students undertaking the module. Although the main focus was interdisciplinarity, the module was a working example of the ways in which students are treated as researchers rather than simply students who happen to be learning in a research-rich environment. The module itself evolved in collaborative ways and had creative collaboration between students at the heart of its pedagogy and assessment. It is therefore useful to draw on the module to illustrate the possibilities for student engagement.

What makes the module interesting from the perspective of student engagement are the implications for teaching and learning that creating such an interdisciplinary module leads to. In the initial phase of the module, different visiting experts came every week to the group seminar to teach on their particular area of expertise relating to Faust. For example, there were visiting experts in Economics, German, Neuroscience, Theology, Sociology, Business Studies and Law. During the seminars in which a visiting tutor led the session, the module convenor himself sat in a circle amongst the students, placing himself as a fellow learner, not just an imparter of knowledge. He explained his reasons for this:

> I try to negotiate on a weekly basis what my status is within the group, and it's very interesting to try and observe that, but I am very clear that when someone comes in to teach the group... that I am then part of the group and learning with the group.
>
> (Paul Prescott, interview, November 2009)

This challenges the 'deficit model' of students being in intellectual arrears compared to lecturers and it cuts right to the heart of student engagement with regard to the relationship between student and teacher.

In all aspects of the module, including assessment, there was, as Paul put it, "a strong onus on the students to devise their own research agenda" (Interview, November 2009). Students were put into the role of researchers and then encouraged to pursue their own interests, being told to 'write about what interests you' for the first assessed essay, in stark contrast to the usual procedure of being given a list of approved titles or themes to choose from. As one student put it, "If you have a particular interest you can pursue it further; it's left up to us to take it a step further" (Focus group, November 2009). The assessment for the module was split between an individual portfolio of work built up over the course of the module, the assessed essay and a group project. The project was again left mainly to the students themselves to design and produce, the only requirements being that it was related to Faust and that it had an output that had a physical presence and could be released into the public domain: the module outline specifies "an original adaptation (stage, film, radio), an installation, or an exhibition."[*] In terms of both the teaching and learning and the modes of assessment, there was an unusually high degree of negotiation and student autonomy. Paul articulated two key benefits that he hoped students would gain from this:

> One would be the obvious benefit... of being exposed to different backgrounds, different ways of seeing, different sets of knowledge, different assumptions, all of which you could quite easily go through university without being exposed to. The second benefit, which is a kind of corollary of that, is that that would lead to a greater degree of reflexivity and of self-awareness, that is, of the assumptions that the students were bringing into the classroom as it were.
>
> (Interview, November 2009)

His hopes appear to have been realised. In the student focus group, one member of the class talked about having freedom "to think beyond the boundaries... of our course, specifically, but also beyond our thinking, like we're forced to think differently". The module not only recognised, but *depended upon*, students' individual and collective abilities to (a) generate ideas and knowledge (relating to Faust) and (b) make strategic decisions, for example in devising appropriate forms of assessment for their group projects. The emphasis on a 'public' output as one of the assessments indicates that the students' research is being taken seriously and the

---

* An online summary of the module and assessment can be accessed at <http://www2.warwick.ac.uk/fac/arts/english/undergraduate/current/modules/fulllist/special/interdisciplinaryandcreativecollaboration>

expectations of what they are able to produce is high. Such an emphasis is in keeping with the tenets of critical pedagogy in which students' own ideas and knowledges are validated (Freire, 1970) and the role of the teacher is to have (and express) faith in their capabilities (Rancière, 1991). Such a model of working also has important implications for knowledge itself. In the Faust module, where interdisciplinary input contributed to the collaborative building of knowledge, it is implicitly recognised that knowledge is not 'out there' in the form of 'right answers' embedded in a course outline and delivered lectures. Rather, it is contingent and unpredictable, able to be viewed, constructed and deconstructed from many different (and maybe oppositional) perspectives.

The Kings–Warwick final report, *Creating a 21st Century Curriculum* (2010, p.166), recommends that "student learning, the student experience and student engagement are put at the heart of all planning, teaching and review" and we can hardly find a better example of this than the Faust module; but it is important to bear in mind the challenges, both institutional and practical, in following through on this recommendation. Even at the early planning stages of Faust, there were institutional hurdles with setting a module that needed approval from all departments and needed to meet the assessment needs of all students. There were difficulties attracting a good mix of students from all departments, not just the English and other Arts students that one might expect. The perceived 'risks' of being 'creative', 'collaborative' and working beyond the security of one's own discipline are much greater for some students than for others. As well as being hard work – "a steep learning curve" – engagement is (or feels) risky: for all involved. For the students who decided to take the module, the greatest source of anxiety was assessment methods. We see then that one of the potential problems in engaging students in curriculum on a fundamental level is ensuring that they are not put off by the 'risk factor' of having to take increased responsibility for their own assessment and of having to create and research, rather than just regurgitate facts and opinions that have been imparted to them by their lecturer.

In creating the module, Paul Prescott was fully aware of the ways in which normative assumptions about pedagogy and assessment are built into the expectations of students and staff. He talked about the challenges of:

> trying to suspend some habits of learning which are predicated on individual achievement; the notion that success can be measured on the basis of a very rigid curriculum delivered by a single authority figure, downloaded as it were into the individual student and the student knows exactly what he or she has to do in order to get the pat on the back and the 2.1 or the 1st… a lot of… students… teachers as well, are quite understandably addicted to this model, are normalised to it. It's so routine in our culture… and you know so far I've found that it has, what's the word, *unsettled* some of the students who are concerned about structure, concerned about assessment methods that they are encountering for the first time, and that's completely understandable.

Despite this, the Faust module worked because students who had opted to study on it were themselves attuned to the idea of risk and felt it to be worthwhile. One student summed up the prevailing attitude: "If you're doing Faust, you can't afford to be too scared… It is a risk" (Focus group, November 2009). Despite the anxieties around the novel form of assessment, there was agreement that the risks involved were positive intellectually and creatively. One student described the module as follows:

> It's like a journey… it all culminates in our Faust Project. And we don't know, we haven't got a clue what that's going to be yet… it's completely up to us… so it's nice to know that there's a bit of uncertainty, but we know we're going to achieve something.

Some students wanted a greater depth into each disciplinary perspective but the unprompted response to the module was very positive. Whether students in general want to be engaged in a meaningful way in developing their curricula or not is a difficult question to answer. Certainly it requires more effort to take an active approach to university education; but it is only through great effort and struggle that meaningful progress is made.

That students taking the Faust module were free, in collaboration with their teachers, to develop their own syllabus and assessment methods, and to work fluidly across accepted boundaries between disciplines and between teaching and research, raises important questions about how such a module can be considered 'accountable' within the Quality Assurance

Agency (QAA) framework. This requires the host department to state the intended learning outcomes, syllabus and assessment methods for all modules and have these 'approved' by the university. As discussed in Taylor and Wilding (2009, p.3), the stated learning outcomes are in turn strongly influenced by the QAA's published benchmark statements for each discipline, which could be seen as "a mechanism for a dominant group to articulate a code of practice that will be clear to that group and difficult to comprehend by others". The critical, reflective, collaborative approach to the shaping and evaluation of learning outcomes and assessment methods adopted in the Faust module on the other hand has student engagement as an essential component.

This tension between the dynamic nature of the Faust module's curriculum and pedagogy and the static 'quality' framework in which it uneasily sits may well contribute to the students' feeling that the module is 'risky'. The Faust students were simultaneously positioned as fee-paying consumers of a module and as producers of that module. Being more attuned to a curriculum governed by the 'cycle' of accountability, the students found themselves to be subverting the cycle and creating curriculum that Apple (1993, p.144) would see as a "symbolic, material, and human environment that is ongoingly reconstructed".

Some conclusions: beyond Faust

Regarding students as agents of ongoing reconstruction of curricula in the face of an establishment struggling to solidify the nature of a discipline in a benchmark statement, or capture the character of an institution by stating graduate attributes or capabilities, resonates beyond the Faust module. Our collaborative action research team was tasked with exploring the different 'capabilities' highlighted by the Kings–Warwick proposal. As highlighted by others, including Anna Jones within the Kings–Warwick project, seeking to define graduate capabilities is inherently problematic.

> Whilst it would be easy to adopt a prescribed set of graduate attributes, drawing on some of the many lists that exist, to do so risks repeating the mistakes of others.
>
> (Kings–Warwick, 2010, p.109)

Instead, our team sought to engage critically with the discourses of our institutions around the different strands (research-led learning environment, interdisciplinary study, globally-oriented curriculum, community engagement and academic literacy) and probe their nature through qualitative research. As well as producing an extensive written report, the student researchers made a documentary film presenting key findings. As a snapshot of the complexity of students' experience of curricula, the film is compelling. However, it contains no simple answers for those seeking to define graduate capabilities and thus has limited value in the 'student-as-consumer' paradigm.

The evidence from our research on the Kings–Warwick project further supported our arguments that undergraduate students should not be regarded as learners coming into an existing research environment but as potential and actual researchers who are themselves producers of the intellectual cultures they inhabit. This shift requires a re-conceptualisation of students as producers of knowledge and of teaching, learning, research and administrative environments as dynamic and always in a state of emergence and change. Student engagement is central to realising this dynamism. Dynamic processes that encourage ongoing reflection on and critique of curricula and pedagogy by students and staff are more productive, risky though this may appear.

Looking back 30 years or more, it could be said that students took big risks in choosing their institution and course, since there was little information available beyond the (largely unaudited) prospectus and from word of mouth. However, the risk was low in another sense, since the state paid fees for all students and living costs for many. Insofar as universities could maintain their 'reputation', recruitment was assured and the risks were low. As maintenance grants evaporated and students were 'investing' more in their higher education, the risks of failure grew for students. The wrong choice of institution or course started to bear a financial penalty. McCulloch (2009, pp.172–3) describes how the sector responded to this by appealing to the consumer rights movement of the 1970s. Universities provided auditable information about themselves and their courses and students gained the right to complain. McCulloch (2009, p.173) has highlighted the positive aspects of these changes, in particular, "aspects of the accountability and responsiveness that all universities should exhibit".

Reading McCulloch's (2009) critique of the student-as-consumer paradigm, one can see that the 'cycle' model of feedback and response has become an arms race. Students have been expected to risk ever more money for their higher education, while the penalty to universities for failing to deliver has escalated beyond student complaints, to financial penalties administered by league tables that impact on recruitment and to the courts, where students challenge the decisions of exam boards. Moving from a consumerism view of higher education to a culture of student engagement presents its own risks but, importantly, such risk-taking is *productive*, as exemplified by our case study. Our vision of universities which take student engagement seriously asks academics to sit with the students, like the Faust module leader, placing themselves in the same role as them, as fellow learners and as collaborators in the ongoing reconstruction of curricula and pedagogy. In the words of Kagwe, one of the undergraduate researchers on the Kings–Warwick project:

> I see myself more now as both a learner and contributor to the education process. The concept of academic literacy has made me realise that my education should equip me to engage not just with my lecturers but also with practitioners, employers, local and international communities. Consequently, I have gained an appreciation for the different components of higher education and the importance of constantly reviewing and even challenging the role of teachers, researchers and students in this environment.
>
> (Mockridge et al., 2009, p.19)

We would suggest that anyone committed to student engagement in the terms we have presented in this chapter – wherever they are positioned in the university – takes and creates opportunities for such interventions in the critical and urgent debates about what higher education is and may become.

References

Amsler, S. (2011) *To the Students (Who Were) in Occupation at Birmingham University, Campaign for the Public University*. Retrieved from <http://publicuniversity.org.uk/2011/01/17/to-the-students-in-occupation-at-birmingham-university>

Apple, M. (1993) *Official Knowledge* (New York: Routledge).

Bowman, P. (2010) *Cut the Shock Doctrine. Radicalize Common Sense.* Retrieved from <http://cardiff.academia.edu/PaulBowman/Papers/340931/Cut_the_Shock_Doctrine_Radicalize_Common_Sense>

Brennan, J. and Williams, R. (2003) *Collecting and Using Student Feedback – a Guide to Good Practice* (York: Learning and Teaching Support Network).

Callender, C. (2010) 'The 2010 Comprehensive Spending Review and Higher Education', Campaign for the Public University. Retrieved from <http://publicuniversity.org.uk/wp-content/uploads/2010/11/Callender.pdf>

Cheng, J.H.S. and Marsh, H.W. (2010) 'National Student Survey: Are Differences Between Universities and Courses Reliable and Meaningful?' *Oxford Review of Education*, 36/6, pp.693–712.

CHERI (2009) (Little, B., Locke, W., Scesca, A. and William, R.) *Report to HEFCE on Student Engagement, February 2009*. Retrieved from <http://www.hefce.ac.uk/pubs/rdreports/2009/rd03_09/rd03_09.pdf>

Daily Politics Show, The (2010) Discussion with Professor Greg Philo on alternatives to cuts in public funding, BBC2, 15 September. Retrieved from <http://www.youtube.com/watch?v=Pmmf-cLnuq0>

Finlayson, A. (2010) 'Britain, Greet the Age of Privatised Higher Education', *Our Kingdom*. Retrieved from <http://www.opendemocracy.net/ourkingdom/alan-finlayson/britain-greet-age-of-privatised-higher-education>

Freire, P. (1970) *Pedagogy of the Oppressed* (London: Penguin).

Holmwood, J. (2011) 'Code of practice needed to prevent degree-course mis-selling', blog entry on *Research Blogs*. Retrieved from <http://exquisitelife.researchresearch.com/exquisite_life/2011/02/code-of-practice-needed-to-halt-degree-course-mis-selling-.html>

Kings–Warwick (2010) *Creating a 21st Century Curriculum: The Kings–Warwick Project*. Retrieved from <http://kingslearning.info/kwp/attachments/134_KWP-Creating_a_21st_Century_Curriculum_Final_Report.pdf.pdf>

Lambert, C. (2009) 'Pedagogies of Participation in Higher Education: A Case for Research-Based Learning', *Pedagogy, Culture and Society*, 17/3, pp.295–309.

Mablin, L. (2010) 'We Are No Longer the Post-Ideological Generation; We Are Now the Generation at the Heart of the Resistance', blog entry on the International Sociological Association's *Universities in Crisis* site. Retrieved from <http://www.isa-sociology.org/universities-in-crisis>

Mandelson, P. (2009) 'Higher Ambitions', speech to BCI HE Conference, 20 October 2009. Retrieved from <http://webarchive.nationalarchives.

gov.uk/20100407184748/<http://www.bis.gov.uk/News/Speeches/higher-ambitions>

Mann, S.J. (2001) 'Alternative Perspectives on the Student Experience: Alienation and Engagement', *Studies in Higher Education*, 26/1, pp.7–19.

McCulloch, A. (2009) 'The Student as Co-Producer: Learning from Public Administration About the Student-University Relationship', *Studies in Higher Education*, 34/2, pp.171–83.

Mockridge, A., Morris, T., Njoroge, K., Simbuerger, E., Smith, S. and Wilding, D. (2009) 'The Graduate Pledge: Kings College – Warwick Project', The Reinvention Centre for Undergraduate Research. Retrieved from <http://www.warwick.ac.uk/go/reinvention/fundingopps/centreprojects/graduatepledge/the_graduate_pledge_-_report_by_the_reinvention_centre_research_team.pdf>

Naidoo, R. and Jamieson, I. (2005) 'Empowering Participants or Corroding Learning? Towards a Research Agenda on the Impact of Student Consumerism in Higher Education', *Journal of Education Policy*, 20/3, pp.276–81.

Neary, M. and Winn, J. (2009) 'The Student as Producer: Reinventing the Student Experience in Higher Education', in Bell, L., Stevenson, H. and Neary, M. (eds) *The Future of Higher Education: Policy, Pedagogy and the Student Experience* (London: Continuum) pp.192–210.

Prescott, P. (2010) 'New Undergraduate Module "Interdisciplinary and Creative Collaboration: The Faust Project"', Academic Fellowship Interim Report. Retrieved from <http://www2.warwick.ac.uk/fac/soc/sociology/rsw/undergrad/cetl/fundingopps/fellowships/fellows/prescott_final_report.pdf>

Ramsden, P. (2008) *The Future of Higher Education Teaching and the Student Experience*. Retrieved from <http://www.heacademy.ac.uk/resources/detail/ourwork/consultations/paulramsden_teaching_and_student_experience>

Rancière, J. (1991) *The Ignorant Schoolmaster: Five Lessons in Intellectual Emancipation* (Palo Alto: Stanford University Press).

Taylor, P. and Wilding, D. (2009) *Rethinking the Values of Higher Education – the Student as Collaborator and Producer? Undergraduate Research as a Case Study* (Gloucester: The Quality Assurance Agency for Higher Education). Retrieved from <http://www.qaa.ac.uk/students/studentEngagement/Rethinking.pdf>

Toynbee, P. (2010) 'Thatcher's Children Can Lead the Class of '68 Back into Action', *Guardian*, Friday 26 November. Retrieved from <http://www.guardian.co.uk/commentisfree/2010/nov/26/student-protest-public-sector-cuts>

Chapter 13

Still active, after all these years: lifelong engagement with learning

Garnet Grosjean

University of British Columbia, Canada

Much of the research on the concept of intentional learning, or engagement, over the last three decades has focused on students enrolled in higher education (see Pace, 1982; Newble and Clarke, 1986; Chickering and Gamson, 1987; and Kuh et al., 2005). Discussions tend to focus on learning that is attributable to the student, in the contextual environment of the institution. Few studies look at engagement in learning once students leave these institutions and make their way in life as productive, contributing members of their community and society. Of these, only a tiny fraction of studies devote attention to engagement in learning by older people, particularly those who have retired from paid work. This is an important area of consideration at a time when the post-war population bulge of 'baby boomers' is beginning to enter the third age. Many of these individuals are well-educated, financially secure and healthier than previous generations, and they may well alter our understanding of continued engagement with learning.

In this chapter, I argue that engagement in learning is not a finite process, something to be measured as a proxy of quality in studies of student outcomes in higher education. Rather, engagement in learning continues throughout the life course. I will demonstrate how the same indicators (cognitive, affective and conative) used to measure academic engagement of students can be applied to the active engagement of older adults in community life, community activism, volunteerism and informed interest in current events. These activities are all part of civic engagement, which is the bedrock of democratic societies.

Older adults enhance society in many ways, whether through paid employment or through volunteer activities which contribute to the public good. Research indicates that many older individuals prefer to be involved in their communities and that they benefit from civic engagement. The impact of such engagement on the health and wellbeing of older people is an active area of study (Bennett, 2002; Morrow-Howell et al., 2003; Martinson and Minkler, 2006; Hinterlong and Williamson, 2007). Drawn largely from the field of gerontology, these studies link volunteerism with positive health outcomes in later life.

Concurrent studies in the social science literature link civic engagement with lifelong learning (Field, 2003) and lifelong learning with personal growth (Aspin and Chapman, 2001); and examine motivation for learning among older adults (Kim and Merriam, 2004) and the development of a lifelong learning inventory (Crick, Broadfoot and Claxton, 2004). These studies draw similar conclusions to the gerontology research on the benefits accruing to older adults who engage in lifelong learning through civic engagement.

In this chapter I draw on these and other theoretical areas of the literature to provide a contextual framework for the case study of seniors' engagement with learning in a health literacy programme.

Engagement

Defining the term 'engagement' is a critical first step in identifying factors that might directly or indirectly affect it, particularly in the case of older adults. The term 'civic engagement' is often attributed to Putnam (1995), who argued that civic engagement could be defined by an individual's interest in the improvement of community programmes, contemplation of public affairs and knowledge of political elections. He further defined civic engagement as discrete activities and behaviours. Other definitions of civic engagement expand upon this concept. For example, the Pew Charitable Trust (2006) suggests that civic engagement consists of taking an interest in issues of public concern and activities, such as joining a neighbourhood association or participating in community affairs. In the case discussed in this chapter, civic engagement links community involvement and lifelong learning. The seniors we studied were helping themselves and their neighbours to become aware of facilities and resources that could assist them to 'age in place' well into their advanced years.

For the purpose of this chapter, I have synthesised a working definition of seniors' civic engagement in health literacy training programmes from a broad reading of the relevant literature, and define it as a combination of:

- The intentional investment, motivation and commitment of an individual to intentional learning
- The comfort and sense of belonging derived from peers in training programmes
- Satisfaction from contributing to social action in their communities.

This definition encompasses the individual, situational and institutional factors that may impact an individual in the pursuit of lifelong learning through civic engagement.

Learning in the 'third age'

In his ground-breaking book *A Fresh Map of Life*, Peter Laslett (1989) provided a useful four-stage heuristic for considering the different ages and stages of people's lives. The *first age* refers to the early socialisation that takes place in childhood. The *second age* consists of adult maturity, development of careers, earning a living through engagement in work, and child rearing. The *third age* is a time when individuals begin to relinquish the responsibilities of the second age (mainly participation in the workplace) and seek other forms of self-fulfilment and autonomy. The *fourth age* is the final stage of life where individuals may become increasingly dependent on others to maintain life.

While there is an abundance of research on learning in the middle years (the second age), learning in the third age has not received such intensive study and there is little information to be found on the transition from the second to the third age and its impact on learning. Rather than being defined as a particular age range, the third age is the time of life when people have usually completed conventional work and child-rearing responsibilities but still have several decades of active living ahead of them. While onset is chronologically different for each person, the third age is qualitatively distinct from the ages that precede and follow it: the second age, of full-time employment or parenthood, on the one hand; and the fourth age, of greater dependency, on the other. Closer consideration of this transition is needed to understand the impact of ageing on learning.

Overview of the study

Presented here is a Canadian study of learning in the third age (Laslett, 1989), the stage following retirement from active working life, which in many countries occurs around the age of 65. The study reports on an action research project conducted by co-investigators from universities in the province of British Columbia, and the Council of Senior Citizens' Organisations of British Columbia (COSCO). As a faculty member in Adult Education at one of these universities, I was recruited to help develop the project. The executive team of COSCO is drawn from retired professionals and trades people. COSCO's executive team chose to push back against cuts to seniors' health care by recruiting researchers and academics to assist them in developing and implementing a plan of action to change government policies. A three-year demonstration project on Health and Safety Learning (HSL) for seniors was developed and is currently in the second stage of implementation.

The HSL project

The HSL project consists of developing a series of health literacy transfer modules for use in a programme to train activist-seniors, to deliver the modules in their own communities and recruit other seniors for the training. The goal of the project is to establish learning communities throughout British Columbia that will foster an improved quality of life and independent living for older adults well into their advanced years. The final phase of the project will adapt the model for use across Canada.

The HSL project confronts the important role of engaged learning in maintaining the health, quality of life and longevity of older adults, and in preparing individuals to take on new roles in their community and society. In keeping with dominant definitions we chose to define a 'senior' as a person 65 years of age and older, and 'literacy' as a person's ability to understand and employ printed information in daily activities, whether at home, at work or in the community.

Learning and community

The connection between learning and community has a long history in adult education and is supported by theory and research. A deeper understanding of the ways that adult learning and community are intertwined is now required. Particularly in the case of seniors, we need to understand the qualities that communities must possess to best support seniors' continued learning and thereby enhance their quality of life. Beattie et al. (2003) argue that community-based organisations that serve older adults are in a unique position to bridge the gap between the research and practice of healthy ageing. By developing a network of individuals representing the health-care sector, community organisations and the academy, organisations like COSCO create opportunities to enhance the health and wellbeing of seniors.

Many seniors must deal with circumstances and challenges that limit their individual quality of life. With people living longer it becomes increasingly important to overcome limitations and find ways to enhance quality of life through community involvement. We think of this as 'ageing in place' within a broader 'learning community' of seniors. In learning communities, seniors work together to define what is important to them, and develop the networks that are crucial for resilient participation in society.

Developing an action framework

The beginning of any action research project must involve agreement on the aims and objectives of the project or study. The HSL project began with a series of meetings between executive members of COSCO and me, representing the adult education department of BC's senior university. The preliminary meetings enabled COSCO representatives to discuss their ideas for a project to assist senior citizens in the province and to request assistance from university professors in structuring and carrying it out. There was strong agreement during the meetings that this was a community-based research (CBR) project worthy of everyone's involvement. The outcome of the meetings was a joint plan of action to implement a demonstration project, Health and Safety Learning: for seniors by seniors. We formed an advisory group and began to recruit others to assist us, including retired civil servants from relevant provincial ministries.

The plan for the initiative was elegant in its simplicity: funds would be raised to train a cadre of facilitators who would spread out across the province to deliver workshops on various health and safety issues affecting seniors. Participants would be mobilised to press government for changes in health policies that would enhance the lives of older citizens. Once the model was proven successful in British Columbia, facilitators would be trained in every province and territory in Canada creating a national seniors' lobby for positive changes to government policies that affect seniors' health and welfare.

Once the overall vision of the project was decided, manageable objectives were set for designing materials for the workshops and training facilitators to deliver them. Three major components of content were established: information, awareness and commitment. People of every age require access to appropriate oral and written *information* tailored to their literacy levels. Mere provision of information, however, does not ensure the adoption of practices with a positive effect on an individual's health and safety. Therefore, COSCO's workshops would seek to increase participants' *awareness* of opportunities in their community. Finally, COSCO's volunteers would be trained to assist individuals to *commit* to improving their quality of life in order to maintain an independent lifestyle for as long as possible.

Developing the workshops

In designing the workshops for the health literacy programme, there were a number of critical factors regarding adult learning that had to be taken into consideration, including: life experience, level of engagement, learning styles and barriers to, and motivation for, adult learning.

Experience: Older adults have a depth, breadth and variation in previous life experiences not available to younger people (Collins, 2004). Past educational or work experiences may affect how participants perceive that education occurs. Each adult brings to the learning experience preconceived thoughts and feelings that will be influenced by each of these factors. If successfully designed into the workshops and guided by the facilitators during the delivery of the material, former experiences might assist older adults to connect their current learning experience to something learned in the past. This connection may also make the current learning experience more meaningful. On the other hand, past experiences may hinder current attempts if these biases are not recognised as being present. Facilitators can surface these biases by discussing them with the group. This allows individual members to share experiences and the facilitator can use the opportunity to address any erroneous or preconceived ideas that might interfere with learning the new material.

Level of engagement: It is known from previous studies (see Rogers, 1969) that the learning experience is enhanced when an adult learner has control over the nature, timing and direction of the learning process. Older adults express a strong desire to be self-directed, deciding for themselves what and when they want to learn. They will engage in the learning process if they have a goal in mind. The challenge for facilitators, then, is one of encouraging the learner to participate, while at the same time reinforcing the process of learning and realising that the endpoint of the learning may not occur quickly, requiring time for reflection.

Learning styles: Studies of adult learners (Edmunds et al., 1999) indicate that most adults develop a learning style that is based on childhood learning patterns but re-shaped by life experience. For this reason, several approaches-to-learning styles were required when preparing materials for the workshops. Richardson (2005) argues that determining a participant's learning style will help identify the preferred conditions under which instruction is likely to be most effective. This becomes more difficult when dealing with diverse groups in a workshop situation. We chose to focus on the senses that would be involved while processing the information we were presenting. These senses we identified as visual, auditory and kinaesthetic.

Visual learners prefer seeing what they are learning. For example, well-prepared PowerPoint presentations or short video clips can convey information and help participants understand ideas and information better than explanations or lectures (see Jezierski, 2003). If participants are expected to master a skill (such as setting up the equipment and acting as a facilitator for a future group), they require written instructions to supplement visual presentations. Older adults will read and follow clear directions, and appreciate it even more when diagrams are included. Of importance for older adults who are visual learners is the need for the facilitator to create mental images during the delivery of material to assist them in retaining the information.

Auditory learners prefer to hear the message or instruction being given. Some older adults prefer to have someone talk them through a process, rather than reading about it first. Some of these learners may even talk themselves through a task and should be given the freedom to do so when possible. Older adults with this learning style remember verbal instructions well and prefer someone else read the directions to them while they are attempting to learn a skill.

Kinaesthetic learners want to be physically engaged in their learning. For example, when we discuss exercise for older adults, kinaesthetic learners become animated if encouraged to participate in the exercises instead of just being given a description of what to do. These learners often become impatient with too much discussion and a perceived lack of activity. They do well when they are given a task to perform that allows them to 'do something' to assist their learning. So, we must also include activities, consistent with the capabilities of the participants, to keep them engaged.

Barriers to learning: Due to the process of ageing, many older adults have responsibilities that must be balanced against the demands of learning. Because of these responsibilities, some experience barriers to participating in learning due to: (a) lack of time, (b) lack of confidence, (c) scheduling problems or (d) lack of motivation (Lieb, 1991; Rubenson and Desjardins, 2009). Moreover, if they do not perceive a need for the change in behaviour or knowledge, this creates an additional barrier. In designing the training workshops, there was a need to find ways to motivate seniors to attend the workshops, to enhance their reasons for learning and to find ways to decrease barriers.

Motivation for learning: Most adults consider becoming involved in a learning experience to create personal change, whether in their skills, behaviour, knowledge levels, or outlook on the world and current affairs (Adult Education Centre, 2005). These findings supplement the earlier work of Lieb (1991), who identified the following sources of motivation for adult learning:

- Social relationships: to make new friends; to meet a need for associations and friendships
- External expectations: to comply with instructions from someone else; to fulfil recommendations of someone with formal authority
- Social welfare: to improve ability to serve mankind; to improve ability to participate in community work
- Escape/stimulation: to relieve boredom; to provide a break in the routine of home or work
- Cognitive interest: to learn for the sake of learning; to satisfy an inquiring mind.

From Collins (2004) we know that adults learn best when convinced of the need to know the information. In the case of older adults, particularly those who begin to experience health problems associated with ageing, it is often a particular situation that stimulates the motivation to learn. For example, an individual who has been diagnosed with arthritis might be motivated to learn about potential treatments and support organisations.

The COSCO HSL workshops

Preliminary research into seniors' health and welfare issues identified a number of topic areas suitable for COSCO's workshop treatment. 'Falls' was chosen as the initial topic. Falls are the leading cause of fatal and non-fatal injuries to seniors: one in three seniors falls each year; 40 per cent of residential care admissions are fall-related; 84 per cent of injury-related hospitalisations are due to falls; seniors who fall are more likely to fall again (Vancouver Coastal Health, 2005). The older the person, the more likely they are to fall and be seriously injured. Retired health professionals were consulted for assistance in preparing the materials for the workshop.

Facilitator training

The next task was to recruit and train facilitators to deliver the workshop to seniors' groups in the local area. An initial meeting was held with a group of potential recruits where the project was explained in detail and the responsibility of facilitators made clear. Those who chose to commit were invited back for a training session on how to use the audio-visual equipment, how to anticipate questions and the role of a facilitator. Interestingly, these volunteers showed little reluctance to learn how to use computer technology and the PowerPoint programme, even if they had little or no previous experience. This willingness may reflect commitment to their role and our assurance of support with the technology in their initial presentations. As part of the evaluation of the facilitator workshops, it became obvious that facilitator training should be provided in each region of the province. Individuals who received training from COSCO would train regional facilitators. There was now a demand to design a longer 'train-the-trainer' programme of at least one week to prepare a province-wide group of facilitators to present the workshops in their own communities. In preparation for the train-the-trainer programme, the advisory group prepared a facilitators' handbook (including feedback derived from the initial presentations) and a train-the-trainer manual.

Participant selection

In selecting participants for the train-the-trainer programme, we chose to capitalise on the training of existing community leaders rather than identifying and grooming potential leaders from 'outside' the community. Modest finances and limited time dictated this choice. Training leaders already in place would also help to strengthen local resources and reduce costs. Potential participants were selected as a convenience sample (Merriam, 1998; Patton, 2001) of individuals known to be active volunteers in each of the regions of the province. Representatives from retired teachers' associations and similar professions were targeted. Computer literacy was not an essential criterion but familiarity with the use of email was preferred. Two intensive one-week training sessions for 22 participants were held in Vancouver during the pilot test of the workshops. At the time of writing, of the 22 original participants, 18 continue to act as facilitators for the delivery of the workshop modules.

A successful strategy was developed with the early workshops whereby COSCO raised funds to pay transportation costs to bring people from different areas of the province and accommodated them in the same hotel for the week of the workshop. We found that this strengthened group cohesion as participants remained together for the duration of the workshop. Facilitators also stayed at the hotel during the workshop so there were additional opportunities for socialising and discussions 'outside of class'. A room suitable for the size of the group was organised through the hotel, so that no additional transportation was required. Older adults are more sensitive to discomfort so the physical setting, room temperature, lighting and noise level were all optimised for the workshops. Of these, one of the most important factors was providing a comfortable ambient room temperature because older adults tend to chill more easily. Seating arrangements were carefully organised so that those with hearing or visual impairments were accommodated without drawing attention to their impairment.

Provision creates demand

The response to the presentation of the early modules demonstrated that there was a demand that exceeded our initial expectations. Participants began to suggest the need for similar programmes to cover specific areas of health concern for seniors. This required COSCO to raise more money to develop additional programmes and train more facilitators to deliver them. To date, 18 workshop modules have been developed covering a wide range of topics that participants argue are important to seniors. Information on these workshops can be found in Appendix A.

Discussion and conclusions

For many of the facilitators, the motive for involvement in the health literacy workshops was a feeling that they would be able to "give something back". The majority of facilitator trainees were already active in their local area as members of various committees and clubs. Nevertheless, they welcomed the opportunity to become involved in the HSL project.

According to one of the facilitator trainees, "we want to get involved in something that will benefit other seniors in the province." Another suggested that "by becoming involved with this training we are in a position to help older people in our area who do not have access to the information provided in the workshops." Yet others suggested they took the facilitator training "in the hopes they would acquire 'insider' information on health issues and new treatments" that could benefit them in the future. For some, the decision to participate in the training workshops was for 'social reasons'. These individuals considered they were already well informed about seniors' health issues and were ageing well, but looked forward to making new friendships through facilitating the workshops. Some individuals admitted during informal discussions the need for new connections following the death of a spouse; adjusting to living alone was a topic of discussion among participants during many workshops. One participant suggested that participating in the HSL workshops was "an opportunity to get out and make some new contacts, rather than sitting at home alone." What this individual is describing is the importance of civic engagement.

From a modest beginning, HSL so far trained 18 facilitators who have presented 248 workshops to 4,154 people in all regions of the province. We consider this uptake an indicator of success. However, the overall success of COSCO's health and safety initiative will be judged by its ability to achieve three objectives: (1) to create a change in seniors' behaviour (safer, more confident seniors in their own homes; decreased burden on the health care system); (2) to assist in the development of active health and safety support communities and networks among seniors throughout the province; and (3) to mobilise seniors to become more active in their demands on government and policy makers (inspire and motivate seniors' advocates), thereby effecting significant changes in health-care policy for seniors.

Evaluation strategies are currently underway to measure the success of the programme. Each of the 4,000-plus workshop participants completed a detailed evaluation form. COSCO is now seeking funds to hire two graduate research assistants to enter these data into a database so they can be analysed. We also plan to conduct focus groups drawn from those who completed the programme. The focus groups will allow us to elicit information that demonstrates a behavioural change attributable to participation in the HSL programme.

In summary, to promote the HSL project, COSCO developed a vision to empower increasing numbers of seniors to take charge of their health and safety. The organisation recruited a group of motivated project leaders who could inspire others to contribute actively to this initiative, as well as expand it over time. COSCO assessed the need for relevant content to increase seniors' awareness of available resources; enlisted support from health authorities and academic partners in the planning and delivery of workshops; and successfully raised the required project funding from granting agencies.

With the proportion of older adults increasing at a faster rate than younger cohorts, elders will have a significant impact on the shape of future societies. Perceptions of ageing are becoming more positive, as numbers increase. But as the ageing curve moves out, it becomes important to find practical ways to enable seniors to maintain their quality of life throughout the third age and beyond. Active community-based learning, as a strategy of lifelong learning, provides the practical tools required. It is inspired by the insight that 'you don't stop learning when you grow old; you grow old when you stop learning.' The participants in the HSL study demonstrate their intentional engagement with learning not only by completing the programme successfully but also by returning to their home communities to present workshops on health and safety for seniors, and by recruiting potential future participants.

Appendix A:

Brief description of 18 modules developed for delivery in the Health Literacy Programme for Seniors.

Falls prevention: This workshop identifies many of the hazards that contribute to the likelihood of seniors falling in their homes or outside in their communities. Safeguards are recommended and exercises to improve balance and strength are demonstrated.

Safety in the home: Participants are given a detailed checklist of potential dangers that may be encountered in every room in the home, as well as outside the home and in the community. Fire hazards, medication use and childproofing the home are all reviewed. Safety devices are shown and tips for effective renovations are provided.

Osteoporosis – the silent thief: This bone disease is often the underlying cause of falls, which can be devastating in their impact on quality of life for seniors. The workshop examines the causes of the disease and the risk factors contributing to an individual's susceptibility. Some of the most recent treatment options are discussed.

Creating an age-friendly community: The importance of the role of seniors in promoting the World Health Organisation's age-friendly community goals cannot be overemphasised. This workshop is designed to assist individuals and groups to promote and achieve the kind of community environments that lead to health and wellbeing, not only for older adults but also for all citizens.

Healthy eating for seniors: Canada's revised Food Guide provides the basis for this workshop. The guide is reviewed in detail and participants are shown how to use the information found on food labels to assist them in making choices of appropriate foods to purchase.

Pensions and tax options: Involuntary separation, caregiver and disability tax rules are presented and discussed. This workshop describes the potential pension benefits that may be available if a couple undergoes involuntary separation. The workshop also deals with the rules governing tax allowances for caregivers and people with disabilities. The procedures and application forms for these allowances are reviewed and discussed.

Preventing elder abuse and neglect: After an explanation of the many varieties of abuse and neglect of seniors, participants learn how to identify suspicious signs and symptoms. The potential causes of abuse are reviewed and intervention techniques and sources of assistance are described.

Medication awareness for seniors: The potential misuse of medications affects the health and wellbeing of seniors. In this workshop we provide information about how seniors can interact with doctors and pharmacists to ensure that their medications are appropriately used. Participants are encouraged to develop a partnership relationship with their medical advisors. A short quiz is used to make people aware of possible side effects and drug interactions.

Doing it your way – legal documents you need: This workshop reviews three important legal documents that all seniors (and others) should prepare – Wills; Powers of Attorney; and Representation Agreements. Each of these documents has specific uses and each requires the appointment of someone to see that the provisions are faithfully carried out.

Participants are encouraged to understand the importance of these documents in terms of estate planning and security should disability or incapacity strike.

Understanding osteoarthritis: This debilitating disease is the most common form of arthritis. The workshop describes the symptoms and recommends ways in which people can cope with the effects of deterioration of cartilage in their joints. Self-management strategies are explained and various therapies are reviewed.

Emergency preparedness for seniors: When disaster strikes, older adults need to be ready to take the necessary measures to survive for lengthy periods of time, sometimes without assistance. The topics covered include: preparation and storage of emergency survival kits; understanding safety procedures in dangerous situations; and where, when and how to seek help.

Fraud and scams: Whether by telephone, mail or in person, frauds and scams are proliferating and can have devastating effects on the lives and health of seniors. This workshop investigates the ways in which people are taken in by schemers whose sole purpose is to rob them of their money, identity or possessions. As frequent victims of scams and fraud, seniors need to be aware of how to protect themselves. The theme explored in the workshop is 'If it seems too good to be true, then it probably isn't true'.

Dealing with stress: None of us can lead totally stress-free lives and perhaps we shouldn't want to. However, excessive stress harms the quality of life of many seniors. This workshop will assist in identifying and handling sources of stress. Effects of stress are examined and techniques for stress relief taught.

Chronic diseases: Four of the most common diseases that affect the health of senior adults are: cancer; diabetes; heart disease; and lung disease. This workshop assists participants to identify the warning signs of these diseases. Early recognition is emphasised and appropriate resources for information and assistance are presented.

Mental health: Many seniors are probably more frightened of losing their mental health than their physical health. In this workshop we concentrate on ways in which people can contribute to their own mental health, ways in which the brain can be stimulated to remain healthy. Attention is also given to warning signs of potential illness.

Caregiving: Many seniors undertake the care of family members or friends and sometimes the workload and stress involved can do harm to the caregiver. This workshop examines the causes of caregiver burn-out and suggests how it may be avoided. Sources of assistance are reviewed.

Social connectedness: As people age, the importance of staying socially active cannot be overemphasised. Loneliness can be a killer. In this workshop we examine the social determinants of health to assist participants to determine the level of social connectedness they need and how to achieve it.

Addiction and seniors: There are three major types of addiction that seniors may need to deal with: alcohol abuse; gambling addiction; and medication abuse. Risk factors leading to addiction are examined and suggestions are given for ways to approach a friend or family member when you suspect addiction.

References

Adult Education Centre (2005) *Facilitation Skills: Working with Adult Leaders* (Dublin: University College Dublin). Retrieved from <http://www.ucd.ie/adulted/resources//facil_adnrogog.htm>

Aspin, D. and Chapman, J. (2001) 'Lifelong Learning: Concepts, Theories and Values', paper presented at SCUTREA, 31st Annual Conference, 3–5 July, University of East London.

Beattie, B.L., Whitelaw, N., Metter, M. and Turner, D. (2003) 'A Vision for Older Adults and Health Promotion', *American Journal of Health Promotion,* 18, pp.200–4.

Bennett, K.M. (2002) 'Low Level Social Engagement as a Precursor of Mortality among People in Later Life', *Age and Aging,* 31, pp.165–8.

Chickering, A.W. and Gamson, Z.F. (1987) 'Seven Principles for Good Practice in Undergraduate Education', *American Association of Higher Education Bulletin,* 39/7, pp.3–7.

Collins, J. (2004) 'Education Techniques for Lifelong Learning: Principles of Adult Learning', *RadioGraphics,* 24, pp.1,483–9.

Crick, R.D., Broadfoot, P. and Claxton, G. (2004) 'Developing an Effective Lifelong Learning Inventory: The ELLI Project', *Assessment in Education,* 11/3, pp.247–72.

Edmunds, C., Lowe, K., Murray, M. and Seymour, A. (1999) *The Ultimate Educator,* National Victim Assistance Academy (Advanced) (Washington: US Department of Justice, Office for Victims of Crime).

Field, J. (2003) 'Civic Engagement and Lifelong Learning: Survey Findings on Social Capital and Attitudes Towards Learning', *Studies in the Education of Adults*, 35/2, pp.142–56.

Hinterlong, J.E. and Williamson, A. (2007) 'The Effects of Civic Engagement of Current and Future Cohorts of Older Adults', *Generations*, 30/4, pp.10–17.

Jezierski, J. (2003) Discussion and Demonstration in Series of Orientation Sessions, presented at St. Elizabeth Hospital Medical Center, Lafayette, IN.

Kim, A. and Merriam, S.B. (2004) 'Motivations for Learning among Older Adults in a Learning in Retirement Institute', *Educational Gerontology*, 30, pp.441–55.

Kuh, G.D., Kinzie, J., Schuh, J.H. and Whitt, E.J. (2005) *Student Success in College: Creating Conditions That Matter* (San Francisco: Jossey-Bass).

Laslett, P. (1989) *A Fresh Map of Life: The Emergence of the Third Age* (London: Weidenfeld and Nicolson).

Lieb, S. (1991) *Adult Learning Principles*. Retrieved from <http://honolulu.hawaii.edu/intranet/committees/FacDevCom/guidebk/teachtip/adults-2.htm>

Martinson, M. and Minkler, M. (2006) 'Civic Engagement and Older Adults: A Critical Perspective', *The Gerontologist*, 46/3, pp.318–24.

Merriam, S.B. (1998) *Qualitative Research and Case Study Applications in Education* (San Francisco: Jossey-Bass).

Morrow-Howell, N., Hinterlong, J., Rozario, P.A. and Tang, F. (2003) 'Effects of Volunteering on the Well-Being of Older Adults', *Journal of Gerontology*, 58B/3S, pp.137–45.

Newble, D.I. and Clarke, R.M. (1986) 'The Approaches to Learning of Students in a Traditional and in an Innovative Problem-Based Medical School', *Medical Education*, 20/4, pp.267–73.

Pace, R.C. (1982) *Achievement and the Quality of Student Effort*, report to the Department of Education (Washington, DC).

Patton, M.Q. (2001) *Qualitative Research and Evaluation Methods* (Thousand Oaks: Sage).

Pew Charitable Trust (2006) *Supporting Civic Life* (Philadelphia: The Pew Charitable Trusts).

Putnam, R. (1995) 'Bowling Alone Revisited', *Journal of Democracy*, 6, p.65.

Richardson, V. (2005) 'The diverse learning needs of students', in Billings, D.M. and Halstead, J.A. (eds) *Teaching in Nursing*, 2nd ed. (St. Louis: Elsevier).

Rogers, C.R. (1969) *Freedom to Learn* (Columbus: Merrill).

Rubenson, K. and Desjardins, R. (2009) 'The Impact of Welfare State Regimes on Barriers to Participation in Adult Education: A Bounded Agency Model', *Adult Education Quarterly*, 59/May, pp.187–207.

Vancouver Coastal Health (2005) *Health Link Archives*. Retrieved from <http://www.vch.ca/enewsletter/files/2005-11-01/falls_prevention_stay_in_the_game.html>

Chapter 14

Engaging students with statistics using collaborative project-based approaches

Michelle Sisto[1] and Peter Petocz[2]

[1] *International University of Monaco, Monaco*
[2] *Macquarie University, Australia*

Introduction

In this chapter, we investigate engagement in the context of tertiary courses in statistics, a subject traditionally regarded with trepidation by large numbers of students as being difficult and uninteresting. We present two case studies of the use of collaborative group projects in statistics learning and show how they have contributed to greater student engagement with their studies. On the basis of our experience, we identify the aspects that help to enhance engagement and indicate how the same methods may be applied to other disciplines.

Over the last two decades, introductory statistics courses have steadily gained a place in the core curriculum of a rich variety of programmes in higher education, both at undergraduate and graduate levels. Statistics is utilised in a wide range of fields such as business, finance, psychology, tourism, dentistry and engineering, and while the specific needs of client disciplines vary, there are elements that seem to be common across all introductory courses. Furthermore, with the ever-increasing availability of data, statistical literacy is becoming an important aspect of formal education in all areas. Despite the increase in numbers of students taking statistics as a degree requirement, the vast majority take only a single, required course.

Many students keep their distance from the subject: some put it off for as long as possible, others require multiple attempts to pass and many view statistics more as a hurdle to overcome in order to graduate than as an opportunity to learn about their own personal and professional interests. For many, statistics represents a completely new way of thinking and an unexpected component of their studies and future profession. One student told us in an interview: "Statistics seemed to be something strange and useless. I was studying engineering, and I didn't know why I had to study statistics." As statistics educators, we know that our discipline is intellectually fascinating and practically useful, and we may find it hard to understand why so many students have a quite different view and seem to have such difficulty engaging with the ideas and the practice of statistics.

'Service' courses in statistics, both introductory and later courses, have been the focus of much pedagogical attention. Articles discussing teaching and learning in this context are a continuing theme in forums such as the on-line *Journal of Statistics Education* and the four-yearly *International Conference on Teaching Statistics*. The notion of 'statistics anxiety' – a persistent theme in statistics education and maybe a converse of engagement – makes regular appearances (see, for example, Williams, 2010; DeVaney, 2010).

Changes in approaches to statistics education have grown internationally with calls to move away from a traditional 'cookbook' approach to teaching towards a more data-driven, authentic learning of statistics with a greater focus on statistical thinking and less emphasis on statistical calculations (Garfield et al., 2002). Advances in technology have assisted this process, with statistical packages taking over the role of carrying out calculations, preparing graphical displays and allowing the easy exploration of statistical information. The growth of the Internet has enabled access to vast amounts of data on almost any topic of interest. At the same time, there has been considerable research on better ways of fostering learning – collaborative and active learning, student-centred classrooms, constructive learning, context-driven activities with appropriate technological support – all of which encourage student engagement in learning (see Chance et al., 2007, and Zieffler et al., 2008 for comprehensive summaries). Engaging students in statistics learning should be considerably easier at the end of the first decade of the twenty-first century but, despite these advances, it seems that problems still remain.

In the United States, research at the college level shows that the best predictors of student learning and personal development are the time and energy that students devote to "educationally purposeful activities" (Kuh, 2003). The (US) National Survey of Student Engagement (NSSE) is to some extent founded on "seven principles for good practice in undergraduate education" proposed by Chickering and Gamson (1987). These principles include student–faculty contact, cooperation among students, active learning, prompt feedback, time on task, high expectations, and respect for diverse talents and ways of learning. Collaborative projects in statistics can encompass all seven principles and promote the habits of statistical thinking. Projects provide students with the opportunity to carry out the full steps of a statistical investigation – from developing a research question to designing the data collection method, selecting appropriate ways to describe data, identifying appropriate methods of statistical analysis and communicating research findings. Requiring students to carry out projects in groups increases cooperation amongst students, promotes active learning and enhances the sense of a learning community in the course. In addition, students select a topic and collect data that they find relevant to their own lives and interests, further increasing their engagement.

At the end of the previous century, Kearsley and Schneiderman (1999) tied together the notions of collaborative learning, project-based learning and authentic learning supported by an appropriate technological environment under the title of 'theory of engagement'. At that time, technology may have been important to highlight. However, more than a decade later, the enormous developments in technological support for learning have paradoxically moved it into the background. The current generation of students has grown up in such a technologically rich environment that for them technology is an accepted, expected and natural background aspect of their learning.

There is some evidence (Scott, 2006, p.34) that different disciplines focus on different learning methods or approaches, with each discipline using relatively few of the full range of possible approaches. For instance, case studies are commonly used in business, seminars in the humanities, practical placements in teacher education, inter-professional presentations in the health sciences and laboratory investigations in science. However, other combinations, such as practical placements in humanities or inter-professional presentations in business, are less common. Statistics education has its own favourite (or even traditional) approaches that include sequential presentation of a standard body of theory, solving numerical exercises and (more recently) computer-based laboratories investigating data sets. Scott writes: "an appropriate combination of more interactive, practice-oriented, problem-based methods is what appears to engage students the most" (2006, p.35). Group projects have not been as commonly used in statistics as (say) in management education. One reason might be related to lecturers' concerns about 'covering' a certain body of content, though in practice this seems to be more than compensated for by the increased authenticity of the learning through projects.

Learning statistics

In this chapter, we look at the use of collaborative projects to engage students in learning statistics. But what do we mean when we say we want our students to 'learn statistics'? Within the field of statistics education, the predominant approach during the late twentieth century was based on the cognitivist and constructivist tradition, exemplified by Garfield's (1995) discussion of "how students learn statistics" (and its 'update', Garfield and Ben-Zvi, 2007). The writings of Garfield and her colleagues have represented a strong presence in statistics education, reaching into all aspects of statistics pedagogy. The key ideas that emerge from their research are that students learn by constructing knowledge, by active involvement in and practice with learning activities, by becoming aware of and confronting their misconceptions, and by using technology to visualise and explore data. Students learn to value what they know will be assessed and learn better with consistent and helpful feedback. Various authors (for example, Rumsey, 2002; Chance, 2002; Garfield and Ben-Zvi, 2004) have considered statistical literacy, statistical reasoning and statistical thinking and discussed the implications of each for teaching and assessment. All three components are necessary aspects of learning statistics, quite different to the more traditional focus on being able to carry out statistical procedures. In addition, working groups on teaching statistics have produced professional recommendations for introductory statistics courses. An example is the *Guidelines for Assessment and Instruction in Statistics Education* (GAISE) *College Report* (American Statistical Association, 2005).

An alternative, though not incompatible, view of learning in statistics is the phenomenographic approach. Phenomenography is a qualitative and descriptive research approach that aims to investigate empirically how people experience, understand and ascribe meaning to a specific situation or aspect of reality or phenomenon in the surrounding world (Marton and Booth, 1997). Originally developed as a way of describing the processes and outcomes of learning from the perspective of the learner (Marton and Säljö, 1976), phenomenography has been applied to a broad range of experiences, including conceptions of a specific discipline (for example, law – Reid, Nagarajan and Dortins, 2006), process (for example, scientific intuition – Marton, Fensham and Chaiklin, 1994) or construct (for example, 'environment' – Loughland, Reid and Petocz, 2002). Phenomenographic studies have repeatedly demonstrated a counterintuitive finding: when a group of people experience a phenomenon, they view it in a small number of qualitatively different ways, as opposed to holding a continuum of views. Thus, some people appear to share a way of experiencing the phenomenon, whereas others will understand the same phenomenon in other, quite distinct, ways.

Specific research on conceptions of statistics has shown that students' views of the discipline can be described in three categories (Reid and Petocz, 2002). In the narrowest conception, students focus on techniques; they see statistics as individual mathematical or statistical techniques, or collections of such techniques. In a broader conception, students focus on data; they see statistics in terms of the analysis, interpretation and utilisation of data. In the broadest conception, they focus on meaning; they view statistics as an inclusive tool used to make sense of the world and develop personal meanings. In the phenomenographic approach, the theory of learning statistics focuses on this variation in students' conceptions of statistics and sees learning as the process of moving from narrower and limited to broader and more inclusive views.

A range of phenomenographic research in a variety of disciplines – including statistics – indicates that the broadest and most holistic conceptions of discipline and of learning include an aspect of personal change and a connection with personal and professional life (Petocz and Reid, 2010). Thus, as well as the epistemological aspects focusing on the nature and development of knowledge, the ontological aspects of being and becoming – who the student is, how they think about themselves and how they change during and beyond the course of their studies – are also important (Barnett, 2007). This has clear links to notions of engagement that are developed through working on group projects. In the context of projects, we aim to guide students to the broadest levels of statistical thinking and to offer them an opportunity to develop a 'deep' orientation toward statistics by carrying out the full steps of a statistical investigation that has personal and professional meaning for them. In other words, we help students to *become* statisticians and give them opportunities to *be* statisticians, rather than just studying statistics.

The constructivist ideas of learning in terms of active involvement with authentic materials and the phenomenographic ideas of learning in terms of transforming the learner by broadening their viewpoint have implications for teaching and assessment. These include using real data and problems of relevance to students, promoting collaborative learning, developing students' statistical thinking, stressing conceptual understanding rather than technical facility, using technology for developing concepts as well as analysing data, integrating projects of community importance, and implementing authentic and formative assessment. Collaborative group projects are a vehicle for learning statistics that incorporate many of these ideas. In the context of introductory statistics, the advantages of using projects based on data collected by students themselves and working collaboratively have been documented in the past (for example, Fillebrown, 1994; MacGillivray, 1998; Mackisack, 2002) and more recently (Bingham, 2010). Group projects can deepen students' understanding of statistics, increase their interest in and appreciation of the usefulness of statistics in making decisions, and allow them to investigate questions of personal interest – a key aspect of engagement. Working in groups promotes cooperation among students, active learning and respect for diverse talents and ways of learning – three of the seven principles of good practice in undergraduate education that increase student engagement. In addition, using multiple assessments – self, professor and peer assessments – further enhances student involvement in the learning process. More recent reports have described the contemporary technology-rich context for such learning (Roseth, Garfield and Ben-Zvi, 2008; Sisto, 2009).

In the following sections, we describe and compare approaches to group project work in introductory and advanced statistics courses at a small, private multicultural (English-language) business school in Monaco and a large metropolitan university in Australia. We present our own experiences as teachers of statistics classes and support them by evidence of our students' views and experiences during the process of learning using the group project format. We link these experiences with theories of student engagement and investigate the aspects of group projects that can be successfully used to enhance students' learning experiences. While firmly set in the context of statistics, we will discuss the implications for other related disciplines.

The Monaco experience

The International University of Monaco is a small, private, English-language business school located in the Principality of Monaco. All undergraduate students are required to take a two-course sequence, Introductory Statistics and Advanced Statistics for Business. For the last ten years, group projects have been an integral part of these courses. With upwards of 40 nationalities and 25 first languages among the full-time students, the multicultural make-up of the student body presents particular opportunities and challenges in carrying out group projects.

The learning objectives of our undergraduate programme are to:

- Perform independent projects and research by synthesising data from various sources to reach a reasoned conclusion
- Work effectively in groups
- Communicate effectively in a variety of written and oral forms
- Use commonly available technology proficiently as a tool for making business decisions
- Recognise and discuss the importance of respect for and sensitivity to cultural diversity, and
- Demonstrate an appreciation of the ethical implications of business decisions and actions.

We use group projects to help students reach these objectives while engaging with their studies and the discipline of statistics. Courses meet twice a week for two hours over a 12-week term. Class size is typically between 10 and 25 students and most class meetings are held in a computer lab. Each project has three components: a business memo to communicate results to a non-statistician; an appendix with results clearly summarised for a statistician; and a PowerPoint presentation for an audience assumed to possess some technical knowledge. In addition to carrying out the projects, students are also involved in the assessment process through self and peer assessments.

We make explicit efforts to promote mutual respect and a comfort level that permits carrying out successful teamwork, including providing and receiving constructive criticism. We take time on the first day of class to introduce ourselves, sharing something about the languages we speak, our interests and passions, and our experiences with mathematics and statistics. This helps to create a feeling of community from the first day, allows students to find other classmates with similar interests and gives participants a first experience in speaking to the class. We find that the time spent on introductions promotes peer engagement and enhances the positive group environment. Additionally, we devote some class time to addressing the advantages and challenges of group work, in particular with multicultural groups. Based on work by Hofstede (1997) and Schneider and Barsoux (2003), we guide teams towards developing clear task and process strategies. We have experimented with group formation in several ways, sometimes requiring students to work with a different team for each project and sometimes allowing them to choose their team and stay together for both projects. Both methods have advantages and neither has proven clearly superior.

To enhance student engagement with the projects, they choose their own topic, be it of personal, professional or societal interest. At an initial stage, students must explain what question(s) of interest they hope to answer with their project work. The professor is engaged with each group, helping them to form appropriate research questions and to plan data collection and analysis. Data collection may involve gathering primary data or seeking and retrieving published data from other sources. At the introductory level, the first project is a descriptive statistics project and, as the content knowledge grows, later projects give students the opportunity to go beyond descriptive statistics and examine the statistical significance of relationships between variables and differences amongst groups. Students have chosen to look at topics such as: examining differences in executive compensation by industry sector; looking at relationships between levels of literacy and incidence of AIDS; comparing prices of products of online grocery stores to classic grocery stores; and predicting the jumping capacity of horses based on their height, breed and tail length. One of the greatest pleasures of using projects in courses is the opportunity for instructors to learn about areas of interest to students, thus promoting faculty–student interaction. In cases where students investigate issues of interest to the University, this interaction has at times involved the administration.

Research into engagement suggests that the time and effort students spend on educationally purposeful activities are key ingredients of student engagement. Work on group projects lasts from three to five weeks and students integrate the evolving course material into their projects as the course advances. This allows them to practice and understand the statistical content first on more standard textbook questions, then to apply the new material to their different projects in a broader range of situations. In this way, students are encouraged to expand their notion of statistics from a collection of techniques to a broader conception of statistics as a tool for making meaningful sense of their personal topic of interest.

Projects are assessed by the professor, by the group members and also through peer assessment. While the grade assigned is summative, the methods of assessment are formative. Students receive clear criteria and the grading rubric that the professor and the group use to assess the projects. For each oral presentation, students must evaluate their peers, writing at least two specific positive comments about what went well and two specific comments on how the project presentation could be improved; two of the four comments must be content related and all must be constructive or regenerative. These peer assessments have multiple benefits: students react more positively to feedback from their peers than from their professors; they develop transferrable skills of critical listening and evaluating by carrying out critiques; and they are actively engaged in all presentations, not just their own.

Comments from University end-of-term anonymous course evaluations provide clear evidence of the impact of project work on the students' perception of the course. To the question: "What part of the course did you find most beneficial?", the vast majority of students comment on the benefit of project work for aiding their understanding of statistics and for helping them discover the interest of statistics as a discipline. Here are some typical responses:

> Projects very beneficial, enable us to apply in real life situation what we learn in class.
>
> I found the whole course both stimulating and beneficial. It was most useful to apply the techniques on real business examples.
>
> The most useful part of the course to me is the way the projects are structured. They are intensely related to real life and as a result we explain the significance of our results. If the course were about running models we wouldn't take much away from it because we would forget in six months, however, we won't forget the relation of statistics to real life!

Students were asked about the role of projects in their learning, answering the questions "If there were projects, were they helpful for your learning? If so, how? If not, why not?" In the ten years of using project work, not a single student has responded that projects were not helpful to learning. Here are some examples of their replies:

> The projects were always based on real life data which made them interesting and also demonstrated how statistics is used in real life.
>
> The projects were very beneficial to learning statistics. They helped us learn through a hands on approach. Especially collecting our own data.
>
> Projects were good, especially the first one because it was hard to understand the course in the beginning but after the presentations and the discussions it made [me] understand it.

Some students commented on the time and preparation needed for project work:

> Projects were helpful but required a lot of work in a very little time.
>
> The projects were great and very useful but more practice before doing them would be more helpful.

Other students pointed to the benefits of working in a group learning community:

> The most useful I found was the projects because we were learning more by doing it, asking or teaching our group members and receiving feedback from you.
>
> Projects were really, really helpful as you study from working on the project and you learn from other students in your group. You really do study while working.
>
> I enjoyed the teamwork, some were more difficult than others but we learn a lot: how to be patient, understanding, generous by helping others, humble by learning from others.

Several students focused on the advantages of learning generic skills:

> Ultimately it was the presentation part, we all learnt how to write a memo, professional power point slides and talk in front of the class. I gained confidence in presentation through this class and learnt not to be ashamed because we got to know each other.
>
> I enjoyed presenting the outcomes and results of our studies to the class. Very business and real world related, hence it was useful to learn how to present complex data in an understandable clear way.

Student response to project work is overwhelmingly positive, although several students do comment that projects are time consuming. By fostering peer collaboration and faculty–student interaction, promoting active learning and helping students develop generic and transferable skills such as writing, oral communication and evaluation techniques, projects promote student engagement on many levels. Initially, we introduced project work with the main aim of increasing student learning of statistics by engaging them in the full cycle of statistical enquiry. However, an unexpected and enriching by-product has been the deeper level at which we ourselves now engage with our students by learning about their interests and passions. While requiring a time commitment from professors and students, the increased satisfaction on both sides is well worth the effort.

The Sydney experience

The second-year unit that is the subject of this case study is a one-semester unit in applied statistics with a focus on linear models, offered by the Department of Statistics at Macquarie University, Sydney. Students have previously taken an introductory unit in descriptive and inferential statistics, and applied statistics is an optional extra course attracting 30–50 students each semester. Some, though not all, of these students will choose to major in statistics. The applied statistics unit is built around projects carried out in self-selected groups of two or three students and based on topics chosen by the students.

The unit runs for one semester – three hours per week for 13 weeks. The first few weeks introduce basic theoretical ideas of one-way and two-way analysis of variance and simple and multiple linear regression; and this is followed by more practical classes on collecting, organising and 'cleaning' data. Later in the semester, there are further lectures on technical aspects such as contrasts and power, as well as process aspects such as graphical displays of multidimensional data and report writing. Lectures are supported by tutorials, focussing on processes such as group work and interpreting results, and laboratory classes, which give students guided practice at analysing datasets using Minitab and other statistical packages.

The first technical lectures are just in time for students to form their groups, select their topic, and plan and then collect their data during a mid-semester break. Other lectures are designed to feed into the process just as they are needed. Students work on their project throughout the semester (and it counts for 40 per cent of their assessment in the unit). They obtain feedback at several points; first, they need to submit a project proposal, which is checked, maybe modified and then approved by the lecturer. Later in the semester, during a one-week window, groups may submit a draft version of their project for comment by lecturer or tutor. This is optional (though almost all groups participate) and enables them to identify any serious problems and make any necessary changes at an early stage. Lastly, if the final version of the project is unsatisfactory, students have the option of working further on it to bring it to a passing level; this provision is rarely needed but students seem to feel better knowing that it is there. All work is submitted and marked using the learning management system – paper isn't used at all.

The unit explicitly addresses the development of a range of generic capabilities. These include skills such as team work, information literacy and written communication; although not part of the unit to date, a small increase in the time allocated will allow us to arrange a final 'mini-conference' where groups will present their results to the whole class, an approach used successfully in previous courses (see Petocz and Reid, 2008). Dispositions such as ethics and sustainability are also addressed. Students discuss ethical aspects of statistical work in an early class and are introduced to the University's ethics approval process; in their project proposals they are asked to identify ethical aspects. The lecturer has obtained formal ethics approval and has undertaken to check and approve these ethical aspects of students' projects. In their proposals, students are asked to identify the social or environmental usefulness of the topic they select. This may involve thinking beyond an obvious topic (such as students' drinking patterns) to a broader social context (for example, identification of factors that promote 'binge' drinking).

Students are encouraged to select projects that link with their private interests, their other studies or professional work projects, and to use their project in conjunction with work, studies or community needs elsewhere. This is an explicit decision, built on our research on students' conceptions of statistics (Reid and Petocz, 2002) and its relationship to their perceptions of their future profession (Reid et al., 2011). Topics that student groups have chosen include: levels and causes of addiction to social networking sites such as Facebook; factors affecting the reliability of local train services; relationships between wealth and levels of violence in various countries; and the effects of immigration on the social and economic prosperity of countries. As the final stage, each student writes an individual analysis and reflection on the process of carrying out the project, indicating how their team worked and what specific roles they themselves took and giving advice to the next group of students and lecturer in the course. This encourages the process of self-reflection, another graduate attribute that has important benefits in professional life.

The following comments are taken verbatim from these individual self-reflections. Although it was clear from the marking scheme that students could get equally good results by making positive or negative comments, the vast majority were positive. Anonymous teaching and unit appraisals also supported the positive tenor. One student commented:

> In the past, most group assignments require you all to sign one declaration confirming equal contribution, which isn't very effective [as] most people don't want to offend the other team members by being honest. This way, it is confidential and the marker can get a fairer picture.

Almost all students seem happy with the experience of working in a group:

> I think group projects are an important learning experience, because you get to see everything you've learned from another person's perspective.

> Not only did we keep each other updated with the latest progress, we also helped each other whenever somebody had a problem, and notified each other whenever somebody had a good idea.

> The team had a weekly meeting time set every Wednesday. We would meet at that time and discuss our next step in the project. ...We would also stick together in the tutorials, practicals, and lectures. We even walked to the train-station together after the lecture.

One student had a contrary view (though she also commented on the advantages of group work):

> I feel that group work can detract from the sense of satisfaction one can feel when completing the task alone and that process can be very important for creating a personal confidence in statistical ability.

Many students felt that the practical nature of the project helped them to understand the theory:

> I could literally see the practical applications of statistics, and rather than seeing each individual method as something I had to learn, I saw each method as a tool to accomplish a task I needed it for.

> This project is just like a bridge, that connects techniques and real stuffs together, and when we were working on it, we have better understanding of how the techniques work with real tasks.

They made many comments on the link between their project and their other studies, professional work and personal life:

> This was probably the most useful assignment I have done in my entire uni years. ...I feel 100 per cent more confident now and I think I will do a lot better just because of this course. Honestly.

> The applied statistics project helped me apply my learning in statistical techniques learnt during the lecture, labs and tutorials to the real work data I deal with, in my workplace on a day-to-day basis.

> It gave me a first-hand experience of what it is like to use statistics in real life. It expanded my perception of daily matters, when I started thinking of them in terms of numbers.

Some students commented on dispositional aspects of their learning:

> I feel that the best aspect of our project was that it allowed us to put to practice what we have learnt about statistical analysis by applying it to answer questions of importance to society.

> Having to collect the data brought to my attention some ethical aspects of applied statistics. ...Most of the [participants'] concerns related to how the data would be used after the project was completed and who would see the data.

Some seemed to come closer to the essence of statistics and found extra benefits:

> The project helps me understanding the true meaning of statistics – using in real life to improve people's work or life in certain way.

> And I have to say that now not only are we group mates, we have built friendship during the project as well, which is the extra bit that the project introduced to me.

From the lecturer's viewpoint, it has been a satisfying experience working with groups that have such evident commitment to their study of applied statistics and very rewarding helping them to explore their chosen topics. A big surprise, though, has been the resistance of (most) colleagues to the project-based approach; currently, the unit is still taught in the 'traditional' lecturing format in alternate semesters. This resistance seems to be based on several connected factors: worries about less 'coverage' of content and increased time spent grading and providing feedback; inclusion of generic skills such as communication and dispositions such as ethics; and unfamiliarity (or even unease) with the alternative pedagogical approach.

It seems that the project-based approach utilised in this unit has made a contribution to the level of student engagement with their studies. This is apparent in many of the students' comments quoted earlier. It is also supported by principles of good teaching (Chickering and Gamson, 1987; Zieffler et al., 2008) and the reports from earlier project-based courses (for example, Mackisack, 2002; Bingham, 2010). Further, the connections engendered with students' personal and professional lives argue for increased levels of engagement (Reid et al., 2011).

Conclusion

The essential argument of this chapter is that project-based learning is a powerful way for students to construct an understanding of statistics and to develop broader views of the nature of the discipline and its use in their professional and personal life. We have illustrated our experience in two quite different contexts, with projects in an elective unit (Sydney) and a compulsory one (Monaco). The feedback from both groups of students is overwhelmingly positive and attests to the engagement that results from the approach. We believe that any risks involved in using a project-based approach, particularly in the sense that specific topics may not be 'covered' by all students, are outweighed by the risks of not engaging students with a traditional course structure.

What is the essence of our practical approach to engagement? We have set up conditions under which students carry out authentic learning on problems that are of interest and importance to themselves, be it on a personal, academic or professional basis. These problems are embedded in a social and an intellectual dimension, and are supported by rich technology (for communication as well as for analysis of data and reporting). Further, project work encourages students to develop a range of generic capabilities, such as communication and teamwork, and to engage with other aspects of learning such as ethics and sustainability. Students are in control of the process, particularly in their own choice of topics and groups, and yet their lecturer and tutor support them; the conditions are set up in such a way that students know they are very likely to succeed. In these project-rich courses, students have the opportunity not only to construct their own statistical knowledge but also to work statistically, to *become* statisticians. These components are not new – but we have found them to be effective and we believe that they could be utilised more often in statistics education at all levels. Other statistics educators before us have come to similar conclusions (amongst others, MacGillivray, 1998; Mackisack, 2002; Bingham, 2010). The organisation of our courses satisfies Chickering and Gamson's (1987) principles of good practice in undergraduate education and the *GAISE* recommendations (American Statistical Association, 2005), both associated with higher levels of student engagement.

Similar approaches can be used effectively in related disciplines, particularly those like mathematics that have a strong 'service' role in university studies. Viskic and Petocz (2006) and Barnett et al. (2009) report positive experiences in using projects in mathematics, though the approach is not commonly used in mathematics pedagogy. Disciplines and courses that do not traditionally use project-based learning might benefit by making more use of the approach. Scott (2006, p.34) identified the broad fields of health, education and the humanities as making significantly less use of group projects than science and management/commerce. However, these broad groupings hide the variation between disciplines: in design and engineering education, the group project is standard (see, for example, McDermott, Nafalski and Gol, 2007); and in music education it would seem impractical to prepare and perform an ensemble piece without it. Sometimes, the projects are more extensive class simulations (Lloyd and Butcher, 2006, in the area of environmental science) that may even extend well beyond the boundaries of the class (Vincent and Shepherd, 1998, politics); but they show essentially the same characteristics that we have identified.

The investigation in this chapter highlights the importance of helping students to engage with their learning at an essential level, to move beyond simply learning *about* statistics to actually *becoming* a statistician, a person who uses statistics and thinks statistically (Petocz and Reid, 2010). At the conclusion of their studies, students need to find themselves prepared for their professional role; as Barnett (2007, p.50, with our small modification) states, "The degree in [statistics] confirms that the student has *become*, if only embryonically, a [statistician]." It is our most important role as statistics educators to give each of our students the opportunity to engage fully with our discipline and to become a statistician.

References

American Statistical Association (2005) *Guidelines for Assessment and Instruction in Statistics Education (GAISE) College Report*. Retrieved from <http://www.amstat.org/education/gaise/GAISECollege.htm>

Barnett, J., Lodder, J., Pengelley, D., Pivkina, I. and Ranjan, D. (2009) *Designing Student Projects for Teaching and Learning Discrete Mathematics and Computer Science via Primary Historical Sources*. Retrieved from <http://www.cs.nmsu.edu/historical-projects/Papers/HPM-collected-volume-historical-projects-rev01.pdf>

Barnett, R. (2007) *A Will to Learn: Being a Student in an Age of Uncertainty* (Buckingham: Society for Research in Higher Education, Open University Press).

Bingham, A. (2010) 'Student Attitudes to Real-World Projects in an Introductory Statistics Course', in Reading, C. (ed.) *Proceedings of ICOTS-8 (8th International Conference on Teaching Statistics)* (International Statistical Institute). Retrieved from <http://www.stat.auckland.ac.nz/~iase/publications/icots8/ICOTS8_C203_BINGHAM.pdf>

Chance, B. (2002) 'Components of Statistical Thinking and Implications for Instruction and Assessment', *Journal of Statistics Education*, 10/3. Retrieved from <http://www.amstat.org/publications/jse/v10n3/chance.html>

Chance, B., Ben-Zvi, D., Garfield, J. and Medina, E. (2007) 'The Role of Technology in Improving Student Learning of Statistics', *Technology Innovations in Statistics Education*, 1/1. Retrieved from <http://repositories.cdlib.org/uclastat/cts/tise/vol1/iss1/art2

Chickering, A. and Gamson, Z. (1987) 'Seven Principles for Good Practice in Undergraduate Education', *American Association of Higher Education Bulletin*, 39/7, pp.3–7.

DeVaney, T. (2010) 'Anxiety and Attitude of Graduate Students in On-Campus Vs. Online Statistics Courses', *Journal of Statistics Education*,

18/1. Retrieved from <http://www.amstat.org/publications/jse/v18n1/devaney.pdf>

Fillebrown, S. (1994) 'Using Projects in an Elementary Statistics Course for Non-Science Majors', *Journal of Statistics Education*, 2/2. Retrieved from <http://www.amstat.org/publications/jse/v2n2/fillebrown.html>

Garfield, J. (1995) 'How Students Learn Statistics', *International Statistical Review*, 63/1, pp.25–34. Retrieved from <http://www.stat.auckland.ac.nz/~iase/publications/isr/95.Garfield.pdf>

Garfield, J. and Ben-Zvi, D. (2004) 'Research on Statistical Literacy, Reasoning, and Thinking: Issues, Challenges and Implications', in Ben-Zvi, D. and Garfield, J. (eds) *The Challenge of Developing Statistical Literacy, Reasoning, and Thinking* (Dordrecht: Kluwer) pp.397–409.

Garfield, J. and Ben-Zvi, D. (2007) 'How Students Learn Statistics Revisited: A Current Review of Research on Teaching and Learning Statistics', *International Statistical Review*, 75/3, pp.372–96.

Garfield, J., Hogg, R., Schau, C. and Whittinghill, D. (2002) 'First Courses in Statistical Science: The Status of Educational Reform Efforts', *Journal of Statistics Education*, 10/2. Retrieved from <http://www.amstat.org/publications/jse/v10n2/garfield.html>

Hofstede, G. (1997) *Culture and Organisation: Software of the Mind* (New York: McGraw-Hill).

Kearsley, G. and Schneiderman, B. (1999) *Engagement Theory: A Framework for Technology-Based Teaching and Learning*. Retrieved from <http://home.sprynet.com/~glearsley/engage.htm>.

Kuh, G.D. (2003) *The National Survey of Student Engagement: Conceptual Framework and Overview of Psychometric Properties*. Retrieved from <http://nsse.iub.edu/pdf/conceptual_framework_2003.pdf>

Lloyd, K. and Butcher, M. (2006) 'Re-using Learning Designs: Role Play Adaptations of the Mekong and Ha Long Bay e-Sim', in *Proceedings of the 23rd Annual ASCILITE Conference: Who's Learning? Whose Technology?* (Sydney, 3–6 December 2006). Retrieved from <http://www.ascilite.org.au/conferences/sydney06/proceeding/pdf_papers/p170.pdf>

Loughland, T., Reid, A. and Petocz, P. (2002) 'Young People's Conceptions of Environment: A Phenomenographic Analysis', *Environmental Education Research*, 8/2, pp.187–97.

MacGillivray, H. (1998) *Developing and Synthesizing Statistical Skills for Real Situations Through Student Projects*, International Conference on Teaching Statistics (ICOTS5), International Association for Statistical Education. Retrieved from <http://www.stat.auckland.ac.nz/~iase/publications/2/Topic8n.pdf>

Mackisack, M. (2002) 'What Is the Use of Experiments Conducted by Statistics Students?', *Journal of Statistics Education*, 2/2. Retrieved from <http://www.amstat.org/publications/jse/v2n1/mackisack.html>

Marton, F. and Booth, S. (1997) *Learning and Awareness* (Mahwah: Lawrence Erlbaum).

Marton, F., Fensham, P. and Chaiklin, S. (1994) 'A Nobel's Eye View of Scientific Intuition: Discussions with Nobel Prize-Winners in Physics, Chemistry and Medicine (1970–1986)', *International Journal of Science Education*, 16, pp.457–73.

Marton, F. and Säljö, R. (1976) 'On Qualitative Differences in Learning: I. Outcome and Process', *British Journal of Educational Psychology*, 46, pp.4–11.

McDermott, K., Nafalski, A. and Gol, O. (2007) *Project-Based Teaching in Engineering Programs*, 37th Annual Frontiers in Education Conference – Global Engineering: Knowledge without Borders, Opportunities without Passports, IEEE, 10–13 October, Milwaukee, WI.

Petocz, P. and Reid, A. (2008) 'Evaluating the Internationalised Curriculum', in Hellstén, M. and Reid, A. (eds) *Researching International Pedagogies: Sustainable Practice for Teaching and Learning in Higher Education* (Dordrecht: Springer) pp.27–43.

Petocz, P. and Reid, A. (2010) 'On Becoming a Statistician – A Qualitative View', *International Statistical Review*, 78/2, pp.271–86.

Reid, A., Abrandt Dahlgren, M., Petocz, P. and Dahlgren, L.O. (2011) *From Expert Student to Novice Professional* (Dordrecht: Springer).

Reid, A., Nagarajan, V. and Dortins, E. (2006) 'The Experience of Becoming a Legal Professional', *Higher Education Research and Development*, 25/1, pp.85–99.

Reid, A. and Petocz, P. (2002) 'Students' Conceptions of Statistics: A Phenomenographic Study', *Journal of Statistics Education*, 10/2. Retrieved from <http://www.amstat.org/publications/jse/jse_index.html>

Roseth, C., Garfield, J. and Ben-Zvi, D. (2008) *Collaboration in Learning and Teaching Statistics*. Retrieved from <http://www.amstat.org/publications/jse/v16n1/roseth.pdf>

Rumsey, D. (2002) 'Statistical Literacy as a Goal for Introductory Statistics Courses', *Journal of Statistics Education*, 10/3. Retrieved from <http://www.amstat.org/publications/jse/v10n3/rumsey2.html>

Schneider, S. and Barsoux, J. (2003) *Managing Across Cultures* (2nd edn) (Harlow: Prentice Hall).

Scott, G. (2006) *Accessing the Student Voice: Using CEQuery to Identify What Retains Students and Promotes Engagement in Productive Learning in Australian Higher Education*. Retrieved from <http://www.dest.gov.au/sectors/higher_education/publications_resources/profiles/access_student_voice.htm>

Sisto, M. (2009) 'Can You Explain that in Plain English? Making Statistics Group Projects Work in a Multicultural Setting', *Journal of Statistics Education*, 17/2. Retrieved from <http://www.amstat.org/publications/jse/v17n2/sisto.pdf>

Vincent, A. and Shepherd, J. (1998) 'Experiences in Teaching Middle East Politics via Internet-Based Role-Play Simulations', *Journal of Interactive Media in Education*, 98/11. Retrieved from <http://jime.open.ac.uk/article/1998–11/41>

Viskic, D. and Petocz, P. (2006) 'Adult Students' Views of Mathematics: Reflections on Projects', *Adults Learning Mathematics International Journal*, 1/2, pp.6–15.

Williams, A. (2010) 'Statistics Anxiety and Instructor Immediacy', *Journal of Statistics Education*, 18/2. Retrieved from <http://www.amstat.org/publications/jse/v18n2/williams.pdf>

Zieffler, Z., Garfield, J., Alt, S., Dupuis, D., Holleque, K. and Chang, B. (2008) 'What Does Research Suggest About the Teaching and Learning of Introductory Statistics at the College Level? A Review of the Literature', *Journal of Statistics Education*, 16/2. Retrieved from <http://www.amstat.org/publications/jse/v16n2/zieffler.pdf>

Chapter 15

Engaging with learning: shaping pre-service music education students' understandings of pedagogy through international fieldwork

Peter Dunbar-Hall

Sydney Conservatorium of Music, Australia

Introduction and theoretical background

This discussion concerns ways in which fieldwork had the effect of encouraging a group of 15 Australian music education students to engage with learning on a number of levels. It is based on their reactions to a one-week trip to study music and dance with Balinese musicians in Bali. This fieldwork experience was offered as an alternative to a one-semester subject on the learning and teaching methods of non-Western music cultures. This subject and its alternative fieldwork experience have a number of objectives. They allow students to experience music learning and teaching from a south-east Asian culture, and to do this on authentic instruments; they challenge the hegemony of students' music learning backgrounds; they lead to investigation of culturally shaped learning and teaching styles; they broaden students' pedagogic thinking; they assist students to analyse and critique their own learning; they encourage development of teaching strategies; and they further students' understandings of the importance of music's cultural contexts in music education terms. Simultaneously, the trip affords students the opportunity to prepare themselves as educators able to teach through engaging their students with Asia and Asian cultures, a recent federal government requirement of the Australian education system (Ministerial Council on Education, Employment, Training and Youth Affairs, 2006; Australian Curriculum, Assessment and Reporting Authority, 2010); and, in line with expectations of education in multicultural Australia (Department of Immigration and Multicultural Affairs, 1999), to reflect on communication and understanding between musicians from different cultures, backgrounds and experiences.

Of these objectives, experiencing and analysing pedagogy outside one's own background have become increasingly accepted components of music education training. Among others, the work of Rice (1994) on learning to play Bulgarian instruments in Bulgaria; Solis (2004) on performance groups from a variety of music cultures in university settings; Green (2001, 2008) on how popular musicians learn and on informal music learning; Brand (2006) on music teaching and learning across Asia; and Mackinlay (2007), on Australian Aboriginal women teaching music and dance in an Australian university and how students learn through this, have contributed to this area of interest and research. At the basis of these authors' research is the theory that, like music, methods of music transmission reflect culturally shaped aesthetic positions. Further, that music education should provide not only access to music from diverse cultural contexts but that it should match relevant indigenous teaching and learning methods to this. In music education contexts, this ideology has been given the name 'ethnopedagogy'. The theory of ethnopedagogy:

> postulates that in the same way that music differs from culture to culture, and reflects different applications of musical roles, values, meanings and significances, ways of learning and ways of teaching also differ from location to location, and that these ways of learning and teaching are also culturally loaded and influenced. Further, these different ways of learning and teaching embody aesthetic positions symbiotic with the music under consideration.
>
> (Dunbar-Hall, 2009, p.62)

As this matching of pedagogy to music is now an expectation of music education, the need to involve pre-service students in activities through which these issues of culturally influenced learning and teaching can be raised and critiqued has become a priority in my institution.

This approach to teacher preparation functions on various levels. First is the belief underpinning my work that learning to teach is about learning about learning; that if a student can understand how learning occurs, that understanding can be transformed into designing teaching strategies (see also Biggs, 1999). Second, it relies on students being made aware of learning and of being given ways of identifying and analysing it. Third is the belief that musicians in non-notated music traditions, such as in Bali, utilise alternative ways of acquiring musical skills and repertoires than those found among musicians from Western backgrounds. Finally, the possibility of involving students in learning that was linked closely to other aspects of a culture provided a way into raising the issue of ethnopedagogy with them (Dunbar-Hall, 2009). The fieldwork trip, therefore, could engage students with learning, and with ways of thinking about learning, in many ways.

Methodology

The research for this project relied on three methodological stages that moved from practical involvement in learning Balinese music to discussion and problematising of the pedagogic issues encountered. In this way, the staff member involved modelled a template of practical experience providing material for theorisation about pedagogy for students. Induction into the basics of fieldwork research methods was another way this experience could be seen as connecting students to a specific learning outcome. In its own way, this simple three-stage fieldwork method involved students with learning – in this case, learning how to plan a research process and to apply it in the field.

In the first stage, students were prepared for fieldwork. As the organiser of the fieldwork, I realised that to expect students to cope with musical instruments, playing techniques and tunings foreign to them in the time frame of the trip was unrealistic. To perform on a Balinese *gamelan* (instrumental ensemble), students would need to learn hand and arm techniques, how to negotiate the tuning system of the instruments, the roles of the different instruments in a *gamelan* and the expectations of Balinese teachers. I recognised that students who had not learnt in non-notated, aural transmission settings would have difficulty in locating and applying relevant learning strategies, and would feel 'lost' without printed music to perform from. Additionally, I surmised that students without fieldwork experience needed to know how to work as researchers in the field (see Dunbar-Hall, 2007). In response to the first need, I taught the group on the instruments of a Balinese *gamelan* once a week over the semester preceding fieldwork. This allowed students to: learn to play short pieces of Balinese music; discuss Balinese music and its cultural implications; become accustomed to instruments, tunings and performance expectations of Balinese *gamelan* music; learn terminology and theoretical aspects of Balinese *gamelan* music; watch my fieldwork films from Bali; and read and discuss research literature on Balinese music and its pedagogy. As I used the teaching techniques Balinese musicians had used with me, the students could also experience and react to Balinese ways of teaching that would force them into Balinese ways of learning (Dunbar-Hall and Adnyana, 2004).

To address the second need (for students to learn basic fieldwork methods), students were set tasks to complete while in Bali:

- Attendance at and documentation of performances
- A visit to a museum
- Maintaining a journal about specific aspects of the experience, and
- Annotating teaching and learning strategies.

Students were given hints about issues they needed to observe and discuss:

- Local customs
- Cultural tourism in the village they would be in
- The purposes of music events
- Types of *gamelans* observed, and
- Aspects of dance.

By annotating teaching and learning strategies, students were being led to identify how the Balinese teachers worked and how they, as learners, were responding.

Through these requirements, students were engaged in experience, observation, interpretation of events, self-reflection and linking field-work to the expectations of their training. There was also an intention to provide students with the means to fulfil Australian music classroom syllabus expectations that music be taught in schools so that pupils cover "the historical, the sociological, the notational and the analytical aspects of music" while "investigating... the cultural contexts of music" (NSW Board of Studies, 2009, p.21). The formalised, documented results of these tasks became the assessable assignments of the field-work experience.

The second stage of the research took place in Bali. Here students studied music and dance with members of Cudamani, a performing group from the southern Balinese village of Pengosekan (Cudamani.org), attended nightly performances across a range of genres of Balinese music and dance (including *kecak, legong, wayang kulit,* popular music) and visited a museum with extensive teaching and performing programmes. Students' learning, both in Bali and in Australia before fieldwork, was filmed for the production of research-based teaching resources, both by the students themselves and by staff accompanying students on the trip.

On returning from fieldwork, students were asked to reflect on the experience and particularly to think about teaching strategies, their learning and how the experience had affected their perceptions of music education. Reflection took the form of a written assignment and constituted the third stage of the process. To help students focus on issues of pedagogy, they were given a set of questions before fieldwork (see Table 15.1 below). These covered: analysis of teaching and learning activities; generic issues of pedagogy; and topics that would encourage self-evaluation. The questions implied the need to adapt what had been understood for use in students' future teaching careers. In their references to students as simultaneously learners, future teachers, curriculum planners and analysts of pedagogy, the questions raise the issue of a music educator as occupier of multiple identities (see Gee, 2000–1; Hill, 2006) and this was discussed with students and made explicit to them.

Questions about learning in Bali	Theoretical perspectives
What teaching strategies did you experience and/or observe?	Identifying teaching strategies.
What problems did you face in learning?	Self-reflection as a learner.
How did you overcome learning problems?	Self-analysis; thinking about learning as problem solving.
How did the experience, as an example of music education, differ from those of your background?	Comparing fieldwork learning to previous learning.
What were the benefits of learning Balinese music and dance in Bali?	Thinking about music and music learning within their original cultural contexts and why this might be important.
What changes did the experience bring about in your thinking about (i) music education in general, (ii) about teaching, (iii) about learning?	Self-reflection as practitioner; thinking about pedagogy; separating teaching from learning, and critiquing each.
How will the experience be used in (i) your own teaching, (ii) your own learning?	Projecting/applying current learning into future learning and teaching.

Table 15.1: Questions about learning in Bali and their theoretical perspectives

Student reactions to fieldwork experience

In their reflections, students provided a range of reactions to the fieldwork trip, identifying and discussing a range of teaching strategies, many of which were novel to them:

- Dependence on aural memory
- Group teaching (Balinese teachers work as teams, not as individuals)
- Reliance on student choice (of what instrument to learn/play)
- No notation
- Students were expected to copy teachers in a rote manner
- Teachers played on various instruments as needed

- Lack of verbal interaction
- Use of repetition
- Teaching was non-confrontational and inclusive
- Music was presented holistically (not broken down into individual parts).

Much of this list challenges the ways students were used to learning, as Western music pedagogy is usually notation based (unlike the teaching and learning of many non-Western cultures), delivered by a single teacher (unlike Balinese teaching which is delivered by a teaching team), teacher directed (whereas in Balinese music learning, learners are expected to be in charge of much of the pedagogic space), usually on one instrument (not across a range of them) and atomistic (music in Western contexts is often broken up into small component parts, but in Balinese learning music is treated holistically). Identifying a key characteristic of the teaching, one student wrote:

> there was minimal talking... with maximum playing, which... for me, resulted in maximum learning and absorption of the music.

While another student, seeking similarities and differences between her past music learning experiences and those in Bali, noted that:

> the way we learnt music in Bali was very different to any lesson or ensemble I had previously experienced. This was a situation where we were taught both in a group, and by a group of teachers. In a way it could be considered similar to an ensemble rehearsal with tutors and a main leader. However, in these situations the main source of information is the sheet music, and the students will also learn their parts separately. In Bali, everything was learnt from observing the teachers, who played not from the score but from their memory and watching their leader, who would often change things as he proceeded... there was also little explaining, and more music making.

As was intended by the questions posed, some of the Balinese teaching strategies led to students' learning problems. For example, one student commented on a range of 'challenges', specifically listing listening/hearing skills, musical memory, orientation within a piece of music and the technicalities of performing:

> with anything that is new there are always challenges, and learning Balinese music and dance was no exception. The difficulties I encountered... revolved around three main factors – the ability to hear when the music was to change, the ability to remember what came next in the sequence, and the technical challenges associated with the dance and *gamelan* playing.

Through asking students to think about problems, an implicit link was made between learning and the difficulties posed by a teacher. Dependence on aural memory was identified as something students had not experienced greatly, as their music backgrounds to that point had relied on reading notation. Not having verbal instruction or discussion, but simply being expected to imitate what was happening was also difficult; it became obvious to students that much music teaching in Western contexts relies on large amounts of teacher talk. Difficulties occurred not primarily because of the complexity of the music, tuning of the instruments or *gamelan* performance techniques (although these were mentioned), rather because teaching differed from that in students' backgrounds. In a meta-cognitive fashion, students wrote about how this helped them think about their own learning and how the teaching methods used had forced them to do this. This included self-reliance as learners – as there was no notation, learning necessitated students focussing on themselves to solve problems, remember what to play, work out what was expected and contribute to the sound of the group:

> the student must internalise the music unaided, responding to what they see and hear the teacher playing.

Students wrote about how they overcame these learning problems. For example, being prepared for changes between the sections of a piece was something a number of students noted. They realised that this "seemed... second nature" to the Balinese musicians teaching them but that "each time the transition passage came I was caught off-guard." The solution, for one student, was:

> listening more broadly to the ensemble... this focus on the ensemble rather than individual parts was a focus of [the] experience. Never were one or two parts asked to play separately from the ensemble – any issues were addressed while the entire group was playing... it taught us to listen at a deeper level... an aspect of Balinese teaching that could be incorporated into classroom teaching.

Beyond methods and styles of teaching and learning such as this, students commented on learning Balinese music in Bali and being able to see how music and dance were integral parts of Balinese life. Students saw this as a valuable outcome of the experience and noted how they would teach this:

> if I were to teach Balinese music in the future I would ensure that I linked it to the culture and dance.

Some students, demonstrating how they would use material they had learnt in Bali, thought that this would require adaptation to Australian music classrooms. The lack of authentic Balinese instruments in Australian music classrooms was obvious to students and they discussed how this could be overcome by using other instruments, demonstrating abilities to implement what they had learnt through adapting it to existing infrastructure:

> Producing an authentic experience for students in a Western classroom could prove to be the most difficult aspect of applying Balinese music to your teaching methods. The first major problem is the instruments – glockenspiels, xylophones and metalophones could be used as *gangsa*, cymbals as *ceng-ceng* and bongo drums as *kendang*. Gongs would most likely be hard to obtain in schools, so may have to be left out. However, with these instruments it could be possible to create as reasonably genuine sounding piece.

One student also discovered another aspect of cross-cultural music transfer, avoidance of nomenclature in favour of musical material:

> In terms of instrumentation, tuned percussion instruments such as xylophones would need to be used to imitate the *gamelan*, meaning it

would be important not to focus on the note names but the patterns of the notes.

Students commented on how learning music and dance and seeing performances helped them to understand the learning and its outcome (performance) through an integrated experience. The symbiotic nature of music and dance (experienced by learning to dance one of the pieces of music they were learning to play on *gamelan* instruments) also contributed to their ability to comprehend the characteristics of the music for the dance, the movements of the dance and performances they attended, with numerous students writing in their assignments about seeing dances performed that included steps, hand gestures and eye movements they had learnt.

An unexpected outcome of the trip for some of these students was the ability to use filmed/recorded excerpts of it in their Music Education ePortfolios. These have been introduced as an outcome/end product and simultaneous learning site for Music Education students at my institution, students being expected to collect materials for their ePortfolios throughout the four years of this degree programme (Rowley and Dunbar-Hall, 2009). That large amounts of this trip were filmed allowed students to add evidence of an international study experience to their ePortfolios, allowing the learning in this activity to be utilised across other areas of students' subjects and their outcomes. As an ePortfolio is meant to show a student's musical profile as much as the ability to teach, having a film clip of working on instruments or dancing in Bali was perceived as a way to demonstrate the potential to teach non-Western music and dance and to imply how experience in an authentic learning situation had become part of a student's training as a teacher.

The ability to teach Balinese music in the future was one valid outcome of the trip for some of the students. Some also saw the experience as benefitting their thinking about music pedagogy on two other levels. First, it helped them see that non-Western music is learnt and taught differently from Western music. Beyond that, some commented on how they used the experience to reconceptualise music pedagogy in general as not uniform, reflecting different cultural positions and open to influences from diverse origins:

> The teaching and learning methods... can also be used when teaching music unrelated to Balinese culture [and] this experience changed the way I think about music education in general as it made me realise that there isn't ultimately a perfect way of teaching and learning.

Conclusion

> The Balinese way is that you feel the music in your muscles first by playing and then you do the thinking later. This is... opposite to the teaching and learning I have experienced...

The major intention of the fieldwork was to broaden students' understandings of pedagogy; thus it echoes the work of Kuh et al. (2005), in which a focus on student learning is seen as a trend in current curriculum discourse. Other issues were canvassed, so it had numerous, simultaneous potential outcomes and students' writings produced various music and music education readings of the experience. Specific to the area of their studies, not only were learning music and dance and observing cultural contexts important but, through confronting pedagogy foreign to students' backgrounds, there was an intention of challenging beliefs and actions: implicit anti-canonicism in music education terms was written into the undertaking (see Kalantzis and Cope, 2008). Students were proactively removed from their music pedagogy comfort zones. There was also a wish to expose students to working with an experienced fieldwork researcher, learning how to conduct fieldwork, and demonstration of how music education research is planned, executed and documented. A template of learning experience followed by problematisation and theorisation about pedagogy was provided to the students through the design of the experience.

Much of this aligns with Kuh's (2008) reading of high-impact educational practices. The student experience functioned through creation of a type of learning community: students were a group that worked closely as a unit; they were involved on a daily basis with their lecturer; the fieldwork covered music as both an ethno-musicological object and music as the focus of music pedagogy – this required different cognitive ways of defining music as an object of study. Students were involved in collaborative learning. The experience was at undergraduate level but clearly required students to engage in research; for this they had to be taught basic fieldwork methods and apply these in a real setting. The fieldwork was an example of students working internationally. They were involved in "exploring culture, life experiences and worldviews different from their own". In this way, "field-based 'experiential learning'" became "an instructional strategy" (Kuh, 2008, p.10). Most importantly, a key element of Kuh's definition of high-impact learning, that students had "the opportunity to both *apply* what they are learning in real-world settings and *reflect* in a classroom setting on their... experiences" (ibid.) is demonstrated here by students working with Balinese musicians to the point of a final performance of the music studied and then, on their return, writing about the experience and connecting it to their studies of music as a learning/teaching activity.

Above all, by placing students in a position of responding to a specific type of non-Western music teaching, they were encouraged to think about how they learnt as individuals and to extrapolate from this about how music is learnt and taught. Students' reflections showed that removal from their usual music education contexts could have this effect. Comments such as:

> I was provided with an avenue in which I could consider the idea of music education as a whole and what its main purposes are, as well as contemplate how I may use these new ideas in my own music teaching and learning,

> I have begun to look at my own music learning critically, and question its validity, [and] through reflecting on these experiences, I have questioned my beliefs regarding... music education

indicate that fieldwork can engage students with their own learning and also influence how they think about music as an object of learning and teaching. As one student commented:

> This experience of teaching and learning in Bali has been very rich and has changed how I view teaching and learning.

References

Australian Curriculum, Assessment and Reporting Authority (2010) *Shape of the Australian Curriculum: The Arts* (Sydney: Australian Curriculum, Assessment and Reporting Authority).

Biggs, J. (1999) *Teaching for Quality Learning at University: What the Student Does* (Ballmoor: Open University Press).

Brand, M. (2006) *The Teaching of Music in Nine Asian Nations* (Lewiston: Edwin Meller).

Department of Immigration and Multicultural Affairs (1999) *Australian Multiculturalism for a New Century: Towards Inclusiveness* (Canberra: Commonwealth of Australia).

Dunbar-Hall, P. (2007) 'Research Enhanced Teaching: Lived Research Experience in Bali as the Basis of Teacher Preparation in Australia', *Synergy*, 26, pp.7–12.

Dunbar-Hall, P. (2009) 'Ethnopedagogy: Culturally Contextualised Learning and Teaching as an Agent of Change', *Action, Criticism and Theory for Music Education*, 8/2, pp.61–78.

Dunbar-Hall, P. and Adnyana, W. (2004) 'Expectations and Outcomes of Inter-Cultural Music Education: A Case Study in Teaching and Learning a Balinese Gamelan Instrument', in *Proceedings of the XXVIth Annual Conference of the Australian Association for Research in Music Education*, pp.144–51.

Gee, J. (2000–1) 'Identity as an Analytic Lens for Research in Education', *Review of Research in Education*, 25, pp.99–125.

Green, L. (2001) *How Popular Musicians Learn: A Way Ahead for Music Education* (Aldershot: Ashgate).

Green, L. (2008) *Music, Informal Learning and the School: A New Classroom Pedagogy* (Aldershot: Ashgate).

Hill, M. (2006) 'Representin(g): Negotiating Multiple Roles and Identities in the Field and Behind the Desk', *Qualitative Inquiry*, 12, pp.926–49.

Kalantzis, M. and Cope, B. (2008) *New Learning: Elements of a Science of Learning* (Cambridge: Cambridge University Press).

Kuh, G.D. (2008) *High-Impact Educational Practices: What They Are, Who Has Access to Them, and Why They Matter* (Washington: Association of American Colleges and Universities).

Kuh, G.D., Kinzie, J., Schuh, J. and Whitt, E. (2005) *Student Success in College: Creating Conditions That Matter* (San Francisco: Jossey-Bass).

Mackinlay, E. (2007) *Disturbances and Dislocations: Understanding Teaching and Learning Experiences in Indigenous Australian Women's Music and Dance* (Bern: Peter Lang).
Ministerial Council on Education, Employment, Training and Youth Affairs (2006) *National Statement for Engaging Young Australians with Asia in Australian Schools* (Canberra: Commonwealth of Australia).
NSW Board of Studies (2009) *Music 1 Stage 6 Syllabus*. Retrieved from <http://www.boardofstudies.nsw.edu.au/syllabus_hsc/music-1.html>
Rice, T. (1994) *May It Fill Your Soul: Experiencing Bulgarian Music* (Chicago: University of Chicago Press).
Rowley, J. and Dunbar-Hall, P. (2009) 'Integrating ePortfolios: Putting the Pedagogy in Its Place', in *Proceedings of the 2009 Conference of the Australasian Society for Computers in Learning in Tertiary Education (ASCILITE)*, Auckland, pp.898–901.
Solis, T. (ed.) (2004) *Performing Ethnomusicology: Teaching and Representation in World Music Ensembles* (Berkeley: University of California Press).

Chapter 16

Can the use of technology enhance student engagement?

Becka Colley and Ruth Lefever

University of Bradford, UK

Introduction

The use of technology-enhanced solutions, and in particular social media, has exploded in recent years. The increased availability of mobile devices and the reduced costs associated with data access have meant that more and more people are using the online world as part of their everyday lives. Helping new students adjust quickly to their new educational environment is of the upmost importance. Work undertaken at the University of Bradford has shown that technology can support this process and help students develop a sense of 'belonging'. This chapter explores how higher education institutions could make use of technology to enhance and promote student engagement and help develop the all-important sense of belonging as quickly as possible.

During the last 20 years, higher education has undergone radical and unprecedented change (Education Act, 1992; Dearing Report, 1997; Roberts Report, 2003; Leitch Report, 2006; Browne Report, 2010). Increased student numbers have placed exceptional strain on a system not designed to deliver mass education (Rowley, 2003). Scott (1995) calls this radical change 'massification', which can lead to depersonalisation (Whittaker, 2008). Today's learners enter with very different expectations and assumptions about their experience compared with previous cohorts. These expectations vary dramatically from cohort to cohort and also between cohorts.

These drivers have forced universities to become more strategic about how they enhance the student experience and manage student engagement (Currant and Keenan, 2008). The introduction of fees within the UK has created an interesting tension for institutions that have seen their students become more demanding and forced a more customer-orientated shift towards services (Bekhradnia, 2009). This is expected to become more significant as fee levels increase for entry to higher education in the UK from September 2012.

Understanding 'belonging'

Given this context, helping students adjust quickly and effectively to university life is crucial. This aspect has been researched as part of a project funded by the Higher Education Funding Council for England (HEFCE) and the Paul Hamlyn Foundation looking at 'What works? Strategies for Successful Student Retention'. The HERE (Higher Education Retention and Engagement) project is a collaborative project between three universities: Nottingham Trent (NTU), the lead institution; Bournemouth (BU); and Bradford (UOB) (see Foster et al., Chapter 5, this volume).

As part of a student transition survey, all first years were asked if they had ever considering leaving university and a number cited issues such as not liking the location, feeling homesick and not 'fitting in' amongst their reasons to leave ("Not feeling like I fit in", NTU student comment; "Not fitting into the town", BU student comment). In addition, aspects of their 'student lifestyle' featured as reasons to consider leaving, such as lack of social opportunities, not getting on with flatmates or finding it hard to adjust:

> It was quite hard to adjust at first, to get used to first the university lifestyle and the different surroundings and the different attitudes.
>
> (BU student comment)

Importantly, at all three institutions, making friends and the support of friends and course mates featured very strongly as a reason to stay:

> My new friends have been able to help me get through many hardships, so they are part of the reason why I have been able to stay.
>
> (UoB student comment)

As part of the project's programme explorations, students were asked if they felt part of the university, or if they belonged. At Bradford, 81 per cent of students on a programme with very high rates of retention said they did, compared to only 56 per cent and 38 per cent on other programmes that had less high rates. The latter programme sample was made up of small joint honours programmes with high numbers of students who had not selected the course as their first choice and, as one staff member noted:

> We don't do anything specifically as a department... they have no clear identity... Many wanted to do the accredited... course but didn't have the points so they are here by default not by choice.

The student interviews stage of the project explored in greater detail issues of whether students felt they belonged and why they believed this to be the case. Understandings and articulations of belonging varied amongst students and yet, for most, feeling a sense of belonging, or fitting in, was an important part of their journey through the first year.

Interestingly, those students who had never considered leaving university (non-doubters) all felt that they belonged and were able to describe the time when they first felt they belonged to the university. They also expressed their sense of belonging quite strongly:

> I think it starts when you walk down the street and you see someone and you go hey... I know them from University and that's what made me feel like it [like I belonged].
>
> (NTU student comment)

> I don't feel left out... I am... comfortable with the course 'cos I know everyone and I am getting to know the lecturers and everything as well... [and] everyone on the... course... At the start you feel a bit left out 'cos you are like unsure of what you are doing, but then like

> now I am much more comfortable and I do feel as though I belong with the University and the course.
>
> (UoB student comment)

> Yeah I do [belong to the University]... I would say we were made for each other... I was born for this... I won't picture myself doing anything different, it just wouldn't work for me.
>
> (UoB student comment)

Overall, the interviews revealed that belonging was, at times, related to being involved, feeling cared about or linked to recognition. Comments from students who had experienced doubts about whether to remain at university (doubters) indicated issues in these areas:

> I don't see myself getting involved as much as I would have done... I don't seem very involved with the University to be honest.
>
> (NTU student comment)

> They don't care, so I don't care, that's my feeling about NTU.
>
> (NTU student comment)

> Probably if I see my tutor on the road, he wouldn't recognise me, that I'm in his seminar group.
>
> (NTU student comment)

> People not knowing your name or your lecturers not knowing your name, or you are not meeting up as your course group... perhaps [I] don't feel I belong to the University perhaps as much as my friends here...
>
> (UoB student comment)

Not belonging could be seen to be potentially problematic, especially if students were experiencing difficulties at university, as a doubter explained:

> I think it would help to feel like you belong more, especially if you are struggling it would help. I think it is easier to give up when you don't feel like you belong in a way.
>
> (UoB student comment)

Across the interviews, belonging was perceived from different, and yet interconnected, aspects of the student experience. Belonging was articulated as belonging to other people, the course or school, the department, a community, the university or to a number of these, including being able to achieve personal goals through the course. However, issues concerning feeling left out were also raised, such as at certain social events or because of other groups established that were not inclusive.

From the findings of research it is therefore clear that institutions need to be able to help students to belong as quickly as possible. This is where the use of technology can help. Recent reports into how students use technology (JISC, 2009; HEFCE, 2011; NUS, 2010) show just how embedded the online lifestyle is for many, with significant numbers of students accessing the Internet on a daily basis. A recent survey at the University of Bradford found that 90 per cent of respondents reported using a computer on a daily basis, with significant numbers using a mobile phone or smartphone to access online social media, such as Facebook, Twitter and others, daily.

The student journey and lifecycle

The process of belonging is complex and begins at different times for different individuals. It is useful, therefore, to reflect on the student lifecycle in order to identify different points at which interventions can be made. At Bradford, the original student lifecycle model (HEFCE, 2001) has been developed into four different areas to reflect the different aspects of the student journey. These four areas of focus are:

- Application
- Pre-entry and transition
- Support during the course
- Moving on.

Appropriate support, to encourage belonging, has been identified across each of these different lifecycles with social media and online resources forming a significant aspect of this approach.

Develop Me!

Thinking about the extended student lifecycle led to the introduction of a university-wide approach to transition, induction and ongoing support at the University of Bradford. Called *Develop Me!*, the model was first piloted in 2006. Since then it has grown considerably in response to feedback from staff and students. *Develop Me!* currently consists of five different strands. These are:

- A **social network**, hosted in Ning and found online at: <http://developme.ning.com>
- Our in-house Skills and Personal Reflective Activity (**SaPRA**) focuses on helping students to identify their levels of confidence in different skill areas such as academic reading, academic writing, communication skills and so on. SaPRA utilises an e-portfolio.
- **Online skills development resources**. These resources provide 24/7 help and support to students who have identified that they need to develop a particular skill area. Students interact with the resources in a number of different ways for example as a result of a 121 intervention with an LDU adviser, after completing SaPRA or after attending an LDU workshop.
- **Mobile guides**. Originally, mobile guides were developed that could be accessed on any type of mobile phone. In 2009, an app was developed which meant that smartphone users were able to download all the content for free. The app provides students with information about the University in an easy-to-access format.
- **Research into the student experience**. We have been actively researching the student experience at Bradford since 2005. This research has been fundamental to the implementation and refinement of the *Develop Me!* approach. Without regular feedback from the student body, we would feel less confident that our approach is meeting the needs of students. However, because we have such an

open dialogue with the student body, we are confident that what we are doing is meeting their needs and doing so in a way that they want it to be done. Many universities have developed social networks in the last few years but we are especially proud of the way in which we have done this at Bradford as it has been truly student led.

Using technology to enhance student engagement

Building technology-focused solutions for supporting students is the natural next step of *Develop Me!* Reflecting on feedback from students, which highlighted how important it has been to them to make friends and develop a sense of belonging to the institution, has meant that staff are using different aspects of social media in different ways to support the student experience and promote student engagement. Technology allows individuals to take control of the learning environment and not be constrained by physical pressures such as competing activities, conflicts in room bookings, difficulties with transport and so on. Using technology also allows students and staff to access support and communities at a time and place that is convenient to them, utilising their own choice of tools.

Given the wide and varied applications of technology to the student experience, the following two case studies highlight how this has been achieved outside of the *Develop Me!* context. Both case studies use tools that are not part of the *Develop Me!* approach and demonstrate how different staff at different universities are using technology to support the student experience.

Case study one examines an academic staff member at a pre-1992 university within a technology-rich degree programme who uses social media to connect with students. Case study two looks at a professional services support adviser who uses email to provide support to students.

Readers are asked to reflect on the examples outlined and identify how they could incorporate aspects into their own working practices.

Case Study One:
Social media (Twitter and Facebook)

Overview	Chris is a lecturer in Computer Games at a medium-sized pre-1992 university in the UK.
What social media do you use?	I use Facebook and Twitter, with my Twitter account automatically linked to my Facebook page so that all tweets are entered as status updates on Facebook by default. While this may seem to be spamming many of my students with double updates and information, I have found that some students – usually the younger ones in stages 1 and 2 – are very happy to engage on Facebook, but others – mature students and students in stage 3 or higher – prefer the relative anonymity and distance of Twitter. In many ways though, the uses are related which is why they are in a single case study.
How do you use it?	I use Twitter almost exclusively for general, blanket information and linking to subject specific information on the games industry. For example, when I saw that many of my students were struggling with technical issues in Maya (a 3D graphics program) close to a major deadline, I posted a top-three list of hints and tips on keeping data clean and avoiding crashing the software. Similarly when I encounter interesting subject articles online, I tweet the links with a hash-tag #oneformystudents. This allows students to search recent links easily and to sort them from any personal tweets I may send. As such this is mostly a one-way communication tool, although some older students do re-tweet or direct-message me in Twitter on a sporadic basis. I use Facebook in the same capacity – thanks to the cross posting of tweets to Facebook – but also as a tool in the pastoral care of my students. Students are free to add me as friends: I never approach them, but always accept if they request friend status. This gives the students control over how much of their lives they wish to share with me (and I with them!), and allows them to message me out of hours, comment on my professional portfolio and status updates, and for me to comment on their University-related status updates or posted work. In this sense, Facebook is much more of a two-way communication tool.

Why do you use it?	Facebook is currently the preferred method of communication among my students. Many of them do not check their University emails daily, but will be highly active on Facebook throughout the day, finding this mode of communication less formal and with a faster turnaround for urgent messages. For example, one of my students had been suffering mental health issues and using Facebook was able to ask me for urgent help one evening, "off the record". I am certain that had it not been for Facebook something quite drastic could have happened. On the flipside, it does mean that I feel pressure to reply to student messages out of hours and over weekends, and so some tutor discretion is required. Twitter is a very powerful tool within the game development subject area, as many industry specialists and game developers are highly active on Twitter, making it very easy to re-tweet breaking industry news and developer articles to keep students informed of current technology, markets and practice. I also use these tweets to help engender a collaborative working environment and knowledge sharing among the cohort that mirrors that of industry. Being an ex industry professional I know how powerful the industry network is, and want my students to be part of it right from the start. One of my students was able to network her way into some work experience doing QA testing for a local developer, which shows just how empowering networking can be.
How long have you used this approach for?	I have used Facebook with my students for professional reasons for the last four months, although I have been using it for personal and industry networking for two years or more. It should be noted that this use with students wasn't something I engineered, but that it happened organically as students requested friend status and the department cohorts began to gel as a whole. At first I felt that a line had been crossed between my personal and my professional life, but soon realised that to the students this barrier is simply not perceived. By gently reminding them that it is the weekend, or that two a.m. might not be a time when I wish to check information, or give feedback, it is usually enough to manage their expectations and so far there have been no real misuses of the medium on their part.

	My use of Twitter with the students started approximately nine months ago, when students found my username and started to follow me for industry news. At this point, this was mostly the final year and master's students who were much more industry aware than the earlier stages of undergraduate cohorts. Gradually as my followers increased, so did my student followers and when I synced my Twitter account to Facebook, it all started to work together, although it must be said that I get much more of a response from the Facebook versions of my tweets than I do on Twitter itself. The majority of my Twitter traffic is from other professionals in the games, CGI and education fields.
What evidence do you have that it helps promote and support student engagement?	Facebook is a major part of the lives of many of my students. They talk to each other, they post their University projects for comment and glory, they arrange social events with each other and have undeniably brought the cohort closer together with its use. My part in this is just a small part of their everyday lives, but I believe that it is expected that their tutors will be just as much a part of their online lives as they are of their offline ones. This belief is supported by the casual and natural way that they communicate with me on Facebook, in the same way they communicate with each other. Recently, I de-friended one of my students on Facebook. This was because he had posted exceptionally personal information about drug use that I felt was none of my business to know. Thinking it to be no big deal, but best just to take a step back in our online communications, I was shocked when this student approached me at his next tutorial and shakily asked why I had de-friended him. What I had perceived as a retreat to a more professional online relationship with my student had been a very personal insult to him. He asked if I didn't like him anymore, or if he had offended me in some way. At no point had it occurred to him that I might see a boundary between the personal and professional sides of our lives. I explained my reasons and immediately re-friended him, but secretly chose to hide his updates in my data feed to avoid any such embarrassment in the future, while still giving him the means to contact me out of hours et cetera.

Reflections and conclusions about using social media?	This Facebook de-friending incident is a clear indicator to me that social media use and online availability of tutors outside of the campus network is expected, and that not being part of it would be seen as actively erecting barriers between the cohort and the faculty. Students simply do not perceive the boundaries between personal and professional lives lived in an online world in the same way that staff do. As there is already an expectation of staff to be available to students in an informal capacity in and out of office hours, and it is likely that these expectations will increase as the cost of their education increases, social media present a relatively un-intrusive way of blurring the boundaries and delivering "more for less", without adding to hours in the office or availability on campus. Having said that, any blurring of boundaries between personal and professional lives has to be in the hands of the individual. In many ways it is a gift that can only be given freely, and even if it is in some ways expected by the student, staff must have the freedom to decline.
Tips and advice for those considering it?	1. Be prepared to self-edit online communications about your personal life even more than you already do. 2. Be prepared for the student cohort not to do so, and please turn a blind eye when necessary. 3. Be clear about boundaries of when it is OK and when it isn't OK to contact you out of hours, and be consistent. 4. Don't poke your nose in where it isn't wanted, but be passively available if it is. 5. If all else fails, prune your live data feed as needed.

Case Study Two: Email feedback on assignment writing

Overview	Louise is a Learning Skills Adviser at a large post-1992 university in the UK.
What social media do you use?	For ten years we have successfully offered an email support service where students from across the University can submit a piece of work in progress for our detailed feedback. This is particularly useful for placement students and those based on remote campuses, as well as simply offering another point of access to suit different learners' timetables and preferences. Some users express that they are happier for us to look closely at their writing and give very specific comments rather than discuss their writing in more general terms perhaps more typical of a face-to-face encounter – although our team aims to an extent to do both in both settings. Increasing demand for this well-received and well-reputed service can bring to the fore some challenging tensions between practicalities, resources and pedagogy. The limitations of feedback when given on a 'one-way street' basis and in the nature of email as a relatively slow platform for conversation raise questions about how the pedagogical principles of facilitative rather than didactic teaching for user empowerment, autonomy and active learning can meaningfully shape and drive as well as underpin this kind of electronic 'exchange', when dialogue generally goes not further than submission and one response.
How do you use it?	Any student may approach us without prior or subsequent contact. Work used to be submitted as either a full assignment text attachment or some or all of one pasted into an email. Since we have always had to limit our input for practical, policy and pedagogical reasons, we have recently designed an online submission form to ensure that the oft-omitted basic details are supplied to do with extract context, assignment title, brief, length and type, programme, year of study and priority writing concerns; and we are explicit about only offering comment on approximately 400 words. We aim to help the users of the service identify and understand the strengths and weaknesses in this extract of their writing in order to be able to apply the same practical tips and principles to improve the rest of their work autonomously.

	The submission is sent automatically to our shared team email account and whichever advisor is on LEARN duty that day will respond to all enquiries, so that turnaround is very rapid. We generally spend up to an hour on each student's submission, offering detailed feedback using Microsoft Word's 'comments' facility. We might pick up purely formal or more substantive issues, and find ourselves having to prioritise carefully so as not to either take too much time or overwhelm the student. An example of a typical comment related to a highlighted sentence might be 'Why? What is the significance of this fact, how does it relate to the following sentence and what are the implications in relation to the title?' This includes time spent on writing an accompanying email discussing the particular issues more broadly and offering strategies to help with editing such as: developing ideas and analysis by asking questions; using frameworks and models to help with organisation and structure; and finding advice from other guides and resources to improve writing, referencing and language skills. There is no fixed number of times any individual can use this service but we each use our professional judgment, log everything we do, do not comment on successive extracts from the same assignment and offer less depth whilst also explicitly encouraging independence if a user seems to begin to rely on us as an 'essay checking service' for a number of assignments. This occasionally encounters resistance, but not serious complaint.
Why do you use it?	Our 10–25% response rate on evaluation of this service (now systematised and comparable between years, conducted through Survey Monkey) is almost 100% positive, with any constructive criticism almost always being about wanting more or wishing they had learnt of it sooner. The following two comments offered by students are very typical in tone and content of optional feedback given by them to us as part of our routine evaluation: it "was extremely helpful and it made me rather motivated to keep going to improve my work"; "Before I received your email I was concentrating on getting references right and including factual information in my essay. You really made a valuable point that I must also include my own thoughts to show that I have understood the topic I was discussing! Thank you soooo much and keep up the good work! A very grateful student." There is concern about the widespread confusion about proofreading (what it is and the hope that we offer it) and we do not provide explicit terms of service; but nonetheless our last evaluation resulted in 100% positive responses regarding how we met expectations.

	Recent evaluation also includes 100% affirmative response to our questioning of whether users understood our comments and were able to apply our suggestions, but we don't usually have an opportunity to actually witness whether learners are developing a deep understanding of writing processes or whether our 'interaction' has helped more than superficially, despite some reports of measurable improvements in marks. This questionnaire evaluation system does not currently lend itself to further dialogue and anonymity means that the practitioner rarely knows how an individual user has received our feedback. This can easily undermine the practitioner's confidence and morale, and working remotely in a relatively monologic medium that can incline the user toward transmission model pedagogy and tutor–pupil inequality is perhaps the greatest challenge.
What evidence do you have that it helps promote and support student engagement?	However, laboriously paying attention to detail and unearthing strengths in a students' writing, whilst perhaps less holistic than the communication in a face to face interaction, can be tightly targeted and focused and so very rewarding when a student seems engaged. When students engage more in the process, their learning is more active: if in a tutorial they express concerns about, say, being too descriptive, they are usually right in their impression, but even if they are not and we contradict them in this, our feedback can be all the more empowering if they have made the connection first themselves. Phil Race (2010) illustrates this in his practice of inviting students to appraise their own work before hearing his feedback, which he finds encourages their criticality and self-reflection: he reports that when asked to estimate the mark he will award their work, the majority are very close. This should increase their confidence, sense of responsibility and thus improve autonomy as well as writing ability.
Reflections and conclusions about using social media?	So engagement seems to be essential for the benefit of both parties. A key to this might be in the user taking ownership of, or more responsibility for, the interaction. One step could be in preparing better before submission. Our current form gives them the opportunity to tick boxes to prioritise their writing concerns, and offers an optional space for any additional contextual information or comment. The students who might benefit from this small focussing task the most are not generally the ones who use it. One suggestion for improvement in this is that we could offer a set of generic questions to help them reflect critically on their work before seeing us and/or be required or at least invited to write a synopsis. Another key could be in our opening channels more explicitly for follow-up, as our emails very rarely receive any response.

Tips and advice for those considering it?	Part of the solution might lie in the way we conceptualise the feedback process: it could be helpful to consider it as cyclical, requiring exchange and response in order to encourage 'deep' learning approaches (Van de Ridder et al., 2008). The practitioner must develop considerable expertise in terms of expression, sensitivity, questioning and so on in the language of and approach to feedback, taking into account the parameters of the medium used; but in addition it is worth exploring other technologies that may better support interactivity. The Jing screen-capture tool may allow him or her to cover more ground in less time and offer friendly verbal support via voice recordings that could, with permission, be shared online to benefit a wider audience. Wikis or chat fora could be valuable for students to post work for our and/or peer comment and discussion, which among other things could be very empowering. This labour-intensive service that benefits a few could perhaps benefit from evolving into something more 'sociable', ideally where students can support each other and thus learn very actively by teaching (Biggs, 2007). Rather than a one-way street, a *learning conversation?*

Aspects of belonging

From our research, the following aspects of belonging were highlighted. Suggestions for possible positive actions that can utilise technology are identified which have been shown to help foster a sense of belonging for students in the first year:

Interaction or identification with others – social belonging

Belonging socially has emerged as a key theme – in terms of having friends and/or groups or networks to interact or identify with. In some cases this was described as knowing people "like me", yet most importantly it highlights the importance of students knowing someone and them being known. These social connections, and recognising or knowing other people, appear to be able to influence whether students feel that they belong; and fostering the opportunity to make friends and establish groups seems to be important in establishing belonging.

I feel a great sense of belonging amongst my group and my friends.
(UoB student comment)

Yeah, very much so yeah... oh it matters a lot that you are part of the group... [that] don't run away when you come near so you have a reliable network, and that's important in any group.
(UoB student comment)

I am from a different country and... I have been here for... three years but I still don't feel like I am at home in this country because I haven't been here so long and I just feel like without all my friends I would just feel like alien or something.
(UoB student comment)

As long as my group of friends are there then it is really good, 'cos otherwise I go to the lecture and 'cos people are speaking their own languages to each other and so you are sat there and people are having a conversation round you in a completely different language...
(UoB student comment)

I feel better now because I feel like I know where everything is and I always see someone walking around that I know if I want to stop and talk to them.
(NTU student comment)

You felt like when you were walking in you had someone to say 'Hi' to. Really simple things like that.
(NTU student comment)

Activities to consider

Provide opportunities for students to interact and make friends – to establish group identity/identities. For example socials, events, residentials, which can have online elements – such as advertising, online sign up, FAQs, Q&As and post-events discussion/follow up.

> Identity is really important… That in-group, out-group identity. They are buying into being a student… We have had people who have been transferred in or who have deferred a year or whatever, go to the lab classes and they start to see new students in groups and they work in those groups and they get to feel as though they are part of that group and then they have a much wider spread of friends.
>
> (NTU staff comment)

Use of social networks and/or online networks to help build relationships prior to arrival. This may help those who are anxious about entering HE and help students to feel a sense of belonging early on. Friendship building is an ongoing process and online opportunities can help establish but also consolidate or develop/continue friendships.

> So I actually met a couple of people that were coming to Uni before I got here, so one of my friends, I'm quite good friends with him now… so I met a few people like that and I think it made it easier so going into week one I actually had some friends already and I made a few more friends and then I met friends of friends and it kind of like snowballed like that. Now I can walk around Uni and see maybe two or three people that I can say hi to… that makes me feel a lot more comfortable.
>
> (NTU student comment)

To the department: course/school identity

Students also discussed belonging to the course and department and, in particular, interacting with staff in a positive way. This included when staff made use of social media to make themselves more available.

> For me… feeling… part of family or feeling part of the community is really important, it is important for me not to be just a student… feeling that kind of… human connection and not just people fulfilling their roles and then being very impersonal… I find it really

> encouraging when the lecturers can just be normal human beings and they wave at you and they recognise you and... can just come and have a chat with you and not just be someone far away from you or someone superior to you.
>
> (UoB student comment)

Activities to consider

Attempt to establish a faculty or course sense of belonging – to help students to build a sense of identity and a feeling of 'this is our place'; for instance, through group activities, course socials, societies, online media and so on.

> I would like very briefly to mention that issue of identity. I think that is really important for students and I think they have often come from educational settings where they have had a really clear identity. They have been part of a sixth form, or part of an FE college structure and when they come to university it can be very difficult to, particularly as they do a lot of independent learning, so they are not scheduled 9–5 every day to attend lectures to have the time to develop that identity and I think they do that. I think that is why the induction week is so important. So for example I would in the induction week give them an opportunity to gel together as a group, give them as many group activities as I can, deliberately give them an hour and a quarter break at lunch so they can go off and meet each other. I think HE can over-estimate the opportunities students have to feel the sense of belonging. Not everybody wants to join the football team, or the student union activities and if you don't and you are trying desperately to establish some kind of identity within your course it can be quite difficult. I think that has worked because the students do go out together on socials and they see themselves as being part of the xxx programme. They identify even with students in Year 2 which is quite positive as well. I am wondering whether or not students who are doubters would have difficulty, perhaps one of the characteristics of that student, I don't know because I've not done any research in it, would be that they don't feel that they have course identity so I feel that is very important.
>
> (NTU staff comment)

> Socials are the only way to do it really. We organised the first one this year but missed out a lot of people due to not knowing everyone. If the Uni could organise one for the first month or so that'd work better.
>
> (BU student comment)

Importance of student being taught by/having regular contact with their year tutor (or equivalent) so they have a designated person they know and can go to, that knows them.

> I think that is a big factor in students beginning to feel they belong and they have someone to go to.
>
> (NTU staff comment)

Importance of developing a sense of identity, belonging and purpose and focus for those on those on programmes with lower entry points who may not feel the course was their first choice or for those on those on joint degree programmes who may experience difficulties or inconsistencies with other departments.

Consider having a Student Liaison Officer role – which coordinates social activities and opportunities, information updates and acts as a point of contact for support for students.

> On my course in particular... you actually have a good support system because you have got a student liaison officer [who]... kind of brings everything together, organises events, reminds people about films that are going on, stuff like that... students can go visit them for a cup of tea if they want to.
>
> (UoB student comment)

Recognise and promote the reputation of the course/department – such as its ranking and/or its links with employers to instil a sense of pride.

> Yes, to [the course]... I will be really proud to say that I came to Bradford School of xxx, because the... school is fantastic and I think it is the 3rd in the league table... [and] I have no doubts and no regrets.
>
> (UoB student comment)

Good communication and timely information. Effective use of the learning management system or website, such as for 'just in time' notices.

> [We] help them to belong by providing information on the resources available, encourage them to use the library, IT help and the LDU for support. And to attend events in seminars or via email, we tell them of relevant events.
>
> (UoB staff comment)

Be flexible and aware of and connected to central support services, for example, the accommodation office to help students who are feeling unhappy or isolated in their halls et cetera.

Spaces: to the campus

Having somewhere to feel comfortable – whether to work or study – also emerged as important from the research. Being involved in campus activities or having an awareness of what was going on featured in the students understanding of belonging, as did the need for varied and *inclusive* activities and spaces.

> I remember the first time I came here and I was stood in the atrium I felt like I was on Mars, you know, it was really odd...
>
> (UoB student comment)

> sometimes it is a little bit hard when there is a lot for erm, like can't really explain it, you know when they have free curry nights and stuff you feel like you are maybe a little bit segregated there 'cos there is not people that you know, or... [you] tend to bunch together with people that you already know and then you don't meet new people.
>
> (UoB student comment)

Activities to consider

Provide places to sit, meet people and socialise, including the use of online spaces.

> Really simple things like that. Finding somewhere where I could sit down and have lunch and feel comfortable like I could sit there...
>
> (NTU student comment)

Offer dedicated space for certain courses/students, such as common rooms, labs, teaching rooms, et cetera.

> I think having xxx in this quad and having rooms which unusually are labelled xxx space, dedicated to special kind of teaching rather than it being general help provide an identity for a lot of students. Not all but a lot of students.
>
> (NTU staff comment)

Offer more links between campuses as some students feel separated from the university experience because they are based on a different campus to where the students' union is based.

Hold and effectively publicise university wide social activities or events:

> Yeah I think so, I think now, once you know your way around and you get to know what's going on you do feel a part of it definitely. I do take an interest with what's going on, you know like reading different posters and stuff dotted about, so I do sort of take part and do sort of have a good idea of what's going on.
>
> (UoB student, discussing how they belonged)

Consider students who don't live on campus or locally – so more events between 9–5pm and of a varied nature to appeal to a broad range of students.

> I kind of feel like I am on the outside and that might be something to do... with being off campus so much you know.
>
> (UoB student doubter comment)

> Being a mature student, not living locally and not being on the main campus makes being part of the University really difficult.
>
> (BU student comment)

To the university: institutional belonging

A number of discussions regarding belonging related to knowing how they could get involved and what opportunities had been undertaken. They also reflected as sense of pride in the institution and of its achievements or reputation:

> I love Uni. It's not just a place of study, it's a great social atmosphere, a great social experience and a learning curve, the societies in the union are great and student activism makes Uni special and makes students part of the Uni.
>
> (UoB student comment)

Activities to consider

Encourage students to get involved with university-wide and extracurricular activities, such as clubs and societies and sports teams – to start to "sow the seeds" of that sense of institutional belonging.

> I am part of a few societies so I feel that I am able to represent the University!
>
> (UoB student comment)

> Only as I play badminton – otherwise I would probably feel like I belonged to the School... rather than the University of Bradford.
>
> (UoB student comment)

Good communication from the university and students' union of events and opportunities can help students to feel involved and aware of what's happening.

> [Communication] makes us feel involved and aware of what is happening at Uni.
>
> (BU student comment)

Promote university-wide communal events externally and make them open to other visitors where possible. This may help to develop a sense of identity and pride from what the university does/offers.

Recognise and celebrate student success and achievement publicly across the university and externally via university newspapers and the website. Make use of the marketing team to publicise students' work or involvement in projects and activities:

> That sense of belonging, that I'm a student of the Business School, I'm a student of Bournemouth University, will come only if we have more opportunities to get out to the world that this is what they've done and get back to them, build up the pride... They want this kind of community feeling. They want to feel part of a group and recognised.
>
> (BU staff comment)

Dealing with not belonging

Overall, it is also important to consider what happens when students feel like they don't belong and to develop ways to counter this. Feedback from our research has shown that students feel like an outcast or 'alien' when they don't fit in and this contributes to them being more likely to doubt than those students who feel they do belong. Older students and those who do not live locally were also more likely to identify that they didn't 'fit in' or feel involved in the university. Online measures can help to alleviate these feelings somewhat as students report that it is positive knowing there is something they can contribute to or participate in on the same basis as those students resident on campus or very close to campus or who do not have additional pressures on their lives for example, mature students or student parents.

The research also showed that belonging is not necessarily consistent in that students felt they could belong to friends or a group but not the university, or not the area. Belonging can change in different circumstances and it is also important to acknowledge that belonging is not always important – some students do not want or need this from their experience. This is particularly the case for some mature students who, although they felt they had friends and enjoyed the course and studying, came on campus to attend classes, go to the library and so on, but had no interest in social opportunities or wider events et cetera. However, we have found that one of the most active groups engaged in our online space are mature students who reported that they wanted to 'fit in with the institution' and felt that the social network helped them to achieve this.

What does all this mean?

Research and evaluation into how social media are being used has shown that these provide a real benefit to the student experience. Feedback such as "I would have left if it wasn't for the friends I had made on it [*Develop Me !*]" show the power social media can have on helping individuals feel more at home in an otherwise invisible and isolating experience. It can therefore be seen as having the potential to help establish positive experiences of belonging and also enhance engagement. Belonging can be readily associated with engagement and, indeed, Krause (2007) proposes building community and a sense of belonging within institutions as a strategy for enhancing student engagement. If engagement is viewed essentially as involvement (Tinto, 2006), social media can certainly be useful tools in allowing students to be and feel involved – whether interacting with other students or staff or being aware of activities and opportunities. This involvement could help students to establish a sense that they belong to a community or communities at university.

Our work on belonging has highlighted the importance of whether students feel that they belong or not and action that could be taken to support belonging via several different areas or levels of the student experience. Possible alienation can be addressed by making students feel valued and through fostering student integration and positive and supportive student and staff interaction. Further, offering inclusive activities and spaces (physical and virtual) could also be beneficial in helping students to engage, to feel comfortable and that they belong.

Technology has the potential to support belonging in all of these areas. The key issue for institutions is identifying how and where they plan to utilise these tools and to *ensure that they do so effectively*. Creating online spaces for students is easy – a Facebook group can be created in minutes.

The difficulty comes from maintaining and updating such a community to ensure that it remains relevant to the needs of the students and that any questions are answered in a timely fashion; however, the benefits of doing so clearly outweigh any issues of workload.

References

Bekhradnia, B. (2009) *The Academic Experience of Students in English Universities (2009 report)*, Higher Education Policy Institute (Oxford: HEPI).

Biggs, J.B. (2007) *Teaching for Quality Learning at University* (Buckingham: Open University Press).

Browne, E.J.P. (2010) *Securing Sustainable Higher Education (The Browne Review)*. Retrieved from <http://www.bis.gov.uk/assets/biscore/corporate/docs/s/10-1208es-securing-sustainable-higher-education-browne-report-summary.pdf>

Currant, B. and Keenan, C. (2008) 'Evaluating Systematic Transition to HE', *Brookes e-Journal of Learning and Teaching*. Retrieved from <http://bejlt.brookes.ac.uk/article/evaluating_systematic_transition_to_higher_education/>

Dearing, R. (1997) *Higher Education in the Learning Society* (Norwich: Crown Copyright).

Higher Education Funding Council for England (HEFCE) (2001) *Strategies for widening participation in higher education*. Retrieved from <http://www.hefce.ac.uk/pubs/hefce/2001/01_36.htm>

Higher Education Funding Council for England (HEFCE) (2011) *Collaborate to Compete: Seizing the Opportunity of Online Learning for UK Higher Education*. Retrieved from <http://www.hefce.ac.uk/learning/enhance/taskforce/>

JISC (2009) *Effective Practice in a Digital Age*. Retrieved from <http://www.jisc.ac.uk/whatwedo/programmes/elearningpedagogy/practice.aspx>

Krause, K. (2007) 'E-learning and the e-Generation: The Changing Face of Higher Education in the 21st Century', in Lockard, J. and Pegrum, M. (eds) *Brave new classrooms: Educational Democracy and the Internet*, pp.125–40 (New York: Peter Lang Publishing).

Leitch, S. (2006) *Prosperity for All in the Global Economy – World Class Skills* (Norwich: HMSO). Retrieved from <http://www.hm-treasury.gov.uk/leitch_review_index.htm>

National Union of Students (2010) *ICT: Students and Technology Briefing Paper*. Retrieved from <http://www.nusconnect.org.uk/news/article/highereducation/1437/>

Race, P. (2010) *Making Learning Happen: 2nd edition* (London: Sage).

Roberts, G. (2003) *Joint Consultation on the Review of Research Assessment: Consultation by the UK Funding Bodies*. Retrieved from <http://www/ra-review.ac.uk/reprots/roberts/asp>

Rowley, J. (2003) 'Retention: Rhetoric or Realistic Agendas for the Future of Higher Education?', *The International Journal of Educational Management*, 17, pp.248–53.

Scott, P. (1995) *The Meaning of Mass Higher Education* (Buckingham: SRHE/Open University Press).

Tinto, V. (2006) 'Research and Practice of Student Retention: What Next?' *Journal of College Student Retention: Research, Theory and Practice*, 8/1, pp.1–19.

UK Government (1992) *Further and Higher Education Act* (c.13) (Norwich: HMSO).

Van de Ridder, J., Stokking, K., McGagje, W. and Cate, O. (2008) 'What Is Feedback in Clinical Education?', *Medical Education*, 42, pp.189–97.

Whittaker, R. (2008) *Quality Enhancement Themes: The First Year Experience. Transition to and During the First Year* (The Quality Assurance Agency for Higher Education). Retrieved from <http://www.enhancementthemes.ac.uk>

Chapter 17

Students as change agents: student engagement with quality enhancement of learning and teaching

Janice Kay[1], Derfel Owen[2] and Elisabeth Dunne[1]

[1] *University of Exeter, UK*
[2] *Quality Assurance Agency, UK*

Quality enhancement in an uncertain future

A great many changes have been taking place in higher education in England over the last few years. Institutions have had to respond to rapidly changing circumstances and external pressures. Widening participation, the demand for skills and the emergence of the student voice as a powerful force in decision making have encouraged higher education institutions to become more flexible in the way they manage the curriculum and the range of learning opportunities they make available. Alongside a growing interest in student engagement in this ever more complex and shifting environment, there has been a specific and growing concern about the conceptualisation of students as customers or consumers, and the way in which this impacts on attitudes and identity in higher education. There is concern, originating in the USA (see Pace, 1982) but now apparent in the UK that if students conceive themselves as customers, then their behaviours and the ways that they engage with their education will suffer accordingly:

> If students are envisioned only or primarily as consumers, then educators assume the role of panderers, devoted more to immediate satisfaction than to offering the challenge of intellectual independence.
>
> (Schwartzman, 1995, p.220)

Cheney, McMillan and Schwartzman (1997) have long argued that the customer metaphor encourages students to be passive and detached. Furedi (2009) is adamant:

> There is little doubt that encouraging students to think of themselves as customers has fostered a mood in which education is regarded as a commodity that must represent value for money... the reality is that the customer is not always right, especially in higher education. What counts as a good student experience – friendly atmosphere, progressive marking, lots of spoon-feeding, great social life – may have little to do with the provision of a challenging and high-quality education.

Streeting and Wise (2009) argue similarly that a 'students as consumers' model:

> invites students to navigate higher education as a market, making choices and judgements about value for money as they go; it emphasises student satisfaction and calls for institutions to respond to both students' demands, as individual learners, and indeed student demand, in aggregate, in a constantly evolving market.
>
> (p.1)

In comparison:

> viewing students as 'co-producers', not as 'consumers', might help to tackle and resolve these problems. In such a model, students are viewed as essential partners in the production of the knowledge and skills that form the intended learning outcomes of their programmes. They are therefore given responsibility for some of the work involved, and are not passive recipients of a service.
>
> (p.2)

In 2008, Porter – then Vice President for Higher Education, the National Union of Students (NUS) – argued that:

> the relationship in learning between students and academics transcends the customer–provider contract; the opportunities to make the institution and its provision better are so much greater, through the active participation of learners, than anything a business can gain from its customers.

As current President of the NUS, he also quotes evidence that:

> an increasing number of students want to put forward their views about how and what they are taught and assessed. Different students will want to engage in different ways and therefore HE needs to open up the fora through which they can do that.
>
> (2010a)

Recently, new metaphors have been emerging that relate to co-production, collaboration and partnership:

> Co-production requires active engagement with the entire learning process on the part of the student, and sees the student as an active participant in the development of knowledge.
>
> (McCulloch, 2009, p.178)

Ramsden (2008) outlines his view of the student role:

> Student involvement in quality processes should start from the idea of building learning communities. Practically speaking, this involves shaping student expectations of their role as responsible partners who are able to take ownership of quality enhancement with staff and engage with them in dialogue about improving assessment, curriculum and teaching.
>
> (p.16)

The Quality Assurance Agency (QAA) in their current public consultation (open until March 2011) emphasises: "Students [should] have the opportunity to contribute to the shaping of their learning experience." What is important is that these discussions relate to learning and teaching, to assessment and the curriculum. They are about engagement with academic learning rather than those areas that might more usually be associated with customer perspectives. However, as Little et al. (2009) point out, active partnership may not be easily achieved:

> While institutions' rationales for student engagement processes stem from a central concern to enhance the student experience, for many... institutions a 'listening and being responsive' rationale seemed to take precedence over a rationale that emphasised student engagement as being central to creating a cohesive learning community (and hence staff and students being viewed as partners in enhancing learning experiences).
>
> (p.43)

Such arguments come from a different perspective to those that usually appear in the literature on student engagement, yet they pick up on many similar features and echo similar concerns about the relationship of students to their educational experiences. They are also arguments that may become increasingly important in the current political context within the UK. Lord Browne, whose independent review into university funding (2010) recommended lifting the cap on tuition fees, along with an increased graduate contribution and a progressive repayment mechanism, has paved the way for uncertain times in higher education, with MPs voting to raise the tuition cap on fees to £9,000 per year while cutting annual public funding for higher education by £2.9 billion. As stated by the Chair of the Higher Education Funding Council for England, in response to the most recent grant letter on funding higher education in England for 2011–12 and beyond from the Secretary of State for Business, Innovation and Skills: "The funding settlement will be a challenging one for universities and colleges in 2011–12 and also in subsequent years for universities, colleges, students and graduates as the new finance and funding arrangements take effect" (Melville-Ross, 2010). However, it seems likely that students in the UK fees context are likely to become more vociferous. With a marked change in tone, Porter (2010b) claims: "the student vitriol directed against the rise in fees will be poured on their universities". There is little doubt that students will require a more customer-focused and student-centred environment, with swifter, more effective and explicit responses to demands for change:

> I will not stand by and let [student] interests fall into second place behind old-fashioned thinking and approaches, no longer fit for purpose in that world. If we face into the cold and unforgiving winds of a substantially free market, I will not allow students to be let down by weak regulation, permissive of misbehaviour and unfair practices... I will be seeking the necessary policies, structures, and other reforms to bring about a consumer revolution in higher education.
>
> (Porter, 2010c)

Such reform would target the QAA itself: "We cannot seriously believe that the present quality assurance model is sufficient to deal with the cut and thrust of the new market. It is too vague, too slow, and too distant from the student. I believe a firmer and more direct approach to quality monitoring should be taken and I think the QAA should have a totally changed structure and remit" (Porter, 2010c). There may be logic in this; but if such demands lead to a narrow approach to quality management, and if any changes are seen to be compliance-led, then this may not be the best way ahead.

It cannot be assumed that changes in tone are driven only by the financial relationship between students and their institutions. In Scotland, where universities have developed along similar lines to those in the rest of the UK, the financial relationship with students is less direct and pronounced but the commitment to engaging and involving students is deeply rooted in their quality culture. Elsewhere in Europe, it is also apparent that students themselves are deeply sceptical about consumer- and market-driven approaches to higher education; the Bologna process is driving a great deal of change to facilitate mobility and comparability of higher education across Europe (Bologna Declaration, 1999) but is facing significant resistance from students in western European states such as Greece, Germany, Spain (Peres de Pablos, 2008) and Italy (see *Economist*, 2008). The European Students' Union has sought to address the expressed frustrations of students by developing a concept of 'student centred learning', underpinned by a number of principles that students expect higher education institutions to abide by, and defined as representing "both a mind-set and a culture... which take students seriously as active participants in their own learning, fostering transferable skills such as problem-solving, critical thinking and reflective thinking" (Attard et al., 2010).

To date, UK higher education has rejected a command-and-control method of quality assurance and maintained a system that empowers universities to continually review and enhance their provision. If quality assurance comes to be conceived as a process by which a product or service is compared with a predetermined standard, there is a risk that quality enhancement – conceived as a comparison between a current standard and a higher standard being targeted (Inglis, 2005) – will suffer. There is evidence that formal external evaluations that have accountability and compliance as a focus may work against the encouragement of continuous quality improvement of the student experience (Harvey, 2005). Further, Middlehurst (1997) argues that the common belief that quality assurance leads naturally to quality enhancement may be wrong, since accountability and enhancement are not necessarily connected and can even be in direct conflict with each other. Swinglehurst, Russell and Greenhalgh (2008) further support this view in reporting perceptions that quality assurance is focused on inflexible, non-negotiable approaches based on standards, with quality enhancement being seen as a flexible, context-sensitive approach based on building professional knowledge. There is clearly an important difference in terms of promoting institutional change, with the former potentially lending itself best to the narrower conception of 'student as customer' and the latter to the more complex, rich and diverse conception of 'student as collaborator and co-creator'.

The UK QAA currently supports enhancement alongside quality assurance and provides a very broad definition – "the process of taking deliberate steps at institutional level to improve the quality of learning opportunities" (QAA, 2006) – thus offering institutions the opportunity to provide their own definitions. In giving a more precise meaning to enhancement, the Scottish Higher Education Enhancement Committee (SHEEC)* has offered more useful, practical conceptualisations. Their ten 'indicators of enhancement' provide clear terms that above all value student perspectives; four of these, which specifically relate to student engagement, partnership and student-centred learning, are outlined below (pp.3–4).

* The Quality Assurance Agency operates across the United Kingdom to similar principles and values; the requirements of diverse regional and devolved administrations mean that in some respects the emphasis on certain aspects of quality assurance and enhancement may vary.

- Alignment of activities – Promoting a learner-centred and cohesive approach which is aligned with policy and practice and is informed by a systematic understanding of learner expectations, needs and aspirations
- Student engagement in learning – Being active in supporting students to become purposeful partners in their learning and providing them with appropriate opportunities for effective engagement
- Student engagement in processes – Ensuring that all policy, strategy and practice relating to the student learning experience is informed by a continuous engagement and dialogue – both formal and informal – with students
- Quality cultures – Enabling a reflective quality culture to be supported and developed through a framework of staff and student support structures, and by the promotion of approaches to learning and teaching which are aligned with a shared vision of student-centred learning

The explicit emphasis on student participation and involvement seems apposite; if universities are to be more responsive to the possibly rapidly changing requirements of students, it will be important for them to know and to understand their student cohorts as well as they can and to be better attuned to the needs of their students. The most effective way of doing this is to work directly with students and engage them in university processes and procedures. Such an approach seems all the more important given the doubling in student numbers in the UK over the last two decades. Although this expansion has challenged and, in effect, revolutionised the ways in which students are taught and assessed in higher education institutions (see QAA audit reports, 2006–10), it has meant that traditional models of tutoring and person support from academic staff, which were previously an effective means of directly gleaning student views, have been put under considerable strain. The medium of organically picking up student views has effectively been lost, though other vehicles for gaining student opinion have sprung into being, as evidenced by the widespread use and support for the National Student Survey and its recognition as a key institutional driver for enhancement

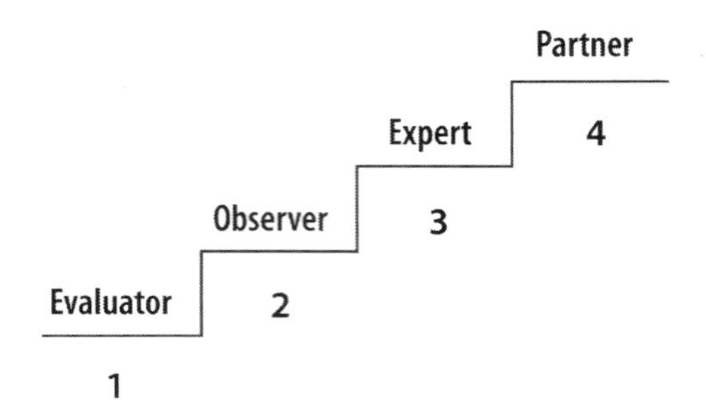

Figure 17.1: Tiers of student engagement in relation to quality enhancement

(Little et al., 2009). However, such surveys have limitations in that they have a limited focus and also fail to create a sense of ownership and empowerment on the part of students. They also tend to fail students by not being explicit about where their contributions have led to change (QAA, 2009); in addition, students often feel that changes are retrospective and have little impact on their continuing education (CHERI, 2003). Hence it is important that universities should seek new and innovative ways to emphasise and harness the energy of students to make a positive difference to their education and to engage them in responsible activity and decision-making processes to support enhancement of the learning environment.

Figure 17.1 sets out four tiers of student engagement that are emerging in institutional approaches to the support of enhancement, moving from 'least actively' (1) to 'most actively' (4) engaged. Although a hierarchy of engagement is intended, it is important to recognise that each of these tiers may be of value in its own right and there may be positive overlap between them.

1. Evaluator – Students show evidence of being engaged with their learning environment and contributing to quality processes through filling in feedback forms, local and national surveys, et cetera; but this form of engagement is comparatively passive and shallow, especially since institutions are likely to make changes with no further input from students.

2. Observers – Students will be invited to engage in meetings where decisions are made about, for example, how to act upon their

feedback (as on school management boards or senior committees of the institution such as Senate or Academic Boards) (Little et al., 2009). However, institutions tend to remain in control of decisions, with student contribution to enhancement processes being minimal; indeed, student presence may be a legitimising factor only.
These two levels of engagement are common and assumed to be regular practice in higher education institutions (HEIs) (QAA, 2009); not engaging students in these ways would be considered unusual.

3. Expert – Here students are considered to be the most expert contributors to discussions and decisions about their own and their peers' learning experience. Whilst replicating the structures present for observer status, practice will be different: students will be fully trained and inducted into institutional culture, invited to undertake research and present papers with their findings, and they may share control and responsibility for meetings and decisions. However, institutions still remain in control of the implementation of change. It is common at this level for close working arrangements to exist between the institution and the student representative body (usually a students' union, guild or association) and that training, research and analysis capacity for its students will be funded through these bodies, but engagement by students remains to some extent limited.

4. Partners – Here many of the characteristics from level 3 will be found; the key difference rests at the stage where decisions are implemented and shared. When working with students as partners, HEIs and students will act as collaborators in a community of practice (Streeting and Wise, 2009), taking responsibility for decision making but also taking a lead, or shared leadership, in implementing changes to the learning and teaching environment and culture. In this way, students are central to the enhancement processes of an institution.

In the context of such debate, the University of Exeter in the UK has recently been working on a major initiative that addresses the challenge and maintains the academic principles of partnership and community. Students have been given the opportunity to engage as change agents, taking the role of fully involved and responsible partners, collaborating to bring about improvements in learning and teaching within their subject areas. In this way, students are formally engaging with the "academic quality" of their programmes "making sure that appropriate and effective teaching, support, assessment and learning opportunities are provided for them" (QAA, 2010b). In policy terms, the Exeter initiative has been designed to fit with conceptualisations of quality enhancement in the spirit of the SHEEC descriptors, with students collaborating in understanding the expectations and needs of their peers, developing a shared view of how their experiences could be improved and taking an active role in enhancing their learning environment.

Students as change agents at the University of Exeter

The student voice is consistently listened to at the University through a variety of means. One of these is through a system of Staff–Student Liaison Committees (SSLCs) in which students can effectively voice what matters to them. This system is not novel and can be found in most HEIs in the UK. As outlined in the national context (Little et al., 2009), there are concerns about the nature of this representation. At times in SSLCs, there have been residual concerns or ideas for improvement in learning and teaching that were consistently returned to by students – although it was not always clear how widespread these concerns were, or whether the more eloquent or strident views of small numbers of committee members were truly representative of the wider cohort. The Change Agents initiative was a practical response to the ongoing challenge of enabling SSLCs to be more effective in managing issues of quality in learning and teaching, and more proactive in bringing about change. In particular, there was a determination to avoid more negative 'customer' attitudes and to view concerns and issues as positive challenges to be resolved, with students leading the way in providing formal recommendations and solutions. However, in order to do this, there was a need for considerably more clarity about the kinds of changes required, why they might be important and for whom. It was important that SSLCs should be more effective in listening to the broader student voice and that they should gain a deeper understanding of the nature of student interests and concerns. In this way, enhancements would be better informed and a response to a broader and more representative group.

Building on these ideas, SSLCs were given the opportunity to take a lead in small-scale action research projects on aspects of learning and teaching in their subject areas. Over a period of two years, 20 small-scale projects have involved undergraduate students working in this way, looking at topics such as assessment and feedback, engagement in lectures, seminar provision, technology development, learning spaces, employability, sustainability, personal and peer-tutoring, and academic writing. Each project not only allowed students to understand more about their learning environment and how it was viewed by their peers but was also designed to provide better opportunities, for both current and future students, to benefit from the enhancements brought about by their fellow students. As appropriate to a research-intensive university such as Exeter, students involved acted as apprentice researchers, deciding on the topic for investigation, developing a research question and planning their own methods of data collection. They designed questionnaire surveys (online, paper or using voting systems), ran focus groups and collected, collated and analysed data from their peers. They then made evidence-based recommendations or provided solutions for change and, where appropriate, put their projects into action. The initiative was co-ordinated by a graduate student, with support and guidance provided through Education Enhancement, making use of the team's expertise in pedagogic research and institutional change. In this way, students could take on the role of 'responsible partner', collaborating with their peers and with appropriate staff to gain data that could be used to promote evidence-based change for enhancement, and a way ahead or course of action based on knowledge and understanding rather than on opinion alone. Each of the projects is written up to provide a series of formal case studies detailing processes and outcomes, with the value of evidence-led change being specifically emphasised. Students have shown total commitment, despite no payment or academic credits for their activity, and most projects have had a widespread impact in the subject areas involved, with some also influencing decision making and practice more widely.

Two examples of student projects are briefly described below, to give a flavour of the ways in which students worked, the impact they had on their learning environment and the potential derived from these projects for greater engagement within their subject area by both current and future student cohorts.

Biosciences

A small group of first- and second-year students addressed the issue of essay writing. It was recognised that Biosciences students tend to struggle with formal writing since their last years in schooling rely largely on multiple-choice responses. What the student research highlighted was just how many students (86 per cent) considered that they struggled with writing and the extent to which they were concerned about this. Ninety-two per cent of second years stated that they did not feel prepared for current academic requirements. Ninety-seven per cent of students said they would find an essay-writing guide useful. A staff member summarises:

> The students showed a mature understanding of the pressures on academic staff from increasing student numbers and research requirements, and so rather than simply asking for more essay writing assignments at level 1, they addressed the question of 'what do I wish I'd known when I wrote my first essay?'

The final outcome from the project was the *Biosciences Essay Writing Guide, Written by Students, for Students*. This included learning outcomes and marking criteria for essay-writing; it was annotated with quotes from staff about good quality writing and common errors, with explanations and examples that brought the information to life. Overall, the look and feel of the booklet was highly professional but with a conversational tone different from any writing guide that staff would have produced, however student-centred their efforts. Copies of the booklet were given to all first-year students as soon as it was completed. Feedback was instantly positive: "A very, very good resource. Just what we need! Brilliant guide to referencing and planning the essay, will be well used!"; "Excellent detail and information… Booklet is a great asset!"; "Brilliant! Covers all the problems that we're likely to come across. This will definitely prove very useful. Thank you." A small follow-up study will be conducted to ascertain whether the booklet is as useful to students as they had expected and whether this impacts on their overall satisfaction or achievement. Other subject areas have been interested in using it as a template for their own disciplines. One academic claims: "The Students as Agents of Change project has revolutionised the way in which we develop tools for learning and teaching and is an excellent way of embedding student involvement through the curriculum."

The University of Exeter Business School

A student-led research project in the Business School – where academic staff have been piloting a range of technologies – has also had significant impact, both on teaching behaviours and on the ways in which students engage. Research findings from a student-designed survey, focus groups and interviews highlighted, for example, that three quarters of the 207 respondents used available video recordings of their lectures when they had difficulties with understanding content; over half indicated that this was an integral part of their revision process; and international students used recordings to support their language development as well as disciplinary learning. Importantly, students were clear that having access to video did not affect lecture attendance and that they preferred to view streamed lectures as a back-up. Students also thought that using an electronic voting system kept them focused in lectures and they appreciated the interactivity it allowed; almost all wanted to use it repeatedly.

Such findings have enabled students, along with the School's Director of Education and other staff, to be confident in pushing strongly for furthering technology use for learning. Since the initial student survey (2008–9), streamed video is far more widespread, and the voting handsets have been used by large numbers of first years, with continuing outstanding feedback from both staff and students. There is observable evidence that (i) the quality of lecturing has improved, with academics reviewing their own videos and recognising areas for improvement; and (ii) using the voting system to diagnose misunderstandings in lectures enables teaching that is better tailored to student needs. For 2010–11, a further 3,000 voting handsets are being used (making a total of 4,000 in total), thus covering all undergraduates and taught postgraduates. The drive cannot be said to be due entirely to the Change Agents project but it has played an important part in promoting change through the provision of evidence.

Sam, the third-year student who ran this project, says: "interpreting the results that we got back from the questionnaire was probably the most interesting part of the project." Another student, Johan, stated: "I think the most exciting part of this project has been that it is possible to make a change even at such a large institution. Before this project I did not expect it to be possible to make a change, but this has shown me that with a little work and dedication you can make things happen." Tim became so immersed in the research aspect that he continued this into a third-year assessed project: "we have already helped to develop more student-centric teaching and learning environments… I would unreservedly recommend getting involved to any proactive individual who has a passion for making a difference and enhancing their student experience and that of others."

Such students were already exceptionally engaged students; but the Change Agents initiative offered them further dimensions that added to their sense of working in authentic ways within the University, enabling professional development and skills for employment, developing confidence and self-knowledge, and prompting new and possibly transformational understandings about how change can be promoted.

Discussion

In the cases outlined above, as with the many other student-led projects, students demonstrate that they can be active decision makers, and even drivers, in institutional change. This has not happened accidentally but has been a planned initiative underpinned by a strong belief in the potential of students to act responsibly, to understand the need for evidence-based change and to have the capacity to provide recommendations and solutions to issues. This gives a new meaning to student engagement with the curriculum; small numbers of students have an opportunity to take on an active leadership role, many become involved in the research processes and many more – both students and staff – gain from the impact of the project. However, a multitude of issues and challenges lie ahead.

Changing institutional ethos through student engagement within authentic communities of practice

According to Wenger, McDermott and Snyder (2002), "Communities of practice are groups of people who share a concern, a set of problems, or a passion about a topic, and who deepen their knowledge and expertise in this area by interacting on an ongoing basis" (p.4). In addition, "these people... meet because they find value in their interactions... They help each other solve problems. They discuss their situations, their aspirations, and their needs. They ponder common issues, explore ideas, and act as sounding boards" (pp.4–5). The Change Agents projects are beginning to operate in this kind of realm. The community is transient as students and staff join and leave, but there is commitment, excitement over the development and change of learning and teaching, and a building legacy of research that can be scrutinised by all – as well as continuing learning about strategies for change in particular contexts. In terms of the conceptualisation of a community of practice, the three key characteristics are supported through Change Agents: (i) there is a shared domain (topic or theme to be addressed and advanced); (ii) there is a growing community (members motivated by a mutual interest in the domain); and (iii) there is a practice (ideas, tools, expertise, knowledge and shared resources) that serves to move the field of inquiry forward (Wenger, 1998; Wenger, McDermott and Snyder, 2002). Above all, the discussions are taking place in an authentic arena. Authentic activity is claimed to be of particular importance for learners, allowing understanding of the ways in which practitioners act meaningfully and purposefully in professional contexts (Brown, Collins and Duguid, 1989). Further to this, the students who engage with the initiative could be said to enter into a form of cognitive apprenticeship (Collins, Brown and Newman, 1989), becoming involved in the interactions and activities that characterise authentic educational enhancement and change, and that are so very different from their usual degree learning.

Importantly, in terms of educational enhancement, "More than a 'community of learners', a community of practice is also a 'community that learns'" (Pór, n.d.). This again characterises exactly what the Change Agents initiative is about: individual learning as students engage with transformational experiences; institutional learning through research that illuminates problems in new and unanticipated ways; and the sharing of this learning amongst the community. Yet, however persuasive the concept of a community of practice, it needs solid foundations on which to continue to flourish. The 'domain', the 'community' and the 'practice' need to be valued by the university, with conversations about learning and teaching not just creating small pockets of enthusiasm but being the norm, supported through university structures, with the expectation that staff and students will continuously be involved in collaborating on projects and implementing outcomes.

One means by which this can be supported, though still on a small scale, is through offering credit to students who become involved as change agents. There are currently discussions about embedding the concept of students bringing about change into a module run through the University of Exeter Business School. It is well placed in this context, because of the existing interest in organisational change and the expertise of staff in this area, but the module would be open to all students. Plans to date are that it would include a drawing together of theory on change along with learning from practical experiences either within the University or in the local community.

Questions of scale

In terms of institutional enhancement, the Change Agents initiative is premised on the belief that small incremental steps in bringing about change, especially at the level of the discipline, can have a powerful impact (Seel, 2000). Overall, it demonstrates in important ways that students can, want to, and will engage with pedagogy and that they want to play an active part in leading innovation. What is yet unknown is the extent to which this kind of involvement can be scaled up or in any way become transformational for a whole institution, with student engagement taking on powerful new meanings that change the culture and ethos of their university. It can easily be argued that students involved to date have been deeply involved in their projects, have created outstanding outcomes, have appreciated the skills they learned and have had an impact on the broader community of learners. Yet does this mean that more, or all, students should be involved in Change Agents projects, and in what depth and how? Or is it more important that students understand the language and the message and feel empowered even if they do not want to engage individually with the processes of change? Is the leadership element something that needs to be preserved, with small groups or individuals taking the greatest responsibility? As Streeting and Wise (2009) ask:

> What should we do about students who just want to follow their course and have a good time? Convincing such students that they should want to be 'co-producers' might be seen as the greatest challenge?
>
> (p.3)

Institutional scale will be dependent on 'selling' the idea of the project more broadly through fitting with strategic planning and key institutional drivers. For Exeter, this would mean, for example, maintaining a high position in national student satisfaction ratings; providing a major USP at a time when the University needs to stand out from the crowd; the potential for establishing Exeter as distinctive, and attracting the best tariff students; the potential for providing students with employability skills, including leadership; demonstrating commitment to students in times of considerable change; continually improving the student experience and engagement with their learning (quality assurance and enhancement) in areas that are selected by and are most meaningful to students, and hence the University beginning to see 'engagement' through the eyes of the student; improving the ethos and culture of the University by promoting collaborative partnership, creative exchanges and communities of learners; and raising the University's profile in the sector as one that embraces change and innovation. However, gaining acceptance of these drivers does not lead to any clear pathways for change.

On a practical level, the Students' Guild and the University will be working to embed the 'Students as Change Agents' project more securely into life at Exeter. A broader series of research initiatives, to be known under the umbrella of 'ExChange', is designed to reinforce collaborative partnerships between students and staff across the University. For example, SSLCs will become known as 'ExChanges' designed to highlight an expectation for creative exchange of ideas and collaborative decision-making processes between staff and students. Projects will include institution-wide research initiatives as well as supporting suggestions from the Professional Services and the new University Colleges. 'ExChange' will embed a culture of students as engaged collaborators, empowered to lead positive changes across the whole institution.

Linking with quality enhancement

It might be argued that what the student projects cover are aspects of curriculum life that should have been sorted out already through ongoing quality procedures; yet the involvement of students is likely to mean that solutions are more student-focused and different to what staff might have suggested or achieved themselves. If ensuring that students remain deeply engaged with their academic learning is a priority in an increasingly customer-oriented environment, then institutions may need to address aspects of quality assurance and quality enhancement that will continue to draw in students in new and more involved ways. There may, however, be both cultural and procedural risks in this approach, dependent on the nature of activity; institutional sharing and spreading of good practice may be considered relatively low risk whereas enhancement that relates to innovation may be higher risk – and institutions may become more risk averse in difficult, insecure or unstable times. As Raban (2007) argues, conventional approaches to quality management can promote the dissemination of good practice and the improvement of learning and teaching; but such approaches are unlikely to promote deep-level change, or innovative and risk-taking practice that may lead to new curricular and organisational structures.

The Change Agents project, as a new and initially untested initiative built on a 'hunch' as well as experience, was potentially full of risks. However, checks were built in to monitor risk. Each of the individual projects was fairly small in scale and low risk because of the way in which each one was framed. Rather than students expressing dissatisfaction, dwelling on what was wrong, themes of projects were turned around to investigate, for example, what academics were concerned about, or looking to 'good practice' to gain ideas. Existing structures also supported the development of the project: for example, having a central Learning and Teaching team (Education Enhancement, with expertise in areas such as promoting change, strategic planning, pedagogic research and working with students) that took responsibility for managing the overall initiative and that already worked closely with the Students' Guild; having strong student representation; having a graduate placement scheme to recruit from; and having a University Education Strategy that has students at its core and is conducive to new approaches. An additional means of strengthening and reinforcing the Change Agents initiative is through formalising links to existing quality procedures within the University, especially through institutional audit or formal periodic review involving internal and external peers as well as students. For example, the Business School subject review panel praised the School's technological initiatives to aid student learning as well as the Change Agents project, both of which were considered to be 'most impressive' and were highlighted as good practice.

In conclusion, students involved as change agents have engaged in remarkable ways because they are motivated and wanting to engage with their learning environment, to push boundaries and to test themselves in new environments – but also because they have been given the opportunity to do so and have been trusted to work in intelligent ways. They have become immersed in improving quality for the benefit of the University; they have taken responsibility for student-led enhancement and they have worked proactively in collaboration with staff to bring about change. In relation to key aspects of engagement as posited by Solomonides, Reid and Petocz in their Relational Model of Student Engagement (Chapter 1, this volume), students demonstrate that, in working on projects as change agents, they engage with thoroughness and seriousness on their task in ways that are cognitive, affective and conative; they are motivated, they persevere and they give energy and time; they invest in a 'deep' sense. They have a will to learn, both for themselves but also for their organisation; they are confident and imaginative. They gain a sense of what it is like to be a professional within an authentic context and as a member of a community of learners, and they gain deeper understandings of themselves and of their future. They are involved in a journey of 'self-authorship' – a "way of making meaning of oneself and the world" (Baxter Magolda, 1999, p.3). This broad understanding of engagement also links in many ways to Jackson's (2010) notion of 'life-wide learning'. In a holistic sense, the 'Students as Change Agents' initiative offers opportunities for students to become fully engaged in multiple ways through supporting the University in providing quality learning experiences.

What is important in the current climate is that quality does not become associated with endless demands for improvement based on the possibly ever-changing whims and fancies of students (and attempting to satisfy the many students with different ideas of what higher education is and should be about, and who feel they have more power because they are paying high fees). The University, through the engagement of students in leading change, has the potential to be more deeply reflective and professional in the provision of high-quality learning experiences and student satisfaction. In the more testing environment of higher education in the future, it seems imperative that such initiatives can expand and grow, that innovative enhancement can flourish and that students can become ever more deeply involved in developing a learning experience that is complex and rich, and also efficient and appropriately supportive for their needs. In this new environment, students may act as customers or consumers in the sense that they want a quality product; but they can also contribute to that product in collaborative, imaginative, responsible and positive ways.

References

Attard, A., Di Iorio, E., Geven, K. and Santa, R. (2010) *Student-Centred Learning – Toolkit for Students, Staff and Higher Education Institutions* (Brussels: European Students' Union). Retrieved from <http://www.esib.org/documents/publications/SCL_toolkit_ESU_EI.pdf>

Baxter Magolda, M.B. (1999) *Creating Contexts for Learning and Self-Authorship* (Nashville: Vanderbilt University Press).

Bologna Declaration (1999). Retrieved from <http://www.ond.vlaanderen.be/hogeronderwijs/bologna/documents/MDC/BOLOGNA_DECLARATION1.pdf>

Brown, J.S., Collins, A. and Duguid, P. (1989) 'Situated Cognition and the Culture of Learning', *Educational Researcher*, 18/1, pp.32–42.

Cheney, G., McMillan, J. and Schwartzman, R. (1997) 'Should We Buy the "Student-As-Consumer" Metaphor?', *The Montana Professor*, 7/3, pp.8–11.

CHERI (Centre for Higher Education Research and Information) (2003) *Collecting and Using Student Feedback on Quality and Standards of Learning and Teaching in HE*. Retrieved from <http://www.hefce.ac.uk/pubs/rdreports/2003/rd08_03/>

Collins, A., Brown, J. and Newman, S. (1989) 'Cognitive Apprenticeship: Teaching the Crafts of Reading, Writing, and Mathematics', in Resnick, L.B. (ed.) *Knowing, Learning, and Instruction: Essays in Honor of Robert Glaser* (Hillsdale, NJ: Erlbaum Associates) pp.453–94.

Economist (2008) 'Higher Education in Italy – A Case for Change'. Retrieved from <http://www.economist.com/node/12607260?story_id=12607260>

Furedi, F. (2009) 'Now is the Age of the Discontented', *Times Higher Education*, 4 June 2009. Retrieved from <http://www.timeshighereducation.co.uk/story.asp?storycode=406780>

Harvey, L. (2005) 'A History and Critique of Quality Evaluation in the UK', *Quality Assurance in Education*, 13/4, pp.263–76.

Inglis, A. (2005) 'Quality Improvement, Quality Assurance, and Benchmarking: Comparing Two Frameworks for Managing Quality Processes in Open and Distance Learning', *International Review of Research in Open and Distance Learning*, 6/1. Retrieved from <http://www.irrodl.org/index.php/irrodl/article/view/221/304>

Jackson, N. (2010) *Vision*. Retrieved from <http://lifewidelearning.pbworks.com/w/page/17247638/FrontPage>

Little, B., Locke, W., Scesa, A. and Williams, R. (2009) *Report to HEFCE on Student Engagement*. Retrieved from <http://www.hefce.ac.uk/pubs/rdreports/2009/rd03_09>

McCulloch, A. (2009) 'The student as co-producer: learning from public administration about the student–university relationship', Studies in Higher Education, 34/2, pp.171–83.

Melville-Ross, T. (2010) *Grant Announcement for Higher Education 2011–12*. Retrieved from <http://www.hefce.ac.uk/news/hefce/2010/grant1112/>

Middlehurst, R. (1997) 'Enhancing Quality', in Coffield, F. and Williamson, B. (eds) *Repositioning Higher Education* (Buckingham: SRHE and Open University Press) pp.45–56.

NUS (National Union of Students) (2009) *Student Experience Survey*. Retrieved from <http://www.nus.org.uk/PageFiles/4017/NUS_StudentExperienceReport.pdf>

Pace, R.C. (1982) *Achievement and the Quality of Student Effort* (Washington, DC: Department of Education).

Peres de Pablos, S. (2008) 'En el Nombre de "Bolonia"', *El Pais*, Spain. Retrieved from <http://www.elpais.com/articulo/sociedad/nombre/Bolonia/elpepisoc/20081125elpepisoc_1/Tes

Periodic Subject Review Panel (2010) [unpublished] *The University of Exeter Business School*.

Pór, G. (n.d.) Definition: Communities of practice. Retrieved from <http://www.co-i-l.com/coil/knowledge-garden/cop/definitions.shtml>

Porter, A. (2008) 'The Importance of the Learner Voice', *Brookes eJournal of Learning and Teaching*, 2/3. Retrieved from <http://bejlt.brookes.ac.uk/article/the_importance_of_the_learner_voice/>

Porter, A. (2010a) Interview with QAA. Retrieved from <http://www.qaa.ac.uk/podcasts>

Porter, A. (2010b) 'Wrong Direction', *Times Higher Education*, 9–15 December.

Porter, A. (2010c) Presentation to Quality in Higher Education Group meeting, November, London.

QAA (Quality Assurance Agency for Higher Education) (2006–10) *Outcomes from Institutional Audit Reports*. Retrieved from <http://www.qaa.ac.uk/outcomes>

QAA (2009) *Outcomes from Institutional Audit – Student Representation and Feedback Arrangements*. Retrieved from <http://qaa.ac.uk/reviews/institutionalAudit/outcomes/series2/students09.pdf>

QAA (2010a) *Interview*. Retrieved from <http://www.qaa.ac.uk/podcasts>

QAA (2010b) *Consultation on Changes to the Academic Infrastructure*. Retrieved from <http://www.qaa.ac.uk/news/consultation/AI/

Raban, C. (2007) 'Assurance Versus Enhancement: Less is More?', *Journal of Further and Higher Education*, 31/1, pp.77–85.

Ramsden, P. (2008) *The Future of Higher Education Teaching and the Student Experience*. Retrieved from <http://www.dius.gov.uk/higher_education/shape_and_structure/he_debate/~/media/publications/T/teaching_and_student_experience_131008>

Schwartzman, R.O. (1995) 'Are Students Consumers? The Metaphoric Mismatch Between Management and Education', *Education*, 116, pp.215–22.

Seel, R. (2000) 'Culture and Complexity: New Insights on Organisational Change', *Organisations and People*, 7/2, pp.2–9.

SHEEC (Scottish Quality Enhancement Committee) (2008) *Indicators of Enhancement: A Contribution to the Scottish Quality Enhancement Framework: Ten Indicators of Enhancement*. Retrieved from <http://www.enhancementthemes.ac.uk/documents/SHEEC_02Oct08_IofE_rep.pdf>

Streeting, W. and Wise, G. (2009) *Rethinking the Values of Higher Education – Consumption, Partnership, Community?* Retrieved from <http://www.qaa.ac.uk/students/studentEngagement/Rethinking.pdf>

Swinglehurst, D., Russell, J. and Greenhalgh, T. (2008) 'Peer observation of teaching in the online environment: an action research approach', *Journal of Computer Assisted Learning*, 24, pp.383–93.

Wenger, E. (1998) *Communities of Practice: Learning, Meaning, and Identity* (New York: Cambridge University Press).

Wenger, E., McDermott, R. and Snyder, W.M. (2002) *Cultivating Communities of Practice: A Guide to Managing Knowledge* (Boston: Harvard Business School Press).

SECTION 4: POLICY AND IMPLICATIONS

Chapter 18

Reinterpreting quality through assessing student engagement in China

Heidi Ross and Yuhao Cen

Indiana University, USA

> We will improve the evaluation of teaching. We will set up scientific and diverse benchmarks for such evaluation... Teaching quality shall be evaluated with the participation of government, schools, parents and communities. We will keep records of students and improve the assessment of comprehensive quality. Diverse evaluation approaches that help promote student development shall be explored to encourage students to be optimistic and independent and become useful persons.
>
> (Ministry of Education, 2010, Clause 33, Section III)

Introduction

Worldwide there is a growing sense of urgency among scholars and the public for the identification of the factors necessary for quality higher education. Higher education is heralded as key to individual advancement and to national prosperity and security; and its perceived inability to secure those aims generates no end of "crisis" (Fischman, Igo and Rhoten, 2011). Just as Premier Wen Jiabao (2011) warns that China's future hinges on "talents" and creative spirit that will emanate only from fundamental educational reform, President Barak Obama (2011) challenges US institutions to embrace their "Sputnik moment" or be out-innovated, out-educated and out-built.

Set within a summary of policy and institutional contexts of improving the quality of Chinese higher education, this chapter examines a student engagement research and institutional assessment project, the National Survey on Student Engagement-China (NSSE-China), China's first national evaluation instrument that focuses on what students actually do in college and what they think about their experiences. The project, which defines student engagement as the time and energy students devote to educationally sound activities inside and outside of the classroom, was inspired by the widely recognised and globally adapted National Survey of Student Engagement (NSSE) administered by the Indiana University Center for Postsecondary Education. Built on Chickering and Gamson's (1987) seven principles for good practice in undergraduate education,* the NSSE instrument and its Chinese counterpart consist of five benchmarks of student engagement (NSSE, 2001a) including level of academic challenge, active and collaborative learning, student–faculty interaction, enriching educational experiences and supportive campus environments (Kuh, 2003). These benchmarks were created through "a blend of theory and empirical analysis" (NSSE, 2001b) and in a way that facilitates dialogue within the policy arena. As participating institutions seek to convert engagement findings into practices that improve students' educational experiences, each benchmark represents a domain that is actionable through improved educational policies and practices on diverse campuses.

In this chapter we focus primarily on the translation, cultural adaptation and implementation of NSSE-China since 2007 and consider what the project adds to broader efforts to improve educational quality and quality assessment measures across Chinese universities and colleges. Quality as a concept and goal in China is currently shaped by anxiety and confusion about the social purposes, contributions, missions and individual pay off of increasingly diverse and highly stratified tertiary institutions, as well as by preference for quality measures that focus on institutional resources, research output and rankings. Student learning experiences and the effective educational practices that facilitate them

* These principles include student–faculty contact; cooperation among students; active learning; prompt feedback; time on task; high expectations; diverse talents; and ways of learning.

have rarely been systematically studied in China or even used as indicators of institutional quality. While student engagement is but one piece of the effective education puzzle,* it is a piece largely missing from a decade of quality debate within China. NSSE-China emerged from our desire to create a springboard for deepening inquiry into the multiple dimensions of educational quality, to conceptualise educational quality as student-centred and process-oriented, and to interject student experiences and voices into educational quality discussions and research in China.

To this end, in 2007 we received a grant from Indiana University to develop and pilot NSSE-China, in collaboration with colleagues at Tsinghua University, at six Beijing universities. An additional grant from the China Ford Foundation in 2008 allowed the Tsinghua–Indiana team to begin the first empirical analysis of student engagement in China. Activities have included: i) reviewing state policies on quality (*suzhi*) education in relation to cultural, economic, and political reform;† ii) creating and piloting NSSE-China;‡ iii) refining NSSE-China through cognitive interviews; iv) leading institutional capacity-building workshops; v) administering NSSE-China in 28 institutions;§ and vi) disseminating research findings (Ross and Cen, 2009; Ross, Luo and Cen, 2008).

These activities invite reflection upon how student engagement as a concept central to improving educational effectiveness has grown indigenously, travelled globally and been incorporated into Chinese national policy and institutional assessment and improvement protocols. Despite growing use internationally of student engagement as one powerful

---

* For example, Pascarella and Terenzini (2005, p.629) provide a rich summary of the areas of net change attributable to college exposure: academic and cognitive (including critical thinking and principled moral reasoning); psychosocial, attitudes and values; career and economic; and quality of life.

† *Suzhi* education emphasizes fostering innovative spirit and practical ability through independent learning and problem solving, extra-curricular activities and social practice. The realization of *suzhi* often serves as a stark marker of inequity in educational provision and reform across rural and urban regions of China. See Kipnis (2001, 2006) and Murphy (2004).

‡ Data from 1,200 samples at the six universities were collected and analyzed to check data quality, examine response pattern on individual items and track unexpected findings; this resulted in revision of 25% of the survey items.

§ A simple random sample of all undergraduate students at each of the universities yielded a total of 30,306 respondents, with a per institution sample size ranging from 1,000 to 1,500.

measure for educational quality (and institutional improvement), to date there has been little comparative analysis of student engagement, a gap this volume intends to fill.*

Since its establishment in 1999, more than 1,400 baccalaureate-granting institutions in the United States and in Canada have participated in NSSE (National Survey of Student Engagement, 2010a) and since the mid-2000s NSSE has attracted higher education scholars around the world seeking assessment tools and policy levers to address the quality issue in undergraduate education. In the process of 'going global', NSSE has been piloted in South Africa and used systematically in Australia among other countries. Contacts for permission to translate and/or adapt the NSSE instrument to local contexts have come from 14 countries and more have expressed interest.

International studies on student engagement are redefining educational quality, challenging ranking systems and together arguably represent the world's largest database on the undergraduate student experience. Literature on the factors (political change, internal dissatisfaction, negative external evaluation) that prompt educational borrowing and lending – particularly Ochs and Phillips's (2004) four-stage (cross-national attraction, decision, implementation, internalisation) cross-national policy attraction framework – guides our conclusions regarding what policies, forces and institutional practices prompt Chinese institutions to embrace or experiment with student engagement and outcome assessment as an important component of improving educational quality.

An alternative measure for what counts as quality in Chinese higher education: promoting student engagement in an era of massification

China is in the midst of a two-decade revolution in higher education (Ross, Zhang and Zhao, 2011; Hayhoe et al., 2011) that requires alternative understandings and measurements of educational quality (Zha, 2009; Morgan and Wu, 2011; Li, 2010). Fifteen years ago, when less

* A small body of global comparisons of student engagement data exists. For an example see Oxford's Higher Education Policy Institute comparisons online at: <http://www.universityworldnews.com/article.php?story=20100702181629774>

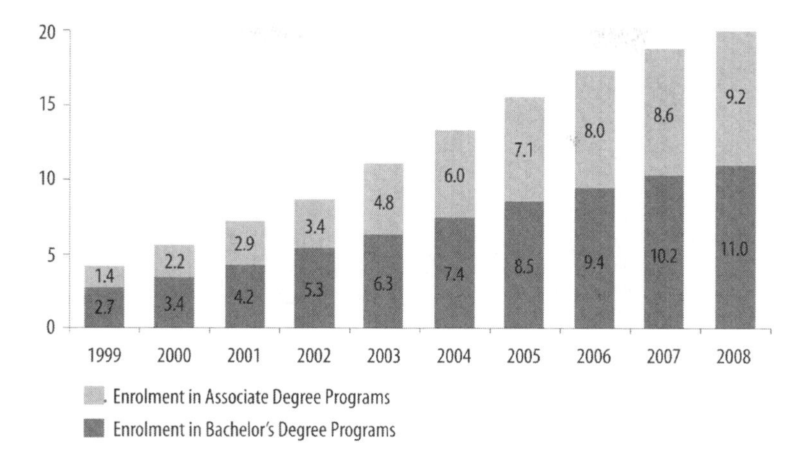

Figure 18.1: Undergraduate enrolment in regular higher educational institutions in China, 1999–2008 (millions)
Data source: Ministry of Education, China

than 5% of the age cohort matriculated to college, graduates were assured permanent employment commensurate with highly selective education. Undergraduate student enrolment at HEIs* has since skyrocketed from 4 million in 1999 to 20.2 million in 2008 (Figure 18.1). These numbers under-represented the total undergraduate population as additional enrolment in adult HEIs and distance education programmes in 2008 was 5.5 million and 3.6 million respectively. The *Tenth Five-year Plan in Education* (2001–5) aimed at a 15% gross enrolment rate for tertiary education by 2005 (Ministry of Education, 2001a); that figure was quickly surpassed, climbing to 23.3% in 2008 (Ministry of Education, 2009); and over 25% in 2010.†

Rapid educational expansion has been accompanied by dramatic institutional stratification, diversification of funding streams and institutional

* Regular higher education institutions (HEIs) are degree-awarding institutions, in contrast with certificate-granting institutions including HEIs for adults and distance education institutions.

† China's gross enrolment rate is calculated by expressing the number of students enrolled at the tertiary level, regardless of age, as a percentage of the population of 18 to 22 year olds (Yang, 2003). Hence, the numerator is larger than the undergraduate enrolment as it also includes that of graduate-level students.

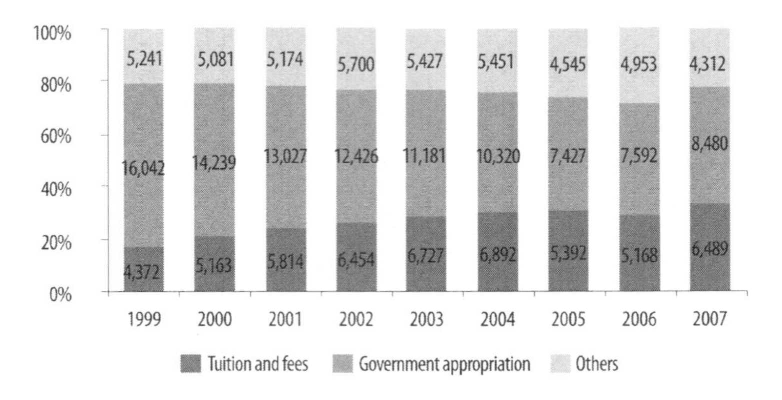

Figure 18.2: Share of educational revenues per student in regular HEIs, 1999–2007, in constant 2007 yuan
Note: "Others" include social endowments, donations and other educational funds
Data source: China Statistical Yearbook, 2001–9

missions, aggressive cost recovery schemes from families desirous of higher education for their children, perceived gaps between graduate expertise and desires and employer demands and compensation, and the quest for world class institutions through mergers, internationalisation and the creation of a Chinese 'Ivy League'. These reforms have sparked a nationwide debate on how to define, measure and achieve educational effectiveness and innovation (Hayhoe and Yan, 2010; Research Group of Graduate Education Quality Evaluation, 2010).

Rapid expansion in China's college population has not been accompanied by proportionate increases in state resources, and institutions have been encouraged to generate income and seek external funding on their own. Tuition and fees, as a primary source of institutional revenue, are increasingly borne by students and their families (Figure 18.2). Meanwhile, student–teacher ratios, a frequently used if problematic proxy for the level of academic attention and mentoring students receive during their college years, nearly doubled during the past decade (Figure 18.3). Furthermore, these figures do not reflect other factors that can conceal problems associated with, or compromise, educational quality, such as institutional over-reporting of full-time teachers, low percentages of full-time teachers holding postgraduate degrees and faculty pressures to juggle

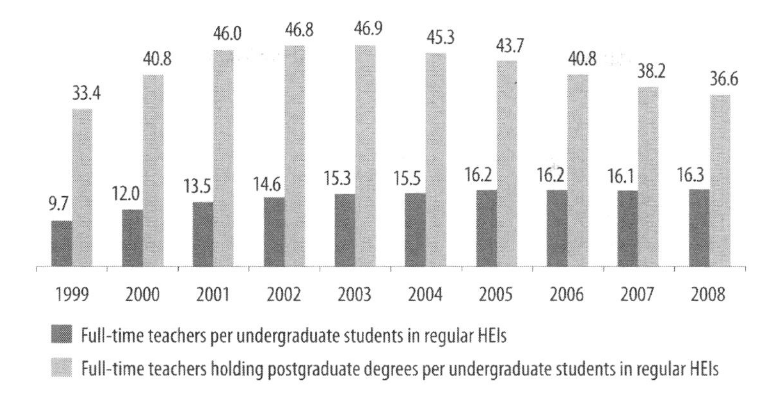

Figure 18.3: Ratio of undergraduate students to full-time teachers in regular HEIs, 1999–2008
Data source: Ministry of Education, China

demands for research productivity and heavy teaching loads (Li, 2009).

In response to growing dissatisfaction with educational quality, the state as the primary provider of higher education to the public has issued and implemented a series of policy initiatives for quality improvement in undergraduate education. National policies related to the quality of undergraduate education first focused on institutional evaluation. A national higher education quality-assurance system was launched in 2002 with a state initiated and sponsored evaluation program, the National Undergraduate Teaching and Learning Evaluation (*Quanguo benke jiaoxue gongzuo shuiping pinggu,* [abbreviated to *Pinggu*]) (Ministry of Education, 2002, 2004). *Pinggu* procedures resemble those of institutional accreditation in the United States, generally consisting of a self-study, on-site visitation by an evaluation team and periodic reviews. However, the programme is administered through the Higher Education Evaluation Center (HEEC) under the auspices of the Ministry of Education (MoE) and thus is attached to the executive and regulatory powers of the state. For example, the HEEC was responsible for constructing a five-year timeline for evaluation and notifying institutions when they were to be evaluated. Institutions failing such evaluations were prohibited by the MoE from admitting new students[*] the following year. By the end of 2008[†], *Pinggu* had evaluated 516 baccalaureate institutions, falling behind the original five-year plan for inspection of a total of 592 institutions (Ministry of Education, 2003).

Undergraduate education evaluation in China also takes place at local levels. Academic and professional associations, higher education institutions and non-governmental ranking institutes and agencies have adopted varied methods for defining and examining the quality of undergraduate education (Cen and Ross, 2009). Together, *Pinggu* and local evaluation efforts have generated a platform for nationwide debate on and beyond evaluation, about what quality undergraduate education is, what counts as evidence of quality, how to measure quality across institutions, how institutions should improve quality and who should serve as the gatekeeper of educational quality.

By the middle of the 2000s, quality discourse had moved to the centre of the undergraduate education policy arena (Ministry of Education, 2001b, 2005, 2007) culminating in *the Eleventh Five-year Plan (2006–2010) in Education* (State Council, 2007)[‡]. By design, the pace of massification has decelerated in the last few years as improving the quality rather than the quantity of higher education has become the mandated priority. Likewise, bringing in fiscal commitment, the policy paper *Opinions on Implementing the National Project of Undergraduate Educational Quality and Educational Reform* (*Gaodeng xuexiao benke jiaoxue zhiliang yu jiaoxue gaige gongcheng,* [abbreviated to *Gongcheng*]) was jointly ratified by the Ministry of Finance and the Ministry of Education (2007). This implementation policy presented problem-solving strategies and tactics (Guba, 1984) to substantiate previous policies of accumulated standing decisions and translated them into grant or award programmes for which

* In China's still relatively centralized higher education system, matriculation quotas for public and private institutions are assigned by the Ministry of Education on an annual basis.

† *Pinggu* has elicited much criticism in the last two years and stands on the verge of complete overhaul.

‡ The central government decreed the Outline of the Eleventh Five-year Plan for National Economic and Social Development of the People's Republic of China on 16 March 2006, with Chapter 7 on Science and Education. The National Eleventh Five-year Plan in Education drafted by the Ministry of Education was approved by the State Council on 18 May 2007.

institutions can compete. Such programmes include programmatic accreditation, curriculum and instruction, practicum learning experiences for students, professional development for teaching faculty, data collection on various aspects of teaching and learning, and institutional partnerships devoted to improving undergraduate teaching (Center for Higher Education Teaching and Learning, 2010).

The importance of such priorities has been affirmed in China's most recent comprehensive educational reform document, the *National Outline for Medium and Long-term Education Reform and Development (2010–2020)* (Ministry of Education, 2010 – hereafter referred to as *Outline*). This outlines key goals for all stages and aspects of education over the next decade. The *Outline's* preamble criticises educational quality as "arrested", students as lacking in their adaptability to the needs of society and innovative, practical and versatile professionals as in short supply. To address these problems, the *Outline* calls for "reform and innovation" in educational quality assessment and evaluation. To ensure quality the *Outline* prescribes tighter supervision and institutional guarantee of the quality of undergraduate teaching, as well as a more participatory approach to teaching evaluation designed to cultivate students who are optimistic, independent and "useful" to society. Although universities are urged to prioritise teaching in their evaluation of faculty evaluation, student experiences and learning outcomes are mentioned only in passing.

In fact, current evaluation and assessment practice in China continues to overlook educational processes and outcomes. Instead, the *Pinggu* and *Gongcheng* projects have channeled national and institutional endeavors toward *inputs* that can be easily quantified (infrastructure, expenditures on undergraduate instruction, instructional materials and proportion of faculty members with doctorates). Based on the questionable assumption that university administrators and faculty are key to understanding and therefore should be held accountable for improving inputs to undergraduate education, both projects neglect the experiences of college students, the presumed beneficiaries of quality education. NSSE-China was designed to remedy the absence of student experience and perspective in educational effectiveness assessment and research.

Localising and implementing NSSE-China: adaptation and institutional capacity building

As summarised above, the NSSE-China instrument was created between 2007 and 2008. After first stage translation and adaptation from the US NSSE survey, the instrument was pretested in China with pilot surveys in the winter of 2007 and further tested with cognitive interviews during the summer of 2008 (Luo, Ross and Cen, 2009; Ross, Luo and Cen, 2008). The second stage of the project, based at the Institute of Educational Research at Tsinghua University and funded by the China Ford Foundation and Tsinghua, set three concurrent goals: introduce, improve and promote the NSSE-China instrument to assess value-added learning of college students; establish a national database on college student engagement in China; and build capacity at local institutions for valid assessment and evidence-based change (Institute of Educational Research, Tsinghua University, 2009).

The NSSE-China instrument elicits self-reported information in five domains: student engagement, learning outcomes, satisfaction, career/educational aspiration and demographic information. Joined by 27 voluntarily participating institutions from different regions of China, NSSE-China is the first college student survey programme that employs probability sampling on a national scale and the data collected set a solid foundation for the creation of a reliable database for both research and policy-making purposes. Just as importantly, the project has initiated significant inter-institutional dialogue and professional development on student experiences in colleges and universities from the bottom up, in marked contrast to the common practice of top-down government-propelled discourse and programmes for improving educational quality.

The NSSE-China research team began the process of survey translation and adaptation by holding close to an old Chinese aphorism about the mandarin orange "that thrives in the south but grows bitter in the north". The US NSSE instrument was designed to examine the effectiveness of common educational activities and practices on US campuses. The survey is centrally administered and the process of administration and analysis has evolved within the changing contexts of US higher education institutional research.* Localising or 'indigenising' the survey to the Chinese context has entailed challenges of adapting the instrument and adjusting the administration process based on what is in the interests of and what is feasible for local institutions. Below we explain how the NSSE-China survey was adapted in the first stage of the project and then administered nationally in the second stage of the project.

Translation and adaptation of the NSSE-China instrument

Translation plays a key role in cross-cultural survey projects, going hand-in-hand with adaptation (Harkness, 2008). We adopted a team approach to this dual process in the first stage of the NSSE-China project. Coordinated by a postdoctoral fellow from Tsinghua University, three Chinese doctoral students specialising in educational policy studies and inquiry met once a week and reviewed the draft translation item by item. The team consulted with a range of expertise including developers of the NSSE instrument, scholars of American higher education and experts on questionnaire design. The draft was pretested in a first round of cognitive interviews before a pilot survey was conducted in six diverse Beijing colleges and universities, representing private, public and different reputational tier institutions in the winter of 2007.† A second round of cognitive

* For example, 33 per cent of participating institutions opted for a paper questionnaire (as well as an on-line option) in 2005; in 2010, this figure declined to 17 per cent and 99 per cent of all NSSE 2010 respondents completed the survey online (NSSE, 2005, 2010b).

† Two striking if tentative observations emerged from the pilot study. First, students in participating private institutions, commonly regarded as being at the lower end of the hierarchy of China's higher education system, evidenced the highest levels of student–faculty interaction and active and collaborative learning. Explanations for these findings appear closely associated with the extent to which faculty and institutions control the numbers of hours each day that students are required to study in form or homeroom classrooms, sometimes in the presence of 'teachers'. Second, unlike in the US, where engagement scores vary within more than between institutions, between-institution variation was larger than within-institution variation. This finding, particularly evident between tier one and tier two and three institutions, suggests that China's most internationally connected tier one institutions' student learning environments, classroom experiences and teacher–student expectations more closely approximate assumptions embedded in NSSE's five benchmarks.

interviews at five institutions of various types and in different regions of China was conducted in the summer of 2008. Findings from the pretests contributed to further revisions of the instrument, which was employed in a full survey in 2009. Survey adaptation fell into four broad categories (Harkness, 2008) that we illustrate below with particularly salient examples that capture both the challenge of translation and adaptation and the fact that in an era of global educational reform and circulation, new pedagogical strategies, structures and services for undergraduate students are increasingly captured through internationally inflected (and often English) vocabularies and grammars of teaching and learning.

Language-driven adaptation. Lexical and structural differences between English and Chinese pose problems in rendering a source question. For example, the Chinese language does not possess a word that directly corresponds to 'presentation' and the common practice in the US of students making in-class presentations has to date not been a frequently used pedagogical and/or assessment strategy in mainland Chinese undergraduate education. In seeking an appropriate Chinese expression to communicate the concept, the team worked with NSSE staff, who paraphrased the practice in multiple ways in English. We finally chose the words '*koutou baogao*', a literal translation of *oral report,* as our closest approximation of 'presentation' and asked Chinese undergraduate students in the field to provide examples of how they understood this activity. Students at an elite university in Beijing and at a branch campus of an overseas institution both described experiences of conducting a prepared talk in front of a classroom of peers and a teacher, often accompanied by visual aids. Interestingly, these students reported that they used the English word *presentation* to refer to the activity not only in response to our question but also in class, as their instructors in assigning the task used the English word. In contrast, students attending an inland university provided imaginative examples of *koutou baogao,* based not on direct experience but rather on their knowledge of such practices from the media and from friends in other institutions. Although their examples indeed captured the meaning of 'presentation', they had themselves never taken part in a 'presentation' and the English word *presentation* looked and felt a bit 'strange' to them. To accommodate this reaction, we decided to retain the Chinese phrase *koutou baogao* in the question and add the English word *presentation* in parentheses.

Adaptation to ensure local coverage of a concept. *Laoshi*, a Chinese word literally translated as *teacher* in English, is an appellation that can and often does refer to any non-peer adult on campus. As such, the reference has a much broader coverage than the English words *faculty, instructor* or *professor* in the US context. Students shared with us their understanding of *laoshi* by describing interactions with instructors who teach academic classes, with thesis advisors in or outside of the university, with *fudaoyuan* or tutors who advise students in out-of-classroom settings, with student (that is peer) organisation advisors and even with administrative staff who are responsible for dormitory and registrar related activities. Interviewees indicated that student interactions with non-academic *laoshi* were more frequent and more influential in their college lives than academic *laoshi*, who were seen as minimally influential and/or somewhat distant. Administrative staff of the institutions in which we conducted interviews expressed their desire and described attempts to build teams of professional staff to support student development. They were particularly interested in our data on student interaction with such *laoshi*. In response to students and student service personnel, we expanded the construct of student and faculty interaction to take these reactions into account and created and tested several items to enrich the construct. This adaptation improved NSSE-China's relevance to students (and to student services personnel) and better captured how students interact with adult others (including senior peers) in the context of Chinese universities.

Adaptation to ensure questions are understood as intended. Choosing appropriate wording to ensure a translated item was understood as intended was an indispensable but challenging task. For example, one survey question asked students to estimate the extent to which "your examinations during the current school year have challenged you to do your best work". The translation team came up with more than one version of this question and agreed that field test respondents should help us understand which version was closest to what was intended. In the pretest of one version (that presented 'challenge' as it is literally meant in English), interviewees responded to the question by explaining the extent to which they regarded their *examinations* as challenging. In response to another Chinese version that retained the superlative form of "do your best work", students interpreted the relationship between examinations and hard work as a one-to-one correspondence and their responses were highly skewed toward the low end of our 7-point scale. Tests of multiple versions of this item were conducted with Chinese college students before we agreed upon a satisfactory translation. In the end, survey respondents' explanations in cognitive interviews were crucial to appropriately rendering this item.

Socio-cultural, system-driven adaptation. The role and mission of a tertiary institution are formed within particular historical, socio-cultural and economic contexts. Differences in the purposes of US and Chinese higher education are consequently reflected in the adaptation process. One of the most obvious examples relevant to NSSE-China's adaptation is the strong role Christian higher education has played in the development of postsecondary education in the US where more than 13 per cent of tertiary institutions identify themselves as religiously affiliated (US Department of Education, 2010). One item in the US NSSE survey asks students how often "you participated in activities to enhance spirituality (worship, meditation, prayer, et cetera)". We doubted whether this question would be relevant to or appropriate to ask to students in Chinese colleges and universities, not because they do not engage in deeply spiritual and/or religious thinking but because this domain has largely been excluded from the mission of mainland postsecondary education since 1949. Only a tiny number of our student interviewees mentioned, in truncated and/or reluctant ways, that someone they knew in college practised a religion. Tertiary institutions in China do not have guiding religious missions or explicit institutional policies regarding the religious practices of domestic students. Therefore, this item was removed from NSSE-China.

Local survey administration

The US NSSE survey is centrally administered through the Center for Survey Research, a partner of Indiana University's Center for Postsecondary Research. The Center collects a population profile from each participating institution, sends invitations for survey participation to sampled students and collects completed questionnaires directly from survey respondents. Central survey administration of NSSE-China proved unfeasible. First, colleges and universities are reluctant to share student population profiles with outsiders for fear of misuse of the information.

Second, as not all institutions keep the mail or email addresses of students in their records, institutions employ different methods for the distribution of information and documents such as surveys to students. Local administration of the NSSE-China survey, agreed upon through conversations with multiple stakeholders and adopted in the full survey administration, represented the NSSE-China project's most significant departure from US NSSE protocol.

At the first national NSSE-China workshop convened in April 2009, institutional researchers from 27 colleges and universities collectively identified and discussed potential obstacles and solutions to survey administration at their own institutions. As an emerging profession in Chinese higher education, institutional researchers come from diverse academic backgrounds and are housed within different academic and administrative units. Examples from the workshop below illustrate how joining the NSSE-China project brought both challenge and enthusiasm to institutional researchers. These examples also illustrate our growing understanding of how important NSSE-China could be not just as a data collection and research project but also as a platform for collaboration in strengthening local institutional research infrastructures and connecting these together to invigorate and encourage deeper and, as our Chinese colleagues, put it 'more scientific' engagement of institutions in the effective learning of their students.

Though the primary purpose of NSSE-China, as we emphasised in our introduction to the workshop, was for institutional diagnosis and improvement, participating institutions were eager to compare themselves with peers. As local survey administration was our most significant procedural 'compromise', we were anxious to insure that the same sampling scheme was employed across participating institutions. Against a backdrop of acknowledgement that haphazard and therefore unusable sampling has been prevalent in much educational research in China, and furthermore that Chinese college students are frequently 'victims snowed under' by poorly designed survey questionnaires, we highlighted the significance of probability sampling to the project and requested a simple random sampling scheme in local survey administration. Presenters demonstrated how to generate random numbers with different software programmes and how to check the samples with the population on selected variables. During discussion sessions, workshop participants worked in groups and on laptops, and practised sample selection. One participant brought an electronic file of his institution's undergraduate population and exclaimed: "We ran the program and it went very well!"

Another participant described, in a brainstorming session regarding methods for distributing and collecting surveys, the possibility of using his institution's well-developed internal mailing system to reach individual students. Another participant responded, "But I believe most colleges and universities do not have such a system and may we use the fudaoyuan system* to collect the surveys instead?" Upon hearing this suggestion, a third workshop participant questioned the approach, worried about the power or influence a *fudaoyuan* might have on student responses: "the hierarchy might imply a type of coercion in eliciting student survey response." A fourth participant then grabbed the microphone and proudly announced, "We've secured financial support from our President's office before coming to this workshop, and we plan to hire several student research assistants to deliver the questionnaire, sealed in an envelope, to sampled undergraduates." By the end of the workshop, all participants had proposed a way for distributing and collecting the survey, taking into account methodological and ethical considerations.

In assisting participants to understand NSSE-China sampling protocol and devise institutionally appropriate and effective strategies for distributing and collecting surveys, the workshop provided an important professional development opportunity for budding and more experienced institutional researchers. One participant recalled that, "the first workshop opened a window of inquiry for me, ranging from technical details in survey administration to the ethical aspect of how to treat our survey respondents with respect and appreciation".

---

* The *fudaoyuan* system, or the tutor system, refers to professional staff members (identified as *laoshi* or teachers by students) who manage and provide non-academic advice and information to a 'form' or cohort of students who share the same major. Most higher education institutions use this system as the communication and regulatory mechanism that links institutional practices, policies and regulations with students.

Internalisation of the NSSE-China project: Tsinghua University

To illustrate how NSSE-China became internalised and then used, after its first full-scale survey run of 2009, we share below select data collected from 1,077 undergraduates at Tsinghua University. Tsinghua is an exceptional institution, one of China's C9 ivy league "985" universities.* Tsinghua attracts top-performing high-school graduates; for the academic year of 2010–11, 40 per cent of the 65 high-school graduates that scored highest on China's College Entrance Exam in their respective provinces enrolled in Tsinghua (Tsinghua Admission, 2010). As a leader of the NSSE-China project and member of the first cohort of 27 participating institutions, Tsinghua desired to compare itself with top-notch US institutions with the goal of improving the quality of the Tsinghua undergraduate education experience.

Comparisons indicated that Tsinghua undergraduates reported much less student–faculty interaction than their US peers. Item by item comparison (Figure 18.4) demonstrated that Tsinghua undergraduates scored significantly lower than their US counterparts in talking with faculty about career plans and in receiving faculty feedback on academic performance: 21.7 per cent of Tsinghua respondents reported that they had *never* received any prompt feedback from faculty on their academic performance and 44.3 per cent *never* had discussions regarding their career plans with a faculty member or an advisor (Luo, Shi and Tu, 2010). In contrast, US figures from NSSE 2009 were about 7 per cent and 20 per cent respectively.

In addition to analysing survey data in relationship to the five benchmarks from the US NSSE survey that were incorporated into NSSE-China, Tsinghua researchers (Luo, Shi and Tu, 2010) also developed five scalelets from the survey items that corresponded to five different but related aspects of undergraduate education at Tsinghua. These included goal attainment

* The "985" designation, currently held by 43 institutions, literally refers to the May 1998 100th anniversary of Peking University, when President Jiang Zimin declared that China must aspire to develop world-class universities. China's 'Ivy League' of nine institutions, whose research funds in 2009 averaged 1.2 billion *yuan* RMB (equalling that of American Association of Universities membership), has been protected from over-expansion and received extraordinary state funding in their race to attain global excellence.

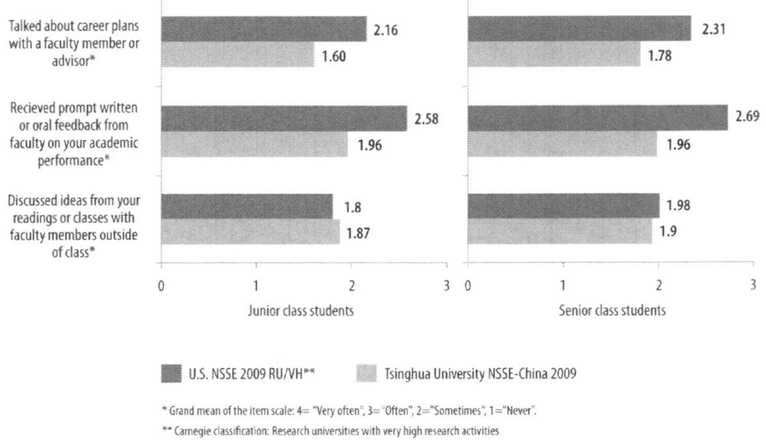

Figure 18.4: Comparing items of student–faculty interaction between Tsinghua undergraduates and US peers
Tsinghua data from Luo, Shi and Tu (2010); US data from NSSE (2009b; 2009c)

in academic curriculum; academic challenge; academic behaviour in class; academic behaviour outside of class; and co-curricular activities. This set of scalelets, originating from the context of Tsinghua undergraduate teaching and learning, proved psychometrically valid and reliable and convincing to institutional and Ministry of Education policy makers and practitioners. From the beginning, some scholars and high-level Tsinghua administrators had expressed a widely shared concern within Chinese academic circles that Chinese researchers must direct greater attention to the development of locally responsive and effective research methodologies and instruments and that 'foreign imports' must be justified and carefully adapted to reflect local discourse and practices. This seemed particularly true for NSSE-China, constructed as it was on a model guided by research findings largely from US higher education, a valued yet problematic primary 'reference system' for Chinese educational reform.

A particularly striking finding emerged from data related to the scalelet representing students' academic behaviour outside of class.* Fully

* Tsinghua scored at least as high as its US parallel research institutions on all five benchmarks except for student–faculty interaction. Compared with the top 10 per cent of US universities, Tsinghua lagged behind on all five benchmarks, except for that of institutional support for students' learning.

30.7 per cent of Tsinghua undergraduates reported having spent more than 30 hours in a typical seven-day week preparing for class. In contrast, at US research universities (with very high research activities) that participated in the NSSE 2009 survey, only 8 per cent of seniors and 6 per cent of first-year students spent more than 30 hours per week on academic study outside of class (NSSE, 2009a). This significant difference was interpreted by Tsinghua researchers to mean, on the one hand, that Tsinghua undergraduates were working much harder than their American peers and, on the other, that the effectiveness of in-class teaching and learning and self-study, and what 'hard work' means for Tsinghua students, needed to be much more carefully understood. Luo, Shi and Tu (2010) illustrated the latter concern by referring to an interview with a regretful student participant who "felt desperate from my first year to my third year in college... as I feel my prime time in life was spent in the self-study room, which I don't think means a lot to me."

These findings and others, obtained through a valid survey instrument and sound procedure for data collection, provided a solid foundation for policy recommendations on improving student–faculty relationships and on reforming the undergraduate programme of studies at Tsinghua. In fact, the Tsinghua report (Luo, Shi and Tu, 2010) has been used as a model for reading and reporting NSSE-China 2009 data for other institutions. The report has also been widely read and commented upon by academic and non-academic readers (Shi, 2009; Xie, 2010) and has begun to shift higher educational institutions, scholars and the wider public's criteria for assessing the quality of higher education toward more student-centred and student-valued outcomes.

In 2010, the NSSE-China project moved to a second round of full survey administration, supported by funding and assistance from Tsinghua University's China Data Center. In addition to 31 voluntarily participating universities and colleges, the NSSE-China team also invited 15 institutions sampled on a national scale. This effort aims at establishing the first nationally representative database of college student experiences in China. Simultaneously, qualitative studies are ongoing, with the intent of digging deeper into student understandings of their college experiences. This research, which includes in-depth interviewing at select participating institutions on students' college experiences that foster learning and growth, extends interpretations of what the

NSSE-China 2009 numbers mean to an intentional inclusion of student voices in the implementation process.

Conclusion

As Chinese post-secondary institutions respond to rapid changes in educational demand, capacity, regulation, social relevance, purpose, accountability and global integration, the NSSE-China project highlights the extent to which educational quality improvement and assessment in China represents what Gita Steiner-Khamsi and her colleagues (2004) have called "real" rather than imagined globalisation; that is, internationalisation based on a nuanced understanding of local needs within a changing global environment, in contrast to "internationality", or the use of global discourse to legitimate local practices. Chinese higher-education quality policies, practices and scholarship have paralleled worldwide trends in assessment (and competition) that were summarised at the 1998 World Conference on Higher Education and continue to be informed by the rich, contentious and increasingly global scholarship on how to define and measure the diverse dimensions of higher-education quality (Dill, 2005; Borden, 2001; Gibbs, 2010; Ewell, 2008; OECD, 2010). Whether we celebrate these trends as building a global scaffold for a "free trade in minds" (Wildavsky, 2010) or criticise them for reconfiguring a global hierarchy consolidating new "empires of knowledge and development" (Altbach and Balan, 2007), calibrating a defensible "global gauge" or "measuring stick"* for educational quality is engaging scholars everywhere. As Nigel Thrift has noted, global discourse on what's wrong with the world's universities shows just how striking their similarities are.† In this context, university administrators in China realise that when education is viewed (and paid for) as a private good, "trust us won't cut it anymore."‡ Coupled with fears that universities aren't 'measuring up' to their responsibility of educating students with twenty-first-century skills, pressures on Chinese postsecondary institutions to justify their

* For global gauge see earlier footnote. "Measuring stick" alludes to the rather dispiriting *Chronicle of Higher Education* September to December 2010 series on quality higher education by that name.

† 15 March 2011

‡ See Kevin Carey, 28 January 2011, *Chronicle of Higher Education*, A 64.

costs and quality to families and students and the state have directed attention toward improving understanding and assessment of student learning experiences and outcomes.*

A four-stage model for explaining cross-national attraction in educational policies formulated by David Phillips and his colleagues (2004) is useful for summarising NSSE-China as a positive example of internalisation in the context of China's move toward global quality assessment. Though originally developed to explain the borrowing of policy, Phillips' framework applies equally well to the borrowing of research approach, methodology and student engagement concept associated with the NSSE-China project.

Motivated by the interlinked questions of why a country is interested in the educational policies and practices in another country and of what the impulses for attraction are, the model posits a number of factors associated with Stage One of the process, *cross-national attraction*. These factors include: 1) political–economic change; 2) system collapse; 3) internal dissatisfaction with current practices; 4) negative external evaluation of current practices; 5) new configurations and alliances; and 6) knowledge and skills innovation. All but the second factor have been shown in our discussion to be relevant to why the concept of student engagement and its definition and measurement through NSSE-China received generally positive reception by Chinese scholars, higher education professionals and policy makers. A greatly expanded, diverse and in some ways chaotic university system; domestic dissatisfaction with educational (e)quality, effectiveness and practical utility, and concomitant pressures to compete for resources and students at home and abroad; widespread external criticism of the Chinese academy, including corruption and lack of autonomy, transparency and creativity; aggressive attention to the building of global partnerships and internationalising environments and opportunities for students and faculty; and national policy focusing on the nurturing of innovation in science and technology are all characteristics of the reform environment in which the 'externalising potential' of NSSE, and its adaptation through NSSE-China, was recognised and supported.

Stage Two of the model, *decision making*, involves how the borrowed

* The most notable example is OECD's Assessment of Higher Education Learning Outcomes (AHELO) initiative. See, for example, Moodie (2010) and Sharma (2010).

practice or policy is used in the decision-making process in its 'transplanted home', for example, to illustrate or suggest a solution to a critical problem or to initiate a particular reform. As noted above, policies associated with higher educational reform in China are geared toward a shift from educational quantity to quality, prompting vigorous debate on higher education assessment. In this context, the NSSE-China concept of student engagement emerged as an exciting springboard for opening up conversations about quality educational processes and outcomes in a context where definitions and assessments of higher education quality were (and are) considered inadequate and unsatisfactory. In addition, examining student engagement and the effective educational practices that support it appeared a promising intervention as Chinese higher education institutions are pressed by stiff competition with overseas and Hong Kong universities for top faculty, students and other markers of world-class education.

Stages Three and Four of the model, *implementation* and *internalisation*, have been illustrated in detail above. While some scholars and senior administrators (with the power of research purse strings) initially expressed scepticism regarding NSSE-China's foreign origins, adequate financial and technical support in the pilot phase, close collaboration among researchers in China and the US, and careful cultural adaptation and eventual indigenisation by a prestigious university allowed the project to thrive. The cultural adaptation process, far from erecting a barrier to project reception and completion, became a key focus of inquiry within the research project. This self-consciously reflexive approach facilitated the internalisation of NSSE-China, which has produced data that are meaningful and actionable to institutions, demonstrably enhanced China's higher-education discourse on student-centred and process-focused quality in higher education, gestated a national database for evidence-based policy making in higher education and provided a platform for professional development and exchange among institutional researchers. Distinct from the *Pinggu* and *Gongcheng* projects that are central-government-led initiatives aiming at enhancing higher-education quality in a top-down manner, the NSSE-China project represents a bottom-up research and reform project that expanded to and improved the research capacities of institutions that care about student learning, the quality of undergraduate education and alternative assessment thinking.

Furthermore, in the process of indigenisation, NSSE-China is serving the needs of many stakeholders. The diverse needs of researchers for different kinds of data on undergraduate education and students, for example, have influenced the form of the survey, which has grown in length as a result of stakeholder interest and funding.

To date, the NSSE-China project has been successful in situating and communicating assessments of educational quality and effectiveness in and through students' experiences and voices; in facilitating student interviews as methods for data collection and for prompting and enhancing student reflection on learning gains; and in focusing attention at the institutional level on what *can* be changed. Factors that promote or impede student learning often fall outside the control of institutions; the NSSE-China project has enabled institutions to anchor quality education assessment and evaluation in evidence from their own experiences and policies. Finally, NSSE-China has strengthened the collective capacities of participating institutions to respond to urgent institutional and national needs. At the 2009 workshop for reauthorisation of China's National Undergraduate Education Evaluation, Ministry of Education officers recommended NSSE-China as a theoretically based, field-tested means to establish a national database in China on college-student learning processes and outcomes.

References

Altbach, P.G. and Balan, J. (eds) (2007) *Transforming Research Universities in Asia and Latin America World Class Worldwide* (Baltimore: The Johns Hopkins University Press).

Arum, R. and Roksa, J. (2011) *Academically Adrift, Limited Learning on College Campuses* (Chicago and London: University of Chicago Press).

Australasian Survey of Student Engagement (AUSSE) (2010) *Student Engagement and the AUSSE*. Retrieved from <http://ausse.acer.edu.au/>

Borden, V. (2001) *Measuring Quality: Choosing Among Surveys and Other Assessments of College Quality*, American Council on Education.

Cen, Y. and Ross, H. (2009) 'Chinese Higher Education and Evaluation in Context', *Chinese Education and Society*, 42/1, pp.3–7.

Center for Higher Education Teaching and Learning (2010) *The national project of undergraduate educational quality and educational reform*. Retrieved from <http://www.zlgc.org/index.aspx>

Chickering, A. and Gamson, Z. (1987) 'Seven Principles for Good Practice in Undergraduate Education', *American Association of Higher Education Bulletin*, 39/7, pp.3–7.

Deng, X. (2009) 'Peking University survey shows: Almost four in ten college students in Beijing unsatisfied with college experiences', *Beijing Youth*. Retrieved from <http://edu.people.com.cn/GB/10123133.html>

Dill, D.D. (2005) *The Public Good, the Public Interest, and Public Higher Education*, Research Program on Public Policy for Academic Quality (PPAQ) Background Paper (Chapel Hill: University of North Carolina). Retrieved from <http://www.unc.edu/ppaq/docs/PublicvsPrivate.pdf>

Evans, N., Forney, D.S., Guido, F.M., Patton, L.D. and Renn, K.A. (2010) *Student Development in College, Theory, Research, and Practice* (2nd edn) (San Francisco: Jossey-Bass).

Ewell, P.T. (2008) 'Assessment and Accountability in America today: Background and Context', *New Directions for Institutional Research*, Special Issue Autumn 2008, pp.7–17.

Fischman, G., Igo, S. and Rhoten, D. (2011) 'Great Expectations, Past Promises, and Golden Ages: Rethinking the "Crisis" of Public Research Universities', in Rhoten, D. and Calhoun, G. (eds) *Knowledge Matters The Public Mission of the Research University* (New York: Columbia University Press) pp.34–66.

Gibbs, G. (2010) *Dimensions of Quality* (York: The Higher Education Academy).

Guba, E.G. (1984) 'The Effect of Definitions of Policy on the Nature and Outcomes of Policy Analysis', *Educational Leadership*, 42/4, pp.63–70.

Harkness, J.A. (2008) 'Comparative Survey Research: Goal and Challenges', in deLeeuw, E.D., Hox, J.J. and Dillman, D.A. (eds) *International Handbook of Survey Methodology* (New York: Taylor and Francis Group).

Hayhoe, R., Li, J., Lin, J. and Zha, Q. (2011) *Portraits of 21st Century Chinese Universities: In the Move to Mass Higher Education 2011* (Hong Kong: Comparative Education Research Centre and Springer).

Hayhoe, R. and Yan, F. (eds) (2010) 'China's universities in the move to mass higher education: The search for equality, quality and diversity', *Special Issue of Frontiers of Education in China*, 5/4, pp.465–577.

Institute of Educational Research, Tsinghua University (2009) *A new approach to quality assurance and evaluation system in higher education in China: An evaluation system centered on student learning and educational process* (Beijing: Ford Foundation).

Jiabao, W. (2011) Comments made during an Internet interview, 27 February 2011, Xinhuanet.com. Retrieved from <http://news.xinhuanet.com/english2010/china/2011-02/27/c_13752018.htm>

Kipnis, A. (2001) 'The Disturbing Educational Discipline of "Peasants"', *China Journal*, 46, pp.1–24.

Kipnis, A. (2006) '*Suzhi*: A Keyword Approach', *China Quarterly*, pp.295–313.

Kipnis, A. (2011) *Governing Educational Desire* (Chicago: University of Chicago Press).

Kuh, G.D. (2003) 'What we're learning about student engagement from NSSE: Benchmarks for effective educational practices', *Change*, 35/2, pp.24–32.

Kuh, G.D., Kinzie, J., Buckley, J.A., Bridges, B.K. and Hayek, J.C. (2007) 'Piecing Together the Student Success Puzzle, Research Propositions, and Recommendations', *ASHE Higher Education Report*, 32/5 (San Francisco: Jossey-Bass).

Kuh, G.D., Kinzie, J., Schuh, J., Whitt, E.J. and associates (2010) *Student Success in College, Creating Conditions that Matter* (San Francisco: Jossey-Bass).

Li, F. (2009) 'An Empirical Study on the Stress of University Faculty', *Journal of Shandong University of Technology* (Social Sciences Edition), 25/1, pp.96–9.

Li, Y. (2010) 'Quality Assurance in Chinese Higher Education', *Research in Comparative and International Education*, 5/1, pp.58–76.

Luo, Y., Ross, H. and Cen, Y. (2009) 'Higher education measurement in the context of globalization – the development of NSSE-China: Cultural adaptation, reliability and validity', *Fudan Education Forum*, 2009/5, pp.12–18.

Luo, Y., Shi, J. and Tu, D. (2010) 'Annual report of Tsinghua undergraduate education survey 2009: Comparing with US top research universities', *Tsinghua Journal of Education*, 30/5, pp.1–13.

Ministry of Education (2001a) *The National Tenth Five-year Plan in Education (33)* (Beijing). Retrieved from <http://www.moe.edu.cn/edoas/website18/level3.jsp?tablename=28&infoid=219>

Ministry of Education (2001b) *Opinions on Enhancing Undergraduate Education and Improving Educational Quality* (Beijing). Retrieved from <http://www.moe.edu.cn/edoas/website18/89/info4489.htm>

Ministry of Education (2002) *The Evaluation Scheme of National Undergraduate Teaching and Learning Evaluation (Tentative)*. Retrieved from <http://www.pgw.ynu.edu.cn/show.php?id=57>

Ministry of Education (2003) *Circular of the General Office of the Ministry of Education on Evaluating Undergraduate Teaching and Learning in 592 Regular Higher Education Institutions (Appendix): Name list and Timeline of Institutions to be Evaluated from 2003 to 2007*. Retrieved from <http://www.pgzx.edu.cn/main/webShowDoc?channel=wjhb_jybsjwj&docID=2005/12/05/1133769809019.xml>

Ministry of Education (2004) *The Evaluation Scheme of National Undergraduate Teaching and Learning Evaluation (Tentative) Revised*, 2004/21. Retrieved from <http://www.moe.edu.cn/edoas/website18/level3.jsp?tablename=1528&infoid=15008>

Ministry of Education (2005) *Opinions on Further Enhancing Undergraduate Education and Improving Educational Quality* (Beijing). Retrieved from <http://www.moe.edu.cn/edoas/website18/31/info13931.htm>

Ministry of Education (2007) *Opinions on Further Deepening Undergraduate Educational Reform and Improving Educational Quality*. Retrieved from <http://www.moe.edu.cn/edoas/website18/level3.jsp?tablename=1196&infoid=25424>

Ministry of Education (2009) *The Statistic Communique of the 2008 National Education Development*. Retrieved from <http://www.moe.gov.cn/edoas/website18/28/info1262244458513828.htm>

Ministry of Education (2010) *National Outline for Medium and Long-term Education Reform and Development (2010–2020)*. Retrieved from <http://www.gov.cn/jrzg/2010-07/29/content_1667143.htm> (English version available online at <http://www.aei.gov.au/AEI/China_Education_Reform_pdf.pdf>)

Ministry of Finance and Ministry of Education (2007) *Opinions on Implementing the National Project of Educational Quality and Educational Reform* (Beijing). Retrieved from <http://www.zlgc.org/Detail.aspx?Id=1048>

Mok, K.H. (2005) *Globalization and Educational Restructuring: University Merging and Changing Governance in China*, Higher Education, 50/1, pp.57–88.

Moodie, G. (2010) 'GLOBAL: Establishing academic standards', *University World News* (28 February 2010). Retrieved from <http://www.universityworldnews.com/article.php?story=20100226130940456>

Morgan, W.J. and Wu, B. (eds) (2011) *Higher Education Reform in China: Beyond the Expansion (China Policy Series)* (London: Routledge).

Murphy, R. (2004) 'Turning Peasants into Modern Chinese Citizens: "Population Quality" Discourse, Demographic Transition, and Primary Education', *China Quarterly*, pp.1–20.

National Survey of Student Engagement (NSSE) (2001a) *Benchmarks of Effective Educational Practice*. Retrieved from <http://nsse.iub.edu/pdf/nsse_benchmarks.pdf>

National Survey of Student Engagement (NSSE) (2001b) *Survey development*. Retrieved March from <http://nsse.iub.edu/html/PsychometricPortfolio_SurveyDevelopment.cfm>

National Survey of Student Engagement (NSSE) (2005) *NSSE 2005 Overview* (Bloomington: Indiana University Center for Postsecondary Research).

National Survey of Student Engagement (NSSE) (2009a) *Assessment for Improvement: Tracking Student Engagement Over Time – Annual Results 2009* (Bloomington: Center for Postsecondary Research).

National Survey of Student Engagement (NSSE) (2009b) *NSSE 2009 grand means: Means and standard deviations by Carnegie Classification, first-year students*. Retrieved from <http://nsse.iub.edu/2009_Institutional_Report/pdf/2009%20FY%20Grand%20Means%20by%20Carn.pdf>

National Survey of Student Engagement (NSSE) (2009c) *NSSE 2009 Grand Means: Means and standard deviations by Carnegie Classification, senior students*. Retrieved from <http://nsse.iub.edu/2009_Institutional_Report/pdf/2009%20SR%20Grand%20Means%20by%20Carn.pdf>

National Survey of Student Engagement (NSSE) (2010a) *Major differences: Examining student engagement by field of study annual results 2010* (Bloomington: Indiana University Center for Postsecondary Research).

National Survey of Student Engagement (NSSE) (2010b) *NSSE 2010 Overview* (Bloomington: Indiana University Center for Postsecondary Research).

Obama, B.H. (2011) *Remarks by the President in State of Union Address* (25 January 2011) (Washington: The White House). Retrieved from <http://www.whitehouse.gov/the-press-office/2011/01/25/remarks-president-state-union-address>

Ochs, K. and Phillips, D. (2004) 'Processes of educational borrowing in historical context', in Phillips, D. and Ochs, K. (eds) *Educational Policy Borrowing: Historical Perspectives. Oxford Studies in Comparative Education* (Oxford: Symposium Books) pp.7–23.

OECD (Organisation for Economic Co-operation and Development) (2010) *Learning our Lesson: Review of Quality Teaching in Higher Education 2010*. Retrieved from <http://www.oecd.org/officialdocuments/displaydocumentpdf?cote=EDU/IMHE/AHELO/GNE(2009)9/FINAL&doclanguage=en>

Pascarella, E.T. and Terenzini, P.T. (2005) *How College Affects Students: a Third Decade of Research* (San Francisco: Jossey-Bass).

Personal communication (2008) Email from Robert Gonyea on global interest in NSSE, 4 February 2008.

Personal communication (2010) A conversation between Yan Luo, Yuhao Cen and Robert Gonyea on the process of the NSSE-China project, 10am, 5 March 2010 at Eigenmann, Bloomington.

Phillips, D. (1989) 'Neither a borrower nor a lender be? The problems of cross-national attraction in education', *Cross-National Attraction in Education, Special Issue, Comparative Education*, 25/3, pp.267–74.

Phillips, D. (2004) 'Toward a theory of policy attraction in education', in Steiner-Khamsi, G. (ed.) *The Global Politics of Educational Borrowing and Lending*, pp.54–68 (New York: Teachers College Press).

Phillips, D. and Ochs, K. (2004) 'Researching policy borrowing: Some methodological problems in comparative education', *British Educational Research Journal*, 30/6, pp.773–84.

Research Group of Graduate Education Quality Evaluation, China (2010) *Educational Research [Jiaoyu Yanjiu]*, 10, pp.60–6.

Rhoten, D. and Calhoun, G. (ed.) (2011) *Knowledge Matters: The Public Mission of the Research University* (New York: Columbia University Press).

Ross, H. and Cen, Y. (eds) (2009) *Chinese Higher Education and Evaluation in Context, Special Issue of Chinese Education and Society*, 42/1.

Ross, H., Luo, Y. and Cen, Y. (2008) 'Assessing Tsinghua university and US universities on learning process indicators: An approach of higher education quality', *Tsinghua Journal of Education*, 29/2, pp.36–42.

Ross, H., Zhang, R. and Zhao, W. (2011) 'The reconfiguration of state–university–student relationships in post/socialist China', in Iveta Silova (ed.) *Post-Socialism is not Dead: (Re)Reading the Global in Comparative Education (International Perspectives on Education and Society, 14)*, pp.299–327.

Sharma, Y. (2010) 'OECD: Higher Education conference attacks rankings', *University World News*, 19 September 2010. Retrieved from <http://www.universityworldnews.com/article.php?story=20100918074720362>

Shi, J. (2009) 'Focus on learning process and investigate on student engagement', *China Education Daily*, 24 November 2009.

South African Survey of Student Engagement (SASSE) (2009) *What is the South African Survey of Student Engagement?* Retrieved from <http://sasse.ufs.ac.za/>

State Council (2007) *Notice of the State Council on the National Eleventh Five-year Plan in Education* (Beijing). Retrieved from <http://202.123.110.5/zwgk/2007-05/23/content_623645.htm>

Steiner-Khamsi, G. (ed.) (2004) *The Global Politics of Borrowing and Lending* (New York: Teachers College Press).

Tsinghua Admission (2010) *Statement of the 2010 undergraduate admission statistics of Tsinghua University*. Retrieved from <http://join-tsinghua.edu.cn/bkzsw/detail.jsp?seq=4030&boardid=26>

US Department of Education (2010) *IPEDS Data Center*. Retrieved from <http://nces.ed.gov/ipeds/datacenter/>

Wildavsky, B. (2010) *The Great Brain Race: How Global Universities are Reshaping our World* (Princeton and Oxford: Princeton University Press).

Xie, R. (2010) 'What are the differences between Tsinghua undergraduate students and top US peers?', *Beijing Daily*, 11 November 2010.

Yang, X. (2003) 'How to calculate the gross enrolment rate of tertiary education in China?', *China Higher Education*, 2003/10, p.36.

Zha, Q. (2009) 'Diversification or homogenization: how governments and markets have combined to (re)shape Chinese higher education in its recent massification process', *Higher Education: The International Journal of Higher Education and Educational Planning*, 58/1, pp.41–58.

Zhang, H. (2005) 'Education index: A bleak and helpless future behind the dream', *China Xiaokang*, pp.14–16.

Chapter 19

Smoke and mirrors: graduate attributes and the implications for student engagement in higher education

Theresa Winchester-Seeto, Agnes Bosanquet and Anna Rowe

Macquarie University, Australia

Discussions of student engagement have gained prominence in universities nationally and internationally in recent years. Simultaneously, statements of graduate attributes have become near ubiquitous for Australian universities. To date, however, there is limited understanding of how the two are linked. Embedding graduate attributes into the curriculum has been ad hoc and Hughes and Barrie (2010) describe the process as sporadic, patchy and lumpy. There has been little exploration of the links or potential links between the intended curriculum (as evidenced by institutional statements of graduate attributes), the enacted curriculum (as graduate attributes are taught within the disciplines and in everyday classroom teaching) and the experienced curriculum (what the student actually encounters) (Marsh and Willis, 2007). As a consequence, the impact of graduate attributes on the student experience is unclear.

Drawing on data from 39 Australian universities over the past 15 years, this chapter examines the relationship between graduate attributes, curriculum development and student engagement. It offers an overview of the intended curriculum of the Australian higher education sector in the 1990s, the early 2000s and the late 2000s and highlights the most important themes and changes evident over this timespan. Internationally, discussions around core competencies, student outcomes and generic, transferable or key skills and capabilities cover much of the same ground as the Australian notion of graduate attributes. See, for example, UNESCO's *World Declaration on Higher Education for the 21st Century* (1998); the findings and recommendations of the Spellings Commission in the United States (US Department of Education, 2006); the Scottish Higher Education Enhancement Committee's (SHEEC) *Graduates for the 21st Century* (2010); and the European Higher Education Area's (EHEA) reports on the first decade of the Bologna Agreement (2010). Three aspects of graduate attributes are explored in detail in this chapter to explain the potential of the intended curriculum for enhancing student engagement: creative and critical thinking; global perspectives; and work-integrated learning.

Student engagement and graduate attributes

Student engagement is a complex notion. Various definitions exist focusing on student motivation, campus experience, organisational enablers, academic support, and intra- and extra-curricular activities (Kuh, 2001; Fredericks, Blumenfeld and Paris, 2004). For the most part, studies of student engagement rely on self-reported outcomes (Krause and Coates, 2008; ACER, 2010). In a recent synthesis of international research on student engagement, Zepke and Leach (2010; see also Chapter 11, this volume) identify four perspectives on student engagement:

- Motivation and agency (engaged students are intrinsically motivated and want to exercise their agency)
- Transactional engagement (students and teachers engage with each other)
- Institutional support (institutions provide an environment conducive to learning)
- Active citizenship (students and institutions work together to enable challenges to social beliefs and practices).

Of these perspectives, the second is the most common focus for studies of student engagement (comprising 55 per cent of the studies reviewed by Zepke and Leach). The relationship between student engagement and graduate attributes encompasses the third and fourth perspectives. In this context, 'institutional support' includes developing policy frameworks for graduate attributes and 'active citizenship' describes the values underpinning graduate attributes such as ethics, social justice, equity, accessibility, environmental sustainability and internationalisation.

Research on graduate attributes is now well established (Barrie, 2006; Bowden et al., 2002; Jones, 2009). A review of the literature around graduate attributes demonstrates four broad conceptions of their purpose: employability; lifelong learning; preparing for an uncertain future; and acting for the social good (Bosanquet, Winchester-Seeto and Rowe, 2010). According to Barrie and Prosser's definition:

> Graduate attributes seek to describe the core outcomes of a higher education. In doing so, they specify an aspect of the institution's contribution to society and carry with them implicit and sometimes explicit assumptions as to the purpose and nature of higher education.
>
> (2004, p.244)

To date, there is little empirical evidence of the impact of graduate attributes on student learning (Winchester-Seeto and Bosanquet, 2009). Various researchers have noted the limited success of curriculum responses to graduate attributes and lack of systematic assessment (Harvey and Kamvounias, 2008; Hughes and Barrie, 2010; Scott, 2008). Research by McInnes (2002) demonstrates that students perceive a gap between university study and the skills required for professional work, and that institutional and sector responses to student needs have been inconsistent. As a way of aligning the intended, enacted and experienced curricula, he argues for "negotiated engagement" (ibid., p.187) in curriculum development that has the potential to engage students in the development, implementation and evaluation of graduate attributes.

Graduate attributes and the intended curriculum

In graduate-attribute statements, higher education institutions articulate their vision of the graduates they seek to produce and the skills, knowledge, values and dispositions they wish to impart. Examination of graduate-attribute statements reveals the intended curriculum for individual institutions and, taken as whole, provides an overview of the sector. It also tracks the influence of community attitudes and concerns, government policy and educational trends across the sector at the time these statements were developed, adopted and ratified. Bosanquet, Winchester-Seeto and Rowe (2010) reported on a pilot study that scrutinised the attribute statements for 13 Australian universities; here, the authors use a similar methodology to examine a larger sample.

This study incorporates both qualitative and quantitative data as lines of evidence, including:

- A thematic analysis of publicly available graduate-attribute statements
- A frequency analysis of the themes in these statements across 15 years
- A word-frequency analysis of the same statements.

Graduate-attribute statements from 39 Australian universities were sourced from publicly available documents including university websites, policy documents and minutes of committee meetings. The search yielded a total of 95 statements of graduate attributes for undergraduates. The statements were sorted into three time slices according to the year they were formally adopted by their institution (or a close approximation): 1996–2000 (31 statements), 2001–5 (30 statements) and 2006–10 (32 statements). Material from each of the 39 universities was drawn upon but, in many cases, statements from all three time slices for each individual university were not available.

While some institutions feature their attributes prominently on websites and make the information readily accessible to students and the general public, others do not. Earlier statements were difficult to retrieve as in most cases they had been removed from university websites. These statements were subsequently sourced from the DEYTA (1999) report, *The Quality of Higher Education* (for statements prior to 2000) and the *Graduate Employability Skills* report (Precision Consultancy, 2007) (for statements between 2001–5). Attribute statements obtained from these reports were not as comprehensive as those sourced from university websites and policy documents.

Thematic analysis

Once the graduate-attribute statements were placed into their relevant time periods, each individual statement was sorted under categories that emerged from the data, using a constant comparative approach (Thorn, 2000). This was an iterative process that grouped similar ideas and looked for similarities as well as any major differences. Not only were the major headings considered but also any explanatory detail. For instance, the major heading might be 'communication' but the detail might list 'written skills' and 'oral skills', as well as some discussion about tailoring the communication for particular audiences. Each of these features was coded and sorted separately.

Frequency analysis

Percentages were calculated for the number of universities that referred to each of the categories in a given time slice. To make comparisons easier, categories were separated into bands:

- Band 1 – category listed by 75–100 per cent of all universities
- Band 2 – category listed by 50–74 per cent of all universities
- Band 3 – category listed by 25–49 per cent of all universities
- Band 4 – category listed by less than 25 per cent of all universities

Table 19.1 shows the results for the top three bands for each time slice. Table 19.2 lists the attributes discussed in this chapter.

Word frequency/tag clouds

Attribute statements for each time slice were analysed, via NVIVO Version 8 word-frequency query, to determine the 100 most frequently used words. These were displayed as tag clouds – a useful visual representation of the data as the relative size of the word reflects the frequency with which it appears. The 100 most frequently used words can be used as a proxy to signify the importance of ideas and language used and comparison of different time slices provides insight into any changes over the entire period. In NVIVO version 8 it is difficult to remove words, such as common English words like 'an' and 'from', from the analysis without resorting to limiting the number of letters in the word. This would, however, distort the analysis and lose potentially important words such as 'we'. In this analysis we therefore used all words, except the names of universities. Figure 19.1 displays the tag cloud for the most recent time slice and Table 19.3 lists the words in common across the three tag clouds as well as any differences.

Percentile band	Graduate Attributes 1990s	%	Graduate Attributes 2000-2005	%	Graduate Attributes 2006-2010	%
Band 1 (75% or more)	Critical/analytical thinking	81	Critical/analytical thinking	92	Critical/analytical thinking	84
	Creative thinking	71	Creative thinking	75	Communication skills	84
			Problem solving	75	Expertise in chosen academic field	78
					Creative thinking	75
Band 2 (74-50%)	Lifelong learning	65	Communication skills	71	Capacity for cooperation/ collaboration	72
	Effective team member	52	Expertise in chosen academic field	58	Problem solving	69
			Lifelong learning	58	Skills in information technology	56
			Identify & retrieve information	54	Identify & retrieve information	53
			Able to work independently	54	Global perspective	53
			Effective team member	50	Social/community responsibility	50
			Capacity for cooperation/ collaboration	50		
			Social/community responsibility	50		

Band 3 (49-25%)	Expertise in chosen academic field	48	Global perspective	46	Ethical member of society	47
	Written skills	48	Understanding of ethics	42	Evaluate information	44
	Oral skills	42	Written skills	42	Sustainability	44
	Identify & retrieve information	42	Oral skills	42	Appreciates & values diversity	44
	Skills in information technology	42	Analyse & synthesise information	42	Lifelong learning	41
	Problem solving	39	Evaluate information	42	Reflection/reflective practice	41
	Communication skills	39	Understanding of social justice	38	Written skills	41
	Professional skills/practice	36	Appreciates & values diversity	38	Effective team member	41
	Application of knowledge/theory	32	Application of knowledge/theory	33	Able to work independently	41
	Analyse & synthesise information	32	Information literacy	33	Thinks locally, nationally, globally	41
	Computer skills	32	Engaged & responsible citizen	33	Oral skills	38
	Effective team leader/s	32	Identify and define problems	29	Application of knowledge/theory	34
	Social/community responsibility	32	Personal development	29	Communicates in appropriate ways for particular purposes	34
	Open-minded	29	Reflection/ reflective practice	29	Understanding of social justice	34
	Capacity for cooperation/ collaboration	29	Ethical responsibility	29	Able to work in culturally/socially diverse environment	31
	Global perspective	29	Computer skills	29	Understanding & respect for indigenous culture	31
	Theoretical knowledge	26	Skills in information technology	29	Autonomous/self directed learner	28
	Discipline specific knowledge/skills for professional practice	26	Interpersonal skills	29	Intellectual curiosity	28
	Self management	26	Thinks locally, nationally, globally	29	Capable of making decisions	28
			Methodological knowledge & skills	25	Cross cultural sensitivity	28

		Ethical standards	25	Commitment to professional development	25
		Able to communicate knowledge and complex concepts	25	Self management	25
		Communicates with computer technologies	25	Ethical behaviour	25
		Environmental responsibility	25	Manages and uses information	25

Table 19.1: Results for the top three bands for each time slice

Graduate Attributes	1990s	2000-2005	2006-2010
Able to work independently		Band 2	Band 3
Appreciate and value diversity		Band 3	Band 3
Capacity for cooperation/collaboration	Band 3	Band 2	Band 2
Communication skills	Band 3	Band 2	Band 1
Creative thinking	Band 1	Band 1	Band 1
Critical/analytical thinking	Band 1	Band 1	Band 1
Cross-cultural sensitivity			Band 3
Effective team leader	Band 3		
Effective team member	Band 2	Band 2	Band 3
Environmental responsibility		Band 3	
Ethical member of society			Band 3
Ethical responsibility		Band 3	
Ethical standards		Band 3	
Expertise in chosen academic field	Band 3	Band 2	Band 1
Global perspective	Band 3	Band 3	Band 2
Engaged and responsible citizen		Band 3	
Lifelong learning	Band 2	Band 2	Band 3
Reflection/ reflective practice		Band 3	Band 3
Understanding and respect for indigenous culture			Band 3
Personal development		Band 3	
Professional skills/practice	Band 3		
Social/community responsibility	Band 3	Band 2	Band 2
Understanding of social justice		Band 3	Band 3
Sustainability			Band 3

Table 19.2: Summary results of selected graduate attributes across each time slice

Findings of the study

Two aspects of the thematic and frequency analyses are immediately obvious. First, there has been a significant increase in the number of graduate attributes tackled by the sector over time. It is unclear whether the curriculum is better defined and articulated than previously or that more content is forced into the curriculum than before. Of course, it is possible that graduate attributes are not reflected in the enacted and experienced curriculum. Second, the 1990s lists, particularly the top three bands, are dominated by attributes that are related to aspects of preparation for professional practice: for example, *critical and analytical thinking, effective team member, communication skills, professional skills* and *lifelong learning*. This theme also dominates the statements in subsequent time slices but the prevalence decreases slightly and many more attributes and themes are added.

In the second time slice, covering 2001–5, in addition to professional preparation there is a re-assertion of traditional academic concerns. The category *expertise in chosen academic field* moves from Band 3 (48 per cent) in the 1990s to Band 2 (58 per cent) in the early 2000s and into Band 1 (78 per cent) in the third time slice. Other categories that increase in popularity into the second time slice include: *global perspective, social/community responsibility, appreciates and values diversity, understanding of social justice, reflection or reflective practice, ethical standards or ethical member of society* and *environmental responsibility* (see Table 19.1).

The third time slice, 2006–10, continues to embrace the themes of professional preparation and traditional academic concerns and these are joined by many other attributes that have continued to increase in importance over the period considered for this study. Notably, *global perspective* and *social/community responsibility* occur in Band 2, meaning between half and three-quarters of universities see these categories as part of their intended curriculum. Other areas that show growth into this time slice are: *sustainability, able to work in culturally and socially diverse environments* and *understanding and respect for indigenous culture*.

Interesting trends can be seen in several categories and themes across the time period, some of which occur in Band 4 and are not captured in the tables. These include a small increase in mention of *research skills*; a slight decrease in *effective team member* but an increase in *capacity for*

Figure 19.1: Tag cloud for 2006–10

cooperation and collaboration; an increasing emphasis on cultural issues such as *cross-cultural sensitivity*; a shift of emphasis from *effective team leader* to *lead others*. The emphasis on the individual, revealed in categories such as *lifelong learning, able to work independently, respect for the rights of the individual, personal development* and *self-improvement*, peaks in the early 2000s and declines thereafter. Notions of community, such as *social/community responsibility, social justice* and *engaged and responsible citizen*, also peak in the early part of the 2000s but tend to remain at about the same level of popularity.

An analysis of the language used in the attribute statements adds support to these observations (Figure 19.1 and Table 19.3). Seventy per cent of the top 100 most frequent words from each time slice are common across the entire period. This may indicate a degree of conformity in the ways universities view their missions. The main changes in the language occur between the 1990s and early 2000s: Table 3 shows that 25 words only occur in the 1990s, with smaller changes thereafter. The 1990s' tag clouds have seven verbs, compared to twelve verbs in the early 2000s and 13 in the late 2000s, perhaps indicating a more action-based approach. The common words cluster around themes of traditional university learning (for example, *intellectual, information, knowledge, thinking*) and professional preparation (for example, *communication, professional, lifelong, skills, problem-solving, work*). Other common themes are *community, creative, culture, ethics, global/international, responsibility, technology* and *values*.

The words unique to the 1990s reinforce the observations from the thematic and frequency analysis. Of particular note are the words *individual* and *workplace* that do not occur in the 100 most frequent words outside this time slice. The subsequent time slices show interesting additional words, indicating shifts in emphasis: *context, contribute, diversity, indigenous* and *research*. The third time slice sees the inclusion of *environment* and *we* for the first time.

Words common across graduate attribute statements 1990s-2010		Words unique to 1990s graduate attributes	Words unique to 2000-2010 graduate attributes	Words unique to 2000-2005 graduate attributes	Words unique to 2006-2010 graduate attributes
ability/able	learning	academic	context/s	local	appreciate
analysis/	life	achieve	contribute	recognize	environment
analyse	lifelong	analysis	diversity	understand	innovative
apply	literacy	chosen	field		opportunities
appropriate	others	creativity	indigenous		we
attributes	own/ours	domain	learning		
awareness	personal	expected	perspectives		
capacity	practice	following	research		
commitment	problem/s	general	students		
communica-	professional	individual	study		
tion	range	learn	through		
community/	relevant	long	within		
communities	respect	more			
creative/	responsibility	one			
creativity	self	oral			
critical/	skills	own			
critically	social	plan			
cultural	solving	practical			
demonstrate	team	qualities			
develop/	technology	sense			
development	thinking	should			
discipline	understanding	standards			
effectively	university	teamwork			
ethical	use	which			
evaluate	values	workplace			
generic	work	written			
global	world				
graduate/s					
information					
intellectual					
international					
issues					
knowledge					

Table 19.3: Word cloud analysis of top 100 words 1990s–2010

Implications for student engagement

Articulating the intended curriculum is a necessary but insufficient first step in engaging students with their learning and with the wider community. Whilst these often grand and exciting ideas remain largely rhetorical, divorced from curriculum design and from what students actually experience on the ground (Bosanquet, Winchester-Seeto and Rowe, 2010), their potential to have impact on student engagement will be minimal. The authors have chosen three aspects to consider in more detail. First, *critical, analytical and creative thinking,* as these categories appear in Band 1 in all three time slices and are thus consistently considered to be important attributes across the sector; second, attributes that include a '*global*' or international aspect, as this has shown a substantial increase in popularity over the fifteen years; and finally, the use of experience-based learning as a curriculum response to the theme of 'preparation for professional practice', which has dominated the higher education agenda across the time span.

Creative and critical thinking

Creative and critical thinking emerged as one of the most frequently reported graduate attributes across all three time slices. Conceptually, however, there is a lack of agreement in the literature about how critical and creative thinking should be defined, making articulation of these skills as explicit learning objectives difficult. More recently there has been a move to combine the teaching of critical and creative thinking in line with the view that these skills are inseparable: creative thinking generates new ideas and possible solutions; critical thinking evaluates and assesses the validity of these ideas (Paul and Elder, 2005). Teaching creative thinking perhaps provides a greater challenge to university educators, not only because of disciplinary differences in how creative thinking is defined but also because of the reluctance of some disciplines to recognise the relevance of creative thinking to their field.

In the top 100 words featured in graduate-attribute statements, the term *creative* appears across all three time slices, whilst *creativity* appears only in the 1990s. *Innovation* appears for the first time in the top 100 words during 2006–10. Our findings suggest that while there is a stable emphasis on the cognitive processes involved in creative thinking, the end product (that is, creativity) is less of a focus from 2000 onwards. This may reflect a change in emphasis from the employability agenda of the 1990s to the recent focus on fostering graduates who are active citizens. Alternatively, it may mirror changing pedagogical perceptions of creativity and creative thinking. Traditionally creativity was defined and measured in terms of its outcomes; currently the focus is on the processes involved (Craft, 2003; McWilliam and Dawson, 2008).

Previous research has linked student engagement to critical and creative thinking but there is a notable lack of research in this area (Carini, Kuh and Klein, 2006). Thus, identifying an explicit relationship is challenging. However, some studies have found that many of the pedagogic practices used to teach critical and creative skills also enhance student engagement. In a review of the literature on critical thinking, Pithers and Soden (2000) identified the following teaching methods as effective: metacognitive and student-centred approaches, and self-regulated collaborative learning environments. Specific methods and approaches have also been linked to creative thinking. Examples include: an emphasis on learning for understanding rather than for content mastery (that is, on the process of learning rather than the outputs); the use of cooperative, socially integrative styles of teaching; and challenging students with real, demanding and exciting work (Cropley, 2001; Jackson, 2005; Knight, 2002; McWilliam and Dawson, 2008). The teacher–student relationship in particular has been identified as a central element in the development of creative thinking skills (Cole, Sugioka and Yamagata-Lynch, 1999). Empirical evidence supports the use of many of these methods in enhancing student engagement, particularly collaborative/cooperative learning.

The effectiveness of small group learning has received widespread attention in the literature and a positive link has been found between student engagement, higher order cognitive activities and collaborative learning (Smith et al., 2005; Umbach and Wawrzynski, 2005). There is strong experimental and correlational evidence that students engage in more complex cognitive activities when they are exposed to differing and opposing viewpoints during group learning activities (Reason, Cox and Quaye, 2010). Prince (2004) reports several meta-analyses that suggest that small group learning promotes a broad range of learning objectives, many of which are key aspects of student engagement. Enhanced interpersonal skills and perceptions of increased social support are two such examples. Both positively impact on student retention, particularly for students of under-represented groups (Prince, 2004). Smith et al. (2005) cite numerous studies that provide strong support for the positive impact of small group learning on student engagement in terms of students' academic performance, psychological adjustment at university, relationship building and positive attitudes towards learning. They also report a positive relationship between critical thinking and student participation, teacher encouragement and student interaction (Smith et al., 2005). Given the importance of relationships to the development of creative thinking in particular, small group learning is crucial to engaging students in this regard, resulting in improved social adjustment to university, integration into university life and sense of belonging with the institution (Prince, 2004; Smith et al., 2005; Tinto, 2010).

There is a growing body of evidence that engaging undergraduate students in research develops both creative and critical skills (Brew, 2009; Healey and Jenkins, 2009). Coincidentally, our study demonstrates a rising prominence of *research* as a category in graduate-attribute statements, particularly in the last five years. Hu, Scheuch, Schwartz, Gayles and Li (2008) cite a number of US studies that demonstrate the positive effects of participation by undergraduate students in research and creative activities on engagement, particularly in relation to personal skills and dispositions (for example, increased confidence and self-efficacy, broader career and study aspirations, communication skills, and emotional growth).

Many of the pedagogic practices outlined above are part of an active learning approach that aims to involve students much more in the learning process than traditional methods do. There is considerable empirical support for the success of active learning methods, particularly in enhancing conceptual understanding and addressing misconceptions (Prince, 2004). Some studies point to the role of one particular form, problem-based learning (PBL), in enhancing critical and problem-solving skills (Prince, 2004). PBL includes aspects of both active and small group learning and it seems reasonable to assume that PBL will enhance engagement of students with their studies, each other and potentially the institution. Recent literature on teaching creative thinking also emphasises the need to move away from traditional lecture-based formats which involve an instructive teaching style, to an active learning environment where students are encouraged to be autonomous, self-regulated learners (Duron, Limbach and Waugh, 2006; Jankowska and Atlay, 2008).

Global perspective

Over the last fifteen years, *global perspective(s)* as a graduate attribute has steadily increased in popularity, so that it is now part of the intended curriculum of more than half of Australian universities. Clifford and Joseph (2005) define global perspectives as building intercultural competence, as well as gaining skills in critical and reflective thinking and developing values and ethics of equity and social justice. Institutional descriptions incorporate multiple concepts including: internationalisation, global citizenship, intercultural awareness, globalisation, cross-cultural competency, social responsibility, inclusivity, diversity, sustainability, leadership, multiculturalism, participation and community engagement. Interestingly, many institutions include local and national issues, such as recognising and valuing indigenous perspectives, in the global perspective category.

Related graduate attributes, including *social/community responsibility, appreciate/value diversity, social justice* and *good citizen/citizenship*, also show an increase over time. Evident here is a transformative philosophy of higher education that asks students to "think, argue and act out alternative visions of the world" (Hanson, 2010, p.84). Leask says that an internationalised curriculum "must, at a minimum, cater to the rapidly changing and divergent needs of all students as global citizens" (2008, p.12). Despite this call to action, the multiplicity of terms – many of them ambiguous, contested or value-laden notions – creates conceptual fuzziness and negatively impacts on understandings of global perspectives in the intended, enacted and experienced curriculum.

Calls to change university curricula to incorporate global and intercultural perspectives into the student learning experience are widespread. This is driven by a number of factors, including government strategy – in Australia, the *Bradley Review of Higher Education* endorsed internationalising the delivery and content of courses (Bradley et al., 2008) – and demands from employers and professional bodies. For example, the Business and Higher Education Round Table notes the need for students to become internationally competitive graduates and global leaders (Hager, Holland and Beckett, 2002). Hanson refers to the "need for radical reform of curricula to foster engaged global citizenship" (2010, p.70). Leask, writing about internationalising the curriculum, similarly emphasises the requirements for "radical, rather than incremental, innovation – that is, new ways of conceptualising knowledge and the curriculum" (2008, p.13). Davies, Evans and Reid (2005) are more explicit in their call for educational revolution:

> We believe that national citizenship is now being weakened and that a new form of education is necessary... The long established frameworks associated with the relationship between statehood and education are... ready to be dismantled.
>
> (p.69)

Despite such lofty sentiments, Lunn notes that the extent to which global perspectives are developed depends for the most part on "individual enthusiasm and discretion" (2008, p.231). Academic resistance towards global perspectives as a graduate attribute, for instance, in relation to its conceptual ambiguity and implicit values and assumptions about the nature of higher education, has been well documented in the literature (Radloff et al., 2008; Shiel, 2006). In embedding a global perspective, university educators have taken a moderate approach to curriculum development. Many have focussed on teaching and learning strategies and assessment tasks at the individual unit level. For example, including international content on reading lists; providing culturally diverse case studies and examples; addressing issues of social justice, sustainability, equity, human rights and globalisation in course content; as well as utilising diverse teaching and learning strategies such as collaborative learning, critical reflection tasks, role plays and peer evaluation (Whalley, 1997). As with creative and critical thinking, previous research has linked student engagement to learning experiences where students engage with cultural diversity (Prince, 2004; Reason, Cox and Quaye, 2010). Extra-curricular experiential learning activities (for example, study abroad programmes; work-integrated learning in international contexts; and engagement with diverse community groups) offer an opportunity for students to develop this aspect of global perspectives. Evaluations of such programmes suggest significant benefits to students, particularly in relation to employability (Mohajeri, Norris and Gillespie, 2008; Fuller and Scott, 2009). For the most part, however, developing a global perspective finds its strongest expression in the intended curriculum.

There are multiple challenges for student engagement here. First, the proliferation of ideas and topics under the umbrella *global perspectives* makes developing strategic curriculum approaches and measuring their impact on student learning difficult. Second, building global perspectives through extra-curricular activities raises concerns about equity and access for students. Third, several researchers have noted challenges for students, in that experiential and transformational learning can cause discomfort or result in conflict (Clifford and Joseph, 2005; Krause, 2005).

For global perspectives as a graduate attribute to impact positively on student engagement, it is imperative for curricula to respond to the broader context of internationalisation and social inclusion in higher education. This includes recognising the complex challenges of and interactions between: the education of international students; offshore teaching; cotutelle programmes; international research partnerships and outside studies programmes; increasing community and industry engagement; higher mobility of staff and students between institutions; the massification or democratisation of higher education; international benchmarking; sector-wide funding pressures; and an increasing emphasis on measuring the standards and quality of research, teaching and learning and contributions to the community (Lunn, 2008; Leask, 2008). It also means responding to the diversity of student cohorts – students from families and communities who have not participated in higher education in the past; with disabilities; from low socio-economic status backgrounds; balancing study with paid work or caring responsibilities; mature age; off-campus students – to ensure that teaching global perspectives is not simply a part of the intended curriculum but is part of the enacted and experienced curriculum for all students.

Experience-based learning

The theme of *preparation for professional practice* has dominated graduate-attribute statements since they were first adopted in the 1990s and shows no sign of declining in popularity. The principal enacted curriculum response to date has been the increasing incorporation of experience-based learning (EBL) into the curriculum, for instance cooperative education and work-integrated learning in the US (Sovilla and Varty, 2004), Australia (Patrick et al., 2009) and New Zealand (Coll et al., 2009).

Work-integrated learning (WIL) and other similar ventures, such as cooperative education, work-based learning and practice-based learning, are viewed as "teaching and learning approach[es] which have the potential to provide a rich, active and contextualised learning experience for students which contributes to their engagement in learning" (McLennan, 2008, p.2). Research suggests that these programmes provide many benefits for students, as evidenced by lists collated by Dressler and Keeling (2004). In terms of student engagement, several benefits stand out: improved motivation to learn; increased commitment to educational goals and attachment to their university; increased adaptation to university life; higher retention rate; increased teamwork, sense of purpose and cooperation; and improved interpersonal relationships. The list demonstrates the potential of this style of learning to impact student engagement positively at many levels, such as engagement with studies, other students and the institution.

The reasons for the profound effect of EBL on students, their learning and engagement are not always clear. The effect, however, seems to extend beyond the particular experience, as this quote from a member of senior management at an Australian university demonstrates:

> Getting students experience in the work place is often very motivating – especially for students who aren't necessarily the highest achievers. That's why we have seen more courses taking up WIL [work-integrated learning]... as a mechanism to retain and let students see they are going somewhere.
>
> (Patrick et al., 2009, p.18)

As our study of graduate attributes shows, there has been a massive increase in popularity over the past fifteen years in the categories of *social/community responsibility* and *social justice*. In the United States, service learning has been used for many decades to address these concepts and as "a teaching strategy that enhances students' learning of academic content by engaging them in authentic activities in which they apply the content of the course to address identified needs in the local and broader community" (Furco, 2001, p.67). The balance between learning of academic content and community service varies from programme to programme.

In Australia, there is increased interest in using this style of learning, with its emphasis on mutual benefit for students, the educational institution and the partners and, most importantly, community service and engagement. One example is the Macquarie University Participation and Community Engagement initiative (PACE) that will allow all students to undertake a range of EBL activities, including service-learning opportunities, for credit and as part of their core curriculum. The Australian Catholic University for a number of years has required all students to undertake 120 hours of unpaid community service as a course requirement (Clinton and Thomas, 2010).

Astin et al. (2000) reported the results of a large scale, longitudinal study of college undergraduates and compared the results of students who participated in community service during their course with those of students who did not. They found that service participation showed significant positive effects on: academic performance, values, self-efficacy, leadership, choice of a service career and plans to participate in service after college. Analysis of their qualitative data suggests that service learning is effective because it facilitates several things, amongst which is increased engagement in the classroom experience. That is, there appears to be some spillover effect from the experience itself into other, more traditional teaching methods. The work of Astin et al. (2000) broadens the conception of student engagement benefits of service learning to include engagement with the wider community, outside the university, as well as engagement with learning and the institution.

In tandem with the rise in popularity of *social/community responsibility* as an attribute, is an increase in prominence of *reflection* and *reflective practice*. This category moves from Band 4 in the 1990s to Band 3, with the attribute appearing in 29 per cent of universities in the early 2000s and up to 41 per cent of universities in the late 2000s. Reflection is used extensively in most forms of EBL to support student learning (Coulson et al., 2010), particularly to connect field or work experience and community service with university learning (Boud and Walker, 1998; Astin et al., 2000), and is considered to be a necessary skill for professional practice (see, for example, McNamara, 2009). Because it is thought to have the capacity to challenge underlying beliefs, attitudes and values, it is often used in service learning (Coulson et al., 2010).

Billett's research (2009) suggests reflection before, during and after practical experience contributes to the development of the 'agentic professional', that is one who is pro-active and critically engaged. As reflection so clearly supports learning in EBL, it is an important component of any curriculum and teaching practice in this arena and contributes to the overall efficacy of EBL in promoting student engagement at all levels.

Conclusion

Universities are very good at articulating grand ideas about what their students will achieve. It is much harder to move from good intentions to offering a curriculum and teaching practices that will achieve these intentions. In this chapter we have explored some examples of curriculum approaches that not only respond to this challenge but have also been shown to have a positive impact on student engagement, such as small group teaching, undergraduate research, active learning, service learning and other forms of experience-based education. In these areas, graduate-attribute statements may be a way to drive positive curriculum changes.

Other, more nebulous attributes such as having a *global perspective* have proven to be more elusive and more difficult to embed in the curriculum. Indeed many of the attributes that are growing in popularity offer similar difficulties, for example *sustainability, ethics* and *cross-cultural sensitivity*. Failure to find ways of teaching these concepts and values will waste opportunities to help students engage effectively with the wider community.

Student engagement at all levels has consistently been shown to be a significant factor in the success of students in higher education. Moreover, it is now recognised and explored in the processes and metrics that are used to measure the success of institutions. It is therefore important for universities to ensure that their policies, curriculum and teaching practices promote such engagement or, at the very least, do not inhibit it.

References

Astin, A.W., Vogelgesang, L.J., Ikeda, E.K. and Yee, J.A. (2000) *How Service Learning Affects Students* (Los Angeles: Higher Education Research Institute, University of California). Retrieved from <http://www.heri.ucla.edu/PDFs/HSLAS/HSLAS.pdf>

Australian Council for Educational Research (ACER) (2010) *Doing More for Learning: Enhancing Engagement and Outcomes*. Retrieved from <http://ausse.acer.edu.au/images/docs/AUSSE_2009_Student_Engagement_Report.pdf>

Barrie, S.C. (2006) 'Understanding What We Mean by the Generic Attributes of Graduates', *Higher Education*, 51, pp.215–41.

Barrie, S.C. and Prosser, M. (2004) 'Generic Graduate Attributes: Citizens for an Uncertain Future', *Higher Education Research and Development*, 23/3, pp.243–6.

Billett, S. (2009) *Developing Agentic Professionals through Practice-Based Pedagogies*, Final report for the ALTC Associate Fellowship. Retrieved from <http://www.altc.edu.au>

Bosanquet, A., Winchester-Seeto, T. and Rowe, A. (2010) 'Changing Perceptions Underpinning Graduate Attributes: A Pilot Study', in Devlin, M., Nagy, J. and Lichtenberg, A. (eds) *Research and Development in Higher Education: Reshaping Higher Education*, 33, pp.105–17. 33rd HERDSA Annual International Conference, Melbourne, July 2010. Retrieved from <http://www.herdsa.org.au/wp-content/.../HERDSA2010_Bosanquet_A.pdf>

Boud, D. and Walker, D. (1998) 'Promoting Reflection in Professional Courses: The Challenge of Context', *Studies in Higher Education*, 23/2, pp.191–206.

Bowden, J., Hart, G., King, B., Trigwell, K. and Watts, O. (2002) *Generic Capabilities of ATN University Graduates* (Teaching and Learning Committee, Australian Technology Network). Retrieved from <http://www.clt.uts.edu.au/ATN.grad.cap.project.index.html>

Bradley, D., Noonan, P., Nugent, H. and Sacles, B. (2008) *Review of Australian Higher Education Final Report* (Canberra: Department of Education, Employment and Workplace Relations). Retrieved from <http://www.deewr.gov.au/HigherEducation/Review/Pages/ReviewofAustralianHigherEducationReport.aspx>

Brew, A. (2009) *Enhancing Undergraduate Experiences Through Research and Inquiry*, 32nd HERDSA Annual International Conference, Darwin,

July. Retrieved from <http://www.mq.edu.au/ltc/altc/ug_research/dissemination.htm>

Carini, R.M., Kuh, G.D. and Klein, S.P. (2006) 'Student Engagement and Student Learning: Testing the Linkages', *Research in Higher Education*, 47/1, pp.1–32.

Clifford, V. and Joseph, C. (2005) *Internationalisation of the Curriculum: An Investigation of the Pedagogical Practices at Monash University* (Melbourne: Monash University).

Clinton, I. and Thomas, T. (2010) 'Learning in the Community: Student Experience of Community Service', in Campbell, M. (ed.) *Work Integrated Learning – Responding to Challenges: Proceedings of the 2010 ACEN National Conference*, Perth, 29 September – 1 October 2010, pp.82–91.

Cole, D.G., Sugioka, H.L. and Yamagata-Lynch, L. (1999) 'Supportive Classroom Environments for Creativity in Higher Education', *Journal of Creative Behavior*, 33/4, pp.277–93.

Coll, R.K., Eames, C., Parku, L., Lay, M., Ayling, D., Hodges, D., Ram, S., Bhat, R., Fleming, F., Ferkins, L., Wiersman, C. and Martin, A. (2009) *An Exploration of the Pedagogies Employed to Integrate Knowledge in Work-Integrated Learning in New Zealand Higher Education Institutions*, Final Report, Teaching and Learning Research Initiative. Retrieved from <http://www.tlri.org.nz/assets/A_Project-PDFs/9263–Finalreport.pdf>

Coulson, D., Harvey, M., Winchester-Seeto, T. and Mackaway, J. (2010) 'Exploring Evidence for the Role of Reflection for Learning Through Participation', in Campbell, M. (ed.) *Work Integrated Learning – Responding to Challenges: Proceedings of the 2010 ACEN National Conference*, Perth, 29 September – 1 October 2010, pp.92–103.

Craft, A. (2003) 'The Limits to Creativity in Education: Dilemmas for the Educator', *British Journal of Educational Studies*, 51/2, pp.113–27.

Cropley, A.J. (2001) *Creativity in Education and Learning: A Guide for Teachers and Educators* (London: Kogan Page).

Davies, I., Evans, M. and Reid, A. (2005) 'Globalising Citizenship Education? A Critique of "Global Education" and "Citizenship Education"', *British Journal of Educational Studies*, 53/1, pp.66–89.

DEYTA (1999) *The Quality of Higher Education* (Canberra: Higher Education Division, Commonwealth of Australia). Retrieved from <http://www.dest.gov.au/archive/highered/pubs/quality/contents.htm#contents>

Dressler, S. and Keeling, A.E. (2004) 'Student Benefits of Cooperative Education', in Coll, R. and Eames, C. (eds) *International Handbook for Cooperative Education: An International Perspective on the Theory, Research and Practice of Work-Integrated Learning* (Boston, MA: World Association for Cooperative Education) pp.217–36.

Duron, R., Limbach, B. and Waugh, W. (2006) 'Critical Thinking Framework for Any Discipline', *International Journal of Teaching and Learning in Higher Education*, 17/2, pp.160–6.

EHEA (2010) *European Higher Education Area: the Official Bologna Process Website 2010–2012*. Retrieved from <http://www.ehea.info/>

Fredericks, J., Blumenfeld, P. and Paris, A. (2004) 'School Engagement: Potential of the Concept, and State of the Evidence', *Review of Educational Research*, 74/1, pp.59–109.

Fuller, T. and Scott, G. (2009) 'Employable Global Graduates: The "Edge" that Makes the Difference', in *Teaching and Learning for Global Graduates: Proceedings of the 18th Annual Teaching Learning Forum*, 29–30 January, Curtin University of Technology, Perth. Retrieved from <http://otl.curtin.edu.au/tlf/tlf2009/refereed/fuller.html>

Furco, A. (2001) 'Advancing Service Learning at Research Universities', in Canada, M. and Speck, B.W. (eds) *Developing and Implementing Service Learning Programs* (San Francisco: Jossey-Bass) pp.67–78.

Hager, P., Holland, S. and Beckett, D. (2002) *Enhancing the Learning and Employability of Graduates: The Role of Generic Skills* (B-HERT Position Paper) (Melbourne, Australia: Business/Higher Education Round Table).

Hanson, L. (2010) 'Global Citizenship, Global Health, and the Internationalization of Curriculum: A Study of Transformative Potential', *Journal of Studies in International Education*, 14/1, pp.70–88.

Harvey, A. and Kamvounias, P. (2008) 'Bridging the Implementation Gap: A Teacher-As-Learner Approach to Teaching and Learning Policy', *Higher Education Research and Development*, 27/1, pp.31–41.

Healey, M. and Jenkins, A. (2009) 'Developing Undergraduate Research and Inquiry', *Higher Education Academy*. Retrieved from <http://www.heacademy.ac.uk/assets/import%20assets%20here/documents/ourwork/research/DevelopingUndergraduateResearchandInquiry.pdf>

Hu, S., Scheuch, K., Schwartz, R.A., Gayles, J.G. and Li, S. (2008) 'Reinventing Undergraduate Education: Engaging College Students in Research and Creative Activities', *ASHE Higher Education Report*, 33/4.

Hughes, C. and Barrie, S. (2010) 'Influences on the Assessment of Graduate Attributes in Higher Education', *Assessment and Evaluation in Higher Education*, 35/3, pp.325–34.

Jackson, N. (2005) 'Making Higher Education a More Creative Place', *Journal for the Enhancement of Learning and Teaching*, 2/1, pp.14–25.

Jankowska, M. and Atlay, M. (2008) 'Use of Creative Space in Enhancing Students' Engagement', *Innovations in Education and Teaching International*, 45/3, pp.271–9.

Jones, A. (2009) 'Redisciplining Generic Attributes: The Disciplinary Context in Focus', *Studies in Higher Education*, 34/1, pp.85–100.

Knight, P. (2002) 'Notes on a Creative Curriculum', *Palatine Working Paper: Notes Prepared for the Imaginative Curriculum Project*, HEA, UK. Retrieved from <http://www.palatine.ac.uk/files/943.pdf>

Krause, K. (2005) *Understanding and Promoting Student Engagement in University Learning Communities*, paper presented at the James Cook University Symposium, 21–22 September, Townsville/Cairns. Retrieved from <http://www.cshe.unimelb.edu.au/pdfs/Stud_eng.pdf>

Krause, K. and Coates, H. (2008) 'Students' Engagement in First-Year University', *Assessment and Evaluation in Higher Education*, 33/5, pp.493–505.

Kuh, G.D. (2001) *Assessing What Really Matters to Student Learning: Inside the National Survey of Student Engagement*. Retrieved from <http://cpr.iub.edu/uploads/Assessing_What_Really_Matters_To_Student_Learning_(Kuh,%202001).pdf>

Leask, B. (2008) 'Internationalisation, Globalisation and Curriculum Innovation', in Hellsten, M. and Reid, A. (eds) *Researching International Pedagogies: Sustainable Practice for Teaching and Learning in Higher Education* (Dordrecht: Springer) pp.9–26.

Lunn, J. (2008) 'Global Perspectives in Higher Education: Taking the Agenda Forward in the United Kingdom', *Journal of Studies in International Education*, 12/3, pp.231–54.

Marsh, C.J. and Willis, G. (2007) *Curriculum: Alternative Approaches, Ongoing Issues* (4th edn) (Upper Saddle River, NJ: Merrill Prentice Hall).

McInnis, C. (2002) 'Signs of Disengagement? Responding to the Changing Work and Study Patterns of Full-Time Undergraduates in Australian Universities', in Enders, J. and Fulton, O. (eds) *Higher Education in a Globalising World: International Trends and Mutual Observations* (Dordrecht: Kluwer Academic) pp.175–90.

McLennan, B. (2008) *Work-Integrated Learning (WIL) in Australian Universities: The Challenges of Mainstreaming WIL*, paper presented at the Career Development Learning – Maximising the Contribution of Work Integrated Learning to the Student Experience, NAGCAS Symposium, Melbourne, Australia, 2008. Retrieved from <http://tls.vu.edu.au/vucollege/LiWC/resources/NAGCASpaper-final10June08.pdf>

McNamara, J. (2009) *A Collaborative Model for Learning and Assessment of Legal Placements*, paper presented at WACE 16th World Conference, Vancouver.

McWilliam, E. and Dawson, S. (2008) 'Teaching for Creativity: Towards Sustainable and Replicable Pedagogical Practice', *Higher Education*, 56, pp.633–43.

Mohajeri Norris, E. and Gillespie, J. (2008) 'How Study Abroad Shapes Global Careers: Evidence from the United States', *Journal of Studies in International Education*, 13/3, pp.382–97.

Patrick, C., Peach, D., Pocknee, C., Webb, F., Fletcher, M. and Pretto, G. (2009) *The WIL [Work Integrated Learning] Report: A National Scoping Study*, Australian Learning and Teaching Council (ALTC) Final Report (Brisbane: Queensland University of Technology). Retrieved from <http://www.acen.edu.au>

Paul, R. and Elder, L. (2005) *The Thinker's Guide to Critical and Creative Thinking* (Tomales, CA: Foundation for Critical Thinking).

Pithers, R.T. and Soden, R. (2000) 'Critical Thinking in Education: A Review', *Educational Research*, 42/3, pp.237–49.

Precision Consultancy (2007) *Graduate Employability Skills: A Report Prepared for the Business, Industry and Higher Education Collaboration Council* (Canberra: Commonwealth of Australia). Retrieved from <http://www.dest.gov.au/NR/rdonlyres/E58EFDBE-BA83–430E-A541–2E91BCB59DF1/20214/GraduateEmployabilitySkillsFINALREPORT1.pdf>

Prince, M. (2004) 'Does *Active Learning* Work? A Review of the Research', *Journal of Engineering Education*, 93/3, pp.223–31.

Radloff, A., de la Harpe, B., Dalton, H., Thomas, J. and Lawson, A. (2008) 'Assessing Graduate Attributes: Engaging Academic Staff and Their Students', *ATN Assessment 08: Engaging Students with Assessment*. Retrieved from <http://www.ojs.unisa.edu.au/index.php/atna/article/view/342/279>

Reason, R.D., Cox, B.E. and Quaye, B.R.L. (2010) 'Faculty and Institutional Factors That Promote Student Encounters with Difference in First-Year Courses', *The Review of Higher Education*, 33/3, pp.391–414.

Scott, G. (2008) *University Student Engagement and Satisfaction with Learning and Teaching* (Canberra: DEEWR). Retrieved from <http://www.deewr.gov.au/HigherEducation/Review/Documents/Scott.pdf>

SHEEC (2010) *Graduates for the 21st Century: Integrating the Enhancement Themes*. Retrieved from <http://www.enhancementthemes.ac.uk/themes/21stCGraduates/

Shiel, C. (2006) 'Developing the Global Citizen', *Academy Exchange*, 6: 18–20.

Smith, K.A., Sheppard, S.D., Johnson, D.W. and Johnson, R.T. (2005) 'Pedagogies of Engagement: Classroom-Based Practices', *Journal of Engineering Education*, 94/1, pp.87–101.

Sovilla, E.S. and Varty, J.W. (2004) 'Cooperative Education in the USA, Past and Present: Some Lessons Learned', in Coll, R.K. and Eames, C. (eds) *International Handbook for Cooperative Education: An International Perspective of the Theory, Research and Practice of Work-Integrated Learning* (Boston: World Association for Cooperative Education) pp.3–16.

Thorn, S. (2000) 'Data Analysis in Qualitative Research', *Evidence Based Nursing*, 3, pp.68–70.

Tinto, V. (2010) 'From Theory to Action: Exploring the Institutional Conditions for Student Retention', in Smart, J.C. (ed.) *Higher Education: Handbook of Theory and Research*, Vol. 25 (London: Springer) pp.51–89. Retrieved from <http://www.springerlink.com/content/t038280147422014/fulltext.pdf>

Umbach, P.D. and Wawrzynski, M.R. (2005) 'Faculty Do Matter: The Role of College Faculty in Student Learning and Engagement', *Research in Higher Education*, 46/2, pp.153–84.

UNESCO (1998) *World Declaration on Higher Education for the Twenty-First Century: Vision and Action*. Retrieved from <http://www.unesco.org/education/educprog/wche/declaration_eng.htm>

US Department of Education (2006) *A Test of Leadership: Charting the Future of US Higher Education* (Washington, DC). Retrieved from <http://www2.ed.gov/about/bdscomm/list/hiedfuture/reports/final-report.pdf>

Whalley, T. (1997) *Best Practice Guidelines for Internationalizing the Curriculum* (Victoria, BC: Ministry of Education, Skills and Training). Retrieved from <http://www.jcu.edu.au/teaching/idc/groups/public/documents/ebook/jcuprd_018292.pdf>

Winchester-Seeto, T. and Bosanquet, A. (2009) *Will Students Notice the Difference? Embedding Graduate Capabilities in the Curriculum*, 32nd HERDSA Annual International Conference, Darwin, July. Retrieved from <http://www.herdsa.org.au/wp-content/.../HERDSA2009_Winchester-Seeto_T.pdf>

Zepke, N. and Leach, L. (2010) 'Improving Student Engagement: 10 Proposals for Action', *Active Learning in Higher Education*, 11/3, pp.167–77.

Chapter 20

Discourse and dialogue in student engagement

Angela Voerman and Ian Solomonides

Macquarie University, Australia

The idea of student engagement has grown from a number of strategies of inquiry into the experience of university students: those designed to explore the ways in which students encounter the everyday practices and experiences of university; those designed to map a developmental process associated with university attendance; and those that more generally look to measure the efficacy of university learning. Some of these inquiries have looked closely at the behaviours associated with study, learning and participation in university communities. It is these in particular that have been mobilised at institutional and policy levels in developing and monitoring processes of quality enhancement and assurance, criteria that might be related to funding, benchmarking between institutions and the meeting of national agendas in the production of citizen workers.

The need to understand the experience and worth of a 'university education' has been driven by important questions about the value of university in determining the courses of individual lives. As such, these questions play into the deep concerns that have preoccupied researchers in Britain, the United States, Australia and many other places about the ways in which education can lead to greater social equity and inclusion, and the distribution of the value that university education can give to individuals (OECD, 2009). Studies that look at the experience of the first year of university implicitly look at what makes students either stay or drop out, interrogating contextual aspects of higher education that impact upon the decisions of individuals to stay or go (Thomas, 2002; Gibbs, 2010); and sometimes these inquiries can take on a broader historical or social perspective as they address the changing nature of the world for which higher education is meant to prepare students (Barnett, 2007; Bock, 2005). There are already tensions, then, between an inquiry driven by concerns about the ways in which individuals interact with the contexts of higher education; normative understandings of the place of higher education in producing and maintaining certain kinds of understanding; and the production of individuals with particular views of knowledge and its relationship to the social and economic world. These sometimes-divergent aims are envisioned in the Australian government's recent policy statements:

> Self-fulfilment, personal development and the pursuit of knowledge as an end in itself; the provision of skills of critical analysis and independent thought to support full participation in civil society, the preparation of leaders for diverse global environments; and support for a highly productive and professional labour force should be key features of Australia's higher education.
>
> (DEEWR, 2009b, p.7)

In support of the above, student engagement has been identified as an important component of the notion of quality in higher education. The Australian government has made the purpose of this more explicit in the measures that it proposes to include in the framework for higher education performance funding. In March 2008 (DEEWR, 2008), the government initiated a review to examine the future direction of the higher education sector known as the Bradley Review, after the chair of the panel, Emeritus Professor Denise Bradley, former Vice-Chancellor and President of the University of South Australia. The review recommended that:

> comparative information about institutional performance on the Course Experience Questionnaire and the Australasian Survey of Student Engagement should be published... as well as broad details of actions taken by institutions to address issues identified through student feedback.
>
> (DEEWR, 2008, p.xxvii)

To put it plainly, the government was concerned about falling behind other OECD countries and saw it necessary to develop robust measures of student engagement and satisfaction to encourage universities to develop themselves towards these ends.

Engagement embraces a variety of constructs of the ways in which students relate to learning. Behavioural notions of engagement, for example, recognise that effective learning requires an active process on the part of an individual (Markwell, 2007; Frederiks, Blumenfeld and Paris, 2004; Kuh, 2009). Being active can mean formal academic activities, such as attendance at classes, completion of set work, time spent 'on task'; but it can also mean participation in more informal aspects of university life including socialising on campus, living on campus, engaging in student and sporting groups or just doing work with peers or teachers. Some behavioural measures also look at engagement in what is loosely termed 'culture'. But what drives the wish to be active, to behave in these ways; and what does being active in these ways lead to within individuals?

Other models of engagement explore the emotional and cognitive domains, sometimes overlapping and blurring conceptually. Emotional engagement can relate to positive or negative feelings about peers, lecturers or administrative and support staff, about the content or ways of learning and about place. It encompasses the general principle of engagement as a sense of belonging but it is also inextricably linked with ways of learning. The emotional responses that students have to encountering ways of learning and knowledge-making challenge the rituals and strategies with which they approach difficult and new problems (Perkins, 2007).

What is evident is a complexity of the demands placed on the concept of engagement: from individual to society-wide engagement; from the practices at an individual's desk to the benchmarking of institutions. If these are the high stakes of the concept, it is vital to interrogate the measures that are meant to foster it.

As a case study, then, we will explore the results of a piloting of the Australasian University Survey of Student Engagement (AUSSE) (see Coates, 2010) across a sample of two faculties (Business and Humanities) at a major Australian university. The questions raised in practice relate to the ways in which such measures can be used to drive critical reflection on the implementation of university curricula. In particular, the efficacy of measuring student engagement in different disciplinary environments will be explored, as will the possible disaggregation of institutional results to the level of individual faculties. We must also ask what norms of learning and teaching are existing measures of student engagement built on and implicitly reinforcing. Indeed, as engagement measures are increasingly referred to in making comparisons between institutions of different nations (Coates, 2010) we must also ask whether they are sensitive to variations in the ways in which students live out the intersections between life, learning and work within these different countries and contexts.

The use of engagement measures does pose a bit of an existential crisis for universities. What does it mean to 'engage with engagement measures'? What are the limits on the influence that engagement measures can have on what students actually experience in the classroom and can the use of engagement measures actually enhance the experience of students? In other words, can they interact in a positive way with the practice of teaching and in the design of the university's physical, social and intellectual environs? More importantly, do enhancement strategies employed in everyday practice show up as improvements in engagement measures?

There is reason to be sceptical about these questions; for example, Koljatic and Kuh (2001) reported a longitudinal study that demonstrated minimal variation in the frequency of involvement in three key educational practices: cooperation with peers, active learning and faculty–student interaction. Nevertheless, there has been a proliferation of surveys that attempt to interrogate and measure the experience of students at university (Barrie, Ginns and Symons, 2008). What stands as a dilemma from these studies is whether the language of assessment used by researchers, teachers, support staff and others is asking the questions that have full bearing on what engagement means in practice to students.

Our own attempt to explore this was in a sample of Macquarie University faculties and departments. Within a wider context of curriculum renewal and based on the piloting of the AUSSE, a project was designed to enhance the critical reflection and pedagogic practice of staff and to promote some collaboration in research with interested students. The challenges of this project were (a) to communicate the idea of a survey of student engagement and (b) to investigate how staff structuring of teaching and learning activities might be related to the survey responses and to student demands and expectations.

There are two ways in which the AUSSE has been used at Macquarie. The Australian Council for Educational Research (ACER) administers it annually by email to a sample of students. This is the conventional institutionalised way of administering such surveys and is modelled upon the way in which the NSSE has evolved in the United States. An alternative way is described in this chapter – one that is dynamically linked with practice but that has significant implications in terms of resources, most significantly, time.

A group of staff and student collaborators, active and engaged honours and postgraduate students, was convened in the Faculty of Arts (a large humanities faculty). Students enrolled in first-year units were the subjects so that we could start to think about the way in which engagement was linked with the emerging study patterns that students start to follow through their degrees. This also allowed for the project to concentrate on establishing a dialogue with the convenors of first-year units. For purposes of comparison, the AUSSE was also administered to a large cohort of students in the Business Faculty. Three stages in this project will be described:

- Initial exploration of the AUSSE questions and explorations of the terrain of engagement in the interested departments
- Administration of the AUSSE and
- Using the information from the AUSSE.

Initial exploration of the AUSSE questions and explorations of the terrain of engagement in the interested departments

To develop a sense of ownership in the study, we started by canvassing the idea of engagement by discussing the questions that comprise the AUSSE and thinking about how relevant they were to Macquarie students. Most discussion focussed upon the 28 items in the first section of the survey that report the frequencies of various learning behaviours and interactions. This was quite challenging for staff because in effect the survey proposes norms of desirable practice that sometimes collide with what academics perceive as good scholarship within a particular discipline. To illustrate this, several items invite students to reflect on online educational tasks, access to the library or the exchange of emails with staff, such as:

About how often have you:

- Asked questions or contributed to discussions in class or online?
- Used library resources on campus or online?
- Used email or a forum to communicate with teaching staff?

There were extensive and heated discussions about the value of online repositories or activities – such as pictures of objects, access to readings, access to the library and other more interactive kinds of learning materials. In some kinds of scholarship it is access to and interaction with, and perhaps construction of, real objects that is intrinsic to the scholarship. It is possible then that hours in the library, museum, laboratory or workshop can be viewed as intrinsic to the field. And perhaps this is seen as going hand in hand with a kind of apprenticeship model around the interaction between lecturer and student. That means that staff maintaining a contrary pedagogy have to defend against the idea that there 'should' be online discussion, collaboration or access to the ideas and materials of the course for those who cannot attend the campus. The dilemma in the context of this discussion is what the relationship between staff and student demand should be. What such arguments begin to articulate is the complexity of discipline-based perspectives of engagement.

Another aspect of this preparation or pre-implementation phase was to look further at the ways in which staff and students perceived engagement. As the example shown above demonstrates, there was already a sense from student feedback that some of the expectations within disciplinary cultures did not align with student demands. What does this lack of alignment mean for students? Does engagement mean that they need somehow to be inducted into the ways in which staff view the desirable disciplinary behaviours or feel attachment and belonging in a disciplinary space? What are the limits around which various scholastic practices should be defended?

Discussion of the items in the survey was quite productive. Course leaders also decided to go through the same process with the tutors teaching the course. The AUSSE questions, then, functioned as foci for developing conversations about teaching and teaching practice. This remains a nagging question because the *petitio principii* implied here is that the process of discussion and reflection is essentially a good and productive one that leads to improvement. At the start of this section, we mentioned the study that looks at the negligible impact of many years of using student feedback upon some key practices that focus on interaction. We have to ask whether the act of discussion does have a bearing on the potential climate for student engagement and upon practice, and we have to wonder what engagement measures are actually measuring.

But what did engagement mean to the participants? We decided at this stage to do a qualitative study within the group, asking the staff and postgraduate student-tutors about their own images of engagement. We did this by exploring how they got to be where they are, on the basis that they were an embodiment of successful engagement in study. They were asked to describe their journeys as scholars, to recall their experience as students, to think about mentors that they had been supported by and then to describe what they considered engagement to be.

A number of characteristics were revealed in this discussion that, at face value, are unsurprising and consistent with the relational model of student engagement presented earlier (Solomonides, Reid and Petocz, Chapter 1, this volume). The most consistent of these was the passionate and all-consuming identity with a discipline. These participants constructed their trajectories into academic life by recounting narratives of academic success and conviction that often began in childhood. For example, in describing their professional formation, one member of the group said:

> Okay, well, for me it came through a childhood passion for archaeology and I wanted to be an archaeologist since I was 12. I never left this path, I always pursued it... so I went to, finished high school, went to university, did my doctoral degree and in, during my studies I worked professionally in the area and so when I finished my PhD I then proceeded to go on a post-doc for two years to North America and while I was there in my last year I saw the job advertisement here at Macquarie. I applied for it and I got it and that was all 12 years ago and here I am.
>
> (Subject 1)

> ...very quickly I started working within the department and doing little bits, little works, little jobs, and then from that basically I never left. I guess I've never left university from that point on, so I did my degree; before I finished my degree, they encouraged me to continue and do honours. Once I did honours, that was the first first-class honours that they had in the department, so they pushed me to continue onwards and into more post-graduate studies, at the same time, giving me any sort of job that I could possibly have at the time, and as I say, I never left.
>
> (Subject 4)

> My world of interest. As a kid, I was a nerd, you know. I really wanted to be a scientist. That's what I wanted to do. But at the same time I found that I always had an interest in humanities. I suppose that was an academic interest at school. But also from... I came from a traditional, scholarly... family. So I was sort of infused with sort of the classics and those stories and from classic literature and so forth. So I grew up with these stories of kingdoms slogging out and sort of warriors fighting and all that sort of business. So I guess I had two paths to get to where I am today. I had that sort of formal path of education, but also that cultural tradition.
>
> (Subject 3)

Another strong characteristic of academic staff related to their understanding of engagement as being a project of self-direction. Subject 4 above relates his pursuit of study to the encouragement of his lecturers and of a key colleague. This is in contrast with a notion of engagement that sees the love of study as a steady state, as something completely inner:

> So I just did two third of a second BA, filled up with units that I had not known about and I just wanted to do for pure enjoyment. I was a very self-directed learner and I did not see that as being, laying the foundations for a career by any means.
>
> (Subject 1)

> I don't think it's separate from my whole life. It's not just a job, if that's what you're asking. It's not just a nine to five. I guess I'm

> detached in the way that it can be a nine to five thing, in the sense that, as a job, I can switch off and go home and what have you. But no. It's sort of – I think it's one of those things that's sort of inside you that it's what you want to do, it's what you are. When I'm at home reading for pleasure for example, I might be reading something related to my interests. If that's what you mean.
>
> (Subject 3)

A third characteristic of these lecturers was ambivalence about their academic success or a reluctance to attribute it to mentoring. This is a crucial point to explore because of what it may mean about how the role of a teacher is conceived. How do lecturers understand the ways in which engagement measures assume that engagement is fostered? One of the outcomes of the engagement research centred on the NSSE and the work of George Kuh has been the publication *High Impact Educational Practices* (Kuh, 2008). The characteristics reported by Kuh as fostering increased rates of engagement and retention are for the most part focused around active learning and the scaffolding of relationships, learning communities that link students with other students, and students with lecturers:

- First-year seminars and experiences
- Common intellectual experiences
- Learning communities
- Writing intensive courses
- Collaborative assignments and projects
- Undergraduate Research
- Diversity/global Learning
- Service Learning, community-based Learning
- Internships
- Capstone courses and projects.

(Kuh, 2008)

Items in the AUSSE that explore this, and that challenge lecturing staff in many ways, include:

About how often have you:

- Participated in a community-based project as part of your study?
- Talked about your career plans with teaching staff or advisors?
- Discussed ideas from your readings with teaching staff outside class?
- Worked harder than you could to meet the teacher/tutor's standards or expectations?

Which of the following have you done or do you plan to do before you graduate from this institution?

- Practicum, internship, fieldwork or clinical placement
- Industry placement or work experience
- Community service or volunteer work
- Participating in a study group or learning community
- Work in a research project with a staff member outside of course requirements
- Study a foreign language
- Study abroad or student exchange
- Culminating final-year experience (for example, honours thesis, comprehensive exam, etc.)
- Independent study or self-designed major

All of these items assume an active involvement on the part of lecturers both in providing rich social learning experiences, in maintaining and developing links between the lives of students on campus, within a discipline and in the context of a life beyond university. Learning here is an activity around making meaning of one's self as well as of a growing disciplinary expertise (see for example, Barnett, 2007). Lecturers are aware of the need that students have for contact with them but it is often contextualised as an issue of control and of managing workload:

> They do, they tend to come up and talk to me afterwards and particularly if they are having problems. The older, more confident students

> will do that. The middle-aged people in particular. I do explain to them – if they want me to do something that I do not think is useful for them such as giving them entire scripts of my lectures – I try and explain that they need to learn to take their own notes, it is part of the process. I do respond to them but I do not automatically do what they ask me to do. It is mainly one-to-one after the lecture that that happens. Or they email me, because I put my email on all the documents. And quite often they do not want to contact the tutors, they want to go straight to the top and contact me.
>
> (Subject 1)

Now it would be very easy here to characterise this discussion as being centred on the mismatch between student needs and expectations and lecturers' visions of learning and engagement. A student participant in the project reported that it was not until her third year at university that a staff member called her by her name. While it is evident that there are these mismatches, there are also issues around educational cultures that are inherent in the structure of the AUSSE.

The AUSSE has been developed for use in Australia through the work of ACER and Hamish Coates. Its origin is in the extensive work of two American Institutions, the National Center for Higher Education Management Systems (NCHEMS) and the Center for Postsecondary Research and School of Education at Indiana University, led at the time by George Kuh. As such, it contains the story of an educational culture that is centred upon university as primarily an on-campus residential experience. In addition, students often share a core curriculum of study in liberal arts, most notably the development of writing and speaking skills. Whilst the ideal of the administration of the AUSSE is to provide comparative rankings of engagement between universities both nationally and internationally, in practice the assumptions underpinning this measure are often difficult and confronting for lecturers concentrating on one particular discipline.

The survey concentrates on the behaviours that constitute the life of the student. This is done through the prism of time: time on task with work, reading, writing, preparation and participation in class; but also time spent on travel, work, family responsibilities, rest and relaxation. It is possible to interpret this in an instrumental way as saying that less social life and relaxation and more time on academic task mean higher engagement. There is also the potential for these measures to contain a vision of the whole person of the student. Such an idea of engagement "helps to develop habits of the mind and heart that enlarge their capacity for continuous learning and personal development" (Kuh, 2003 in Kuh, 2009, p.5). Is this asking too much in the context of practice? Can the responses to the survey contain an indication of this enlargement of mind?

Questions raised by administering the engagement survey

It is becoming less the norm for surveys around satisfaction and engagement to be administered face to face. In this study, however, the cooperation of individual lecturers with the encouragement of faculty leadership meant that we had the opportunity to administer the survey to reasonably large cohorts of students (1,520 students in total across two faculties, representing approximately 10 per cent of the student group). It was useful to get feedback from the students as they completed the survey and especially useful to observe how long some students took to complete the survey properly. There was, as one might expect, considerable variation between cohorts of students being able to comprehend the questions. Many students were observed to need the dictionary, primarily those whose first language is not English. In addition, the rate of missing data toward the end of the survey saw students across the board becoming weary of the length of the survey. Many students were also sceptical about the use of identifying data such as their student number. They were, however, very positive about being asked about their experience at university. Finally, we need to note that those who completed the survey were only those who attended lectures. We did not sample those who chose not to attend lectures, those who were studying in flexible or distance mode or, for that matter, those who could not manage to complete the survey.

What have we actually learnt from the administration of the survey? What can we say are the links between engagement measures and the outcomes of students at university? After commissioning an initial statistical exploration of our results, we have some scepticism about the links between engagement measures and possible outcomes. We also observe the limited efficacy of the engagement scales structured into the AUSSE

(Petocz, 2009). We do not intend in this chapter to explore the statistics fully but it appears that there are grounds to be sceptical about the predictive validity of such measures, sometimes because of doubts about the self-reporting of student experience (Pike, 1999) and more critical explorations of the statistical validity of the instruments (see, for example, Korzekwa, 2010).

It seems that the most important (and statistically significant) factors, as measured by the AUSSE scales and the statements made by students about whether they would attend Macquarie if they were to start over again, were the following. Firstly, the likelihood of a student having a positive view of their experience or to wishing to repeat it depended on which faculty they were in. Secondly, if they had done better (as measured by their average grade), they had a more positive experience and were more inclined to repeat it. Thirdly, if they viewed the academic challenge to be higher, they were more likely to report a positive experience and re-attendance intentions. Finally, a more supportive learning experience made for more positive overall experience and there were possible small effects of work-integrated learning or staff–student interaction on re-attendance, but not in the expected direction. Overall grade seems to be a good predictor of overall experience and re-attendance; it appears to measure ability to a certain extent, with some limited measure of application or engagement itself. There may be an assumption that if students reported a positive educational experience and re-attendance intentions then they were more engaged with their studies – but this is an assumption that needs empirical and theoretical support.

So what other forms of data might we look at to make sense of or enhance what we have found in the AUSSE? We return here to the student members of the team. What drew these students to the project was their involvement in a mentoring group founded by students to support and mentor other students in their discipline or in the transition-to-university programme run centrally in the university. In their explorations of what university means to them (and of what engagement means), they explore much more directly the ways in which they make meaning of their lives. As one of the student-tutors described:

> I mean, I'm just the typical Uni student who does casual work wherever, but it does have a big place in my life. When I see people who

> are like family members who I haven't seen in a while, it's always brought up, what I'm doing, so it's a big part of my life. I suppose that by kind of default, Uni then is a big part of my life as well. And I do a lot of things at Uni. I work with the mentors. I do volunteer stuff here; I work with the PR department and stuff, so yeah, don't ask about the long-term plan.
>
> (Subject 6)

And when others were asked, "So in terms of your own engagement then, what would it take to make you feel that you want to keep on doing what you're doing?" one replied:

> To have someone ask me how I am. To have someone ask me how it's going and to say ask the question is there anything I can do? That's it. But obviously for them to be real, not for them be "are you okay?", okay I've asked that question, "anything you need?", okay I've asked that question. It has to be real and obviously I suppose – you know I'm not talking about a utopian situation here – I also understand that personality has got an enormous amount to do with it.
>
> (Subject 5)

> Doing this time like we're doing at the legal centre has been really good because I'm thinking for a while: "Gosh I'm never going to make it. I'm not a competitive person. I'm not interested in the corporate world. I'm not going to have a life. I'm not going to get a job. I'm not going to be any good." But at the legal centre they deal with people a lot more and I find that would keep me going. I could do that for life. People come in with problems and you solve them, it's great. It's different every day so that's fabulous. It's given me some hope. Sorry did I go off the question there?
>
> (Subject 7)

These students, then, are searching for authenticity and purposefulness in the conduct of their life both in the university environment but also in the context of a future life that they are building. They are actively building identity, making meaning, internalising the actions, roles and functions that they perform at university (Castells, 2004, pp.5–12).

Conclusion

We are left to reflect on both the transcendental and the prosaic; the need for hope and meaning, the wish to do things that one loves, the need to have a life and be useful. Returning to our statistical analysis, the most predictive and statistically significant responses related to student satisfaction and to whether they would make the decision to come to the same institution again if they had the chance. What is it that these questions contain for students? Could it be that what they allow students to express is a plain measure of happiness, of social integration? Other work points to the importance of students developing supportive friendship networks to sustain them when difficulties arise and of unhappiness when this does not occur (Yorke and Longden, 2008, p.48).

Finally, there is the issue of the boundaries between the world of the university and work, boundaries that are more and more permeable for most students. Research does show that full-time students working up to eight hours a week are equally as likely to complete as those who do not work. After this, they become progressively less likely to complete the more hours they spend at work (Polidano and Zakirova, 2011, p.8). However, "full time students who find a job they would like as a career while studying are estimated to be around four percentage points more likely to complete study than those who do not work in a career job" (Polidano and Zakirova, 2011, p.9). The student-tutors who took part in our study had been initiated into the university as a workplace to a greater or lesser extent. They were in the enviable position of having a working life within the context of their study. But this is not the case for the majority of students. We know that the majority of them do have some work and that many of them have little time for relaxation or socialising. What we cannot tell is what this means to them and what it means to the way in which they encounter their study.

We also need to be mindful of the ways in which lecturers approach the interrogation of these measures. All tutors were deeply committed to the practice of their particular disciplines and yet the engagement measures ask students to reflect upon their whole university experience, something that in the Australian unitised system can straddle a number of disciplines, especially in the first year. The environment of university teaching increasingly requires an intensification of accountability.

Engagement measures bring with them the promise of ways of tabulating and measuring improvement. The piloting of the AUSSE did provide the context for useful and enriching dialogue about learning and teaching; it remains unclear, however, whether it measures what it sets out to.

Engagement is dynamically shaped by changing and competing aspirations and needs, feelings and senses of students, whilst the broader institutional environment has inherent tensions related to the potential of engagement and measures of engagement that objectify the student (in other words, by observable behaviours). We should perhaps align more of the understanding of student engagement with paradigms where learning is seen as transformational and the student is the agent of making meaning and governance of learning. Similarly, there is room to explore a more transcendental, ontological aspect similar to the Weberian notion of enchantment for students and staff (Weber, 1946, 2002; Jenkins, 2000). In short, we support more attention to the affective elements of engagement and involvement discussed elsewhere in this book.

References

Barnett, R. (2007) *A Will To Learn* (Maidenhead: Open University Press).

Barrie, S., Ginns, P. and Symons, R. (2008) 'Student Surveys on Teaching and Learning: Final Report', in Chalmers, D., *Rewarding and Recognising Quality Teaching and Learning in Higher Education: Teaching Quality Indicators Project* (Chippendale: Carrick Institute). Retrieved from <http://www.catl.uwa.edu.au/__.../Student_Surveys_on_Teaching_and_Learning.pdf>

Bock, D. (2005) *Our Underachieving Colleges: A Candid Look at How Much Students Learn and Why They Should Be Learning More* (Princeton: Princeton University Press).

Castells, M. (2004) *The Power of Identity* (Carlton: Blackwell).

Coates, H. (2010) 'Development of the Australasian Survey of Student Engagement (AUSSE)', *Higher Education*, 60/1, pp.1–17.

DEEWR (Department of Education, Employment and Workplace Relations) (2008) *Review of Australian Higher Education Final Report* (Canberra: Commonwealth of Australia). Retrieved from <http://www.deewr.gov.au/HigherEducation/Review/Documents/PDF/Higher%20Education%20Review_one%20document_02.pdf>

DEEWR (Department of Education, Employment and Workplace Relations) (2009a) *An Indicator Framework for Higher Education Performance Funding* (Canberra: Commonwealth of Australia). Retrieved from <http://www.deewr.gov.au/HigherEducation/Documents/HIEDPerformanceFunding.pdf>

DEEWR (Department of Education, Employment and Workplace Relations) (2009b) *Transforming Australia's Higher Education System* (Canberra: Commonwealth of Australia). Retrieved from <http://www.deewr.gov.au/HigherEducation/Documents/PDF/Additional%20Report%20-%20Transforming%20Aus%20Higher%20ED_webaw.pdf>

Fredricks, J.A., Blumenfeld, P.C. and Paris, A.H. (2004) 'School Engagement: Potential of the Concept, State of the Evidence', *Review of Educational Research*, 74/1, pp.59–109.

Gibbs, G. (2010) *Dimensions of Quality* (York: Higher Education Academy). Retrieved from <http://www.heacademy.ac.uk/assets/York/documents/ourwork/evidence_informed_practice/Dimensions_of_Quality.pdf>

Jenkins, R. (2000) 'Disenchantment, Enchantment and Re-Enchantment: Max Weber at the Millennium', *Max Weber Studies*, 1, pp.11–32.

Koljatic, M. and Kuh, G.D. (2001) 'A Longitudinal Assessment of College Student Engagement in Good Practices in Undergraduate Education', *Higher Education*, 42, pp.351–71.

Korzekwa, A.M. (2010) *An Examination of the Predictive Validity of Student Engagement Benchmarks and Scalelets*, Thesis for Master of Arts, Educational Psychology (Albuquerque: University of New Mexico).

Kuh, G.D. (2008) *High Impact Educational Practices: What They Are, Who Has Access to Them, and Why They Matter* (Washington: Association of American Colleges and Universities).

Kuh, G.D. (2009) 'The National Survey of Student Engagement: Conceptual and Empirical Foundations', *New Directions for Institutional Research*, 141/Spring, pp.5–20.

Markwell, D. (2007) 'The Challenge of Student Engagement', *Keynote Address – Teaching and Learning Forum 2007* (Perth: University of Western Australia). Retrieved from <http://www.catl.uwa.edu.au/CATLyst/current/1/don_markwell>

OECD (Organisation for Economic Co-operation and Development) (2009) *Education at a Glance 2009: Summary of Findings*. Retrieved from <http://www.oecd.org/document/24/0,3343,en_2649_39263238_43586328_1_1_1_1,00.html>

Perkins, D. (2007) 'Theories of Difficulty', in Entwistle, N. and Tomlinson, P. (eds) *Student Learning and University Teaching* (Leicester: British Psychological Society) pp.31–48.

Petocz, P. (2009) *Unpublished Report on Investigation of AUSSE Data* (Sydney: Macquarie University).

Pike, G.R. (1999) 'The Constant Error of the Halo in Educational Outcomes Research', *Research in Higher Education,* 40/1, pp.61–86.

Polidano, C. and Zakirova, R. (2011) *Outcomes from Combining Work and Tertiary Study,* Research Report. Retrieved from <http://www.ncver.edu.au/publications/2320.html>

Porter, S.R. (2006) 'Institutional Structures and Student Engagement', *Research in Higher Education,* 47/5, pp.521–58.

Thomas, L. (2002) 'Student Retention in Higher Education: The Role of Institutional Habitus', *Journal of Education Policy,* 17/4, pp.423–42.

Weber, M. (1946) 'Science as a Vocation', in Gerth, H.H. and Mills, C.W. (eds and translators) *From Max Weber: Essays in Sociology* (New York: Oxford University Press) pp.129–56.

Weber, M. (2002) *The Protestant Ethic and the Spirit of Capitalism* (Kalberg, S., trans.) (Oxford: Blackwell).

Yorke, M. and Longden, B. (2008) *The First Year Experience of Higher Education in the UK: Final Report* (York: Higher Education Academy).

Chapter 21

Student engagement: a messy policy challenge in higher education

Kerri-Lee Krause

Griffith Institute for Higher Education

Introduction

This chapter explores the student engagement construct through a policy lens. It examines the policy and politics of engagement from an institutional and national quality assurance and enhancement perspective. The chapter opens with a brief overview of the history of the student engagement movement in the United States and, subsequently, Australia. Discussion then turns to the meaning of 'engagement' in a mass higher education environment where a one-size-fits-all approach to engagement is unsustainable. The focus of the chapter lies in an analysis of how the idea of student engagement is manifesting itself in national- and institution-level policy in the Australian higher education sector. Based on this analysis, I argue that student engagement represents a messy or 'wicked' policy challenge confronting the sector. The chapter closes by exploring the implications of this 'wicked' policy problem at institutional and national levels.

Engagement in a higher education policy context

The notion of student engagement is increasingly evident in the higher education lexicon of many OECD nations. This is particularly the case in North America where Kuh's (2002) conceptual framework for the National Survey of Student Engagement (NSSE) was informed by the long history of student experience research in the United States. This empirical work is based on the principle that what students do during their university experience is more important than who they are, where they have come from, or which institution they attend (Kuh, 2002). Astin's (1985) theory of student involvement contends that students learn by being involved. In turn, involvement in educationally oriented activities positively contributes to a range of outcomes including persistence, satisfaction, achievement and academic success (Astin, 1985, 1993; Goodsell, Maher and Tinto, 1992; Kuh and Vesper, 1997; Pascarella and Terenzini, 2005). Kuh's empirical approach to student engagement has attracted widespread interest in North America and has now spread to countries such as the United Kingdom, South Africa and Japan. In Australasia, the Australian Centre for Educational Research (ACER) adapted Kuh's instrument to develop the Australian Survey of Student Engagement (AUSSE).

Complementing these national-level questionnaires – primarily designed for benchmarking purposes – are institution-level surveys of the student experience, along with the nationally mandated Course Experience Questionnaire that is administered post-graduation. International organisations like *i-graduate* are also seeking to make their mark by offering a suite of 'barometer' instruments and benchmarking services. The International Student Barometer is one such example.

Each of these instruments is administered at different times during the academic year and for various purposes. Not all measure student engagement. Some are more satisfaction-oriented; yet all provide universities with different types of information about the extent to which their students are engaged with dimensions of the institution, with learning, with its people and its services. It is beyond the scope of this chapter to debate the relative merits of student satisfaction surveys compared with instruments like the NSSE or the AUSSE, which include indicators of time on task to gauge the extent of student involvement in a range of curricular and extra-curricular activities. Suffice to say that universities confront many challenges when trying to decide which surveys to use, how often, with which students and to what end. Survey fatigue and low response rates pose a significant problem for institutions seeking to develop evidence-based approaches to policy and faced with an increasingly diverse plethora of survey options.

Of interest in this chapter is how the data emerging from these surveys are shaping approaches to policy development at institutional and national levels. What does an analysis of policy documents reveal about how Australian universities are interpreting student engagement and its role in the higher education landscape? How are national policy developments in Australia reflecting the international interest in student engagement and the broader issue of the student experience? Before addressing these questions, there is merit in considering some of the connotations of student engagement in the context of a mass higher education system.

Engagement: not always what it seems

The surveys of student engagement are behavioural in their focus. Both the NSSE and the AUSSE gather data on how much time students spend on activities such as interacting with peers and teaching staff, amount of time spent on study, class projects, extra-curricular activities and the like. These data are useful in their place but one needs to be cautious about perceiving 'engagement' as a one-size-fits-all notion that can be captured in quantitative data representing students' time on task (Krause and Coates, 2008).

Based on the national studies of the Australian first-year experience over the past ten years (James, Krause and Jennings, 2010), I have challenged a one-size-fits-all approach to student engagement (Krause, 2005, forthcoming (b)). For some students, engagement with university studies is a battle and a challenge rather than a positive, fulfilling experience. To 'engage' with university in the various ways conceived by the surveys of student engagement – for instance, through group-based assessment tasks, one-to-one interactions with academic staff or through online interactions – may involve coming to terms with new ways of learning and interacting that may prove uncomfortable, even confronting for some, particularly in their first year of university study. Assumptions about engagement need to be challenged in light of the diverse linguistic and cultural backgrounds students bring to the university learning environment. A few examples are discussed here for illustrative purposes.

In the Australian Survey of Student Engagement, students are asked to comment on the frequency with which they engage in behaviours such as those outlined in the following items:

- Had conversations with students who are very different to you in terms of their religious beliefs, political opinions or personal values (section 1)
- Talked about your career plans with teaching staff or advisors (section 1)
- Worked with teaching staff on activities other than coursework (for example, committees, orientation, student organisations, etc.) (section 1)
- Attended an art exhibition, play, dance, music, theatre or other performance (section 6)
- Participating in extracurricular activities (for example, organisations, campus publications, student associations, clubs and societies, sports, etc.) (section 9).

These items assume that students possess the social and cultural capital – and the associated confidence – to talk about "career plans with teaching staff or advisors" or to work with "teaching staff on activities other than coursework". While some may argue that the purpose of a university education includes developing students' confidence to engage in such activities, when faced with these questions in their first year, some students may find the experience a daunting one. In such cases, there is merit in looking beyond behavioural measures of time on task, to appreciate the range of ways in which students from various cultural, linguistic and social backgrounds engage, using diverse approaches that may not necessarily be captured through western-oriented constructs such as 'engagement', as depicted in the NSSE and the AUSSE.

Attending art exhibitions and participating in student associations and clubs may also lie outside the zone of comfort and familiarity of students who have not been exposed to such experiences prior to coming to university. While these experiences might prove enriching for some, they may be unfamiliar, even confronting, for others. For those entering higher education from under-represented backgrounds, the approach to learning, information about subject choices, availability of support resources and the requisite coping strategies may not be in place, leaving some students feeling isolated and overwhelmed (Forsyth and Furlong, 2003; Thomas and Quinn, 2007). Similarly, for those entering Australian universities as international students, widely accepted approaches to 'engagement' in the Australian context may assume prerequisite ways of relating and behaving that are not necessarily familiar to students from international backgrounds (Neri and Ville, 2008). The first year is clearly a time for developing students' engagement capabilities but at the same time it is important to ensure that widely held assumptions about optimal approaches to engagement for diverse student cohorts are challenged and reviewed. This is particularly important as the sector opens its doors to increasingly diverse student cohorts. The fact that student engagement cannot be taken for granted as a 'given', operating in similar ways for all students, across all institutions, renders it a wicked or messy policy problem, as discussed in the next section.

The messy policy challenges of student engagement

The notion of wicked problems was introduced by Rittel and Webber (1973) in the context of urban planning where such issues as safety, aesthetics and ease of movement represent a few of the more intractable challenges facing urban planners. Unlike tame, well-defined problems, the wicked variety tend to be ill-defined and changeable; views on solutions vary widely; the problem-solving process typically involves diverse parties with strong vested interests; and today's apparent solution is no guarantee of tomorrow's success. These types of problems tend to be resistant to attempts at achieving resolution (Briggs, 2007) and often require new approaches to engaging with problems, particularly in relation to policy. Wicked or messy problems tend to be most apparent when organisations are subject to constant change or unprecedented challenges (Camillus, 2008, p.100). This seems an apt description of the state of play in higher education internationally at the present time. Elsewhere, I have referred to the wicked problem of quality in higher education as a related messy policy problem (Krause, forthcoming (a)). Typically, stakeholders disagree on such matters as the kinds of factors contributing to messy problems and how to manage them. In addressing messy policy issues, one also needs to be cognisant of conflicting goals and vested interests that often mean that "trade-offs between conflicting goals" (Briggs, 2007, p.204) are necessary.

In the context of contemporary policy development, Ney (2009, p.5) argues that messy challenges require a new "toolbox" because they are typically "shrouded in uncertainty" and are shaped by an array of interconnected factors. While Ney's work concerns itself with policy in such areas as transport and health, these descriptors aptly capture the challenges facing those involved in higher education policy development at both national and institutional levels.

Designing and implementing policy that is responsive to paradigm shifts in the higher education landscape, including notable changes in the ways in which students engage with higher education, is arguably one of the messier policy challenges facing governments and universities. This section explores some of the ways in which the Australian government and institutions are grappling with this challenge. Student engagement has implications for macro-level policy settings that shape accountability and funding arrangements. At the same time, disciplinary and departmental groups are tackling the challenge of how best to engage students at the local level.

Student engagement: a national policy context

Australia finds itself on the brink of a new era in higher education. The federal government has introduced several initiatives that have significant implications for measurement, monitoring and reporting of the quality of the student experience and students' engagement with learning and institutions. A significant shift to a student demand-driven system from 2012 places the spotlight on the effectiveness of institutional strategies for communicating the success with which they support the quality of students' experiences and outcomes. With an apparent focus on student as consumer and client in a student demand-driven system, the emphasis on demonstrable evidence of quality in the student experience will be more important than ever.

The new Tertiary Education Quality and Standards Agency (TEQSA) will commence in 2011, placing emphasis on institutions' capacity to demonstrate that they have in place robust processes for assuring standards in a range of areas, including learning and teaching. The quality of the student experience and outcomes will undoubtedly form part of the evidence trail an institution would wish to bring to bear as part of any TEQSA review process.

In addition to these changes to quality assurance and funding arrangements, the national government has also introduced a system of mission-based compacts, based on individually negotiated targets that are intended to reflect the differentiated missions of universities across the sector. Closely allied to this development is the introduction of a new suite of indicators underpinning performance-based funding for learning and teaching. In late 2009, a discussion paper (DEEWR, 2009) with a proposed indicator framework was released. In that paper, both student engagement and student satisfaction were highlighted as important dimensions of the student experience. The proposed reward-funding model to be applied across the sector comprises three performance categories, one of which is 'student experience' (Randall, 2010). Indicators of quality in this category will include domestic undergraduate students' satisfaction with the teaching they experienced during their undergraduate programme, along with overall satisfaction with their experience, as measured by the Course Experience Questionnaire.

A new instrument is also under development – the University Experience Survey. The introduction of this survey instrument further highlights the messiness of the policy challenge of measuring and monitoring the quality of the student experience. Up to now, the Course Experience Questionnaire has been a long-standing performance indicator in the sector but there is much concern about the lagged nature of this indicator. Consistent with the characteristics of wicked problems, yesterday's solution is insufficient for addressing the needs of the current context where new approaches are required to monitor the rapidly changing patterns of student engagement with university learning. Views on ways to address this challenge vary widely across the sector and, as Ney (2009) points out, the attempts at resolving the policy challenge will involve an array of interconnected factors and stakeholders.

In the first instance, it is expected that the new University Experience Survey will be piloted among first-year students with a view to gathering more immediate data about how effectively universities are supporting the quality of the student experience in the first year. The commissioning of this new survey reflects a renewed government focus on gathering timely data that arguably may be used for both quality assurance and enhancement purposes. It is too early to predict whether or not the proposed instrument will be used as a national indicator. At the time of writing, it remains a proposed indicator to be developed for potential longer-term use (DEEWR, 2010). The evolving nature of these performance indicators once again reinforces the messy nature of the policy problem at hand.

It is beyond the scope of this chapter to analyse these and related policy developments in further depth. Nevertheless, it is evident that while Australian government policy makers attach high importance to metrics that will capture the quality of the student experience, engagement and outcomes, there is no simple solution for this policy problem. Complexities such as the diversity of the student body, the diversity of institutions and the multidimensional nature of the student experience render this a particularly messy policy challenge. The most that quantitative measures might hope to achieve is a proxy for the quality of students' educational experiences in institutional settings. Having identified the dangers of a one-size-fits-all approach to student engagement earlier in this chapter, the policy dilemma inherent in trying to measure and summarise in a single figure the effectiveness of universities' efforts to enhance the student experience becomes a truly wicked one. Within this complex national policy environment, how are universities approaching the issue of student engagement in their policy statements? This is the focus of the next section.

Institutional approaches to the messy policy challenge of student engagement

This section examines how Australian universities are grappling with the messy policy challenges inherent in addressing the issue of student engagement in the sector. Questions that universities may ask themselves as they develop policy in this regard include the following:

- Is the language of 'student engagement' fit for purpose in our institution or are there alternatives, such as 'student experience'?
- Assuming that the quality of the student experience and student

engagement are priorities, how do we reflect this in our institutional policy statements?

- How do we then enact this strategic priority at all levels of the institution?
- What data sources are optimal for evidencing our progress in enhancing the quality of the student experience and student engagement?
- How does a focus on student engagement help us to respond to the national policy agenda and its emphasis on demonstrating evidence of the quality of student outcomes?

In order to understand how Australian universities are dealing with these key policy questions, a desktop analysis was undertaken of relevant policy documents available on Australian university websites. The analysis was limited to institution-level strategic plans and/or learning and teaching strategies (or equivalent) accessible within three clicks of the homepage. Analysis did not include department- or faculty-level plans. The focus of analysis was on how universities depict themselves in relation to the student experience and the extent to which student engagement features in the language of institutional strategic planning and policy documents.

Analysis reveals a somewhat mixed picture of how the sector reflects its understanding of the role of student engagement in institutional policy documents. Of the 39 university websites reviewed, 69 per cent (n=27) make explicit reference to the student experience either in their institutional strategic plan or their learning and teaching strategy or both. Of these institutions, 44 per cent (n=12) use the language of engagement, referring to learner or student engagement in their institution-level policy documents. Illustrative policy statements relating to student engagement include: *improve student engagement in a high quality campus community* (University of Western Australia); *encouraging student engagement* (University of New South Wales); create an *engaging student experience* (University of Wollongong); and facilitate *engaged learning experiences* (University of Western Sydney).

This rudimentary analysis suggests that, while the language of student engagement is not yet infused in the majority of Australian university policy statements, over two-thirds of institutions acknowledge the importance of the student experience in their policies. I would argue that it is not so much the terminology of student engagement that matters but rather the ways in which institutions demonstrate their commitment to engaging students in a range of ways. An analysis of those universities making policy-level references to the student experience reveals three main institutional levers for engaging students and enhancing their experiences. These levers are: the curriculum, institutional infrastructure (both physical and virtual) and university support services.

Those institutions referring to the curriculum as a key avenue for engaging students refer to:

- Setting a curriculum that engages students (University of New South Wales)
- Develop[ing] a suite of engaged learning models associated with the acquisition of UWS graduate attributes (University of Western Sydney)
- Engaging experiential approaches to delivery that allow students to apply their learning (Swinburne University)
- Relevant programmes taught in ways that engage our students (Edith Cowan University) and
- Enhanced curriculum design (Queensland University of Technology).

Some universities refer explicitly to the importance of institutional infrastructure as an important means of engaging students. References to infrastructure include physical dimensions (for example, campus facilities, food outlets) and a virtual dimension (for example, online learning management systems). For instance, Griffith University values an "excellent campus environment" while Central Queensland University emphasises the importance of "a stimulating learning environment that promotes learner engagement [and] is supported by appropriate technology infrastructure and services."

Learner support services represent a third lever for engaging students in the university learning environment. For example, Flinders University mentions the importance of "effective support services"; Bond University refers to its value of "nurtur[ing] the Bond student experience through student support"; Curtin, on the other hand, refers to the importance of "consistent standards in service delivery".

These brief excerpts from university policy documents highlight a range of ways in which institutions are attempting to come to terms with the messy problem of student engagement in higher education. There is no uniformity in their approach. Some use the terminology of engagement, others appear to use the terms 'enhancement', 'experience' and 'engagement' synonymously. Three key levers for engaging students are evident in these documents, as outlined above. A small minority of institutions refer to the coordination of these engagement dimensions. For instance the University of Adelaide speaks of the need to: "Enhance the learning experience of students with a coordinated approach to improving student support services and amenities, the quality and currency of the curricula and the teaching skills of staff." Griffith University also makes reference to a: "Coherent whole-of-university approach to improving the quality of the student experience."

The wickedness of the student engagement problem intensifies as one analyses the ways in which institutional policy documents attribute responsibility for student engagement. Many universities assume the responsibility for student engagement in their policy documents, stating that they will: "achieve superior engagement"; "maximise student engagement"; "improve student engagement"; "embed engaged learning" and will "effectively engage students". In other words, the responsibility for engagement apparently lies with the institution. Other universities are more circumspect in their approach, stating that they will "encourage" student engagement; "ensure that students have access to engaged learning experiences"; "monitor the scope and scale of engaged learning"; and "foster an enriching student experience". There was little evidence in the available documents of statements of mutual responsibility for engagement between students and the institution.

In summary, an analysis of strategic policy statements among Australian universities suggests that some are using the language of engagement, though less than a third explicitly refer to engagement in the policy documents analysed for the purposes of this study. More than two-thirds mention the importance of the student experience in their publicly available online learning and teaching policy statements. As noted, the interest in this chapter is not limited to whether or not universities use the term 'student engagement' but lies in whether their policy statements reflect an appreciation of the complexity of the construct and its various dimensions. There is some evidence of a growing understanding of these dimensions, which are summarised and elaborated in the section to follow.

A systems approach to interpreting the student engagement problem

Figure 1 summarises some of the key findings of this chapter's analysis of national and institutional policy attempts to come to terms with the messy problem of student engagement.

The figure draws attention to the fact that universities operate in a national context. External drivers have a significant impact on institutional operations. These include social, economic and political drivers such as the state of the economy, labour market forces and political stability. Closely connected to these drivers are those relating to community and industry expectations of higher education and associated beliefs about the purposes and outcomes of higher education. A third, inter-connected set of drivers is that relating to national policy making. Specifically in the higher education context these might include policies regarding assurance of quality and standards, the role of regulatory bodies such as the new Tertiary Education Quality and Standards Agency or the employability imperative. Several dimensions of this policy environment have been discussed in this chapter. Each of these sets of drivers has a significant bearing on the ways in which universities operate. Similarly, there should be reciprocal connections between universities, their communities, industry stakeholders and the broader socio-economic, political and policy environment. Possibilities for establishing and maintaining these connections are signified by the gaps in the circle surrounding the institutional dimensions.

Within the institution, the analysis of online university policy documents highlights several dimensions of student engagement. The three key levers for student engagement highlighted in this analysis are: curriculum design and delivery; the physical and virtual infrastructure of the institution (including online learning management systems and physical

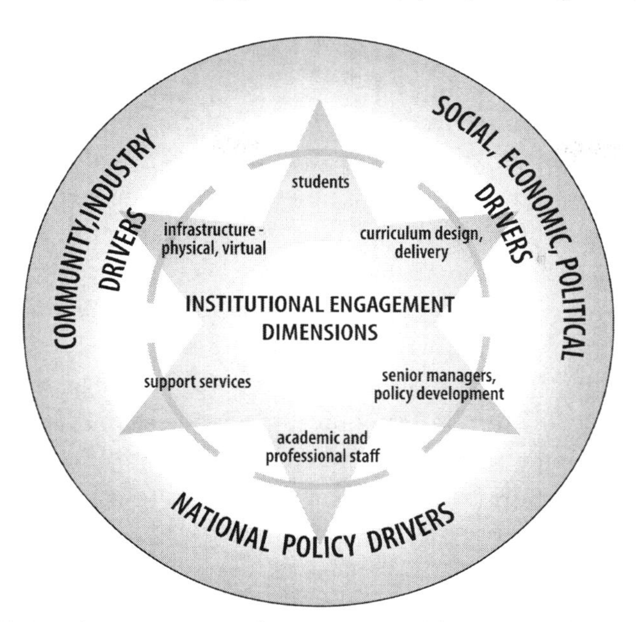

Figure 21.1: A systems approach to institutional dimensions of student engagement in higher education

campus environments); and support services which include libraries, learning support and the like. Key players in the system are: students and staff, both professional and academic. Another set of key players is the senior management team and those responsible for policy making in relation to the student experience. If these people are not engaged and in touch with the other dimensions of this system as they develop institutional policies, the system will falter at best and fail at worst.

The glue holding such a system together must be a focus on the quality of the student experience, whether or not it is articulated in the language of engagement. Such a system would need to be characterised by a quality management framework comprising both quality assurance and enhancement elements. As noted earlier in this chapter, while the proposed national indicator framework to be used in Australia from 2011 is primarily driven by a quality assurance imperative, there is scope for a complementary focus on enhancement, particularly in the student experience category. Further implications of this systems approach for institutions and the wider national context are considered in the final section of the chapter.

Implications and concluding remarks

This chapter has examined student engagement from a national and institutional policy perspective, using the Australian higher education sector as a national case study. A fruitful avenue for further investigation would be a cross-national comparative analysis of the ways in which universities in such nations as Japan, South Africa and the UK use the language of engagement in their policy documents and strategic planning statements, particularly in relation to the quality of the student experience. Equally important is an analysis of whether or not the higher education sector internationally demonstrates an appreciation of the complexity of student engagement and its application to specific student cohorts.

This chapter has drawn on data from national studies of Australian universities to argue for the importance of appreciating the fact that not all students engage in the same way. For some, engagement with institutionally acceptable ways of knowing, being and doing can be a battle rather than a positive experience. The challenge is for institutions to engage in socio-culturally sensitive policy making that respects the diversity of student experiences and backgrounds, including diversity in the range and nature of social and cultural capital that individuals bring to the university learning environment. This is but one of the factors contributing to the argument that student engagement represents a wicked policy problem in higher education. Once again, the merits of an international comparative study in this regard are considerable.

Wicked or messy problems tend to be ill defined; they involve a complex array of factors and vested interests, with an equally complex range of views about potential solutions and strategies. Rather than trying to 'solve' messy problems, the challenge is to aim for some form of resolution, where possible. This chapter has examined ways in which the Australian higher education sector is coming to terms with the messiness of measuring, monitoring and planning for student engagement across the sector. The national government is tackling the issue of developing indicators in relation to the quality of the student experience, including a proposed new instrument to capture elements of the student experience in the first year. Institutions, on the other hand, have been shown to be relatively diverse in their approach to policy making with respect to student engagement. Less than one-third of Australian universities refer to engagement in their policy documents, though more than two-thirds draw attention to the importance of the student experience in their institutional policy statements. A more telling finding is the diverse range of approaches to managing, monitoring and enhancing the student experience evident in these documents.

The wicked challenges inherent in developing, monitoring and sustaining responsive higher education policies in relation to student engagement are no less apparent in other nations which are grappling with the messiness of student-demand-driven systems and the drive to widen participation. For instance, in the United Kingdom, the Higher Education Funding Council for England (HEFCE) commissioned a study on student engagement (Little et al., 2009), seeking to understand more about systemic approaches to enhancing student learning experiences. In this report, the authors acknowledge the complexity of the issue of engaging students as the student body continues to diversify. The report also raises the issue of clarifying and communicating the purposes of student engagement. This, in itself, represents a messy challenge as the rationale may vary considerably depending on stakeholders and contexts. South Africa faces a particularly challenging set of policy issues in relation to the improvement of the higher education sector in that country. These include addressing issues of student under-preparedness among a diverse student population; improving student success rates and motivation to succeed; and addressing social cohesion across institutions of higher education (Strydom and Mentz, 2010). In their report on a pilot study of the South African Survey of Student Engagement, Strydom and Mentz (2010, p.v) speak of the "seemingly intractable" issues facing South African policy makers in relation to higher education participation and improvement.

As the higher education sector continues to grapple internationally with what it is to engage undergraduate students successfully in the twenty-first century, it will be particularly important not to underestimate the challenge this represents, both from a practical and a policy perspective. The challenge for governments and university leaders is to acknowledge the obvious tensions underlying a desire to capture the quality of the student experience through a proxy measure such as that of student engagement. These policy challenges, which exist in the context of a declining resource base and a high-stakes accountability environment, have all the characteristics of 'wickedity' (Bore and Wright, 2009; Camillus, 2008; Watson, 2000). Yet they cannot be ignored – they require ongoing debate and our most creative thinking as a sector. Dynamic and innovative leadership at both government and institution levels is particularly important in order to progress the debates and manage the wicked policy issues in informed and visionary ways. Recognising the messy nature of these challenges is an important starting point for ensuring that policy responses are sufficiently sensitive to context, evidence based and robust.

References

Astin, A. (1985) *Achieving Educational Excellence: A Critical Assessment of Priorities and Practices in Higher Education* (San Francisco: Jossey-Bass).

Astin, A. (1993) *What Matters in College? Four Critical Years Revisited* (San Francisco: Jossey-Bass).

Bore, A. and Wright, N. (2009) 'The Wicked and Complex in Education: Developing a Transdisciplinary Perspective for Policy Formulation, Implementation and Professional Practice', *Journal of Education for Teaching*, 35/3, pp.241–56.

Briggs, L. (2007) *Tackling Wicked Problems: A Public Policy Perspective* (Canberra: Public Service Commission). Retrieved from <http://www.apsc.gov.au/publications07/wickedproblems.htm>

Camillus, J.C. (2008) 'Strategy as a Wicked Problem', *Harvard Business Review*, May, pp.99–106.

DEEWR (2009) *An Indicator Framework for Higher Education Performance Funding: Discussion Paper*. Retrieved from <http://www.deewr.gov.au/HigherEducation/Pages/IndicatorFramework.aspx>

DEEWR (2010) *Compacts and Performance Funding Overview*. Retrieved from <http://www.deewr.gov.au/HigherEducation/Policy/Pages/Compacts.aspx>

Forsyth, A. and Furlong, A. (2003) 'Access to Higher Education and Disadvantaged Young People', *British Educational Research Journal*, 29/2, pp.205–25.

Goodsell, A., Maher, M. and Tinto, V. (eds) (1992) *Collaborative Learning: A Sourcebook for Higher Education* (University Park: National Center on Postsecondary Teaching, Learning and Assessment, the Pennsylvania State University).

James, R., Krause, K. and Jennings, C. (2010) *The First Year Experience in Australian Universities: Findings from 1994–2009* (Melbourne: CSHE).

Krause, K. (2005) *Engaged, Inert or Otherwise Occupied? Deconstructing the 21st Century Undergraduate Student*, keynote paper presented at James Cook University Symposium: Sharing Scholarship in Learning and Teaching – Engaging Students, James Cook University, Qld, 21–22 September 2005. Retrieved from <http://www.griffith.edu.au/gihe/staff/kerri-lee-krause>

Krause, K. (forthcoming (a)) 'The Wicked Problem of Quality in Higher Education', *Higher Education Research and Development*.

Krause, K. (forthcoming (b)) 'Transforming the Learning Experience to Engage Students', in Thomas, L. and Tight, M. (eds) *Institutional Transformation to Engage a Diverse Student Body* (Bingley: Emerald Group).

Krause, K. and Coates, H. (2008) 'Students' Engagement in First Year University', *Assessment and Evaluation in Higher Education*, 33/5, pp.493–505.

Kuh, G.D. (2002) *The National Survey of Student Engagement: Conceptual Framework and Overview of Psychometric Properties*. Retrieved from <nsse.iub.edu/pdf/conceptual_framework_2003.pdf>

Kuh, G.D. and Vesper, N. (1997) 'A Comparison of Student Experiences with Good Practices in Undergraduate Education Between 1990 and 1994', *The Review of Higher Education*, 21, pp.43–61.

Little, B., Locke, W., Scesa, A. and Williams, R. (2009) *Report to HEFCE on Student Engagement* (Bristol: HEFCE).

Neri, F. and Ville, S. (2008) 'Social Capital Renewal and the Academic Performance of International Students in Australia', *Journal of Socio-Economics*, 37/4, pp.15–38.

Ney, S. (2009) *Resolving Messy Policy Problems: Handling Conflict in Environmental, Transport, Health and Ageing Policy* (London: Earthscan).

Pascarella, E.T. and Terenzini, P.T. (2005) *How College Affects Students: Vol. 2, A Third Decade of Research* (San Francisco: Jossey-Bass).

Randall, J. (2010) *Compacts and Performance Funding: Information Session*. Retrieved from <http://www.deewr.gov.au/HigherEducation/Policy/Documents/InformationSessionPresentation.pdf>

Rittel, H.W.J. and Webber, M.M. (1973) 'Dilemmas in a General Theory of Planning', *Policy Sciences*, 4, pp.155–69.

Strydom, J.F. and Mentz, M. (2010) *South African Survey of Student Engagement (SASSE) – Focusing the Student Experience on Success through Student Engagement* (Pretoria: The South African Council on Higher Education).

Thomas, E. and Quinn, J. (2007) *First Generation Entry into Higher Education* (Maidenhead: Open University Press).

Watson, D. (2000) 'Managing in Higher Education: The "Wicked Issues"', *Higher Education Quarterly*, 54/1, pp.5–21.

Summary

The nature of the elephant: metaphors for student engagement

Ian Solomonides[1], Anna Reid[2] and Peter Petocz[1]

[1] *Macquarie University, Australia*
[2] *Sydney Conservatorium of Music, Australia*

Introduction

A modern version of an old Indian story describes how a group of tourists in an African game park have each taken photographs of an animal lurking in thick vegetation. Each of the pictures looks quite different – one looks like a large snake, one like a tree and others look like a wall, a rope, a hand fan and a plastic pipe. Of course, they have all photographed various parts of an elephant – trunk, leg, side, tail, ear and tusk – although each of them is convinced that the creature is quite different. The story illustrates the limits of individual perception, the need to be tolerant of other people's ideas and the folly of holding on inflexibly to a particular view. It reminds us of the benefits of cooperation: when all the photos are put together, a clearer picture of the animal emerges. The story can also be applied to our investigation of student engagement. The various chapters in this book have shown a diversity of views about the nature and properties of engagement, as different authors have looked at various parts of the elephant. In this final chapter, we want to summarise these diverse views of engagement and attempt to put them together to get an overall idea of the beast.

In setting out to write this book, we knew that the various authors would illustrate numerous interpretations and applications of engagement. The authors have explored the psychology, application and interpretation of student engagement in various contexts: individual, discipline, departmental, institutional and at the level of national policy. Coates makes the point:

> The term 'engagement' has many semantic connotations and requires qualification. Depending on the context, it can describe processes with different temporal, existential, directional and moral characteristics. Engagement can refer to something that happens in the past, present or future, and to something of either limited or ongoing duration. It can refer to objects or subjects, be they groups or individuals, although logically it requires at least two entities. Depending on the entities involved, it can involve unidirectional, bidirectional or multidirectional connections. Engagement is not essentially an evaluative term and it can be morally positive, neutral or negative.
>
> (2006, p.16)

Faced with such complexity, it can be helpful to highlight various metaphors for the notion of student engagement. These metaphors represent a way of framing the varied meanings that we assign to student engagement and the different ways in which we think about the concept. There are many examples in the academic literature of the use of metaphor as a rhetorical device for thinking about some problem. On the basis of interviews with senior academics, Brew (2001) has identified metaphors of academic research, distinguishing the 'domino', 'trading', 'layer' and 'journey' views. Burton (2008) gives an interesting case study of using the metaphor of 'superhero' with a university class as a device for investigating ethical behaviour in organisations. Chapman (1997) investigates the 'community', 'adventure' and 'game' metaphors for trainee teachers' problem solving in mathematics, while Williams and Wade (2007) utilise the 'number line' as a metaphor for explaining the workplace use of a spreadsheet formula for estimating gas usage. As we were putting this chapter together, we received an email invitation to attend a talk by one of the authors of a recently published book (Spicer and Alvesson, 2010) on metaphors for leaders – classified as 'gardener', 'buddy', 'saint', 'cyborg', 'commander' or 'bully'. Metaphors can help us to expand our thinking about student engagement, though they can also have limiting effects if we forget that they represent only one part of the elephant. Hutchings (2007) uses the 'elephant in the room' metaphor in discussing the role of theory in the scholarship of teaching and learning, later saying that:

> many different kinds of work, representing a wide range of traditions and contexts, can come in contact with one another, find fertile cross currents, and bring fresh insights and resources to the ongoing conversation about how to strengthen our students' learning.
>
> (Hutchings, 2007, p.3)

The various views of student engagement that we have seen in the chapters of this book are presented and discussed next. Each view is linked with a metaphor that highlights some aspect of engagement. Each view is also exemplified by one or more of the chapters, referred to under the names of their authors (and the chapter numbers). The authors of each chapter used as an example may also hold other views of engagement as well as the one under discussion. Indeed, they may not even agree with the view being discussed, although they will have put forward some aspect of it in their chapter.

A dichotomous view of engagement

The simplest view of engagement is a dichotomous one: students are either engaged or not. Maybe the marriage metaphor is the most appropriate here (as discussed in Reid and Solomonides, 2007): it highlights the joy of being in the state, the need for commitment and the necessity to push through the difficult times. David (Chapter 10) identifies engagement with recruitment into university, in the context of widening participation from the viewpoint of equity and feminism. For Nelson, Kift and Clarke (Chapter 6), the dichotomous idea is retention: students who are engaged will stay at university, others will leave. However, like Sambell (Chapter 9) and Winchester-Seeto, Bosanquet and Rowe (Chapter 19), they discuss the need for careful enactment of strategies to support engagement if they are to be realised.

Colley and Lefever (Chapter 16) put forward similar dichotomies (or the 'connections' referred to by Coates (2006) above) based on the notion of belonging, in all its various aspects – belonging to the department, to the institution or to a social group generally, though it is more likely that these are multidirectional in nature. Sambell (Chapter 9) includes the distinction between a deep approach to learning, characteristic of students who are engaged, and a surface approach to learning, shown by students who are not engaged. She also evokes the affective dimension of learning, something that is somewhat under-represented in the literature and was the focus of earlier work leading to this book (see Reid and Solomonides, 2007). Taylor et al. (Chapter 12) present an interesting contrast between students as consumers and as producers, with the latter view representing engagement. Two members of their team are student 'producers', illustrating how students and teachers can work in partnership on the co-construction of knowledge and the reconstruction of curricula. Similar arguments are put forward by Sambell (Chapter 9) and Kay, Owen and Dunne (Chapter 17).

Support during the difficult times is also referred to by several authors: Bryson and Hardy (Chapter 2), Foster et al. (Chapter 5), Leach and Zepke (Chapter 11), Colley and Lefever (Chapter 16) and others refer to the importance of social or community networks in the support of engagement. The combination of increasing student numbers and distance education may mean that this is one area in particular that might benefit from institutional support rather than being left to chance.

Engagement as a measured quantity

At the other extreme is the view of engagement as a measured quantity – the notion of time on task, or time spent on particular educationally relevant activities, as measured by surveys such as the NSSE or AUSSE. A useful metaphor here is that of the petrol tank: it highlights the benefits of greater engagement, in terms of being able to go further, and also the limiting nature of low engagement – or even the 'empty tank' of a complete lack of engagement. A number of our chapters refer to this view. Krause (Chapter 21) critiques behavioural questionnaires and performance indicators more broadly, in the context of policy, and discusses the development of a new University Experience Survey. This issue of judging student experience against a proxy measure of quality vexes several authors, Voerman and Solomonides (Chapter 20) included, who challenge the assumptions of the AUSSE in terms of which activities should be included as part of a measurement of engagement – maybe different ones for different disciplines. Webster and Chan (Chapter 8) talk about the development of an engagement scale in a survey of Hong Kong students' reactions to changed educational conditions. For them, the value of measurement is in being able to show effects of interventions aimed at improving student engagement and learning. Ross and Cen (Chapter 18), in reporting the development of the NSSE-China describe the various measures within the instrument but go on to discuss the broader impact of the project in engendering conversations about student engagement in an increasingly diverse higher education system. This diverted attention from other measurements such as institutional reputation, resources, research and other rankings, thus igniting a debate about student and staff experiences previously missing from national discussions on quality. At a more modest level, Voerman and Solomonides (Chapter 20) show how having conversations about the AUSSE perhaps did more to promote departmental thinking about engagement than did the application of the instrument itself. Similarly, (Elizabeth) Reid and Solomonides (Chapter 7) describe the opportunity afforded for reflection by discussing engagement and capability.

Newbery (Chapter 3) writes that "student engagement is not an either–or phenomenon, but rather a matter of degree", a statement that seems to imply a measured view of engagement. Newbery also comments on another aspect of the engagement literature, that is, the tendency to apply postmodern jargon to what might be some already established and quite fundamental concepts within teaching and learning. Michell (2009a, b) reminds us that only quantitative attributes can be measured and points out that the common psychological approach of measuring ordered attributes such as intelligence or wellbeing (with psychological tests) involves the mistaken assumption that such attributes are inherently quantitative – he calls this the "psychometricians' fallacy". Even some physical attributes such as hardness have not been demonstrated to be quantitative; while different degrees of hardness can be ordered, there is no way of measuring the property. Does this apply to the notion of engagement? It may be that student engagement is not a quantitative notion but rather an ordinal one.

Engagement as an ordered phenomenon

In the ordinal view of student engagement, there are different states of engagement that can be ranged from least ordered to most ordered but that cannot be measured. An appropriate metaphor here is the ziggurat – a stepped pyramid with progressively higher levels of the type built in ancient Mesopotamia. The metaphor reminds us that there is a better view from a higher level and that this view takes in the views from the lower levels. Kay, Owen and Dunne (Chapter 17) use a step model (a more familiar ziggurat) to talk about student engagement with university quality processes, from the role of evaluator, through those of observer and expert, to the role of partner. This again evokes the ideas of partnership and community alluded to by many of the authors. Foster et al. (Chapter 5) examine engagement using the notion of doubting, identifying four groups: the disengaged, minimally engaged, falsely engaged and engaged. Newbery (Chapter 3) identifies motivation as an important component of engagement and distinguishes five ordered types of motivation: external, introjected, identified and integrated regulation (all forms of extrinsic motivation) and, at the highest level, intrinsic motivation. Gordon, Reid and Petocz (Chapter 4) present views of students and teachers illustrating an ordinal model of engagement: formal, disciplinary and essential. Their model is derived from a phenomenographic approach, which most commonly results in ordinal outcomes.

A categorical view of engagement

An alternative view of student engagement is that it comprises a series of unordered categories. Reid and Solomonides (2007) presented such an unordered view derived from a phenomenographic investigation of design students' experience of engagement and creativity (Figure 1.1 in Chapter 1 is based on this original research). The students in their interviews identified aspects of engagement as being represented by their sense of artistry, sense of being a designer, sense of transformation and sense of being within a specific context. These came together to form their identity – their sense of being. An appropriate metaphor here is the artist's palette: a desired colour can be obtained by combining a number of different colours in various proportions. In the same way, different visions of engagement can be obtained by combining various components. The 'outcome space' from phenomenographic research is typically ordinal, as mentioned previously; but by having the components in Figure 1.1 organised in equally weighted categories, we wanted to represent the various foci students may have relative to engagement at any one time and, by association, the things that it is worth investing time and effort in supporting. Several authors in this book have provided suggestions for what institutions and teachers might focus on in attempts to enhance student engagement.

In the chapters of this book, several categorical views of engagement are presented. Krause (Chapter 21) talks of engaging students through curriculum, university infrastructure and support services, three distinct aspects or channels of engagement. Winchester-Seeto, Bosanquet and Rowe (Chapter 19) identify various aspects of engagement – motivation and agency, transactional, institutional support, active citizenship – in their examination of the link between graduate attributes and student engagement. (Elizabeth) Reid and Solomonides (Chapter 7) also investigate this link, based on a series of interviews with students, and show that students from different faculties find more engagement in different graduate capabilities – scholarship, ethics and sustainability, and career skills; moreover, this view changes from student to student, especially where the students are either recent school-completers or more mature-aged entrants. This last point alone hints at the problems of viewing engagement as a fixed phenomenon applicable to all students irrespective of maturation, culture, gender and so on. Leach and Zepke (Chapter 11) present a categorical model comprising six perspectives on engagement: motivation and agency, student–teacher interaction, student–student interaction, institutional support, active citizenship and support of family and friends.

A naive view of engagement

Around the views that we have identified there are two further ways in which our authors have treated the notion of engagement. The first of these could be described as the naive view; the application of a generally accepted and well-understood concept of engagement that does not undergo any further scrutiny or scepticism. The metaphor of the bathroom door might be appropriate here; the sign says 'engaged' and the occupant's privacy is respected. This view is exemplified by several of our chapter authors because they wish to focus their writing on some pedagogical aspects, without problematising student engagement further. Dunbar-Hall (Chapter 15) gives a fascinating description of a field trip to Bali designed to give music students the opportunity to learn *gamelan* and in the meantime expose them to quite different pedagogical practices such as oral learning and the primacy of group work. Grosjean (Chapter 13) talks of the commitment to learning shown by retiree participants in a community health education program, thus investigating the idea of civic engagement. He points out that such civic commitment is the bedrock of democratic societies and perhaps there are lessons here for those institutions seeking to position themselves as partners in community engagement. Sisto and Petocz (Chapter 14) describe the effect of a pedagogical approach – project-based learning – on their students' engagement, using this naive view of engagement. Winchester-Seeto, Bosanquet and Rowe (Chapter 19) point out that graduate attributes can have a strong effect on engagement, again interpreted in a generally agreed sense. However, unless capability development is integrated into the curriculum and the experience of the student, it is unlikely to be realised; Krause (Chapter 21) makes similar points.

The multidimensional view of engagement

At the other extreme, several authors base their chapters on a multidimensional view of engagement that combines diverse aspects of students' experience. In some cases, this multidimensional view could be built up by combining the previous notions of engagement – the dichotomous, measured, ordered and categorical, and maybe even the naive view. In this way, they are able to see the whole elephant (or at least, many aspects of the elephant) – which in this context is the obvious metaphor! Some of these chapters have been mentioned earlier but here we concentrate on their multidimensional approach to student engagement.

Nelson, Kift and Clarke (Chapter 6) present a model of engagement as the sum total of all aspects of student experience, an extension of the well-known 3P (Presage-Process-Product) model of Biggs (1987). Their notion and application of transition pedagogy is a response to this view. Bryson and Hardy (Chapter 2) combine many aspects of student background and experience in their analysis of five students' personal stories of university study and, in doing so, show how engagement is a dynamic aspect of student lives neither predictably robust nor fragile. Similarly, Leach and Zepke's (Chapter 11) multidimensional categorical model of engagement that we mentioned previously illustrates this dynamism and could also be used to exemplify this category, as could Voerman and Solomonides' (Chapter 20) exploration of life stories of successful academics and student peer mentors as exemplars of people showing high engagement.

Some of the chapters that illustrate such a multidimensional view of engagement are built around innovative pedagogical projects that engage students with the whole range of academic life, not only the learning, and are often related in the words and experiences of the participants. For example, Kay, Owen and Dunne (Chapter 17) and Sambell (Chapter 9) utilise many dimensions of engagement in their descriptions of student volunteers participating in the university community by designing learning guides and materials for earlier-year students. Taylor et al. (Chapter 12) take this a step further, including students as researchers and course designers in their description of the Faust project. Here the notion of student agency returns and illustrates the approach afforded by critical inquiry referred to by Newbery (Chapter 3). Many recent authors (Healey and Jenkins, 2009; Brew, 2010; Ramsden, 2008; Gibbs, 2010; Kuh, 2008, to name a few) have called for and promoted the involvement of students in research and other similar activities that authenticate learning and are deemed to support student engagement. Similarly, the chapters of Sambell; Kay, Owen and Dunne; and Taylor et al. challenge the view of students as consumers, putting forward instead the idea that students are productive and active agents in the educational endeavour and their development as citizens. This is the reconstruction of the student (and of higher education) called for in the work of Neary (2008, 2010; Neary and Winn, 2009) and has links with the promotion of critical enquiry by Newbery (Chapter 3) as pedagogy to support the 'ontological turn' called for by Barnett (2004) and Dall'Alba and Barnacle (2007).

Overall then, we are left with the multi-component and interrelated nature of student engagement and the resultant variety of purposes to which it is put to work. The phenomenon continues to be viewed in a variety of ways depending on the perspective of the stakeholder and the value of the stakes. What is clear, though, is the theme running throughout this book: in order to make use of engagement in quality enhancement we need to have conversations about it, in a partnership with policy makers, practitioners and, above all, students. Failing to do so will render student engagement as no more than a proxy measure for quality; and yet it is clear, through the chapters in this book and reports from elsewhere, that it can be so much more – indeed, for some authors, a clarion call for change. Considering the complete collection of chapters in this book, the shape and nature of the elephant starts to become clear.

References

Barnett, R. (2004) 'Learning for an Unknown Future', *Higher Education Research and Development*, 23/3, pp.247–60.

Biggs, J.B. (1987) *Student Approaches to Learning and Studying* (Hawthorn: Australian Council for Educational Research).

Brew, A. (2001) 'Conceptions of research: a phenomenographic study', *Studies in Higher Education*, 26/3, pp.271–85.

Brew, A. (2010) 'Enhancing Undergraduate Engagement through Research and Inquiry', *Australian Learning and Teaching Council National Teaching Fellow Report*. Retrieved from <http://www.altc.edu.au/resource-enhancing-undergraduate-engagement-research-enquiry-macquarie-2010>

Burton, C. (2008) 'Superhero as metaphor: using creative pedagogies to engage', *International Journal for the Scholarship of Teaching and Learning*, 2/2. Retrieved from <http://academics.georgiasouthern.edu/ijsotl/v2n2/articles/PDFs/Article_Burton.pdf>

Chapman, O. (1997) 'Metaphors in the teaching of mathematical problem solving', *Educational Studies in Mathematics*, 32/3, pp.201–28.

Coates, H. (2006) *Student Engagement in Campus-based and Online Education: University connections* (Abingdon: Routledge).

Dall'Alba, G. and Barnacle, R. (2007) 'An Ontological Turn for Higher Education', *Studies in Higher Education*, 32/6, pp.679–91.

Gibbs, G. (2010) *Dimensions of Quality* (York: Higher Education Academy). Retrieved from <http://www.heacademy.ac.uk/assets/York/documents/ourwork/evidence_informed_practice/Dimensions_of_Quality.pdf>

Healey, M. and Jenkins, A. (2009) *Developing undergraduate research and inquiry* (York: Higher Education Academy). Retrieved from <http://www.heacademy.ac.uk/assets/York/documents/resources/publications/DevelopingUndergraduate_Final.pdf>

Hutchings, P. (2007) 'Theory: the elephant in the scholarship of teaching and learning room', *International Journal for the Scholarship of Teaching and*

Learning, 1/1. Retrieved from <http://academics.georgiasouthern.edu/ijsotl/v1n1/essays/hutchings/IJ_Hutchings.pdf>

Kuh, G.D. (2008) *High Impact Educational Practices: What They Are, Who Has Access to Them, and Why They Matter* (Washington: Association of American Colleges and Universities).

Michell, J. (2009a) 'The psychometricians' fallacy: too clever by half?' *British Journal of Mathematical and Statistical Psychology*, 61/1, pp.41–55.

Michell, J. (2009b) 'The quantity/quality interchange: a blind spot on the highway of science', in Toomela, A. and Valsiner, J. (eds) *Methodological Thinking in Psychology: 60 years gone astray?* (Charlotte: Information Age Publishing) pp.45–68.

Neary, M. (2008) 'Student as producer – risk, responsibility and rich learning environments in higher education', in Barlow, J., Louw, G. and Price, M. (eds) *Social purpose and creativity – integrating learning in the real world. Articles from the Learning and Teaching Conference 2008*. Retrieved from <http://staffcentral.brighton.ac.uk/clt/events/conf/2009/Post-conf.%2708%20spreads%20.pdf>

Neary, M. (2010) 'Student as Producer: A Pedagogy for the Avant-Garde', *Learning Exchange*, 1/1. Retrieved from <http://learningexchange.westminster.ac.uk/index.php/lej/article/view/15>

Neary, M. and Winn, J. (2009) 'The student as producer: reinventing the student experience in higher education', in Bell, L., Stevenson, H. and Neary, M. (eds) *The future of higher education: policy, pedagogy and the student experience* (London: Continuum). Retrieved from <http://eprints.lincoln.ac.uk/1675/>

Ramsden, P. (2008) *The Future of Higher Education Teaching and the Student Experience*. Retrieved from <http://www.heacademy.ac.uk/resources/detail/ourwork/consultations/paulramsden_teaching_and_student_experience>

Reid, A., Abrandt Dahlgren, M., Petocz, P. and Dahlgren, L.O. (2011) *From Expert Student to Novice Professional* (Dordrecht: Springer).

Reid, A. and Solomonides, I. (2007) 'Design students' experience of engagement and creativity', *Art, Design and Communication in Higher Education*, 6/1, pp.27–39.

Spicer, A. and Alvesson, M. (2010) *Metaphors We Lead By: Understanding leadership in the real world* (London: Routledge).

Williams, J. and Wade, G. (2007) 'Metaphors and models in translation between college and workplace mathematics', *Educational Studies in Mathematics*, 64/3, pp.345–71.

Contributor biographies

Agnes Bosanquet is an early career researcher with a PhD in Cultural Studies. Her PhD performed an autoethnographic response to Luce Irigaray's philosophy of sexual difference, transcendence and the mother/daughter relation. From her research in Cultural Studies, Agnes values critical theory, creative methodologies and questions about power relations, discourses and practices of inclusion and exclusion, locations of knowledge and constructions of subjectivity. As an Academic Developer in the Learning and Teaching Centre, Macquarie University, Agnes applies this critical perspective to her research, which explores changing academic roles and identities, theories and models of curriculum and graduate attributes.

Natalie Bates is a Research and Knowledge Exchange Officer at Bournemouth University. During the HERE! (Higher Education Retention and Engagement) project Natalie worked as a Research Assistant at Bournemouth University and was involved in a number of externally funded projects that explored the first year experience of students at university and their transition to higher education, in particular the role of friendship in student transition and its influence on students who have doubts in their first year of study. Natalie holds professional and academic qualifications in teaching and lifelong learning and her research interests include the international transfer of learning and professional skills to the UK.

Colin Bryson is Director of the Combined honours Centre at Newcastle University. He began his career as a Marine Biologist before becoming an employment researcher then a lecturer in various Business Schools. As his responsibilities started to encompass more learning, teaching and educational development he decided to become a scholar in that field. He has become a leading advocate of student engagement in UK higher education. He gained a National Teaching Fellowship in recognition of that work. He is cofounder and chair of RAISE (Researching, Advancing and Inspiring Student Engagement). He espouses putting student engagement at the centre of education and tries to put that into practice that in his day job by working with students in a partnership model through co-design of curriculum and co-management of the student experience via peer models and student involvement.

Yuhao Cen received her BA from Beijing University in 2006 and her Ph.D. in Educational Policy Studies at Indiana University-Bloomington in 2012. Her research interests include student learning and college experiences of Chinese undergraduate students, effective educational experiences in undergraduate education, and education research methodology. Yuhao has been working on a project on student engagement in Chinese higher education with Dr Heidi Ross and colleagues at Tsinghua University since 2007, and has published and presented internationally on the project. She has taught educational inquiry at Indiana University-Bloomington and Tsinghua University. Yuhao was a recipient of the prestigious Chinese Government Award for Outstanding Students Abroad and the Overseas Young Chinese Forum Gregory C. and Paula K. Chow Teaching Fellowship. Yuhao joins the Graduate School of Education at Shanghai Jiaotong University as an Assistant Professor in 2012.

Wincy Chan is a PhD candidate of the Faculty of Education, University of Hong Kong. She has worked in the Faculties of Education, Medicine, and Social Sciences in universities in Canada and Hong Kong. The major theme of her research is that of studying the well-being of adolescents. She has conducted research on risk behaviours and suicide, and the development and evaluation of psycho-educational programs on coping skills and resilience enhancement. Her current research projects include the study of social cognitive learning; with particular interests in the efficacy of course designs and outcome based approaches on generic skills development in higher education. She teaches research methods, educational psychology, and forensic sciences at undergraduate and postgraduate levels.

Professor John Clarke is an Adjunct Professor associated with Student Success and Retention in the Learning and Teaching Unit at QUT (Queensland University of Technology). From 2007-2009, John was the Project Manager of the Transitions-In Project at QUT that focussed on facilitating the transition into QUT of commencing students and that interest has continued as a Co-Editor of the International Journal of the First Year in Higher Education. Prior to the Project Manager role, he was an Associate Professor in the Faculty of Education at QUT where he co-ordinated the Doctor of Education program. John has a history of working and researching in the fields of classroom learning and interaction and learning environments, particularly at the tertiary level, and also has an interest in social science research methodology and its application to learning environment research.

Becka Colley is the Dean of Students at the University of Bradford, she has created an innovative approach to supporting skills development at Bradford which includes the development of the SaPRA (Skills and Personal Reflective Activity) tool and the Develop Me! approach to skills activities. She has a keen interest in student engagement and is active in researching the student experience of e-learning, transition to University and initial engagement with Higher Education. Her current research is focusing on digital literacy. Becka was awarded a National Teaching Fellowship in 2010.

Dr Miriam E. David, AcSS, FRSA is Professor Emerita of Sociology of Education and was, until recently, Professor (2005-2010) and Associate Director (Higher Education) of the ESRC's (Economic and Social Research Council) Teaching & Learning Research Programme (2004-2009) at the Institute of Education University of London. She is a visiting professor in the Centre for Higher Education & Equity Research (CHEER) in the School of Education and Social Work at the University of Sussex. She was formerly a Professor at London South Bank (1988-97); University of the Arts (1997-9) and Keele University (1999 – 2005). She has a world-class reputation for her feminist social research on families, gender, social diversity and inequalities across education, including widening participation into higher education. She has published 25 books and reports, and 160 articles or chapters, including an intellectual biography in 2003 entitled, Personal and Political: Feminisms, Sociology and Family Lives, (Trentham Books).

Peter Dunbar-Hall is an Honorary Associate Professor at Sydney Conservatorium of Music, University of Sydney, where he was a full-time member of staff between 1989 and 2011. During his time at Sydney Conservatorium of Music, Peter was Chair of the Music Education Unit and following that Associate Dean (Graduate Studies). In addition to a series of school-based texts on music, he is the author of the biography of Australian soprano, Strella Wilson, and co-author of Deadly Sounds, Deadly Places: Contemporary Aboriginal Music in Australia. Since 1990 Peter has been a performing member of Sydney based Balinese gamelan group, Sekaa Gong Tirta Sinar, and has studied Balinese music extensively with Balinese musicians in Bali.

Elisabeth Dunne is Head of Project Development within Education Enhancement at the University of Exeter, UK. Her career has been devoted to the promotion of innovation, change and strategic development in education, including initial teacher training as well as a range of ground-breaking initiatives across the University. A major focus has always been on improving the student experience and developing student skills, as well as on understanding the processes of change, including the development of evidence-based practice and working with students as change agents. She has coordinated and directed many projects on aspects of learning and teaching of national interest, including Video-Conferencing, Audio-Feedback, Distance Learning, Integrating Technology across the Exeter Business School, and Augmented Reality. She is currently directing projects on Digital Literacy, e-Assessment and Feedback, Reciprocal Shadowing and Students as Change Agents.

Ed Foster's work is all about helping students to become effective learners in higher education. This is done through a range of practical outputs; he co-ordinates Nottingham Trent University's Welcome Week programme and jointly leads the development of the institutional induction strategy. From 2011, all course inductions had online content and pre-arrival activities. Ed's research interests in US models of the first year experience and the findings from the Higher Education Retention and Engagement project directly led to the creation of an extended academic tutorial programme for all new first years students at his institution. Ed heads the learning development team in the library leading a team of staff and student mentors.

Sue Gordon is a Senior Lecturer in the Mathematics Learning Centre (and Honorary Adjunct to the Faculty of Education and Social Work) at The University of Sydney, in Australia. Sue's area of expertise is teaching and learning in higher education, particularly in the disciplines of mathematics and statistics. Her research is closely linked to her teaching and informs her teaching practice. Sue's research interests include statistics education and pedagogy in higher education. Current and previous projects (many with Peter Petocz and Anna Reid) include seminal research on students' conceptions of mathematics and mathematics learning, researching teachers' and students' experiences of learning statistics, exploring teachers' conceptions of student diversity in their classes, investigating mathematics bridging courses and early support of students in mathematics and using statistical approaches for research in creative and qualitative disciplines.

Garnet Grosjean is a Lecturer in the Department of Educational Studies and Academic Coordinator for the Doctor of Educational Leadership and Policy program at the University of British Columbia, where he teaches post-graduate courses and supervises students. He is also the International Coordinator of an online Intercontinental Master of Education program on Adult Learning and Global Change. He is a strong proponent of peer learning throughout the life course. His research and writing focus on higher education and the changing economy; lifelong learning; the social organization of learning; and policy and practice implications of experiential learning programs. He is co-editor with two colleagues (Hans Schuetze and William Bruneau) of a recent book on University Governance and Reform Policy (Palgrave Macmillan).

Christine Hardy is a Principal Lecturer in the School of Art and Design, Nottingham Trent University. She has a PhD from Nottingham University in adult reading, published in 2008 entitled To Read or not to Read: Adult Reading Habits and Motivations. Christine's recent teaching is focused on research methods and academic writing with post-graduate students. She also works across the academy leading pedagogic research and student induction. Her current research interest, and the subject of publications and conference presentations, is student engagement. This includes transitions, academic writing and internationalisation, taking a student perspective. She is co-founder of the international RAISE network (Researching, advancing and inspiring student engagement). She is a Fellow of the Higher Education Academy.

Professor Janice Kay is Deputy Vice Chancellor at the University of Exeter in the UK. She has two portfolios: strategic responsibility for education and line management responsibility for the College of Humanities and the Peninsula College of Medicine and Dentistry. She has been responsible for the strategic development of the University Science Strategy, and has also recently overseen the new national and regional Arts and Culture strategy, which links strongly with the university's excellent Humanities disciplines. She speaks nationally on graduate employment matters, widening access and admissions, and the student experience. She chairs the 1994 Group of research-intensive universities Student Experience Policy Group and is a Board Member of the Higher Education Academy.

Chris Keenan is a learning and teaching fellow at Bournemouth University where her main role is as an education developer. Her area of research is transition into higher education and she is currently leading two projects looking at transition to higher education STEM (Science, Technology, Engineering and Mathematics) programmes and the role of Peer Assisted Learning on higher education science, technology, engineering and mathematics programmes. Chris is also Chair of the Association of Learning Development in Higher Education.

Professor Kerri-Lee Krause is Pro Vice-Chancellor (Education) and Professor of Higher Education at the University of Western Sydney. Her portfolio responsibilities focus on enhancing the quality of learning, teaching and academic quality across the University. She is internationally recognised for her research on the contemporary undergraduate student experience and implications for quality and standards. At UWS her role connects the quality of the student experience and outcomes with capacity-building for academic staff. Higher education policy is her research focus, including extensive work on the changing student experience, the evolving nature of academic work and implications for quality and standards in higher education.

Sally Kift is a Professor of Law at Queensland University of Technology, where she has served as Law Faculty Assistant Dean, Teaching & Learning (2001-2006). She was QUT's foundational Director, First Year Experience (2006-2007). Sally is a national Teaching Award winner (2003) and national Program Award winner (2007). She was awarded a Senior Fellowship by the Australian Learning and Teaching Council (ALTC) in 2006 to investigate the first year experience and is currently an ALTC Discipline Scholar in Law. In May 2012, Sally will take up the role of Deputy Vice-Chancellor (Academic) at James Cook University, Australia.

Cath Lambert is Associate Professor in Sociology at the University of Warwick. She works in the areas of critical pedagogy, and gender and education. She has published on teacher identities, students' political engagement, educational space and pedagogic art. Her most recent work focuses on the generation and critical exploration of alternative spaces for the production of knowledge, both inside and beyond formal educational institutions. She has an interest in the development of 'sensory' methods and methodologies that might help us to understand how knowledge is lived, felt and experienced in embodied and sensory ways. Alongside published work she also communicates some of her research, often produced collaboratively with students, in the form of documentary film and art installation.

Sarah Lawther is part of the Learning Development Team, based in Nottingham Trent University's library. She is a trained researcher who supported the Higher Education Retention and Engagement project. Prior to this, she carried out research on student transition into the first year. This research informs the work undertaken by a team to support staff and students at Nottingham Trent University, UK. Sarah is also involved in the practical support provided to staff and students such as Welcome Week, the annual Student Writing and Transition Symposium, and the development of resources and staff workshops in areas such as induction, transition and retention.

Dr Linda Leach is a Senior Lecturer in the College of Education at Massey University. She has been teaching adults since the late 1970s, in non-formal, community contexts as well as in two polytechnics and one university. She currently coordinates postgraduate programmes in adult education and tertiary teaching, and teaches about adult learning at both undergraduate and post-graduate level. Linda's research focuses on learning and teaching in the tertiary sector. She has been a joint project director for projects funded by the Ministry of Education, the Teaching and Learning Research Initiative, the New Zealand Qualifications Authority and the Institutes of Technology and Polytechnics of New Zealand Foundation Education Forum. These included studies on academic development and student support, student retention, foundation learning, student engagement, adult literacy, language and numeracy, student decision-making, and standards-based assessment. Linda has published widely on adult learning and teaching topics.

Ruth Lefever joined the University of Bradford as a Research Associate in 2009 having come from a role and position focused on welfare and retention. Her previous research covered the first year experience, withdrawals, student representation, widening participation, internationalisation and student resilience. Ruth's current research at Bradford continues to focus on the student experience and includes projects on student retention and engagement, supporting transitions into and through university as well as student feedback and student experience policy. Her particular interests include qualitative research, student friendships and community building, notions of belonging and gender issues.

Alex Mockridge is a current full-time undergraduate student at The University of Warwick, studying for a four-year Masters of Mathematics, Operational Research, Statistics and Economics degree, which reflects his broad range of interests. He spent part of his time in 2009-2010 employed by The Reinvention Centre at the University as part of a team of four undergraduate and two postgraduate researchers, working on a joint research project between King's College London and Warwick on the development of graduate capabilities from research-intensive Universities. In 2010 he received a Warwick Advantage Award, partly for his work for The Reinvention Centre. More recently, Alex has joined another collaborative research team in Warwick's Institute for Advanced Teaching and Learning. The project is investigating how small and medium enterprises in the areas of science, technology, engineering and mathematics can better integrate with university curricula.

Professor Karen Nelson is the Director, Student Success and Retention at Queensland University of Technology. From 2008-2010 she was the Director, First Year Experience and responsibility for the First Year Experience activities now falls within her wider portfolio. Karen leads a series of university wide initiatives that are designed to enhance student success and are having measurable impacts on student engagement and retention. She is currently the leader of two national research projects and a team member in a third project. Karen's higher education research interests focus on student engagement in higher education, student retention, the first year experience, and institutional research and responses relating to these topics. She presents and consults nationally and internationally in these areas of interest.

Glenn Newbery is a lecturer in psychology at the University of Western Sydney, where he teaches courses in the history and philosophy of psychology, critical thinking, research methods, personality, motivation, and sport and exercise psychology. He gained his PhD in 2006 from the University of Sydney. His current research interests are in motivation theory, psychoanalytic theory, and sport and exercise psychology. He has published in the areas of sport psychology, motivation, research methods, and personality.

Derfel Owen is Student Engagement and Participation Development Manager at the University of Exeter, UK. He studied British Politics and Legislative Studies at the University of Hull where he went on to become President of the Students' Union and was then elected to the National Executive Committee of the NUS where he led efforts to improve students' union governance and their relationships with partner universities. He then joined Goldsmiths, University of London, as Student Support and Development Manager, to improve personal and professional development opportunities for students and to oversee the development of effective advice and representation structures. In 2007, Derfel joined the Quality Assurance Agency (QAA) where he led improvements in student engagement and participation and pioneered new approaches to communication and engagement, including launching the QAA podcast series, QAAtv, utilising social media, student-led publications and a substantial redevelopment of QAA's website.

Peter Petocz is Associate Professor in the Department of Statistics at Macquarie University, Sydney. He divides his time between professional work as an applied statistician, mostly in health-related areas, and pedagogical research in statistics and mathematics education. He has authored text books and video-based learning resources for statistics learning, written widely in the field of statistics pedagogy, and held a position as editor of Statistics Education Research Journal for several years. He has worked with Anna Reid and Sue Gordon on several research projects, including teachers' approaches to teaching service statistics, their conceptions of student diversity in their classes, and the role of statistical approaches in research in creative disciplines. His investigations of the process of 'Becoming a Mathematician' have culminated in publication of a research monograph by Springer, co-authored with Anna Reid and another colleague.

Anna Reid is Professor of Music and Associate Dean of Learning and Teaching at the Sydney Conservatorium of Music, a faculty of the University of Sydney. She has had an academic career in music and music education, and professional development at tertiary level, working at several universities in Sydney. She has a wide range of qualitative research interests spanning a diversity of disciplines, including design, law, mathematics and music. Her research focuses broadly on the professional formation of students through their university studies, and their conceptions of their discipline and various dispositions such as creativity, particularly in the context of performing and visual arts. Springer has recently published her book 'From Expert Student to Novice Professional', co-authored with Peter Petocz and two Swedish colleagues.

Elizabeth Reid is a doctoral candidate and tutor in Modern History at Macquarie University. Her primary research is in the use of clothing to create religious and social identities in Renaissance Europe. Previously, she completed a Bachelor of Creative Arts at the University of Wollongong, followed by Honours in Art History at the University of Sydney. From 2008-2011 Elizabeth worked as a Research Assistant for two projects at Macquarie University. The first was based in the department of Psychology, conducting interviews to facilitate the development of tools to aid effective communication and provide support for international PhD candidates and their supervisors. The second researched the engagement of first-year students from various departments with higher education, and forms the basis of a chapter in the current publication.

Heidi Ross is Director of the East Asian Studies Center and Professor of Educational Policy Studies at Indiana University. She also co-directs the Australian National University-Indiana University Pan Asia Institute. Heidi earned her PhD in Educational Foundations, Policy, and Administration at the University of Michigan. She has taught and consulted at numerous institutions in East Asia and has served as president of the Comparative and International Education Society, co-editor of Comparative Education Review, and Chair of Educational Studies and Director of Asian Studies at Colgate University. Ross has published widely on Chinese education, gender and schooling, and qualitative research methodology, and her books include China Learns English (Yale), The Ethnographic Eye (Garland), and Taking Teaching Seriously (Paradigm). She is currently leading two field-based projects on student engagement in Chinese higher education and girls' educational access and attainment in rural Shaanxi. In 2011 Ross received Indiana University's prestigious Presidential Award for excellence in teaching, and in 2012 Indiana University's Ryan Award for her leadership in international studies.

Anna D. Rowe is a doctoral student in the Department of Marketing and Management and research assistant in the Learning and Teaching Centre, Macquarie University, Australia. Her research focus is university student and lecturer perceptions of the role and functionality of emotions in learning. She is particularly interested in the social dimensions of teaching and learning in areas such as assessment and feedback. Other research areas include graduate attributes, social inclusion within higher education and work-integrated learning. She is currently investigating the role of host supervisors in work-integrated learning as part of a collaborative research project.

Kay Sambell is currently Professor of Learning and Teaching in the School of Health, Community and Education Studies at Northumbria University, UK. A committed university teacher with over twenty years' classroom experience, Kay continues to work with large groups of students, putting new pedagogic principles into practice. She specialises in assessment for learning. In 2002 she was awarded a National Teaching Fellowship for her research and development work on innovative assessment to support student learning. Since then she has directed a wide range of funded learning and teaching initiatives, developing, researching and disseminating practical, evidence-informed ideas about improving student learning via assessment. In 2005 Kay became a Director of Northumbria University's centre for excellence in Assessment for Learning, where she led on student engagement and enhancement.

Michelle Sisto is a Professor of Mathematics and Statistics and the Special Advisor to the Dean on Teaching and Learning at the International University of Monaco in the Principality of Monaco, where she has been since 1998. Her publications and research interests are in the fields of statistics education research, quantitative methods, statistics applied to management, and in finance. Michelle completed her undergraduate work at Georgetown University, masters at the University of Nice, and she is currently finishing a PhD in Finance program at the EDHEC (Ecole Des Hautes Etudes Commerciales du Nord) Business School.

Ian Solomonides is Associate Professor and Director of the Learning and Teaching Centre at Macquarie University, Sydney, responsible for Academic Development, Educational Design, Learning Systems and Services, Accessibility Services, and Student Evaluation in the University. Originally from the UK, he worked on various learning and teaching enhancement projects in the disciplines of engineering and design. He has maintained a strong practical and research interest in the student experience throughout his academic career to focus on student engagement and teaching standards in higher education. He is an Executive Member of the Council of Australian Directors of Academic Development.

Paul Taylor studied for a BSc and PhD in Chemistry at the University of Durham before spending two years as a postdoctoral fellow at the University of Geneva. He moved to Warwick as a Lecturer in 1991 and is currently a Reader in Organic Chemistry as well as Director of the Institute for Advanced Teaching & Learning. Paul's scientific interests are varied and include interdisciplinary projects both with Engineers and with Biologists. He teaches organic chemistry to undergraduate chemists with a particular focus on the practice of the subject in the laboratory. As Director of the Reinvention Centre, Paul was engaged in HEFCE-funded (Higher Education Funding Council for England) research into Learning in a Research-rich Environment. The engagement of student researchers on this project led to a model of collaborative, student engaged research that underpins all Paul's current work, for example an Higher Education Academy funded study of Student Engagement Surveys in the UK and funded programmes around enterprise.

Angela Voerman manages the development of central services to promote student engagement at Macquarie University. She has a particular interest in strategies designed to blur the boundaries between social and learning environments both within the university and between the university and the wider community. Central to this is research that interrogates the experience of students at university, and that locates the voice of students within the professional development of university staff. Angela has also assisted in the development of projects that promote the links between Aboriginal and Torres Strait Islander Communities and university learning. She also has a broader interest in the integration of an understanding of the diversity of students into the design of curricula across a range of disciplinary practice.

Beverley Webster is currently the Director of the Teaching and Learning Unit in the Faculty of Business and Economics at the University of Melbourne. Her experience in higher education since 1997 includes working in Faculties of Business and Law, Health Sciences, Mathematics and Science and Education in Western Australia till 2005. She worked at the University of Hong Kong from 2005 to 2011 where she held roles including Associate Dean Research Higher Degrees, Acting Executive Director of the Centre for Enhancement of Teaching and Learning and the Graduate School Course Coordinator. Her research over the last 5 years has focused on student learning in higher education; in particular the first year experience, assessment and outcomes based approaches. Her primary teaching area is in research methods and more specifically quantitative research methods but includes many management and finance subjects.

Danny Wilding is an Account Executive at Political Lobbying and Media Relations in London. Danny joined PLMR in 2011 from another London-based public affairs and communications agency. During his time there he was heavily involved in providing public affairs and PR support to a number of companies, charities and organisations across the green technology, healthcare, energy and sport and leisure sectors. Prior to entering public affairs Danny was Research Associate at the Institute for Advanced Teaching and Learning at the University of Warwick whilst undertaking his MA in Social Research part-time. In this role he took responsibility for the designing and managing of research projects into the policy and practices of higher education, co-authoring a number of publications. Danny has previously worked as an auditor for the Quality Assurance Agency and graduated with a BA in Sociology and Social Policy from the University of Warwick.

Dr Theresa Winchester-Seeto is the Academic Director of Participation in the Faculty of Human Sciences at Macquarie University. She is also a Senior Lecturer in the Learning and Teaching Centre, where her main research interests include pedagogy of experience-based learning, graduate attributes and cross-cultural supervision. Recent projects include research on student assessment in work-integrated learning, the role of the host supervisor and the development of effective curriculum for Learning Through Participation. She is also part of a Macquarie University group partnering with other universities to address a commissioned Project on assessing the impact of work-integrated learning (WIL) on student work readiness. Theresa has researched and written several papers on the background of Graduate Attributes and their impact on higher education, as well as being part of a recent project on cross-cultural higher degree research supervision.

Associate Professor Nick Zepke works at Massey University in New Zealand. His field of research is adult, higher and lifelong education. In this field he researches in three interrelated areas: learner centred teaching, policy studies, and futures studies. Research has been empirical through funded projects such as the Teaching and Learning Research Initiative (TLRI), New Zealand Qualifications Authority (NZQA) and the New Zealand Ministry of Education and theoretical in classroom, policy and futures studies. The chapter co-authored in this book is based on results from a funded TLRI project that investigated student engagement in their first year of study across nine tertiary education institutions. This research has been disseminated widely, including in a joint article with Linda Leach presenting an engagement framework in the journal Active Learning in Higher Education, currently the most read article in that journal.